MS 1701trilogy/10/16/13
183,034 words

The Irwin Glass Trilogy: Betrayal Retribution Burnt Out

by
Harley L.   Sachs

Ebook ISBN 9781939381392
Paperback ISBN 9781939381408

Harley L. Sachs

Books by Harley L. Sachs:

Novels

Queer Company
Never Trust a Talking Horse
The Gold Chromosome
Murder by Mail (Scratch—Out!)
Ben Zakkai's Coffin
The Search for Jesse Bram
The Mystery Club Solves a Murder
The Mystery Club and the Dead Doctor
The Mystery Club and the Hidden Witness
The Mystery Club and the Serial Widow
Deliver me from Evil
White Slave
Conspiracy!
Murder in the Keweenaw
The Lollipop Murder
Betrayal
Retribution
Burnt Out
Sam in Love

Collections of short fiction

Ahoy! Quarterdeck!
A Troll for Christmas and other stories
Threads of the Covenant: The Jews of Red Jacket
Misplaced Persons

Non-Fiction

How to Write the Technical Article and get it Published
Freelance Non-Fiction Articles
IS
Chilly-Chilly BANG! How We Freelanced Through Europe's Coldest Winter in a VW with a Kid
Essays and Columns: 1992-2011

Cartoons

Hunting the Mail Buoy and other hazards to navigation

Harley L. Sachs

For Ulla

The Irwin Glass Trilogy

Table of Contents

Harley L. Sachs

Book One: Betrayal

Part One

She came through the doors of the American Library in Moscow, a dark-haired, gorgeous woman in a long coat with her Slavic face framed by a fur collar. It was one of those first impressions that imprint on your mind and stay with you forever. Stunning, like being struck by lightning. I remember Dante is said to have seen Beatrice only once as a young girl, and she haunted him forever. It was like that with me and Svetlana. Standing with a tray of shots of sour mash American bourbon I took one look at her and was smitten. It was a look that has haunted me ever since like a blessing, an enigma, and a curse.

My interest in Russia began when I was only ten. I was just a kid, but what happens when we are ten years old can set the pattern for an entire life. As a ten year old I found an old shoe box of family pictures in the attic of our South Bend, Indiana home. There was a shoe box with a medal in it, a purple heart, and a picture of my dad in uniform, standing with a bunch of buddies in a tropical place I guessed was Vietnam. I knew my dad had been in Vietnam, but he never talked about it. I knew when he saw homeless vets begging on the street he always gave them a dollar. He didn't wear one of those baseball caps emblazoned with "Vietnam" or "veteran." He wanted to forget all about it, never talked about the war. I didn't even know where Vietnam was.

What struck me even more than my Dad's army photo was a cracked, yellowing portrait of a shabby-looking man posing uncomfortably in a studio. On the back of the photo was some printing I couldn't read, and the address of the studio, I guessed, and the city, Moscva. I showed the picture to my dad, who was irritated that I'd been going through the stuff in the attic. "That's your paternal great grandfather Isaac Melamed," he explained. "I think he fled Russia to escape conscription for twenty-five years among the Cossacks."

That's all he told me. There was also an old letter in the box of photos written in a foreign cursive text and small, so whoever wrote it could get the most on a single sheet of what must have been expensive, very thin paper. Someone had removed the stamp from the envelope and the postmark was illegible. I wanted to read the crabbed handwriting, and felt like if I couldn't read it—no one else in the family could— I was denying part of our ancestry. All I knew then was it was Russian. I didn't know if it was from Isaac Melamed or some other relative. It was a mystery.

I loved mysteries. I used to read kids' books, like the *Mystery of the Spanish Treasure* and stuff like that. This was a real mystery. What was that forgotten or hidden past? As a kid I did not know about family genealogy and my parents didn't care. Busy making a living and involved in their own day to day existence, my folks had no interest in family history.

I figured out that Moscva was Moscow and I found it in our atlas. I didn't know anyone who could translate Russian. Even if I did, I wanted to read the Russian letter myself. The South Bend library didn't have much about Russia, but what little I found intrigued me even more.

Having no other particular interest, when I went to Indiana University in Bloomington I majored in Russian Language and Literature. It turned out that I had a knack for foreign language. Other students just memorized vocabulary and grammar. I embraced it. After four years I could almost pass for a native speaker, except for lapses of an American accent. There are some things you can learn only in the country itself. It followed logically to get a Masters in International Relations.

My father taught high school social studies in South Bend, was forced by a shuffle of personnel and budget shortfalls to take early retirement and while I was away at grad school moved to a double wide in Ocala, Florida The irony was that after all that preparation the shoe box of family photos, dad's medal, the Moscow photograph and the letter in Russian, the original catalyst, were left behind in the South

Bend attic for whoever moved into the house. I guess dad didn't care, was too busy, or didn't want to remember.

I took the Foreign Service exam. My Russian language skills got me the five point bonus and I passed even though I had to detect subtle nuances in editorials in Pravda and Isvestia. My Russian language fluency pointed me in the direction of the then Soviet Union

Though President Reagan and Gorbachev were talking about arms control, the cold war was still on. It's different today. Back then the American embassy in Moscow had been bombarded with microwave transmissions that forced them to cover all the windows with aluminum shutters. The transmissions hadn't been intended as an attack on the health of the personnel inside, but to activate the bugs planted in the walls, the furniture, and so on by the KGB snoops.

I was apolitical. I had not voted for Reagan. In grad school I had not bothered to register. But the State Department wasn't supposed to lean toward one party affiliation or another, so being neutral was a good thing.

As part of my studies I had read "Will the Soviet Union Survive until 1984?" That year had passed and the Soviet Union was still intact. Gorbachev seemed to be going strong with his Glasnoz, Openness, policy.

Getting to Russia was the fulfillment of a dream, the achievement I had worked for through six years of college. I wanted a posting to somewhere in the Soviet Union. The only job for which there was an opening was at the USIA library in Moscow and I took it, hoping to move up in the Foreign Service later. The main thing was to get into the system even though the job at the American library was not a perfect fit.

So here I was at last, in Moscow. Wow! It was a thrill for me to stand in Red Square, the site of all those displays of military might in the May Day parades. The Soviets were smart, making Lenin's tomb the platform for the reviewing dignitaries. Troops passing on parade were saluting both Lenin and the Soviet leaders, a powerful symbol.

But the Russia I found wasn't quite the world I had imagined when reading *Crime and Punishment.* That was nineteenth century czarist St. Petersburg. Dostoevsky's

Russia was before the telephone, when to reach someone across town you sent a telegram which was then delivered by some poor functionary in a shabby uniform.

This was the Soviet world of palatial Metro stations, crowded busses, and Russians who looked at me with envy when I returned to my billet with groceries from the American commissary. Russia had food shortages, and the affluent capitalist Americans were both resented and envied. The xenophobic Soviets regarded all foreigners as spies. Well, I was not a spy, and when riding the busses hid my purchases out of shame for my relative affluence.

What the American library needed most was someone who knew contemporary American literature. In grad school I had been so busy with Russian and Soviet literature and International Studies that I was weak on American lit.

The library director, Susan Lutz, would have preferred someone else. I realized that, but did not take the incipient hostility seriously. I saw the library job, while not terribly prestigious in itself, as a stepping stone.

Until I got tripped by a beautiful woman and a glass of vodka.

Ironic how one night of indiscretion can ruin your life.

The embassy settled me in a cramped, fourth floor, studio apartment, what the British call a bed-sit in an old Soviet-style building, with a kitchen no bigger than a walk-in closet. Like many others of the period, the building was constructed of prefabricated concrete slabs thrown together like a child's Lego kit. The elevator was so slow and unreliable that I preferred to climb the stairs rather than risk being caught between floors. The faucet in the bathroom dripped and getting a cracked window replaced took a flurry of forms, applications, and delays. The radiator sometimes made funny noises, but provided little heat. The tiles in the hallway had started to fall apart as soon as the building was finished, even before, and only a few remained to hint at what had been promised once as something grand. The Soviets didn't seem to understand the necessity for maintenance.

It was the tangible proof of the Russian joke about Marxism, "We pretend to work and they pretend to pay us." Communism promised freedom to work but that didn't mean the worker did very much. The revolution might have freed the serfs but it didn't change the slave mentality.

The furniture in my apartment was embassy supplied. Before I moved in, the security squad sniffed the place for electronic bugs, not that I was privy to any information the Sovs, as the slang went, might want to collect. The spooks had found one bug hidden in the door of the armoire that served as a clothes closet and another behind a picture of the Kremlin. If it weren't for the fact that it was on an outside wall, one couldn't be certain that the mirror in the bathroom wasn't actually one way, permitting snoops behind the wall to see what went on inside. That was the price for living in a Soviet police state. As in Orwell's *1984*, Big Brother was watching. What I didn't realize was that there were other watchers.

I had brought along my favorite books, Russian dictionaries, recent Russian literature and classics. I loved Gogol's *Dead Souls* and identified with Akaky Akakyveich, the scheming hero who tried to beat the system but was, in the end, just a hopeless shit, what the name epitomized, roughly translated "Little Shit Head, the son of Shit." I was closer to that role than I realized.

Aside from my skeletal library, I had one pot, one pan, and did my own cooking on a two burner gas hot plate. The sink had only one faucet, cold water, but I realized my cooking accommodations were better than the average Muskovite. They generally shared a Primus kerosene stove in a hallway with several other families. Try to imagine a hallway with the pervasive smell of a kerosene stove and cooked cabbage.

The only modern touch about the embassy billet was the electronic keys that replaced ordinary door locks. My key was programmed to trigger the street entrance and the door to my apartment, but no other. There were no surveillance cameras like those around the embassy building. It didn't matter to me that every time my key was used the computers noted my comings if not my goings.

That kind of surveillance was something I could shrug off, since I was, after all, only a clerk in the library. If the KGB wanted to follow me when I stood in line at the bakery for a loaf of Russian black bread, so what? I wasn't anyone they would be interested in. Or so I thought.

Catering to the tastes of Soviet readers, the library had works by Mark Twain, Howard Fast, John Steinbeck, and American leftist authors. Though not an American, Dickens was another favorite for his emphasis on social change. And of course there was the expected collection of travel books exploiting the beauty of the American National Parks, American history, and copies of the US Constitution and related documents so curious Russians could get a feeling for the American way. What the female Russian visitors always asked for were magazines like *Vogue*. *Playboy* was forbidden as Russians saw it as decadent and immoral.

The event that called for the reception at the library was a display of American art. It was not original art, but reproductions, decently framed, but not the real thing that Russians respected. The library director, my supervisor, was Susan Lutz, a forty-year old, Jewish New Yorker, daughter of an art dealer. In her late thirties she had lost the freshness of youth and had acquired the downward wrinkles of someone who frowned too much. Her straight, short hair was lifeless in spite of the availability of American cosmetics in the commissary. She knew that Soviets were proud of being cultured. The worst insult they could give someone was *Nyet kultorny*, that someone lacked culture.

It was an attitude that had rubbed off on Ms Lutz . (I never felt comfortable calling her Susan.) She didn't think I had much culture, either, coming as I did from the Midwest. To New Yorkers everything west of the Hudson was Indian country and people from Indiana were cultural savages, Hoosier yokels. She cringed when I missed the literary allusions to American writers that she dropped into her conversation. She'd wanted to call me Holden, an allusion not too far off the mark and I didn't get it at first until I remembered the book from high school. Anyone who didn't know Salinger and *Catcher in the Rye* she considered a doofus. I considered her to be a name-dropping snob.

When I started the job the first thing she did after showing me the library was to take me on a tour of the Kremlin's museum to admire art of the old Czarist days.

Adding to the undercurrent of conflict, Lutz had been in Moscow for a year but did not know Russian. That I did was to her not just an asset to our work in the library, but a threat. It rankled that I could read the blurbs under the Kremlin art displays and she could not. After all, she was the guide, not me.

I found it ironic that while treasuring the Kremlin art the Soviets also put it down as the product of exploited serfs. With them everything had to be seen through the lens of Marxism-Leninism.

Lutz was also a micromanager who tended to count the pencils and keep everything under lock and key. That might be because after a year in Moscow she knew that some commodities were so scarce that if someone's light bulb burned out at home a Russian would take it to their job site and switch it for one that worked. She didn't want visitors to the American library to snitch the light bulbs. Someone in the army would have called her a tight ass.

Clearly, if she'd been in charge of hiring, I would not have been a candidate. She would leap at the chance to replace me with someone more to her liking.

Lutz set up the exhibit of American art. The opening was to be preceded by a sneak preview for dignitaries. She reminded me to look my best and would have dressed me herself if she'd been my mother or my wife, which she wasn't. "Remember," she said, "we can expect the Minister of Culture to be here and the ambassador may make some opening remarks." I would put on my best suit and tie and be sure to wear an American flag lapel pin. My best suit was a pin striped, single breasted wool with lined trousers that my mother picked out before I left for Russia.

Even though Lutz had prepped me with information about the artists on display, which made me nervous, for I was no art critic myself, I looked forward to the social occasion. I hadn't met the ambassador, a Texas tycoon who got the job for having made major contributions to Reagan's campaign. Who might the Russian dignitaries who came to the reception be? Higher ups from the Ministry of Culture? Representatives of the Kremlin's art collection? True to form,

I could expect someone from the KGB, keeping an eye on the guests.

In a police state everyone watched everyone else. If someone showed too much of an interest in the United States there was the suspicion that they might want to defect. And of course, the so-called political officers (read CIA) at the Embassy would have someone there, too, watching the watchers. Had I been more experienced, I would have noticed which visitors avoided political talk, stuck to the weather, or possibly sports, innocuous subjects that didn't reveal political leanings, true feelings or intentions.

The result was that there was an undercurrent of caution, artificial conviviality. Lutz could welcome the visitors in English, but I did so in fluent Russian. She knew Russians wanted to practice their English; I didn't realize that showing off my fluency in front of her was a put down she resented. I had not learned caution.

The special reception pre-viewing the exhibit was for dignitaries, a cocktail party where I would act as a sort of junior host, seeing that everyone got to sample tidbits supplied from the commissary. Appealing to the taste of the visitors was a supply of California wines and Kentucky sour mash bourbon, cheese and crackers, of course.

I was convinced that the main interest of the Soviet guests was the food and the drink, not the books or the art reproductions. That didn't matter. The idea was to get potential customers in the door. If they came once, they might come again. It all seemed harmless enough at my level. I wasn't playing cat and mouse with potential defectors or the KGB. I was just the young American passing around a tray of drinks and seeing that glasses were filled. Right? Harmless? Maybe not.

The Soviet guests arrived, surreptitiously photographed by someone from the embassy posing as a journalist. Susan Lutz was dressed in her finest, not quite a ball gown, feminine but official, form fitting but high in the collar. She welcomed the Minister of Culture, a middle-aged apparatchik in one of those ubiquitous, innocuous, double-breasted suits. Comrade Oblomov had added a flower in his lapel. His assistant, in a similar, black suit, wore a colorful display of medals on his breast. I hadn't studied Soviet military medals, couldn't distinguish a Hero of the Soviet Union award from the Russian version of a Purple Heart like my Dad got in Vietnam.

On Lutz's signal, I offered a tray of drinks, Jim Beam whiskey in shot glasses. Oblomov eyed them with suspicion, but quickly downed two. At that rate the commissary would have to order a few more cases to be shipped in on the weekly embassy plane.

The library wasn't large and the space quickly filled. I noticed a couple that came in together, a small, athletic, bald man in a leather jacket and a taller, dark-haired woman in a coat with a fur collar, even though it wasn't yet winter. I understood the hierarchy well enough to spot a party member with access to the special state stores. I categorized her as a party member's wife or possibly the bald man's daughter, for she was clearly years younger.

I offered them drinks. The bald man took a pass. The woman gave me a mischievous look and asked, in English "No vodka?"

"Kentucky sour mash bourbon. Something special you won't find in Moscow."

She feigned insult. "In Moscow you can get everything." Her arched eyebrows suggested that "everything" included women, and wouldn't I be interested?

I sensed she was coming on to me and switched to Russian. "I suppose so, if you have the price. I haven't been here long enough."

"Oh, you speak Russian. Have you been here long?"

"Only a few weeks. A month."

"You are what you call a quick study?"

"I studied Russian at university."

"Where?"

"Indiana."

She didn't know Indiana. "They taught you well, those Indians."

"No. Indiana is a state in the Midwest."

"Ah." She laughed. "Excuse me."

When she laughed she had dimples in her cheeks but tried to cover her mouth. Perhaps she wanted to hide a stainless steel tooth, common in those days. She had a Slavic face, wide-jawed, but her lips, heavily lipsticked a dark red, reminded me of French girls. I got a whiff of her seductive perfume, not that godawful overpowering toilet water some Russian women wore and could almost knock you out with in the close quarters of a Moscow bus. She obviously had access to more expensive scents. In the special stores reserved for party members one could buy French perfumes.

"I'm Irwin Glass," I offered. "Assistant to the library director, Ms Lutz ." I gestured in the direction of my boss who was showing the Minister of Culture one of the framed prints of American art. It was that famous late night painting of people seen through the window of a diner, a portrait of loneliness and isolation. I don't remember the name of the artist. Oblomov had the look of someone who thought American art was decadent, about as appealing as a puddle of vomit on the street.

"Irvin," she said, having difficulty with the W. "I am Svetlana." She didn't give her patronymic. Americans weren't as stiff and formal or, if you will, stilted as Europeans. Was Svetlana being deliberately anonymous or using the informal atmosphere of the American library as an excuse to cut loose from social protocol?

She took one of the glasses of bourbon and cautiously sipped. "You should try our vodka, Irvin," she said and winked.

I caught the invitation. She was flirting. "I'd like that. Any time."

She nodded and smiled. "Perhaps later. You like to dance?"

"Sure."

"Moscow has some nice places for a party." Then she moved away into the crowd, leaving me wondering, interested.

Putting down the tray of drinks, I followed her. "It's rather warm here. Would you like to hang up your coat?"

She turned, pleased that I had noticed. "Very kind."

I helped her slip the coat off. She was wearing a party dress held up with spaghetti straps, deep cleavage that invited a peek down between her ample breasts.   She noticed that I was staring.

Embarrassed, I stammered, "I'll hang your coat in the office," and escaped into the crowd.

Susan Lutz saw the encounter.   "She's quite a dish. Don't forget the drinks.   You're a host, not a guest."

I hung Svetlana's coat on a clothes rack in the office and returned to the drinks tray.   Someone had finished off all but two of the shots of bourbon.   Those Russians might prefer vodka, but anything with alcohol, especially free drinks, was an invitation to a binge.   I found a diminishing supply of clean glasses in the office and opened another bottle of Jim Beam.   I sensed that when the drinks were gone the crowd would disappear as quickly.

They did.   It was all very polite, but there was no disguising the fact that it was the refreshments that had lured the Russians to the American library, not the art and not the books.

A man who might have been a taxi driver came through the doors, spoke with the bald man who had arrived with Svetlana.   Svetlana joined them and there was what looked to me like an arGument.   Svetlana was obviously displeased. Her escort excused himself and left, leaving her at the door.

I approached her.   "Did your date desert you?"

"He's not my date."

"Boy friend?"

"Not exactly.   Someone from the office."

"Your boss?"

"He thinks so." She bit her lip, clearly angry.

I didn't ask what office that might be and afterwards regretted not being curious enough.   I assumed she was from the Ministry of Culture.

"Do you need someone to see you home? I'm almost finished here."

She considered, sighed, seemed to have put the dispute, whatever it was, behind her.   "I promised you some of our vodka."

Had she? Had she promised that? "Well, I'm not much of a drinker." I had already helped myself to two shots of Jim

Beam and was feeling a bit light headed. "I'll just get your coat."

She let me help her into it and brushed against me when I smoothed it over her shoulders, seeing that her hair wasn't trapped under the fur collar. Again I caught the heady fragrance of her perfume. I felt disoriented.

Lutz was watching curiously. Even though she was my boss, that man/woman thing was always present. If I wanted to go off with some Russian tart, that was my headache, and if I screwed up, well, she'd have an excuse to replace me with someone more to her liking. "I'll lock up," she said. "You're free to go."

At least I wouldn't have to wash the empty shot glasses and clean up after the party, I thought. I hadn't had a date or been alone with a beautiful woman since I arrived in Moscow. What were Russian women like? What did they expect? I didn't know how to interpret her signals.

I followed Svetlana out onto the dark, Moscow street. Why wasn't I surprised that a black taxi was waiting at the curb?

I held the door for her while she got in the back seat. I settled in beside her.

It was an old Moskovitch, the Soviet equivalent of the Volkswagen people's car except the Soviets didn't know how to put a car together so everything fit. Unlike American taxis it had no meter, no displayed driver's shield posted above the dash board. When the door slammed it sounded like the lid of a garbage can. I hadn't heard Svetlana's instructions to the driver and we drove off at once.

Svetlana snuggled up to me and possessively put her hand on my thigh. I hadn't expected that. She asked, "You like to dance?"

"I haven't had much time since I got here."

"I know a good place."

I was hesitant. I didn't have many rubles on me and I was afraid I might not be able to pay the tab. How much would the taxi cost and where were we going? What would this little adventure lead to? Would I take her up to my studio apartment? Gosh, I remembered I hadn't made my bed. The place was a mess.

17

I wondered where she lived. She looked like a party member, might have a swell apartment, but she might also have a roommate, or even a husband. I didn't know her at all. Why was she coming on to me? I was good looking enough. Maybe she thought, with my access to the US commissary, I might get her a carton of Marlboros. Some women might have that motivation, but she didn't look the type. She was too elegant.

What I did sense was that she was willing and that got me excited. She wasn't just talking about a taste of vodka. That stuff had all the character of grain alcohol, about as appetizing as Sterno. Where was all this leading? Just a casual foray into Moscow's night life? Or something more serious? I'd heard that some women were collectors, as in "Have you ever had sex with a Nigerian? A Chinese? An American?" Was I another trophy to be counted amidst her conquests? She certainly wasn't taking her time about it.

I did realize I didn't have any condoms and had no clue where to get some. Did they sell them at the embassy commissary? Having zero sex life, I hadn't thought to ask.

While all this was going through my mind the hand on my thigh had moved up toward my crotch. Steady, now. I didn't want to get out of the cab in a public place with an obvious hard on.

I recognized Red Square and in a moment we had pulled up in front of the old Metropol Hotel. Even at that hour a couple of bored KGB watchers were loitering outside the entrance, smoking those awful Russian cigarettes, mostly a paper tube with a little tobacco at the end, while they waited for someone to tail.

Before I could reach for my wallet, Svetlana had dispatched the driver and we went inside, our presence duly noted by the watchers on the front steps.

The Metropol was Moscow's grand old place with potted plants in the lobby and plaster statuary. When I had first arrived in Moscow, before being assigned the apartment, I'd been put up in a new high rise, modern hotel for a couple of nights. The Metropol, by contrast, had the look of something that had stood since before the Revolution. It showed the dignity and wear of an old dowager like some Paris expatriate Russian countess down on her luck.

The sound of Soviet-style jazz came from the ballroom and I followed Svetlana to it. She paused in the doorway, surveyed the evening crowd of young people. "*Stylagi*," she sniffed.

It was the term for young show-offs, the scions of party members, Russia's current generation of parasitic youth that, in spite of the 1917 revolution and subsequent purges, sprouted up like weeds amidst the ruins of aspirations for a worker's Marxist utopian paradise.

"Not your style?" I asked.

"Let's get that vodka I promised you," Svetlana said, and took my arm. I thought she'd show me the bar, but she led me to the elevator and took me up to the fifth floor.

In the elevator she kissed me on the cheek. "I like you Irvin. You are a nice boy."

Not exactly a boy any more, I thought, mildly insulted, but she looked a few years older than I was, with the desirability of a mature woman who knows what she wants.

In my ignorance I thought that there must be a private party room, sort of a VIP lounge or something. I didn't know the Metropol, being so new in Moscow. I did know that at the hotel where I had first stayed there were some obvious whores who hung around the bar looking for tricks. Moscow had its seamy side.

In the fifth floor hallway an old woman sat at her post, watching. She was like so many babushkas I had seen sitting on front steps and keeping an eye on the streets. It was one way for Soviets to provide full employment for the elderly. The watcher nodded to Svetlana as we passed.

It was no VIP lounge that I in my ignorance and confusion had somehow expected. It was an ordinary hotel room with a double bed, chandelier, bureau with a large mirror, and as Svetlana had promised, a bottle of vodka and two glasses beside it on the varnished table. When had she ordered that? Was that the Moscow equivalent of a minibar?

What was I getting into? I was caught between my lust and my suspicion. I looked up at an air vent near the ceiling and wondered why a wire, much painted over, led up the wall

19

and into the vent.   I pulled out of my thoughts when Svetlana handed me her coat with the fur collar.   "There's a hanger over there."

I hung up Svetlana's coat and when I turned she had already filled a glass and handed it to me.   "Your health, Irvin.   *Nosdvravja.*"

That my last clear memory.   The drink hit me like a hammer.   What followed was a jumble of impressions. Under that dress with the spaghetti straps she wore nothing at all.

When she slid off my trousers and saw my erection she groaned with pleasurable anticipation.   I took a swallow of the vodka and barely had time to set the glass on the bureau in front of that big mirror when she was on me like a tiger.

. . .

I came into semi-consciousness feeling cold and hung over.   I was lying... where? On the pavement.   Where were my clothes? I was in my underwear, shoes, no socks.   I pulled myself up on my knees and tried to clear my head. Where was I?

I was somewhere out on the street, but had no idea where.   Before I could stand up, shivering, I heard the sound of a van's engine and before I could muster a protest two men in uniform lifted me up and shoved me into the back.

In the darkness of the lurching van I could hear other men.   One was singing something out of tune.   Another wretched.   There was an acrid smell of sweat, dirty clothes, and vomit.

It was the drunk wagon, the detail that patrolled the Moscow streets every night, picking up the residue of Russia's alcoholic disease.   The van stopped.   When the doors opened I saw we were outside a precinct.   Several militiamen half dragged their quarry into the building and into the drunk tank where we could sleep it off until we were sober enough to be released, if we were released.

What did they do with drunks? Send them to the Gulag? I remembered the Russian black humor, the guy who arrives at a Soviet prison on a five year sentence and is asked, "What are you in for?" Answer: "Nothing." Reply: "For nothing you get ten years."

The steel door slammed shut. It had a peephole at eye level, and a little door down at the bottom.

There was no toilet, just a bucket, and it was already full of piss and vomit, the contents foul enough to make a healthy man puke.

Someone was kind enough to toss me a smelly blanket that might be full of fleas but offered a modicum of warmth. The steel cots, little more than built-in shelves, no mattresses, were already occupied. I dragged myself as far as I could from the slop bucket and passed out in a corner on the floor.

In the morning the little flap at the bottom of the solid steel door opened and someone slid in a tray with tin cups, a can of luke warm tea, and a battered metal plate with some hunks of black bread.

Grateful that I could speak Russian, I hammered at the door and called the guard. "I'm an American. Will someone please call the American embassy?"

The cover of peephole was slid aside; then a key turned in the lock and the door opened.

The guard was a woman, possibly in her fifties, with hard features that said she had seen it all and didn't like any of it. She looked little better off than the derelicts in the cell and might have been a burnt out whore herself, her looks gone. She had the makings of a mustache and her uniform collar was undone. "Your papers?"

I showed her that I was in my Tee shirt and boxer shorts. "No papers. I've been robbed. They took my clothes." I realized that whoever had dressed me put my under shorts on backwards.

The guard shrugged, an expression that said, 'Tough shit.' "No papers."

"Look," I said, desperate. I had to get out of there. My watch was gone, too, a cheap Timex, but I knew I was supposed to be at work. "I'm an American." I showed her the waist band label of my boxer shorts. "See? Fruit of the Loom. American."

She gave me a quizzical look. "You try to sell me your underwear?"

"No. I'm trying to get you to phone the American embassy. I work at the American library." Maybe if she

21

thought I had diplomatic immunity she'd let me go to avoid an international incident.

"Very good."

That could mean anything, like it was very good that, being a capitalist-fascist, I belonged in jail. She slammed the door, went away, came back, and unlocked.

The grey hallway was dimly lit by a series of lamps, one burnt out, another buzzing because of a bad connection or a failing filament. I followed the guard, the blanket around my shoulders, my shoes untied. At least they hadn't taken away the laces. Sometimes they did that, didn't they? To prevent disconsolate prisoners from hanging themselves?

I was taken into a dreary office that reeked of cigarette smoke. An unhappy-looking policeman—was he a sergeant?--pointed to the old-fashioned telephone on the desk.

I had to ask for a directory, for I didn't know the number. The policeman on duty reluctantly handed over a battered, hard bound, Moscow phone book. I was again glad I knew Russian, for anyone else would have been stymied by the Cyrillic alphabet. I got through. "This is Irwin Glass from the USIA library. I've been mugged and my clothes stolen. Can you send someone down here..." I turned to the duty officer. "Where are we?"

The female guard, who was watching with intense curiosity, told me the name of the precinct and the address.

"I'll need some pants, at least. If someone can get me back to my apartment I can get cleaned up and dressed." Then I remembered. "Crap. They got my key, my wallet, my passport, everything. I'll need someone from security to get into the building."

It took an hour before someone showed up. My escort was an athletic, tough-looking guy I thought I recognized as one of the embassy's marine guards. He brought a set of janitor's coveralls that obviously belonged to someone who weighed a hundred pounds more than I did and was six inches shorter.

"What the hell happened to you?" my escort asked.

"I don't remember."

"Don't tell me. She offered you a glass of vodka and you passed out."

"Does this happen all the time?"

"Let's just say it happens."

I felt like a fool. I was hung over and humiliated. I'd liked Svetlana, but of course I didn't know her from any whore at that hotel. What next? Would I come down with a disease? For all the trouble I was now in, I had at least been laid, or thought I had. It was all a jumble.

"I can't take you to your place. First you'll have to be debriefed."

"Debriefed?"

The marine looked me in the eye. "This is Russia, Mr. Glass. The Cold war is still on, or did you forget?"

In the embassy car I remembered to tie my shoes. I hadn't shaved or washed, felt that the stink of the drunk tank clung to me. I didn't want to see anybody in that condition, but I'd have to go through this humiliation.

I was led to an office on an upper floor of the embassy. Because of the aluminum shield covers on the windows there was no outside light. I thought I remembered the man behind the desk as the security officer who had conducted an orientation session when I and a couple of others had first arrived.

We had been told that life in Moscow was different. This was not Paris or Stockholm and certainly not London. This was a police state. I might not be privy to any state secrets but the Sovs—that was the first time I'd heard the CIA slang—didn't know that and they regarded everyone at the embassy as potential prey. They were always looking for someone they could recruit.

Too bad I, in my excitement at being in Russia, hadn't paid enough attention. I felt like an utter fool. It was like being sent to the principal's office for having pissed my pants.

The man behind the desk squinted at me over the tops of his glasses. "Jesus, Glass, you look like hell. What happened to you?"

I was glad I hadn't seen myself in a mirror. I felt my face and knew I needed a shave. "I don't know exactly."

"The militia said they picked you up half naked on Gorky Street."

"I wasn't naked. I was in my underwear."

"Fair enough. So how did you get there?"

"I have no idea."

Except for a single manila folder, the desk top was bare of any papers. A sign on the safe built into the wall said "Locked." A narrow cot was set up under the shielded window, the blanket rolled military style at the foot end.

"I'm Robert. How about a cup of coffee? I've got some APCs." He shoved a couple of white tablets across the desk. "All purpose capsules. Caffeine and aspirin. Might clear your head."

There was a carafe and a supply of Styrofoam cups on top of a steel filing cabinet. "Robert" poured a cup and set it down in front of me.

Lifting the cup, I realized my hands were shaking. My eyes didn't focus. The coffee wasn't hot. I swallowed a couple of the pills, vaguely hoped they weren't some sort of truth tablet. After last night I didn't know what to expect.

"Sorry we don't have any donuts or pastry. Maybe you can get something in the canteen later. I don't suppose they fed you anything in the drunk tank."

"Black bread and cold tea."

"Know what they served in the Lubyanka?"

The Lubyanka was Moscow's infamous prison.

"No." Did "Robert" know the menu in Moscow's KGB headquarters?

"A bullet in the back of the head." "Robert" was in his forties, a streak of early grey at his temples, heavy brows, possibly of Italian extraction. He'd hung his suit jacket over the back of his chair and loosened his tie. The collar of his white shirt was unbuttoned. The sum of his appearance was that he practically lived in that office. "So tell me how you got in the drunk tank."

"I work at the USIA library. We had a reception for the opening of the art display. I was handing out the drinks."

"Robert" pointed to the manila folder. "I know that. How did you get from the library to the second precinct?"

"One of the visitors to the library invited me out for a drink."

"Who was that?"

"She said her name was Svetlana. Came in with a bald guy in a leather jacket. He left early and I offered to see the lady home."

"Robert" pursed his lips sardonically. "How very gallant of you. Do you think you could recognize that couple? Or were you too drunk?"

"I wasn't drunk."

"You had a couple of shots of bourbon, maybe more."

How did he know that? How many of the visitors were really embassy snoops?

"Well… I had a couple of shots but I wasn't drunk."

"Robert" opened a desk drawer and took out a folder full of photographs. "Sit down. Take a look at these. See if you can identify them."

What I really wanted was to get back to my apartment and have a shave and a shower. I hoped this time the water would be more than luke warm.

The office was stuffy and when I unzipped the top of the borrowed coverall I could smell a residue of musk and residual sex that reminded me of Svetlana. She'd practically devoured me. I wondered, as I tried to remember what had happened, if she was a nymphomaniac or simply starved for sex.

I was sternly interrupted. "Focus, Irwin. Come on. Look at the photographs."

I had hardly slept on that concrete floor among the derelict drunks of Moscow. My head was still hung over from the vodka or whatever had been put into it. My mouth felt like my tongue was swollen and full of cotton. Exhausted, I tried to focus on the pictures. They were all black and white eight by tens.

I'd thought the embassy photographer was taking shots for a news release or the newsletter. Now it was obvious the pictures were a record of attendance, not just for a news report. Someone must have been up half the night developing and printing those in the embassy darkroom.

"That's Oblomov, the Minister of Culture. The guy with the medals on his chest is probably his assistant."

Except for a shot of the ambassador toasting minister Oblomov, I didn't recognize any of the others. There was Susan Lutz, looking very much the hostess in that dress. If she'd worn pearls or diamond earrings she's have looked like royalty. "Oh, that's the bald guy and Svetlana." They'd been caught as they entered the library. The bald man hadn't opened the door for her, but entered first, she trailing behind like a dog on a leash.

"Did you speak to them?"

"I offered drinks. I remember the man refused, which I thought kind of odd. The Russians couldn't wait to sample that bourbon."

"Robert" took the picture of the bald man and tapped it. "This is Putinsky, a KGB officer."

"What about Svetlana?"

"Robert" wasn't sure. "We don't know her but I'll find out. Putinsky might have brought her along as bait. "So you left with her. Then what?"

"She took me up to a room in the Metropol for a drink."

"And you got laid, right?"

Feeling foolish, like a kid caught in the bathroom with dirty pictures, I nodded.

"Weren't you warned about the honey pot?"

"Honey pot? We only offered cheese and crackers."

"Don't be dense, Glass. The honey pot is an old ploy. Get you into bed for sex and get you to reveal state secrets."

Besides feeling groggy and hung over I felt stupid. "I don't know any state secrets."

"Robert" shook his head. "Where do they find these guys?" he muttered. "That's for you to know and them to find out."

"I guess so. I didn't tell Svetlana, or whatever her name is, anything."

"Well I hope the sex was worth it, Glass. Cost you your suit, your passport, the key to your apartment, and your reputation. Susan Lutz is convinced you are a hopeless drunk and can't wait to see you fired and on your way back to the States."

"Oh, shit."

"Yes.   And by now the KGB have used your key, searched your apartment and helped themselves to your blue jeans and anything else they fancy.   Now that we've got you back I'll have your key code changed.   You'll get a new entrance key and we'll have to issue you a new passport.   I have to warn you.   It will only be valid for return to the United States.   You won't be able to travel with it.   You are now an official security risk, a known fuck up."

"Am I fired?"

"Not yet.   Just take this as a warning.   Don't get seduced by KGB women or you'll be fucked in more ways than one."

"Yes, sir."

"Now I'll have one of the crew take you back to your place.   We'll have to screen the place for bugs again."

I stammered, "It won't happen again." I'd hardly got to Moscow and I was already on the verge of being sent home in disgrace.

As I went out the door "Robert" called after me.   "If you see Putinsky again, stay away from him.   He's poison."

I couldn't wait to get out of the building, I felt so ashamed of myself.   This time I was accompanied by two technicians who carried their spook tools.   They were young, one slender, the other with a pizza and beer belly, but they were all business, didn't talk.

As soon as they let themselves into my place they got to work.   They were systematic, working their way around the apartment inch by inch while I stood in the middle of the single room, stunned, in shock.

As "Robert" had guessed, someone had been in the tiny apartment.   My clothes, fortunately, were still in the armoire, though someone had swiped my newest jockey shorts from my underwear drawer.   Would they be sold or kept as a souvenir? The letters I had saved from my parents in Ocala had been in a drawer, bundled with a rubber band, but the rubber band was gone.   The letters had probably been photographed.

The KGB snoops had probably photographed every page of my address book, so would know where my parents

27

lived, all of my near relatives, my friends from graduate school. That was private stuff I didn't share with anyone.

The photo of my parents by their Florida swimming pool had been taken out of its frame. Maybe the snoops had thought something was hidden behind it. More than ever, I felt violated, my personal space no longer my own.

My Yashika 35 millimeter camera was in its leather case, but when I took it out to inspect it I discovered the exposure counter was at zero. The KGB had taken the exposed film. What would they find when they developed it? Just some tourist-type pictures, Red Square, pictures I'd taken when Susan took me on a tour of the Kremlin.

We had visited Lenin's tomb, saw the glass coffin with the revolutionary leader, and learned that Stalin had been in the tomb, too, but after his cruelty to his own people had been exposed, his body had been removed. In the end, even Stalin had been purged. A nice irony, that.

I was relieved to find that my stash of a few Rubles and my savings of three hundred dollars in US currency was still in the envelope with my socks. I might not have my wallet, but I still had enough Russian money for the bus to get back to the library.

The Soviets had wasted no time. The sniffer team found three electronic bugs. Unscrewing a vent, they even found a hidden camera. Finally, they packed up their gear.

"You can use the bathroom now. You can leave the building but you can't get back in until you're issued a new key."

"Thanks. Do you guys have to do this all the time?"

The sniffer with the belly shrugged. "It's like a game of hide and seek. This is a war zone, after all."

His partner added, "At least they're not shooting."

"Thanks a lot." I'd hoped that my stint in Russia would be exciting fun not Spy versus Spy, like the cartoon in *Mad Magazine*.

As the team went out the door the tall one added, "Just keep out of trouble. If things get too serious you might conveniently fall out of the window or into the Moscow River. It happens."

The door shut behind them.

I slipped out of the borrowed coverall and my underwear. Hoping there were no other hidden cameras, I gave the finger to the vent that the sniffer team had replaced, and took a shower.

Looking back, I did remember that wire leading up the wall to the vent in the Metropol hotel room. Svetlana must have known it was there. After all, she was a Soviet. She'd been with Putinsky of the KGB. She must have known our coupling had been photographed or filmed.

Standing before the bathroom mirror while I waited for the water to run warm, I looked at my reflection. I looked awful, like I'd, well, slept on the floor of a Moscow drunk tank. What were those marks on my chest, my neck? Lipstick? She'd kissed me.

That was odd. I had no personal experience, but I'd heard that whores don't kiss. Kissing was for someone they cared about, not some john who paid cash.

Why the hell had she done it? Gone with me? Was that her job? Had that Putinsky ordered her to do the honey pot thing? What was their relationship? She'd said he was from the office, but that might have been just a dodge.

I wished I could remember what had happened after that glass of vodka. I did have a clear image of her standing naked. She looked vulnerable even though she was clearly in control.

Did she kiss me because she was aroused or were her embraces an act of defiance for the camera I was now sure had been observing?

Now that the embassy sweepers had detected a camera, I realized the Metropol hotel room must have had a camera, too. Was that mirror over the bureau a one way window? Some peeping tom probably was watching and getting his own jollies off while Svetlana and I did the dirty.

If I'd known that I'd have opted out right away. I'm no exhibitionist. Sex is a private thing. I had no aspirations for being a porn star. If anything, I was shy, not a womanizer, not always hitting on women. I had no pick up lines for bars and seldom drank.

I felt stupid. I was just a fall guy, a chump, a victim.

A victim of what? Of Svetlana? The KGB? Or was I betrayed by my own naivete and lust? There was nothing as stupid as an erect penis.

I swore I'd never take another drink of vodka.

. . .

What the hell time was it? I missed my digital Timex, but remembered I had a keepsake, an old analog watch with a leather strap and a cracked crystal. It was still in my bureau, had been overlooked by the Soviet burglars or not worth stealing. I wound it, but without a clock didn't know what time to set it at. I left the apartment as soon as I could pull myself together.

I still felt hammered. What a night! Hung over and sleepless. It was difficult to face Susan Lutz when I arrived, late, at the library. The vestiges of the reception the night before had been removed. The shot glasses and empty bourbon bottles were gone.

Susan, unpacking a box of new books, gave me a knowing look. "I hear you spent the night in the drunk tank."

I gave her an open hand gesture of helplessness and near supplication. "News travels fast." I must be a subject of gossip in all the embassy hallways. It was a closed community. Though divided by function and Government Service rank, the marine guards tending to hang out with each other, and so on, the low level clerks crossed department lines, sharing gossip during coffee breaks.

The library staff, located a few blocks away, was somewhat out of the loop, but Susan Lutz had been there a year, had her contacts. She had probably reported when I didn't show up for work on time. That had to be how she found out. "I was drugged. They say to never turn your back on your drink in case someone puts something into it."

Susan agreed. "I thought that was a precaution against date rape."

"I guess there's more than one way to be violated."

"So? Was it worth it?" She was asking me about sex. Might have been because she wanted to hear a hot story, second hand titillation she could share with others, or was it her way of showing her superiority? She hadn't been made a fool of. I had.

"I don't want to talk about it." I felt ashamed of myself. I didn't want to be interrogated by Susan Lutz. How had the word gotten out? The driver who picked me up at the police station wasn't sworn to secrecy. Damn. No doubt my condition in my underwear with that filthy prison blanket around my shoulders had been a pitiful sight.

"Robert" had the story. "Robert" wouldn't gossip around the embassy offices, though I was certain that at the next briefing for newcomers my failure would be used as an example of what not to do in Moscow, a story without revealing my name. I hoped.

I didn't look forward to facing knowing looks and whispers in the embassy hallways. Best to avoid them, shut up, stonewall, and hope people forgot about it. Considering the large Moscow staff, there was bound to be some fresh gossip soon to push my own misadventure into the background.

Susan let me leave early enough to go back to the embassy, return the coveralls, and be issued a new door key. The replacement passport was not yet ready. To be without ID papers which you were supposed to have on your person at all times was not good. You might be stopped at any time by the ever-patrolling Moscow militia, have to give explanations and excuses and maybe be hauled in to the nearest precinct for your identity to be verified. Or try to bluff your way through, pretend not to understand Russian, say you were a tourist and that Intourist had your passport. One could gamble on the militiamen's own fears of causing trouble in a hierarchy where anyone could be denounced.

For the next two days my life returned to normal. I thought, I hoped, it was all over. I took the same crowded bus to the library, conscious that I was clearly a foreigner. I pretended not to know Russian so I could eavesdrop and hear the comments of other passengers. Some viewed me with curiosity, others with suspicion. Russians who were sensitive to the dangers of association with foreigners avoided me. Perhaps those remembered the days of the Moscow purges when the slightest suspicion could get you sent to the

Gulag. A few regulars recognized me and had lost interest. Sometimes a student would speak to me, wanting to practice their English, but they were often stuck after the first couple of textbook sentences.

I was used to checking the street when I left the apartment to see if I could spot any watchers. It was like a game of hide and seek or gotcha. The third morning after the hotel incident, when I left the apartment to walk to the bus stop a black Volga sedan was idling at the curb. The door opened and a man in a shabby overcoat got out, carrying a package wrapped in brown paper and tied with coarse string.

"This for you," the man said in heavily accented English.

"What?" I asked, taking the bundle, but the man had slipped quickly back into the car and drove off before I could say thanks.

The parcel wasn't heavy, felt like a bundle of laundry. I tore open a corner and peeked at the contents. I recognized the material. It was my suit.

I didn't want to open the package on the street or on the bus, so waited until I got to the American library.

Susan Lutz gave me the once over as I came in. She was always checking my choice of clothes, as if she were my mother or my wife. The white shirt and tie were obligatory. She apparently approved of my sport coat and slacks. She asked, "What's the package?"

"Don't know," I said, and went back into the office to open it. I knew where Susan stashed her scissors. I hoped the parcel wouldn't explode when I cut the string.

As I suspected, it was my suit. Not only that, but my shirt had been laundered and ironed, folded neatly with my best necktie. It was a relief to get it back, but it was also a surprise. An American suit might fetch a good price on the street, maybe not as much as the blue jeans coveted by the *Stylagi*, but a prize nevertheless. Someone had kept my American flag lapel pin as a souvenir. Susan had a supply of those.

It didn't make sense. If I was meant to be robbed, I'd wake up in the hotel room with no money and no papers. That was what whores wanted, wasn't it? Svetlana wouldn't have taken my clothes and then returned them. Svetlana couldn't have carried me bodily out of the hotel, past the old lady guarding the hallway and the watchers outside the entrance—if they still hung around at that hour—and into a car. It hadn't been Svetlana who dropped me like garbage on the Gorky Street sidewalk. She'd need to have help.

Something was going on that didn't fit the pattern "Robert" described.

Whoever had carried me out of the hotel could as easily have dropped me in the Moscow River, as I'd been warned. I hadn't done anything to deserve that, but being humiliated and left among the drunks was an act of what? Revenge? Whose?

Maybe it was just to show me that I was garbage, an exhibition of power. I hadn't been beaten up, either. Why not? Maybe humiliating me was enough. I felt I was being jerked around like a doll on a string.

I checked the pants pockets of the suit. My wallet wasn't there. Nor was my passport which I usually carried zipped in the jacket inside pocket. But there was something in there, a piece of folded paper.

It was a typed note in Russian. "My dear Irwin. I am sorry they took your clothes, but thanks God I am able to return them. I did not trust anyone with your money or your passport. I will return them if you will join me for dinner at the Bolshoi restaurant at seven o'clock tonight. Your Svetlana."

My Svetlana? The note was not signed, just typed. It could have been written by anybody. Was it another trap? Did it really come from Svetlana? Well, I'd better go, if I expected to get my passport and wallet back, with or without the few rubles. And what about my Timex watch? I'd better let "Robert" know, just in case.

The library did not possess one of those precious and scarce Moscow phone books like the one I'd seen at the police precinct. The embassy number was on a card in the library office. I dialed the switch board, asked to be directed to "Robert."

The operator didn't know any Robert. Which Robert?

"This is Irwin Glass at the USIA library.   I was debriefed by a guy who called himself Robert."

"Oh."

I was connected, but aware that all the phones were tapped.   How should I phrase this in case some Sov was listening in? "This is Irwin Glass.   Surprise, surprise, I've got my suit back, but not my wallet or passport.   Svetlana's invited me to dinner tonight at the Bolshoi restaurant to return them.   Seven o'clock.   Want to come along and meet her?" Some back-up would help.   Maybe if "Robert" saw her he'd be convinced she was OK.   Wishful thinking.

"What did she do, phone you?"

"No.   My clothes were returned.   I found a typed note in the pocket of my suit."

"The Bolshoi at seven?"

"Right."

"I'm not going to get involved in your romance, Glass. But go ahead and keep the date."

"Well, I'm not sure..." What if it was another trap?

"You'll be all right.   I'll see to it."

Did that mean the embassy would send someone to keep a discreet eye on me? "Robert" had told me I was a security risk.   Maybe from now on, besides being followed everywhere by KGB watchers, I'd be trailing a CIA spook as well, a little parade like the Pied Piper, even if all I was doing was standing in line to buy a loaf of bread.

One thing certain, I wasn't going to drink anything unless it was a bottle of sparkling lemonade that I opened myself.

I had never been to the Bolshoi restaurant.   When I hung up the phone I asked Susan.   "You know the Bolshoi restaurant?"

She did.   "It's a very fancy place near the Revolution metro station." She'd overheard my conversation.   "You're going to see your Svetlana again?"

I shrugged. *Damn that woman.   She'd be gossiping with all the embassy clerks about my love life and snickering that I was tossed out in my underwear.* "She's going to return my passport."

Susan gave me a knowing look. Clearly I had risen in her estimation from being a mere flunky to some sort of womanizer. "You must be hot stuff, Irwin."

"Not me. I think she drugged me and took my money."

"Oh? And took your clothes, dumped you in the street, then returned the clothes. Maybe she has a guilty conscience."

I sighed. I didn't want to speculate about this stuff, especially not with Susan Lutz. She was not my friend. She was my boss, a boss who would never have hired me in the first place. Anything I told her might turn up in a negative personnel report. What she wanted was someone with a degree in library science.

"I don't know the woman," I said. "I was only going to see her home. She offered me a drink. That's all."

Susan laughed. It was not a kind laugh. It was more of a sardonic snort. "And then offered to have your suit cleaned and pressed? You are really something, Irwin. Well, you go have that dinner and give me a full report."

What did she want? A news release for the daily scuttlebutt? No way.

In spite of the night in the drunk tank, I could not get out of my mind that flash of memory of Svetlana naked. There was another flash… of Svetlana straddling me on the bed, riding me like a horse. Had she been putting on a show for the watchers or enjoying herself? Maybe both. Maybe more. People didn't do things for only one reason. Motivations were complicated.

I had to admit my own motives were complicated, too. I needed my passport and wallet. I wanted to see her again if for nothing more than an explanation. Face to face I might understand her motivation. "My dear Irwin" she had written. Was that a Russian convention, or a genuine indication of affection? One might write "Dear Sir," but it was not a statement of endearment.

As for dinner at the Bloshoi? I hoped it wasn't too expensive. Some of those places were restricted for Russia's power elite like the grocery stores for party members. From what I gathered already, Russia might be billed as the workers' paradise, but no worker ever got into a place like that except to scrub the floors or bus the tables.

After work I returned to the apartment carrying the suit in the remains of the brown paper wrapping. I put it on after checking all the pockets in case there might be other notes or clues to what had happened. Then I studied my tourist map of Moscow to see the best route to the Revolution metro station.

It was already dark and chilly. In an American city I might be afraid of muggers, but in Moscow, with all the secret police hanging around, I in effect had bodyguards who saw everything. It was an invitation to paranoia if you couldn't dismiss the watchers as part of the scenery.

The street lights came on early. Winter would be closing in soon with the bitter cold that defeated the German army in World War II. My first week in town I had bought a Russian winter jacket with a collar of fake fur at the famous Gum department store. To give the standard hat a feature to distinguish it from others, I pinned a souvenir Russian red star to the front of it. Unfortunately the coat wouldn't fit over my suit jacket. In the future if I were going out dressed for a party I would need an overcoat.

Leaving the apartment, I checked as usual for watchers, saw none, and walked to the nearest metro station. I felt conspicuous. Even if I had been wearing that Russian jacket, I knew from my studies of international relations that Americans walked funny. Americans had aimlessness to their gait. Unlike Europeans, they were used to making eye contact with strangers. Germans tended to march. Russians, on the other hand, plodded along, studiously avoiding others.

I had no difficulty finding the Bolshoi restaurant. It was on the second floor of a commercial building. I hesitated at the entrance, aware that I had no coat to check. I was early. It was only twenty minutes to seven.

The gate keeper, a man dressed in an impeccable, black suit and bow tie, spotted me immediately as an American who didn't belong, perhaps a tourist, and addressed me in stilted, British English. "Good evening, sir. Can I help you?"

I preferred Russian. "I'm expecting someone." *Damn, I didn't know Svetlana's last name. What could I say? Svetlana was a common name.* "Maybe you have a reservation for an Irwin Glass?"

The gate keeper checked a handwritten list. "Sorry, sir."

"Maybe you can find me a quiet table for two."

"Will that be for dinner?" He had a menu ready.

"Eventually."

It was a high class place. Table cloths, wine glasses, tableware set for several courses. There was even a three piece orchestra. Someone was playing a piano. The head waiter guided me to a table between a potted palm and an erotic statue of a comely girl only partially draped. How appropriate, I thought, for a tryst with the svelte Svetlana.

With my back to the wall, I studied the room, wondering where Svetlana was. She was already late, but I didn't know how punctual a person she was. After all, I didn't know her. We had hardly spoken. It was one of those incendiary things, one look and flames. It was not love at first sight, but the attraction was unmistakable, at least from my side. She had that look that turned me on. Maybe it was her perfume, some packaged pheromone, love potion in a small bottle. I didn't wear any scents other than Old Spice deodorant. I wasn't egotistical enough to think my looks knocked women dead. She had probably been ordered to seduce me. It was all a mystery.

I wondered, too, if "Robert" would show up to keep an eye on me. I saw no one I recognized, no one in the restaurant who looked like an American. A group of three businessmen were working their way through several bottles of wine. An apparatchik with a much younger woman was showing off, trying to impress his date. I wondered if she might be a Moscow call girl imported from one of the satellite countries, Poland or Rumania.

For a moment I half expected Susan Lutz to show up to spy on me, but she wasn't that brazen. She'd wait until I got to work the next day and try to winkle information out of me. Didn't Lutz know it wasn't gentlemanly for a man to kiss and tell? I knew women gossiped in the ladies' room. Men seldom spoke in toilets. Even though the embassy women might speculate about how I ended up on the sidewalk of Moscow in my jockey shorts, I wasn't going to feed their curiosity.

Killing time, I studied the menu. It was pretty expensive. The only item I recognized on it was beef stroganoff. I had turned to the wine list and was studying it when someone sat down at my table. I looked up, startled.

It wasn't Svetlana. It was Putinsky, the bald man who had shown up with her at the library reception. No leather jacket this time.

He spoke English with an accent partly British, partly Russian. "May I join you, Mr. Glass?"

I tried to pretend I didn't know who he was, then feigned a recollection. "You were at the library reception, weren't you? We weren't introduced, but I remember you didn't want to try our sour mash bourbon."

"I do not touch alcohol."

I nodded. "After that night I'm a teetotaler myself."

"Teetotaler?" Putinsky didn't know the word.

"Not a drinker. I've sworn off."

Putinsky agreed. "A wise choice. Excuse me. I'm Vladimir."

"That would be Vlady to your friends?"

Putinsky actually laughed, an embarrassed smile that was restrained enough not to show his teeth or open his mouth. He was putting on the charm. "Only to my mother."

I got down to business. "I was supposed to meet your friend Svetlana here. She should be here any minute."

Putinsky, or Vladimir as he was calling himself, tilted his bald head in a gesture of regret. "Svetlana can't come. She is what you call..." He searched for the English word. "Indisposed."

"She was supposed to return my passport."

"Ah, yes. Well, that I have for you." Putinsky reached under his chair. He was carrying a well worn leather briefcase, the kind I had seen on the bus. Russian workers didn't carry lunch pails like Americans. They carried briefcases. A briefcase could hold bottles of beer, sandwiches, a change of shoes, anything, even an AK47 with a folding stock.

Opening the catch, Putinsky took out my green American passport and my wallet. "This is yours, too."

Grateful, I took possession. I opened my passport to inspect it. It didn't appear to be tampered with. The stamped Soviet visa was as before. What would Putinsky and the KGB do with my passport? Extract the personal information? Make some infrared mark to alert Russian customs and border guards? The world of secret police and espionage was totally foreign to me. Maybe the secret police would use my identification papers to make some counterfeits.

I would check the contents of the wallet later. It wouldn't do to appear too suspicious. I just hoped Svetlana, or whoever, had left me some rubles.

"Alright?" Putinsky asked.

I nodded. "What about my wrist watch?"

"Someone must have kept it as a souvenir," Putinsky said, but he didn't put the briefcase away.

"Or maybe a trophy?"

Putinsky smiled and joked, "Who can you trust nowadays?"

I remembered that a pair of my jocky shorts had been taken from the apartment. "Then I guess we're done here," I said, ready to leave. "Robert" had said Putinsky was poison, a KGB officer. Just being at the same table made me uncomfortable.

"Oh, no, Irwin. You can at least stay for dinner as my guest. Order anything you like. I do not want to appear unfriendly."

"Are you the one who dumped me in the street? That wasn't very friendly."

A guileless response. "Is that what happened to you?"

"I think you know very well."

"What do you know, Irwin Glass?"

I kept my hands on the table cloth. "I know only never to drink any more vodka and not to accept drinks from beautiful, strange women."

"Well, it takes only one time." Putinsky gave me a hollow laugh, man to man. "Let's say you are not a virgin any more."

I felt himself blushing. "I wasn't that."

Putinsky opened the briefcase again. "What do you think of these, Irwin Glass?"

Putinsky extracted half a dozen photographs.

I already knew what to expect. I was alerted by the bugs and the camera the sniffer crew had found in my apartment. I remembered the wired air vent in the Metropol hotel, the big mirror which was probably one way glass. This was Moscow, and there I was, photographed in all my naked glory with Svetlana looking not at me but right at the hidden camera.

It was not as I remembered it, but then, I hardly remembered anything, being under whatever influence. "Too bad I was half snookered. This looks like fun."

"Snookered?"

"Potted. Out of it. She drugged me, didn't she?"

Putinsky or Vladimir didn't want a lesson in American slang. "What matters, Irwin, is what might happen if your superiors at the American embassy saw these. Or your boss, Miss Lutz."

"I think my boss would have a lot of fun passing around some dirty pictures."

Putinsky raised his almost hairless eyebrows. "Oh? I would like to learn more about your Miss Lutz."

"Why is that?"

"We like to know everything we can about everyone."

"She's just a librarian. I am only her assistant."

Putinsky shook his head. "You are more important than that, my dear Irwin."

My dear Irwin? That's what the note said. Maybe Putinsky wrote it himself. "I don't think so." I said, feeling very much the mouse being toyed with by the cat before the final bite to the neck.

Putinsky changed the subject. "How much do you earn as an assistant?"

"I'm only a GS7, but I get a housing allowance and extra pay because Moscow is considered a hardship post."

Putinsky was genuinely offended. "Moscow a hardship post? But everyone in the Soviet Union wants to live in

Moscow. That's why we must restrict movement to the city. Otherwise we would be overwhelmed by immigrants."

"That's not how our government sees it." I tried to make light of the subject. "Maybe because there's no baseball or basketball here."

Putinsky shook his head. "Back to my point, Irwin. I think you could use some extra money, yes? What you call under the table. No tax."

"For what?"

"You could write for me a little something about your boss Miss Lutz. Her habits, her interests, if she is a Republican or a Democrat, things like that."

"You're building a dossier on Susan Lutz?" It seemed ludicrous, but who knew what went on in the mind of the KGB?

"We're interested in everyone," Putinsky said. "I'll pay you a hundred dollars, US money. I can even have someone put it in a bank account for you in Washington, DC. A little nest egg when you go back to America."

I was inclined to say no at once, but thought about "Robert." "Robert" had said I was a security risk, having been dumb enough to fall into the honey pot. Maybe if I found out something about Putinsky and his motives I might redeem myself. "I'd have to think about that." What was Putinsky up to? Seemed innocuous enough, a paragraph or two about Susan Lutz. Maybe I could make something up that was outrageous that couldn't do anyone any damage.

Putinsky turned one of the photographs over and wrote a number on the back. "The photographs are for you, just a souvenir of your hot night with Svetlana, a reminder of what might happen if these somehow found their way to your personnel director. I have the negatives, of course. I'm writing my private phone number here. Call me in a day or two when you have Miss Lutz's report and I will arrange to meet you and pay you for your trouble."

My hands were trembling when I lifted them from the white tablecloth to take possession of the six photos.

"I think you will want an envelope for those," Putinsky said. "People in the metro are too curious." He extracted an envelope of poor quality paper.

I put the photos away.

Putinsky dropped his conspiratorial demeanor. "Very good. Now that's settled. Enough of business. I know you do not drink, but have you tasted our wonderful red caviar?"

I had no appetite. My stomach was churning from the anxiety of meeting with this dangerous KGB officer. I realized, suddenly, that the Bolshoi was probably not the sort of place Putinsky frequented, either, and that the man was on an expense account. To refuse dinner would have denied Putinsky the luxury of an evening out at government expense. In that sense, for me to accept made the dinner my treat. Turning the tables, I said, "Dinner. Yes. Anything you like," and winked. We were now co-conspirators. Who was recruiting who?

The Russian red caviar on rich, white bread flavored with coriander and slathered with butter was delicious. The red caviar, unlike the black, salty stuff from Sturgeon, was salmon roe cured in salt. The golden fish eggs popped under my tongue like nectar. The beef in the main course was tender, done to perfection, though the vegetables were overcooked, on the edge of mush.

For dessert I chose a small dish of ice cream to clear my pallet.

The waiter, a grey-haired man who looked like he might be one of the few intact World War II Russian veterans, brought the bill. Putinsky showed some ID, and signed it, no cash. When the waiter saw Putinsky's identification he was visible shaken.

Fear was an ingredient inescapable in a police state.

In the United States I'd have offered to pay the tip, but I knew service was included in the bill. "Thanks for the meal," I said when I felt it was not too early to make my escape. Someone else might have stayed for a cognac. Neither of us drank, each for our own reasons.

"You can find your way back to your apartment on your own?"

"Sure." I realized that though Putinsky probably had his own car and driver, it would be imprudent to be dropped off in front of the US Embassy personnel's quarters by the KGB.

I could hardly wait to get out of the restaurant. Outside, on the dark Moscow streets, every passerby seemed suspicious. Which were the watchers? Had "Robert" sent some to spy on me the whole evening?

It was too bad Svetlana hadn't come. I wanted to see her and get an explanation. It would have been an awkward conversation. After a night of intimacy, strangers might feel embarrassed, like "Who are you" and "What have I done?" Would she be ashamed? Or was sex with me just another trick and I another john?

It was a one night stand and I was not someone for one night stands. My father had warned me of consequences. The encounter with Svetlana was a fluke. I did not make a habit of casual or promiscuous sex, not that I had that much opportunity. I was not promiscuous, not one of those tomcats always on the prowl. I imagined that some people got together just for sex and preferred to make no connection afterwards. It was just sexual gratification, no commitments, no emotional investment. Not my style.

In my case, not being a tomcat, I felt attached. I'd been smitten by the French look of her mouth, the fragrance of her perfume, the look in her eyes. Was it love at first sight, that romantic cliché? Or lust as first look? I wanted to believe that Svetlana didn't get me into bed just because she was ordered by Putinsky. It might be wishful thinking; I was just a chump, after all. I should forget the whole thing as a meaningless quickie.

Of course, I couldn't. Putinsky and his six photographs meant that I would never forget. The images of sex were already burned into my memory. I had blundered and now I was in the KGB net.

I lay in bed, listening to that ineffectual radiator making mysterious noises. I studied the photographs and wondered what to do next. It took a long time to fall asleep.

Early the next morning I left the apartment and instead of taking the bus to the library went directly to the US Embassy. The offices were not yet open. I had to show ID in order to pass the marine guard. In the hallways a few early birds were clutching their morning cups of coffee and stared at me like they knew who I was, the guy who'd been in the drunk tank. I went upstairs to "Robert's" office.

"Robert" was already at his desk, drinking coffee and smoking Marlboros. Several butts were in the ash tray. He was obviously a chain smoker. "Robert" looked over the tops of his glasses. "I expected you. How was your dinner with Putinsky?"

"So you know Svetlana didn't show up."

"I couldn't let you walk into the spider's nest alone."

"Then you know Putinsky gave me these." I sat down in the visitor's chair and shoved the envelope with the photos across the desk.

"Robert" took out the pictures and studied them. "Irwin, Irwin, you naughty boy."

"Not lucky?"

"Robert" laughed. "That, too. Mind if I keep these?"

I did mind. "Why don't you make yourself a set for your files? There's a phone number on the back of one. Putinsky's number."

"Ah. What's he want? What's his offer?"

I explained.

"Robert" was thoughtful. "Interesting. Go ahead and do a couple of paragraphs about Susan Lutz, but let me see them before you make a delivery. I want to know everything that goes on between you and Putinsky. We can feed him some disinformation, see if we can turn him."

"Turn him?"

"Get him to work for us."

My chest felt tight. When I swallowed I could feel the aftertaste of my breakfast. I shouldn't have wolfed down those scrambled eggs in my haste to make an early departure.

What did they call it? Double agent? Pretending to work for one spy agency while actually working for another, and trusted by neither?

This is not what I had in mind when I majored in International Relations. Intercultural relations were my speed, not flirting with the Soviet Secret Police. "I don't know if I can do that."

"Robert" snubbed out his cigarette. "You can do it, Glass. Just act normally. Don't start walking around like you're overcome with guilt and suspicion."

"But I am overcome with guilt and suspicion."

"Robert" clearly was enjoying this. What had looked at first like just another dumb employee getting drunk and thrown in the tank with some Russian alcoholics was developing into a significant operation. "Just relax, Glass. Don't drink any more vodka. Or anything else."

"Coffee, just coffee from now on." I got up from the chair. "I'll write a couple of paragraphs about Susan Lutz and bring them to you. And you'll give me back the photos."

"And don't mention this on the telephone."

"Understood." I gave "Robert" a mock salute.

"And don't write your mother or anyone else about your little escapade with Svetlana. Not even in the pouch mail."

When would I have shared this kind of stuff with my mother? Maybe "Robert's" relationship with his own parents was more open than my own. In fact, I had no one to share adventures with. I hadn't made any friends in Moscow. The newbies I'd had flown in with from Washington and sat with during the orientation sessions had all gone their separate ways. My only confidante was "Robert" and I didn't even know his real name.

I returned to the USIA library, arriving just as Susan was opening up. "You're early," she said with some surprise.

"Making up for the other morning."

Trying to be casual, I started asking questions for information I could put in my report for Putinsky. I learned that Susan had a bachelor's degree from CCNY, City College of New York, and a Masters in Library Science from Columbia. Her father was an art dealer in Manhattan and sometimes did restoration of damaged paintings. Her mother was a docent at the Metropolitan.

That sort of information seemed harmless enough. I wondered if Putinsky wanted a report in Russian or in English. The library didn't have a Cyrillic typewriter. I didn't have any typewriter at all. Though the embassy was going over to computers and word processors, I didn't know how to use those. I would have to write it all out in longhand.

I chose to prepare the report for Putinsky in Russian. If Susan saw it she would not know what it was.

When she saw me writing she asked, "What's that, a love letter?"

So she was still interested in my liaison with Svetlana. "In a manner of speaking."

Her reaction was simply arched eyebrows. Since, so far as I knew, she had no love life of her own she wanted to feed on mine. That supposition might be the sort of thing Putinsky wanted. Maybe he'd have someone try to seduce her, the male version of the honey pot, make Susan Lutz the mistress of some dashing KGB operative.

I finished the report during coffee break and at lunch took it to the embassy.

"Robert" was in the canteen having a hamburger and a Coke. He was sitting alone. It was a noisy place, the clatter of plates and cutlery, the hubbub of voices, occasional laughter.

Hoping no one recognized me as the jerk who had been picked up drunk in his underwear, I handed over the hand written report on Susan Lutz. "You want this typed?"

"Robert" puzzled over it. Apparently he knew Russian, too. "Would it be normal for you to type?"

"We don't have a Cyrillic machine."

"Then keep it like this. Your Russian is pretty good. I like the occasional misspelled word."

"That wasn't intentional."

"It wouldn't do for you to hand Putinsky a perfect report. He'd think it was done by a professional. I'll make a Xerox copy. Come up to the office after work and I'll return the photos. Then you can phone your contact and set up a meeting."

"OK."

"And don't visit me here in the canteen." "Robert" made a gesture with his eyes to the burger bar. A Russian woman in a soiled white coat was serving up the sandwiches. "We never know if there's a mole here."

"A mole?"

"You are a babe in the woods, aren't you, Glass? We try to vet the Russian employees, but we never can be sure of them. There's always the possibility that the opposition will threaten to imprison their family members if our staff don't cooperate. We have to burn our carbons and leave nothing on the desk at the end of the day."

The library didn't have that need for security. Susan didn't mind of someone stole a book. The purpose of the library was to disseminate information about America. But she did keep the spare light bulbs under lock and key. "I don't think I could live like that," Irwin said.

"You will have to, Glass. This is Moscow."

Have to? No wonder this was a hardship post. Lack of baseball had nothing to do with it.

After work I picked up the original of my report on Susan Lutz and the photographs. "Robert" was satisfied with the report. It was, he said, harmless. I thought I was safe, since what I had written had been cleared for release. Then I went to the nearest Metro station to find a public telephone. I rode down a long escalator into the palatial depths. The tile walls and décor were relics of the Stalinist days, heavy handed Soviet art, gilded and imperial, to give the workers of the world the feeling that they were living in grand style under a frieze depicting members of the politburo. One of the faces in the tile had been removed. When Stalin purged you, he even took your picture off the Metro walls.

Aware that I was spotted by the usual plain clothes watcher at the station, I found a bank of public telephones. The watcher took another phone booth in the bank, kept a suspicious eye on me, and was probably notifying the exchange to tap all the calls.

I dialed Putinsky's number. I held the receiver tight to my ear and covered the other to muffle the scream of the wheels of the passing subway. Someone picked up at the other end. I said, "I have the report for Vladimir."

I did not recognize the voice.

"Go to the Heroes of the Revolution workingman's café at ten past seven. Vladimir will meet you."

I was given the address.

For this meeting I wore the Russian jacket I'd bought at Gum. Though winter had not quite come on I even put on the fake fur hat with ear flaps and the red star souvenir pin.

In order to create boulevards out of the rabbit warren of streets in old Moscow entire blocks had been torn out, leaving paths for streets so wide that only an athletic broken field runner could cross without being wiped out by some speeding car. The workingman's café was on an unimproved side street filled with potholes and going back to gravel. The dilapidated buildings were pre-revolution, unpainted, the clapboard siding checked and in some places falling off. The Heroes of the Revolution café was not in much better shape. In spite of the grandiose name, the sign over the stained door said simply "food."

I was early, so walked up and down the street. My back-up wristwatch with the cracked crystal seemed to be losing time. As soon as I could I'd stop in at the commissary, or maybe shop at GUM for a genuine Soviet watch. They were good at making knockoffs that looked great, but might not work very well. In making their work quotas, Russians skimped on quality.

It was like that famous sham that had been engineered for who was it? Czar Nicholas? Katherine the Great? Who made a trip down the river and saw happy villagers cavorting, except from one passed village to the next didn't notice that it was the same dancers? The Russians had spiffed up the Moscow boulevards and public buildings foreign tourists might see, but they had skipped the side street with the Revolution Café.

What a dump. I hoped I was on time as I pushed open the battered door and went inside. The café smelled like rancid fat and looked like a good place to contract food poisoning.

It was a quiet time of day or maybe even the Russians wouldn't eat there. A couple of old men in shabby clothes were playing dominos. That was it except for a table at the back.

Putinsky, again in his leather jacket, was sitting with a cup of coffee and his back to the wall. He gave me a nod of recognition. "What have you got for me?"

I sat down at the table and noticed that it was uneven and wobbled. Was one leg too short or was the floor buckled? I took out the hand written report on Susan Lutz.

Putinsky studied it like one of my old professors evaluating a badly written research paper. "You could have given me more details. Was your boss ever married? Does she have any brothers or sisters? What are her politics?"

I didn't know. I hadn't wanted to go into much detail. Susan's life was her own, wasn't it? Why should I pry into it? She'd been flattered that I had asked questions, surprised that I had any interest. She thought I was genuinely interested in her. As far as I could guess, she hadn't suspected any ulterior motive. "I guess you will need a follow-up report."

"This will do for now. I owe you some money for this." He showed me a crisp hundred dollar bill but didn't hand it over.

I didn't want Putinsky's money.

"It is better if you do not start spending more than your job pays. It would attract suspicion. Instead, I will deposit this in your US account."

That about freaked me out. Did Putinsky know that much about me? I had closed my old savings account before leaving the country. Did he know about my checking account? My checks on the bank in Indiana were no use in Russia.

Putinsky pushed a card across the greasy café table at me. It was a printed form in English. "With this I will open an account for you at the Riggs bank in Washington. I need your signature, your social security number, and your mother's maiden name." Putinsky provided a fountain pen, a Russian imitation of a Parker.

That was quick. In the short time since I had seen Putinsky at the Bolshoi Restaurant he had procured an account application form from the Riggs bank. Or maybe he had a supply of such cards already on hand for cases like this, probably for accounts at other banks as well.

I studied the form. It looked authentic, with places for joint owners of the account to sign. Putinsky must have connections to be able to get such forms from Washington. Probably someone from the Russian embassy there had to go down to the bank and pick up a supply to be used when necessary, then turned in the signed form at the bank to open an account.

I filled out the card and handed it over. I was about to return the pen when Putinsky asked me to sign something else. "I will deposit the hundred US dollars in the account as I promised, but I need a receipt." He was pretending to be apologetic. "Our accountants, you see. They are afraid I will steal the money."

"Doesn't anyone trust anyone in your business?"

Putinsky clearly didn't like that and flashed a steely look that said "Don't go there." "Bureaucrats, Irwin. Bookkeepers. Sorry."

I had seen the hundred dollar bill, but now Putinsky had taken it back. "How do I know that you are really making a deposit?"

"Trust me, my dear Irwin. My word is as good as gold."

Fat chance. Aware that I was stepping off a cliff, I signed the receipt for the one hundred dollars he hadn't actually given me, put the cap back on the pen, and slid it and the receipt across to Putinsky.

"Very good," Putinsky said. "We must not leave together. You go ahead. Find out more about Miss Lutz and call me in a week. Is that alright?"

"I guess."

"This can be very important for you, Irwin. And remember, we have those photographs. We want you to stay out of trouble."

The hell you do, I thought. I was in more trouble than I could ever have imagined.

As I made my way back to the nearest Metro station I wondered, *why is Putinsky interested in me? I'm a nobody.* But maybe the man thought of me as a small deposit that would grow with interest as I advanced in the state department ranks. Or maybe Putinsky was a victim of his own bean counters, had to fulfill a quota. So many Americans recruited in a year if he was to keep his job. If Putinsky succeeded, would he have his picture posted at the KGB office as "Agent of the month"? If that was it, I was just a commodity, the hundred bucks, real or otherwise, mere play money in the Soviet game of world Monopoly.

I'd better report back to "Robert."

"So, he made you sign a receipt?" "Robert" said when I arrived at his office at the American embassy. He made a quick phone call, adjusted his tie and pulled his jacket off the back of his chair. "Robert" stood up. "We'll have to talk about this in a secure room. Follow me."

The US Embassy didn't have a "cone of silence" like in the television series "Get Smart" but it did have a secure, windowless room with a vault-like door. It was a small, claustrophobic space with a conference table, six chairs, no other furniture, the only decoration a large map of the Soviet Union. The atmosphere was stuffy, airless.

Two other men were already assembled. One was much older than "Robert", had a shock of white hair like some Biblical prophet, and was clearly the senior on the team. The second looked like a wrestler with a thick neck and large chest. He was someone I would not like to encounter in a dark alley. I was not introduced.

"Tell him your story, Irwin. They already know it, but they want to hear it from you."

"Where should I begin?"

"At the beginning."

"Well, it was the big reception at the library for the opening of the display of American art. You know how the Russians are about culture."

"We know that."

"Well, uh, Putinsky came in with this pretty woman. I offered her drinks and she was coming on to me."

"Coming on to you?"

"Well, you know, flirting."

The white-haired man broke in. "So she invited you up to her room at the Metropol?"

"No. She asked if I liked to dance. It was the end of the evening and Susan Lutz said it was OK if I left. So I did."

"How did you get to the hotel?"

"By taxi."

"Taxi?"

"Yeh. There was one waiting outside the library."

"Did it have a sign on it, 'taxi'?"

"I didn't notice. I don't think so."

My interrogators looked at each other. "Robert" speculated. "A KGB car. You were set up, Glass."

I gave a helpless gesture. "How was I to know that? Now that I think about it, the driver seemed to know where to go. I never heard her tell him our destination."

The three interrogators nodded. "So you went dancing?"

"No. The ball room was full of *stylagi*. So we went upstairs."

"And you had sex."

"She gave me a glass of vodka and I buzzed out."

Having to repeat the story of my encounter with Svetlana and being dumped on a Moscow street in my under shorts was embarrassing enough. I assumed they had all seen the photographs.

"Something's not right here," the white-haired senior officer said. "All they had to do was take the pictures and leave you in the room to sleep it off. Doesn't make sense that they'd dump you in the street. Why do you think that happened, Glass?"

"I don't know. Afterwards someone returned my clothes. I didn't get everything back. Not my passport or apartment key. Someone pinched my wrist watch. Oh, yeh, and my lapel pin."

Then I described in detail my two meetings with Vladimir Putinsky.

The older of the three men extracted a tobacco pipe from his jacket pocket, would have lit it, but looked around the room and thought the better for it. The secure room had no ventilation. "You realize, Mr. Glass, that by signing Putinsky's receipt you are now a paid Soviet agent and a criminal under the Official Secrets Act."

Jesus. It sounded like I was headed for Leavenworth Federal Prison. "I only did this because 'Robert' told me to."

"He told you to take money? sign a receipt?"

I felt trapped. "Well, no."

The senior man turned to "Robert." "Has he signed the Act?"

"No."

I asked, "What act?"

"The Official Secrets Act.   You don't have Secret clearance, do you?"

I didn't know.   "I'm just a library clerk."

The muscular man stood up.   "I'll get a copy," and left the secure room.

"Has he been sworn?"

"Robert" shook his head.

"Well, then, get on with it."

"Robert" sighed and stood up, said to me, "Repeat after me: I—state your name—swear to defend the Constitution of the United States of America against all enemies, foreign and domestic."

I swore.   *What enemies?* I wondered who the domestic enemies might be.   Could they be government officials who bent the constitution and committed treason? Was this a vestige of the old McCarthy era when paranoid senators saw commies under every bed?

But of course, this was Moscow, and there really were commies under every bed, or rather, listening at the walls and taking pictures through one way mirrors.

The muscular man with the big shoulders returned with a sheet of paper.   "Sign this."

It was a document in fine print, extract from some government regulation or other.   *How could I have time to read this?* "You expect me to read this?"

"Just sign it," Robert said.

I complied.   Now I'd signed Putinsky's receipt *and* the Secrets Act.   Was the signature for the KGB an act of treason?

"Robert" took the signed document.   "We understand. Putinsky figures he has you in the bag.   The fact that he picked you out tells us something."

"What?"

The older man smiled.   "Since you're just a GS7 means the Sovs are scraping the bottom of the barrel.   If you were the military attaché, that'd be something else."

My mouth was dry. So now in their eyes I was a bona fide Soviet agent, a traitor to my country.

"We're also interested in the kind of information Putinsky is asking for. Tells us his plans. Like, if he wanted to know the combination of a safe you'd know he was planning a burglary, stuff like that."

I asked, "Why does he want to know about Susan Lutz?"

"Robert" answered. "We don't know yet. Maybe this was just a test, something preliminary, to get you locked onto their payroll."

Shit. I hadn't bargained for this when I took that Foreign Service exam. I hoped I might get posted to someplace where I could perfect my language skills, see the world. I had no grandiose goals like becoming the undersecretary to the chief assistant of the deputy ambassador to Chad.

"What do I do next?"

The senior man put the unlit pipe back in his pocket. "I don't want you to start lurking around and acting suspicious. You don't know any trade craft. Let Putinsky show you how the KGB does it. That will be helpful for us. See yourself as a kind of a decoy."

"A decoy?" That meant I was expendable, the goat in the cage waiting to be swallowed by the snake.

"Just play it cool, Glass. Go along with Putinsky for the time being."

"You think Susan Lutz should seduce him with bourbon, then toss him out on the street in his underwear after you take his picture?"

All three men laughed. "Susan Lutz? Not Putinsky's type, I think. Besides, he's not that dumb."

But I am, I thought. So they thought I was a stupid jerk and an enemy of my country. It wouldn't take them much to hand me over to the FBI as Soviet spy. Putinsky might think he had leverage with those six compromising photographs, but the pictures were nothing compared with my signature on a bank account to conceal Soviet payoffs.

"I'm not a decoy," I protested. "I don't want any part of this."

The senior security officer glowered at me. The white haired guy, who I guessed was the head of station, gave me a fierce look, like some picture in a Bible showing Moses with his staff. "You are part of this, Glass. Do as you're told."

I was trapped.

The senior man wasn't through. "You have your passport on you?"

"Yes, sir."

"Hand it over."

I unzipped the inside pocket of my jacket and took out my precious American passport. An American passport is like gold. Some people would give anything for one.

The man examined it, turned all the pages, and put it in his pocket. "I'll return this to you later." Then he turned to the others. "I think we're done for now." He stood up.

I watched the two men leave.

"I need a cigarette," "Robert" said. "I hate this room."

In the elevator I could only think, *"How the hell am I going to get out of this?"*

In the next few days I discreetly tried to slip personal questions into my conversations with Susan. I didn't want to do her any damage, but I also didn't know what use the KGB would have for what seemed to me to be innocuous information. I didn't like gossip, yet this was worse. It wasn't talking behind Susan's back like I imagined she did when laughing with other women about my escapade with Svetlana. This was actually writing a report on her.

It was a betrayal of confidence. I was pretending to be her friend, when I was actually working against her interests. How would Putinsky use this information?

Yet I could not warn her. I couldn't tell her that I was handing over personal information to the KGB for money, even if it was with the approval of embassy security. She'd never trust me with anything.

I was not a rat, not a whistle blower. I was caught in the middle of a cold war duel and likely to be shot down in the crossfire. Which would it be? Tossed out of my window or into the Moscow River, or sent to a Federal prison for espionage?

With great reluctance, I wrote the second report and handed it to "Robert" for clearance. He got an OK. What I had written was innocuous, but I didn't know what was important to Putinsky and what wasn't. Feeling sick to my stomach, I phoned Putinsky's number a week later.

"You know Gorky Park?

"Yes." I had never been there but had seen it on my city map and pictures of families having a sunny Sunday outing. It was a huge park, the sort of destination for lovers who had no chances for privacy, lovers and spies having a tryst.

Putinsky described the location of a specific park bench. "Meet me there tomorrow evening at six thirty-five. You have a new report for me?"

"Yes."

"I have the pass book for your savings account at the Washington bank. So you can see I made that deposit for you. You can trust me."

Trust me? Anyone who said that was not to be trusted. What if the passbook was a fake? The KGB could forge anything. Besides, I didn't want the money. I wanted no part of this.

Just to be on the safe side and cover my ass, as they said in the office, I stopped in at the embassy to inform "Robert" of what was going on.

The secretary at the security office stopped me. She was a blond wearing heavy makeup, her carefully coiffed hair down to her shoulders. I had heard that women looking for a man wore their hair long. Women satisfied with their position in life, women not on the make, had their hair short. Susan Lutz had short hair. Maybe Susan, at forty, had given up looking.

It embarrassed me to have to speak with "Robert's" gatekeeper, for I was reasonably sure that she, too, had seen the incriminating photographs. I could tell by her knowing look that she was part of that inevitable circle of gossips in the embassy hallways. "He's not in," she told me.

With no other option, I wrote the details of the planned Gorky Park meeting with Putinsky on a slip of paper, sealed it in an envelope, and left it with her. "See that he gets this. It's important."

By six o'clock Gorky park was dark. It was not that happy place depicted in the Intourist brochures. No children cavorted on the grass. A mist was forming at the base of the trees, a bit of fog that condensed almost like a drizzle. Was it going to rain on this meeting? I hoped not.

The inadequate street lights left only pools of brightness separated by sinister expanses of darkness. Gorky Park was a fine place to commit a murder and leave a victim in the shrubbery. I hoped "Robert" read my message and had sent someone to keep a discreet eye on our meeting, perhaps take some infra-red photos as evidence.

I was nervous and scared. My first meeting with Putinsky had been in a brightly lit, posh restaurant. The second meeting was in a run down café on a side street. Now it was in a dark park. This was definitely downhill. My mouth was dry. If only I'd been able to talk with "Robert" face to face, not just leave a note. No telling whether he got it or not.

I entered the park and was sure that I wasn't followed. This time I wished I were. When I walked the Moscow streets I wasn't afraid of being mugged or robbed because I knew I was watched wherever I went. But I also figured that most of the watchers were like typical government employees. They quit at five o'clock. If I wanted to avoid them I could slip out of my apartment very early in the morning or late in the evening. Maybe by now the watchers had gone home to their dinners.

I didn't like this one bit. Following Putinsky's instructions, I found the bench. It was damp from the mist. Where was Putinsky? Hiding in the bushes?

"You are very punctual," a voice said from behind me.

I turned. It was Putinsky in a raincoat like some flasher. He was, as far as I could tell in the gloom, alone. "Someone stole my watch at the Metropol but I bought a new one at Gum, an imitation Rolex."

"Ah, yes, your digital. How much did it cost you? I can reimburse you."

"So what will you do then? Take it out of someone's salary?"

"They steal," Putinsky admitted.

So, he was admitting that it was his crew that had carried me out of the hotel.   At least they dressed me in my underwear.   I could have been dumped buck naked.   Why not steal the suit? If American blue jeans could fetch a nice price on the street, what about my wool suit? Did someone have second thoughts? Pang of conscience? It could have been Svetlana who returned the clothes after all.   Maybe she felt sorry for my situation.   There was no way of knowing.   Maybe returning the suit was a token of good faith to persuade me to go along with their plan.   It was so confusing.

"Did you bring the report on Susan Lutz?"

"Yes.   Do you have the passbook for my account at the Riggs bank? Trade ya."

Putinsky had the passbook in his pocket.

I handed over the Lutz report and took the passbook. It looked authentic.   There was a notation of a $100 deposit. Was it genuine? If I showed up in Washington at the Riggs bank would the clerk confirm its authenticity? I no longer knew what to believe.

Putinksy wanted the passbook back.   "I will need this for your next deposit."

So first he shows me a hundred bucks, but doesn't hand it over.   Now he shows me a bank deposit book, and takes it back.   I had nothing.   It was like a goddamned shell game. Now you see it, now you don't, I was beginning to get pissed off.

Putinsky had a small, pocket flashlight and was scrutinizing my report.   He wasn't satisfied.   "You can do better than this, my dear Irwin."

Again with the "my dear Irwin," except this was dripping with sarcasm.

"This is shit."

Shit? "You're right," I said.

"You expect me to pay you for this?"

"I don't expect you to pay me for anything, Putinsky. This whole business is shit."

The KGB agent crumpled the Lutz report.   "Putinsky? You know my name? I am Vladimir.   I never told you my name."

Damn.   As they say in the spy business, I'd just blown my cover.   "I've known from the start who you are, ever since the reception at the library." That wasn't exactly true. I'd been told later who Putinsky was when "Robert" showed me pictures of the guests at the reception.

My memory of that loyalty oath and the Secrets Act was fresh.   For espionage against the United States I could be sentenced to thirty years in a Federal prison.   I was not going to get in any deeper than this.   So what if all I gave Putinsky was shit? "You think you can blackmail me to betray my country?"

"So now you are a patriot?"

I seldom lose my temper, but now I was angry.   For a moment I forgot that I was alone in the darkness of Gorky Park with a dangerous KGB officer and God knows how many of his hidden thugs ready waiting to stuff me in a sack. "I'm not a patriot and I am not a traitor, either.   I am not your pet American."

Putinsky stood up and I did the same.   I was taller and outweighed the smaller Russian by a good twenty pounds, but I was no athlete.   The most exercise I got was climbing the four flights to my apartment.   For all I knew, Putinsky might be an expert at hand to hand fighting, or was armed.

"I own you, Irwin Glass." He held up the crumpled Lutz report.   "What about the photographs of you and Svetlana?"

"Copies are all over the embassy by now.   They have no value."

"You are a fool, Irwin."

"Fuck you, Putinsky." Half expecting to be shot in the back, I started walking swiftly for the park entrance.   I wasn't sure I could remember the layout of those serpentine paths, but I had to get away.

Behind me I heard Putinsky laugh.   "You can't escape, Irwin Glass.   I'll come after you.   You are a dead man."

There was no sound of a pistol being fired.   If I was a dead man, this was not the place for my demise.   But how long would it take before Putinsky got his act together and had his revenge?

I hid in the bushes until I saw a bus coming, then stepped out into the light of a street lamp to flag it down.

There were few passengers. I gradually relaxed. When I changed busses to get to my apartment I was almost calm.

Then I realized that if the KGB knew my destination they didn't have to follow me. They could simply wait outside the embassy billets for me to arrive.

I saw no one on the street outside the embassy billets. No car idled at the curb. I let myself into the building, climbed the deserted stairway, and listened outside my door. Silence. I half expected to be ambushed when I got inside. There was no one.

I did not sleep until well past midnight and woke up stiff and sore as if I'd been lying on a stick.

I did not go to the library the next morning, but to the embassy to report to "Robert." This time the blonde receptionist let me pass.

"Robert" was typing a report at his desk. Though the embassy now had electronic word processors, "Robert" still used a typewriter, an IBM Selectric. "Robert" typed with only two fingers, but was fast, like an old journalist batting out a story for a deadline.

"Did you get my note?"

"Note?" Robert looked up, puzzled. "No."

Disappointed, I sat down in the guest chair. "I saw Putinsky last night. He set up a meeting in Gorky Park. I gave him the Lutz report and he said it was shit. I told him to fuck himself. I quit."

"You what?"

"I quit. I'm not going to do this."

"You can't quit, Glass. We need you to get to Putinsky."

"I told him the photos will do him no good, that everyone in the embassy has seen them. No blackmail. He says he owns me. He says I'm a dead man."

"Robert" turned off the Selectric and stood up, suddenly fuming. "You stupid son of a bitch. You've fucked up the operation, Glass. I needed this operation. We had a chance to run you as a double agent, feed Putinsky a bunch of misinformation, get to him."

"I don't want to be a double agent, whatever that is."

"Robert" tried to control his temper. "Look, Glass, the Sovs are a lot better at this than we are. There's always some stupid lefty who tosses some stolen secret document over the wall of the Russian embassy and offers to sell out his country for money. When they do that our agents over here get killed. You understand?"

"I don't want to get killed. I just want to do my library job."

"Christ, Glass. I had a good thing going here and you've queered it. If we could have turned Putinsky we'd have an inside track to what goes on inside the KGB. You understand that?"

"That's not my line of work."

"Robert" sat down again. He was clearly pissed off at me. I wanted nothing to do with his spy versus spy games. I didn't want to be anybody's pawn in a game of international political intrigue. I just wanted a nice State Department job, maybe helping immigrants get visas, stuff like that. "Robert" wanted to turn me into some sort of James Bond. What would he do next? Give me license to kill people? My hands were shaking, but I had to stand up to him, angry as he was.

"I wish you hadn't done that, Glass. Putinsky now has two choices. He can pick you up and haul you off to the Lubyanka for interrogation or he can have you whacked."

"Why should he interrogate me?"

"He'll want to know who you talked to here at the embassy, how we reacted, what our procedures are. You met the station chief."

"Station chief?"

"My boss, the guy with the white hair, no names, please. Putinsky will want to know everything he can wring out of you. When he's done you'll simply disappear."

"That would cause an international incident."

"Robert" shook his head. "It would if you were a consular officer with diplomatic immunity." What he meant to say was "You're a nobody."

I was silent, my mind a confusion. I had heard about the Lubyanka. That's where prisoners got shot in the back of the head, like Beria. One minute you were a top Soviet official. Next someone denounced you and you were sent to the Gulag or simply shot.

Even if you did nothing wrong, as the Soviet joke went, you got ten years in the Gulag.

"What do I do now?"

"Robert" shook his head. "We had a good thing here, Glass. We were going to train you up. You've let us down."

"What do I do now? Just go back to the library?"

"We can't risk that. Putinsky is suspected of engineering assassinations. He has lots of choices. Poison gas was used for a killing in Germany, an exploding capsule in the face of the victim. Then there was the umbrella poked in a guy's leg in London, a little pellet shot into the victim's leg. You know what Ricin is? It's a poison from the castor plant. A tiny amount will kill you. Or he can simply throw you from your apartment window. Putinsky's threat has to be taken seriously. He's a vengeful guy."

If "Robert" wanted to scare me, he had succeeded. What did "Robert" already know about Vladimir Putinsky that he hadn't told? I felt helpless. My hands were shaking. I dried my sweaty palms on my thighs. "What am I going to do?"

"For one, you aren't going back to your apartment. And you aren't going back to the library. I don't have enough personnel to provide you with a bodyguard. You're not that important." "Robert" gestured toward the narrow cot against the wall under the blanked out window. "You'll stay here for now. I'll get you out on the next flight."

"What, with Aeroflot?" That was the Russian airline.

"You'd never make it though customs. Putinsky's men would be waiting for you. We have a weekly plane that flies the military attaché and the diplomatic pouch. Lucky for you, it happens to be in Moscow today."

"What about my stuff?"

"I'll have all your belongings packed up and shipped to you in the States. Where should I send it?"

I didn't remember the street address of my parents' place in Florida. "I can't remember the address. It's in my address book at the apartment." Now I couldn't fetch it myself. It was dawning on me that I was like a stranded tourist whose bags were lost by the airline. At least my passport was at the embassy. But I had no dollars on me.

"You probably gave it to us when you notified who should be contacted in case of an emergency."

I remembered. "It's written in pencil in my passport. Emergency contact information."

I had visited my folks in Ocala before starting the job in Moscow and knew their quarters were cramped, crowded with furniture, family heirlooms my mother didn't want to part with when they left South Bend.

The double wide in Ocala had a lanai, a screened in add-on typical of Floridian homes. The weather there was conducive to outdoor living. My folks didn't have a pool, but the complex where they lived did. My boxes of books would have to be stacked in the lanai until I found a new job and an apartment someplace.

"Will I be home free then?"

"Robert" shook his head. "Don't count on it. Putinsky thinks he owns you."

"What's what he said," I remembered. "I own you."

"He may try to use you as a sleeper."

"A sleeper?"

"An agent he activates later. They send people in to build their cover stories, then wait for instructions. Sometimes it takes years."

"Years?"

"This is going to hang over your head forever, Glass. But for now, let's get you someplace safe."

"Don't I even get to pack?"

"You can buy a razor and toothbrush at the commissary."

"I don't have any clothes, just what I've got on, this Russian jacket and hat."

"Robert" pointed a finger at me. "Don't start whining at me, Glass. And don't get any ideas of sneaking out for a little shopping trip at Gum. Give me your underwear size and I'll send Ingrid shopping for some whitey tighties."

"When does the plane leave?"

"Tonight. That'll get you to Rhine Main in the morning. It's not a fast plane."

"Do I have to wear a leather helmet and goggles?"

"Don't be funny, Glass. Ever worn a parachute?"

"No."

"It's an old C-46, precursor to the C47. The air force calls them flying coffins. That should appeal to your suicidal impulses."

"What about my passport?"

"The station chief still has it. You won't need it to get out of Russia. The Sovs hate to see us leaving with the embassy pouch. They think we're smuggling the czarist jewels, but they can't do anything about it. We just thumb our noses."

"Where's the plane fly to?"

"Frankfurt am Main, Germany. You can get a SAC flight from there to Andrews."

"Then what?"

"Robert" paused to light one of his Marlboros. He did it with a Zippo lighter that he flipped with one hand. He took a drag on the cigarette and, as he exhaled the smoke, said, "You'll report to personnel at State."

"Will I be reassigned?"

"If reassignment is all you get you'll be lucky. You're a security risk. You don't strike me as being very lucky." The smile was not friendly.

"Robert" was clearly enjoying this, venting his anger.

"What'll I do now?"

"You've passed the civil service exam. Maybe the Forest Service will hire you to put out forest fires."

I heard him mutter, "asshole." I couldn't see myself as a smoke eater. What was I qualified for? Who cared about my Russian language and literature specialty? Or my degree in International Relations? I would have to start all over again, rebuild my life. All because of that damned glass of vodka. "That stinks," I protested, pulling myself together after the initial shock. "Security risk? I only did that Lutz report because you approved it. You approved of my meetings with Putinsky."

"I didn't give you permission to quit, to tell Putinsky to go fuck himself. You blew it, Glass."

"So now I'm a security risk?"

"Robert's" grin was evil. "Ain't that too bad. You betrayed your country, Glass."

Betrayed? "I didn't betray anyone. What are you going to do, turn me over to the FBI?"

"You aren't worth the trouble."

I covered my face. How could anyone be so vindictive? If anyone had been betrayed, it was me. All along the line. Svetlana lured me to the Metropol. Now "Robert." The irony was, the only person who had been straight with me was Vladimir Putinsky. Putinsky was playing it by the book. Blackmail was a conventional tool. Getting me to accept payment for a report and sign a receipt must be standard KGB procedure.

I had appeared, at least, to agree to provide the KGB with personal information about Susan Lutz, then reneged. No wonder Putinsky was mad. Ironic as it seemed, I had not only betrayed Susan's confidence, I had betrayed Putinsky. I was thoroughly rattled and confused. What kind of a world was this?

What would happen when I got to Washington? Would I be reassigned to some clerical post? I didn't see myself as a security risk. It wasn't like I'd gone to the Soviets on my own volition to sell secrets. I hadn't sneaked around. Everything I'd done was with the full knowledge of the department, except, of course, whatever happened once I got in that Metropol hotel room.

Would there be a disciplinary hearing? A board of review? If so, who would vouch for me? Nobody. I couldn't call in Putinsky or Svetlana to testify that I'd been drugged at the Metropol. Susan Lutz had told me it was OK to leave the library with Svetlana, but she would be glad to replace me with someone who knew libraries and American literature. Being fluent in Russian wasn't enough for her. If "Robert" provided the personnel office at State with copies of the incriminating photographs I'd be sunk.

"Can I at least go back to my place and pick up some stuff?"

"Not alone," "Robert" insisted. "I don't have the men to go along and ride shotgun. We're short staffed here. We have more important things to do than baby sit you, Glass. Stay right here," "Robert" left the office to confer with the white-haired station chief.

I wasn't going to wait for the secretary to shop for me. I slipped out and went down to the commissary to buy essentials for the flight back to the States, shaving stuff and a change of underwear. Though I had no dollars on me, I told them to put the purchase on my account. The bill would be applied to my next paycheck, if there was one.

What if I wasn't reassigned, as "Robert" suggested, but actually fired? What about that scenario? Now I was overwhelmed with worry. I had very little money. I had only walking around cash in rubles in my wallet. I had kept that checking account at the bank in Bloomington, Indiana but it had a small balance, a couple of hundred bucks. The check book was back in my apartment.

I had no home in Indiana. At Indiana University I'd stayed in graduate student housing. I'd left all that behind when I took the government job. My parents had sold the house in South Bend. Did they have a spare room in that double wide in Ocala, Florida where I might hang out until I found a job?

If I was fired, what would I tell my folks? I really did feel like Akaky Akakveyich, except there were no dead souls to buy to beat the system. Leaving Moscow, I'd be a fugitive with Putinsky after me like Porfiry Petrovich, the detective in *Crime and Punishment* who finally gets Raskolnikov to confess. At least, once in the States, there was no risk of being sent to Siberia.

Being back in the States would put thousands of miles between me and the KGB. I didn't want to believe they'd go after me, call me out as a potential sleeper agent. If they really had photographed every page of my address book, they could easily track me down.

Even in the United States I wouldn't be safe. There probably wouldn't be KGB watchers lurking outside my door to follow me wherever I went but there might be new watchers, the FBI tailing me as a Soviet agent while they gathered enough evidence to put me on trial.

Dejected, sitting alone, I forced myself to eat a hamburger for lunch in the embassy café, not that I had much appetite. The Russians didn't know how to bake an American style burger bun.

The white-haired station chief joined me. "Here's your passport."

"Thanks."

"It's valid only for direct return to the United States."

Sure enough. It was stamped that way. They were treating me like some sort of fugitive. I guess I was.

The station chief got up to leave. "A word of warning, Glass. Robert is a tough adversary. You've crossed him and spoiled his plans. You don't want him as your enemy. You screw up again and he'll have your ass. He'll track you down like a pack of bloodhounds."

"Thanks for the warning." After that I couldn't finish my hamburger. It tasted like death.

Susan Lutz would be pissed that I didn't show up for work. "Robert" wouldn't let me phone to tell her I had to leave the country. The phones were not secure. She didn't leave the library for lunch at the embassy cafe, but packed a sandwich and a bottle of carbonated lemonade. When I didn't show up she'd probably assume I'd gotten drunk again or shacked up with some Russian babe and was back in some precinct holding tank with the wretched Moscow alcoholics. I felt wretched myself.

I had a lot of time to think while waiting for that flight. It was too bad that the six photographs were back in my apartment. Maybe if I had a chance to study them I might find some clue to that puzzle the station chief had pondered: namely why had I been tossed out on the street when all the KGB needed were the photographs?

As the early Autumn darkness fell on Moscow "Robert" got ready to take me to the airport.

I had time to think about that trip back to the States. How long would the layover be in Frankfurt? I had never been to Germany. If I had a few days, I might play the role of tourist. I suggested that to "Robert."

"You can't leave the Frankfurt air base," "Robert" said. "With your passport you can't clear German customs." He was clearly enjoying this, maliciously teasing me, playing on my fears. "Even if you could, Soviet agents in Germany might be waiting for you."

"I don't believe that."

"And don't get any ideas about bugging out, escaping to some European country. With your passport stamped 'for immediate return to the United States. You can't go anywhere but back home."

"But I don't have a home. My folks sold the house. They live in Florida now."

"It's a new world for you, Glass, like being in the Witness Protection Program, except you're not getting a new name or a stipend to tide you over while you get into a new identity."

I remembered my meager checking account in the Bloomington bank. How long would that balance last? A month? "If I get fired, will I get severance pay?"

"I doubt it."

I had to fight back. Though I'd been in government service only a short time, I'd learned some of the ropes. "I'm not fired yet. You have to fix me up with travel documents and per diem cash. I can't do anything with a few Russian Rubles."

"Robert" relented. "Spoken like a true civil servant." He was reluctant. "I'll get you something." He left the office, came back an hour later with an envelope. "Here's your travel voucher and forty bucks a day for five days."

"Thanks." I looked in the envelope to make sure the money was there, two one-hundred dollar bills. They looked new. The last hundred dollar bill I'd seen was the one Putinsky showed me, then took back.

"Robert" looked at his watch. "Let's get going. We'll dress you in a flight suit so you look like one of the crew."

So, I was just being dumped, discarded like a piece of rotten fruit. "At least you're not making me change my name."

"Robert" shook his head. "Your name is Mudd." It was a reference to Doctor Mudd who unwittingly gave first aid to

John Wilkes Booth, Lincoln's assassin, and was sent to prison on the Dry Tortugas, his reputation destroyed forever.

With my purchases of toiletries and a change of underwear in an innocuous plastic garbage bag, redneck Masonite, I got into an embassy car for the run to the Moscow airport. Along with a cart loaded with mysterious Embassy freight, we passed reluctant Russian customs guards and pushed to the side of a waiting C-46, a twin engine prop plane of World War II vintage. It was a tired old transport, the aluminum skin tarnished and corroded. It was so old it was probably left over from the Berlin air lift and might still be full of coal dust. Besides the tail number the only marking was a small American flag stenciled on the tail.

"Robert" got on the plane with me and showed me how to put on a seat parachute that doubled as a cushion. "This ring is the rip cord. Make sure the straps are tight. If there's any play in the crotch and you have to jump the shock when the chute opens will crush your balls."

"Thanks a lot."

"The pilot has to fly an approved course so you don't get shot down by the Soviet air force."

"That's a relief."

One of the engines cranked over with a rumble, a roar, and a cloud of exhaust. "Robert" got ready to leave the plane. In the open door he shouted over the roar of the propellers. "By the way. Don't harbor any fantasies about another hot night with Svetlana. The boys checked her out. Her full name is Svetlana Ivanovna Putinsky. She's his wife."

With a wave, "Robert" slammed the door to the old transport. The copilot latched it and showed me to a bucket seat on the right side of the plane. In the center was the cargo, lashed down with heavy straps.

I wondered what was in the cargo. Beluga caviar? Vodka? Parts of a stolen Soviet cruise missile?

"You'll need your winter jacket and cap, sir," the copilot advised. "The rear of the plane isn't heated. It's not pressurized, either, so we can't fly over ten thousand feet. Put on these headphones so you can hear instructions from the cockpit in case you have to bail out."

69

Bail out? If I didn't break my neck landing in some Russian field, would the xenophobic Soviets who found me shoot me as a spy? What would I tell them? That I was an agent for the KGB and they should just ask Potinsky for a reference? Such wild, desperate fantasies.

This was certainly no luxury flight. I was suddenly in need of a toilet, but saw no such facility. Before I could ask, I heard the engines throttle up, felt the plane start its taxi.

The C-46 took off. I looked out the scarred plastic window to see Moscow falling away. I had looked forward to being in Russia, the land of my great grandfather, and invested all that time to learn the language. Now it was over. Fearful as I was of Putinsky and his minions, I had liked Moscow, enjoyed talking with Russians not afraid to speak with a foreigner. Moscow reeked with history. With so many crippled veterans of what the Soviets called the War Against the Fascists, the memory of World War II was still fresh.

It was the land of Dostoevsky, Tolstoy, Gogol, Turgenev, those authors I had read with such fervor. I hoped when "Robert's" crew packed up my stuff they wouldn't leave my books behind.

It wasn't until we reached cruising altitude that I had time to ponder "Robert's" parting shot. So, Svetlana was Putinsky's wife. What kind of a man pimped for his own wife? What kind of a wife would submit to that humiliation? It gave me a lot to think about on the long flight to Frankfurt am Main. Many questions, no answers.

The plane landed in Berlin to refuel and unload some of the freight. I was allowed to get off the plane and find a bathroom, but returned, listening to the sounds of machinery, of vehicles passing, the roar of fighter jets taking off.

At Frankfurt am Main Autumn was not as far advanced as in chilly Moscow. I was too warm in my Russian winter jacket and hat. I didn't know what to do next, but was directed to the operations office to get on a list for a SAC flight carrying dependents and troops on leave back to the States. My jacket and hat with the red star got some attention. When the operations clerk, an air force non-com in uniform who was due for a haircut, saw my travel papers and the passport stamped only for direct return to the United States, he asked, "So you were in Russia. You get kicked out? What did you do?"

I didn't want to tell my story. "I stole a library book."

The clerk shook his head. "I get it. You must be CIA. A need to know deal. I hear they drink a lot of vodka there."

I nodded. "If you ever get to Moscow, don't accept any drinks from anybody."

I got priority seating because of the strong wording in my documents to report immediately to the State Department.

The airliner chartered for SAC wasn't deluxe. No drinks were served. The passengers, a mixed bag of troops on emergency leave, dependents going home, and a couple of men on leave, got box meals. It was another long military flight.

I sat beside a highly pregnant dependent wife, a German bride, who took the aisle seat because she had to make frequent trips to the toilet. She wore too much makeup, spoke with a thick accent in halting English. She would have preferred German, but the only foreign language I knew was Russian.

She wanted to tell me her life story. She was from Schwetzingen, a little town outside Heidelberg, had met her future husband, a sergeant, in the famous park there, and on and on and on. Her ultimate destination was a little town in North Dakota.

I had to smile. If the Germans were anything like the Russians, they thought America was New York City. Boy, was she in for a surprise. How long would she last in Grand Forks?

All I wanted to do was sleep. I had already been traveling twenty-four hours.

Eventually I landed at Andrews air force base outside Washington, DC jetlagged, exhausted, and depressed. I needed a shower. At least I had a tooth brush, razor and shaving cream in my plastic sack. That helped. I felt totally out of place in my Russian jacket and fake fur hat with my meager belongings in a garbage bag. Putting on my Russian accent I could pretend to be a refugee who stowed away, or

71

maybe a Soviet defector being spirited away to safety in the USA. I didn't do that. I didn't need to arouse any more suspicions about my loyalty or integrity.

It was just past eight in the morning and raining in Washington, warm with a humidity that hit me in the face like a steamed towel as I went down the steps and onto the tarmac. I took off the jacket and carried it over my arm, stuffed the hat in the garbage bag with my toilet kit.

The SAC passengers had to go through customs. In line beside the German bride I was mistaken for her husband, which I denied. Were we carrying any food? Some Americans who acquired a taste for German sausage tried to smuggle some back, but it was confiscated. No, I had nothing to declare.

The customs agent, an older, humorless man in uniform and badge, checked my passport. "You've been in the Soviet Union. How come this is stamped for immediate return to the United States?"

"I got denounced by the KGB."

"That a joke?" The agent didn't like jokes.

"I wish it were."

"Any checked baggage?"

"Nope." I showed my plastic sack. "Just this. I left in a hurry."

The agent looked inside the sack, reached in and pulled out the hat as if it were a dead skunk. Once he realized it was only a hat, the fur fake and not some prohibited animal pelt, he was satisfied.

It's a good thing I'm not carrying those photos from the Metropol, I thought. *They'd probably confiscate them as pornography.*

Had I bought anything while abroad? "Just this imitation Rolex." I showed my wrist.

The agent's face showed an expression of surprised recognition. "Wait a minute. Mr. Glass. I think I've got you on a list." He consulted a clip board. "Yes. Go to that office over there. Someone's waiting for you."

Like a lamb led to the slaughter, I dragged myself to the office indicated. So I had an escort. What would it be? FBI? Someone from the State Department? At this stage of the game I didn't care.   I just wanted a bed someplace and about two days sleep.

I was recognized by a dark haired, good looking woman in a short, pale blue rain jacket with a hood.   She was sipping coffee from a paper cup.   Her lipstick was the same shade as Svetlana's.   It gave me a shock, a feeling of deja vu.   "You're Irwin Glass?"

"What's left of him."

"Follow me."

I followed her.   Where were we going?   "I need a shower," I said.

"I'll get you checked into the Marriot."

"Just so it's not the Metropol."

"What?"

"And no pictures, please."

"I don't get it."   We had reached the parking garage.

"Private joke."   Apparently I had not been preceded by the incriminating photographs.   They were something this go-fer person didn't need to know.

She didn't introduce herself but checked me into the hotel.   A reservation had been made in my name.   In the elevator I asked, "How much is the room?   I only have a couple of hundred American dollars per diem money."

"It's on a contract," she said.   "Don't worry about it." She didn't let me out of her sight until I made it to the room, then didn't go inside.   I half expected her to stand guard in the hallway to make sure I didn't make a run for it.   "I'll give you an hour.   Have you had breakfast?"

"No."

"Then meet me in the coffee shop."

I was so tired I had difficulty focusing on her face.   "We going over to State to check in?"

"Not yet.   It's still early.   Why don't you have some breakfast? You're not due until 10:00."

"At State?"

"That's tomorrow.   This morning you're to take a Polygraph."

I leaned against the door to the hotel room to keep from collapsing.   Forty eight hours of travel with little sleep was too much.   "Polly Graph?"

"You haven't had a lie detector test before?"

"No, but I had my fingerprints taken."

"We can do that, too."

She left.

What the hell, I thought. *Why do I have to take a lie detector test?* Two days of travel and now this.   I was not only exhausted.   I was angry.   They were treating me like a fugitive, what the cops call a person of interest. All that was missing was handcuffs or one of those electronic tethers.

It was time that I called my parents. I puzzled over the hotel instructions for long distance calls, realized I didn't know my parents' number in Ocala.   Fortunately the information operator found Kenneth Glass and put me through.

All I got was an answering machine.   "We can't come to the phone just now.   Leave your name and number and we'll get back to you."

I couldn't be certain that I had the right Kenneth Glass, or that my message might simply be deleted by some stranger, so was cryptic.   "This is Irwin.   I'm in Washington, DC at the Marriot hotel.   I hope you can put me up for a few days.   I'll let you know when I'm coming." I wasn't going to explain anything more than that to an answering machine.

Even face to face, what was I going to tell my folks? Certainly not that I'd been seduced in Moscow and dumped nearly naked in the street.   If I mentioned being thrown in the drunk tank they'd be so appalled they'd simply stop listening.   They had never been very communicative, certainly not about my sex life.   They were not that kind of parents.   I'd never had the birds and bees lecture when I was a kid.

My father hadn't wanted to know about family history, not anything about the great grandfather who came from Russia.   After years of high school teaching Dad had been bored, tired of baby sitting impudent, unruly teenagers.   His main interest since they moved to Florida was golf, not international relations.   My mom made quilts.   Neither of my folks read books.   Classic Russian literature was to them a great mystery of no more interest than Egyptian hieroglyphics.   To my mother, Erna Glass, *War and Peace* was just a fat book of over a thousand pages. She didn't even pick up Harlequin romances. Her idea of literature was a grocery store copy of *Good Housekeeping*, mainly for the recipes.

I'd have to figure out a suitably evasive but credible story to tell them. It wouldn't be productive to get into that business with Putinsky and the KGB.

I hung up the phone, but saved the bit of hotel note paper with the Ocala number. Only then did I turn my attention to the amenities of the first class hotel.

It was a pleasant change of scene to use plumbing that worked and to walk on a carpet that wasn't threadbare and prewar. In Moscow everything seemed worn out. Maintenance. That was the difference. In America if it was worn out it was thrown out and replaced. Russia was too poor for such luxuries.

I showered in real hot water, used the little bottle of shampoo the hotel provided, and felt more presentable. In fresh underwear I was beginning to feel human again. I left the Russian coat and hat in the room when I went down to the coffee shop to find my keeper in the blue rain jacket.

She was having breakfast herself. She was a take charge person. "I ordered orange juice for you, coffee, scrambled eggs and toast."

"Thanks." I was so tired, I was afraid I'd fall asleep in my plate. I was definitely not my chatty self. When I questioned the necessity for a polygraph she was non-committal. I was to follow orders and not ask questions.

When the waitress came with the check my keeper asked for my hotel key and put both our meals on the bill.

It reminded me of Putinsky at the Bolshoi restaurant taking advantage of the KGB expense account. I guessed that bureaucrats were the same everywhere, Communist or Capitalist.

The coffee helped. Breakfast gave me some energy and I was more alert, sitting beside her on the front seat of a government car. She was a skillful driver who knew her way around Washington. In my exhaustion my imagination was running wild. Did she also do classic car chases like in the movies? Tail escaping Russian spies? But it was an ordinary automobile. No special radio or electronics. In minutes she accompanied me to an unmarked office in the lower floor of an anonymous office building.

The only furnishings were a well-used table and two old office chairs. My anonymous guide introduced me to the technician and left. The technician looked bored.

The hotel breakfast had been good, but I was feeling pushed around. I'd been forced to leave Moscow without packing, not allowed to leave Rhine Main airport, escorted everywhere like a prisoner. "Why do I have to do this?" I demanded.

"Orders."

"Bullshit."

Now it was the technician's turn to be testy. "Are you refusing?"

"Do I have a choice?"

"If you refuse it's assumed you have something to hide."

"So if I refuse I'm automatically guilty of something?"

"Could be."

"What a lot of crap."

I was reluctantly parked in a chair beside what looked like a portable EKG machine. The technician spoke mainly in monosyllables. No conversation. Electrodes were stuck on my body and a strap snugged around my chest. My pulse and breathing were recorded on a scrolling roll pf paper like an earthquake detector. I was not supposed to watch.

The operator had obviously done this so many times it had become a dreary exercise. I sensed that the job was a dead end, my test just another of perhaps hundreds. I was instructed to answer questions simply yes or no.

The first ones were easy and asked in a monotone. "Is your name Irwin Glass?"

"Yes."

"Were you born on..." and gave the date.

"Yes."

"Did you study at Indiana University?"

"Yes."

"Have you stolen any money from the government?"

That must have been the shocker to see how I reacted. "No."

"Are you a Soviet agent?"

That jolted me. "No."

"Have you ever worked for the KGB?"

Now I was stuck. Had I? I had written that report on Susan Lutz. Had I been paid by Putinsky? My answer was a very hesitant "Yes, but…"

"No, 'but' Mr. Glass. Just answer the questions with a yes or no."

"OK, but you don't understand…"

"Just yes or no, Mr. Glass."

I could see this was not going well.

"Have you ever received money from the Soviet Union?"

I had been promised the hundred dollars, but hadn't taken it. It was supposedly deposited in the Riggs bank. I didn't actually receive money. Did the bank deposit count? Was it even real? "No."

The technician had a list and had more questions meant to rattle me. Was I a homosexual?

"No."

Did I ever masturbate?

I asked, "Doesn't everyone?"

"Just yes or no, Mr. Glass."

Well, maybe I did. Sometimes. "Yes."

By the end of the test I felt totally humiliated. The way the questions were put the answers made me look like a jerk-off pervert who was a traitor to his country on the payroll of the Soviet Union. "Robert" had been sarcastic, but knew the circumstances of the situation in Moscow. Too bad "Robert" wasn't there to back me up.

The technician unhooked the wires and the belt, gave me a bit of tissue to wipe off the jelly used to make the connections for the electrodes on my skin. Then he phoned for someone to pick me up. "You're done for now."

I got up, put my shirt back on. "What's next?"

The technician shrugged. He didn't need to know. "I just do the polygraphs. Have a nice day."

A nice day? It had been a long time since I heard that one. I was definitely not having a nice day. One thing for sure. I was not going to the Marriot bar for happy hour. If someone offered me a drink of anything alcoholic I'd puke.

I was picked up by someone else, this time a neatly buttoned kid in a jacket and an attempt at a mustache to make him look older. It was back to the hotel. My only instruction was to report to the State Department personnel office the next day at 9:00 AM.

I didn't know Washington, but I did want to buy a clean shirt and a pair of pants. I had forgotten to buy socks at the Embassy commissary. I'd need a few pairs of those, too, and a suitcase. I didn't want to keep dragging that garbage bag with my stuff. The hotel had a store, the typical place where you can buy souvenir items like a shirt that said "My folks went to Washington DC and all I got was this lousy shirt." Maybe I could put all my purchases on the hotel bill along with that breakfast for two. Those two one hundred dollar bills weren't going to last long.

No telling when my stuff would arrive in Ocala. To avoid pilferage by underpaid Russian workers, would the Moscow crew load my belongings on that old C-46 along with the diplomatic pouch? How long would that take?

And where was the Riggs bank? Did I really have an account there? Did Putinsky actually have some embassy flunky in Washington deposit the deadly hundred dollar payoff? The deposit book he showed me could have been a fake put together in the Lubyanka forgery department. It wasn't only that I might need the money, even if it was tainted. I needed to make sure.

I dropped my purchases back in the room, asked the hotel cashier to change the two one-hundred dollar bills into twenties, and stepped out of the hotel to find a taxi. "Riggs bank. Know where that is?"

The unshaven driver looked Slavic and spoke with an accent. On a hunch I addressed him in Russian.

The driver was not surprised, but then Washington with all its embassies and foreign legations was full of people who spoke languages other than English. Still, snagging a Russian immigrant driver apparently by chance gave me a creepy feeling. The night I left the library with Svetlana a car had been waiting with another Russian driver.

Was this paranoia? Was this the long arm of Vladimir Putinsky reaching all the way to Washington, DC? Would the driver calmly turn around with a silenced pistol and shoot me in the face? I was ready to duck.

The taxi pulled up in front of the Riggs bank. "*Spaseeba*," I said and handed over a twenty, waited for change. "*Dasvidanya*."

I did not have the savings deposit book, which Putinsky had shown me but kept.   At least I did have my American passport as ID.   I asked to see the manager and was led into an office.   The name plate on the desk said R.   Plotnik, and in smaller letters, Assistant Manager.   Plotnik wore a black suit, pale blue shirt, a silver and black striped tie and a studied, bland expression.   Plotnik was either deeply tanned or of mixed race.   "What can I do for you?"

"An account was opened for me.   I'm Irwin Glass." I held out my passport, keeping my thumb over the stamp that said "Valid only for immediate return to the United States." "You should have a savings account set up in my name."

Plotnik checked his computer monitor.   "No Irwin Glass.   What's your Social Security number?"

I gave it.

No luck.

"But I signed the registration card, gave my mother's maiden name.   Supposed to have a balance of a hundred dollars."

"I'm sorry, Mr.   Glass, we don't have an account here under your name."

"Maybe it's a checking account."

Plotnik looked suspicious, as if he suspected a con job. "You are not in our system.   Maybe you are in the wrong bank."

Screwed again, I thought.   "I guess it's a mistake." As I turned to go I remembered the polygraph question.   Had I ever received money from the Soviet Union? I hadn't been sure when I was asked, and couldn't remember how I answered.   Now the answer was definitely "no' but I couldn't go back and change my answer even if I knew how to find the polygraph office.

I speculated that Putinsky hadn't had time for someone to make the deposit and send the deposit book to Moscow by courier, so he simply had someone make a fake passbook with the hundred dollars entered.   I'd been conned and betrayed.

I couldn't trust anyone.   I hoped that the polygraph had no bearing on my meeting at the State department the next day.   From what I'd heard about Washington bureaucracy, the FBI didn't talk to the CIA and the CIA husbanded their information so cautiously that they didn't share with anyone. Who had done the polygraph? The CIA? State? The FBI? I needed to know, but the cliché was that you were never told anything you didn't need to know, and they were the judge of that need, not me.

I would have to wait until the next morning.

That was fine with me.   I took another cab back to the hotel, this one driven by a displaced Israeli who wanted to turn the short hop into an expensive tour of the city.

"Just the Marriot," I insisted.

Once back in the room I drew the blinds against the pale, Washington sun, collapsed on the bed and slept.

The next morning I took another cab over to the State Department and checked in at the personnel office.   I felt rested but nervous about my fate.   I was let into yet another office.   This one, unlike the anonymous, rented space where I'd had the polygraph, showed personal signs.   The personnel officer, Peter Kenney, had a framed diploma on the wall from Duke University, framed pictures of a pretty wife and two children, even a close up picture of a yellow Labrador retriever.

I reasoned that a man who loved his family and his dog would be sympathetic to my rather complicated problem.

Kenney, a man in his early forties, was dressed in a white shirt with a button down collar and a jacket with an American flag lapel pin.   He wore aviator style glasses, bifocals, I noticed, the badge of someone in middle age.

"Did you have a nice flight?" Kenney asked, not that he seemed to care.

"A boring flight," I conceded.   "The best kind.   Except the army wife next to me didn't stop talking."

Kenney wasn't interested. He consulted a manila personnel file on the desk, leafed through several documents and reports. Finally he said, "I have bad news for you, Mr. Glass. Your supervisor at the library…" he checked the report for the name. "Susan Lutz, says you are an alcoholic and a womanizer."

"That's not true."

"She says you know almost nothing of American literature, which is the library's main purpose. She also reports that you haven't been coming in on time, that you've been distracted, and that you were picked up by the Moscow police on the street, that you were drunk and in your underwear. That right?"

"I was drugged." I hoped against all hope that the manila personnel file didn't include the six photos of me having sex with Svetlana. Didn't seem to be. That was a relief.

Kenney wasn't finished. "You had a polygraph yesterday, a lie detector test. That right?"

"Yes."

"You flunked."

I protested. "I heard those tests aren't reliable."

"That may be, but I have a fax here from the CIA station chief in Moscow. It says you were recruited by the KGB and accepted money from a Soviet agent."

"That's not true." At least I knew that there was no account at the Riggs bank. "I was never paid."

"Says here that you signed a receipt."

"It was part of the act. 'Robert' approved of everything."

"Who is Robert?"

"That's the name he gave at the embassy."

"No Robert mentioned here."

"Maybe he didn't tell me his real name."

Kenney picked up a pencil and clicked it against his teeth. "And you wrote a report on Susan Lutz and sold it to the Soviets."

"With Robert's approval," I insisted. "He reviewed and approved every word. I didn't pass any secrets."

Kenney shook his head. "So you say. There's nothing in this report about that. You realize this stuff has also gone to the FBI. You are likely to be prosecuted as a Soviet agent."

My mouth was dry. My tongue wanted to stick to the roof of my mouth. "I was supposed to become a double agent. I refused. This is all a misunderstanding."

Kenney shook his head. "That's your story."

"Jesus. Putinsky, the KGB guy, said he'll kill me, that I'm a dead man."

"Some imagination, Glass. You've been watching too many spy movies."

I protested, "But it's true."

"Sure you're not having a nervous breakdown? Maybe you need a psychiatrist."

It was all I could do not to shout at the man. "I'm not having a nervous breakdown."

Kenney was having none of it. "Take it easy, Glass. The federal prosecutors will decide if they want to charge you. That's not my job. Maybe you can plead insanity."

At that I could only shake my head in sheer exasperation. What did it take to convince this man?

Kenney was not finished. "One thing sure: you can never get a security clearance."

I took a deep breath and tried to contain my anger. "So what happens now? Am I to be reassigned?"

"Are you serious, Glass? You actually think you can continue to work for the federal government? You're fired."

It was what I expected but didn't want to accept. I felt like I was drowning. What the hell was I going to do now? Were they going to dump me on the streets of Washington, DC among the beggars and homeless? I stammered, "I... I have some vacation time accrued." It was a weak arGument.

"The gall of this guy! You don't deserve anything, Glass. You may go to a federal prison for espionage and you're quibbling about vacation pay?" Kenney hesitated, reconsidered. "I can provide you with a travel voucher and some per diem money. So where do you want to go?"

"To Ocala, Florida where my folks live. I guess I'll hang out there until I find another job. I don't suppose I can get a letter of recommendation."

Kenney actually laughed. He rocked back in his swivel chair, looked up at the ceiling and pretended to dictate, "This will introduce Mr. Irwin Glass. He only worked for us for a few months and proved to be an alcoholic womanizer who voluntarily signed on with the Soviet Secret Police as a spy for Russia." Kenney sat up again. "I doubt if even Burger King will hire you to sweep the floor on that one. Go down to the travel office and pick up a voucher."

I was reluctant to accept Kenney's verdict. "Don't I get a chance to appeal?"

"You can try. If you weren't a civil servant you could be fired without cause or warning and hustled out of the office without notice. Happens all the time."

"Don't I get two weeks severance pay?"

Kenney sighed. "Yes, and payroll will reimburse you for lost vacation time. Now get out of my office."

Plunged in gloom, I waited in the travel and payroll offices for the paperwork to be completed. Then I returned to the hotel to phone my parents, the airlines and make a reservation.

I arrived back at my room in the Marriot and stood, still in shock, trying to put it all together in my mind. Did any flights go to Ocala? Ocala was in the middle of Florida. Would I fly to Orlando? Tampa? Gainseville? Which airline flew there? I should have asked at the travel office at State, but I was so confused, shocked, and befuddled that I forgot.

Could my father pick me up? I didn't possess a credit card. I probably couldn't get one, since I didn't have a job and was homeless. My Indiana driver's license was back at the apartment in Moscow, presumably being packed up with all my belongings. Hertz wouldn't rent a car for cash and I couldn't drive without a license.

All these problems were boiling in my mind as I browsed the yellow pages of the Washington, DC phone book when there was a knock at the door. Now what? I opened the door to see two men in the hallway. For a frightening, irrational moment I thought Putinsky had sent a couple of assassins. "What is it?"

"FBI. We need to ask you some questions. Can we come in?" Just as Mormon missionaries travel in pairs, dressed in suits, white shirts, and ties, the two agents wore suits that might have been bought off the same rack. The only difference was the color of their ties. They were grey men, chosen because they were so nondescript and average that they could disappear in a crowd without being noticed. The only thing missing was sunglasses. Secret Service and FBI watchers wore sunglasses so you couldn't see their eyes and figure out where they were looking.

One agent was a couple of inches taller than the other. He flashed his ID and I asked to examine it more closely. I could not tell if their identification was real or forged. "So you are Phelps and this is Adams? What do you want? How did you know I was here?"

"We know everything," the second agent, Adams, said.

"Then you don't have to ask me anything," I said, recovering my senses.

"Can we sit down?"

There was only one chair and I took it. The agents sat on the bed, moving aside the clothes I had left there when I changed into the new slacks I'd bought in the hotel shop. "I thought the FBI, CIA, and State didn't talk to one another. So what do you want to know that you don't already?"

"Why don't you tell us?"

I repeated the whole story, how I got to Moscow, the reception for the art exhibit, the meeting with Svetlana, the encounter at the Metropol, the night in the drunk tank, the return of my clothes, the meetings with Putinsky, the man who called himself Robert, even the six incriminating photographs. The more often I told my story, the more absurd it sounded to me, like it was someone else's story, not mine. I felt like a disembodied spirit, an uprooted plant, a lost soul.

Phelps wanted more details. "So you accepted payment from the Soviet agent and signed a receipt?"

"It was all part of the act," I explained. "Except there was no payment. I went to the Riggs bank today to check on it. Putinsky never opened the account and never made the deposit. I never received any money from the Russians and I was never a Soviet agent."

"But you did write a report on your boss, Ms Lutz ."

84

"Only with the approval of the man at the embassy."

The two agents looked at each other. Phelps shook his head. "I don't think we have enough to charge you, Mr. Glass. You can be of great help to us if your story is true. We need to know where you are at all times. This Putinsky is likely to want to maintain the connection."

"You mean, he'll want to kill me?"

"That's unlikely. You are not a sufficient threat, but he may want to turn you into a sleeper agent."

"I can't believe that."

Agent Adams wasn't taking any chances. "When you get to Florida, check in with the FBI office in Tampa. If Putinsky tries to contact you we want to know about it."

I acquiesced. "I guess I can do that. Am I home free?"

"These things never go away, Mr. Glass. As long as someone somewhere in the government still thinks you are a Soviet agent, your file is always open."

"But I haven't been arrested or convicted of anything."

"True, but a background check can turn up this situation. It's not like there's a warrant out for your arrest, but you have to behave yourself. You are a suspicious character, Mr. Glass, what they call a person of interest."

It might have been simpler if everyone told the truth. Unfortunately, there were people who were vindictive, who had their own agendas, like Susan Lutz who wanted to get rid of me and didn't mind calling me a drunk and a womanizer. Maybe she was jealous. Maybe she wanted to be the one who had a nice fuck in a Moscow hotel, maybe even with souvenir pictures, and this was her revenge. Go figure.

What was "Robert's" motivation? To play me like a pawn in a chess game of spy versus spy? And then be mad when I opted out?

In spite of having written those innocuous reports on Susan, I didn't think he betrayed her. Well, not seriously. She wasn't the victim. I was. I felt used. By everyone. It just wasn't fair.

"I didn't think I was an interesting person," I said. "You guys should go after someone real."

"That's not up to us to decide."

So the two agents were, like the old Nazis at the Nuremberg war crimes trials claimed as a defense, "Just following orders." Whose?

Phelps got up off the bed and smoothed the coverlet. "Have a nice flight to Florida. And remember to check in with the Tampa office. Just to dot all the i's and cross all the t's."

They left.

I turned to the task of getting a flight reservation so I could call my father and arrange to be met at an airport in Florida.

...

I stuffed the Moscow jacket and hat in the new carryon suitcase I'd bought at the Marriot, checked out, and took the hotel shuttle to Dulles for my flight to Tampa. I was still experiencing culture shock. After months in Moscow with its shortages, poverty, bad food, and the ever presence of KGB watchers, here were crowds of Americans who did not live in fear of having their conversations recorded, of being watched by their neighbors, of being denounced.

They were still serving meals on the planes in those days. My meal on the flight, in spite of conventional complaints by American passengers, was pretty good. In included a fresh apple. When in Moscow had I ever found an edible apple?

My folks were waiting at the airport when I came out among the tourists and Florida vacationers. My dad, Kenneth Glass, looked fit for his age, was deeply tanned from his hours on the golf course. Both of my parents had made the transition from Midwestern South Bend, Indiana to the Florida milieu. Dad had on a pair of chartreuse slacks and a gaudy, short sleeved shirt only a golfer would wear. My mom, Erna Glass, wore a white blouse with gold trim and a pair of pedal pushers she was much too old for.

Dad didn't say much until we left the airport and were on the highway north toward Ocala. "So are you on leave? You've only been at the Moscow job for a couple of months."

I didn't know where to start and wasn't about to tell my parents about the business with Svetlana. "Didn't work out, Dad. Moscow wasn't what I expected."

"You mean after all that studying Russian stuff you got to Russia and didn't like it?"

"It wasn't that. I got in trouble with the Soviet Secret Police. I've been sent home for my own safety."

My father took his eyes off the road. "What were you doing? Playing James Bond? I thought you had a job at the American library."

"I did."

"So what's that got to do with the Secret Police? What do they call it, the KGG?"

"KGB." At the mention of the KGB I looked back to see if we were being followed. My paranoia was kicking in again. "It's had different names under different regimes, NKVD, stuff like that."

My mother had other interests. "How long will you be staying with us? Are you on vacation?"

"Not exactly. I don't know." I didn't want to admit I was fired. "Call it indefinite leave. You have a spare bedroom. I thought I might stay there."

"Oh, that won't do. I've taken that room for my quilting. That's where I have my sewing machine and all my materials. You can sleep in the lanai. There's a cot there."

I remembered the lanai, a fancy name for an enclosed sun porch. It was open most of the time for fresh air, but the windows could be shut when it rained. There were no curtains. I couldn't forget Putinsky's shout in Gorky Park, "You're a dead man!" If I were sleeping on a cot in the lanai in full view of the street, Putinsky's assassin might pop me with a silenced pistol shot from a passing car. No poisoned umbrella pellet needed.

"What about your books and stuff?" my father asked. "We don't have an attic or a basement."

"The embassy is packing it all up and sending it." I remembered the crates loaded in the back of the C-46 from Moscow. Maybe those were someone's personal effects, not just caviar and duty free vodka as I'd suspected.

My father grumbled, "It's going to be crowded."

I could see my presence was not very welcome. It had been years since I lived at home. My folks were used to having an empty nest. When I left for graduate school they had rented out my room in South Bend to a Notre Dame student. On Christmas vacation I had to sleep on a couch in the basement rec room.

"I'll start looking for a job right away."

"A job?" My father was startled. "I thought you were on leave or something."

"I was fired."

"Goddamit, Erwin, I was never fired from any job in my whole life."

I was ashamed and apologetic. "Not my fault. Stuff... (I almost said shit) happens."

That killed our conversation.

I was not home free, as I'd hoped. Being fired made me persona non grata even to them.

An FBI agent visited all the neighbors, asking questions about me. This infuriated my father. He fumed, "They think you're a damned commie! We're just getting to know these people."

The last stroke fell when I returned from the post office. I'd been mailing a dozen copies of my resume, such as it was, with application letters. I was met by my father who took me into the master bedroom. "What the hell is this?" he asked.

"What the hell is what?"

"This mail came for you." He held up a government manila envelope, penalty for private use $300, the postmark illegible. "I thought it was from the State Department to reinstate you, but it only enclosed this letter." The enclosure was an envelope on cheap, foreign stationery with a Russian stamp. It was addressed to Irwin Glass at the American library.

Attached to the Russian letter was a yellow Post-it note. "I warned you about this. If someone shows up with the other half, report in at once or you'll be arrested." It was signed simply "R."

The flap on the Russian letter was already loose, like it had been steamed open and not resealed. "You opened my mail?"

My father protested. "It was already open. How do you explain the picture? Who is 'R'?"

"'R' is the guy who kicked me out of Moscow."

I studied the photograph. It was one of the dreaded six photographs taken at the Metropol, the one with Svetlana straddling me, naked. Like a rider posting on the saddle of a cantering horse, she had bounced ecstatically on my penis. That I was crocked half out of my mind and delirious didn't show on my face, but there was no mistaking my identity.

The top section of the photo with Svetlana's face and bare shoulders had been torn off, leaving a jagged edge.

I could only mumble, "Oh, Jesus." My parents were never meant to see those photos.

"There's a note along with it, but it's not in English." My dad couldn't read Russian.

My knees were weak and I sat down. My hands shaking, I unfolded the cheap, anonymous paper. "My dear Irwin," it began. Again with the "dear Irwin." Was this Putinsky being cute or Svetlana? If it had been spoken, Svetlana would have mispronounced my name. She couldn't handle the W's. The note said simply, "Keep this photo. You will need it when someone contacts you." That was it.

So, whoever contacted me would show the matching piece with Svetlana's face. Putinsky wasn't through with me. He thought he could still force me to be a sleeper agent.

It was a mixed signal. All this time in Ocala I had slept fitfully, waking during the night every time the lights from a passing car swept over me. If Putinsky were going to make good on that threat to kill me, why send the photo? Someone was working at cross purposes.

"So?" my father demanded. "What's it say?"

"I think it's from a girl friend."

Dad smiled. "You son of gun, Irwin. Sowing wild oats, were you? I didn't think you had it in you."

"It's complicated. She's the wife of a KGB officer. That's why I had to leave Russia." It was a plausible excuse, one a man like my father could believe.

He laughed. "Like they say, let me die at age ninety, shot by a jealous husband."

"I'm not ninety yet, Dad. At this rate, I'll never make it."

The photograph established a different relationship between me and my dad, but it renewed my determination to leave Ocala. I didn't want my parents to be caught in the crossfire. A visit from the FBI was bad enough. People among the retirees had little to do but gossip. I was not confident that my father might not share the story of the pornographic photo with his golf partners and brag how his son had cuckolded an officer of the Soviet Secret Police and had to leave the country for his own safety. The only secure secret was known to only one person who didn't talk.

I did not report the arrival of the torn photograph to the Tampa FBI office. I wanted to put plenty of space between myself and the government. I guessed that when the envelope arrived at the American library Susan Lutz simply handed it over, unopened, to embassy security for forwarding. Then "Robert" got his hands on it. That was how it got into a government envelope.

"Robert," or whoever he was, might have put a copy of the Russian note in a follow up report to the FBI. I hoped not. I was gambling on the notorious compartmentation that separated the US intelligence agencies, each protecting their own territory. If they did not share information, I might be safe. I hoped that "Robert" would typically keep the information about the torn photo within his own agency and not notify the FBI. They didn't need to know about it, did they?

I turned my attention to finding a job. What would I do? My Russian was fluent, but my own writing in the language was not literary. I did not have the skills to approximate in English the nuances, rhythms and allusions of an original Russian text. I could hardly get a job as a translator for a New York publisher. What was to translate? Solzhenitsyn's *Gulag Archipelago* excepted, Russian authors were not popular.

There were some Russian émigrés in Florida. Maybe the local hospital needed someone to translate. At best that would be a temporary, on call position, not a regular job.

My personal effects were delivered in several wooden crates I had to pry open with a borrowed crowbar. Nothing was missing. Even the six original Metropol photographs were intact.   Someone had even packed the pot and pan from the apartment, and those were embassy property.

I left the books in their crate and unpacked only my clothes.   The Russian jacket and hat went into the crate.   I didn't need those in Florida.

Could I teach? I had a Master's degree, but not a certificate to teach in a K-12 system like my father.   As a graduate student I'd had an assistantship, teaching one basic course a term.   This was not the time of year to apply for a university job.   What to do in the meantime?

I would have to start my life over.

Part Two

What followed my return to the United States was a series of unsatisfactory jobs. I applied for a cashier's job at an Ocala department store, but was overqualified. The personnel manager had only a high school education and saw me as a potential competitor for her own job.

After that rejection I didn't mention my Masters in International Relations. Nobody needed to hire a full time Russian speaker. A degree in Russian looked suspicious in a society where the memory of the McCarthy witch hunt for communists was still fresh. To get a nothing, minimum wage job I had to be a nobody.

While in college I had read mostly Russian literature or textbooks. There was little time for any other reading. I really knew nothing of espionage and what they call trade craft. All I'd heard were terms like "double agent" and "recognition signal" so I went to the library in search of books about spies and spying. I learned that the "honey pot" tactic I had fallen for was classic Mata Hari stuff. I read about dead drops and cutouts. I also realized that Ian Fleming's James Bond was a comic book figure. In the movies about Bond many people were killed, but nobody got hurt. It was all gadgetry, cars that turned into submarines and the like. The fiction was plot driven, not about character, and the villains were hollow caricatures. The real world, the one I was in, was different. The real world was about paranoia, fear, and in my case depression and loneliness. I had no one to turn to, no "handler" to encourage me.

Reporting to the FBI office in Tampa of my whereabouts was met simply with confusion. At that time the FBI weren't communicating with the CIA or the State Department or even their own branch offices. When I checked in with the Tampa office as the Washington FBI guys had required I was treated like some quack or nut case. In Florida it was Cubans they were interested in, and were too busy to follow up. Reporting my whereabouts was, I felt, a waste of time, a formality I'd as soon dispense with.

The Irwin Glass Trilogy

I bought an old Volkswagen bus from a broke hippie who had come to Florida for the easy life in the sunshine. It was painted with gaudy flowers and peace symbols and needed constant care but it could hold my stuff in the original crates that had been flown from Moscow. Armed with various versions of my resume, prepared on my father's computer, I drove to Bloomington to revisit my old department at Indiana University. If I enrolled in the Ph.D. program I might get an assistantship to cover basic living expenses, but I no longer had a stomach for student status and poverty. I'd been out in the so called real world. Compared to that, being a student seemed superficial, insulated, even demeaning.

Thanks to a tip from my mother's pastor at her church in Ocala, I landed a job at Indianapolis Christian, a small, struggling college in Indiana. The administration which consisted of the president, his secretary, and a part time dean, had grandiose ideas but the school was not accredited. At Indianapolis Christian I shared an office a few hours a week and felt like a welfare case. It reminded me of my graduate assistantship days at IU. It was a shit job that paid only enough for me to rent a room in the damp basement of a private home. It was worse than that bed-sit in Moscow. I didn't even have a kitchen, just a microwave to heat up TV dinners.

I hadn't given up on the demand for registration with the FBI, not yet. As instructed, as soon as I was settled in on that miserable teaching job I stopped in at the Indianapolis office of the FBI for my obligatory check-in. The office was in the Federal Building, the entrances watched by strategically placed surveillance cameras. Inside I had to show a picture ID before the guards would let me in.

After Tampa, I figured it was just a meaningless formality. I did get to see someone, an agent about my age, white shirt, tie, and shoulder holster. When I told him I was Irwin Glass and was supposed to check in he asked me into an office. He didn't want to talk in front of the receptionist.

The FBI must get lots of nut cases, so he was wary. "Why do you have to check in with us? You on parole or something? This isn't a parole office."

"I got kicked out of my job in Moscow because I refused to work as a double agent."

The FBI guy smirked. "You been reading spy novels, Mr. Glass?"

"I'm just supposed to let you know I'm in town. I'm teaching at Indianapolis Christian."

"Never heard of it."

"It's a shit job, but it's work."

He asked me for my Social Security number and logged in on his computer. I sat down and waited.

The agent's attitude changed when he found my record. He swiveled in his chair and looked at me with new respect. Obviously he no longer thought I was some sort of nut who read spy novels and lived in some fantasy world. "Who is Robert?"

That gave me a sick feeling in my stomach. "He's CIA. He claims I'm a paid Soviet agent."

"Are you?" Nothing like asking the direct question.

"No. It's all a misunderstanding."

"You involved in any political activity?"

"None. I'm not even registered to vote." I gave him my Indianapolis address and phone number and he let me go. He seemed satisfied that I was a rational person, not some escapee from an asylum or candidate for one but he took down the information I gave him.

What was in my computer record with the FBI? There was no way for me to find out, but one thing was clear. Bulldog "Robert" was sniffing at my tail. Hell with him.

I didn't go back to the FBI and they didn't contact me. The job at Indianapolis Christian was not tenure track and lasted only one year. I would have to look elsewhere for any kind of future. At least I was gaining some classroom experience even if I taught fewer than ten students at a time. I had to rebuild my resume, to put the failed State Department job in the background.

Tenure track jobs required a so-called terminal degree, a Ph.D. Even a tenure track position, if I could land one, had a five year probationary period. That meant publication in scholarly journals and, possibly, research grants. I had no ideas worthy of a grant proposal. If not awarded tenure after five years you were out.

Adjunct instructors were second class citizens. They got no committee assignments, were not expected to publish or attend professional association meetings. Like the janitors, they were simply the help, invisible and expendable.

I became one of a sad company of itinerant college instructors, always temporarily employed, no benefits, paid by the course and moving like a solitary gypsy from one college campus to another. Like some skilled handyman, my professional role as "teacher" meant I could teach any entry level course. Just give me the textbook and time enough to be two chapters ahead of the students. God forbid some smart student would read three chapters ahead and leave me befuddled.

Some such teaching hacks actually read the textbook to the class, like story time in kindergarten. At least I didn't do that, but I did learn enough of teaching methods to make it look like I knew the subject.

After the year at Indianapolis Christian I landed a job at Southern Illinois University in Carbondale. It looked like I was finally achieving some credibility. The dean, a smooth talking administrator in his fifties with an immaculate haircut and an expensive suit, gave a sales pitch worthy of a used car salesman. SIU was an up and coming university, he said, and bragged about the sports teams. I signed a one year renewable contract. I did not expect to have to sign a loyalty oath, but I did. Perhaps the powers at SIU were afraid of Communists and other subversives.

The oath was approximately the same that I swore to when I was hired by the government, that I swore to uphold the Constitution and defend it against all enemies, foreign and domestic. In spite of "Robert's" assertions that the business with Vladimir Putinsky made me a spy for the Soviet Union, I did not see myself as an enemy of the Constitution, foreign or domestic. I signed.

Fortunately, in my interview with the SIU dean I was not asked about his brief sojourn in the Soviet Union or my brief employment with the State Department. I did not have to be evasive about my reasons for leaving government service. That failure to ask me showed that the dean was all show and little depth, that the loyalty oath was just a formality.

I suspected that the loyalty oath might be used as an excuse to fire some instructor who demonstrated publicly or otherwise against American military activity, whether in Vietnam, Iraq, or anywhere else. If Susan Lutz could exaggerate my one night in the Moscow drunk tank and call me an alcoholic and womanizer, what false claim might be made against me if I marched in an anti war protest?

By now I was aware that all anti-war protests were photographed. The FBI was looking for agitators who moved from campus to campus stirring up trouble. I stayed in the background, carried no signs, and gave no speeches, but I did look up the number of the FBI in the Carbondale phone book and called in to register. It was just a formality, I assured the person I spoke with, but I was obliged to stay in touch. I figured that would be enough, but I got a call back.

My record had pursued me. I was asked why I left Indianapolis Christian. Again, was I involved in any political activity? None. No marching in demonstrations? No.

This time there was no mention of "Robert," but I felt he was still watching, expecting me to be a sleeper spy awakened.

Another surprise at SIU was the requirement that I sign a non fraternization agreement. I was not to invite a student to my apartment, though I could invite an entire class. Nor was I to be seen alone with a student in some bar, on a picnic, or other place. I was, simply put, not to date any student. The reason, as the dean put it, was that professors were authority figures who could take advantage of a student's vulnerability. There was to be no hanky panky with the students, male or female.

I had to admit that at Indianapolis Christian I had a couple of female students who were cute. One had flirted with me. I had suspected that some girls might flirt with a professor in order to get a better grade, but I was mature enough to see through that sort of mischief. Some students might be unscrupulous enough to try to get me into a compromising situation and then blackmail me for an A in the course. It could be the college version of the Moscow honey pot ploy, minus the bugged hotel room and the incriminating photographs. I did not want to get into a "she said, he said" confrontation in which the male was always presumed to be the guilty party. It would be like being denounced to the Secret Police with no recourse other than the Gulag or Coventry.

I had already experienced that sort of trap when the prize was more important than just a grade in a course. I had the pictures to prove it. Like some Israeli who survived the Holocaust, I swore "Never again." No, sir, there would be no fraternization or hanky panky with the SIU students.

I was promised a couple of sections of beginning Russian language and was hungry enough to believe it, only to be told after I moved all my stuff into an apartment above a store on Carbondale's main street that the classes didn't make the minimum enrollment. Unlike Indianapolis Christian, SIU had standards. SIU wouldn't run an undergraduate class with only five or six students. Could I teach English Composition instead? I had no choice. The old Volkswagen needed an engine rebuild and wouldn't survive another job hunt. Sure. I could teach home economics cooking classes if necessary, just so I had a job.

My office on the SIU campus was shared with a pretty blonde, Marg Cole, and we had a brief romance. There was nothing in the fraternization agreement prohibiting romance with a fellow faculty member. I had fantasies about marriage and having kids, maybe a boy and a girl. I was tired of being a celibate bachelor. Since I didn't drink, certainly not vodka, and not even beer, I didn't frequent the Carbondale bars where I might pick up some companionship.

Marg Cole was nice. Together we bicycled around campus. Was it love? Or was I reading too much into the relationship? It was convenient, not passionate.

Unfortunately, Marg decided to join the Peace Corps. We broke up when I made an excuse not to join with her. The truth was I remembered I could never work for the government again, could never get a security clearance, and was viewed as untrustworthy. If I did apply for the Peace Corps, loyalty oath or none, someone might turn up the old State Department personnel record and I'd be out.

Marg wrote me from her post in Kenya, but the letters

became shorter and infrequent.   Finally she announced that she was getting married to another Peace Corps volunteer. That was that.

There was no future for me at SIU as an adjunct instructor.   Teaching Southern Illinois farm kids English Composition and the evils of comma splices was a bore. Hadn't I myself made errors in subject-verb agreement? Did it matter?

I had to move on.   I tried networking with every old classmate I could remember, attended the Modern Language Association annual meeting in Chicago at my own expense, left my resume with everyone who might have a connection.

The Chicago based American College Bureau, which used to place college teachers in jobs on a commission basis, went bankrupt in a period of declining enrollments and funding.

After Southern Illinois, I did five years in my old home town, South Bend, at the IU-PU joint campus of Indiana and Purdue Universities.

Remembering the order I'd been given by the agents in Washington, I dutifully registered with the South Bend FBI office figuring they had forgotten about me.   I acted casual, like it was just a formality.   It wasn't like I was a registered sex offender or something like that.   I wasn't on parole.   I wasn't a criminal.   But I sensed that the FBI agent I spoke with suspected I was hiding something.   What if he pursued it? Was "Robert" in the information loop? Still?

South Bend was my home town, but I had not made many friends at Riley High School, possibly because my father taught there.   As a teacher's kid I was suspect, not invited to illicit beer parties at Pinhook Park.   In the years since graduation the few pals I did have had dispersed to other cities around the country.   South Bend was no longer my home.

IU-PU also had a loyalty agreement, but no rule against fraternization, not that I was tempted.   But in my fifth year there I was told the contract would not be renewed.   IU-PU needed a high percentage of terminal degrees on the staff.   I was told it was an accreditation thing.   I would have to look again for another job.

Nobody wanted to hire someone with a Masters in Russian and International Relations.

I had reached an important passage in life. I was forty. Forty meant it was now or never. I was not going to pursue a Ph.D. I was about to be over the hill except I had never got to the top of it.

Before it was too late I thought I would try business. The Soviet Union had collapsed. I figured Vladimir Putinsky was out of the picture as the country reorganized. He was probably no longer KGB but a salesman for luxury automobles and no longer interested in me. The collapse of the bankrupt Soviet Union opened the doors to speculative trade. The old apparatchiks shifted gears and became the new Russian mafia. There was money to be made for an American who spoke Russian. It was common for American government officials to go into business jobs for more money. Could I find a niche there?

Again the feelers went out. Surely some American companies would be interested in hiring someone who knew Russian and international relations.

I got a web site and posted my resume on the Internet. At last I got an interview.

It looked promising. After several phone calls I was provided free transportation to New York, met at Kennedy airport by a driver who held up a sign "Glass", and taken directly to an office for the interview with IJAG corporation. IJAG had a web site but the description of what they did was innocuous and vague, full of terms like "cutting edge technology" without mentioning what technology.

Arriving for the interview, dressed in a new blazer and necktie bought for the occasion, I sensed there was something that wasn't kosher. So much can be deduced from furnishings and bulletin boards. IJAG had no bulletin board. The premises reminded me of that rented office in Washington where I had failed the polygraph. I decided the lack of anything personal was what made me suspicious. The office had no family photos on display, no framed diploma, not even architectural renderings of a future factory. The furniture was new and looked rented. Was this a front? A cover organization that masked some nefarious activity, perhaps CIA? I had no interest in under cover work.   I'd been bitten once.

The woman who interviewed me was in her mid-thirties, her blonde hair shoulder length.   The name plate on the desk said simply "Personnel" and she said her name was Miss Olsen.   By that time I had had many unsatisfactory interviews.   This interviewer looked more like a receptionist, not a mid-level executive.   Olsen was thorough, had a checklist, asked me questions about my resume, asked about my brief position in the State Department but it was perfunctory and routine, no special emphasis or even interest.

Then she asked the key question.   "Would you be willing to work abroad?"

"What country are we talking about?"

"Do you think you'd like to work in Poland?"

I didn't know Polish, but after the long Russian occupation, I was sure my Russian would be useful in Poland. "I think so."

"You'll need a passport, of course."

That was it.   My American passport, which had expired, had been stamped only for immediate return to the United States.   Could I get another one to work outside the country? Without a passport I could not travel abroad except to Canada or Mexico where a valid driver's license was sufficient proof of residence.   Was I still tainted by that incident in Moscow? Was I still, after so many years, regarded as a security risk?

"I can't travel behind the Iron Curtain."

The interviewer was surprised.   "There is no more Iron Curtain, Mr.   Glass.   That's past history.   Nothing should prevent you from working in Poland."

"I'm not so sure.   I had to leave Moscow on short notice for my own safety and my passport was marked valid only for immediate return.   That was years ago."

Miss Olsen wasn't giving up so quickly.   "You can apply for another, not mention past history."

"You mean lie about it?"

"You don't have to lie.   Just don't tell the passport people what they don't need to know."

There it was again, that "need to know" business.   What

100

was IJAG? A CIA cover?

"You want this job, don't you?"

She had been evasive about what my duties would be if hired. If she would have me be evasive about this, what else? What the hell?

"Well, I can apply for a new passport."

"Why don't you do that and get back to me?"

Even if I didn't get the job, whatever it was, it was worth the test.

I flew back to South Bend, had the required glossy photos taken, had a notarized copy made of my birth certificate, went through the whole regamarole of forms, signatures, and a check for the fee. I filed an application for the new passport.

After a maddening delay, the passport application came back refused. The letter was polite but cryptic. I could not be issued a passport for travel outside the United States. No reason was given. It was like running into a stone wall of bureaucracy.

Until then I had not had any plans for foreign travel. When Marge joined the Peace Corps I hadn't thought about the passport thing, just that I couldn't take a government job. Since then I'd been too busy eking out a living in poorly paid jobs, grateful that I had not been sick, for I had no health insurance. Now the very denial of the freedom to travel abroad made me angry and bewildered. Did I have any recourse? Even if I did fight through rolls of Washington red tape, by then the job opportunity would have disappeared.

I tried to call the IJAG office with the bad news, but the phone was disconnected and a letter to the attention of Miss Olsen came back as undeliverable. I never found out whether the company was legitimate or even existed. Maybe it was a con job, one of those schemes some employers used to get people who work their asses off for a so-called probationary period when there was no intention of offering a permanent job.

Maybe it was a scam, like those advertised "earn money at home" deals or, worse, a scheme to mail parcels which in fact contained stolen goods, making the sender a co-conspirator for a criminal gang and liable for prison.

Someone was always trying to game the system. Hadn't I been promised to teach sections of Russian, only to be told there would be none? I'd been exploited.

Then came 9/11. The fifteen Moslem suicide terrorists not only knocked down the World Trade Center in New York and killed over three thousand Americans but they turned the United States on its ear in a fit of national paranoia.

In that state of national emergency I had to look for yet another job. The old hippie Volkswagen had died long before. Now I owned a used, white Ford pickup truck with a box on the back where I could load my recycled wooden crates that had accompanied me from school to school for years.

There was a job opening at Michigan Institute of Technology in Portage Lake, a small town near Lake Superior. Could I fly up for an interview? Sure. I'd love to. Where the hell was Portage Lake, Michigan? I used my computer mapping program to search for it and was surprised to find how remote Portage Lake, Michigan was. It was about six hundred miles north of South Bend. I could fly up from Chicago, skipping the inconvenient short flight from South Bend to Midway and the hassle of getting from there to O'Hare.

A United flight would get me to the Houghton County airport about 2:30 in the afternoon.   I needed to be at O'Hare by noon to go through security.

I packed a bag for a couple of nights and set off early in the morning to drive the pickup truck to Chicago.   I hated the drive.   The I-94 was congested with eighteen wheelers belching diesel exhaust and the Dan Ryan expressway was in continuous repair.

I parked my truck in the long term lot, took the shuttle bus to the terminal and the United Airlines check-in.   It was crowded.   While I waited in line I ruminated about what Portage Lake, Michigan must be like.   I had looked up Michigan Institute of Technology on the Internet.   Portage Lake was the place where professional hockey got its start. Besides having a hockey team, the school had a ski hill. The location looked ideal, though the winters in the Upper

Peninsula were long. Hell, it was a job. I'd work anywhere.

At last I got to the United desk to check in.

The clerk, an uncertain, clean shaven young man, was a trainee. He had to consult with another employee, an older woman, who stood behind him and walked him through each step.

"I have a reservation," I explained.

The trainee couldn't find it.

The woman intervened. I noticed her name tag said Shebulsky. Her tag had two little stickers, wing-shaped awards for service. She busied herself at the keyboard, frowned, and called a supervisor.

A much older man came to the desk. He shouldered the trainee and Shebulsky aside. A few clicks of the keyboard later and he asked, "You are Irwin Glass?"

"Yes. I'm flying up to Portage Lake for a job interview."

The man shook his head. "I'm sorry, Mr. Glass. You're not flying with anyone. We have you on the No fly list. Homeland Security."

"What?" I was starting to panic. "There must be some mistake."

"If there's a mistake, it's not ours, Mr. Glass. You'll have to check with Homeland Security."

"How do I do that? I need this job."

"Beats me, Mr. Glass. Now if you'll just step out of line."

"But this is ridiculous. Do I look like a Moslem terrorist?"

"I can understand you are upset, Mr. Glass, but if you're on the list there's nothing we can do about it. Now step out of line or I'll have to call security."

Defeated, I wheeled my carry-on bag away from the United desk and went in search of someone from Homeland Security. Was someone else named Irwin Glass a Moslem terrorist or one of the FBI's ten most wanted men? Didn't seem likely.

I had checked in with the FBI when I got the job in South Bend. Nobody should be thinking I had gone into hiding like some parolee who skips. Paranoia causes people to imagine all sorts of improbable threats. Who's paranoia? Mine or the FBI's?

The security guard didn't know anything. The No fly list came out of Washington. Maybe I could appeal. What did that require? Months of paperwork? By then I'd have missed out on the job.

I didn't believe it was a coincidence. Some computer database digging through past records had hit my name and put me on the list automatically. It had to be a bureaucratic mistake, as the computer jockeys said, garbage in, garbage out. It had happened to others. I'd read about such cases in the South Bend Tribune, innocent people who could not get on an airplane, people whose names were the same as some potential terrorist, but they couldn't get off that damned list.

Maybe it was a domino effect. That erroneous report that I was a Soviet agent had made its way to the passport department and now to Homeland Security. It was exasperating, but there was nothing I could do about it. What next? I felt like I was again in a police state. The difference between the USA and the defunct Soviet Union was that nobody followed me wherever I went. Or did they?

I phoned the MIT department head to postpone my interview until the next day, took the shuttle back to the long term lot, checked out my pickup truck, then drove north, stopping for gas and road maps of Wisconsin and Michigan.

It took ten hours, a long time to ruminate over who or what put me on a no fly list, how I might get off, if at all, and what limits on my air travel might mean. I could not fly to Florida to see my folks. Neither was in very good shape. How many days would it take to drive all the way to Florida? Especially if I got the job so far north.

When I was in Russia people had internal passports and had to get police permission to travel more than fifty miles from their residence. Would Homeland Security also prohibit me from getting on a train or a bus? What next? Road blocks at every state line crossing?

Whatever had happened to American freedom? Freedom to come and go as you pleased without having to check in with the police, to sign in at a hotel without the police picking up the registry? To travel without a permit was not uniquely American, but it was important. That was what freedom was all about, and someone had taken mine away.

My gas station road map showed that the highway I was driving on, US41, was historical, began at Copper Harbor, Michigan and ended down in Florida. At a place called L'Anse I got my first glimpse of Lake Superior, shimmering silvery in the moonlight. The air off the lake smelled clean and fresh.

I arrived in the Upper Peninsula town of Portage Lake at nearly midnight. The single main street was deserted, but there was a vacancy light on at the Downtowner Motel overlooking the waterfront. It took some time to arouse the clerk. I checked in, exhausted.

Before the interview the next day I took a walk around the town and the campus. It was an attractive place. The downtown looked a bit seedy with a number of empty store fronts and ornate sandstone facades with dates like 1885. What could you expect from an old mining town, a place with a history? There had been copper mines, all now closed. I read the historical plaques posted here and there, discovered the hockey stadium. I took a walk on the waterfront saw the marina on the other side of the waterway that, according to the road map, separated the Keweenaw peninsula from the rest of the U.P.

There was only one traffic light. *This is a good place*, I thought. *I could settle down here.*

The interview at MIT went well. The department head was Dr. Waarala, a name typical of the Finnish population in the Copper Country. This time I was to teach English as a foreign language for the large number of students from abroad. Michigan Institute of Technology, known by the locals as Portage Tech or simply Da Tech, as the clerk at the Downtowner motel had called it when I explained why I was there, had a large number of foreign students and faculty. There was a continuous need for a teacher of English as a Second Language, a course most faculty with the so-called terminal degree didn't want to teach. Maybe it was faculty boredom that had persuaded the curriculum committee to drop traditional English Comp courses. As long as Da Tech had so many foreign students, English as a Second Language

promised job security.   Others might think of me as a
teaching hack, locked in as I was in Freshman level courses,
but I would enjoy working with foreign students.   They
would promise more variety and sophistication than the
poorly motivated farm kids I taught at Southern Illinois.   I
was tired of short term jobs.   Maybe, for once, this was a job
that might stick.

It would be a full time position, with benefits, a one year
renewable contract, but as usual not tenure track.   Da Tech
didn't require a loyalty oath, but they did have a no
fraternization agreement.   Sex with a student meant instant
dismissal.   Dating a student meant a reprimand.   Flagrant
violation and you were out.

I understood.   There would be no problem with
fraternization.   I was too old and too careful for that.

What about housing? The department head, Doctor
Waarala said, "One of my neighbors is Dr.   Kosinsky.
You'd like him.   He's a Russian Jew who is leaving on
sabbatical to spend a year in Israel at the Technion.   Maybe
you can rent his house."

I asked for Kosinsky's office address and was directed to
the Electrical Engineering building.   I found Dr.   Kosinsky
on the second floor.

Kosinsky was a stocky, round faced, athletic man about
fifty wearing a tweed jacket that was too small for him and
wasn't buttoned.   Kosinsky obviously wasn't terribly
interested in fashion.   He wore a turtleneck sweater with a
stretched-out neck and faded blue jeans.   His wild hair had
touches of grey.   When I addressed him in Russian the
professor was startled.   Perhaps, he, too, feared anyone who
might be from the KGB.   "You speak Russian?"

"I majored in Russian Language and Literature at
Indiana University.   That was a long time ago.   When did
you come to the United States?"

"After the Soviet Union collapsed.   They let the Jews
out."

I remembered that the USSR at one time had more than
two million Jews.   Of course, with religion officially
suppressed under Communism, Jews were considered a
nationality, like Ukrainian, and their only connection with

their religious heritage was a stamp on their internal passports. "I'm looking for a place to rent. I understand you are going away for a sabbatical."

Kosinski wasn't yet ready to talk about that. "Have you been to Russia?"

"I worked in Moscow at the American library for a short time."

"Only a short time?"

"I got in trouble with the KGB and had to leave."

Kosinsky understood that. He apparently saw we were kindred spirits.

He must be a refusenik, I thought. *Fired from his job when he asked to leave the country.*

"Yes, my house is to rent. I will not charge you very much. You will have to pay for the utilities of course. Do you like cats?"

I had never had a cat.

"It will be good if you care for my cat. I cannot take her with me to Israel."

If I could arrange for housing so quickly and at such a decent rent, I'd be glad to baby sit a cat.

"But no subletting. I do not want you renting one of the rooms to some student. Students can destroy a house."

"No sub letting. I understand."

I was given a tour of the house, an old three story affair with a steep, double roof, gas heat, and a bathroom with an old cast iron bathtub on gilded feet shaped like lion's claws. There was a spare bedroom.

I was invited to join Kosinsky for dinner at his home. Kosinsky was not married, baked his own bread, and quickly fried up a couple of pork chops and potatoes. Obviously having a internal Soviet passport stamped "Jew" didn't mean he kept the dietary codes.

Kosinsky treated me almost like a relative. He did not have much opportunity to talk to someone in his native language. I was invited to stay the night before my return to South Bend. We had, after all, a shared experience of life under Communism. I understood the black humor typical of Soviet expatriates. "Call me Avrom," Kosinsky said. "Since we are almost landsmen." We were simpatico.

The only jarring note was my polite refusal to have a glass of vodka with my host. I explained that I didn't drink, not even beer. It was rude not to drink with a fellow Russian, but the very sight of Vodka brought back too many bad memories.

I felt a huge sense of relief at my arrangements. In spite of the glitch about not being able to fly, everything else was falling nicely into place.

I was now over forty. Signing the no fraternization agreement was unnecessary. I wasn't interested in fooling around with any student. I certainly wasn't going to fall into the honey pot and get blackmailed for a grade.

I seldom had an opportunity for sex. I had passed that critical mid-life crisis. In spite of the rejuvenating effect of the new job and new surroundings, I was beginning to feel old and washed up. I had almost given up hope of ever marrying or having a family. It was depressing, but that had been my life up to now. Maybe I might meet some female faculty member.

I did not mention to Dr. Waarala that I was on the No fly list. Employers were interested only in the last ten years of employment. I had dropped my brief government service from my resume. As long as I kept a low profile and did my job well, there was hope.

This job might last only five years and by then I'd be so old that some employers wouldn't touch me. Though I was not someone who couldn't hold a job more than a few months, my employment history showed no firm career commitment, either. After forty-five a prospective employee might not be a good prospect for health benefits. By then there were probably what the health insurance companies called preexisting conditions. I'd worry about that later. I was in good health. For the time being I had a job and a place to live, thank God, even if I was on the damned No fly list.

A new beginning was what I thought when I threw my carry on bag onto the passenger seat of the old pickup truck and headed south. New job, new place to live. Things were looking up.

. . .

The Irwin Glass Trilogy

Professor Kosinsky wanted me in the house before he left for Israel so there would be someone there to feed the cat. I packed all my belongings in the back of the pickup and said goodbye to South Bend. It was an easy departure. My few high school friends had moved away. Urban renewal had changed the landscape. The family that bought my parents' old house had put on new siding and a deck. It didn't resemble the home it had once been. I had no sentimental connection to my old home town. Like Thomas Wolfe said, you can't go home again.

I'd experienced the intensity and seriousness of dealing with the KGB and the FBI, a sort of fugitive pursued by Vladimir Putinsky and the sinister "Robert." I realized I had not recovered from the psychological wounds of what happened in Russia and those consequences, the betrayals all along the line.

I'd become like those World War II prisoners or Holocaust survivors, forever imprinted by their experience. I was so ashamed of how I'd been duped, I would not talk about it to anyone. I held back so much of myself that I'd become hard to know.

Maybe when I got up to Portage Lake I would be a new Irwin Glass. With the truck loaded, I looked forward to the trip north.

To avoid the horror of driving through or around Chicago, I chose the longer route through Michigan, across the Big Mac suspension bridge over the Straits of Mackinac and across the vastness of the U.P. forests. The detour gave me a chance to experience those woodlands and the beaches of Lake Michigan's north shore. It was beautiful country, unlike the cornfields of Indiana or Southern Illinois.

Professor Kosinsky and I were together in the Portage Lake house only one day before I drove him to the Houghton County airport for the first leg of his long journey to the Middle East. Then I returned to the old mining era house to unpack and settle in.

The four wooden crates that had followed me from Moscow years before were so durable that instead of being nailed shut, the lids were now hinged with my books and papers. I lugged them upstairs to the back bedroom.

It was a three story house, and Kosinsky had his office on the top floor, which was off limits. I had the second floor with the master bedroom at the front. The back bedroom would be my home office. I stacked the crates to be used as impromptu bookshelves for my collection of classic Russian and Soviet literature.

Among the books was the original envelope with the six damning photographs, plus the torn one I'd received with the warning note. It had been a long time since I looked at those photos.

Sitting on the spare bed, I studied them. I was still smitten by Svetlana Putinsky. Looking at the pictures, I had a strange affinity for the woman even though she had betrayed me. We had hardly spoken, yet I felt a connection. Perhaps it was my imagination, a what-if fantasy. She was a beautiful woman with a wicked gleam in her eyes, and a fetching smile. When I first saw the photos of the two of us in the nude I thought she must be starved for sex, or a nymphomaniac. Then I reconsidered, since she obviously knew she was being photographed at the time. It must have been an act, I thought, for the sake of the cameras and the blackmail scheme. If it was an act, why did she look like she was enjoying herself? It was pretty convincing.

Then again, she could as well have simulated sex for the cameras. She didn't have to be penetrated. Maybe when she saw me naked she'd been aroused. I still couldn't understand it.

I was certain that she hadn't been the one to carry me out of the hotel room, and down to the Moscow street to be transported to wherever I was dumped. Had she been the one who dressed me in my underwear and shoes? It was difficult to reconstruct the scenario.

In some other country I might have been killed, the photos used in a demand for ransom for someone already dead. But this hadn't been a kidnapping. It was just a setup. But why dumped in the street like trash? Putinsky's scheme would have been just as effective if I had been left to sleep it off and wake up hung over in the Metropol the next morning.

And what about the torn photo and the note? It had been years since that was forwarded to my parents' address in

110

Ocala in that government envelope. Surely I must be forgotten by now. With the Cold war over, I was a closed case. Now that I was in Portage Lake, should I report to the local FBI office? Was there even an FBI agent stationed in such a small town? Probably not. I decided to hell with it. I would not report in as I had in other towns where I worked. The Moscow business had been almost twenty years ago. I was done with it.

As soon as I was unpacked and visited a grocery store to stock up on food, I reported in to Dr. Waarala to be assigned office space and be told the department protocols, the password for the assigned desktop computer, the policy on photocopies, etc.

"I'm afraid you'll have to share an office," Waarala said. "We're remodeling, making some space for the language lab and the grad students. For the time being you'll be sharing with Dr. Hartshorn."

Though each faculty office door had a small window so one could look in to see if anyone was in, most of the faculty taped paper, clippings, or announcements over their windows.

Turned out, the faculty member I was to share with worked in the language section of the Humanities Department. Hartshorn had already taken the desk with the view of the campus, marking the territory with an engraved name plate. I didn't have a name plate of my own, not yet.

Waarala had said "Doctor Hartshorn." Was the department head making the same mistake students often did, assuming that all faculty had the so-called terminal degree, a term that suggested death, or was Waarala reminding me that I had only a Masters? If Hartshorn was senior faculty, would there be some conflict about faculty status, since I was only an instructor? I had run into problems with the pecking order of faculty when I was at SIU. I hoped Da Tech was as laid back as the localism for the school's name suggested.

Was this Hartshorn male or female? A newbie like myself, or an established faculty member with tenure?

My curiosity was soon satisfied. Hartshorn turned out to be an assistant professor, Ivy, mother French, father German, her subject German. Yes, there were a still few students who chose German for a foreign language, though it was now more important to learn Chinese. Russian had been dropped from the curriculum for lack of interest years ago.

Ivy Hartshorn was vivacious, bouncy, bubbling with humor. She didn't take much care of her hair, which looked like she'd been riding in a convertible with the top down. As it turned out, she didn't drive a convertible, but a cherry red Tracker, the poor man's Jeep, with a ski rack on the roof. Not that she drove it much, for her apartment was five minutes from campus by bicycle, or a bit longer on cross country skis which she would occasionally use when conditions were right.

Like Kosinsky, she wore faded blue jeans, which seemed to be the faculty uniform at Da Tech. Instead of a blouse, she wore a faded, mostly red, cotton flannel lumberjack shirt. Surely, I reasoned, she wouldn't teach her classes in that outfit, but classes hadn't yet begun. At Indiana University when I was a grad student there was a dress code. Faculty never wore jeans at the office.

Ivy had taken her junior year abroad at the University of Heidelberg. Between her bachelor's and Ph.D. she'd lived in Berlin to build her fluency in German, was actually there when the Wall came down. She had a piece of it, a nondescript chunk of concrete, as a souvenir on her desk.

She was, I realized, a flirt. I hoped she didn't flirt with the students or she'd be snared by the anti fraternization rule. The first thing she asked me was if I was married. When I said I wasn't, she followed quickly with, "Are you gay?"

I was not that either.

"What do you do?" she asked. "Tie it in a knot?"

Embarrassed, I laughed. "Restraint," I said, then tried to take the initiative. "Are you married?"

"I haven't found my dream man yet." Sitting on the edge of the better desk she took on a more serious demeanor, not so easy because she was short enough so her feet didn't reach the floor. It made her look like a little girl. "I'm thirty five. Maybe I'd better get busy. Biological clock and all that."

"I know the feeling well," I confided. "I wanted to have a family, but things haven't worked out."

112

"Don't give up," she advised. "You might get lucky yet."

"I'm afraid I'm an unlucky person. For me things always seem to go wrong."

"How's that?"

"I'd rather not go into it." I didn't want to tell anybody I'd been denied a passport and put on the No fly list. I needed to change the subject. "Have you been here at Michigan Institute of Technology very long?"

"Two years."

"Tenure track?"

"Tough to get here if you're in a subject not conducive to research grants and publishing."

"Maybe you could write a textbook."

"Boring," Ivy said.

"What about translations? Or editing an anthology of German literature?"

"Good idea."

"Maybe you're too busy having fun." I suggested. "What do people around here do for fun?"

"We have six months of snow here, so I ski cross country. I hate snowmobiles, noisy, smelly things. How can you enjoy the beauty of nature when you're roaring through the woods?"

I had never skied, so asked about other alternatives.

She explained that besides hockey the primary means of student entertainment at Da Tech was to hang out in the local bars. Having sworn off drinking any alcoholic beverages I didn't go to bars and discovered long before that if I gave a party and there was no booze, people lost interest. If you didn't drink, people regarded you as something of a drudge.

"I'm afraid I don't drink," I admitted.

"Not even an occasional glass of wine?"

"It's sort of a phobia."

"You're afraid of losing control."

That was a perception I hadn't thought about. She was smart. "I'll have to think about that."

Ivy cocked her head thoughtfully. "Maybe I can cure you." That sounded like an invitation. She was flirting.

Well, why not? Ivy was cute.   I liked that.   "I do drink coffee.   How about a cup?"

"We can go to the student union." She hopped down from the desk.   "It's quiet now.   Students haven't arrived for the Fall semester."

At the Student Union, not having a beer to do the ritual, she made a show of locking arms with our coffee cups. "*Brudershaft*," she said.   "Old German custom.   Now you can call me Ivy.   Ivy is something my aunt calls me."

"Ivy." I liked that.   "As in clinging? I'm just Irwin." It was a good beginning.

I would learn later that she loved to play Scrabble and usually won, except she sometimes tried to foist German words on me if she picked some without umlauts.

. . .

The mixed bag of foreign students and a reluctant Chinese professor who'd been ordered to brush up his English or else were a good test of my training in international relations.   Though I might sit on the classroom desk when lecturing, I was careful not to cross my legs or show my shoe soles to the Arab students.

The Chinese graduate students and their spouses were earnest, but their English preparation before they left their country was largely rote.   In China students repeated stock phrases in unison.   Then there was the pronunciation.

There were other nuances they didn't get.   Few understood the difference between "Do you have any questions?" which anticipated a negative, no questions, and "What questions do you have?" which encouraged them.

For students whose native languages were highly inflected, the nuances in English caused by word placement in a sentence befuddled some.   "I only told you I loved you" versus "I told only you that I loved you" drew blank looks.

Others whose native language was inflected tended to drop definite articles.   In the case of Yoopers whose heritage was Finnish, the tendency was to skip prepositions in sentences like "You go town, hey?"

The fall quarter went well.   The sections were graded pass/fail which made grading easier.   I didn't have to decide between a B minus and a C plus.   I had no problems with students whose cultures demanded an A and never a B. But I still had trouble getting the Arabs to do their homework. They had come to the United States to learn engineering, not the nuances of "any" versus "some."

Some students were humble and easy to please, if not sincere. Others could be arrogant. I was acutely aware that the foreign student who came to class unprepared and ill dressed might be the one who returned to his home country to be Prime Minister or at least a member of parliament. That was something the Yooper students, those natives of the Upper Peninsula who made up forty percent of the student body, didn't understand.

Future Prime Ministers or not, in the classroom I was king. If I didn't show a firm hand I'd utterly lose control. I was relieved when the grades were turned in and I could enjoy the break between quarters.

The snow had, typically, come early, a flurry in September, intermittent ground cover in October. By Thanksgiving the Copper Country had a good start on the six months of winter. My next door neighbor, Department Head Waarala, showed me how to use Kosinsky's snow blower with its electric start, the trick of spraying the outlet with Pam so heavy, wet snow wouldn't stick. Waarala explained the method used for shifting snow with a snow scoop, the region's alternative to ineffective snow shovels.

Ivy Hartshorn was a seasoned transplant to the UP and introduced me to cross country skiing on the trails maintained by the university. She would stand her skis in the corner of our office where the snow melted into a puddle behind the door. I had never skied. South Bend had no skiable hills and no cross country trails when there was snow. SIU was too far south for skiing. Ivy explained the difference between cross country and slalom skis and lectured me on the difference in bindings.

Under her tutelage, I found a serviceable pair of cross country skis and poles at the Goodwill store and bought some boots. She was a patient instructor, didn't laugh when I fell on the trails. After a couple of hours on the Tech Trails we would return to her apartment near campus for hot chocolate and, yes, a snuggle. Our sharing of an office had become a romance even though she had an irritating habit of keeping the phone on her own desk.   For a change, life was good.

Something was amiss at the start of the winter quarter. Occupied with the new class lists, seating charts, lesson plans and my syllabus, I was too preoccupied to notice, but Ivy was suspicious.

"Who's that girl who hangs around in the hallway outside our office? She one of your students?"

"What girl?" I hadn't paid any attention.

Our door was closed.   Ivy pulled off the paper we'd taped over the little window and looked out.   "That girl. The one in the storm coat with the hood."

I went to the window.   "Looks like the old jacket I bought at Gum."

"Gum?"

"The famous department store in Moscow.   Same place I bought that fake fur hat I wear when we go skiing."

Ivy took her turn at the window.   "She's not wearing a hat."

When in Moscow, before that business with Putinsky, I had not been afraid to walk right up to whoever was following me on the street or on the bus and confront him. It was something no fearful Soviet would have dared.   "I'll go out and speak to her."

That surprised Ivy.

I approached the mystery girl.   She was sitting on the floor, leaning against the wall and pretending to study.   She was pretty, wore dark lipstick on rosebud lips.   "Are you waiting to see me?"

She looked up, locked eyes with me.   "You are professor Glass?"

"Not professor.   I'm just an instructor."

"Irvin Glass?"

There it was.   She'd mispronounced my name.   Who else had done that? Some students had trouble with W's and V's.   German students did that.   "Irwin."

"I saw your resume on Internet."

She'd dropped the definite article.   So she was one of the foreign students, but not in my class.   Why bother

116

looking up my resume? Few students went to that trouble. Only the most well organized and thorough did some sort of background check on their professors before signing up for a section. The most some did was to check the published student evaluations. Mine had been just average, the usual ass-kissing praises and the occasional disgruntled disparagement by someone who didn't get a top score.

"You're not in any of my classes."

"No. My mother told me to look you up."

"I don't understand. I've only been here one quarter. She couldn't have been one of my students, unless it was in South Bend."

"At IU/PU?"

"Yes." How did she know that? But that was in my posted resume. I had put it up on the Internet when I was hunting for a job. But I also had a blog and had hoped by networking on the Internet I might find a lead to better employment. Anyone could read it. "Was your mother a student at IU/PU?"

"No. My mother is dead. Breast cancer."

"Sorry to hear that. What about your father?"

The girl shrugged. "Is complicated. Divorced."

Again I detected a foreign aberration. She had an accent. On a hunch, I switched to Russian. "You speak Russian?"

"*Da.*" Suddenly uncomfortable, she stood up. "We talk again, *Doktor* Glass. Not now." She walked away.

"Strange," I said to Ivy when I closed the office door. "She said her mother told her to look me up. She's Russian. I don't get it."

"Who is she?"

"Damn. I didn't ask."

Ivy raised her eyes. "Irwin, I think you have a groupie."

"Not possible. I've never seen her before."

"You've better be careful. I don't like competition."

"Ivy, that kid is half my age. Don't be silly."

"Be careful, honey. She struck me as being too earnest."

"You've nothing to worry about," I reassured her. But I wasn't reassured. The girl's attention wasn't welcome. It

117

brought back old memories I had tried to suppress. My Moscow paranoia had been a mere ember of another life. Now it was flaming up again.

The Russian girl did not sit outside my door again, but I saw her waiting outside my ten o'clock section when I came out. Curious, I walked up to her and spoke to her in Russian. I needed the practice. I seldom had an opportunity to speak the language and was conscious of my American accent. "You said your mother told you to look me up." People often did such things as in 'You're going to America? I once met someone from New York.' But I didn't know anyone in Russia. This had to be a mistake or some mistaken coincidence.

"Yes. She gave me something to show you."

"Really?" What could that be?

She was carrying a back pack, unzipped an inner pocket and pulled out something in a plastic, protective cover. She held it out to me. It was the torn upper half of a photograph.

I recognized it instantly. I had mulled over the original often enough. "You'd better come to my office. The hallway isn't the place to discuss this."

She followed me upstairs to the bank of faculty offices. I unlocked the door and let her in. Thankfully Ivy wasn't in. I realized my hands were shaking. It had been years ago when "Robert" warned me about this. To steady myself, I sat down in my swivel chair and looked across the top of the torn photo at the girl. "Who gave you this? Your mother?"

She hesitated, unwilling to answer or unsure of what answer she should give.

"Have you seen the rest of this picture?"

"No. Only this piece."

Her piece showed only her mother from the cleavage up. The rest of the picture, the half I had in my underwear drawer with the others, showed a naked woman straddling a dazed and naked Irwin Glass. It was not a picture a mother would show her daughter, but then Katya said she had only seen the top portion. What about the others in that incriminating set?

"The last time I saw this it came from Vladimir

Putinsky."

"Vladimir Putinsky my mother's husband. Ex husband. Now he is Putin."

"What? *That* Putin? He's come up in the world?"

The girl shook her head. "Not that Putin. Vladimir Putin, Putinksy like you say, was my mother's husband."

"Did he, Putin or Putinsky, give you the picture or did your mother?"

"My mother. Svetlana Putinsky."

"Svetlana gave this to you? I would expect it would come from him, but they were working together, right?"

She nodded.

She was letting me draw my own conclusions, right or wrong. So she was Putinsky's daughter. Small world. "It's been a long time. What does Putinsky want from me?" As Alice said in Wonderland, curiou ser and curioser. I was confused. "OK." I started over. "So Vladimir gave you this picture?"

"No. My mother stole it from his files."

"What did she expect? To make me a sleeper agent?"

"What is sleeper agent?"

"A spy for the Soviets."

"No spy."

"But you say your mother is dead."

"Yes. Before she die she say I must find you. Show you this photograph as proof."

Proof of what? This is a damned peculiar way to set up an introduction, I thought. Did this girl know what was in the bottom half of the torn photo? The piece she'd given me showed only head and shoulders of Svetlana Putinsky, not the lower half of a naked Svetlana straddling a naked Irwin Glass.

"What's your name?"

"Katya, In American Kathy. In Russian Katarina Vladovna Putinsky."

So. It was Katarina the daughter of Vladimir, family name Putinsky. It would be no huge surprise if a foreign student was asked to look up an old friend in America, but Svetlana was hardly a friend, and certainly Vladimir was not. Hell, he wanted me dead. That was a long time ago. Some people have long memories. What was this strange girl

119

supposed to do? Poison my coffee for telling her father to go fuck himself? This was no chance meeting. She'd hunted me down. For a moment I was afraid of her. "You have some ID? Your passport?"

She was ready and produced a Russian passport from the pocket of her backpack. She handed it over.

I opened it up, saw the picture, name, date of birth, the US immigration stamp. The immigration stamp had to be authentic, but could I trust the passport itself? Was her identity authentic? Or had Putinsky or Putin picked any girl who would pose as my daughter, some agent recruited and trained up with her back story? The Soviet intelligence services could provide her with any number of false passports from any country. I couldn't believe any of it. I returned the passport, not convinced. "You have a student visa?" She could have entered the country on a visitor's visa. How long did it take to get a student visa? What did immigration require before they would issue one?

And why me? If the Russians wanted to send in an agent posing as a student, that was easy. They didn't need Irwin Glass to provide the girl with cover.

Yet whoever sent her had gone through a great deal of trouble and preparation. The deathbed request from a dying mother was a good story, if it were true. What if it was true? That the Putinskys had divorced? The kid would be on her own, far away from her home country, gambling that somehow the torn half of a photograph would serve as a solid introduction, and then what? What did she expect?

Katarina said I wasn't supposed to be a sleeper spy. Maybe she was a spy herself. Seemed a bit young to be an assassin, but then I had never known an assassin, not that I knew of.

Shit. This was going to be trouble. I thought I was through with it. Now I regretted not having located the local Upper Peninsula FBI office to check in as I had years before. I thought I was done with all that nastiness, the concealment of the reason I'd left government service, the avoidance of telling people I couldn't get a passport or fly in an airplane. It was like being a registered sex offender who declined to register and could be picked up any time when they rounded up the usual suspects.   This could ruin the life I was building at Michigan Institute of Technology.

I had not mentioned any of that old history to Ivy.   She might not be happy about this brush with the KGB, certainly not with the label of my being a Soviet agent, no matter how ridiculous that had been in my own mind.   It was what other people thought that mattered, not the truth.   It made me angry.

"But you said your mother is dead.   And divorced from Putinsky." In the years since my expulsion from government service I had done some reading about spies and spying.   I was familiar with some of the tradecraft of what "Robert" would call "the business." "Why this recognition signal?"

Someone else might have asked the meaning of that term.   Katya asked, "How else would you know who I am?"

"Know who you are?" I scoffed.   "Putinsky could send anyone with this piece of a photograph.   That may prove you've come from him, but it doesn't prove who you are. This is all a KGB scam." Now I was angry.   Best to get rid of this kid right away.   "I am not going to work for your country.   "I'll turn you in to the FBI." I took the telephone from Ivy's desk and picked up the receiver.   I didn't know the number, but I could look it up.   Must be in the phone book for the Western Upper Peninsula.   With all the foreign students on campus, especially the Chinese, there must be some spies among them, and the FBI must have a presence somewhere I could reach.

"No!" Katya pleaded.   "Is not like that." She hesitated, her lips trembling.   She was starting to cry.   She took a deep breath before continuing.   "You are my father."

"What?"

"You are my real father."

I dropped the phone and studied the girl's face for the first time.   I saw a resemblance to Svetlana, the same eyes, the same French-looking mouth.   She was biting her lip, had sat down weakly in the visitor's chair, her arms crossed defensively.   She was breathing heavily and starting to sob.

What was she? Some kind of a nut case? "You say I am your father? How is that possible? Vladimir Putinsky is your father."

Katya fumbled in the pocket of her Russian jacket for a handkerchief. She shifted to English. Maybe in English it was easier for her to reveal details too uncomfortable in her own language. "Is complicated. My mother explain before she die in hospital. My mother learn that Putinsky cannot have children. He a very bad man. Brutal. He force my mother to take you to old Metropol hotel for pictures." She couldn't remember the right word.

"For blackmail," I suggested.

"Yes, for what you say blackmail. To make you Soviet agent."

Could she be bona fide? No one else knew those details, unless she somehow had access to CIA, FBI, or State Department files. Maybe there was a mole at the embassy who passed on the details of my expulsion. Surely the details of my misadventure in Moscow were secret, buried in some file but available only to those with a need to know. How else would I turn up on the no fly list? Once you become suspicious, everyone is a potential informant and a traitor.

"That doesn't make me your father," I said. "You could be anybody Putinsky sent. Why should I believe your cover story?" I could understand that for Putinsky to force his wife to pose for nude pictures was a betrayal of their marriage vows, but for Putinsky, a devoted Communist KGB agent, the end justified the means, even if it meant humiliating his wife.

Unless she was already a whore, beyond humiliation.

In that case, why me? How many dumb clucks like me had fallen for Svetlana's honey pot trap? Half a dozen? Any one of them might be the father of her child. Svetlana had said, "I like you, Irvin. You are a nice boy." Maybe I was the only one she remembered.

I tried to recall the six incriminating photos. They were at home in the bottom of the underwear drawer of my bureau. In light of this new information I would get them out and study them again. Svetlana had mugged for the camera. There was a "that will teach you" look in her expression.

Yes, it was complicated. I guessed, I imagined, that she was forced to pose naked for the cameras, so to get even she deliberately had real sex, not just a simulation for Putinsky's blackmail photos. I could guess that Putinsky, furious at that betrayal, had carried me, drunk and groggy, out to the street. That made sense. Under other circumstances and in other cultures, I might have been killed for having sex with the man's wife, but that wouldn't serve the purpose of the KGB. They wanted a live agent, not a dead one. Not then.

Had Svetlana become pregnant because of that domestic conflict? I did remember that I had no condoms, but did not remember whether or not she had helped me put one on. I had heard that condoms were in short supply in Russia. Svetlana could not have anticipated getting pregnant. But even if the sex had produced a pregnancy, the typical Russian solution was an abortion. If Putinsky couldn't have children, Svetlana's being pregnant by me was one way for her to have a child. And then she could hold that knowledge as the ultimate pay-back to her domineering husband. "It's not your kid! You are impotent!" That would show him.

And I was in the middle, the live shuttlecock in a badminton game of gotcha. I wasn't the first bozo to have a one night stand that backfired as a paternity suit. It could happen to anyone. *Why me?*

That was the scenario I guessed. I didn't know if my guess was accurate. It was just another possibility. More likely, this girl was given the name and cover story and sent to force me to provide her with a legitimate identity to slip into the United States and stay for whatever nefarious reasons. Faculty at Michigan Institute of Technology had lots of government grants for research with military applications. The research facility out at the county airport was off limits to foreigners.

Even if she actually was my birth daughter, which I did not believe, why send Katya to America? What gain was there in that? Did Svetlana really expect me to accept the girl? She must have been desperate.

But I knew people do things for many reasons. I tried to put myself in Svetlana's position, dying, if that story were true, divorced, and with a daughter with no means of support in a country where the economy was falling apart. None of the old Soviet guarantees, pensions, jobs, and economic structure, however artificial under Marxism-Leninism, remained. Desperate war veterans were selling their medals to tourists on the streets of Moscow for money to buy food. Sending Katya to America might be Svetlana's only hope.

I hadn't known Svetlana. We had hardly spoken before she gave me that fatal glass of vodka. But thanks to Putinsky's organization, she'd know plenty. Maybe she had pangs of conscious when I was fired and summarily deported to the United States, my nascent career ruined.

I shook my head, trying to make sense of it all. I looked out the window at the campus in the grip of winter. Every day the lake effect snow from Lake Superior added a few inches of new stuff which, Ivy had assured me, would not melt until April or May. Students from Da Tech, bundled in their storm coats and boots, were trudging through the Copper Country snow to class. Out there life was normal, routine. Here in my shared office, nothing was normal or routine.

I asked , "When did your mother tell you this?"

"In hospital."

"How long did Putinsky know that he was not your real father?"

She didn't know. "Putin not come to hospital. Divorce a long time ago."

"So you're stuck."

"Stuck? Not understand."

"Either that or this is a put up job by the KGB, that you are just an imposter, that this is another trap. It's a trick to get another agent into the United States. You are on a student visa, right?"

She was confused. "Yes, student visa."

"Do you plan to get a degree here at MIT? Or is this just a trick to get into the country and then disappear?"

"I come to find you."

"You went to a lot of trouble to do it. Why didn't you just send me a letter? Telephone?"

Katya shook her head. "Putin is powerful man."

Was Vladimir Putinsky so vindictive that he would take his revenge on his own daughter, or his alleged daughter, or whoever? Or on the daughter of the wife who had betrayed him?

Putinsky had shouted "You're a dead man!" in Gorky Park when I backed out of the KGB scheme that "Robert" had encouraged. Putinsky had a bad temper, a vindictive streak. It had been a serious threat.

I realized from my intercultural studies that there were people who never forgot. Afghans held vendettas for generations. Hell, Christians were still seeking revenge against Jews for killing Christ. So why not Putinsky making a victim out of an innocent daughter? There were no illegitimate children, only illegitimate parents.

Too bad for Katya. If she really was my daughter she'd gambled everything to connect with me. It was a long shot. Visa applications, an air ticket, all that. And if I just told her to piss off? What then? She'd be stuck even worse than I was when I was fired from the State Department. At least I had my folks in Florida to turn to. What did Katya have? Nothing. My anger suddenly dissipated. I was filled with compassion for the girl. I didn't see her as my daughter. That would take a totally new mind set. But I did have sympathy for her dilemma.

Hadn't I been caught in a bind in a foreign country? At least when I got to Moscow I'd had a job and an embassy that was supposed to stand behind me, to protect me. Had I worked for an American company I might have been dumped with no means of returning to the States. At least the State Department had rescued me and put me on a plane to Florida. My meager personal effects weren't left on the curb to be scavenged by passers by, as happened to some people in the States who were evicted. I hadn't become a homeless person, broke, in a foreign land.

Did Katya have a round trip ticket, or was this a one way deal? Would the Russian embassy send her home to Moscow? With no parents, no job, what would she do then? She must have gambled everything on this one bet: that I'd accept her. And then what?

Even if Katya's father wasn't Putin or Putinsky as she claimed, she might be still hung out to dry, as expendable as I was when the State Department spit me out like a piece of spoiled meat.

Victims had to stick together. I held up the piece of the torn photo. "Do you know what the rest of this picture is?"

"No."

"It's a sordid business. I don't know if I should show it to you." I had seen the six incriminating photographs so many times that they had lost their initial shock effect. To me, in spite of the faded recollections of intimacy, they were no longer pictures of myself. They might as well be photos of pictures in an art museum, mere erotic curiosities and impersonal.

They would not be the same for this girl. What was she? Eighteen years old? A kid. How would she react if she saw photos of her mother having sex with the then young Irwin Glass? How would anyone else interpret my decision to show them to her? I could just see the headline in the student newspaper: "Old instructor shows dirty pictures to a student less than half his age." And is fired. I had better be discreet. I held up the piece of photograph. "Can I keep this? I don't have the rest of the picture here. I need to see if this is a match. Come to my office tomorrow."

"What you want me do now?" Katya asked. She had played her last card. What next was up to me.

"I'll have to think about it. Come back tomorrow."

She left, leaving me in a daze, mulling over the possibilities, the probabilities, the impossibilities of my situation. I didn't know what to believe.

Ivy came back to the office and found me there. With the onset of winter she had replaced the faded blue jeans with wool slacks or ski pants. Today it was ski pants and the hard, noisy boots that fit the cross country bindings. Ivy wore no makeup. She didn't have to look glamorous to teach beginning German. Teutonic, maybe, not Wagnerian, though occasionally, like today, she'd done her hair in Brunhilda pigtails with a wool head band that kept her forehead and ears warm. She dropped her back pack and papers on her desk and looked at me with curiosity. "What happened to you? You look like you've seen a ghost."

I tried to focus. "That girl. The one who's been stalking me?"

"What about her?"

126

"Her name is Katarina Putin or Putinsky. Russian." There was no diplomatic way to say it, so I spoke plainly. "She says she is my daughter."

Ivy wasn't buying it. She took off the head band and wiped her forehead. "That's a new one. I've heard of students getting a crush on their instructors, but not making them out to be father figures."

"She's not my student."

Ivy slipped off her jacket and hung it on the hook behind the door. "You should send her to the Dean of Students' office. She obviously needs counseling."

"It's not that simple," I said. "Look at this." I handed over the piece of photograph with Svetlana's face. "That's her mother."

"Head and shoulders," Ivy said. "Looks like she might be naked."

"She was," I said. "This is what spies call a recognition signal. I have the other half of the photo back at my place. Guess who's in the bottom half? Me."

"You?"

"Her mother and I were, well, together. That was about nineteen years ago, so it is possible that the girl's claim that I'm her father is true. The picture was taken to incriminate me."

"How?"

"For blackmail."

"Do I get to see it?" Unlike most women, she liked erotic pictures but didn't care for X-rated romance novels.

"It's a long story, sweetie." I normally didn't call Ivy "sweetie" but just now I needed to reinforce our relationship. "Nobody here knows it and I haven't told you. Why don't you come to my place for dinner and I'll tell you the whole story? I'll even show you the rest of this picture."

"How could I refuse? Do you also have etchings?"

"I'll keep you in suspense."

"Pervert."

"Don't flatter me. I'll pick up a couple of steaks at Jim's grocery on the way back from class."

Ivy was thoughtful. "When were you in Russia?"

"Nineteen years ago. I had a job there."

127

"What was the job? Knocking up Russian women?"

"Hardly. I had a menial job at the American library. Got seduced." I gave her a palms-up gesture. "It happens all the time in this country. Some guy has a one night stand and gets stuck with a paternity case and child support."

I was afraid this might kill my romance with Ivy. Being a "man with a secret past" might strike some women as mysterious and intriguing, but not revealing the details of my background was a deception. It was like suddenly telling your wife that you've been married before, have kids, and never told her, or that you were gay. Not a good thing.

"You think the Russians want child support? Can they do that."

"It's not a paternity case. Hell, the girl's already eighteen and an adult. Even if there were a paternity case, even if she is my daughter, which I don't believe, there's not going to be some kind of award for child support. She's not my responsibility, even if she does claim to be my daughter."

"Do you feel like a father?"

"Me? Well, it's not too late, Ivy. I want children. You know, babies, watching them learn to walk, see them off to kindergarten, the whole parenting bit. I could take that role. I'll embrace it when the time comes. But this... this is ridiculous. I don't know this Katya, if that's her real name. For all I know, she's a trained Soviet agent."

"If she is, you'd better notify the FBI."

I sighed. "That's another part I haven't told you. I'm supposed to register with the local FBI office, but I haven't. I thought this was all over."

Ivy was stunned. "Why should you register with the FBI? You'd better start from the beginning."

"Supper at my place tonight. I have to go to class."

She looked at me with new interest. "You are a man of mystery. You have a secret past."

Maybe she wasn't having bad second thoughts about me after all. Being a man of mystery might be a good thing, not that I was going to make up spy stories and pretend to be some sort of James Bond. I knew enough from personal experience and wide reading about "the business" as they called it, to know that most espionage was mostly tedious reading in a variety of sources and trying to come to conclusions not obviously apparent. What I had done, or almost done, was so minor it could have been a joke if it hadn't had such consequences.

I slipped the deadly half photo into my briefcase and made my way to class. It was going to be hard to focus on the differences between "some" and "any" for those foreign students.

I splurged on a couple of T-bones and frozen Tater-tots at Jim's grocery on my way back to the house. I had salad makings in the fridge. It was a fifteen minute walk down the snow-packed streets—sidewalks weren't plowed in Portage Lake--that gave me some exercise and allowed me to avoid shoveling my truck out of the snow. The single garage behind the house was taken up by Kosinsky's car for the winter. I did have to fire up the snow blower to break a path through the daily snow bank pushed into the driveway by the city plow.

Next door, the light was on in Waarala's kitchen and Mrs. W was busy cooking their dinner. She saw me and waved. It was convenient that Professor Kosinsky lived next door. Otherwise Waarala might not have known the house was for rent. But it also meant that when Ivy stayed overnight and we left in the morning together, we were noticed. Everyone in the department knew we were a couple.

Portage Lake was a small town. People talked. What else did they have to do when snowed in half the year? If I gave one of the faculty wives a lift home from Wal-Mart, we'd be seen and the subject of gossip and speculation.

At least Michigan wasn't like Wisconsin where, I'd heard, if an unmarried couple spent the night together they could get an honest to God ticket for "fornication."

Ivy was on time, shook the snow off her stylish LL Bean winter jacket and hung it up inside the front door on a hook beside my old Moscow jacket. "So what's this about the picture?"

"Steaks will be ready in a couple of minutes," I said. "Eat first. The photo is very graphic. Once you see it you may lose your appetite."

"For what? Steak or sex?"

"You might get the wrong idea about me."

"I don't get it."

"You will. I made a tossed salad. Vinegar and oil OK?"

Fortunately we both liked our meat medium. Well done might have dried the steaks out or reduced them to ash.

We skipped dessert, cleared the kitchen table, and I went upstairs to the bedroom to retrieve the photograph. I thought about the other five. *It's too much,* I thought. I took out the bottom half of the torn photo to show Ivy the match, plus the original complete photo just as proof. I didn't want to show Ivy the others. Though we had been intimate, I was hesitant to show her all six explicit pictures. My mother had always told me it wasn't proper to kiss and tell.

Ivy had been, as some said, around the block a few times and wasn't shy about showing herself naked, but I was uneasy about how she'd react seeing pictures of me in bed with another woman.

Ivy might get the idea that I secretly took pictures of us in bed. I'd heard that some people did that sort of thing. Home videos, and such. If I had, would I show those to my next girl friend? For what purpose? Best to use only the one which had been used for the recognition signal. That was bad enough. The worst case scenarios were people who posted, to their everlasting shame, nude photos of themselves on the Internet.

We were sitting across the table. As a dramatic touch, I first took Katya's piece of the photo out of the plastic and laid it on the kitchen table. "That's Svetlana Putinsky. The rest of the photo is me." Then I took out the bottom half. The tear was deliberately ragged so only the mate to the top half would make a perfect match.

Then I showed the original, complete print.

Ivy recognized me naked on the double bed in the old Metropol. "You've aged."

"Hell, I was what, twenty five? Barely out of college then."

"What were you? Drunk?"

"Vodka. Might have been spiked. That's why I don't

130

drink any more.   The whole thing was a setup.   The photos were supposed to be used to blackmail me to work for the Soviets or risk a scandal.   It's an old trick.   "

"You said there are six photos."

"I'd rather not show you the rest."

"I'm a big girl.   I can handle it.   Are you being shy, Irwin?"

"Let's say so.   The photos look like a series from an instructive sex manual or the Kama Sutra.   Let's leave it at that for now."

I then went on to tell her the rest of the story, of being dumped on the Moscow street, put in the drunk tank, the return of my suit, the meeting with Putinsky at the Bolshoi restaurant.   I skipped the bit about signing the receipt for the hundred dollars never paid.   But I did dwell on the report "Robert" had never shown me: Susan Lutz's claim that I was a drunk and a womanizer.   "Can you imagine that?" I asked Ivy.   "Me? A drunk and a womanizer?"

Ivy shook her head.   "Maybe you were a drunk--- once."

"Never.   I had a shot of sour mash whiskey that night. The vodka, or whatever she put in it, knocked me flat.   How can you doubt me?"

"You might have changed your ways, Irwin.   The old Irwin Glass and the new one, the Irwin on the Wagon."

It brought back that sinking feeling in my stomach. "Susan Lutz betrayed me.   She was my boss at the library. She could have said simply that I wasn't suitable for the job, that I didn't know enough about American literature to sell it to the Russians.   She didn't have to lie."

Ivy agreed that it was too bad.   "Some people have a nasty streak."

"Or a vengeful one."

"Maybe this Lutz was jealous.   You look pretty hot in this photo."

Putinsky had been vengeful, that shout "You're a dead man, Irwin Glass." "Ivy, promise me, you'll never betray me."

"I won't tell lies about you, Irwin." Ivy looked at me like she was seeing a stranger for the first time.   "Except for your being a poor Scrabble player and a beginner skier, I don't know much about you.   I couldn't say you were never a

131

drunk because I don't know anything about that. You have a mysterious past."

"It's not one I'm proud of."

"Ah, but it's very romantic, don't you think? Irwin Glass, secret agent?"

"I never was a secret agent."

"Soviet spy, then?"

"Hardly. Sucker, maybe. Like the Russians used to say, 'We pretend to work and they pretend to pay us.' Putinsky said he was depositing a hundred bucks in a Washington DC account at the Riggs bank, but he never did. He probably kept the money himself, cheating his own system."

"Did he put the money in a Washington bank?"

"No. I checked."

"Nice irony," Ivy commented. "So what are you going to do now? You going to show Katya these pictures?"

"My God, not all of them." I slid the photos, the torn one and the original, back into the old envelope. I had saved the original envelopes, the one with the Russian stamp and the government envelope used to forward it to Ocala along with the note in Russian. I wasn't about to destroy evidence I might need if the old case ever got me into court. What was the statute of limitations on espionage?

"But I will show her the matching bottom half, just so she knows I believe that part of her story."

"Then what?"

"I don't know."

"I mean," Ivy said. "If she really is your daughter what then?"

I was finding it hard to be coherent. "You mean, if we, well, I mean if you and I got married, could you deal with my already having a kid? Well, I mean, she's not a kid. Jeeze, Ivy, this complicates things."

"We haven't talked about marriage."

"No. But we've both thought about it, haven't we, without saying anything?"

She wasn't going to admit that. Whatever past romances Ivy had had, relationships that failed for one reason or another, she wasn't saying. "Let's play it by ear, like they say. OK? No commitment. Not just yet. First let's get this

Katya thing straightened out."

"I wish I knew how." I tried to turn the conversation. "So do you have a secret past?"

Ivy arched her brows. "You think I'm going to tell you about my past lovers? I'm not going there, Irwin, dear."

"Sorry. None of my business."

"If I'd had an affair with Rudolf Valentino you might not survive the comparison. Best not to ask."

"Gotcha."

She didn't stay the night. The news of my previously hidden past had raised a barrier of doubt between us. I was not the person she thought I was. I'd become a stranger. If she couldn't accept my reluctance to tell people my unfortunate secret, that might be the end of our relationship.

Ivy's past was her private business. The hint of other affairs made her more, not less alluring to me. How well do two people ever know one another? A couple might marry after a long courtship only to discover that one never puts the cap back on the toothpaste and the other has a compulsion about orderliness. One couple I had known at SIU had split up because she had a habit of twisting a lock of her hair and he couldn't stand it. Someone who truly loved you accepted your quirks.

I brought the two halves of the photograph with me to the office the next day. The student who claimed to be Katya Putinsky or Putin showed up as expected.

Katya was nervous and hesitant. She was obviously under stress. Even though hers was the matching half of the photo, that didn't prove her identity. It could all be a KGB setup.

I was suspicious. I didn't show her the reconstructed photo right away. "Do you have your passport?"

She did, and handed it over with some hesitation as if she were afraid I wouldn't give it back. It was different from the old internal passports the Soviets had provided every citizen after the age of sixteen. I studied it carefully, turning the pages, noted the visa stamp, the "admitted" stamp put there when she came through customs into the United States. In the days before the EU the stamps in a passport were a paper trail of a person's travels. With borders open people were free to move from country to country without border crossing stamps. Nowadays a passport could be innocuous.

The girl's document looked genuine, but I was no expert on how to tell a real passport from a faked one. This might easily be fabricated in some KGB office. Besides this one, she might have others, for Britain, Argentina, Germany, whatever. In my world of suspicion and subterfuge nothing could be trusted as authentic, except, of course, the two matching halves of the torn photograph.

The only thing I could be certain of was that the photograph in my briefcase was the one taken at the Metropol.

I had put the reconstructed photo in the plastic cover she'd carried and showed it to her with some hesitation. I was not accustomed to showing sexy photographs to coeds. I knew it was improper, but in this case it had to be done. "This is Svetlana Putinsky or the woman who called herself that, and me."

The scene was graphic, but could have been posed. Svetlana was straddling me. Her ample breasts were depicted, but aside from some pubic hair you couldn't call it a crotch shot.

Katya wasn't shocked, though I caught a hint of blush. Perhaps she had never seen her mother—if that was her mother—naked. The photo showed little more of me than might be visible if I were wearing a Speedo brief bathing suit. Svetlana was sitting on my private parts.

Katya asked, "You believe me now?"

This was it, the big gamble for her. She had come a long way, at great expense and with much preparation. This could be the make or break moment.

I handed back her passport. "I believe the photograph is genuine. That doesn't make you my daughter."

At that moment the office door opened. One of Ivy's German students came barging in, breathless, and started to ask, "Is Doctor Hartshorn..." then stopped, staring at the photograph of a sexual act. "Oh."

"Hartshorn is in class," I said, trying to cover the photo, but it was too late.

"I'll come back later," the girl said. "It's about her

134

quiz." She disappeared in a swirl of red storm coat and hood.

I apologized. "I should have locked the door." Ivy hadn't put back the paper cover over the little window. Anybody could be standing out there in the hall, watching what I was doing alone in my office with a female student. That was why instructors were cautioned to leave the door open during conferences with students of the opposite sex.

Ivy's student was probably headed for Waarala's office. Maybe not. Maybe she would simply tell other students that she had surprised Professor Glass showing dirty pictures to one of the coeds. What was worse? Gossip and rumors among the students, or a direct accusation lodged with the department head? Did it make any difference? Either way, I'd be in trouble again, just when I was beginning to feel at home in the Copper Country and looking forward to years of employment at Portage Tech.

If I were called on the carpet, what would I tell Waarala? That Katya Putin was my daughter? No one would believe me.

I didn't believe it myself.

"My office isn't the place for this," I said. "We have to talk someplace private. I need to know more about you and your mother. I need to know your story."

What I needed was verification. Was her cover story simply memorized? Would my pursuit of details lead to inconsistencies that might trip up an imposter? I had read about interrogation. Often interrogators worked in pairs, playing good cop, bad cop. I had no partner for such a tactic. Maybe I could enlist Ivy.

The girl suggested, "What about the student union?"

"Too public." We should not meet on campus. "There's an internet café downtown. How about meeting me there?" But the internet café was frequented by geeky Tech students with their laptops. That wouldn't do, either. "On second thought do you know where the Portage Lake public library is? Downtown?" Few Tech students hung out at the public library. Da Tech had a huge library with lots of space for students looking for a place to study. They didn't need or use the city's public facilities. I explained how to get to the Portage Lake library, a fifteen minute walk from campus.

The public library was open until eight. It was a new building on the waterfront, across from the county marina. The library had a heavily frequented bank of computers near the circulation desk, but at the far end of the building, beyond the children's section, out of the traffic, there were soft chairs and a study table shielded behind bookcases but with fine views of the Keweenaw waterway.

The waterway had frozen by the first of December, but the ice wasn't safe enough yet for the snowmobilers who came up north from as far south as Indiana to enjoy their sport. It was snowing, as usual, a fine precipitation almost like an ice fog that partly obscured the view of the two level lift bridge that connected the Keweenaw peninsula with the rest of the UP. In the wintry dark, there wasn't much to be seen of traffic on the bridge, but the red lights atop the towers that supported it could just be made out if you knew where to look.

Katya was late. She came in with snow on the shoulders and hood of her storm coat. She took off her coat and eased into the overstuffed chair I had moved close to mine. She was wearing a wool sweater that suggested her breasts were as ample as her mother's. That was a physical feature she shared, along with those eyes and her rosebud lips.

We sat knees to knees and spoke softly, carrying on our conversation in Russian in case someone might chance to overhear us. "Why did you come to Portage Lake, Michigan? It's a long way from Moscow and there are better engineering schools, more famous ones."

"I came to find you," she said, her eyes searching my face for some sign of sympathy or understanding.

"You could have written me a letter. How did you find me?"

"First you were in Indiana."

"That was my last five years," I admitted.

"I wrote to you there at..."

"At IU/PU?"

"Yes. But the letter came back. It was marked 'not here.'

"You could have telephoned," I suggested, but I

136

wondered how difficult it would be for her to make a long distance call to South Bend, Indiana from Moscow. "Or sent an email."

"No email listed."

"That's possibly because I was only an adjunct instructor." I wasn't exactly *persona non grata* at IU/PU but I was a third class citizen, hardly on the department roster, and shared an office with a couple of grad students. "So you finally located me through my resume, Googled me."

I hadn't posted my resume on the web until I had to look for another job, not having achieved bona fide status in South Bend.

"Yes." Katya smiled, eyes that resembled her mother's in those fatal photographs. I remembered her mother's disarming, flirtatious look.

"And then you applied as a student here? You could have traveled on a visitor's visa."

"Is better that I am student."

Better in what way? I wondered. Visas are temporary. "I can't see you spending all that money and going through all that trouble of enrolling at Michigan Tech just to find me. Doesn't make sense."

"My mother said…" Here she lowered her eyes. I was being too intense in my questioning, almost threatening. I wasn't being fair.

"Said what?"

"She said you could not refuse me."

"Refuse you? I don't know you. The photograph you showed me doesn't prove that I am your birth father. Just because she says I am your birth father is no proof. She may have had other boy friends beside Vladimir Putinsky." I said 'boy friends' out of charity. Who knew how many others she had trapped in those KGB schemes? I might be one of half a dozen.

"Mama said a woman knows."

She had me there. Still, it seemed to me very improbable that a girl of eighteen would travel half way around the world on the gamble that a man she never met wouldn't slam a door in her face, refuse her, reject her and leave her stranded. There had to be some other reason.

I was reminded of her father.   Vladimir Putinsky, or
Putin as she said he'd changed his name to.   Putinsky could
have picked any comely young agent to send to the United
States and pose as my daughter, using the piece of
photograph as the recognition signal..   That didn't make this
Katya my daughter.   She could be a spy, another setup to
trap me.   I had enough trouble already, still on the books
someplace as a would-be paid Soviet agent.   Hadn't I been
ruined enough?

I had to dig into her cover story.   "Tell me where you
lived in Moscow."

"We had big apartment."

"Not typical of the usual Muskovite," I commented.
"When I was there the housing shortage was pretty bad.   A
three bedroom apartment would have three families living in
it and a bed in the hallway."

Katya knew that.   "Putinsky was KGB.   Party
member."

"So you were privileged."

She shrugged.   "After the end of Soviet Union things
changed."

"It must have been difficult for your father.   Did he
keep his old job?"

"Same job, I think.   Different title.   No more KGB."

"And your mother?"

"She was not happy.   They argue all the time."

"What about?"

She didn't know.   "Sometimes he hit her."

She told me that as a child she had not understood.
"When I was twelve they had big fight.   After that Vladimir
did not speak to me.   I didn't understand."

Katya rushed through her story as if she had rehearsed it.
She said that only when her mother was dying did the
explanation come for the divorce.   Physically and mentally
abused, Svetlana had taunted Vladimir that Katya was not his
daughter.   A mother always knows a child is hers.   A father
can never be entirely certain.   Putinsky, never a doting father,
said he'd been suspicious all along, as they had no other
children and Svetlana had never become pregnant again.
"He was so angry he divorced my Mama," Katya said,

tearfully. "He tore up my birth certificate because it named him, Vladimir Putinsky, as my father."

"Then you have no birth certificate? Didn't you need it for your student visa?" That was just my guess. I had never applied for a student visa. I wondered if a duplicate could be ordered from some Russian office. If would be helpful to have Katya's birth certificate to prove her identity. I knew how difficult it could be to fight the Soviet bureaucracy when on the scene. I imagined it to be improbable at best if I tried to get a copy from across the ocean.

"New birth paper," Katya said. "I never see real one. New one says 'father unknown.'"

"Could he do that?" But I remembered that in the Soviet Union when you were purged the government could even remove your face from the tiled mosaic in the ceiling of the Metro station. Putinsky was a powerful person who knew the system. He could get the registry to produce a birth certificate for Katya with any name on it that he pleased. The KGB could forge any document, even the passport Katya had showed me. Was her identity genuine?

I had to ask her. "What do you want of me?"

Katya hung her head. "I have no family but you."

It's a good sob story, I thought, trying to shield myself. I suspected this was an elaborate con job by Vladimir Putinsky or Putin as he now called himself. Still, if Katya was acting, she was convincing. That didn't mean I felt like a parent. Nevertheless, I had sympathy for the girl's situation. If this was a scam, she was another victim of Vladimir Putinsky, sent on a wild goose chase to the wilds of Upper Michigan. If I rejected her story, what then? Would she go back to Russia, defeated, and to what fate? But if her story were true, her mother dead, her father rejecting her, who did she have for family?

I had no brothers or sisters and my parents, down in Ocala, were far away. Unable to get on a plane, I was far removed from what little family I had. When they died I'd be an orphan. Imagine, Katya crossing to a distant land on the hope that when she got there she would be accepted. What a gamble on her part. What a risk! She must be desperate. If I rejected her, told her to just piss off, what would become of her? When I was fired from my job I at least had a ticket back to the States, a bit of per diem money to get me home. If I rejected Katya, what did she have? Some fall back position? I couldn't figuratively dump her out on the street as had been done to me. In my soft-hearted way I wanted to believe Katya was sincere. I didn't detect any cynicism as I might have if dealing with Vladimir. "What will you do if I am not your father?"

Katya's eyes were moist. "I don't know."

She must be awfully impulsive to take such a gamble, but wasn't that typical of a teenager? So many ran away from home and soon become homeless, broke, easy prey for pimps and drug dealers.

What I was still uncertain about was why Svetlana had dwelled at all on our brief encounter. Blackmailing me was all business for Putinsky. It wasn't for Svetlana.

I considered another scenario, that I had unwittingly and unknowingly given Svetlana a child, and she had probably unintentionally participated in my ruination. My refusal to cooperate with Putinsky and with "Robert" was my own doing. Did Svetlana have a guilty conscience? Was that why my clothes were returned? Was sending Katya across the ocean to me a way of saying she was sorry? If so, it was a damned unusual sort of apology. Katya mentioned no other relatives. Sending her to the USA might have been Svetlana's last chance of providing her daughter with a family.

By then it was nearly closing time. Our conversation was interrupted by Mrs. Hawthorne, the librarian. Mrs. Hawthorne was usually friendly. At this hour she was tired, wanted the patrons to clear out so she could go home. She knew me, but not the girl. "Closing time, Mr. Glass."

"We were just leaving."

Mrs. Hawthorne was curious. "And this is…?" she started to say, but cut it off as being too nosy.

"One of my students," I explained and regretted it instantly. "Well, not my own student. One of our foreign students."

Then I remembered that Mrs. Hawthorne's husband was the head of the Electrical Engineering department. Portage Lake, Michigan was a small town, indeed.

Everything interlocked.

We got up together, put on our coats, and were the last patrons to leave.

"I'll give you a lift back to the dorm," I offered. "My pickup's right outside. Where do you live?"

"Coed Hall."

I had to shift some student papers off the passenger seat. I was suddenly embarrassed by the clutter. The window ice scraper and snow brush were on the floor along with a paper coffee cup and an empty soda can. "Sorry about the mess."

I didn't drive up to the front door of the dormitory, but stopped in the parking lot. "I hope you don't mind getting out here. It's not a good idea for a student to be seen riding with a faculty member."

"I understand," she said in Russian. "Goodbye."

She moved off into the falling snow toward the back entrance to the coed dorm.

I put the pickup in reverse and backed out. I hoped we hadn't been seen, but of course, we had.

I needed some advice. As soon as I got back to the house I phoned Ivy at her apartment. "I met with Katya at the library downtown."

"How did it go?"

"I asked her about her life in Moscow, about her mother. Checking her cover story."

"And?"

"I don't know. She tells a good story. She's either sincere or a good actor."

"So, do you think she's your daughter?"

"I think she thinks she is. Trouble is, how do I know I wasn't just one of many dupes who got seduced for the incriminating pictures? The honey pot ploy is a well known spy trick. If that's the case, there's no telling who else could be her father."

Ivy agreed. "That's true."

"In that case, picking me out from several candidates, I may be a bad choice. Svetlana may simply have lied to Katya, a deathbed deception, not a confession."

"That's possible, too."

"Or Svetlana simply had a fantasy. That she deceived

herself."

Ivy was sympathetic. "Oh, Irwin, you are in a muddle."

"No kidding. The librarian finally threw us out. Now I realize that the librarian's husband is a faculty member."

"You're thinking of the anti-fraternization agreement," Ivy said.

"That, too. I have to think she might well be my birth daughter but I don't know what to do about it."

"Nobody's going to believe you," Ivy said. "Frankly, I don't. Look at it this way: she's pretty, she has a thing for you, and..."

I interrupted. "Whatever that is."

"And anyone would assume you're taking advantage of her vulnerability. You should go to the Dean of Student's office."

"And do what? Denounce her? She's come to me in confidence."

"So what do you want to do? Protect her and lose your job? You have a low sense of self-preservation, Irwin."

"Something like that happened to me." I remembered Lutz's false report to the Embassy personnel officer. "I don't want to betray her."

"Then don't. You figure it out, Irwin. It's your problem."

"I was hoping you'd be more supportive."

"Let's not quarrel about this, Irwin. You have to find a way to cover your ass before Waarala or the Dean come down on your head."

"Sounds like a mixed metaphor."

"This is not a problem for your English as a foreign language class."

"Right. I'll try to figure out a way to approach this."

"Just don't do anything in writing," Ivy advised. "You don't want to get into a memo war."

Puzzling about the problem kept me awake for hours.

After my morning class the next day I dropped in at the Dean's office. Dean Sheldon was a local Yooper, wife of a descendent of one of the founders of the town. Her job was a vestige of paternalism and the local old boy's network still remaining in the administration in spite of the importation of new blood.

Dean Sheldon wore a subdued, brown skirt and jacket outfit over heavy tights that for professional women substituted for the long underwear that was obligatory in the Copper Country winter. She didn't know me, since I was a mere instructor, bottom rung of the Humanities department in a college of engineering and technology. I had to introduce myself.

"I'm Irwin Glass, instructor of English as a second language for our foreign students and some faculty. I have a problem."

Doctor Sheldon, in listening mode, sat back in her office chair. "What problem?"

"One of the foreign students—not one of mine—seems to have a fixation."

"Fixation?"

"She thinks I'm her father."

Dean Sheldon suppressed a laugh. "That's a new one. I've heard of students having a crush on their instructors, but not a father fixation."

"I guess when I was in kindergarten I might have accidentally called my teacher Mom, but I'm no kindergarten teacher."

"You think she needs a psychiatrist? We have a counselor here who could help her."

That seemed too extreme. Katya didn't strike me as neurotic, but then, I'm no psychiatrist. Certainly she was troubled and anxious about her situation. Who wouldn't be? "I don't want to suggest that she's mentally ill. That would be cruel. You never know what will send some students over the edge."

Dean Sheldon tapped a pencil on the desk, first the pointed end, then the eraser end. "Humor her. You could pretend to go along with her fantasy. Go to the campus sick bay and ask about getting a DNA test."

"I don't want to do this on campus. Confidentiality and all that."

"Then ask up at the hospital in Hancock. They could take samples and send them to a lab. When the results come back you'll have proof that she is not your daughter. That

143

should convince her.   By the way, what's her name?"
Sheldon was ready to write it down, the pencil ready.

"I'd rather not say.   She's a Russian foreign student."

The dean looked up from her paper.   "Russian? Have
you been to Russia?"

"Yes.   A long time ago." I had not put the failed foreign
service job in my resume when I applied for the position at
Da Tech.

"Oh? Sow any wild oats there?"

"Not that I know of." I turned to leave.   "Thanks for
the suggestion."

"You understand I have to put this in my daily contact
report."

"That's all right." As long as I hadn't mentioned Katya's
name, the fact that I had discussed the paternity question
should adequately cover my ass, as Ivy had suggested.   I
wasn't exactly keeping this alleged fraternization a secret.

Yes, a DNA sample would conclusively prove that Katya
was not my daughter.   Then I'd be off the hook and could
hand her off to the campus psychological counselor.

But what if the sample proved that I was her biological
father? This was just as much a gamble for Katya as it was for
me.   If Katya was, in fact, my birth child, what then? Did I
have any responsibility for an adult daughter I didn't even
know? What might that be?

It was like those college guys who were sperm donors
for extra money, then got tracked down years later by the
resulting offspring who wanted to know if they had siblings
or were at risk of some congenital disorder.   Some sperm
donors weren't interested.   Others cared, but there was no
real need for bonding, no responsibilities.

This wasn't quite that impersonal, not a case of artificial
insemination.   Did I have any legal obligation? I had to go
over all the "what ifs." Like, how would Ivy react if Katya's
story were true? What would that do to our relationship? I
felt like the suitor who reveals that, like it or not, he already
has a child.   Love me, love my kid.   How would Ivy like
being a step mother to a Russian girl who, frankly, was
prettier than her?

Katya was pretty, had a good figure that reminded me of

Svetlana, but she was only eighteen, for God's sake. I quickly admitted that the age difference wouldn't hinder some men from taking advantage of a girl's vulnerability. I had to concede that, being a reasonably virile man, I was vulnerable, too. Katya was, well, a good looking babe. How many step fathers had been guilty of molesting girls in the family? The local *Mining Gazette* carried such stories of incest. How much did it matter if you were innocent and were falsely accused? In cases of he said-she said, the man was always assumed to be guilty. That was why the anti fraternization agreement was so important.

Deeply troubled, distracted and confused, I slogged through the fresh snow from the Administration and Student Services, the ASS building, to the Humanities offices half way across the campus. I had resurrected my old Moscow jacket and fake fur hat. Since arriving in the Copper Country I'd acquired a pair of stout waffle stompers, the name given boots with soles that left waffle-like footprints in the snow.

I barely acknowledged the greetings of a couple of foreign students.

When I came up in the elevator to the second floor offices I did notice that a couple of the female students in the hallway gave me looks like I'd interrupted a clandestine conversation. Maybe that was my old paranoia. I was not important enough, I told myself without conviction, to be the subject of student gossip.

There was a pink envelope in my mail box and a brief note: "See me. Waarala."

The executive secretary, Mrs. Houghton, another of those historic, local names, possibly a descendent of Douglass Houghton, the state geologist who first discovered commercially accessible copper on the Keweenaw, gave me a cold look.

"Doctor Waarala wants to see me."

Waarala was ensconced like king on the hill behind his desk in the corner office. It was the only office with a carpet. His book cases were laden with textbooks. His Ph.D. was framed and displayed on the wall like a physician's shingle. Waarala did not look pleased. "Close the door."

I closed it and, realizing that I felt weak in the knees, sat down in the visitor's chair.

Waarala normally put on a friendly face, was usually cordial to everyone, and aware that Humanities was a low priority department subject to poor faculty raises and even cuts in staff. Humanities was expendable. Anything that gave the administration an excuse to shift Humanities money to Engineering was a threat.

"There's a rumor, Irwin, that you may be dating one of your students, the Russian girl."

"Katarina Putin," I offered. I didn't use the familiar version of her name. "I'm not dating her."

"Someone saw you showing an obscene photo to the Putin girl."

I tried to explain. "That's a long story."

Waarala leaned back, the skeptical look on his face already showing that he wasn't likely to believe anything I said. "Tell it."

"The photo was taken of me and Katarina's mother in Moscow. Katarina was given the upper portion to match up with my half as a recognition signal."

"Recognition signal? I don't get it."

"When I was working in Moscow I got conned by the KGB."

"What do you mean, conned?"

"Seduced. They call it the honey pot trick."

"Honey pot?"

"They seduce some dumb cluck and take incriminating photographs. I was the dumb cluck."

"I didn't know you worked in Moscow. It's not in your resume."

"I was only there about a month. Then everything fell apart. The KGB tried to get me to work for them as a Soviet agent." I wasn't about to go any further with the story, not say I'd reported on a fellow employee and was allegedly paid for the service.

Waarala actually laughed. "You're reading too many spy novels, Glass. What is this cock and bull story you're telling me?"

"I'm not kidding. It was a long time ago. A one night

stand. Could happen to anybody." Was that a way to shrug off a paternity case?

"This is not the kind of excuse I thought you'd come up with, Glass. You have a sick imagination."

"No," I protested. "It's true. The kid thinks I'm her father."

"Her father?"

"I've just come from Dean Sheldon's office. She suggested I get a DNA test so we can lay this thing to rest."

"I'll admit that is an original excuse, Glass. You realize you signed a non-fraternization agreement."

"It's not fraternization. You wouldn't forbid a man from meeting his own daughter in private, would you?"

Waarala shook his head in disbelief. "Usually when some old guy shows up in a fancy hotel with a bimbo he says she's his niece."

"Katya is not my niece."

"Katya? I thought you said her name is Katarina."

"Katarina, Katya. It's the same as Robert, Bobby in English. Katya is the familiar version."

"So you are familiar with this girl?"

I let the insinuation pass. "I don't think she's my daughter, but she thinks so and I have to prove to her that she isn't. Do you know a local lab where I can get a DNA test?"

Waarala was set back. "You are a funny guy, Glass. You have any other daughters in our student body?"

"I don't believe I have any daughters at all."

"Well, you get that DNA test or your excuse is diddly poop. I don't want to lose your position, and you don't want to lose your job."

"Yes, sir." I got up to leave, more correctly, to escape.

"Some time you must come over to the house and tell Martha and me the rest of this honey pot story."

"Really, Dr. Waarala, I'd rather not." I was glad Waarala didn't demand to see the photograph. It was bad enough to have students whispering in the halls about dirty pictures. I didn't want to be the butt of campus-wide snickering.

Back in my office I made some phone calls. I called the Medical Care Facility, got nowhere. Called the hospital and was told it was possible for a doctor there to take a DNA swab and send it to a lab, but it might be expensive. The price was about three hundred dollars. Ouch.

"It's a paternity case," I explained, realizing that the mere mention of paternity might set the tongues wagging. "I have to use the results in court if necessary, so it has to be official, whichever way it goes."

I didn't know who I was talking to and had immediately forgotten her name. She asked, "Do you have a lawyer? Sometimes we do this on a court order. Then it's cheaper."

"I don't have a lawyer. I'm sure this will never go to court. If the result is negative that ends it."

"Bring the other party with you to the hospital and Dr. Jenkins will take the samples."

"I'll get hold of the, er, other party, and come up."

As I hung up I heard the nurse mutter a derisive, "Men!"

So men were always the guilty parties, eh? I didn't feel like the cause of all this. I saw myself as a victim. Hell, I'd always been the victim. Svetlana, Vladimir, Susan Lutz, and "Robert" (or whatever his real name was) had all dumped on me for whatever personal reasons. I even suspected that somehow I'd offended the bored clerk that gave me the polygraph. Or maybe if everyone passed their polygraphs the agency that paid for the tests wouldn't feel they were getting their money's worth unless someone flunked once in awhile. How had I flunked that? Didn't make sense. And the whole business cascaded down on my head. I felt like the kid with a sign on his back saying "kick me."

This DNA test should set things straight and get me off the hook forever.

I didn't even know Katya's phone number, but she was in the coed dorm. I called the switchboard, got her number. Another girl answered. "Yah?" Sounded like a Yooper.

"I'm trying to reach Katya Putin."

"Who's this?"

"One of her instructors."

"This about her exam?"

"Just tell her she needs to call Mr. Glass, please." I gave the girl my extension number.

148

"You could send her an email," the roommate suggested. "She's kputin@mit.edu."

"I'll do that, too, but please ask her to call me. It's very important."

"You betcha," the roommate said.

Email. I did that, too, but since emails were saved in the system all I wrote was, "See me ASAP. I. Glass." I hoped she knew what ASAP meant.

So much for now. What next? Ivy's CYA, Cover Your Ass, tactic was wise. She obviously had more experience with survival in organizations like Da Tech. I realized I had better finally fulfill my obligation to check in with the local FBI office.

The phone book's only number for the FBI was an office in Marquette, a hundred miles away. Marquette was an old mining town, port for lake freighters picking up iron ore pellets from the huge iron mines in Ishpeming. It was also the site of Northern Michigan University, but there was no other industry.

I reached the FBI office, got only an answering machine, so left my name and number. "This is Irwin Glass at Michigan Institute of Technology in Portage Lake. I'm supposed to check in. So I'm checking in. I'm usually at this number on Tuesdays and Thursdays." I gave my home number. I didn't want the FBI agent, whoever that was, identifying himself to the office secretary. Tongues were already wagging.

When Ivy came back to our office after her German 101 class I told her about my visit to Dean Sheldon's office and Waarala's warning.

Ivy beamed at me. "I told you to see the Dean. What did she say?"

"Get a DNA test. But it will cost about three hundred bucks."

"Cheap enough if it gets that girl off your back. When are you going to get the test?"

"As soon as I can reach Katya I'll drive her up to the hospital. All they do is take a swab of saliva, I guess. Send it to a lab."

"Good. Then our lives will be normal again."

149

"I don't think my life has ever been normal."

"Did you tell your folks that they might have a grandchild?"

I sat back in his chair. "My mother would love that. It's too early. I wouldn't want to get their hopes up. My dad already thinks I live a wild life. He's seen the photos."

"Oh? You never showed me the other photos besides the one you pieced together." She gave me a skeptical look.

So, she remembered that. Teasing me, she deliberately imitated a Russian accent and mispronounced my name. "You do have your secrets, Irvin."

"I didn't want to get you too excited."

"Hey, I don't mind being excited."

"I'll show you next time you come to the house."

"I can hardly wait."

"Another thing," I added. "I'm supposed to check in with the FBI whenever I change addresses."

"Really? Why? You're not a registered sex offender, are you?" She rolled her eyes. "I didn't think you had it in you."

"If I were, it would be a local registry, city cops. The FBI thing is just a formality."

"I wouldn't think any contact with the FBI would be just a formality. Why do you have to do that?"

"It's old stuff. Not important now. It was all a mistake. Twenty years ago they thought I was a paid Soviet agent. Now I'm stuck with the label. I phoned the FBI office in Marquette, left a message. I suppose they'll call back."

"Irwin Glass, Man of Mystery."

"Anything to keep you interested." I liked this familiar give and take with Ivy. A little spice kept our relationship from going stale. I wouldn't show her the remaining five photos until the time was right.

. . .

Katya called me at home that evening. She had an exam coming up in a engineering class, and was anxious. "I need to have us tested for DNA," I explained, speaking in Russian but using the English spelling for the DNA test. "I know you believe you are my birth daughter, but my department head says I'd better prove it. We have this anti-fraternization

150

agreement." I didn't know the Russian word for fraternization.

She didn't know what fraternization was. It was a new English word for her.

I explained, "I'm not supposed to have personal contact with the students. If someone thinks I'm dating you I could lose my job. It's important that we do this."

"I understand. What is DNA test?"

"They just take a sample of saliva and compare the genes and stuff."

"Is not a blood test?"

"No. Just a little wipe in the mouth with a cotton swab. It will prove whether you are my daughter or not."

"You don't believe me." She was clearly upset.

"I have to do it. You don't want me to be fired, do you?"

"No."

"So just take this test."

She didn't sound like she was afraid of the test, but I wasn't sure. After all, I didn't know Katya. She had told me her cover story, but that wasn't enough. It might as well have been recited from a memorized script. I wasn't sure how I should react to her reaction to taking a DNA test. If she were pretending to be my daughter, one of Putinsky's under cover schemes, the DNA test would blow the operation. If that were the case she should be afraid of being exposed as a fraud and beg off. She spoke slowly and deliberately, weighing her words. Maybe she was just a good actress. Maybe she was bluffing. If the test proved she was not my daughter she might just claim the test was faulty.

Could a DNA test be trusted? Could a polygraph? I'd already had one bad test experience.

I arranged to pick her up during our break between classes the next day.

The Portage hospital was at the top of the hill across the Keweenaw Waterway from Portage Lake. Head-high ridges of snow had been pushed to the side of the parking lot by the plows. There was no bare pavement and would not be until spring.

A senior citizen volunteer in a blue uniform met us

inside the front entrance and directed us to Dr.   Jenkins'
office.   We sat in the waiting room, scrutinized suspiciously
by the nurse as if we were an unmarried couple and this
might be a pregnancy test.   Katya absently leafed through an
old copy of *Redbook* and pretended to read.

I noted the sign on the wall, "Respect patient
confidentiality" but I wasn't confident that someone would
not talk.   Portage Lake was such a small town.   Secrets were
hard to keep.

I asked the receptionist if my health insurance might
cover the DNA test, but it didn't.   I'd be billed.   What good
was health insurance if it didn't cover everything?

Taking the DNA swabs took only a couple of minutes, a
cotton swab in each of our mouths, the samples put safely
into sterile test tubes for shipment to a lab.   Katya submitted.
Either she didn't fully understand the impact the results
might reveal, or she was indifferent, or pretended to be too
distracted by her pending engineering test to focus.   She was
pensive and silent.

On the way back, as my pickup truck approached the
massive lift bridge that connected the Keweenaw Peninsula
with the rest of the U.P.   I heard Katya sob.

"What's the matter?" On the Portage Lake side of the
bridge I pulled into the parking lot of the Holiday gas station.
"What is it, Katya?"

"You are Irvin Glass, yes?"

"Sure."

"The Irvin Glass who study at Indiana University,
Russian language."

"Yes."

"And get Master's Degree at Indiana University in
International Relations?"

"That's me."

"There is no other Irvin Glass?"

I shut off the engine and looked at her.   Her face was
wet with tears.   "If you Google me you'll find several people
with the name Irwin Glass, but I'm the only one who got
those degrees at IU"

Katya covered her face with her hands.   "I like you.   I
want you to be my papa.   But what if my mother lie to me?"

"You mean, there might be someone else who could as easily be your birth father?" I had thought of that. Putinsky was not above using his wife in other honey pot schemes. I might not be the only possible father.

I was suddenly overcome with sympathy for the girl. Her tears had that effect on me. I almost cried myself. If Katya's mother lied to her and sent her off on a futile, expensive, and emotionally draining expedition to the wilds of northern Michigan in search of a spurious birth father, it was an act of cruelty. I didn't want to believe Svetlana was capable of such a dirty trick, but if the story had been a death bed confession, Svetlana, in her pain and delirium, might have picked the wrong man.

I put my arm around Katya and drew her close. I could feel her shoulders shuddering. "Katya, please. Just wait for the DNA test. Whatever the result, I'll do what I can for you, maybe help you find your real birth father, if that's the case." It was a rash promise. How would I do that?

This time I drove the truck right up in front of her dorm. It was no longer a secret that I was seeing this student. I didn't expect that she would put her arms around me and kiss me before she got out of the pickup. "Thank you, papa."

I was touched, then froze as I saw a passing student had noticed the embrace.

I figured that the call back from the FBI would be routine. It wasn't.

I was at home, sitting in the upstairs back bedroom I'd made into a study, a slab of plywood on top of the old crates from Moscow as a desk. I had a cup of fresh coffee beside me while I prepared a lesson plan, a tricky quiz on some of the nuances of English. I'd been peeved at the superior attitude of a couple of my wise ass Arab students and wanted to trip them up.

The phone rang.

I crossed the room to pick it up. "Hello?"

"This is Agent Wilkins in the Marquette FBI office. You called, said you need to check in. What's this about?"

"About twenty years ago I worked for the State Department in Moscow. Even though the CIA officer approved everything I did, when I backed out of a deal with

153

the KGB I got sent home."

"Wait a minute. KGB? What is this? You are Irwin Glass, you say? What's your Social Security number?"

I gave it. "You must have me in your computer someplace."

The FBI agent was obviously skeptical. He must get plenty of crank calls from nut cases. "What's this about the KGB?"

I hated having to tell all of this again. I wasn't proud of my past mistake and didn't like to repeat the story. People talked, exaggerated, embellished a single fact into a blown up melodrama. "The KGB tried to trick me into working for them. I pretended to cooperate and accepted payment—which was never made—for a report the CIA officer approved. But I didn't want to be a double agent so I quit. The KGB guy, Vladimir Putinsky, was pissed off, said he'd kill me. The American security guy screwed me over, said I was a paid Soviet agent, and now I can't get a passport." Thinking back on it again, I suspected that the reason I was sent home at once was because of the risk that Putinsky would pick me up, torture me, and find out how things worked inside the embassy. "Now I'm even on the damned No fly list. And I'm supposed to check in whenever I move. So here we go: I'm at Michigan Institute of Technology in Portage Lake, teaching in the Humanities department. Is this enough for you?"

"I guess so. I'll have to check the computer files."

"Can you get me off the No fly list? I'd like to be able to visit my folks in Florida. I'd hate to have to drive. It would take days." Ocala was over a thousand miles away. Just driving out of the UP in the winter was a challenge.

"That's up to Homeland Security. Anything else? You sound like you're got something else to tell me. You hiding something?"

I hesitated. "Well, yes. I was sent half of a photograph some years ago, saying I'd be approached by someone with the other half. It's a recognition signal. You know what that is?"

"Sure. So someone showed up?"

"Yeh. A Russian student. She says she's Putinsky's

daughter but that I am her birth father."

Agent Wilkins was skeptical. "Sounds like a bullshit story to me."

"What? Hers or mine?"

"Maybe both. So what's her name?"

"Katarina Putinsky, Katya. Might be shortened to simply Putin. We just had a DNA test to see if her claim is true."

"And she's supposedly the daughter of this KGB guy?"

"Right. She's here on a student visa."

"Interesting," Wilkins said. There was a pause. "She's trying to prove you are her birth parent?"

"That's what she claims."

"Do you believe her?"

"I don't know what to believe. It is possible."

Wilkins paused again. "You realize if she really is your birth daughter she's an American citizen."

"I hadn't thought of that." That added another dimension to the business.

"I want to interview this Putinsky girl. Don't mention our conversation to her. I'll just show up in Portage Lake. Give me her address."

I gave it, along with Katya's phone number. I felt both relieved and apprehensive. For a change I was relieved that I had some support from the FBI. Wilkins might not believe a word of what I said, but it was necessary to check out the story.

But I also was worried for Katya's sake. She was vulnerable, tentative, and afraid. She was out on a limb. If her story was true, everything depended on my accepting her. Her mother was dead, Putinsky, now Putin, out of the picture. She had nobody but me, her alleged birth father, to cling to. Though I was skeptical, I had to know the truth, one way or the other.

I had heard of imposters who played elaborate scams on rich people to get their money, but I wasn't rich. I was merely eking out an existence in a job with little future.

It was hard to concentrate on writing mundane quiz questions when this was hanging over my head.

Just to cover my tracks, I called the department head.

"We've had the DNA tests.'

"Good," Waarala said. "When do you get the results?"

"I don't know. Maybe a couple of weeks."

"Let me know what you find out."

"Absolutely. Oh, Dr. Waarala, I'd appreciate it if all this stays between us." I didn't trust Waarala's secretary. What else did the office staffs have to talk about during their coffee and lunch breaks but university gossip?

Still in telephone mode, I called Ivy at her apartment. "Can you come over tonight?"

Ivy had given an exam, needed to grade papers.

"Bring them with you. I'll cook you something nice."

Ivy understood. "You feeling lonely?"

"For you? All the time."

"Convince me."

"Want to see some dirty pictures? I never did show you the other five in the set."

"Show me your etchings?" She laughed.

"Why not. You might get some ideas." I had a need to be close to someone. It wasn't only that I wanted to talk about my problem with someone sympathetic. Katya's hug and her unexpected kiss reminded me that I needed some companionship. The whole business made me uncertain and afraid.

I didn't know what Wilkins would do with the information, whether he would treat my registration as routine or pounce on my story like a cat that found a mouse to play with. Certainly Katya's situation was not routine. Wilkins would have to report, and that report would trigger an investigation. Did the FBI have the resources to waste time on a case like this? Wasn't it an offense to file a false report with the police? Could I go to jail if Wilkins was convinced that my story about Katya was a lie and I was wasting his time?

Poor Katya. She was so sincere and troubled. What would the other kids in the dorm think when the FBI came around, asking questions like they did in Ocala when they visited my parents' neighbors? It might remind her of the old Soviet days when everyone was afraid of the secret police. Maybe she had been too young then to be aware of the fears adults had. In the old Soviet Union, everyone was afraid of everyone else. No one could be trusted.

Then again, living with Putinsky, KGB activities must have been second nature. Were the children of KGB officers like US Army brats, thinking that because their parents were ranking officers their children had insiders' privileges? I could only guess and imagine.

I turned my thoughts to supper. What did I have in the house that I could whip into something special? Since I didn't drink, was not a wine snob or someone who compared the quality of the Portage Lake microbrews I had no alcoholic beverages in the house. Those were not my choice of vice. I wasn't one of those guys always on the make, treating women as prey or trophies. I realized if I had any vices it might be food.

I had to admit that I'd taken an interest in food. I sometimes watched the Iron Chef on television, but Portage Lake, being so remote, didn't have much in the way of exotic ingredients in the grocery stores. Jim's Market catered to the foreign students, so had curries and some grains I didn't recognize, but I wasn't into curries.

I could make some Russian *piroshky*. I'd eaten greasy *piroshky* sold on the street in Moscow, but I was too health conscious to eat something with that much fat. Ivy wouldn't go for those, either.

I puzzled over the contents of my larder and settled on beef stroganoff. It was a suitable dish to go with my Russian story.

Ivy's Tracker was just short enough to fit into the driveway in the space between the back of my pickup and the snow banks that hid the street.

I let her in and hung her jacket inside the door. She took off her boots and padded around in her stocking feet. Giving me a hello kiss, she said, "So where are the pictures?"

"Dinner first." I started setting the kitchen table, aware that across the yard my kitchen window was in view of the Waarala's. I drew the curtains. "I called the FBI in Marquette. The agent there's going to interview Katya."

"You're coming on this a bit heavy, aren't you? I mean, first the Dean of Students, then the DNA test, now the

FBI?"

"Hey, you told me to see the Dean."

Ivy knew where I kept the water glasses and set them out. "True enough. But the FBI? Aren't you being hasty? The kid's just a neurotic with a father fixation."

"I don't think so." I checked the pot on the stove. The water would be boiling soon for the noodles. "Honey, this business has been going on for a long time. If I hadn't been in Russia... well, that Putinsky is a scary guy. I believe he was capable of tearing up the girl's original birth certificate and issuing one saying 'father unknown,' which makes Katya a bastard."

"If he did that, why not list you as the father?"

I shrugged. "Maybe he didn't want to accept Svetlana's story that it was me."

Ivy was wearing a thin sweater that enhanced her perky breasts. I suspected that she wasn't wearing a bra under it. "How do you get yourself in such trouble, Irwin?"

"Maybe it's my karma."

I concentrated on the meal, then, after putting the dishes in Kosinsky's dish washer, went upstairs to the bedroom where the fatal photographs were hidden under the underwear in my drawer. The envelope from the Moscow embassy was there.

"This is the one you saw," I said, showing the two halves, now taped together. "And this is the original."

"Uh, huh. She was some dish."

"Very sexy woman."

"I can see how you fell for it."

I showed Ivy the others, spreading them out on the bed.

"She made sure your face was turned toward the camera."

"I hadn't thought about that."

"Some gymnastics. Gave you a blow job, too."

"Might have been to keep me going," I mused. "You know, if you're drunk, you can't get it up." The conversation was turning me on.

"I can see you don't need encouragement now."

"It's not a gun in my pocket."

Ivy pulled off her sweater. As I had suspected—hoped

—she had dispensed with the bra.

"You aren't going commando, are you?"

"I can do you better than that Svetlana did."

I smiled. This is what I needed. "Show me."

She did, and then some.

We took an intimate shower together afterwards. Soaping each other's private parts was erotic and arousing. Toweling myself off, I was reminded of my fatal encounter with Svetlana Putinsky. "I didn't ask you," I began cautiously. "Are you on the pill?" I hadn't used a condom, assumed she was protected. It was an assumption I should not have made.

Ivy wrapped the guest towel around her loins, not covering her breasts. "Would it make a difference to you?"

I swallowed. "I'm forty-four. I wouldn't want to be surprised when I'm sixty four by a student who claims to be my son or daughter."

"You mean one is enough?"

"God yes. I wouldn't want to cause any surprise pregnancies."

Ivy put her arms around my shoulder. "I've thought about having a child, husband or not. I can't wait forever, and I do want children. But I know that life is tough for single parents."

"You can count on me to do the right thing," I said.

"You going to 'do the right thing' if Katya turns out to be your daughter?"

"That's the way I was brought up. I don't know, though, what I'm expected to do if she really is my daughter."

"You're a decent guy, Irwin. I wouldn't trick you."

"I hope not."

I finished drying myself. "So what is this, I mean, our sex?" She hadn't said whether she was on the pill or not. "Are we playing Russian roulette?"

"Not Russian, I hope."

"My Dad says if the cook spoils the meal he has to eat it himself. You want me to be your chef?"

"Is this a proposal?"

"Well, you could do worse."

"Don't sell yourself short, Irwin. I think you'll make a

great husband."

"I'm at that stage in life when it's now nor never," I admitted, aware that I sounded like this thing with Ivy might be my last chance.

"Me, too. Some people throw themselves headlong into marriage and regret it afterwards. I've seen that. Others are more rational, if not passionate. What about you?"

"I think we could be a good couple."

Ivy wasn't ready to commit. "Let's think about that. See how things work out."

"Fair enough. I just needed to know how we stand."

Was this a pre-engagement? I wasn't certain.

It might have been a test of my domestic potential, for Ivy reminded me that one was supposed to clean the cat's litter box. I had to admit that, not having had pets before, I fed Kosinsky's cat, but wasn't as responsible as I should have been. Cats sleep about twenty hours a day. They aren't as attentive and playful as dogs. The reminder about taking care of the cat litter was a hint that if we were married I'd have to clean up my bachelor ways.

Her parting shot as she went out the door to her parked Tracker was, "Just to put your mind at rest, I am on the pill, but I can come off any time you're ready."

...

For the next two or three days life returned to normal. I put together a suitably challenging quiz that did catch up the two insolent Kuwaiti students. The hockey season was proving successful for Da Tech's team. That was the topic of hallway conversation. Preparations were under way for Winter Carnival, the annual ice statue contest. Katya stayed away from my office. Then FBI Agent Wilkins showed up.

Wilkins was an athletic man in his late forties. Like any Yooper, he didn't wear the standard agent's overcoat you'd expect to see in Chicago or some other city. He wore a wool watch cap and a heavy storm coat. When Wilkins took off the coat I saw the man carried a sidearm, probably had to be prepared if something came up on short notice. He carried a well worn briefcase. Wilkins had a strong jaw and a crooked nose that might have been a hockey trophy. "I need to compare your story with what this Katarina Putinsky told me."

"So you did interview her."

"She tells a good story. Showed me her passport and her birth certificate. But it's in Russian, of course, and I can't read it."

"If you have a copy I can translate it for you," I offered.

"Matter of fact, I do." Wilkins took out a file folder and showed me a Xerographic copy.

I studied it. "Says the mother is Svetlana Putinsky and the father is unknown."

"You believe it?"

"Her father is a KGB officer. He could produce any forgery."

"Makes it more difficult."

"Could you make me a copy of that?" I asked, handing it back.

"No can do. Evidence. You can ask her yourself."

"OK."

"So tell me your story again, from the beginning. You mind if I record this?" Wilkins took out a small tape recorder.

"Go ahead." I saw to it that the office door was locked. Then it all began over again. This time, I concentrated on my victim status, how I was sent back to the states in the clothes I stood up in, with a plastic garbage bag for luggage, arriving broke in Washington. I made a point of telling how the Riggs bank had no record of any account in my name, and no payment, that I was not a paid Soviet agent and never had been, and could I now be taken off the No fly list? Could I be issued a passport?

I knew Wilkins would have the tape transcribed and compare his version with whatever could be dug up out of other files. "Will the CIA send you their version?"

"Since 9/11 there's better cooperation, but this is an old case, Mr. Glass. Anything written down is probably buried in some catacomb in Langley, Virginia. Nowadays we're too busy chasing Moslem terrorists."

I thought about some of my foreign students. "There are some candidates here on campus."

"I know that," Wilkins said, but went no further in that direction.

"OK," I said, sensing we were finished. "What if Katya really is my daughter? What do I do then?" What were my responsibilities? Was I obligated to her in any way? She was of age, after all.

"You can ask that she be issued a prima facia document."

"What's prima facia?"

"Prima facia evidence is a document that establishes a fact. It will indicate she's the daughter of an American citizen and entitled to US citizenship."

"She's on a student visa now. Can't work."

Wilkins was putting away the tape recorder. "Once she's a citizen you can get her a social security card, driver's license, the whole package."

"US passport?"

"You'll have to get a true translation of the birth certificate, but sure. She'll be able to get a passport."

I shook my head. It was ironic. "That's more than I can get. My last application for a passport was refused."

"Refused?"

'Yes. I'm still on the books as a paid Soviet agent. I'm supposedly a security risk."

"Maybe that can be fixed," Wilkins offered. "These things take time."

"It's been twenty years already," I lamented.

"Not that long," the agent promised. "Might take months. Someone has to dig up the old records."

I had visions of the movie *Secrets of the Lost Ark* in which the tablets of the original Ten Commandments are boxed and tucked away amidst acres and acres of underground storage, never to be seen again.

"What about Katya?"

"I'll see if her story checks out. And you be sure to tell me the results of that DNA test. Everything hangs on that."

"Make me a copy of Katya's birth certificate and I'll translate it for you. I'll even have it notarized if you want."

With that promise Wilkins relented. We ran a Xerographic duplicate of the Russian document on the office machine. It took me only a few minutes to prepare a translation.

Before Wilkins left he had one more question. "Who is Robert?"

I was stunned. "What?"

"The name turns up in your file."

So my old nemesis was still at it. "Code name of a CIA operative. He must be retired by now. He's the guy who got me kicked out of Moscow and claimed I was a paid Soviet agent. Is he still around?"

"Either that or someone else is using the same code name. Not likely. Causes confusion."

That was one man I never wanted to see again. "You think he'll show up?"

Wilkins didn't know or wouldn't say.

I had to wait.

Not knowing what I might tell Katya about the FBI visit, I didn't call her, but she showed up at my office, perturbed. She wore her usual winter jacket but had added to her wardrobe a pair of rather stylish, red boots that didn't look very practical for the Copper Country. Maybe she'd gone shopping. She came right out and asked in Russian, "Did you denounce me to your secret police?"

I responded in kind. "What? This isn't Russia. We don't have secret police."

"You have many police. City police. County police. State police."

"It's the United States, Katya. United, but separate." I didn't know the Russian equivalents and had to switch back to English. "Each state has its own government, even its own army, what we call the National Guard. Then there's the federal police, the treasury agents who deal with counterfeiting, the INS—immigration and naturalization—the firearms and drug enforcement agency, the border patrol, and the Secret Service which protects the president."

"Then your CIA and FBI," Katya added. She had done her homework.

"Not to mention the rent-a-cops."

She didn't know rent-a-cops.

"Private security guards, like you see at the mall. There are more rent-a-cops than all the official police put together."

Katya shook her head. "And you call old Soviet Union

163

a police state."

I had to agree.   "And the UP of Michigan is our own Gulag where Michigan puts most of its own prisoners.   The United States has more people in prison than any other country, even the old Soviet Union."

"Did you send the FBI?"

I couldn't pretend I didn't know.   "Every foreign student is checked," I guessed.   "Ever since 9/11 we are afraid of terrorism.   How did you get to Portage Lake? You flew, didn't you?"

Katya nodded.

"And you got checked at the airport, baggage x-rayed, shoes off, right?"

"Yes."

"So don't be surprised if you are questioned."

That troubled her.   "I thought America is free country."

"You can travel anywhere you want.   You don't have to register with the police." But of course, I did.   I did have to register, and I could not travel abroad without a passport.   I couldn't even get on a plane, though Katya could.   At least I could get in my truck and drive to Florida if I wanted to. There were no checkpoints at the Wisconsin border, at least not yet.

"What does the FBI want from me?" she asked.

I couldn't say.   "I don't know.   I do know that if the DNA test says you are truly my daughter, you will be entitled to US citizenship.   You will be able to work without a permit.   I never asked you: how are your finances? Don't you have to show you have enough money for tuition before you can get a student visa? This isn't Russia.   College tuition is expensive."

"Tuition, yes, I paid."

Where did she get that? From her mother's money? "Did you have an inheritance?"

Either she didn't understand inheritance or didn't want to say.   "Books are very expensive.   I do not have much money," she admitted, sitting in my guest chair and looking down at her new boots.

If she didn't have much money, what did she do, shop? Some women had a thing for boots and shoes.   Could a foreign student get a credit card? A student loan? "Do you have a credit card?"

"No."

"Bank account?"

She didn't answer.

I'd heard that Jews who finally got exit permission could take no money out of Russia. If that applied to all émigrés, no wonder she was broke.

I wondered how someone without a tax ID number opened a bank account. I'd have to ask down at the Wells Fargo. What did she do? Arrived with a wad of cash which she was quickly spending? Many students, out on their own for the first time, had no idea how to manage their finances.

What now, I wondered. *Is she going to ask me to finance her education? Pay her expenses at Da Tech? Is that what this is all about? Is this what my being her birth father meant?* She was over eighteen, an adult. She was not my responsibility. Even if she was my daughter-- which I didn't believe-- I wasn't obligated to provide her with financial support. If she wanted that she should have picked on someone rich to be her father, not a mere Humanities instructor, the lowest paid full time Tech faculty. I expected the DNA test to be negative. I assumed it would be. Then this whole charade would be over. My head was full of unanswered "What ifs." There was only a very small chance that the one night with Svetlana Putinsky in the old Metropol Hotel had borne any fruit other than the ruination of my career. But what if it did? What then?

"I do not think you will have any trouble with the FBI," I reassured her. "Just tell the truth." Telling her that made me feel like a hypocrite. I had always told the truth, and what had it got me? I felt like a misfit. Maybe I should, like that Greek cynic Diogenes, live in a tub and go around with a lighted lantern looking for an honest man. "Just do your homework and forget about it. We should have the DNA test result in a few days. Don't worry."

Katya seemed reassured. She got up, crossed to my side of the desk, and kissed me on the cheek. "Thank you, Papa."

Was this wishful thinking on her part, or was she working on my emotions? For Russians, kissing was a custom. Politicians bussed both cheeks of their equals before continuing with their plots and power plays. It could be the kiss of death.

. . .

A few days later I got the call at the office. I was Friday morning. "This is Dr. Jenkins' nurse. Your DNA test is ready."

I took a deep breath. "What's the result?"

"We don't give out that information over the phone. You and your partner will have to come to the office."

"She's not my partner," I corrected.

The nurse was reading off a chart. "Oh, yes. Katarina Vladovna Putinsky. What is she, a student?"

"Yes. I'll get hold of her and come to the hospital right away."

"Better make it today before four o'clock. We're closed over the weekend."

I didn't want to wait over the weekend for the DNA results. I dialed Katya's number. No answer. She and her roommate were both out. Where was she? In class? I didn't know her class schedule. I called the dormitory resident counselor. "This is Irwin Glass in the Humanities Department. I need to get hold of Katarina Putinsky right away. Will you put a note on her door or something? It's urgent."

"Is this about the fraternization case?"

"What fraternization case?" Had rumors gotten that far? I didn't wait for an answer. "It's a private matter," I insisted. "Family business. We have to get up to the hospital before four o'clock."

"I'll tell her."

"Tell her to call me. She has the number. Irwin Glass, Humanities."

"Will do." She hung up.

Someone knocked at my office door. It was Doctor Waarala's secretary, Mrs. Houghton, a picture of superior self-importance. "Dr. Waarala says you're to meet with him and the Dean on Monday."

"What for?"

"It's a hearing on your fraternization case."

166

"I thought he was going to wait until the DNA test came back." I didn't like Waarala's secretary. She had a smug attitude. She treated senior faculty with respect, but I was a nothing in her estimation. Though I was the only faculty member who taught English as a second language, it was a pass fail course, only one credit, not required on any of the curricula for graduation. I was expendable.

"The DNA test is ready," I said with a false expression of bravado. "I'm picking up the results today. On Monday we'll be able to lay this whole business to rest." Whatever the outcome. Either I was, indeed, Katya's birth father, or she could be passed on to the campus psychiatrist as a neurotic kid with a father fixation. Either way, I'd be exonerated—I hoped.

Pensive, nervous, and anxious for fear of missing Katya, I didn't dare leave the office except to go to class. Where was Katya? Why hadn't she called? When I did go to my class I was distracted. This was the English language section with the Kuwaiti students. They were rich playboys. The African students were serious and dedicated. The brightest was an Indonesian who, if in Kuwait, would have been treated like dirt. In his own country he might well end up as Prime Minister. The only female in the section was a girl from India who had started the Fall term in a sari and sandals but soon adapted to the Copper Country climate. She had ditched her original clothes, but still wore a diamond in one nostril.

It was different with the Chinese students. They were serious, dedicated, laughed at my jokes when they got them, likely to be emotional, even cry if they did not do well. I had to be careful not to cause a Chinese to lose face. I had to adapt my teaching methods to the cultures of the students. Today I could not concentrate on the class material, went through the exercises like an automaton. I dismissed the class a few minutes early.

When I got back to my office Ivy was there with Katya. "I'm glad you made it," I said, looking at my watch. "The DNA test result is ready. We have to go to the hospital right away."

"Can I come along?" Ivy asked.

167

"For moral support?"

"Sure." It would be comforting for Ivy to be there. If we were to be married and the DNA test were positive, we'd all be family. Good grief! It was a disconcerting idea I would have to get used to. I was torn between my concern for Katya's welfare and my need to be rid of this business, to send the girl on her way. Hand her over to the Dean of Students and the campus counselors. Let me get on with my life. Get Mrs. Houghton and the department head off my back. Stop all the gossip and whispering in the halls so I could concentrate on my job.

We would have to squeeze into my pickup in the Humanities parking lot. I brushed the fresh snow off the windshield and ran the engine until the defroster cleared the glass. There were seat belts for only two. Katya sat in the middle.

At the hospital we passed the senior citizen volunteer gatekeepers and went directly to Dr. Jenkins' office. It was nearly four o'clock and the impatient receptionist was getting ready to pack up for the weekend.

Doctor Jenkins called me and Katya into an examination room. I asked if Ivy might come along, too, which was permitted.

Jenkins, in his white coat and stethoscope, looked tired. He began, "I don't know whether you will be happy about this or not." He took the DNA report from a folder. "The lab says there is no doubt of patrimony. Mr. Glass, you are definitely the birth father of Katarina Putinsky."

Katya gasped. Was it shock or relief?

The news hit me like a baseball bat. Katya's story had been, I hoped, unbelievable. I admitted it was an unlikely possibility, but a possibility nonetheless. I had humored Katya, even entertained the idea that she might be my daughter in spite of the long odds, but I didn't want to be reminded of that Moscow incident that ruined my State Department career and pursued me ever since. Considering the impact of this news, Dr. Jenkins might be delivering a verdict of a terminal illness. My life was going to be changed again. "Hundred percent sure?"

"It's not like a blood test," Dr. Jenkins explained.

"With DNA there is no doubt."

I had done the test to stop the rumors and be exonerated from claims of fraternization. After what happened with Svetlana I was afraid of entanglements. It had affected my relationships with other women. My love affair while at SIU had also ended in disaster. My relationship with Ivy was a step toward recovery. Now my troubles were back.

I focused on the details, suppressed my feelings. I remembered what Wilkins, the FBI agent had told me. "I'll need copies of the report. They will establish Katya's identity. The DNA report can be used as proof of citizenship."

Dr. Jenkins didn't understand. "Citizenship?"

"Yes. I'm told officially that the DNA report will be prima fascia evidence." I had not used the term before.

"I'll have my secretary make you several copies."

"Can she notarize them?"

"I think you can get that done at the front office."

"Thank you, doctor."

Katya clung to me as we left the building. She was crying. The resolution of this long quest had been a huge release. All the tension and anxiety were lifted. "You are my Papa."

"Looks like it," I admitted. I had often thought about having children, had never been married. Now suddenly I had a daughter, but she was grown up. There was no bond, not the kind of connection established from birth. In spite of my sympathy for her situation I didn't love her. Daughterhood would normally be earned by degrees, from birth to diapers, first words, nursery school-- all those stages of childhood development leading to adulthood. Katya came as a finished package without a background in common. Our only connection was a one night stand in the Metropol hotel in Moscow.

I rationalized that this was not so uncommon. It could happen to any man who had a brief affair quickly forgotten, only to be stuck with a paternity case. There were even sperm donors who were confronted years later by their inadvertent progeny. There were actually legal paternity cases pending that surprised the men who in college had made some extra money by selling their sperm, thinking there would be no consequences. Hadn't the donors realized that by selling sperm there would be issue and they would be technically fathers of any number of children they never saw?

As for paternity and legal obligations appertaining thereto, Katya was an adult. I shouldn't have any child support to pay to Svetlana. Svetlana was dead. Vladimir Putinsky, or Putin as she said he now called himself, was out of the picture. That made Katya even more dependent on me. Did she have any relatives back in Russia? No siblings? No doting aunts?

The old Soviet Union, decimated by war, hampered by a housing shortage and a practice of abortion as contraception, meant small families, children with no aunts or uncles, no brothers or sisters. The generation Katya came from was often spoiled. What had Svetlana called them at the Metropol? *Stylagi*. The spoiled scions of party members and elite. What had they become now that the Soviet Union had collapsed? Were the *stylagi* the new Russian mafia? Was that the crowd Katya had grown up with?

I didn't know her. Katya had told me her story, but our relationship was superficial. It was partly because I didn't believe her story, didn't want to be too close to her with that threat of disciplinary action for fraternization hanging over my head. She was a mystery.

She seemed to be a nice kid, earnest, sincere, a good student. Having graduated from a Russian gymnasium she already had the equivalent of at least one year of college work. She was better prepared than most American freshmen. She should do well.

"This is like your birthday," I suggested when we got back in my truck. "Is this an occasion for a celebration?" I didn't add, "Or for mourning?"

"I think I need a drink," Katya said. "You have any vodka?"

That was a surprise. Of course, the drinking laws in Russia were different than in Michigan. Was Katya, like many students, a binge drinker? Did she drink at all? Apparently so. I was so far removed from that scene that it was foreign to me. I shuddered. "No vodka." That was how I got into all that trouble in the beginning. "I don't drink. Maybe you and Ivy here can share a bottle of wine to toast your new identity. We'll stop at Jim's market and you can pick something out. Maybe champagne?"

It was the first time Katya had been to my house and I, aware that Mrs. Waarala could see my front door from her kitchen window, was glad that Ivy was with us.

We were met by the cat. The cat rubbed against Katya's calf, approved, and retreated to the living room sofa.

"This is your house?" Katya asked, looking around with approval.

"It's a rental. Professor Kosinsky is away in Israel at the Technion."

"It is big house for one person," Katya said. She was speaking from the Moscow frame of reference where a three bedroom apartment would house three families.

"Two bedrooms on the second floor. I don't know what's on the top floor. Off limits. Kosinsky's office." The door to the attic, third floor office was locked and I didn't have the key.

It wasn't appropriate to drink without something to eat with it. The Russian custom was a bit of bread along with a glass of vodka. I had no vodka, of course. What would go with champagne? I found some cheddar cheese in the fridge and the remains of a box of crackers. While Ivy and Katya watched I set out a plate. Kosinsky's furnishings did not include champagne glasses designed for sniffing the tingle of the bubbles. Champagne drunk from wine goblets that didn't match was hardly festive. We sat around the kitchen table and I observed.

"*Nozdrovya,*" Katya said, holding up her glass. She was offended that I did not drink.

I relented. "Maybe a little." I poured a half inch of champagne and sipped.

Before driving Katya back to her dorm I gave her one of the copies of the DNA report. "This is yours. You will need it."

"Is my name now Katarina Glass?"

"I don't think so. If you want to you can probably call yourself Katarina Glass-Putin, one of those hyphenated names."

She didn't like the sound of it.

The three of us piled into the front seat of my Ford. I dropped Katya at the dorm and pulled around into the Humanities parking lot for Ivy to pick up her Tracker. Before getting out of the pickup she asked, "What's next?"

"I hope this doesn't affect us, I mean, you and me."

"Depends," Ivy said. Like her sparring with me over pill or no pill, she wasn't going to commit. Perhaps she'd had failed romances in the past. I never asked her about that. Forbidden territory.

Did two people ever know one another? Ultimately there was always the skin barrier. The closest you both got to being inside one skin was during intercourse, to become one flesh, but in spite of coupling, there was no fusion. There was always a degree of separation.

That degree of separation could be a good thing. The spark of playful sparring and teasing added spice as long as it didn't cross the line into genuine conflict. I wondered if I could be comfortable with Ivy long term. This business with Katya being my birth daughter might be a test that made or broke my relationship with Ivy.

I'd passed that critical age forty, the passage in life when you realize this is it: now is the time to get that Ph.D. or sail around the world, or have that last great adventure, for life was half over. What could I expect beyond this? The encroaching infirmities of old age? I had already acquired a bit of a paunch. I had lost whatever muscle tone I had in my twenties. I was a late bloomer but I realized that at forty-four it was now or maybe never. The same went for Ivy. If she wanted a marriage and children, it would soon be too late.

Returning to my house, I sat on the bed for a long time looking at the DNA report and studying the fatal photographs. I had been thinner then, better looking. In twenty years the photographs had lost all shock effect, had no erotic impact. I saw Katya's resemblance to her mother, but I didn't think the girl shared any of my features.

What time on Monday was I supposed to confront the department head and the dean? I should have no trouble defending myself with the DNA report. I didn't anticipate other ramifications of my new role as Katya's birth father. The DNA report should solve my problems with the administration.

The appointment with the department head was after my early class. Armed with the DNA test report, I announced myself to the head's secretary and was told to go on in.

As befitted a laid back Yooper, Dr. Waarala was usually casually dressed, but this morning he wore a jacket and tie. That might have been for the benefit of Dean Sheldon.

Sheldon was already in Waarala's office, looking severe and pugnacious. Outranking Waarala in the administration pecking order, she opened the proceedings. "You signed the non-fraternization agreement and understand you are not to have a personal relationship with any student. You cannot have a student visit you in your home unless you invite an entire class. But you were seen on Friday with Katarina Putinsky at your home. This is a clear violation."

"We weren't alone. Doctor Hartshorn was with us."

"That's immaterial. What were you doing?"

I cleared his throat. "It was sort of a celebration. The DNA test result is in. You remember, you suggested I have a DNA test to prove Katya was just a neurotic kid who needed counseling and not my daughter."

"Yes, I remember that."

I produced a copy of the DNA report. "Turns out, she actually is my daughter."

Dean Sheldon studied it, looked confused, passed the copy on to Dr. Waarala. "How is that possible?"

"It's a long story I don't want to go into. I had a brief relationship with Katya's mother in Moscow when I worked in the State Department."

Dean Sheldon wrinkled her forehead in puzzlement. "I got your resume from the personnel department. There's nothing in it about your working in the State Department."

"It was a long time ago. There's nothing in my resume that isn't true. It's not padded with lies. I simply omitted that item as irrelevant to a teaching position application."

"So this makes Katarina Putinsky your birth daughter?"

"Yep. And there's no rule against a faculty member entertaining his daughter in his own home."

Waarala seemed to be enjoying this. He clearly didn't like Dean Sheldon or having her lord over him and his staff in his own office. "Can't deny that."

I felt glad that Waarala was on my side.

"Well, then," Dean Sheldon said and held up the copy of the test report. "May I keep this?"

"That's a private document. It's a confidential medical record."

Sheldon changed the subject. "Since you are the girl's birth father, perhaps I can broach another subject. It's about Katarina's role as a student."

"You mean her grades? She's not my student. Aren't her grades between her and her professors? Student confidentiality and all that?"

"I know that a parent can't ask to see a student's grades, stupid as that rule may seem. This is a financial issue."

"How's that?"

"She hasn't paid her dorm fees."

"Are you suggesting I pay them? She's an adult. If a parent can't see a student's grades, is a parent responsible for a student's expenses?"

"As a foreign student, she's not eligible for a student loan."

"She can't get a job as a foreigner on a student visa."

"That's right," Waarala put in. "The INS will pounce on any foreign student caught working here."

"What about a scholarship?"

"That's possible," Dr. Sheldon admitted, "But a scholarship would apply to tuition, books, that sort of thing."

"If she's the daughter of a faculty member, isn't she entitled to reduced tuition? Seems I read something about that in the Faculty Handbook. Maybe now she can get a rebate and use the money for her dorm costs."

"Not likely. As your daughter she can get reduced tuition next term. If she doesn't pay her dorm fees she'll have to move out. We require freshmen to live on campus unless…"

"Unless what?"

"Unless she moves in with you."

Oops. I hadn't thought that far ahead. I hadn't even

174

considered that Katya would live with me. It was more than I could handle just considering that she was or was not my birth daughter. Kosinsky had rented me the house on condition that I didn't sublet to any students.

"Well, I do have a spare bedroom." I imagined having to deal with a pretty girl, essentially a stranger, moving in, sharing the bathroom, a level of intimacy I in my years of bachelorhood had never had to deal with. Ivy had slept over on occasion, but in spite of our romance there was still that awkwardness. It was an old house. The only bathroom was on the second floor.

"Why don't you talk to Katarina?"

"Is she broke?" I wondered how she handled her money. Did she have a local account at the Wells Fargo? Had she inherited something from Svetlana, enough to pay for a ticket to the United States, make that payment of non-resident tuition? Where did her money come from?

"You'll have to ask her," Dean Sheldon said.

Dr. Waarala broke in. "Dorothy, I think that the accusations of fraternization are past history. If Irwin wants to give his daughter a fatherly good bye kiss in the parking lot, that's nobody's business." Implying, *none of your business, either, Sheldon*. Waarala was plainly enjoying the opportunity to put down the dean.

So I had been seen in the dorm parking lot, and reported. I would have to make some public gesture that once and for all killed all the gossip. Or would there be some residue? People could be so malicious, so willing to believe the worst. I could not forget Susan Lutz's claim that I was an alcoholic and a womanizer. I had never been able to confront her, to prove her wrong. People might even accuse me of incest. Good God. I would have to dispel all such nonsense. If Ivy and I were officially engaged to be married, that might deflect other rumors.

I called Katya right away. This time I caught her at her dorm room. "I have to talk to you, Katya. Can I come to the dorm?"

She sounded confused, surprised. "Yes. You must tell the counselor first."

Of course, there were rules about men on the women's

floor. I put on my old Russian jacket and fake fur hat and crossed the highway to the coed dormitory. It had been years since I was in a dorm. When I was at IU years before one had to shout "Man in the hall" in case one of the college girls came out of the shower wearing only a towel or nothing at all.

"I've come to visit my daughter," I announced to the gatekeeper, and was sent up to the third floor. I felt awkward in the residence hall, out of my element.

Katya's door was open. It was a typical dorm room, bunk beds, two desks, posters of rock stars taped on the concrete block walls. There was one bureau she apparently shared with her roommate. Who got the top drawers? I wondered. First come, first dibs. On the top of the bureau was an electric corn popper and in the corner a small refrigerator. The roommate's desk had a Dell laptop and a stuffed Husky sled dog mascot with a little sweater bearing the MIT school logo. Katya's desk was Spartan, the only personal touch a framed photograph I recognized, Svetlana and Vladimir Putinsky. I guessed it was an old photo, probably taken before their divorce, a remembrance of happier times before the blow-up when Svetlana revealed that Vladimir was not Katya's birth father. That betrayal must have been a terrible blow to the man's ego.

Katya was wearing a sweater, jeans, and slippers. Under her bed I saw the new, red leather boots I had noticed before. If Katya was broke, how could she shop for those new boots? I speculated that for some women shopping was more important than eating. Maybe she thought she was putting on weight and was trying to take it off. Typically students living in the dorms put on ten or twenty pounds the first year because of the abundance of food and unlimited seconds. The dorms hadn't been that generous when I was a student at IU Was she starving herself? She looked thin. She had none of that baby fat around the chin that was so typical of girls her age. Was she eating enough? Was I starting to behave like a concerned parent?

I supposed one could warm soup in the popcorn popper, or boil water for tea. Engineering students were resourceful. They might not be permitted hot plates or microwaves, but I had heard that one resourceful electrical engineering student had jury rigged a hot dog cooker that consisted only of a board with two nails wired to an electric cord. A hot dog impaled on the nails would be essentially electrocuted. That's what criminals meant when someone got the electric chair: they were actually cooked by the high voltage. Of course, the hot dog gadget wasn't to be plugged in until the sausage was in place on the nails or the "cook" might be fried as well.

Not wishing to be overheard by Katya's neighbors, I shut the door and spoke to her in Russian. "Thanks to the DNA test the fraternization business is over. I spoke with the dean of students about your situation. She tells me that you haven't paid your rent, that you don't have a meal ticket. Is that true?"

"Yes." She was embarrassed. "Some trouble with my bank account."

Where was she getting her money? Wire transfers from Russia? How did that work?

Katya was a freshman and required to live on campus. Had she been a sophomore she could get a room in a rental house with a bunch of other students and cut her expenses, do her own cooking, and the like. So many students lived on Raman noodles it had become a joke. If she had family, say, an older sibling who lived off campus, she could move in with them. But she had no family except, well, me. She was stuck. She wasn't exactly stranded on Mars with no way of getting back to Earth, but she was alone in a foreign country and running out of money, or so she claimed. I felt obligated to do something for her. I valued my privacy, but not to offer Katya shelter would be selfish. "You could move in with me. Even if you are a freshman you can live off campus with a relative."

She hadn't expected that. "I don't know." Perhaps she envisioned the cramped quarters she'd seen in Moscow. I might be her father, but she was not prepared to sleep in the same room.

"I have a spare bedroom. It's nicer than this. I can show you. Then you can think about what you want to do."

"All right. When?"

177

"Now, if you have time. Do you have a class?"

"Not until this afternoon. I have a two o'clock."

"Then come."

She accompanied me across the highway to the parking lot. There was an unseasonal thaw, the air damp, the snow banks sagging, showing the alternating layers of stamp sand and snow that recorded the different storms as they accumulated. The snow banks would not disappear until April. Vestigial snow might linger in the northern woods as late as June.

Arriving at the Kosinsky house, I took Katya upstairs. She had only seen the kitchen and living room before this. "Excuse the mess," I apologized. I had spread some student papers on the spare bed. "You see, I have a nice library of Russian and Soviet literature, some in Russian. You can use this desk. I know it is crude, but it works for me." I was eager to show her the spacious closet. Prof. Kosinsky's winter wardrobe was shifted to one side. He would not need waffle stompers at the Technion in the Negev desert. "Plenty of room."

"It is very good," Katya said. She was uneasy. "What do I pay you?"

"Pay me? Nothing. Am I not your papa?"

Perhaps she had not thought that far beyond simply confirming her mother's claim that Putinsky was not her real father.

"Yes. I will do this."

"Good. But there are other matters."

"What matters?"

"Since you are my daughter, you do not have to go by the rules of foreign student visas. You can get a job to earn your tuition money. There are jobs for students on campus or in one of the local stores. Wal-Mart and the grocery stores hire Tech students."

"What kind of job?"

"Cashier I suppose."

"I must have papers to do such work."

I hadn't thought of that. "You will need a social security number." For that she would need a birth certificate. I could see a flurry of paperwork ahead of us. A driver's license would be enough, but that was complicated, too.

"Do you have an international driver's license?"

"No. How do I get driver's license?"

"You'd have to pass the driver's test."

Katya shrugged. Did she know how to drive? Would I have to give her lessons? Driving in the Copper Country snow took skill and practice. Then I remembered that, thanks to illegal immigration and homeland security, to get a driver's license you now needed a birth certificate, proof of US citizenship or a green card issued to legal immigrants. Proof of residence, such as rent receipts and utility bills was no longer enough. Her birth certificate was Russian, said "father unknown." With the DNA test, she'd have enough, I hoped. But then she would also have to have a copy of my birth certificate or my old, expired, passport—where was it? —as proof that she was the daughter of a US citizen. I did have a copy of my own birth certificate.

"Perhaps the easiest would be for you to get a US passport."

"How do I get passport?"

Of course, she was used to having an internal passport. It was an element of the old Soviet police state. "The United States doesn't have an internal passport, or a national identity card. At least not yet. First let's get you moved."

"When?"

"Ask at the dormitory office."

I returned Katya to the dorm in time for her to get ready for her two o'clock class.

On my way home after my own classes I stopped at the county court house and picked up the application form for a passport, saw that for Katya to claim proof of citizenship through birth abroad to one US citizen parent she would need a consular report (Form FS-240), whatever that was, a foreign certificate of birth and proof of the citizenship of her parent. Those seemed clear enough, but the application also demanded an affidavit showing all of my periods and places of residence abroad before her birth. I'd been in Russia only about a month. Would that satisfy the passport bureaucrats? Or would that be a red flag suggesting that this was a scheme to sneak a foreigner into the country? I had not been around

179

when Katya was born, didn't even know she existed until she showed up at my university office.

I did find my old passport, souvenir of a bad dream, with that fatal stamp, "valid only for immediate return to the United States." If the county clerk asked about the restriction I might have to tell my own unpleasant story all over again. Merely saying I had gotten in trouble with the KGB might be enough. Some people lacked curiosity, were satisfied with the first answer and didn't follow up with more questions. I wasn't telling anyone that I was regarded as a paid Soviet agent, couldn't get a new passport for myself, and was on the no fly list. I could fall back on the "need to know" excuse, say it was all classified information, the old joke, "If I told you I'd have to kill you." It was Vlaldimir Putinsky who had threatened to kill me. Ironic that Katya was eligible for a US passport and I was not.

Katya and I went through the whole routine. Filled out the passport application. Gathered up the essential documents, including a sworn and notarized true translation of her Russian birth certificate, a copy of my own, had the prescribed pair of photographs taken at a studio downtown, and swore before the county clerk that all the statements were true. The only kicker was the affidavit showing my residence abroad. One month. Would the passport office balk at that as insufficient evidence of fatherhood? How long did it take to start a baby? Five minutes? The father didn't have to stick around for nine months waiting for the delivery.

I was shocked at how expensive the passport fee now was. Americans might be free to travel abroad, but not if they were too poor to even pay that fee.

No longer living alone, it would be intimidating to have Katya in the back bedroom if Ivy came over to spend the night. My bed squeaked loud enough for me and Ivy to break out in laughter. For sex, we might have to meet at her apartment near the campus, leaving Katya alone in the house.

I broached the subject at the office when Ivy was between classes. "You realize, honey, that you could be Katya's stepmother. How do you feel about that?"

"We're not married yet, Irwin."

"I mean, well, let's say we are married. What then?"

Ivy was wearing a turtle neck sweater over matching slacks, but her hair was pulled back. It wasn't very flattering, but she wasn't supposed to look alluring to her mostly male students. "She's eighteen. She'll soon be out on her own. It's not as if I'd be raising her, going through seventh grade puberty, badgering her about dressing properly for school, stuff like that. She's her own responsibility."

"I guess so. I have a daughter in name only. She's more like a foster child. She's really a stranger."

"That's right. A stranger in the house. Sounds like the title of a bad movie."

"More like a roommate," I admitted. I had shown Katya how to run the washer and drier. When I did a load myself I would have to adapt to seeing panties and bras along with my tee shirts and shorts. At least my own mother had taught me not to mix colored with whites.

I had never had a sister. I wasn't used to living with a pretty eighteen year old who was nonchalant about being seen in her pajamas. If Ivy walked around in a loose bathrobe or even naked when we were alone, I enjoyed that but I hadn't adapted to the role of fatherhood. Would I be comfortable buying a package of tampons at the grocery store?

I hadn't mentioned any of the business with Katya to my parents. The whole idea of having a child out of wedlock was something my mother would never approve of, but dad had seen the photo taken at the Metropol years ago. We'd not talked about it since, but he wouldn't have forgotten. It wouldn't be such a total surprise to my father that something had come of that crazy night in Moscow. Until the results of the DNA tests were in there was no point in saying anything. It was time I told my folks.

I phoned Ocala and got my father on the phone. "Are you sitting down?"

"Why? You got some bad news?"

"That depends. What would you say if I told you you're a grandpa?"

"I would ask if you were married. Irwin, you're not an unwed father are you?"

"Not married yet, but you remember that picture from

181

Moscow?"

"How could I forget?"

"Turns out the lady got pregnant. And didn't abort, which you'd expect. So now it turns out that I have a daughter. Lovely girl. Student here at Da Tech. No kidding, dad. DNA test confirms it. I'll send you a picture as soon as I can."

There was a long silence while the news sank in. Finally my father came back on. He was clearly rattled. "I, I have news for you, too. You remember that box of old pictures you found in the attic when you were a kid?"

"Yeh, the one with the Russian letter nobody could read. What about it? It was lost, wasn't it?"

"It had my Purple Heart medal in it, and pictures from Vietnam. A veteran found the box at a garage sale, saw the medal, and decided to track me down. You know how the Vietnam vets are. They support each other. Comrades in arms."

"You never wanted to talk about Vietnam."

"No. But the vets organization is persistent. You know, Irwin, when we came back people spat on us and called us baby killers. Now the vets are sticking up for each other. Closure, they call it. The man who found the pictures and the medal, his name is Chuck--Charlie-- Sanders. He's a veteran, too, and tracked me down. He's sending me the box of pictures and my medal."

"That's great." I remembered the old photograph of my great grandfather Melamed. "Is that old Russian letter with it?"

"I don't know. If it is, I'll send it."

"Great. What do you think Mom will do when she finds out she has an eighteen year old grand daughter she never met?"

"Better late than never, Irwin. You sure she's really your daughter?"

"No doubt of it."

"Oh, my." He hung up.

I still had to notify my landlord about Katya. I remembered that I had agreed not to sublet to students. Professor Kosinsky would not be happy to learn that his tenant had a guest living with him. Should I call? I had never placed a phone call to Israel. The only mailing address I had for Kosinsky was the Technion. My rent payments went directly to the professor's account at the Wells Fargo bank downtown. Turned out, I didn't have to wait. Kosinsky called me.

It was early in the morning, already late in the day in Israel when the phone rang. A voice in Russian said, "This is Avrom, Avrom Kosinsky."

"How are you? How's everything at the Technion?"

"Very good, very good. I have for you a favor to ask."

"What's that?" Perhaps Kosinsky needed some of his winter clothes after all.

"My cousin is flying to Portage Lake for a job interview. He is also engineer, Russian like me. Now he lives in Israel. Can you pick him up at the airport? He needs a place to stay for a couple of days while he has the interview. He can sleep in the back bedroom."

"Sure. But, ah, there is a complication. My daughter is staying with me."

"Your daughter? You not say you have a daughter."

"I didn't know it myself. It's a long story. She's Russian."

"You have a Russian daughter? How is this possible?"

"A surprise souvenir of an old love affair." That was a close to the truth as I wanted to go.

"You were a naughty boy, Irwin?"

"Things happen." I would have said "shit happens" but Katya wasn't in that category. "So what is your cousin's name, and what flight is he coming in on?"

"He is Mordechai Melamed."

"Melamed? My great grandfather was a Melamed, also from Russia."

"Then perhaps you are related. But you are not Jewish?"

"No."

"So your bedroom is occupied. No matter. I have a spare bed on the top floor where my office is. Mordechai can sleep there. The key to the top floor is hanging in the broom closet by the back door."

"OK."

"What is your daughter's name?"

"Katarina. Katya. She will be glad to have someone else to speak Russian with."

"So. Katarina Glass."

I didn't correct him. Putinsky sounded a lot like Putin, another Rusian official. Might not go down well with a Russian Jewish visitor or with my refusenik landlord.

"How will I recognize your cousin?"

"Is no problem. He moved to Israel and turned Orthodox. It happens. Some Jews visit Jerusalem and… they call it Jerusalem syndrome."

What did that mean? Was my visitor to be dressed in a big black hat and long caftan?

I wrote down the United airlines flight number. The plane got in from Chicago after midnight. Dr. Melamed would be jet lagged and bone tired. I would check on the bed upstairs, see that there was clean linen and a towel. "If he has time I'll show your cousin the campus, take him on a little tour."

"That would be nice. How is my cat?"

"OK. She sleeps a lot."

"Don't over feed her. I do not like fat cats. That is a joke, Irwin."

"Yes." I pretended to laugh.

Kosinsky hung up.

Well, that was a complication. I would have to lay on some groceries. What would I feed my Orthodox Jewish guest? Not bacon and eggs. If Dr. Melamed was an adopted Israeli he would expect lots of salads, hummus. What else did Israelis eat? Falafel? I didn't know how to make falafel. I had seen it in the grocery store health food department. There must be instructions on the box.

How would Katya feel about having a Russian-Jewish visitor in the house? I would soon find out.

At breakfast, making Katya some American pancakes, I announced, "We'll be having a guest for a couple of days."

"Oh?" She was mildly curious, already thinking about getting to her class on time.

"Like Professor Kosinsky he is also a Russian Jew, but

now he lives in Israel."

Now I had her attention. "A refusenik."

"I suppose so." Before the collapse of the Soviet Union the Jewish population was 2.4 million. After the collapse they were free to leave the country. Only about five hundred thousand remained.

"Why is he coming?"

"Job interview. He's a relative of Professor Kosinsky, electrical engineering."

"Where will he sleep? On the couch?"

"There's a spare bed on the top floor."

"Oh."

"Just remember not to clutter the bathroom with shampoo and makeup stuff."

"No problem."

But I sensed that she was uncomfortable. I didn't know if she was uneasy about a stranger in the house or that the visitor would be another Russian and a Jew at that.

As the time for Dr. Melamed's arrival approached, I tidied up the front seat of my pickup truck, swept out the stamp sand grit I'd tracked in off the streets and the sidewalks on campus. I hoped my foreign visitor wasn't expecting a Cadillac. At eleven thirty I set off for the airport a mere seven miles away.

That late at night the streets of Portage Lake and Hancock on the other side of the waterway were deserted. The snows that had melted in the early thaw during the day had formed puddles and wet spots were freezing during the night, making driving risky, but by now I was used to such obstacles. As long as vestiges of the frozen snow banks remained there was little danger of sliding off the road. It was a tough climate for cars which may be why the Copper Country roads were full of beaters, dented and rusty hand me down vehicles dealers down south didn't want.

At the top of the hill outside Hancock there was fog. Could the plane land at all?

A few sleepy people were waiting at the Houghton County airport terminal. The Keweenaw's isolation had deepened with the disappearance of Northwest airlines. Now only two flights came in a day, one arriving after midnight.   Unable to fly myself, I wasn't familiar with the new schedule.   I guessed that the night plane went out early the next morning, giving the crew only a few hours sleep at a nearby motel.

After a delay as the pilots waited for a hole in the fog, bright landing lights appeared under the dark clouds south of the runway.   Soon the United jet landed and taxied up to the terminal.   I had no idea what my visitor looked like.   It would be someone foreign.   A black caftan in the UP would be bizarre.

My anxiety was quickly dissipated, for coming through the door to the tarmac were a handful of locals greeted by relatives, an Asian, probably a Chinese student returning from a job interview, and a stocky, swarthy, bearded man in his fifties wearing a skull cap.   How could I miss? "Professor Melamed?" In Russian, I added, "I'm Irwin Glass, your host. Doctor Kosinsky sent me to pick you up."

"Very kind."

We shook hands.   Melamed had only a carryon and followed me out to the parking lot.   He didn't seem disappointed to be fetched in a pickup truck.   "Not a Toyota?" he asked, snapping on the seat belt.

"Ford."

"In Israel there are many Toyotas. And Jeepskies."

"Jeeps?"

"Yes.   In Hebrew Jeepskim.   It is combination of the American Jeep, the Russian diminutive and the Hebrew plural. We are an international people."

"Funny."

"How is it you speak such good Russian?"

"I studied it in the university.   And I worked for a time in Moscow."

Melamed gave me a sidelong look.   "So what were you? A spy?"

I almost choked.   "Afraid not.   I worked at the American library."

"Ah, so."

Fortunately Melamed didn't ask more.   "I have a room for you on the top floor.   My daughter has the back bedroom.   She is also Russian."

"Really? An American with a Russian daughter?"

"It's a long story."

Melamed yawned. "When I have had some sleep you must tell it. I have been traveling almost…" He looked at his watch, couldn't read it in the dark of the pickup's cab, pressed the button that lit up the dial… "Forty eight hours What time is it here?"

"Past midnight."

"I must reset my watch." Melamed spoke no more, closed his eyes, and had to be roused when I pulled into the driveway. The tires crunched on the refrozen snow.

I carried Melamed's bag up the stairs, showed my visitor the bathroom, told him which towel to use. Katya's door was closed. She was already asleep.

On the top floor I showed my guest the spare bed. "I have a class in the morning. You will probably want to sleep. If I have already left for the university, just help yourself to anything you find in the refrigerator."

"Thank you. What did you say? Irvin?"

"Irwin."

"Irwin. Yes." He, too, had trouble with the W sound. It looked like Melamed was about to collapse onto the bed without bothering to even take off his shoes. "Then I shall meet your Russian daughter. What is her name?"

"Katarina. Katya."

"Just so." But Melamed's eyes were already glazing over.

When I came downstairs for breakfast that morning Melamed was already up, his beard trimmed. He had wasted no time to find the television set in the living room and had it tuned to the news, the sound low enough not to disturb anyone still asleep.

"You're up," I said, "Watching the news?"

"We Israelis are what you call news junkies."

"I expected you to sleep until noon."

"I have appointment at ten o'clock. At electrical engineering. They plan for me a full day."

"I hope you have the energy for it." I remembered that my forced return to the United States had taken forty-eight hours, leaving me dead tired and zombified. I wondered at the energy of this much older man. How could he manage a job interview when jet lagged? "I'll make you some breakfast. What about dinner tonight?"

Melamed shook his head. "The department head is taking me to dinner and then there is a reception at someone's home. I do not remember the name. But tomorrow night I am free. I take you and your daughter to dinner. Then I leave the next day very early."

"Where to?"

"San Francisco. Another interview. This time Stanford."

I envied my guest's credentials. Israel had more engineers and scientists per capita than any other country. They had more patents, and the Jews had a remarkable record in Nobel prizes. A man like Melamed could almost write his own ticket.

Melamed turned away from the television. "When I first come to Israel I am astonished. The first thing people ask is 'Are you a millionaire?' Then 'How much do you pay in rent? How much money do you make?'"

"We never ask that."

Melamed smiled. "You are no millionaire. How much does Kosinsky charge you for rent in this old house?"

"Three hundred a month, but then there are the utilities. It costs that much to heat the place in winter. And there is the electricity, the television cable, telephone…"

"And how much do you make? What are you? Assistant professor?"

"No. Instructor. But I am full time, with benefits."

"Benefits? Ah, health insurance. That is very important in America. And your Russian daughter. You pay her expenses? Her tuition?"

"I've arranged for reduced tuition for her and she boards with me."

"You don't give her money?"

After all my own expenses, I had little left. I tried to save something against the day when this job would end, but it was not much. "No."

"So she came to America with a big, what you call, a nest egg?"

"I don't know."

"Does her mother send her money?"

"Her mother's dead."

Melamed was suspicious. "Strange story."

"She did not know I was her birth father. When the story came out, her mother divorced."

"I see. What about her father, her other father? Does he send her money?"

I had never thought to ask. One didn't ask such things, not in the States. This was not Israel. Your salary, your rent, your assets were always private. "I don't think so."

Melamed suggested, "Perhaps she has an inheritance."

I had no idea. I assumed, perhaps incorrectly, that to come to the States on a student visa one had to have a return ticket, some proof of solvency. But the Dean had said Katya was broke, couldn't afford the dormitory meal plan or the monthly rent.

I knew what it was to be broke. Hadn't I been kicked out of Moscow to arrive without assets, with barely the clothes I stood in? I had adjusted. My parents had helped me get started. I had all those half assed jobs and gradually built up a resume. It was tough, but I managed. I assumed Katya could do the same.

I had been too inhibited to ask Katya for any details about finances. When I had quietly asked Susan Lutz about her life, interests, and so on for that report to give—to sell—to Vladimir Putinsky, I'd had an ulterior motive. Selling that information was a betrayal of Susan's confidence. Ever since then I had not liked to ask people questions about themselves. I certainly would never ask "Are you a millionaire? How much do you earn?" It was unthinkable.

Katya came down to breakfast in her pajamas. She'd borrowed my robe which hung on a hook inside the bathroom door. She paused in the kitchen doorway when she saw our visitor and modestly tightened the belt of the bathrobe.

"Good morning."

I spoke to her in Russian. "This is our guest, Professor Kosinsky's cousin from Israel, Mr. Melamed. Want some toast?"

Melamed studied her with curiosity. "You are Russian

189

daughter? Remarkable." He turned to me with a sly smile.
"You have daughters from other countries as well, Irvin?"

"One is enough."

"And where in Russia are you from, Katarina?" So, he remembered her name. He had not been that tired when I picked him up. Melamed was sharper than he looked, even when exhausted by such a long flight.

"Moscow."

"What part of the city?"

Katya hesitated, uncertain, then named a street.

"Ah. Near the university." So, Melamed knew Moscow. He sipped the coffee I had poured for him, added two spoons of sugar. "I am from Leningrad, now again St. Petersburg. And where did you go to school, Miss Katarina?"

The question made Katya uncomfortable. "At a private technical school. I studied engineering."

Melamed laughed, turned to me. "In Russia everyone wishes to be an engineer. The porter calls himself a domestic engineer. But you will be a real engineer, yes Katarina?"

She answered, "Electrical," but clearly didn't like to be asked or her education made fun of.

"High voltage or low voltage?" It was something I had not thought to ask.

"Low voltage," Katya answered. "I will study computer chips."

"Yes. Everything gets smaller and smaller these days. My specialty is solar power and nanotechnology."

Katya didn't know much about solar power or nanotechnology. Russian educators, those who had no money for laboratories or equipment, concentrated on subjects that could be taught with chalk and a blackboard, which meant mathematics, theoretical physics and engineering.

Melamed wasn't finished. "So what else did you study? Marxism-Leninism? Dialectical materialism?"

Katya shook her head. "With the end of the Soviet Union classes in Communist theory are no longer so popular."

190

"Perhaps only with the older faculty?" Melamed was familiar with those types.

"Yes. We had one old comrade. A war veteran. A real Stalinist."

"I would think they have all retired by now," Melamed suggested. "But unfortunately a Russian pension today means poverty. One cannot afford to retire."

I sensed that Melamed was interrogating my daughter and listened carefully. What was on Melamed's mind? Did he doubt that Katya was a bone fide student? Or perhaps that she, being a freshman, had little true understanding of the courses to follow?

Melamed looked at his watch. "I must get to my interview. Can you drive me, Irvin? Or perhaps I can call a taxi."

"I'll drive you." I preferred to walk to campus. It took only fifteen minutes, in cold weather not much longer than it took to warm up the pickup enough for the defrosters to clear the windshield.

Melamed was gone all day on a tight schedule. He did not return until late in the evening, delivered by Doctor Waarala.

When Melamed came in Katya and I were sitting on the sofa watching the evening news. She had already dressed for bed, no robe this time, and when Melamed came in the door she excused herself and retreated upstairs. Was it because she was shy or didn't she want to be questioned again by our visitor?

"Busy day," I commented. "Do you think you'll get the job?"

Melamed took off his suit jacket and loosened his tie. Clearly he was not used to wearing a necktie and was glad to get rid of it. "It is possible, but it will be for one year only as what you call an adjunct."

I was familiar with the Tech administration's goals. "They'll want you to bring in research money."

"They wish me to sign a patent agreement. I am not sure I like that. I have similar obligations back in Israel. But American universities pay more than in Israel and of course, you do not pay here very much taxes."

191

"I suppose so." Being in the Humanities department, I wasn't expected to bring in research money to pay for my salary and the university's overhead. My teaching load was strictly service courses.

"Your Katarina interests me," Melamed said. "What about her mother?"

"Her mother is dead. Breast cancer."

"Sad for the girl. Lucky for her she has her American father. Were you married to her mother? Excuse me for asking. We Israelis are impolite."

"It was a brief relationship." I didn't want to say how brief. "I imagine you may have had some affairs in your youth."

Melamed sank back on the sofa next to me. The TV program had switched to the weather report. Melamed nodded. "They say a bachelor is a man who has no children to speak of."

"You could say this is one of them," I admitted. "Katya was quite a surprise."

"I can imagine. You were in contact with her mother?"

"No. Katya found me."

"Interesting. What were you doing in Moscow when you met her mother?"

"I was working at the American library."

"Oh yes, you told me that. What happened?"

"There was some trouble and I was sent back to the States."

"Trouble? Did you try to sell your American blue jeans?"

"Nothing like that. Trouble with the secret police."

"Too bad. It took me a long time to get out of Russia. At first I was fired from my job because I asked for an exit visa. Only after the Soviet Union collapsed did the gates open. They didn't want us Jews in and they didn't want to let us Jews out. You know, the Russians always hated the Jews. You say your grandfather Melamed was from Russia?"

"Great grandfather."

Melamed made some mental calculations. "That would be before the Revolution, perhaps in the time of the pogroms. Many Jews left in those days. Is this all you have in your news broadcasts, the weather?"

192

"I'm afraid so. Weather and sports."

Melamed turned and studied my face. "It must have been quite a surprise for you to learn you had a Russian daughter."

"I didn't believe it myself until we had a DNA test. She is definitely my daughter."

"A DNA test? Very good. You are a cautious person, Professor Glass. That is necessary. You must always be careful when dealing with the Russians."

"How well I know."

Melamed got up. "I am still jet lagged and it has been a long day. There will be more tomorrow. I am to give a guest lecture for the department. But remember, I will take you and your Katarina to dinner. Since I do not know the city, you can name a good place. OK?"

"Fine. I suggest a restaurant that serves Lake Trout. There is a fish place downtown. We can walk there."

"And then the next morning I am on my way. The early morning flight. I will take a taxi."

"Oh no," I protested. "I'll drive you. It will be no trouble."

"Good night."

Melamed was gone all day. Katya had her classes and I had three sections of English as a Second Language. I'd hoped some day to teach beginning Russian, but there was no demand even though at one time years before someone had taught it.

Again Waarala dropped Professor Melamed off after work. I answered the knock at the door and let him in.

"I have a little present for your Katarina," Melamed said. Somehow during the day of meetings he had stopped at the university bookstore. "This is for you," he announced to Katya.

She opened the plastic bag. Inside was a stuffed bear with a little sweater bearing the university MIT logo.

I asked, "What will you call him?"

She didn't know. The gift was a surprise. Was she embarrassed, or simply shy? Had she, as a little girl, slept with her doll or teddy bear? Certainly if she had, when flying to the United States there was no space in her baggage for such a thing. I knew that some of the female students, what we used to call coeds, had mascots. It was common to see some little stuffed animal hanging from a backpack. When I was still able to fly I had seen girls her age in airports carrying well worn stuffed animal companions. Katya had no such thing. The stuffed MIT bear brought out another facet of her somewhat enigmatic personality. She hugged it.

Still standing inside the entrance of the house with its coat hooks and boots parked where snow could melt off harmlessly, I took down my fake fur Russian hat with the earflaps and removed the red star pin. "Put this on him. That makes him a Russian bear."

"Thank you," Katarina covered the MIT logo with the souvenir pin. Looking at Melamed with his beard and skull cap, she hesitated as if trying to decide whether the gift deserved a hug, a handshake, or a typical kiss on both cheeks. She decided on the air kiss, a quick cheek to cheek sanitary embrace. "I think Ivan is good name for a Russian bear."

It had been an unseasonably warm afternoon and the streets were again wet with melting snow. At least the thick snow pack had been scraped away and one could see pavement again. It would be weeks before the sidewalks, used for storage of snow pushed off the streets, would be passable again. We had to walk in the street until we got downtown.

At Captain Jake's Fish House we were seated at a table at the back. Built into the wall between the dining area and the kitchen were portholes that were actually fish tanks. It gave the impression that the restaurant was under water. We ordered broiled Lake Trout and salads. Melamed ordered a beer, Katya coffee. I settled for ice water.

When the food came Professor Melamed surprised me and Katya by saying a Hebrew blessing over the bread. Then, between bites, he continued his questioning of Katya. "Tell me about your mother. What did she do?"

"She worked in an office with my father, I mean, her husband. That was before their divorce."

"But Irvin here is your father. I do not understand."

"Irvin is my birth father. My mother's husband was Vladimir Putinsky. He has shortened his name. Now he is

Putin."

"Putin? Not *that* Putin?"

Katya put down her fork. "If he were *that* Putin, I would not have such troubles with my dormitory bills. No, that Putin is no relation."

"She was broke," I explained. "That's why she moved out of the dorm and stays with me."

"Interesting."

"I am now American citizen," Katya said proudly.

"Yes," I added. "She's even applied for a passport."

"I am impressed," Professor Melamed said, and took a swallow of beer. "Some people would kill for an American passport. An authentic one, I mean."

I explained, "She gets her citizenship because she is the daughter of an American."

"Remarkable." Melamed smiled. "I am an Israeli citizen because of the Law of the Return. This is also remarkable, as I never before had set foot in the country."

We finished our fish and declined an offer of dessert. Always concerned about time, perhaps because he had passed through so many time zones and found it hard to make the adjustment, Melamed again looked at his watch. "So late! I must be up very early. My plane for Chicago leaves about five thirty tomorrow. What time must I be at the airport, Irvin?"

"Quarter to five, I think."

"And you still wish to drive me to the airport?"

"Absolutely. You are my guest."

"I have imposed upon you. Thank you. Shall we go?"

Melamed paid the bill with a credit card, refused my offer to leave the tip, and we walked back to the house.

Carrying Ivan the bear, Katya disappeared immediately to her room.

I was looking forward to telling Ivy about my hosting. Melamed was an interesting man even though he was persistent in asking questions. There were many questions not asked, questions I would like to have answers to myself.

It was too late to call Ivy and tell her about the dinner and my house guest. That could wait until the next day. I set my alarm clock for four fifteen and tried to go to sleep.

I had hardly closed my eyes after sleeplessly pondering Melamed and all those questions when the alarm went off. I dressed quickly, didn't bother to shave, and quietly went downstairs to put on a pot of coffee. Professor Melamed wasn't up yet, so I climbed to the top floor and knocked.

Melamed was only partly dressed, trousers and a sleeveless, athletic undershirt, bare arms except for phylacteries, those leather boxes, one on the forehead, the other with a strap wound around the left arm. He was at his morning prayers. I didn't interrupt him.

Until I had my coffee, I didn't feel like talking. I was too groggy for conversation. Silently, we drove to the Houghton County airport.

The jet that had come in the night before was parked outside the terminal. I stood back and waited while Melamed checked in. I wanted to wait until the plane was safely off. The call to board came and the passengers, all looking like they had been dragged from their beds for that early departure, lined up.

I stood alongside. Making small talk I said, "I hope your interview at Stanford is a success."

"We shall see."

We had almost reached the security guard. Melamed had his boarding pass and Israeli passport ready. He turned to me. "About your Katarina," he began. "Be cautious, Irvin, my friend. She is KGB. I can smell it."

Then he was past Homeland Security and gone.

Stunned, I watched through the windows as Melamed and the other passengers crossed the tarmac and climbed the stairs to board the United flight. KGB? Was that possible? But Katya really was my birth daughter. She was only eighteen. Melamed, a survivor of the collapse of the old Soviet Union and all the difficulties of emigrating from the police state, had to be paranoid. I knew that feeling well. Hadn't I feared Putinsky might make good on his threat, "You're a dead man, Glass!" That somehow Putinsky would send someone with a silenced pistol, a poisoned umbrella, or an ampoule of cyanide gas had been my nightmare many years ago. In the interval since, I'd been convinced that the threat shouted in Gorky park was just a moment of anger.

Katya was no assassin. She had not been sent to kill me. That was absurd.

Katya was a nice kid. I'd been living with her for weeks. I had gotten used to having a young woman in the house. I had never shared my home with a sister or a girl friend. Now I was used to seeing tights hanging up to dry in the bathroom and finding panties in the clothes hamper. At first I did her laundry, but after I showed her how to use the machines she insisted on doing it herself. Though I would not admit to such impulses myself, I could see how some step fathers molested the girls in their households.

Katya called me her papa and I truly felt affection for her, if not fatherly love. With her and Ivy I felt we were a family. I was not just an over the hill bachelor with a half ass career and a sorry past. It had been a long, difficult, frustrating crawl up the hill to build a new life. I was beginning to feel fulfilled.

I had been plagued by anxiety and loneliness, feelings of worthlessness and depression. I'd felt hopeless in my search for steady employment, something beyond teaching a few courses, no benefits, no tenure, no hope. Now at last I was, did I dare say it? Happy.

The happiness was short lived. Dr. Melamed must not have been what he seemed. Were all Israeli visiting professors also agents for the Mossad? Did they share information with the CIA? I got a phone call late at night, a voice I didn't recognize. "How's my sleeper agent?"

"What? Who's this?" For a second I thought it might be Vladimir Putinsky, a sinister voice from the past.

"Robert. I hear you have a Russian daughter."

"News travels fast. I thought you'd have retired by now."

"Well, Glass, it's complicated. Not that you were any help. I don't like loose ends. You're a loose end."

"And you're a loose cannon. I'm not the same guy you kicked out of Moscow. You ruined my career." I could feel the old anger rising.

"You ruined mine, Glass."

"Bullshit."

"That aside, so she showed up with the recognition

signal?"

"Right, but not to activate me as a sleeper agent."

"So you say."

"Ask Wilkins of the FBI in Marquette. It's all on the up and up."

"Good cover story."

"Why don't you get off my back, Robert? It's over. You're wasting your time. I am not a Soviet agent and you know damned well I never was."

"What about this Katarina girl?"

"She isn't, either. She's a sweet kid. Now leave me alone. Go play golf or something. Like they say up here in the Copper Country, "265Go Florida." I'd have added 'Go fuck yourself' but I didn't know if the call was being recorded. Last time I told someone to go fuck himself he told me I was a dead man. Got to be careful who you tell things like that. I hung up and hoped he wouldn't call again.

Katya had three more years to study at Da Tech. I would see if I could get her a PELL grant. She could find a part time job and integrate with the other students, be a real American. KGB? That was ridiculous. Melamed, a Russian emigree, was living in his own difficult past. Israelis lived forever in the shadow of the Holocaust. Melamed not only remembered that war against the Fascists, as the Soviets called it, but the oppression of being a refusenik. Perhaps he looked under his bed to see if someone were hiding there, listening.

. . .

By degrees, Ivy and I had grown together. We were a couple. It was not an infatuation or convenient, casual sex. With her playful exuberance she had revived my sense of humor. We were seriously involved. It was now an unspoken assumption that we would marry. Ivy would beat her biological clock and I, with Ivy and Katya, would finally be established in a settled life. We were family. It was wonderful, a cause for celebration.

It was the end of the term. Finals were the next week, but my pass/fail courses needed no final exams. Ivy had devised a package of German tests. She joked that from term to term the questions were the same but the answers had changed.

"Let's have a party," I suggested. "Celebrate the end of term. Announce our engagement and introduce Katya to the department as my real daughter. Dispel all those rumors and gossip with one event."

"Aren't you going to buy me a ring?"

I hadn't thought of that. "We'll pick something out."

"Who shall we invite?"

"The whole Humanities department. Make it an open house. I'll run off an invitation and put it in everyone's box."

"Even Waarala's secretary?"

"Definitely the secretaries, the grapevine gossips. And the Dean of Students. Got to shut them up once and for all."

"Sounds good to me."

"Feeding all those people will be a challenge."

"Make it a pot luck," Ivy suggested. "If you do hamburgers and hot dogs and a keg of beer, other people can bring snacks and cookies. "And by the way, the answer is yes."

"Yes what?"

"Yes, marriage."

"You want to be Mrs. Glass?"

"Hartshorn-Glass, or keep my professional name."

"Whatever."

"I wonder what Katya will think of me as her stepmother?"

"She's an adult. I don't think she's going to call you Mama."

"It will be interesting to see how she reacts," Ivy suggested.

I had no answer for that. I knew there could be difficulties with stepmother relations with step daughters. Coming from a stable family, parents happily married, I had no experience with such conflicts. My parents had come to an agreement: my father could play golf as long as my mother had the spare bedroom for her quilting. To each his own.

Telling my mother about Katya had been an exercise in diplomacy and tact. Only my father knew about that business with Svetlana.   My mother was, well, prudish about men having affairs or one night stands, but I had figured out long ago from calculating their anniversary and my date of birth that she was pregnant when they got married.   I would never have considered showing her those incriminating photographs which I still had hidden in my bureau under the underwear.   News that Mom was a grandmother bought a mixed reaction from her--shock, pleasure, and admonition at the circumstances.

The details of the story of me and Svetlana Putinsky were strictly between me and my father.   News without equivocation was the announcement of my engagement to Ivy.   "I'm getting married."

Ivy and I told Katya our news over dinner in the Kosinsky kitchen.   "We're getting married," I announced as I dished up pieces of apple pie I'd bought at the Econo Foods grocery.

"We?" Katya was distracted.

"Ivy and me.   How would you like Ivy here as a stepmother?"

"I do not know this word, 'stepmother.'"

I didn't remember the Russian equivalent.   I did remember the song from the movie *Birds of a Feather* about a gay couple and their son.   "We are family," I began in an off key rendition.   "What do you think?"

"I think it is good.   I have news, too.   My American passport has come," she announced proudly.   She showed the heavy envelope it had come in and passed the document around for us to examine.

I looked at it with a twinge of envy.   An American passport is a precious document.   I could not get a passport. My Russian kid was more free to travel than I was.   I couldn't even get on an airplane.   If she wanted to, she could fly to Russia with it.   But of course, she could have done that at any time on her own Russian passport-- and she didn't need a visa.

I shared in her triumph.   "Now you can get a social security card and a driver's license.   You can look for a job at the university.   No more student visa restrictions. Congratulations."

"Thank you, papa. You are very good to me." She kissed me.

Flushed, I said, "Hey, what's a papa to do? We will have a party to celebrate our engagement and your citizenship. Do you have any friends you'd like to invite to our party?"

Katya shook her head. She had not dated, not even once even though she'd been asked. She was more mature and serious than other freshmen, more sophisticated and worldly wise than the Yooper kids who made up forty percent of the student body. The only other Russian speaker among the foreign students was from the Ukraine and he distrusted all Russians. The male-female ratio of students at Da Tech was still lopsided in spite of the increase in girls going to college. Now the majority of students at most American colleges was female.

Katya had been invited to some fraternity parties, but knew they were notorious for binge drinking. Coeds were known to have been plied with beer and then taken advantage of, a polite term for rape. Katya wanted none of it.

She was a serious student. I thought she was even too absorbed in her books. She seemed more interested in her relationship with me. She could be exuberant, as she was when announcing her passport's arrival, but mostly she was quiet, reserved, even cautious. She seemed to always be on her guard.

That might have been because she was uncertain about her finances, afraid to fail a course, or nervous about her status while waiting for that precious passport. Until it came, she had no stability.

I wrote up a brief invitation to the open house on Friday night to celebrate the end of term and announce our engagement. It was a pot luck. I would provide burgers, brats and beer. If anyone wanted something harder than beer it was BYOB. I would also introduce everyone to my daughter Katarina.

The three of us drove in the pickup to Jim's grocery where the frat boys usually picked up their kegs of beer. We didn't know how many people might show up, but reasoned that any supplies left over could go into Kosinsky's ample deep freeze. "Ketchup and mustard," Ivy reminded me as we filled a shopping cart.

"And chips," Katya added.

"We will need plastic cups," Ivy reminded. Preparations were exciting.

Ivy moved her Tracker to the top of the driveway near the closed garage door. We would need all the parking space we could make room for. Though the snow banks that encroached on the street had receded, it was necessary to leave room on the street for a fire truck to pass. At least this was one night when it would not snow, requiring the city plows to pass unhindered. All night parking restrictions were still in force.

Katya did her share of setting up. The guests arrived.

I did not know all of the department faculty. I had seen them all, of course, at various meetings, but the only committee I was on was foreign languages, a small segment of the humanities mix. Ivy, more active in department and campus politics, knew everyone. She took up her position as greeter, introducing everyone to Katarina, who grew more and more reserved. Katya was out of her depth among those strangers.

Someone had brought a couple of music CDs and put them in Professor Kosinsky's player. The music boomed out. It was past eleven o'clock when, at the moment when the level of noise had increased because of the effect of beer on people's ability to hear, Ivy and I made our announcement.

"We're getting married."

Applause and congratulations all around.

Almost as if on cue, there was a knock at the door. Katya went to the door, opened it, and gasped. It was the police, a Portage Lake cop who looked like he could not have been on the force very long. In my mid forties, I was already noticing that the police were beginning to look like kids in dress up uniforms.

The officer had probably expected a crowd of raucous students. He was surprised to find adult faculty. "There's been a complaint because of the noise. You'll have to quiet down."

I asked, "Who complained?"

"The students in the house across the street."

That was a switch. Usually it was the student parties that made such a racket. "We'll quiet down," I said. "Doctor Hartshorn and I are celebrating our engagement."

"Congratulations. Take this as a warning. I don't want to ticket anyone for disturbing the peace."

One of the inebriated assistant professors, I remembered as Jack something or other, approached the policeman with a glass. "Want a beer?"

"No thanks."

I shut the door, went to the audio player and turned it off. "Katya has an announcement tonight, too. She's got her American citizenship." I looked around, but Katya had disappeared. I'd expected her to show her passport like a hockey trophy.

What was she? Spooked by the policeman? Or overcome with shyness?

"She's gone to bed," Ivy explained.

"It's time we did, too," I said, my mind on sex.

The guests dispersed. The last left, leaving behind a sudden silence. Ivy and I took one look at the chaos and decided we would clean up the mess in the morning, gather up the empty plastic cups, return the now empty keg for the deposit.

Katya's bedroom door was closed. "She must be asleep," I said and we tiptoed past it.

Then Ivy and I, the lights out, eased into bed naked for our own celebration of our engagement.

We slept late, but it was a Saturday and the term was over. No classes. At Portage Lake's north latitude dawn and dusk came on slowly and it was usually overcast. There could be more snow as late as May. Looking out the bedroom window for a glimpse at the weather, I saw there was a light in the Waarala's kitchen window next door and remembered I was naked. I hoped Mrs. Waarala wasn't watching. Ivy's Tracker was parked next to the garage door but my truck... my white Ford pickup, was missing. "The truck's gone."

"What? You think it's stolen?"

"I don't know." I slipped on my pajamas and went to

203

Katya's door. I knocked softly, then called "Katya?" No answer. I opened the door.

No one.

The bathroom door was open, the usual signal that it was available. I called downstairs, "Katya?"

No answer.

Ivy had wrapped herself in my bathrobe. "Isn't she here?"

"Not in the house. Where could she be?"

"Maybe she's gone someplace in the pickup."

"She can't drive. She doesn't have a license."

"Well, she's not here and no truck, either."

We returned to Katya's bedrooom. No sign of her. The bed was made. Kosinsky's winter wardrobe had been shifted aside. Katya's clothes were gone.

"She's gone."

In fact, nothing of Katya remained. Her toiletries had been removed from the bathroom. It was as if she'd never been there.

Ivy checked the waste basket. There were a few discarded papers in it. "Look at this," she said, and held up an envelope.

I examined it. The return address was the Riggs bank. "Riggs bank. Same bank Putinsky was supposed to deposit the money he promised me." Maybe the old fox had been skimming from others, setting up a nest egg for his daughter or for himself if things got too hot in the new Russia.

"But he never opened the account?"

"No. But he could have opened an account there for Katya."

"Why would he? You said Putinsky had divorced his wife."

"That's Katya's story, that when Vladimir found out Katya wasn't his daughter he got mad and dumped his wife."

"But he could have opened an account for her before that."

"Right. We don't know the timetable. Anyway, Katya said she was broke, couldn't pay her bills at the dorm."

"That's her story. Anyway, this is just an envelope. There's no bank statement. If there was a statement it might show she had a zero balance."

"She must have something or she wouldn't have skipped. Couldn't have. Where would she go? How could she live?"

Ivy was puzzled, too. "Do you think the announcement of our engagement freaked her out? That she didn't want to be a third wheel?"

"Or didn't want you as a step mother? I doubt it. She likes you."

"That's what she says. I don't really know her, Irwin."

"I guess I don't either. I'd better call the police."

"On what grounds? Katya's an adult," Ivy reminded me. "She's not a minor. If she leaves home, she has a right to."

"Come on, Ivy. Not without telling us first."

"You want to report her as a missing person?"

"Not yet. She might come back."

"I don't know," Ivy said. "She's taken the teddy bear." She sat on the bed. "Well, if you want to be mean about it, you can tell the police the truck's been stolen."

"You're right.   There's something wrong here. Reporting the truck as missing is probably the least I can do. If they find her she can say she borrowed it. Kids do that all the time, don't they?"

"It's your call, Irwin. She's your daughter."

"If she just went shopping, she wouldn't take all her stuff with her."

"Shopping? The stores aren't even open yet. You want to wait awhile and see if she changes her mind? She might phone."

"I think I'll call the police right now. How far can she have gone? There's not that much gas in the tank." I realized at once that was a dumb remark. Katya could always fill the tank, if she had any money. She never seemed to have any cash. So far as I knew, she didn't have a checkbook or even a credit card. I never pried into her finances. I should have taken Melamed's advice, acted like an Israeli, "Are you a millionaire? How much money do you make?" Now I felt like a fool.

I looked up the number and called the police. Then, trying to focus on something we knew, Ivy and I showered and got dressed.   I needed fresh jockey shorts and

205

discovered my underwear drawer had been disturbed. I made a hurried search. "She's taken the pictures."

"What pictures?"

"You know, *the* pictures. The six Metropol pictures." *Removed the evidence.*

"When would she have done that?"

"Any time. It's not like I look at them frequently. They were just in the underwear drawer, been there for God knows how long." We went downstairs to clean up the mess from the party.

About noon the phone rang. Hoping it was Katya, I answered it. "Yes?"

"Mr. Glass?"

"Speaking."

"This is the State Police in Calumet. We've found your truck."

"Where is it?"

"At the airport. Someone drove it into a snow bank, but it doesn't seem to be damaged."

"I'll be right there."

"It's locked. You'd better bring the keys."

I hadn't told the police about Katya or that she might have borrowed the pickup without permission. She had taken the ignition key from the hook inside the front door, but I always carried a spare in my wallet in case I locked myself out.

Ivy and I grabbed our jackets and got into her Tracker for the short drive to the airport. With only two flights a day, the County airport was deserted. A few cars were parked in the long term area, some dirty with the remains of the last snowfall.

We had to drive all the way around the lot before we spotted the truck jammed into the remains of a snow bank near the car rental parking section.

As the State Police had reported, the pickup was locked, but there was no damage, no sign that it had sideswiped an obstacle. The keys were still in the ignition.

Looking in the driver's side window I spotted something on the seat, a piece of paper. A note?

Fumbling with my spare key, I unlocked the door and

reached in.

"What is it?" Ivy asked.

I held it up to her. It had been written hastily with a ball point pen on a piece of recycled paper.

"It's in Russian," Ivy said. "What's it say?"

Tying to control my emotions, I took a deep breath. "She says 'Thanks.'"

"Just thanks?"

"It's a little more than that. Actually, she writes, 'Comrade Glass. Thank you. Love, Katarina Volovna Putinsky.' How about that?"

"Not Katya?"

"No. It's formal--name, patronymic, family name."

"And Comrade? She actually calls you comrade?"

"She may be my daughter, but she's Putinsky's daughter, too. He's devious."

"What do you mean?"

"Professor Melamed told me she was KGB. I didn't believe him. The State Department accused me of being a paid Soviet agent. She addresses me as Comrade so I can't show this to the FBI without incriminating myself. Clever."

"Irwin, you need help. Maybe it's her idea of a joke. You're paranoid."

"Old habits. I bet she went out on the early plane."

"Where to?"

"The United flight only goes to Chicago. After that...? Anywhere. Damn." I felt crushed. I had invested so much in her, risked my job, accepted her, made her my family. Had Katya simply bolted on an impulse, or was the whole business an elaborate scam planned in advance? I had gone through all that worry, stress, and preparation. Now this. Betrayed again. I felt destroyed.

Ivy put her arm around me.

I sniffled, pulled out my handkerchief and blew my nose. I didn't want her to know I was crying with frustration, disappointment and, yes, heart break

Ivy tried to console me. "Now you are acting like a parent. At least she took Ivan with her with his red star pin. She does love you, papa Glass."

As usual, I was confused. Would Katya come back?

Where had she gone? Even if I knew, I couldn't hop on a plane and pursue her. Was it Vladimir Putinsky's doing? An elaborate plot? Some kind of revenge? Was Vladimir trying to get his daughter safely out of the country? Russia with its mafia was a dangerous place. There was no telling. The DNA test was the only thing I knew for certain. She couldn't have faked that. Looking back, I didn't know what to believe. Maybe that claim that her parents had divorced was a lie. Maybe Svetlana had not died of breast cancer after all. There was no knowing the truth.

I always told the truth. My mother had drummed into me "Oh, what an ugly web we weave when first we practice to deceive." Lies had to be backed up by other lies and you ended up in a confused mess of contradictions. Lying was not part of my nature. Maybe I was naïve, gullible.

If you grew up in a family of musicians, music would come naturally. If your parents were police, you grew up with cop talk. Vladimir Putinsky was KGB and Katya's was a world of fear, deception, and secrecy. I shouldn't be surprised by her behavior. I had misjudged her, saw her as another eighteen year old kid, but that was my own frame of reference. She was not like those American freshmen fresh out of high school with a background of computer games, high school sports, and television sitcoms. My mistake. She was Russian. I had been in Russia only a couple of months and that was a long time ago. What did I know? "I'll drive the truck back," I told Ivy. "You follow me."

Back at the house I was in a state of shock, dismay, hurt. I was confused, angry, upset, even heartsick by Katya's disappearance. Everything in my mind was a jumble, and that wasn't the end of it.

The morning mail brought a letter from my father in Ocala. In it was the old photograph of my great grandfather Isaac Melamed. The picture was smaller than I remembered, but back then I was only ten years old. The silver emulsion had tarnished to a sepia tan that was starting to turn to powder. A few rubs and the image might disappear entirely.

"Look," I told Ivy. "This is my great grandfather."

"Amazing that the picture turned up."

"Not so amazing. Some vet found the box of photos

with Dad's Purple Heart.   With the Internet you can track down anyone."

Dad enclosed the letter, too, the Russian letter that had so fascinated me and set me off on a career of foreign language study that carried me to Moscow.   Now, in spite of its being in a foreign script, I could read it.

Ivy was burning with curiosity.   "What does it say?"

"It's from Melamed's fiancé.   Apparently he promised to send for her as soon as he had enough money for a ticket. Barring that, she asks him to return to Russia.   But with World War I and the Revolution, he never did."

"What if he had?"

I had to laugh.   "The road not taken.   He married someone else, and here I am."

"Yes, here you are." She hugged me.

"You know, Ivy. It's funny. We think we have control of our lives.   Then something sets us off.   If it weren't for this letter, I'd have never studied Russian, never gone to Moscow, and Katya would not exist.   Funny how things work out."

Book two: Retribution

With my fiancée Ivy Hartshorn by my side I stood shivering with the cold or with trepidation in the airport parking lot. My aging Ford pickup was where the Michigan State Police had found it, abandoned. The officer had told me to bring my spare key, because the truck was locked. On the seat we found a carefully written, but brief note. It said simply, "Thanks, Comrade," in Russian, and was signed Katarina Volodna Putinsky. Katya. My daughter. She was gone.

Why not, "Goodbye papa?" Or "Sorry, Daddy?" Some trick, calling me "Comrade." How about that as a farewell to her birth father? I was not a Communist. My job with the State Department in Moscow had lasted only a couple of months and ended abruptly when I was seduced by Katya's mother so the KGB could try to blackmail me. That was nearly twenty years ago, but had a surprise consequence: Katya. The DNA test had confirmed my patrimony only a couple of months ago.

What I had not anticipated when she claimed I was her parent was that, as the child of a US citizen, she could claim US citizenship. I provided the passport office with an affidavit showing that I had, indeed, been in Russia at the time of her conception. Surprise: I not only had a Russian daughter, but she was a US citizen. A US passport was her ticket to a new life in America. It had hardly arrived when she disappeared. That left me with what? A note calling me comrade as if I was part of some kind of Communist plot?

All those old betrayals had come down on my head again to threaten the life I had rebuilt after years of poorly paid academic jobs. I felt like a registered sex offender who gets picked up as one of the usual suspects whenever someone, no matter how far away or unconnected, fondles a nursery school kid. Why me?

"Comrade," indeed. She knew what she was doing. If she'd called me "papa" I might have thought her disappearance was simply an act of a quirky teenager who felt a need to strike out on her own. Now, with those old troubles revived, I was in a bind again, like she was blackmailing me to do nothing to stop her. What's a parent to do?

The Ford started with no trouble. I was so befuddled I could hardly keep the truck on the road. Ivy, in her cherry red Tracker, followed me from the Houghton County airport back to the house in Portage Lake.

Except for some vestigial banks of ugly snow blackened by the stamp sand the road crews spread on the streets, there was little to remind us of the long Keweenaw winter that was finally ending. Back in the house I rented from Professor Kostinsky, who was soon to return from a stint at the Technion in Israel, I wondered aloud, "What do I do now?"

Ivy assumed I was asking her. "You think you should call that FBI guy in Marquette?"

To cover my indecision I made a prolonged fuss with hanging my old Russian jacket neatly on the hook inside the front door. I didn't want to alert the FBI. "Wilson?"

Agent Wilson isn't like your typical FBI agent in dark glasses and an overcoat. He's a Yooper, complete with a handlebar mustache and an American eagle belt buckle the size of a saucer. Last time I saw him he was a bit shabby in a hip length storm coat loose enough to conceal a shoulder holster and sidearm. I like him, but he is mostly all business. "Katya hasn't been gone for more than a few hours. She's not what the police would call a missing person. At least not yet. Besides, it's not an FBI matter."

"You sure?" Ivy busied herself with the coffee maker. She likes her coffee strong. "The FBI's going to think Katya's a suspicious person."

"You mean a person of suspicion?" I quickly added, "Sorry. One of those problems I spring on my foreign students."

Ivy gave me one of her piercing looks that says "What do you think I am, stupid?" "In words you won't misunderstand, Irwin, the FBI is going to think this whole Katya business is a KGB scam and you are aiding and abetting. They haven't given up on that old claim that you are a paid Soviet agent."

'You're right," I admitted. The threat of a stint in a Federal prison still hung over my head. I wondered what my old nemesis, the mysterious "Robert" would think about this new development. I had hoped "Robert" was put out to pasture in retirement, but he seemed to cling to me as his pet case or pet peeve. "Let's wait a few days. Maybe Katya will show up. But you're right. I'd better notify Wilson."

"Just to cover your ass?"

"That, too. But it doesn't save me from worrying about Katya." I had just begun to be used to being a parent. I'd made the adjustment to having a pretty girl living with me, all those intimate details like women's underwear in the laundry and bottles of lotions and potions in the bathroom. I'd had plenty of pretty coeds in my classes before, but I hadn't fraternized or even had a live-in girl friend. I was a lone bachelor, even if it hadn't been by design. Katya was a great kid. I loved having her around. "She is my daughter, after all. Her being gone is, well, I don't know what to think." I felt deserted, abandoned.

"Maybe she thinks she's a third wheel, doesn't want to interfere with our personal life."

I put my arms around Ivy. "Could be." I was suddenly overcome with a sense of loss. "You won't desert me, will you?"

"Not as long as you behave yourself. No new claims that some student is your daughter. Sure you don't have any other accidental babies?"

"A bachelor has no children to speak of, but I can assure you there's aren't any other surprises like that."

But I was mistaken. There were other surprises to come.

I looked up the number of the FBI office in Marquette, a hundred miles away. Marquette is the largest town in the Upper Peninsula, down to about twenty-seven thousand after the close of the old cold war air base. It's the only UP town big enough to warrant an FBI office. Agent Wilson is the guy who realized Katya would be entitled to US citizenship if the DNA test proved she was my birth daughter. He wasn't in, but I left a message on his answering machine. "This is Irwin Glass in Portage Lake. My daughter, Katya, you know, the Russian girl who turned out to be my daughter, has

212

disappeared. Just thought you'd want a heads up."

Not that I expected the FBI to put out an all points bulletin to track her down. She was an adult. She could take off if she wanted to. There were no suggestions of foul play. Kids disappear all the time. Probably the most I could do was put out a call for help on Facebook or Twitter. The cops wouldn't do anything. I suppose the most I could hope for was to put her face on milk cartons as a missing person—if I had her picture. The only pictures we'd taken of her were used for her passport application.

I couldn't chase Katya if I knew where she'd gone because I'm on the no-fly list, another consequence of that business in Moscow. In these days of computers and Google once you have a record somewhere it floats around and can never be erased. Like I tell my students: never get arrested for anything. Once you've a record it will pursue you and you'll never get a decent job. My troubles with the CIA and KGB hadn't been in newspapers or court records, but I suspected "Robert" had poisoned the well, as they say. He'd claimed I was a paid soviet agent. The label stuck.

Paid? I couldn't forget that sleight of hand trick. Now you see it, now you don't. Katya's father, Vladimir Putinsky, a KGB officer, had shown me the hundred dollar bill, said he would deposit it in the Riggs bank, but the money was never handed over and the account never existed. That didn't matter to "Robert" or whatever his real name was. He'd denounced me as a paid Soviet agent and the false report followed me ever afterward. Somewhere along the line my name had come up as a person of suspicion, and just to be on the safe side Homeland Security had declared me a no-fly person.

Sometimes I feel like the kid who's had a sign pinned on his back saying "kick me."

So now Katya was gone. Where? I'd had no contact with Vladimir Putinsky, ever since that night in Gorky Park when he said I was a dead man for refusing to be his agent. What was I supposed to do now? Tell him Katya was missing? Write him a letter c/o the KGB, Moscow, Russia? Since the collapse of the Soviet Union there was no more KGB. The agency had changed its name again. It had been the Cheka,

213

GRU, NKVD, and KGB, but now? How would I address a letter even if I wrote one? Should I tell Putinsky that Katya had disappeared? Maybe she was supposed to. Maybe it was Vladimir's scheme to plant an agent in the United States. If I did write to him the letter was sure to be intercepted because the FBI was watching me. They'd think I was part of the plot.

I was stuck again. My name is Irwin Glass. Kick me.

It wasn't fair. I liked Katya. She made me feel like a Dad. I had even begun to love her. She reminded me of her mother, who was gorgeous. When the DNA test proved Katya was my daughter and she said she was broke I let her move in with me. She could, even though as a freshman and was supposed to live in the dorms. A student can live at home with her parent, no?

Agent Wilson called me back the next day. I explained the situation. His response? "Katya's disappearance is not FBI business. I'm more concerned about other matters at Michigan Tech."

"I suppose you think there are spies among the students from Communist countries—Russia and China—or terrorists from the Moslem countries."

Like they say in diplomatic circles, Wilson would neither confirm nor deny. That my daughter had skipped town wasn't his concern. His only concession was, "Let me know if she shows up." I think he only said it to make me feel he cared.

Again I was being hung out to dry.

At least I had someone to confide in. Ivy and I were now engaged and could think about a wedding.

A week went by, a month, then another with no call from Katya, not even a post card. Ivy and I planned our wedding for the end of spring term. It would be a simple affair, a chance for our parents to meet.

What was awkward was my parents hadn't met Katya and I had to make excuses. I could only say Katya was out of town and would miss the wedding, a genuine disappointment. My mother had wanted a grandchild, and Katya, in spite of the odd circumstances of my patrimony, almost fit the bill. Except she was gone, a phantom granddaughter. Mom suspected Katya was a fantasy. Dad, always the academician, had wanted proof and got a copy of the DNA test. Ever since that business in Moscow and the FBI snoops bothering their Ocala neighbors, I was suspect, even to my own parents.

It was time for me and Ivy to look for a place to live as a couple. My landlord was returning from Israel. Ivy's apartment near campus was too small as we both, being faculty, needed work space at home.

It was not easy for me to give up on Katya. She was like a promise made and then broken. I felt terrible, empty, like someone had stolen a kidney or something. Part of me was gone. I tried to not dwell on that betrayal, to put it behind me, to move on, as they say. In the preparations for the wedding I almost succeeded. Then I got a letter from the IRS. I showed the letter to Ivy. "Look at this. The IRS says I haven't declared the interest income for my account in Washington, DC."

Ivy asked, "Do you have an account in a Washington bank?"

I studied the IRS letter. "I'm supposed to call somebody at Internal Revenue."

Ivy suggested, "Maybe it's a stolen identity."

"Possible." I called the IRS number and after a long wait got connected. I was told it was interest on an account at the Riggs bank.

"But I don't have an account with the Riggs bank," I protested. But then I remembered. Vladimir Putinsky had said he was going to deposit that elusive hundred bucks in a savings account for me in Washington. When I returned to the United States in disgrace I stopped in at the Riggs bank to check. No account. That confirmed I was never paid as a Soviet agent, not one cent. I thought that let me off the hook, but it was too late. A negative doesn't prove a positive. I was told that not having the account didn't prove that I hadn't accepted payment in cash and lied about it. The State Department records said I'd been paid, even though it wasn't true.

I tried to reconstruct. Maybe Putinsky did set up the account after I was fired. I'd filled out the bank's account application form, provided my social security number and mother's maiden name, typical bank stuff, but I was back in the states before he had time for someone from the Soviet embassy to set it up. "I guess I'd better call the Riggs bank," I said. "There can't be that much interest on the lousy hundred bucks which I was never paid. Must be a piddly amount." I mumbled, "Some zealot at the IRS is making trouble. You'd think that after these years the account would have been declared a dormant and shut down. You know how the banks are. If an account is dormant they start charging a monthly fee until the money's all gone. So why does it still exist?"

I had to go through the whole recorded routine. For Spanish press one. It was maddening. Finally I got through to a real person. The clerk sounded bored and tired. For all I knew she was in India or the Philippines. What time was it there? "I'm being charged by the IRS for taxes not paid on interest on money I don't have at the Riggs bank," I explained.

"Name? Social security number? Mother's maiden name?"

I gave the clerk all that but I didn't know the account number.

The clerk found it. "You're the first name on that account," the clerk explained.

"What do you mean, the first name?"

"It's a joint account."

I could already guess. "And the other person is Katarina Putinsky?"

"Putin. Katarina Putin," she corrected.

"Her father shortened it. He's not THAT Putin." Hardly able to breathe, I asked, "What's the balance in the account?"

"Seven hundred and fifty thousand dollars."

If I were the fainting type I'd have hit the floor. "What?"

She repeated the amount. It took me a minute to catch my breath. "Where do you send the statements? I haven't received any."

"The statements were being sent to Portland. Oregon, but they came back. We don't forward statements. Have you considered our on line banking option? You can access your account any time."

So Katya had been in Portland, my first real clue. If I chose on line banking, Katya could access the account from anywhere and I would never know where she was. "I want you to send the statements to me from now on," I insisted, and gave the clerk my address.

The information was duly noted.

"How have withdrawals been made from the account?"

"From ATM machines."

"Can I have a record of those?"

"The information on the statements only shows the date and the amount, if that's any help."

I had an idea. "I'd like to open a separate checking account and move most of that money to the account in my name only. Can I do that?"

"Yes, sir. But our checking accounts pay no interest."

"It's the interest that got me in trouble with the IRS." I set it up, ordered a supply of checks. "On the checks I don't want my full name. Just I. Glass. No address, no driver's license number, no phone number. None of that stuff."

Moving the money out of savings should smoke Katya out. She couldn't access the checking account. She'd have to come back to me when she ran out of cash. It was my only hold on her.

Then I had second thoughts. Where had that much money come from? Vladimir had used my identity to open a bona fide account at the Riggs bank. He was probably skimming, embezzling, or otherwise getting money out of Russia. I had very little banking experience, certainly not international. Was cash smuggled in the embassy pouch and deposited a bit at a time by some partner in Washington, or was it done by wire transfer?

One thing certain: it was not my money even though the account was in my name. I had moved it to another account in my name only. I was laundering money, probably stolen money. It was stealing, wasn't it? Or would the IRS and the FBI figure I was being paid off by the Soviets for unknown services rendered? How could I explain that?

I told Ivy, "Surprise: I have more than seven hundred thousand dollars in an account in Washington,"

"It's enough to buy a house," she said, then quickly added, "Where did you get that much money?"

"It's not mine. It's Katya's or her father's. Or God

knows whose."

Always an honest person, Ivy said, "You can't spend it."

"Of course not. I'll pay the IRS the tax and penalty out of that account and we'll wait and see what happens. Katya's going to be surprised when her ATM withdrawals are refused for insufficient funds. Then she's going to call."

"Or Putinsky is going to send someone after you."

"Oh, shit." I remembered what he said in Gorky Park: "You're a dead man." "What do I do now?"

"Sit tight," Ivy suggested.

"You think I should notify Agent Wilson?"

Ivy shook her head. She'd had her hair cut short, no more option of Pippi Longstocking pigtails. She'd found her man. She didn't need to wear her hair long. "Like they say, Irwin, let sleeping dogs lie."

We made arrangements for the wedding and debated on whether to put a down payment down on an old house remaining from the copper mining days or simply rent an apartment large enough to accommodate our joint foreign language libraries. Ivy had a ton of German books and mine were Russian. She had furniture—a futon that made into a single bed, a desk, and a chest of drawers--and I had no more than would fit in the back of my Ford pickup truck.

We sent out invitations, arranged for my parents to fly in and stay at the Super 8 motel down on the waterfront. We could hold the reception in the party room there. It was going to cost a bit, but then I had that huge balance in the Riggs bank. Why not? Let that be Putinsky's wedding gift. If I had to pay the taxes I might as well spend some of it.

Did that make me an embezzler? It might if the account was for some hockey club and I was the treasurer, but I don't play anything but Scrabble.

My folks flew in from Ocala, Florida and I sprung for the air tickets. Ivy's parents drove up from Chicago, the long haul I had made for the initial job interview at Michigan Tech, only in the Hartshorns' Volvo station wagon with cruise control it was a more comfortable ride than my old Ford pickup. Both parties were surprised that we could pay for their rooms in the Super 8. Thank you, Vladimir Putinsky, or whoever.

218

Was I living beyond my means? Would this spending of that mysterious money trigger an investigation, like what happened when that turncoat American spy spent money from selling secrets on sport cars and a house bigger than government pay could ever justify? I hoped not. I hadn't sold any secrets. I didn't know any, unless it was the answers to my last exam in English as a Second Language.

My folks occasionally attend a Methodist church in Ocala and Ivy's parents are Lutheran. Ivy and I go to no church but have friends among the Portage Lake Unitarians, so settled on a very secular non-denominational ceremony on the deck of the Super 8, no bridesmaids or fancy dress necessary. They say "something borrowed, something blue," for the bride. My mother still had the veil from her own wedding. As a wedding gift she had made us one of her gorgeous quilts, her hobby.

Ivy's father, Tomas Hartshorn, is a descendent of Swiss immigrants, and his hobby in his retirement, adhering to an old world tradition, is clock making. Besides assembling grandfather clocks from kits he has an extensive wood shop in his Chicago basement where he makes cuckoo clocks. Appropriately, his wedding gift to us was a hand made cuckoo clock. Not my taste in time pieces, but what better to give than something you cherish yourself?

The dress code in the UP is casual rustic and I never wear a suit or even a jacket when I teach. For sentimental reasons I wore the wool suit my mother had picked out for me before I left for Russia, the one I'd been wearing in Moscow the night I got seduced. I had put on some weight in the twenty years since, so the jacket was too snug to button over my stomach and I had the pants let out an inch, but I wanted to wear it. No rented tux for the Super 8.

We had a surprise guest. Agent Wilson showed up at the wedding reception in his handlebar mustache, brass belt buckle, and an ill fitting sport jacket.

I wondered why he showed up. I handed Wilson a glass of champagne in one of those disposable plastic flutes. "You come to congratulate us?"

Agent Wilson doesn't smile much, but he tried. "That, too, Glass. But this is business. You hear about the murder in

Washington?"

"Which murder? I thought Washington was the murder capital."

Wilson corrected me. "That's Detroit or maybe New Orleans. This was several weeks ago. A man was found hanging from a bridge over the Potomac."

I hadn't seen the story. The local Daily Mining Gazette carries hockey scores and reports on the latest drunk drivers, not D.C. murders. "What was it? Suicide?"

"The victim was a chauffeur at the Russian Embassy. No diplomatic immunity, so the DC police investigated."

"Should I be interested?" I'd heard that so many people in the District had CD stickers on their cars the cops had trouble enforcing parking tickets. I could imagine they had to get clearance in order to investigate a murder. "What are you getting at?"

"Your name came up."

"What?"

"When the detectives searched the chauffeur's apartment they found papers with your name on them. Something to do with an account at a D.C. bank. You know anything about that?"

As they say, the penny dropped. "Let me guess. The Riggs bank?"

Wilson sipped the champagne. "Tell me more."

"Let's go inside," I suggested. "Too much of a crowd out here." I led him through the doors to the Super 8 swimming pool. A couple of kids were splashing and shouting, but otherwise we were on our own.

"The Riggs bank was where Vladimir Putinsky was supposed to deposit the hundred bucks I was never paid. How did my name show up in an investigation of the murder of an embassy chauffeur?"

"I don't know the details," Wilson admitted. "The Soviets used to use chauffeurs as cover jobs for their agents. It has something to do with deposits that were or were not made to your account at the Riggs bank."

"Were or were not?"

Wilson had finished his drink and was looking for a place to throw away the plastic flute. I spotted a trash can and pointed to it. "Well, that's the mystery. The investigators found receipts showing that a large sum of money was deposited in increments to a savings account in your name, but when they checked it out the money wasn't in the account. Know anything about that?"

"Did they find out if it was an account in my name only or was it joint?"

Wilson shrugged his shoulders to adjust the fit of his sports jacket. Either it was a poor fit or it bound on his ever present weapon. "What is it you're not telling me, Glass?"

"I got a letter from the IRS dunning me for interest on a savings account at the Riggs bank. I didn't even know there was an account in my name. Turns out my daughter's name was added to it. Joint account."

"Your Russian daughter."

"Right. Katya, who disappeared last spring. I think Putinsky was using that account to supply his daughter, our daughter, I guess, with expense money."

"Expensive daughter. The deposit slips the detectives found added up to seven hundred thousand."

So Wilson knew that much, except I knew the money wasn't there and where I'd stashed it. "That's the thing," I admitted. "Could be it wasn't just for Katya's pocket money. Putinsky may have been shifting money out of Russia for some other purpose and hiding it. Or Katya is working somewhere on some secret mission. Honestly, I have no idea."

"So where did the money go? I'm told most of it disappeared."

At that point I could have suggested the chauffeur stole it, which might be the reason he was murdered. If that were the case, maybe I had blood on my hands. That was not a pleasant prospect I would have to think about later. "I moved the money to force Katya to contact me when she runs out of cash. After all, she's my daughter.'

"Did she contact you?"

"Nope."

"Didn't you think that was an awful lot of pocket change for a kid?"

"Well, sure, but I just wanted to find Katya. I didn't

think about anything else."

Wilson shook his head. "So that's your cover story for laundering money?"

"I'm not laundering money. I'm only trying to find my daughter. What other options did I have? Seemed like a good idea at the time."

Wilson licked his lips. Maybe he was thinking of a refill of the champagne. "Apparently somebody thought the chauffeur had stolen it. So now he's dead. That's one theory."

I speculated further. "You know, this doesn't have to be a KGB thing. Since the collapse of the Soviet Union the Russian Mafia have taken over. Putinsky may have gone over to the dark side, not that he was ever a force for good."

Wilson didn't catch the Star Wars allusion. I had to put it in terms a cop could understand. "There's a narrow line between being an undercover cop inside the mob and the temptation of a criminal lifestyle."

"You think the money that went into your and Katya's account was Russian Mafia money?"

I could only shrug.

Wilson smiled at me from under his handlebar mustache. "So you moved the money? You've got more guts than I took you for, Glass."

I gave him an open hands gesture. "I'm just an ordinary guy."

"Or dumb. In Detroit you can get killed for twenty bucks."

I didn't want to think about that and tried to turn it into a joke. "In the Copper Country we don't come that cheap."

The door to the party room opened and my father came out. "So there you are. We've been looking for you. Pictures, Irwin. Pictures."

I turned to Wilson. "They're taking the wedding pictures. I have to go."

Before I got away Wilson asked, "Have you ever heard from that Putinsky?"

"No."

"I think you can expect to. Or from one of his people."

"If I do I'll call you."

Wilson held me by the sleeve, the long arm of the law.

"You should know that money laundering is a federal crime."

"Thanks for the warning. I do know that anybody can deposit money into anyone's account. What if I deposited fifty thousand in Agent Wilson's account? You'd have to pay income tax on everything over $13,000--gift tax."

The remark actually shook Wilson. "You wouldn't do that."

"It would look like a bribe, wouldn't it? Hush money to get you off my back."

Wilson didn't like that. He wasn't someone to push around. "Careful, Glass. You making some sort of a threat? You're on thin ice as it is."

I shook my head. "You mean, like passing on a large sum of Soviet blood money? Now I think you understand how I could be in deep shit for doing nothing at all. Imagine Agent Wilson put on the No-fly list for taking money from a known Soviet agent. That would make us partners in the eyes of some parties."

"You mean like your friend who calls himself Robert?"

"You got it. Anyway, don't worry. I'm just trying to make a point."

"Point taken."

I wouldn't say I was playing hard ball, but I'd been kicked around enough. Wilson looked at me as if I'd grown a couple of inches. I reassured him. It occurred to me if I moved the money into Wilson's account he'd be next on the list of victims along with that chauffeur. I didn't want that to happen. God knows if things went really sour I'd need him in my corner. "You know I've always been cooperative," I said, and followed my Dad back onto the Super 8 deck for the wedding pictures.

The photographer was setting up. It was a beautiful day, one of those special Copper Country blue sky days in a summer sandwiched between late winter and early winter. Several of the university sailing club Lasers were taking advantage of a light breeze. All was peace and tranquility, no lurking KGB assassins. I hoped.

As we posed for the family portrait my father asked, "Who was the man you were talking to?"

"Agent Wilson," I explained. "FBI."

My father was worried, but not as worried as I was. "I thought that business was all over with."

I shook my head. "With some people, Dad, it's never over."

We took another pose, camera flashed.

Not able to keep my mouth shut I whispered to my Dad, "Agent Wilson thinks I'm connected to the murder of a Russian chauffeur in Washington." I grinned.

Dad's eyes opened wide, new wrinkles in his Ocala golf tan. "So are you?"

"When was I in Washington? How could I even get there? Drive my old pickup? I don't do murder."

"Irwin Glass. Man of mystery." He no longer thought of me as his little kid.

I gave my father a closer look. "You should have your doctor look at the dark patch on your ear lobe, Pop. Skin cancer is no joke."

We were interrupted by my Humanities department head, Dr. Waarala. "I have something for you, Irwin. Forgot all about it. When you celebrated your engagement and your daughter announced she'd got her US Passport, I took her picture." He handed it over. a single print in a plastic sleeve.

There she was, Katya, beaming and holding up that precious document. She had her mother's mouth and eyes and--I could see it now--something of my features in her forehead. "Is this digital? Could I have more copies? You know, the only pictures I had of her were for her passport application."

"Glad to," Waarala said.

I hurried to show the picture to my parents. "That's Katya, taken the night before she disappeared."

My father studied the picture. He remembered the fatal six photographs taken of me in the Metropol Hotel in bed with her mother, the photos Katya stole when she skipped. "Looks like her mother."

My mother hadn't seen those x-rated shots. "And she's never called or even written?"

"I'm still waiting."

"Someone will call," my father reassured me. "Now that you have her photo you can put it on your Facebook account.

Someone will recognize her. She's a missing person."

While the wedding photos were being taken Wilson disappeared. Ivy and I didn't plan on hiding out for a short honeymoon. Maybe we're too old for such romantic notions. The Keweenaw is so remote and hard to get to we concentrated on giving our parents the Cook's tour of the Copper Country, the usual run up to Copper Harbor, the parks and the beaches.

My truck and Ivy's Tracker wouldn't do, but we all fit in the Hartshorns' Volvo station wagon. Ivy's folks drove back to Chicago a couple of days later and we saw my folks off at the airport for the first leg of their trek back to Ocala. Who knew when we'd see them again?

With our parents on their way I had to make plans to move out of Prof. Kostinsky's house. I hadn't forgotten my father's advice to post Katya's photo on my Facebook page. I was hesitant in how to approach it and Googled missing persons. It was appalling to see how many people, mostly young women and children, had disappeared without a trace under mysterious circumstances. In some cases hefty rewards were offered. I was sure Katya hadn't been kidnapped, that she was simply a runaway, if being a runaway could be classified as simple. There are too many reasons for running away, like fear of being molested by a relative or not wanting to do the dishes. Some people make bad decisions for dumb reasons. Maybe I could find out what newspapers are published in Portland, Oregon and post a personal ad as in "please contact." I had a feeling that she was on the move, no longer there. It's a big country. How soon would she run out of money?

Ivy was thinking about the Facebook option. "Facebook isn't secure," she reminded me. "If you reveal too much you risk a stolen identity."

In the end I simply put up Katya's photo on my Facebook photo gallery with a note, "if anyone sees her, please contact me." Nobody responded.

Our lives shifted into a new mode. Professor Kostinsky returned from Israel so I had to vacate. He was glad to see his cat again, though I felt the cat was aloof. Ivy and I were moving into new digs, the contract for rent with an option to buy. It's an old house built before the automobile, so there's no garage for our two vehicles. There might have been a barn or a stable on the property at one time, but that was long gone. Fortunately the house is walking distance from the Tech campus so we needn't be shuffling cars in the driveway that often.

I did get a call a few days into our move, but it wasn't from Katya. We had just had the telephone installed. The phone was on the floor, dark, scarred hardwood that had never been refinished since the day the house was built a hundred years ago. I had to squat down on the floor to answer it. "Hello?"

"Irwin Glass?"

"Yeh, who's this?"

It was someone who said they were at the State Department in Washington, a name I didn't catch and immediately forgot.

Alarm bells. I remembered Agent Wilson's story. "This about that murdered Russian driver?"

Maybe I'd said too much. There was an awkward pause like someone was asking for advice. "We need to ask you a couple of questions, Mr. Glass."

I shifted my position on the floor. Was this about the seven hundred grand I'd moved out of the savings account? I was immediately defensive. "Look, I don't know who you are or even who you claim to be. I'm in the process of moving and we're not even unpacked. Maybe you could send someone around for a face to face, with proper ID, of course. I don't do interviews over the phone."

"Do you think you could come to Washington?"

I almost laughed out loud. "For that you will have to issue me a travel voucher and wings. I'm on the No-fly list." If the caller were legitimate my no-fly status should be known.

That stymied them. Another pause while the voice explored other options. Finally a parting shot: "Does the name Vladimir Putin mean anything to you?"

I guess that was a password I could accept. "Putinsky. What about him?" I guessed that Putinsky must be about sixty. Thanks to Russian state alcoholism the life expectancy of men had dropped to about fifty five. "Is he dead?"

"Mr. Putin lists you as a reference."

Jesus! Now what? "I'm not hiring."

"Mr. Putin isn't looking for a job, Mr. Glass."

"I suppose he wants his money back."

The voice didn't know about that, or claimed ignorance.

Ivy was standing over me with puzzled, irritated look and a cardboard carton of stuff destined for the kitchen. "What is it?"

I covered the mouth peace. "Trouble."

Ivy gave me a worried look. "What are you so angry about?"

"This just pisses me off. It's about Vladimir Putinsky. Why can't those people leave me alone?" I resumed the phone conversation. "If Vladimir Putin is there tell him I want my daughter back."

The voice was not finished. The speaker had a short temper and a voice with a hard edge. "Mr. Glass, let's keep this on a cordial basis. Vladimir Putin says you can vouch for him."

"Vouch for him? That's crazy. I only saw him a couple of times and that was years ago. He ruined my career." I couldn't be anything but a hostile witness.

"Apparently there's more to your relationship than that, Mr. Glass."

I took a deep breath. This wasn't making sense. "So what am I expected to do?"

"We'd like you to write a report giving your impressions of Vladimir Putin."

My impulse was to laugh. "That's ironic. There was a time when he wanted me to write reports on my boss back in Moscow." I couldn't remember her name. "Susan something, Lutz or Butz. It was part of Putinsky's scheme to make me a Soviet Agent."

"That would be it."

"So now it's my turn to write a report on him? That's funny."

"Yes. We're like a character analysis, if you think you can do that."

"So what are you going to do with it? Compare it to

227

other reports?"

"Something like that."

"So what do I get out of it? How about a hundred bucks deposited to my account at the Riggs bank?"

The speaker wasn't aware of my allusion to Putinsky and the fatal hundred dollar bill. "We don't pay for these, Mr. Glass. Payment would taint the results."

"How soon do you want it? Where do I send it? Email, snail mail, or registered?"

I was given the details which I wrote down on the flap of the carton Ivy had been carrying to the kitchen. As a parting shot I asked, "Just what is this all about?"

The reply hit me like a hammer. "Vladimir Putin is asking for political asylum."

I wanted to ask if Putin was in Washington, but the caller hung up.

Ivy was curious. "Did you say Vladimir Putinsky? Who were you talking to?"

"Some clown who claimed to be in some government agency."

"Irwin, you have to be careful with those people."

I tried to stand but my knees were stuck. "Give me a hand up." Once standing, I brushed the dust off my jeans. "They say Vladimir Putin claims me as a reference."

Ivy brushed a stray lock of hair out of her eyes. "What does that mean?"

"What do I know? Something about political asylum. Maybe he wants a job working for the CIA. The world is a funny place. After World War II we hired old Nazis. Maybe post-Soviet Union they're hiring ex KGB officers. They want me to write a report on Putinsky."

"Really?" Ivy looked cute in a baggy Michigan Tech sweat shirt. We'd been painting and the shirt looked like a painter's palette.

"Now I suppose it's my turn to rat him out like happened to me."

Ivy was puzzled. "I don't get it."

"When I got in that trouble in Moscow everyone wrote a report on me. Susan, my boss, called me a drunk and a womanizer. A guy who called himself Robert said I was a paid Soviet Agent. Someone collects all those reports and tries to make sense out of them. Can you imagine working under conditions like that?"

Ivy couldn't. She's straight forward and up front. She's sharp which is why she's so refreshing. She was way ahead of me on this one. "You think Putin has come to this country to find Katya? He could be looking, too."

"I don't know. The way she put it, he disowned her when he found out he wasn't her birth father."

Ivy smoothed down the rumpled sweat shirt. I saw she wasn't wearing a bra. Her nipples made titillating little bumps under the Michigan Tech logo. "Could be, but if whoever killed the chauffeur thinks Katya stole the money, they'll be after her, too. Putin might be coming to her rescue."

"Depends on whose money it is. Maybe Putin stole it from someone else, set himself up a nice little nest egg in that joint account with Katya. I'd better shift the money back and turn off the heat."

"It's probably too late for that, Irwin. Some people are very possessive about their money."

"In the meantime I have this report to write about Putinsky."

"How can you do that? It's been years."

I thought about it. "Well, he has a quick temper. When I refused to cooperate he threatened to kill me."

"Anything else?"

I thought about it. I'd seen him in the American Library, but hadn't actually spoken with him until we met at the Bolshoi Restaurant. That's when he handed over the photos of me in bed with who I now knew was his wife. But afterwards we stuck around for a very nice dinner. I remembered the red caviar. 1 remembered that I guessed he was on an expense account, that the KGB would pick up the tab and we were taking advantage of it. Why not? By accepting the invitation I was, in a sense his host or at least his co-conspirator to rip off the Soviets for a nice meal. How would I describe that in my report?

But then I remembered that when I got to Washington in just the clothes I stood up in, a change of underwear in a plastic garbage bag, my only luggage, I had decided "Screw it" and bought a suitcase and a minimal wardrobe in the Hilton's shop, putting the bill on the room and the State Department's tab. I told myself then that I deserved it, considering the abrupt way I'd been hustled back to the States on short notice with a cancelled passport. It was a self-delusional excuse.

Was my gaming the system any different than Putinsky getting a nice meal at KGB expense? So was I just as much a weasel and exploiter as Putinsky? A bureaucrat is a bureaucrat, is a bureaucrat, political colors and stripes of no consequence.

Maybe we are all corrupt to one degree or other. The person who brings home company ball point pens from the office is stealing or awarding himself a perk. The biggest thieves at Big Box stores aren't the petty-ante shoplifters but the employees who haul away trunk loads from the loading dock. The person who plays solitaire on the office computer is stealing time, which adds up to a lot more money than a few ball point pens. Is anyone a saint?

At what point do we become serious criminals? When seven hundred thousand is laundered into a convenient bank account? Hell, it wasn't my money, but I had to pay taxes on it. There is no black and white. Life is all grey.

So now instead of writing about Susan I was writing about Putinsky. I would have to restrain myself and not taint the objectivity of the report with my old anger. That would not be easy.

The relationship was more complicated in that Putinsky and I have a daughter in common, he her father, me her papa. He may have disowned her and she may have deserted me, but I didn't know if her cover story was true. She might have been coached in how to play on my sympathies. For me to find out I would have to ferret out the truth somehow, not easy if the person you're working with is an inveterate liar accustomed to so much deception that the truth is elusive.

Our rental house was not furnished. We had a mattress on the floor of the bedroom. Ivy had the futon in the living room by the TV, an old desk, some bookcases and a used wardrobe. I stacked my milk crates of Russian books topped with an old door I found in the basement, turning it into a serviceable desk. We found a rather beat-up, wobbly kitchen table and rickety chairs at the Goodwill. The wedding present cuckoo clock went up on the wall near the kitchen door. I'd forgotten to ask my father in law how to disable the irritating cuckoo-cuckoo.

The Putinsky report had priority. Setting up my laptop on my makeshift desk I wrote the report on Putinsky, printed it out, rewrote it, passed it in front of Ivy's sharp eyes, and revised again. I wasn't entirely satisfied with it.

"What you need to do is leave some of it open ended," Ivy explained. "Like those research reports that are somewhat inconclusive and ask for more investigation."

"You mean, like we need another grant."

Ivy gave me her mischievous grin. "I heard you say something about a ticket to Washington and permission to fly."

I chuckled. "You think we can wheedle this into a honeymoon trip at government expense?"

"Why not? We've the summer free."

Summer in Washington, D.C. is humid and hot compared to the clear, cool air of Michigan's Keweenaw. I remembered the bad experience I had with the State Department. "I guess my report on Putinsky has to be tactful. One of those state department documents that means all things to all men."

Ivy's good at that stuff. "Leave some open ended questions. Drop some hints. Send the report and we'll see what happens."

I carried the envelope down to the Portage Lake post office and sent it off to the D.C. post office box address, certified, return receipt requested. Then we waited.

It was summer break. Neither of us was teaching again until the Fall term, so we had some time in case the people in Washington rose to the bait.

It didn't take long before we got another call. Could I travel to Washington?

I was suspicious. I remembered the old KGB tactic of waiting until a quarry was out of town on vacation, like at some Black Sea resort, so they could arrest him on the beach. One minute he's sunbathing in trunks. The next he's gone, whisked away. Could someone be hatching a scheme to blame me somehow for the death of the Russian driver? Or claim I was part of a Russian mafia money laundering scheme? If Putinsky had anything to do with it I could expect the worst. I asked, "How about if my wife and I both fly to Washington? We'll need travel vouchers and a letter to Homeland Security assuring them that I don't plan to blow up the airplane."

To my surprise, they agreed.

"Per diem?"

Agreed. There might be some walking around money.

"How about first class tickets?"

"Don't press your luck, Glass."

"My mother used to say 'You don't ask, you don't get.'"

"Nice try. Vouchers will be sent to you by registered mail and as soon as you have a reservation call this number. You will be met at Dulles."

I had visions of the Hilton, nice meals, time to do some touring in our nation's capital at government expense. I had never seen the Smithsonian. "Where will we be staying?"

"You'll be at the farm."

The farm? In my post-Moscow reading about CIA spooks I'd run into the reference. The so-called farm was a secure training ground in Virginia. Visions of armed guards and a high fence. Maybe if Putinsky was in the country that's where they stashed him for debriefing. Well, I guess we couldn't have everything.

Ivy was pleased at the prospects of a free trip to Washington until I said we'd be staying at "the farm." "The farm? I don't get it. I thought they'd put us up at a nice hotel and while you testified or whatever I could do some touring."

"Doesn't look like it," I admitted with a twinge of guilt. "I think what they call the farm is a CIA training camp."

Ivy's eyes were wide in a growing sense of alarm. "What? What are you getting us into, Irwin?"

I shrugged. "I don't exactly know myself. If Putinsky is in the country they probably have him sequestered for his own safety."

"His what? You mean he's under house arrest?"

"I don't know. These people never tell me anything."

"Irwin, sometimes you worry me. One minute you're

232

Irwin Glass, man of mystery. Next you're Irwin the dupe and dofus."

"I just take it as it comes and hope for the best."

"And you want me to come along on this little adventure?"

"For moral support. Don't you like adventure?"

She was skeptical.

Afraid she'd back out, I tried to persuade her. "Look at it this way, honey. The government wants my help. They're footing the bill. It's not like they're going to arrest us or anything. We haven't done anything illegal."

"What do you mean, 'we' white man?" It was her allusion to a joke about the Lone Ranger and Tonto when they are surrounded by hostile Indians. "You're the one who fiddled that seven hundred thousand."

"Seven hundred and fifty thousand," I corrected, as if that would make any difference. "What do I know?"

"Ignorance of the law is no excuse," she insisted and mocked me with, "You mean robbing banks is against the law. Gee, I didn't know."

"They haven't mentioned the Riggs account," I insisted. "This is supposed to be about Putinsky."

"Katya's father. The KGB guy."

"Yes."

"Is he dangerous?"

"He's not in Russia any more," I pleaded. "He's just a little, bald guy."

"With a nasty temper."

"He must be over sixty. Maybe he's mellowed."

"Ha!" Ivy wasn't happy about being sequestered on "the farm," but suggested there might be horses to ride or a tennis court or maybe a pond with trout in it. She usually looks at the bright side of things. That's good, because I've been stung so many times I anticipate the worst. This time she wasn't so sure.

The travel vouchers came in a heavy, brown envelope "penalty for private use $300." I remembered I'd left a couple of things at Kostinsky's house, mainly my old, Russian storm coat from Gum hanging on that hook behind the front door. The jacket was pretty shabby but had sentimental value. I called Kostinsky to make sure he'd be home and stopped by to pick up the coat.

Prof. Kostinsky was glad to see me and to speak his native Russian, but he was worried. "There was someone looking for you yesterday."

No visitor had contacted me. "Did you tell him my new address?"

Kostinsky was a refusenik who never lost his suspicious nature. "I told him I didn't know your address. I said he should check with the Humanities Department."

Coming out of the old Soviet Union, Kostinsky was used to speaking obliquely. It was a practice we both understood. My residence in Moscow had been short, but memorable. I had not forgotten how some Russians on the busses had been afraid to talk to me while others, apparently students, members of Young Komsomol, had acted like junior KGB pretending to want to practice their limited English. "What are you not telling me?"

Kostinsky and I are on the same wave length, something he appreciates. "Your visitor was very tall, in a long, shiny leather coat. He had snakeskin boots."

Not typical Copper Country garb in June or at any time. "Obviously a foreigner," I said, thinking out loud. "Nobody wears leather coats around here."

Kostinsky smiled. His cat was rubbing against his leg and he picked it up, cradled it in his arms. "Or snakeskin boots. He was Russian. The accent was unmistakable."

A shiver of fear ran up my spine. In Moscow the secret police were grey men who melted into the crowd. They didn't want to be noticed. From what Kostinsky told me, this man was more like John Gotti, the Teflon Don, showing off his status. Gangsters wanted to be noticed and feared. "Russian Mafia?"

Kostinsky's friend Professor Melamed had said Katya smelled like KGB. Now Kostinsky detected something equally sinister. His shrug told me most of what I wanted to know.

"He didn't ask about Katya?"

"Katya?"

"Katarina Putinsky, the Russian student who turned out

to be my daughter. You never met her. She lived with me here for a couple of months before she disappeared."

Now Kostinsky was more worried than ever. "No. I didn't want to tell him anything. I saw that Mrs. Waarala was watching from her kitchen window, so I waved. The man went away."

So Kostinsky's instinct told him he wanted a witness who might identify the unexpected visitor. "Smart."

"Be careful, Irvin."

"I don't look for trouble," I assured him. "It just follows me around."

Kostinsky raised his bushy eyebrows. His year at the Technion had given him a nice Negev Desert tan. "Oh? So what are you not telling me?"

"Katya's father has turned up."

"I thought you are this Katya's father."

"Life is complicated. The government wants me and Ivy to travel to Washington. Vladimir Putinsky is asking for political asylum."

Kostinsky put a fatherly hand on my shoulder. "You are a popular fellow, Irvin. Everyone wants you for something."

I agreed. "Right now I think Ivy and I better get on a plane before Mr. Snakeskin boots catches up with me."

I tossed the old jacket on the seat of my Ford pickup and hurried to our new digs. Most people our age would be well established. In our careers Ivy had tenure at Michigan Institute of Technology; I didn't.

Ivy was trying to make some sense out of the cupboards and the under the counter storage space in the kitchen. We would have a lot of work to do to make the place livable. As a couple we've started late. Ivy's only bed had been that single futon. Sleeping on it together was cozy, but not comfortable. Until we bought a bed we just had that mattress on the floor. At least you couldn't fall out of it.

A bit breathlessly, I said, "I think we should be on the next plane to Washington."

Ivy was surprised. "You mean like today? You just got the vouchers."

"Kostinsky says there was someone looking for me."

"Some student unhappy about a grade?"

Since my classes were graded pass/fail only the most petulant and lazy Kuwaiti was likely to protest a fail. "Maybe the Russian Mafia."

Ivy knows I can appear to be delusional after all my troubles with the KGB, FBI, and Homeland Security. "You sure you're not having a paranoid fit, Irwin?"

"If I'm not paranoid, why are all these people following me?" It was meant to be a joke.

"I can pack in an hour, if that makes you comfortable."

At least we don't own a cat or a dog that needs boarding. We don't even own a goldfish or a parakeet. What should I pack? All papers related to Katya…of course, the DNA test results, what little I had of that joint account at the Riggs bank. I had a few starter checks for the account where I'd moved the money. The printed checks hadn't yet arrived. I didn't want to leave anything behind in the house in case someone searched it while we were gone.

For years people in the Copper Country never locked their doors and left car keys in the ignition, but things had changed. We didn't even have dead bolts on the doors and anyone could knock a window pane out of the back door and let themselves in. One might as well put up a sign "Don't knock. It's open," Not that anyone would want to steal household furnishings bought at the Goodwill. "I think I'll give Wilson a call, just in case."

Ivy was skeptical. "The FBI guy? Suit yourself. I'll go pack a bag."

I'd parked the phone temporarily on a plastic milk crate that would have to do until we got more furniture. For a change, Agent Wilson was at the office in Marquette.

"Hi. It's Irwin Glass in Portage Lake. Just wanted to give you a heads up. The government has lifted the ban on my flying, at least for now. Ivy and I are on our way to Washington. Seems Vladimir Putinsky has asked for political asylum and I'm supposed to be a character witness, if you can believe that."

"Vladimir Putinsky? Refresh my memory."

"The KGB officer who tried to blackmail me years ago."

"With you, Glass, I never know what to believe. I think you live in fantasy land."

I brushed off the impulse to indignation. "It gets complicated. It's possible that there's someone from the Russian Mafia looking for me. Know anything about that?"

"If I did I couldn't tell you."

"There is something you can do that I can't. The person looking for me may also be looking for my daughter. You remember when she disappeared, right?"

"Yes. Right after she got her US passport."

"Well, you should be able to get the airline to check the old manifests. See where she flew to. I mean, besides Chicago. Think Portland, Oregon." Since Northwest no longer flew to Minneapolis and United had bought that airline, the only flights still leaving the Houghton County airport went to Chicago O'Hare. That's where Ivy and I would have to fly, and then change for Washington Dulles.

"Why ask me, Glass? Why don't you hire a detective?"

"What? On instructor's salary? You've got to be kidding."

"You want the FBI to track down your daughter? How do you justify that?" Wilson might humor me, but there were limits to his tolerance.

"Could be a matter of National Security," I suggested. "Katya might be a Russian spy. One of those sleeper agents like the ten that got deported."

Wilson's incredulity was palpable even over the phone. "You mean you're denouncing your Russian daughter as a spy?"

That hurt. "Mr. Wilson, I don't know what to believe. All I know is that the government is paying for me and Ivy to fly to Washington for an interview with Putinsky. Something heavy is going down and I have no clue what it is. But Katya may be in danger. Christ, Wilson, she's my daughter."

"I'll see what I can find out," Wilson finally conceded. That might amount to one perfunctory phone call. As the only agent working out of Marquette, he had his hands full already. Just keeping coordination between the drug enforcement teams tracking down meth labs and God knows what black helicopters sniffing for marijuana plants, plus foreign students who might be terrorists in training, plus the occasional bank robber, smugglers of bear organs into

Canada and who knows what else, Wilson had plenty on his plate. Some people even smuggled old-fashioned five gallon flush toilets into the country. Maybe the possibility of a Russian Mafia hit man that might hang me from the Mackinaw Bridge would be a change of pace for him.

Ivy sensed my nervousness as I booked the flight to Washington. Was I afraid of what might happen there? Or was I spooked by Kostinsky's story of someone looking for me? Could be harmless, but I doubted it. More and more it looked like we were making a run for it, but maybe it was from the frying pan into the proverbial fire. Who knew? I'd be on the five o'clock plane and there was a layover in Chicago. We'd get to Washington very late. I phoned in the arrival time to the number we'd been given, and got ready to leave town.

Just as a precaution, I stopped in at my department head's office. I was lucky to catch him in. Dr. Waarala was dressed for the tennis court.

"Ivy and I are going to be out of town for a few days," I explained. Not that we had to tell anyone if we were taking our vacation elsewhere, but I didn't want us to simply disappear, if that's what was about to happen. "A government agency asks for my presence in an immigration case."

"What agency?"

I was embarrassed not to know, but I played it cool. "We work on a need to know basis," I said, hinting that I might be doing something top secret even if I didn't know what it was. "If someone comes looking for me, just say I'm out of town."

Waarala had been amused by my successful battle with the Dean of Students over Katya's status when I was accused of fraternization. I had earned some respect beyond what might be due to a mere instructor without tenure. "So who's looking for you," Irwin?"

"I think it's someone who thinks I owe him money."

"What are you? Over spent on a credit card? Those collection agencies can be aggressive."

"No credit card. It's all a mistake, but it could be unpleasant. I can give you an emergency phone number, but please keep it confidential."

What would happen if Waarala did call the number? Usually if you call a government office the person who answers states their name or the name of the office you've reached. The number I phoned with the information about the air reservation was answered simply, "Hello." If I asked who was speaking I got an evasion.

Waarala shook his head. "I think you're in the wrong subject, Irwin. Instead of English as a Foreign Language you should be teaching the crime novel."

"Surely not at Michigan Institute of Technology," I suggested. "Not in our curriculum."

"So when are you leaving?"

"This afternoon."

At least Waarala didn't ask me to send him a post card.

Packing was a problem. Business trip or vacation? Would I need a jacket and tie? I didn't know what to expect, except I'd need documentation. I dug out my old, expired passport, the one stamped "For immediate return to the USA" I had already assembled what little paperwork I had from the Riggs bank. In case it was needed for an interview with Vladimir Putinsky I also had an old envelope with the DNA test results.

Beyond that I basically threw some stuff into the carry-on I'd picked up at the Hilton years ago. One can travel indefinitely on the contents of one suitcase if willing to rinse out socks and underwear every night. The luggage was battered. One of the zippers was unreliable, but I always carried a roll of duct tape just in case the whole business fell apart on me.

On the other hand, Ivy is a tidy packer. When she saw my mess she rolled her eyes and muttered something about men. Not knowing how long we would be gone was stressful. It made me feel like a refugee running from some invader, destination unclear, and date of return unknown. All I knew was that we'd be met. What if we weren't? Would we wander aimlessly in confusion in the Washington airport? It wasn't like we could hop in a cab and tell the driver to take us to something called "the farm."

The ticket agent at the Houghton County airport's United desk knew Ivy. "Hello Doctor Hartshorn," was her greeting.

Ivy explained. "This is Carol Kiusku. She took my German 101 class. Her husband is a grad student in Mechanical."

Small world. I said, "Hi," and handed over my government travel papers and an apologetic look. "I'm on the no-fly list, but I've got special permission to travel."

Mrs. Kiusku had never seen such a document and was impressed by the US government letterhead. ROTC officers had often traveled on federal travel vouchers, so she was familiar with those. Kiusku knew enough not to ask questions about the permission letter, but that didn't assuage her curiosity. I was treated with the respect worthy of someone who would be the subject of whispers and nods. She booked our flights. We didn't check any bags, had only our carry-ons.

I showed the letter to the uniformed TSA agent and we boarded the Bombardier Canadian-built jet without incident. No tall foreigners in leather coats or snakeskin boots were on the plane.

Because of my "no-fly" status I had not flown in or out of the U.P. before. Looking down over the forests and lakes I wondered how long we'd be gone. That view soon gave way to a patchwork of farm fields and Wisconsin wetlands as the plane followed the shore of Lake Michigan. Then it was mile after mile of cheek by jowl homes that looked identical even from five thousand feet—the Chicago suburbs.

O'Hare is one of the busiest airports in the country and least pleasant. No people mover sections, no little automatic shuttle. One could almost book a flight from one gate to another, they are so far apart. It's also crowded with hundreds of people rushing to catch their flights. Was our arrival there noticed? There was no way of knowing.

The flight to Washington was packed with fellow sardines. Ivy and I were crammed in the middle section of a jumbo jet, no view of the windows. Even if we had window seats it was dark when we landed at Dulles. Washington, DC is in the Eastern Time zone, same as Washington even though Chicago, which is to our south, is in the Central zone. Much resetting of our watches. Altogether it was a five hour trip.

I hadn't been in an airport in years and had never been at Dulles. My flight out so many years ago had been from National, served by the subway, not far from the Pentagon. Dulles was way out on the Beltway. We were herded like cattle from the plane into a sort of box car lifted up to the plane doors and trundled to the gate like a selection of Jews headed for the gas chambers.

At Dulles I half expected someone to be holding up a sign "Glass" but we were recognized by a kid who looked to be fresh out of college. Sport jacket and tie, a compromise that would fit meeting a VIP or a Tee-shirted tourist. I suspected he had drawn the late airport pickup job nobody with rank wanted. He did insist on identification. I showed my Michigan driver's license. Just to prove I wasn't a pushover I asked to see his, which flustered him. He flashed an ID with a government seal, putting it back in his pocket before I could make out the name of the agency. His said "Thom" something but I didn't trust any alleged government ID. With my computer and Photoshop I could produce an ID that said I was king of Morocco with accompanying text in Arabic.

Ivy gave me a sidelong look and squeezed my hand. I didn't know if she was reassuring me or if she was afraid. We were hit by a cloak of nearly suffocating humidity and heat as we followed "Thom" or whoever to the parking garage. His non-descript silver-grey Honda Accord had a crease along the passenger side and an empty Starbucks coffee cup on the floor of the back seat. Looked like the driver's personal car. I asked the kid, "So where's this farm?"

He jumped, like mention of the place required a secret clearance I didn't have. His only reply was "Not far."

I guessed the information was something we didn't need to know.

I hadn't been out to Dulles before. "Any chance we could stop first at the Riggs bank?" That was one place I needed to visit while we were in D.C. I immediately felt stupid for asking. The bank was long closed. "I thought I might make an after-hours withdrawal."

Ivy snickered.

The kid didn't know the Riggs bank. That he took my

dumb remark seriously suggested he had no sense of humor. "My instructions are to take you right to the farm. Sorry." He didn't sound sorry and didn't speak again.

It was chimney dark as we wound through some woods and were stopped by a gate guard that spoke into his radio before he let us through.

The flood lights showed a big house that might have been a private home or a lodge. It had a reception desk reached only after we passed through two sets of glass doors that gave anyone inside a secure chance to have a good look at us. We passed though a set of detectors and for all I knew might have been x-rayed.

A woman in her sixties and a one style fits all jacket that would have been suitable in a hospital, nursing home, or even a jail greeted us, asked us to sign in after we showed our ID. She was wearing an ID tag on a lanyard around her neck. It had her photo, but no name, just a bar cods. She didn't introduce herself. After we signed in she gave us each a clip on tag identifying us as "guest" and insisted we wear ours at all times. "No electronics," she explained as she confiscated our cell phones and took Ivy's iPad for safe keeping. "You'll get them back later." That done, she took us to a room. Apparently we didn't need keys. "You must be hungry," she said. "Did you have time in Chicago for a meal between flights?"

I admitted we were rushed, only an hour between flights, and about two miles of corridors to fight our way through to the gate.

"The dining room's closed now. I'll have someone bring you some sandwiches. Coffee?"

Ivy likes her coffee. "Please."

Bewildered, we surveyed the room. Though there was a window that revealed a well-lit garden, it wasn't a window one could open. A big mirror over the bureau was a chilling reminder of that trap in the Metropol hotel. I didn't see any wires leading to any air ducts, but assumed that in the years since I'd been in the State Department the bugs had become more sophisticated.

"So this is our honeymoon suite?" Ivy said, dropping her carefully packed bag on a little table for two beside the window. She turned and gave me a reassuring hug. "You're nervous."

I gestured at the mirror. "Last time I had sex in front of a mirror like that Putinsky took a set of x-rated pictures. Remember those?"

"How could I forget?"

"I suppose we could have sex in the shower. I'd like that .Steam it up so no pictures."

"What about moaning?"

I hadn't thought about moaning. "You have to assume everything we say in this room can be recorded and transcribed."

Now she really was worried. "Irwin, what the hell have you got us into?"

That put a damper on any thoughts of a romp. In a few minutes there was a knock at the door.

It was a man in grey hair and a white, waiter's jacket pushing a tea cart loaded with a generous tray of sandwiches, a big thermos of coffee, bottled spring water, and even a couple of pieces of chocolate cake wrapped in plastic wrap. "No vodka," the man said and winked at me.

I was startled but before I could say something he was gone. How did he know my aversion to vodka? Then I remembered. "My God!

Ivy was already examining the contents of one of the wrapped sandwiches. "What?"

"I know that man," I said, thoroughly shaken.

"Really?"

"He once told me his name was 'Robert.'"

I poured two cups of coffee, hoped it wasn't drugged. Ivy opened a wrapped sandwich and said, "Ham and cheese. Who was Robert?"

"My nemesis in Moscow. What's he doing here? I mean, is he one of the interrogators? Why the white jacket? Maybe he retired and is now pretending to be a waiter."

Ivy took a bite of her sandwich. "Is this your latest conspiracy theory?"

I ransacked the dregs of my memory. "I remember when I asked to see him at the embassy the clerk didn't know any 'Robert.' So I don't know if it's a code name or if he's working for one agency inside another. With these people there's always compartmentation. Nobody trusts anybody."

Ivy just shook her head and munched hungrily at her ham and cheese.

"I think it's like the Russians," I mused. "The guy whose cover job is chauffeur is actually the KGB informant watching everybody, maybe has a little deal of his own on the side."

"You mean like making secret bank deposits and ends up hanging from a bridge? Is your sandwich tuna?"

I peered between the layers. "I think it's egg salad."

Ivy shook her head. "Aren't you glad you're just an instructor at Da Tech? You don't even have to worry about intrigues among committees."

"At least at the university if you screw up all they do is fire you. You don't end up hanging from the Portage Lake lift bridge."

We finished the sandwiches, discovered that the waiter had forgotten to provide forks for the chocolate cake.

I was suddenly overcome with the stress of the travel, the jet lag, and the late hour. "Bed," I said.

I dug out my toothbrush, made a rude face at the bathroom mirror in case it was one way glass, and fell into the queen size bed. I was too tired to speculate about what would happen next and didn't want to think about it. Might bring on insomnia from worry and fear.

We were awakened by a gong sounding outside in the hallway. Breakfast was ready. Ivy took first dibs on the shower while I shaved using the minimal toiletries I'd packed in a gallon plastic bag for the airport inspection. Like actors cued to go on stage we took a deep breath and left the room.

There was a different person on reception desk duty and we were told how to find the dining room. Nice buffet on the sideboard, typically American, scrambled eggs, bacon strips, Danish pastries, or little boxes of corn flakes and skim milk for cholesterol phobics. Ivy had an appetite. I was so nervous I put toast and coffee on a tray.

"Over here, Irwin," someone said. We were being gestured at by a pleasant-looking man in his fifties, white short-sleeved shirt, yellow tie, jacket over the back of his chair.

I tried to size him up. How would I remember his face if I saw it in a crowd? I realized I wouldn't unless he wore a cowboy hat with a big peacock feather. One of those grey men. And of course if he were wearing such a hat and I were shadowing him, all he had to do was switch hats with another grey man and I'd follow the hat anywhere. Looking around the dining room at the other tables the few people I saw, men and women, seemed to be of a certain age, and almost uniformly white. It was a community of WASPS. We might have a president of mixed race, but power in America was not yet integrated. No wonder the FBI had such trouble finding agents who knew Arabic or Farsi.

As we took places at the table the grey man in the yellow tie asked, "Did you have a nice flight?" and didn't wait for a reply. He turned to my wife. "So you're Ivy Hartshorn. I should say Doctor Hartshorn."

"Anyone who wants to call me Doctor should also salute. Ivy will do."

He turned to me. "So what is it? Irvin or Irwin?"

"Some foreigners have trouble pronouncing Irwin. Putinsky or Putin as I'm told he now calls himself, says Irvin." I looked around the dining room for the small, bald man, didn't see him. "By the way, is he here at the farm?"

"Sequestered in one of the cottages."

I peeled open one of those little restaurant packages of strawberry jam and spread it on my whole wheat toast. "I suppose so he won't be able to identify any of the others who work here."

"That, too," the man admitted.

"Or run away."

"There'd be no point in that. Vladimir Putin is not a prisoner."

"I suppose as long as he wants something from you it's to his advantage to cooperate."

"Sure."

"You haven't introduced yourself," I said.

"No." No introduction was forthcoming. This was irritating.

"Then you won't mind if Ivy and I call you Yellow Tie?"

That didn't go down well. "Ralph."

Code name made up on the spot, I guessed. "OK, Ralph. Tell us what's the drill? When do I see Putinsky or Putin as I guess he now calls himself?"

"First breakfast," the man who called himself Ralph said. "I just wanted to get acquainted."

"OK. Let's do that," I said. "How do you get this job? Does it go through CIA, FBI, or do you have to have a law degree or maybe a background in police work? Or is this an INS, Immigration and Naturalization agency job?"

"You could say that."

That was not being very forthcoming. I gave Ivy a sidelong glance and turned back to him, pausing to take a sip of coffee. "I assume you know all about me and Ivy. There'd be reports from FBI Agent Wilson in Marquette, the old file from Moscow and the record of my being fired, failing the polygraph, stuff like that."

"There are gaps," Ralph admitted. "What about your relationship with Katarina Putinsky?"

"She lived with me for a couple of months after the DNA test proved she was my birth daughter. FBI Agent Wilson helped her get a US passport." That wasn't exactly true. Wilson had told me she was eligible for US citizenship and what I had to do to apply, but he didn't actually help. My story was making Wilson a coconspirator. "Then she skipped. I have no idea where she is. I was kind of hoping you'd help me find her. That's why I'm here."

Ralph's forehead wrinkled as he gave me a crooked look. "I thought you're here to help us find out what's inside the head of Vladimir Putin."

Ivy had chosen a full breakfast with scrambled eggs and sausages. She smiled through a mouthful of sausage, swallowed, and said, "We're here to have a nice honeymoon at government expense." She's such a tease.

Ralph coughed at that one.

I explained, "People do things for multiple reasons. I'd guess you're here not only to interrogate us over our breakfast but because your job makes you feel like an insider, knowing things other people don't which gives you a sense of power." It was a long speech, but it hit the mark. This was

246

not going well.

"As you say."

"So I'll do what I can to get inside Putin's head and you help me find my daughter. Deal?"

"I'm not in a position to make any deals."

"I get it," I said. "Like the clerk who says 'I don't know, I just work here.'" Flunky bastard.

Ralph wasn't taking notes. I assumed he was wired, that the flower in the vase on the table was probably bugged, and somewhere someone was taking down all of this for transcriptions later. "Tell me, Irwin or Irvin, why is Katarina Putin so important to you? You hardly knew her. She's been gone for how many months? Has she written? Called?"

"No."

"So?"

"So I don't like being conned," I explained. "I don't like being used or taken advantage of. I don't like liars and don't like the kind of life you spooks live."

"Give me a break," Ralph said, suddenly defensive or pretending to be offended. "This is a matter of Homeland Security. I'm serving my country."

"And only following orders," I added, alluding to the old Nazi war criminals' defense.

Ralph asked, "Don't you care about your country?"

"Sure I do, but. I wonder if my country cares about me. I presume you've read the old files. You know I got screwed." I'd joined the Foreign Service because I wanted to serve the country with skills I had that were relatively unusual, my fluency in Russian. Plus grad school. That was a big investment and Robert and his ilk trashed it.

Ralph didn't confirm or deny knowledge of the old files.

I looked him hard in the eye. "Ralph, or whatever your real name is, I am not cannon fodder. I didn't join the military but I swore to defend the constitution against all enemies foreign or domestic. How do I know you are not a domestic enemy of the Constitution?"

He didn't answer.

"Think about it," I said. "If a harmless kid like me gets put on the No-fly list because of someone's whim, what's at play here is a breach of my constitutional rights of freedom.

You think that was a mistake?"

"The No-fly business?"

"Damn right."

Ralph nodded. "I get it. What you want is retribution."

"For starters," I said. "So when do I get to see Vladimir Putinsky? He owes me one."

Ralph—or whoever—shook his head. "So you're bearing a grudge."

No doubt that would go down in his report of our allegedly casual breakfast conversation. "One has to start someplace."

That sort of killed the conversation. I hadn't found out much but had established myself as not a pushover. If anything I'd be classed as a hostile witness.

Ivy was enjoying this but said nothing until after we finished breakfast.

Ralph stood up and suggested a little walk around the grounds. I was to see someone at nine o'clock so there was time to tour the farm.

Outside, Ivy whispered, "You gave him a hard time. You don't want to start off on the wrong foot, Irwin."

"I'm pissed off," I admitted. "This guy's so transparent it's insulting."

We stepped out onto the grounds through a set of French doors. We quickly encountered a security guard with a fierce-looking Doberman on a leash. "Morning," I said and muttered to Ivy, "Don't pet the dog."

She whispered, "Next time I'll save him a breakfast sausage."

It was already hot, Virginia in June. Next time I'd wear the shorts I'd packed. Ivy had a tan blouse and a matching, knee length skirt. She eschews the indecently short skirts that make sitting down an exercise in studied discretion reserved for flaunting teenagers.

We got a tour of the grounds, saw the tennis court where a couple of sweating, middle-aged men with paunches grunted with every serve. There was no one at the swimming pool. I saw no sign of a high fence like you might find at a minimum security prison, but assumed there were detectors defending the perimeter. There were several cottages in a row, reminiscent of Depression era motel cabins. When I was a kid my parents and I stayed in something like that on a trip to Florida before my folks discovered Ocala and made a note of it for their future retirement. Now, of course, they had a double wide with the lanai where I'd slept when I got fired from the Moscow job and sent back in disgrace. The farm was all very pleasant and innocuous until we got within earshot of a firing range and heard small arms fire. Someone was practicing with a submachine gun. Short bursts.

Ralph wore a Bluetooth earpiece and we were called back.

We were met at the French doors by a man and a woman. The woman was about Ivy's age with frown lines at the corners of her mouth like her life was full of things she disapproved of. The man, about forty like myself, but wearing a gaudy Hawaiian shirt, explained that Ivy would be accompanied by the woman and I was to go with him.

"Thanks for the tour 'Ralph,'" I said.

Ralph turned away without a word.

I wasn't happy being separated from Ivy because I depended on her for her wit and moral support. Hers was a light touch compared with my sometimes angry demeanor.

I followed the Hawaiian shirt to an office which was obviously an interrogation room, not a place for other work. That is, no computer, no file cabinet-- just a bare room with a table and two opposing chairs. I didn't see a tape recorder, but assumed it wasn't needed and the place was bugged and watched. My interrogator got down to business. "Let's talk about Vladimir Putin."

"Sure. All I know now is he's asking for political asylum."

"That's one version of the story."

"I'd like to know more of the particulars," I said. "I need a context. What's the background for this? Did he walk into the Moscow embassy, or show up at customs in New York with a visitor's visa?"

The man in the gaudy shirt wore his hair long and if under cover might have posed as someone loitering outside a bar. He thoughtfully pushed the hair back off his forehead. "I'd rather not say. Best that your conversations with Putin aren't tainted by anything you might have read. We want a clean slate, so to speak."

"OK. So how is Putinsky, or Putin as he calls himself these days."

"Retired. He's over sixty now. You knew him when he was in his early forties."

"Then he's already lived longer than Russia's current life expectancy. I understand they're down to about fifty-five for men. Alcoholism."

"Putin doesn't drink."

"I don't, either." My last alcohol was a symbolic glass of champagne at my wedding. Not drinking was one thing Putin and I had in common besides a connection to Katya. "Unusual for a Russian. So when do I see him?"

"Right away."

The man in the Hawaiian shirt left the interrogation room, leaving me to wonder who might be watching behind the one way window and how many might be back there.

There was a quick rap at the door and Vladimir Putinsky came in alone.

This was the guy who had threatened me in Gorky Park and said I was a dead man. He was the reason for my downfall, the blackmailer, and probably the one responsible for my being found drugged in my underwear on a public street in Moscow. My old fear of him and the anger remained until I saw him come in the room.

He had never been a large man and he was now a bit stooped in spite of an effort to hold himself erect. I wondered if he was succumbing to the same sort of bone loss that gave women a widow's hump as their spine's collapsed from osteoporosis. But he also looked like he had a burden on his shoulders. He was weary and didn't look healthy. Putin was wearing a prison gray, cotton, long sleeved shirt too large for him, like they couldn't find his size or maybe issuing him clothes that didn't fit was meant to diminish him.

There were subtle ways to wear a man down. You didn't have to deprive people of sleep or even water board them to break down their will.

My instructions were to "get inside Putin's head" so I guessed a friendly approach would work best. I did not have the stature, authority, or experience to play bad cop with him. I addressed him informally in Russian, partly to put him at ease and partly to confound the eavesdroppers in case they didn't know the language. "Vladimir. It's been a long time."

He managed a weak smile. "You haven't forgotten your Russian, Irvin."

"I'm a bit rusty. I'm afraid my accent is now American."

Putinsky was familiar with the circumstances of an interrogation room and sat down across from me. I assumed he might be uncomfortable, since in his Soviet past it would be he who was in charge. Now I was there to question him. I asked, "So what brings you to America? Running from or running to?"

A smile can convey or conceal many things—pain, chagrin, anxiety, friendliness. I thought his was self-deprecating. His grey eyes shifted to me and to the one way window. "Well, Comrade Irvin, that is like the glass that is half full or half empty, depending on how you look at it."

I liked that, but not the comrade part. "We're not comrades," I corrected him, "but we do have something in common, someone in particular."

"You mean, Katarina."

"Yes. Our daughter." As if two men could share a daughter, but of course they could if one were the step father, or in our case the father of record and the birth father.

"Our daughter?"

"She told me that you divorced her mother when you were told that I was Katarina's birth father."

Putin weighed his words carefully. "That's what she told you?"

Answering a question with another question is not an answer.

"She came to me at the university where I work, Michigan Institute of Technology in Northern Michigan. She said I am her papa."

Putin smiled as if to a private joke. "Really?"

"Our university rules forbid fraternization with students."

Putin didn't understand that, so I had to explain. "In the end we had to take a DNA test. The dean thought Katarina

251

had a father fixation."

"A what?"

"That she had a fantasy about an instructor, except I was not her teacher."

"I see."

Did he? "The DNA test came back proving that she actually is my daughter."

Putin was unflappable. With him, anything was possible. "Remarkable. How convenient."

"I don't get it? Convenient for who?"

Putin only shrugged.

"Maybe because, being my birth child, she could be an American citizen. And she is."

"Very good. Then she is safe."

I didn't know what that meant. "Safe from what?"

Putin cocked his head back and forth, a gesture of equivocation. "She cannot be deported."

I hadn't thought about that. I had only thought that, as a citizen student, she could get a job and cover her expenses. That was before I found out she was on that joint bank account that was full of money. "Well, as soon as she got her passport, she disappeared."

"Disappeared?"

"Ran away." That recollection still hit me in the pit of the stomach.

Putin leaned forward earnestly across the table. "Where is she? Do you know where she is?"

I didn't conceal the recollection of my own anguish at her disappearance. "I wish I knew." We were suddenly two parents worried about our kid.

Putin shook his head. "No telephone? No letters?"

"Nothing. Any idea why she would run away?"

Putin shrugged, but I detected a measure of insincerity. He was concealing something. I changed the subject. What about Svetlana? Your wife."

"So you know that."

Know what? "Katarina, Katya, said Svetlana died from breast cancer. Is that true?"

Putin bowed his head. "It is a sad story."

I agreed, but I was uncertain about what I was agreeing

to. A sad story. Was it a true story? I was so confused I didn't know what to believe. For all I knew, Svetlana was alive and well and ensconced in a luxury apartment in Moscow, or retired to a Dacha in the country. Or dead. "Something I couldn't understand. That business in the Metropol. If she was your wife, why would she go to bed with me for all those photographs?"

A hardness came over him. "Svetlana would do as she was told."

"I presume she was told to pose for those photographs of me in bed with her."

"Of course. Standard procedure."

"Was it standard procedure for her to actually have sex with me?" I thought I had him there.

Putin turned his head, a genuine grin, man to man, and shifted to English. "She said you had a nice cock."

At that I thought I heard someone laughing behind the one way glass.

Now I found myself blushing. I had no comeback for that one. I was not used to discussing my private parts with the husband who had been betrayed. "Katya said you divorced Svetlana when you found out you were not her birth father."

Putin returned to Russian. "That is Katarina's story. Do you know the play by Strindberg, 'The Father'?"

I didn't. I remembered vaguely that Strindberg was Swedish, but my background was in Russian literature. "No."

Putin explained. "In 'The Father' the wife suggests that her husband is not the father of their child, that only a mother knows who the true father is. She does this to drive him mad."

"So did Svetlana drive you mad?"

"There were other reasons," Putin said, still evasive. "One must not let the job interfere with one's personal life."

I had seen the movie "Other People's Lives" in which the East German Stasi agent comes to identify with his quarry. I had read there was a risk, Stockholm Syndrome, for instance, the prisoner falling in love with the jailer, the jailer too sympathetic with the prisoner. Human relations could get in the way of bureaucratic protocol.

Sitting in the interrogation room I felt a sudden kinship with the man who had threatened to kill me. What we had in common were two women, Svetlana and Katarina, and a past, however brief. I remembered that the only one who had been totally honest with me in Moscow was Putinsky. He was straight up. He had a job to do: blackmail me into becoming a Soviet agent. So what if that meant that sleight of hand with the hundred dollars? Maybe I'd been wrong, that he'd intended to pay it all along, that I had been too quick to show up at the Riggs bank to check on it. There hadn't been time to set up the account, what with diplomatic pouches, communications, whatever.

"So have you come to the United States to join Katya?"

Putinsky nodded. "That, too."

"And what else?"

"Troubles in Moscow."

"You don't ask for political asylum just because your daughter is missing," I said. "Tell me about the trouble in Moscow."

"The Soviet Union collapsed after you left."

No cause and effect there. "I'm sure my leaving the country had nothing to do with it."

"Not with the collapse of the government. It did cause for me some difficulty."

"You mean besides with Svetlana?"

Putin's nod was rueful. "What did your report say about me?"

He was talking about back then, could not have known what I'd recently submitted. "I never wrote one. I was thrown out, fired, disposed of like so much garbage. You ruined my career."

Putin appeared to be genuinely apologetic. "Not my intention."

That was nice to know, but not worth much. "So did you get fired, too? Because I refused to cooperate?"

Negative. "Sometimes we succeeded, sometimes not."

So I was just another sacrificial pawn.

"You know, Irvin, it didn't have to happen."

"You mean my losing my job and my career." Did he think I'd have kept it if I went on with the role of double agent that 'Robert' wanted me to play?

"Of course. You remember the photographs?"

"How could I forget?"

Putin shook his head as if he were trying to explain something to a child. "In one case like yours-- the photographs for blackmail-- the counselor officer from Argentina was shown such pictures of himself in bed with two whores. His response was, 'Wonderful! Can you make me half a dozen sets of these?' He would show them to his friends. In such a case, there could be no blackmail. End of story."

I had been naïve and inexperienced and made the wrong choice. Loss of job and career was entirely my fault for being stupid. That rattled me. Putinsky was right.

But this was not supposed to be about me. It was supposed to be about Putinsky. Still dazed by the implications of my mistake in Moscow, I changed the subject. "After the collapse of the Soviet Union, what happened?"

"Chaos. A scramble to pick up the pieces. You may remember--the workers were given stock in their factories. It was like your game of Monopoly. People needed food, not worthless shares, so they traded."

I knew that the old grey market had suddenly surfaced. The old apparatchiks had their alliances, their co-conspirators. The people who stole from the factories had become the owners of the factories. Takers don't necessarily produce anything. Maintenance had never been a Soviet strong point. What mattered was the fulfilled work quota, so and so many finished products, even if they were defective. Detroit auto makers had suffered the same and got whipped by the Japanese. Now Toyota was slipping in quality, too. I guessed it must be a natural cycle. "But the KGB was a government agency, not a factory," I suggested. "What happens when a government agency loses its government authority?"

Putin lifted both hands off the table in a gesture of surrender. "That's me."

"Did you find a new job?" In the film "Other People's Lives" the old Stasi officer ends up delivering mail.

"I survive." Putin wasn't going to say what his job or his

business was.

If that was true he didn't have to be in the States asking for asylum. "You have a pension?"

"A pittance. Moscow is now very expensive."

I remembered that even when I was there one could see crippled veterans hawking their medals for cash for food. One could not exchange an Order of Lenin for a new leg. Wages of war. Did Putinsky have any medals for his KGB service? Did it matter?

I guessed that just as an undercover cop working with gangsters recognizes the clandestine nature of both opposing sides, Putin's skills in the secret police would be of same usefulness to the new strong men, the Russian mafia. He didn't look to me like his survival was that successful. If it were, why wasn't he still in Moscow?

I didn't want to bring up the seven hundred and fifty thousand dollars that appeared mysteriously in my joint account with Katya. Not yet. And I didn't want to mention the murdered chauffeur. I knew nothing about that except that the police had found some evidence linking him to the Riggs account. What I wanted was a lead to where Katya might be, but that was not forthcoming.

"You must tell me about Katarina," Putin said.

He was clearly hungry for information about her. She had told me she had not seen him since her parents divorced, but I didn't know if that was true or not. "She's a lovely girl. Smart. She showed up at Michigan Tech…"

"Michigan Tech?"

"Michigan Institute of Technology. Where I work. I teach now, English as a second language for foreign students."

Putin's expression showed genuine pity. "With all your Russian language and degrees you are teaching such a basic class?" He knew how to find a person's weakness. I was supposed to get inside Putin's head. He'd got into mine, hit on my weakness and vulnerability.

"I'm afraid so."

"You should go into some business, Irvin. You are a smart boy."

I didn't feel smart, not realizing how easily I might have

256

avoided the catastrophe in Moscow. "Not a boy any more. I'm married, by the way."

"You have children?"

"Unless you count Katya, no, not yet."

"It is not too late for you, Irvin." Putin's demeanor said it was too late for him.

I guessed this venture to America was his last shot, like the senior citizen who dreams of a quiet, comfortable retirement, someplace safe. My parents had found that in Ocala, though even a double wide manufactured home with no stairs was getting to be a challenge for my mother's arthritic knees.

There were many reasons for immigrants to want to come to America. Usually it was for greater opportunity. Sometimes it was to escape from a war. Though searching for Katya was a legitimate reason to come to the States, he didn't need political asylum for that. What Putin was doing was a gamble. I guessed he was hoping to trade his insider's information about his KGB career for a safe escape, but from what?

Maybe he had stolen the seven hundred thousand. Ivy had warned me that moving the money might make someone mad, that they would want it back and come after me. It was rash of me, even stupid, to shift it into a personal checking account, but was it Putin seeking restitution, or someone else? Would Putin have ordered a hit on the chauffeur, assuming that was the courier who made the deposits, or was it someone else? Maybe it was simply a coincidence that bank deposit slips had been found in the murdered man's apartment. Might not have anything to do with his murder. Who knew what else the chauffeur might have been involved in?

With watchers hanging on everything we said, I didn't want to get into that money business. Like Ivy had warned me, laundering money is a crime. I could end up in prison. I didn't want to give my hosts at the farm leverage in negotiations with me. Getting inside Putinsky's head was enough, and I hadn't done much of that.

I decided to start over. "Tell me about Svetlana. Did you get a divorce?"

"Yes. Regrettably."

So the man had a conscience after all. "And did she have cancer?"

"Yes." He didn't elaborate.

From what I had read about conditions in Russia, their socialized medicine was a disaster. A nurse practitioner in the United States might be called a doctor in Russia, just as everyone over there even in menial jobs, wanted to be called an engineer. Here we had mammograms, digital imaging, and million dollar diagnostic machines. Svetlana's treatment might have been no more than palliative care.

So far, what little I had learned seemed to fit the story Katya had told me. "If you are given political asylum, what are your plans?"

"Perhaps a small stipend. My English is not so bad. I could lecture at an American university, Soviet history."

College programs ran to fads, flurries of politically expedient courses like Holocaust studies, while other topics were dead. Latin and Greek were no longer taught. No one was offering courses in, say, the Vietnam War. Past history. Current politics suggested that the next academic fad would be courses not in Russian but in Chinese or Arabic. I knew from personal experience that no one wanted to study my subject, Russian. Vladimir Putinsky, unlike Gorbachev, was not famous enough to land an adjunct professorship at Harvard or some other Ivy League university.

We were both at the bottom of the academic ladder. If Putin wanted my advice on how to find an academic job he'd be disappointed. It had taken me years to crawl from Indianapolis Christian and other part time positions to finally arrive at Michigan Tech. Putin didn't look like he had that many years left.

He didn't look healthy. At his age and in his condition, what with our inadequate health insurance programs, no one would dare hire him. Some comedown from being an important KGB officer! Maybe the CIA would hire him as a consultant, but like retired Pentagon generals, his usefulness would fade in a couple of years of being disconnected from his sources.

I looked up at the mirror-like window and the unseen

watchers behind it. "I think it's time for a break," I said. The realization that I took the wrong approach to the incriminating photographs and might have saved my job unhinged me. What I needed was time to collect my wits.

There was a knock at the door and the man in the Hawaiian shirt came in. "Lunch?"

It would not be lunch with Putinsky. We went separate ways as I was guided back to the dining room to reconnect with Ivy.

This time it looked like there would be no buffet, but table service.

Mercifully, we were allowed to eat alone. I did not want to share a table with "Ralph" or any other pseudonymous watcher. "Let's sit somewhere it's noisy," I suggested, hoping that background noise would make it difficult for eavesdroppers. It's pretty intimidating to carry on a conversation when you fear every word may be taken down as some sort of evidence.

I pointed to a small table for two.

"You all right?" I asked.

Ivy looked pale, said nothing.

"They give you a bad time? After all, I'm the one who is supposed to be here. You're along for the ride and the vacation. Did you get interrogated?"

"Stomach upset," Ivy said and rubbed her forehead. She took a compact with a pocket mirror from her purse and studied her face. "Do I look different?"

"You look OK to me. Maybe a little tired."

She closed the compact. "I didn't tell you, but I missed my period. I think maybe I'm pregnant."

"That's wonderful." Was it? I knew Ivy's having a baby was a greater desire than even marrying me. This was news it was going to take a long time to assimilate. "I'm pregnant" set off a jumble of confusing thoughts. Being Katya's "papa" by default or discovery was not the same as the long haul of raising a kid. As an only child I hadn't grown up with siblings, no little brother or sister. I had never had to baby sit or change a diaper. Then there would be the juggling of schedules if Ivy and I both kept our jobs at the university. I knew one couple on the faculty who handed off their kid like

259

a football when one's class ended and the other started.

Ivy looked like she was having trouble trying not to throw up. "Right now it doesn't feel so good."

The person in the white jacket who came to wait on us was not "Robert," as I feared. It was a kid of indefinable mixed race who might be a recruit assigned to kitchen/waiter duty. I guessed the intelligence community was trying to integrate. Was our waiter Korean? Chinese? Vietnamese? He might even have been part Arab or Indian, a true rainbow person.

I asked, "What's on the menu?"

"Two choices: meat sandwich or vegetarian salad."

Ivy said "I think I'll pass. Maybe a glass of milk."

I ordered a hamburger and fries and a clear diet drink, 7-Up or Sprite, whatever they had. While we waited, Ivy asked, "How did it go with Putinsky?"

I was still trying to focus after Ivy's announcement of impending babyhood. "He's not well. Looks old and ill. But he's sharp as ever."

"What do you mean?"

"I'm supposed to figure him out, but I didn't make much progress. He's the kind of guy who can turn you inside out. Very subtle. Made me feel like he was the puppet master and I was Pinocchio."

Ivy was not at her sparkling best. She shook her head as if to get rid of the cobwebs. "I don't get it."

"He made me feel like an utter fool. I guess I am."

"How's that?"

I squinted at her. "You remember the six photographs of me and Svetlana that he used to blackmail me?"

"The ones Katya stole? How could I forget?"

"He pointed out that all I had to do was ask for a bunch of duplicate sets to show to my friends. That would have defused the attempt at blackmail."

That made her laugh. "And you'd have kept your State Department job and might have a career now as an undersecretary to the deputy assistant at the embassy in Baghdad. Car bombs, check points, and suicide bombers."

"Might have been posted to London or Paris."

"But you wouldn't have met me, Irwin."

I agreed that I was on a better path.

"And you still might have learned that you have a daughter named Katarina. Don't forget that."

"Maybe my fate is sealed," I admitted. "Did your interrogator ask about Katya?"

"Yes, she did."

"And?"

"She doubts the story, says it's unlikely. These people always expect the worst and look for conspiracies. I think the people here suspect that Katya was groomed to pretend to be your daughter and use you as a cover story. In spite of the DNA test they think Katya is a sleeper agent and you're part of the plot."

The waiter brought my burger and fries with a side salad I hadn't ordered, and Ivy's glass of milk.

I could just imagine some trumped up charge like that Mohammed kid in Oregon. The FBI could have arrested him at any time, but waited until they had conned him into thinking he was setting off a car bomb to blow up the Portland Christmas tree. Letting, or making the case go that far in order to make headlines and a spectacular arrest must have given some agents big brownie points with the agency while the stupid kid went to prison forever. Was something like that going to happen to me? The FBI agents who saw me in Washington at the hotel years ago said there wasn't enough evidence to charge me with being a paid Soviet agent. Maybe they hadn't given up. If they could make the connection with the seven hundred grand that turned up in that joint account at the Riggs bank, they might be able to make a case before a hanging jury. Why couldn't they go after real spies and criminals? "I smell 'Robert's' hand in this."

Ivy tentatively sipped her milk, wrinkled her nose at it. "You sure he's the one who brought the food last night?"

"Positive."

At the next table a couple of women were laughing at something. One of them pointed at me and said, too loudly, "Nice cock."

She must have been one of those behind the one way glass in the interrogation room. Now I was the butt of jokes. Puppet master Putin knew what he was doing to humiliate me. No one would take anything I had to say seriously.

Ivy was curious when she saw my reaction. "What's that about?"

"Putin and I were talking in Russian, except he shifted to English. I'd asked him something about Svetlana, why she had sex with me at the Metropol instead of just posing for the pictures. Putin quoted her in English. She said I had a nice cock."

Ivy laughed. "You do."

"You never told me that."

"You don't need your ego massaged, Irwin dear."

"I suppose I'm lucky the people here don't have copies of the pictures."

Ivy had momentarily forgotten her queasiness. "I bet they do, Irwin. You know how people are who can't keep a secret. Don't be surprised if you show up on Facebook, Wikileaks, or some porn site."

"Oh, God." What with Putin showing me what a fool I was, and the gossip about my penis, I was ashamed to show my face anywhere. Who was the quarry here, anyway? "I think we should have stayed in Portage Lake."

We were interrupted by Mr. Yellow tie, the man who called himself Ralph. He had a troubled look on his face. Now what? I asked, "What's up?"

"We had a telephone call from your department head at your college."

Damn. I'd hoped Waarala wouldn't use that number. "That would be Dr. Waarala. I gave him the contact number to use only in case of some emergency."

"Ralph" leaned over our table for two and lowered his voice. "Seems there was a break-in at your house."

"Sure it wasn't one of your own snoop teams?"

Ralph shook his head. "If we search your place you'll never know it."

There was no knowing when we'd be back in Portage Lake. "What do we do now?"

"Any idea who might have burgled your place?"

"The only thing I can think of is someone was looking for me, a tall Russian in a long leather coat and snakeskin shoes."

That intrigued Ralph. He fingered his yellow tie. "Tell me about it."

"Professor Kostinsky, my old landlord, a Russian Jew, said a man was looking for me. He suspected the man was Russian Mafia."

Ralph wrinkled his forehead. "Could be a connection with that murdered chauffeur."

Without thinking I added, "And a missing seven hundred thousand dollars."

"I'll notify the local police in Portage Lake to mark the place as a crime scene. What is it? Apartment? House?"

"An old house," Ivy said. "We've barely moved in. There's nothing there worth stealing except maybe our computers."

"Not the latest models," I suggested. There was no market for used computers. With new ones costing about $300, computers had become expendable throwaways. I'd taken with me all the papers I had pertaining to Katya, but of course hadn't removed the hard drive from my laptop. My identity wasn't worth stealing. It would be ironic if someone decided to be Irwin Glass and got arrested for being a paid Soviet agent and couldn't get on an airplane. It would be like impersonating one of the FBI's ten most wanted. There might be something of interest on my hard drive, but if Mr. Snakeskin boots were looking for Katya, there were no clues. "So now what?"

Ralph pondered for a minute. "Might be worth checking. Fingerprints and like that. Do we have your fingerprints on file?"

"You have mine from when I worked for the State Department," I said, "But Ivy…" I turned to Ivy. "Ever had your fingerprints taken?"

She hadn't.

"OK," Ralph said. "We'll have both of you fingerprinted and have some of our people check out your house. Might find something."

This obviously wasn't just about Putinsky asking for asylum. There was that murder, and the missing Katya, and the mysterious source of the money that turned up in my account.

I glanced at Ivy. "I guess it's a good thing we're here at the farm guarded by that nice Doberman and not in Portage Lake."

Ivy suddenly got up. "I think I'm going to be sick," she said, and left the table.

When she came back, more pale than before, we were ushered to an office in the basement of the lodge. The fingerprint equipment was in a little carrying case parked in the corner. The woman who unpacked it was the same lady who had been working the desk when we checked in the night before. This was obviously not her regular duty. She inked Ivy's fingers one at a time and took the impressions one at a time on a card, then repeated it with a palm print. It was a messy business, but there was also a special cleansing cream that took it all off.

I was next. Being fingerprinted made me feel like a criminal, even though I knew it was necessary protocol. "Will these go into the national fingerprint database?"

"Yes."

I didn't feel comfortable having my fingerprints in a database along with felons, terrorists, and other criminals. "Will this record show who took these? I mean, will my fingerprint record lead back to this agency?" I didn't even know what agency was acting as our hosts. Was this a CIA operation? Homeland Security? FBI? Made me feel like this was a secret black box organization hidden inside some labyrinth of agencies within agencies.

"No." She didn't elaborate.

"I'm not feeling so good," Ivy complained. She was still queasy.

"I'll take you back to your room," Ralph suggested.

I asked, "Am I going back to see Putin this afternoon?"

"We're going to have a little confab. Compare notes," Ralph said.

In a conference room with windows off the farm's swimming pool I sat with several members of the team. No introductions. No names, please. There was one woman, about fifty, I guessed, who looked like she never smiled for her mouth was turned down by a perpetual grim frown. My mother used to tell me when I was a kid that when I made a funny face it might freeze that way. In this lady's case I guess the idea had some merit.

Ralph of the yellow necktie was one of the team and there were two others, men in business suits. They wore name tags, too, except without names, just bar codes and their pictures. I could bet these people didn't even tell their wives their real names, they were so cagey. Maybe they told their wives they were computer repairmen always on call, no addresses please. I didn't have enough experience of cops to tell if they were detectives or some corporate middle management. Nor did I know enough of men's fashion to tell the difference between a J. C. Penny jacket off the rack and a thousand dollar custom tailored job. I never wore a jacket at the university. Men's clothing is cookie cutter boring.

One of the men had a military style haircut but that didn't mean he was from military intelligence. Some guys adopt a tough guy look as part of their persona. I saw no tattoos.

The other man had adopted another convention: the Arafat look that had given the old Arab a perpetual look of a four day's growth of beard. To me that just made someone look like he was too lazy to shave. He also had pierced ears with tiny studs I couldn't believe would be real diamonds. He was too old to adopt that younger generation look.

The sum total of my impression was that both would be more comfortable in tee shirts and jeans, an unconvincing affectation intended to let them meld into a crowd of younger men. Those jackets didn't fit the faces and haircuts.

The woman had a legal pad and pen to jot down notes or maybe doodle. She got down to business. "What's your assessment of Vladimir Putin?"

"He used to be Putinsky," I began. "I only met him a few times in Moscow and that was twenty years ago."

"And you haven't had any contact with him since?"

"Not until today."

"What's your version of the Riggs bank thing?"

So they knew all about it, or were faking it to draw me out. "You mean the alleged hundred dollars he was supposed to pay me? It was a scam. Putinsky wanted me to write a report on my boss at the American library, a report I did with clearance from a guy who called himself Robert. Putinsky said he'd deposit a hundred dollars in an account for me at the Riggs bank. He never did, not as far as I ever found out."

"But there is an account in your name at the Riggs bank."

"I guess when I checked on it there hadn't been time for him to open the account."

Ralph interjected. "So you were pegged as a paid Soviet agent."

"That was Robert's doing. He's here at the farm."

They were all uniformly surprised. "What?"

"I saw him. He was the waiter who brought us sandwiches and coffee last night."

Ralph looked at the woman. "Do we have a waiter named Robert?"

She didn't know.

I was guessing. "He's in his sixties now. Maybe he retired from the State Department and wheedled a job here."

Confused, the woman shook her head.

Now it was my turn to have some fun with these people. "Maybe Robert is a mole." With so many agencies jealous of each other's sources of information and unwilling to share files, there must be opportunities for someone to infiltrate the farm, make allusions to permissions or introductions not adequately checked. You could hide a lot behind that old "need to know" caveat. I wondered how many FBI agents spied on NSA employees and vice versa. With compartmentation come suspicion and a lack of trust. Of course, it was the compartmentation, the lack of interagency communication and cooperation that made the 9/11 attack possible. If you couldn't get shared information, maybe you had to get it by subterfuge.

"We have pictures of all the people here at the farm. Mug shots."

"You mean with names?" I didn't expect that.

"For you, Glass, no names. Maybe you could go through those and identify this Robert person."

The frowning woman didn't want to be sidetracked. "Did Putin indicate to you why he wants political asylum?"

I shook my head. "I can't imagine him collecting his

Russian pension in the United States, especially if he's a defector. He thinks he might get a stipend to live on, or maybe act as a consultant. He thinks he might be able to lecture at a university. I think that's unlikely."

"Yes, that's what he told you. That doesn't explain why he left Russia."

I sighed. "He wants to locate our daughter."

The concept confused one of the men in suits. "Your daughter? You both have a daughter?"

"Katarina Putinsky, Katya," I explained. "Vladimir was her father of record, but a DNA test proved that I am her birth parent."

Ralph snorted. "You lead a complicated life, Glass."

I avoided further explanation. I didn't want to get into the Metropol hotel story. "Katya disappeared. He may be hoping to use your resources to find Katya. Putin seems to be looking for her, too. I think he's come to the States to find her, and the political asylum thing is just his ploy to get a job or con you into paying him living expenses."

If that were the case, Putin was pretty clever. He'd have more resources than I did in my futile attempts to find Katya. Until this trip to D.C., I couldn't even get on an airplane. The only clue I'd had from the bank was she'd made a withdrawal from Portland. How could I get there from Upper Michigan? Four or five days drive in my aging pickup truck? Even if I could, she'd be long gone.

One of the men, the one with the buzz haircut, interjected. "You mean like putting him in the Witness Protection program?"

"Something like that."

"Protection from whom?" the frown-faced woman asked.

"Could be from the Russian government, perhaps the Russian mafia. I'm guessing he was behind the money put into my joint account at the Riggs bank. Question is, did he steal it from the Russian state treasury? Or did he take it from the Russian mafia?" I almost bit my tongue. I didn't want to get into money laundering and the penalties thereto attached.

"That's something we need to find out," Ralph said.

I finally decided to come clean about the money. Was

this how people were tricked into confessing? "It's a mystery to me, too. I had no inkling that the account was actually opened and still existed until I got a dunning letter from the IRS threatening penalties for not paying tax on the interest of my saving account."

The woman frowned, or was it her usual expression? "But savings accounts pay almost no interest nowadays. The banks don't even issue a 1099 unless the interest is more than ten dollars." She consulted her notes on the legal pad. "You said Putin was supposed to deposit a hundred dollars. Why would the IRS make a fuss over such a small amount?"

Didn't she already know about the seven hundred and fifty grand? Maybe she forgot. Maybe someone understated the amount so they could somehow get their hands on the difference and keep in for themselves. I was suspicious of everyone. I rubbed my nose in frustration. I didn't want to argue with those people. "One percent on a thousand is ten bucks, but how about a hundred thousand? It adds up."

"Why would anyone keep that much in a saving account? There are better places to keep your assets."

"Not if the purpose of the account is to give Katya access to expense money with an ATM debit card."

The man with the pierced ears thought about that. "An ATM can serve as a cutout."

The other man speculated even further. "She could always phone in for a wire transfer, use the money to buy arms to smuggle abroad."

Where were these guys living? Fantasy land? My voice dripping with sarcasm. I agreed. "Yeh, right." I couldn't imagine my Katya as an arms smuggler. These guys were all nuts.

I did remember from my reading in spy books that a cutout was a wall between two sources so one didn't lead back to the other, like two agents who never meet face to face but use some intermediary. A dead drop could do that, a place where one agent hid the microfilm so another could pick it up on a signal. The signal might be a chalk mark on a mail box, something like that.

I was willing to bet they left secret messages for their wives in old woodpecker nests or under rocks in the park.

"I'll be home late, don't hold dinner," no doubt code words for something else, God knew what.

The woman was on the trail like a bloodhound. "So what happened to the hundred thousand?"

I had to correct her. "Seven hundred and fifty thousand. I moved it. I hoped that if Katya discovered her funds were cut off she'd contact me, her papa, and ask for money."

Ralph muttered, "That was dumb," and I would have agreed, but we both got a sharp look from the two men in suits.

The woman ignored the remark. "Did she?"

"No," I admitted. "Maybe she has other sources. No reason there can't be money stashed in banks all over the place."

Ralph was taking notes on his own pad. "So you don't know where the money came from?"

"I thought it might be Putinsky, that he had some courier at the embassy. You can smuggle quite a bit in the embassy pouch. Doesn't go through customs. When I was flown back to the states it was in the military attaché's plane. There were crates of stuff on board. Might be Beluga caviar, vodka, or parts of some stolen Soviet weaponry. Or cash."

"I guess that will be your next line of questioning," Ralph suggested. "See if you can get something out of Putin."

"What about the girl, this Katarina?" the woman asked.

"My daughter? Sweet kid," I said. "She came to me at the college. She was vulnerable, uncertain, and afraid I'd throw her out of my office. She was genuinely relieved, touched, when the DNA test came through." I remembered her tears of relief and her hugs.

"She's a good actress," the woman commented, and wrote something on her pad.

"I think she's sincere. I'm well, crazy about her. Pride of parentage, I guess. She's all the daughter I might have ever hoped for. That's what it broke me up so badly when she split."

The second guy in a suit had been silent up to now. He commented. "Nothing's as it seems."

"Not me," I said. "What you see is what you get." I was a self portrait of innocence.

269

I looked at the people at the table. Obviously they didn't believe me. I even thought one was about to laugh out loud.

Ralph surprised me by patting me on the shoulder. "You got to be careful, Glass. If someone tells you 'trust me,' don't. If they say, 'to tell the truth,' you should wonder what they've been telling you the rest of the time."

I gave him a wicked grin, "So trust me." I shrugged. "Would I lie?"

I guess they figured I would, for that was the end of the session.

Ralph hadn't forgotten the bit about Robert. He took me to a part of the lodge that was all computers and cubicles. He borrowed a computer terminal, logged on, and found the mug shots, just faces and bar codes. We went though them screen by screen. I didn't recognize any of them. Whoever that "Robert" was, he had slipped under the radar. I suggested, "Maybe he's a visitor."

Ralph didn't think so.

I guess when you are super security conscious you keep thinking about how you could be penetrated.

Ralph was ruminating.

"Another thing," I said when he logged off the mug shot file. "Before I talk to Putin again, I'd like to check on what's happening at the Riggs bank. Any chance for a run into town? I don't suppose there's a bus?"

"Not likely," Ralph said, "but there's a shuttle."

"I need to stop at a pharmacy," I said.

"You can't go into the District alone, of course. I'll have to accompany you."

So he was my keeper. Did he think I'd slip away? Not that I had any friends in D.C. if I wanted to escape what was rapidly becoming a constricting experience. At least this time around I had some cash and a credit card, not like the last time I was in D.C. when I had only two hundred bucks and a garbage bag with a change of underwear. Even if I did decide to skip, grab the money from the bank and try to leave the country, I still had no passport. They had Ivy at the farm. Maybe having her as a potential hostage was insurance in case I balked. No wonder they were willing for her to come along on the trip.

We missed the shuttle, which apparently only ran for shift changes, so Ralph had to use his personal car, a beat up Camry that badly needed a wash. I wondered if older cars made better cover or if government employees were not as well paid as some talk show hosts would have us believe.

Ralph cautioned "You'd better put your guest tag in your pocket."

"Right," I acknowledged. No point in my attracting attention as a conventioneer or other outsider.

We stopped at a mini-mall where there was a Walgreen's drug store. I thought Ralph could just wait for me in his car, but he stuck to me like a guard dog. Maybe he was afraid I'd make a phone call or something. I asked the pharmacist about pregnancy kits and bought a couple.

Ralph had no comment, but I knew he would have to report on everything I said or did. I talked about Portage Lake, about my job at Michigan Tech, the foreign students. He wanted to know how I met Ivy. When we got around to Katya I avoided all the business about the recognition signal and the x-rated photos of me and her mother at the Metropol.

We got to the Riggs bank in mid-afternoon. I was glad that Ralph's old Camry had functioning air conditioning. Washington was a steam bath of humidity just short of spontaneous precipitation. I was prepared for the bank visit. I had the account information in my pocket, and my Michigan driver's license. With Ralph silent at my sleeve as an observer, I talked my way into a banker's office.

It seems to me that bank employees, like policemen, are getting younger and younger. This kid looked like he had barely finished a business degree, or maybe was a student in a summer vacation part time job. At least he had a fresh haircut and had assumed the role of a helpful employee eager to set up a mortgage or a business loan. I explained. "I need to check on the status of my accounts here." I gave him the account numbers and entered my PIN in a little gadget on the desk.

The kid was reluctant for Ralph to see any of the information, and I was glad of that. "You can get all this on line, of course, if you subscribe to our on line banking."

271

I hadn't done that. I wanted copies of statements mailed only to me.

Rather than write down any numbers the kid turned the computer monitor so I could see the entries. The seven hundred and fifty thousand was there in the checking account, minus the tax payments and the withdrawals I made for wedding expenses, thank you very much, whoever. The savings account, which I'd reduced to a minimum balance, showed activity.

I pointed to a number on the screen. "When was that deposit made?"

"A couple of weeks ago."

"Ten thousand dollars?"

"Yes. It was a wire transfer."

He couldn't tell me where it came from. "And the withdrawals? Two hundred and fifty dollars at a time?"

The young banker gave me a suspicious look. "Didn't you make those withdrawals yourself? They were drawn from an ATM machine using your debit card."

"It's a joint account," I explained. "My daughter has access."

The bank kid was satisfied. "Then that explains it."

"Can you tell me what ATM machine was used for the withdrawals?"

He didn't know how to do that. I turned to Ralph. "This is something for your crew. If you can locate the ATM machines, you can not only find the city where she's making the withdrawals. You can see who made them. Every ATM has a camera. Find the tapes and you'll see if Katya made those withdrawals herself or if someone else is using her debit card and my PIN."

Not being part of law enforcement, I couldn't get that information. Maybe I could persuade the government to do that for me.

I could tell that Ralph didn't like the idea of my taking charge, but he had to admit that it was a good idea.

With the information I got from the bank I had something to tell Putin, information I could trade as I tried to wheedle the truth out of him. He wasn't an easy wheedle.

As we were turning to leave, the young banker had a

post script for me. "You're the second person to ask about this account."

"Oh?"

"There was a man in here about a week ago asking about it."

Ralph asked, "FBI?"

"No. We have our rules of confidentiality. If he was bone fide, we could have helped him. He claimed to be a relative, but when I questioned him closely he backed down. Even parents can't get information about family accounts."

I asked, "So the man claimed to be a relative?"

The banker nodded. "Said he was your brother, Mr. Glass. But then wouldn't produce any ID."

"I don't have a brother. What was he wearing?" I was wondering about a long leather coat, but nobody would wear such a thing in Washington heat.

Now Ralph was interested. "Describe him."

The banker scratched his neat haircut. "Very tall guy. Maybe six feet six or taller."

"Did he talk with an accent?"

The banker admitted the man was foreign, but he had no experience at distinguishing foreign accents.

I suggested, "What was he wearing?"

"Suit, but he had the jacket over his shoulders, like a cape."

For hot weather that made sense, though American men didn't do that. "Did he wear unusual shoes?" I was thinking snakeskin boots.

"Never saw his feet."

That didn't get us very far, but it made me nervous. I explained to Ralph, "Before I left Portage Lake my old landlord, Professor Kostinsky, said someone was looking for me, a very tall man in a leather coat and snakeskin boots. Kostinsky thought the man was Russian mafia."

"When you see Putin again, ask him. Maybe he knows the guy."

We left the bank and returned to Ralph's Camry. It was starting to rain. "Looks like you'll get a free car wash," I said.

Ralph wasn't sidetracked. "Did you know about the deposits?"

"Nope. Whatever went on is still going on. When did Putin show up in the States?"

Ralph wasn't sure. "Maybe about the same time the last deposit was made."

"At least we found out that Katya is still alive or someplace."

"Not certain," Ralph said. "If that guy you talked about, the one with the snakeskin boots, caught up with her, he might have the debit card and the PIN."

I hardly dared say it. "And she might be dead."

Washington traffic was dreadful. It made me homesick for the nearly deserted streets of Portage Lake. Ralph was thoughtful as we battled commuters and crossed the Potomac heading for Virginia. "You own a gun, Glass?"

"No. Never used a firearm."

"Never hunted? You weren't in the service."

So he knew I was never drafted. "No."

"Might be wise for you to have some familiarity with firearms."

What did he expect? Did his agency, whichever that might be, expect to send me back to Northern Michigan packing heat, as they say on the crime shows? With a shudder I dismissed fantasies about being issued a Glock and a John Wayne swagger.

I remembered I had heard gunfire at the farm. There was a range somewhere on the property. If the tall Russian who was looking for me was a mafia hit man, maybe I should take advantage of our time in Virginia to get some training.

I tried to dismiss the thought. I didn't know who the mysterious man was or why he wanted to see me. Could have been a relative of one of my foreign students. I didn't have any students who fit the description-- Pakistanis, Kuwaitis, and a couple of Saudi princes but nobody over six feet tall. I didn't know if the man who spoke with Kostinsky was the same one who showed up at the bank. Your imagination and paranoia can set you off into all kinds of illogical fantasies.

We all seem to have a penchant for conspiracy theories. There's lots of absurdity, rumors, and nonsense floating around. Claim the President is a Hottentot or from outer space and you'll find followers who believe it.

This was turning into something a lot more complicated than just an interrogation of Vladimir Putin. There was that chauffeur's murder, which might have no connection at all, except for a few deposit slips. There was Katya's disappearance and the cache of money hidden in my account. And Robert, that skunk, who was still sniffing around and didn't seem to be a part of anything. Plus someone who might be an innocent or could be from the Russian mafia. It all seemed to be converging. That gave me a lot to worry about as we drove back to the farm.

It was quitting time by the time we passed through the gate. I found Ivy in our room, relaxing in bed in front of the flat screen television which was tuned to CNN. "I brought you something," I said, holding out the bag from Walgreen's.

"Oh, a present!" she exclaimed, going into her little girl mode. Her mood changed when she saw the kits. "Thanks, honey."

"Just to make certain," I said. "We've got too much suspense already."

She hopped up to head for the bathroom.

I didn't know much about pregnancy tests other than a woman was supposed to pee on them and then there'd be some sort of indicator.

It didn't take long to get the results but it felt like forever. She emerged with a beaming smile, holding the test up like a torch. "Yes!"

"Congratulations." I was still too bewildered by the implications to focus. My mind was a jumble of thoughts.

"It's too bad we can't make a phone call from here. I can't wait to tell my folks. They've been at me for years for a grandchild."

I was curious about her interview with the resident spooks. "How did it go today?"

"All right. Very friendly." She hesitated, no sure if she should explain further. "They knew about the six Metropol photographs."

I dropped into the single lounge chair. "I suppose these people know what brand of underwear I wear."

"Fruit of the Loom," Ivy joked, just to startle me. "I told them that Katya took the pictures with her when she left. I suspect there are duplicate sets floating around in some file."

"No remarks about my nice cock?"

"Don't flatter yourself, Irwin. You look good naked but you are no porn star."

"Shucks, there goes another career option." I changed the subject. "Ralph thinks I should have some firearms training while we are here."

"What?" Ivy hit the remote and muted the TV. "Are they planning to turn you into a trained assassin?"

"No way. But remember that business of the tall guy with the funny boots? The one who showed up at Kostinsky's?"

She remembered.

"It's possible he showed up at the Riggs bank. I went there this afternoon. There's more money in the savings account, and ATM withdrawals. No idea where the money came from or who used the debit card."

"You're giving me an upset stomach," Ivy said.

"Don't blame me. Blame our baby."

My brain was overloaded with information. I suddenly realized that if there was danger, it wasn't just my ass I had to cover. We were a family now. No wonder so many American households were armed against home invasion. When I was on my own in Moscow and the years afterwards I was my only responsibility. Now I had a wife and a baby on the way. No certainty that Ivy could keep on teaching when the kid was born. My instructor's pay was a spit above poverty level. I wasn't still driving a now dilapidated Ford pickup because I loved my truck. On my salary I couldn't afford something newer. Never mind the seven hundred grand in the account that wasn't mine. When the true owner of that money showed up it would likely disappear.

Someone knocked at the door. It was the frowning lady. This time she introduced herself as Ginger, which might have been another cover name, and asked us to join her at dinner.

I half expected the waiter to be Robert in his white jacket. I wondered where he was. There were enough people at the farm, all secretive as hell, so it would be no surprise to any of them if someone was evasive about his identity or purpose.

Though Ivy had wanted only milk at breakfast, she was suddenly ravenous. I guess pregnancy can turn your metabolism upside down. She ordered a spicy taco salad and it was delivered huge. I ordered a prime rib with a twice-baked potato, something we never have back home. Might as well take advantage of the opportunity. The woman who called herself Ginger ordered grilled trout. Different strokes for different folks.

It was not a social occasion. Ginger lost no time in getting down to it. "Just what's your real reason for being here, Mr. Glass?"

"Irwin."

"Alright, Irwin. Tell me your motivation."

"I was asked to be here to question Putinsky, get inside his head."

"Do you think you can be objective? After what happened in Moscow?"

So she knew all about that. My dossier must be an inch thick. "Sure. It was a long time ago. Emotions pro and con fade over time."

Ginger was adept with a knife and fork, lifted the skin off the trout and set it aside like a surgeon. "Didn't Vladimir Putin ruin your career in the State Department?" She had a southern accent, but I'm not familiar enough with the nuances of different regional dialects to place it.

"That was Robert and my boss Susan. They lied about me in their reports."

Ginger's fork stopped half way to her mouth. "So I could say your motive is to undo the damage they did to you?"

"That, too, but frankly, aside from threatening my death, I have nothing against Vladimir. He was always straight up."

"Really? A KGB officer?"

I dipped a bit of beef in the gravy. "Why not? He was all business. I admit he's evasive and hard to figure."

"And your other motivation?" Ginger asked. "People have multiple reasons for what they do."

"Well of course I'm hoping he knows where our daughter Katya is. I'm hoping for a clue."

Ginger separated the last of the flesh from one side of

the trout and was ready to flip it over. "I understand from Ralph that you'd like us to check out the ATM machines where withdrawals were made on your joint account."

"Why not?"

Ginger shook her head. "That's not our main issue, Irwin. We're after Putin, or Putinsky as you seem to prefer. He could be an asset for us if we can trust him."

At that I had to laugh and nearly choked on my mouthful. "Frankly, he's the only one around here that I could trust."

She didn't like that and her frown was back. "Don't sell us short, Irwin."

Ivy was watching both of us carefully even though she pretended to be concentrating on her salad. "Yes, Irwin. These are nice people. They're just doing their job."

That might be true, but where did their reports about contacts with me go from here? Into some case file to support money laundering charges, or to confirm the old claim that I was a paid Soviet agent? Seven hundred grand could be construed as pretty hefty pay. But for what? I hadn't done anything. I had no access to any information anyone might want. I'm a nobody, just a poor schmuck everyone dumps on. I suppose a skillful poker player can bluff his way to the big score with only a pair of deuces, but I'm no poker player. I didn't even know exactly what game they were playing and what the rules were.

I turned to Ivy. "Maybe we can persuade them that finding Katya should be part of their job, too."

Ginger admitted, "If Putin is running a cell of Russian agents and Katya is one of them, it is certainly within our purview."

That was hard for me to believe. I saw Katya only as a vulnerable kid, away from home, in a foreign country, without friends, with only a tenuous link to me as her only potential family. She certainly went far out on a limb to contact her alleged birth father in a small town in the wilds of northern Michigan. Getting that DNA test result hit her pretty hard. Was it a relief, or a shock? I remembered her crying at the doctor's office. All I knew was she soon got over it and was relieved. Our relationship was accepted. No more nonsense of fraternization and dispute with the Dean of students. Moving in with me in Kostinsky's house gave Katya a safe, secure place. It was a new life for both of us, for Ivy, too.

What I didn't understand was why Katya left as soon as she got her US passport. That still didn't make sense. She had security and her "papa" Glass, so why leave?

The conversation with Ginger had reached an impasse. I finished the prime rib and most of the baked potato, which was slightly burnt. Ivy opted for carrot cake for dessert and we shared a piece. Ginger took a pass and was about to call it a day when I asked, "Any chance I could check my email? I left my laptop back in Michigan. You know how those messages pile up."

"I'll see what I can do," Ginger said, getting up from the table.

We retired to our room. Ivy ruminated about prenatal care and baby stuff. I tried to collect my own thoughts.

Soon after Ginger knocked and let herself in. She was carrying a laptop computer. "I'll get this logged in, but I have to stand by if you don't mind."

Did I have a choice? I asked, "Afraid I might tweet Wikileaks?"

Her frown was back. "That's not funny, Glass."

Obviously the farm had wi-fi. The protocols at Michigan Institute of Technology changed all the time to keep hackers at bay. Someone was always trying to get at research secrets or to change a grade. I logged in at the university web site, passed through the fire walls and finally got to my web mail.

As I feared, there were pages of mail sent to iglass@mit.edu. In spite of the Iron Port spam filter, there was junk. The minute you order something somewhere the cookies tell half the world you might be interested in this or that product. I was always getting offers of one kind or another. But there was one message that stood out because of its cryptic nature. It was from Ivan-G@hotmail.com. I didn't know any Ivan-G. There was no subject line. The message was in Russian. The system didn't do the Cyrillic alphabet very legibly. Translated, it said simply, "I miss you—Ivan."

Who the hell was Ivan?

Ivy saw I was puzzled. "What is it?"

"Do we know anybody called Ivan?"

Ivy thought a moment. "You mean like Ivan the Terrible?"

None of my students was named Ivan, and if there was an Ivan in my classes, I wouldn't be missed. Then I remembered. I turned to Ginger, who was watching over my shoulder. "I think I got a message from a Russian teddy bear."

"What?"

Ivy remembered, too. "Kostinsky's relative, that Russian scientist, gave Katya a mascot stuffed bear. One of those pillow toys sold at the university bookstore with the MIT logo. You remember, Irwin. You pinned that red star souvenir from Russia on it and she named it Ivan."

"Yes. She took it with her when she left."

"Sounds like a recognition signal," Ginger commented.

That language almost convinced me that this business at the farm was a CIA operation.

The only recognition signal I had experienced were the halves of the incriminating photo of me in bed with Svetlana at the Metropol. Katya had produced the top half and I had the matching bottom.

"Where's the message from?" Ginger asked.

"Ivan-G@hotmail.com," I said. "Anybody can get a free hotmail account"

"What about the headers?"

The message headers show the paths the various pieces of an email message take while they are broken into bits, transmitted and then reassembled at the destination. I'm not a computer expert. I don't know how to read those.

"You think this email is from your daughter?"

I didn't know. "Could be. Or maybe I'm getting messages from stuffed teddy bears."

Ginger wanted to know if there were any other suspicious messages in my emails. We went through them but there was nothing suspicious. Of course, the best clandestine message is one that appears to be innocuous, like a lost and found, "Lost, one baby blanket."

"Want to send a reply?" Ivy asked, all business. "Just to

confirm the connection?"

I wasn't sure I should. "Won't the sender trace this back to the farm?"

"It will say it came from MIT.edu," Ginger said.

The laptop hadn't been configured for the Cyrillic typeface so I typed in English, "I miss you, too. Please come home." and clicked on "send." I didn't send our new address.

I would have liked to hang onto that laptop, but without logging off, Ginger took at away. "I'll screen your other emails."

That made me uncomfortable. I remembered that the MIT server would automatically shut down the connection after one hour, and Ginger wouldn't be able to log in again without the passwords and protocol. Then I speculated that that particular laptop might be configured to remember every keystroke, in which case, Ginger or whoever could backtrack. I was sunk. There was no such thing as privacy. Using that information someone at the farm could impersonate me and I'd have no way of knowing what or how.

If the "miss you" message was from Katya, could the email headers reveal her location? Maybe the people who maintained the hotmail list could provide the details, like name, address, date of birth of the account holder. But of course, all that could be faked, set up as an anonymous account and subject to cancellation for breaking the hotmail rules.

I guessed that would give Ginger, Ralph, and the rest of the spooks something else to puzzle over. I supposed I could use another email account, a phony one, to send myself a message just to keep them confused. Not a good idea. Ralph and his cohorts didn't like jokes. It might be funny if the "miss you" email were a red herring, just a diversion to keep them confused. I didn't think so. I told myself, Irwin, you think too much. You worry too much. The simplest explanation was likely the right one. I suspected the Ivan-G message was from Katya and she was having second thoughts for having left so abruptly.

Where was she, and what was she thinking about?

All that mental turmoil didn't make for easy sleeping. Ivy and I went to bed. We share a pair of men's pajamas. I get the bottom and she the top, wearing just a pair of lacy panties under it. I tossed and turned, kept Ivy awake half the night.

It was an early seven o'clock when someone knocked. I groggily put my feet down on the floor and remembered where I was. It was Ralph out in the hall, this time wearing a tie with gold stripes. "We have time for some arms instruction before breakfast," he explained.

"What is it?" Ivy asked, groggy with the sleep that had finally come.

"Ralph wants to teach me how to shoot," I explained. I quickly dressed in my single pair of shorts and a polo shirt. Didn't have time to shave or brush my teeth. Still shaking the sleep out of my head I joined Ralph outside our room.

"Don't forget your ID tag," he cautioned. I went back to get it.

It might not be too early for Ralph, but down in the basement of the lodge the armorer who met us at the firing range didn't look like a morning person. He was a skinny guy who might have been an escapee from the Pennsylvania coal fields and looked hung over, like he had partied too long the night before. Had he been a miner the creases in his face would have been permanently soiled with persistent coal dust. His nasal accent was Appalachian. "You familiar with firearms?"

"Not a bit."

He held up a murderous looking hand gun. "You know enough not to look down the barrel of this and pull the trigger to see if it still works?"

I guess there were people stupid enough to do that— once. I didn't want to admit I might do that myself. "I think I know the difference between a revolver six shooter and a semi-automatic."

I had now invited the contempt of an expert who had met an idiot.

Not having had a shave or a coffee, I tried to focus on the instruction. I was introduced to a pistol, was surprised at how heavy it was, and wondered how cops wore those on their belts without losing their pants or getting a bad back from walking a beat with a lopsided load. Maybe they didn't, since I hadn't seen a cop walking any beat ever. They all rode around in patrol cars. I was shown how to insert a magazine, how the safety worked, was given some careful instruction not to point the damned thing at anyone.

Then I was loaned a pair of sound deadening earmuffs, shown how to hold the weapon and aim it.

Down at the end of the range the target was the silhouette of a man.

It took both hands to steady the heavy weapon while I tried to aim down the top of it. Surprised at how sensitive it was, I pulled the trigger. It went off before I was ready.

Even with the earmuffs I was shocked at how much noise it made. Wowch! The recoil almost made me lose my grip. I didn't know if I'd hit the target at all. Gee, in the old cowboy movies I'd seen in late night reruns, Hopalong Cassidy had managed to shoot a gun right out of the hand of the guy in the black hat. Must have been a helluva a shot. Hoppalong never actually killed anybody in those movies. Just shot guns out of hands--a gentleman in the days before PG13 ratings. No blood and gore. No chain saw massacres, please. In those black and white movie days one could tell the good guys by their white hats.

I was no cowboy crack shot. If I were going to hit a barn door I'd have to be sending four feet in front of it.

The armorer muttered something not very complimentary, positioned my hands on the weapon, told me to take a deep breath and hold it, brace myself and try again.

Three full clips later, I managed to get three or four slugs more or less into the middle of the silhouette. As a marksman I'd do better grading pass/fail English papers.

Feeling very much a failure, I followed Ralph back though the catacombs of the lodge to my room. "I'm afraid shooting is not my thing," I apologized.

"You'll do alright. You just need practice."

"You think I really need this?" I'd been brought to the farm to question Putinsky, not for instruction in the fine art of self defense. I imagined some of the people being trained were learning how to kill with one blow, slit someone's throat, strangle them with a shoelace, or simply shoot their victim between the eyes.

Ivy was ready for breakfast when we got back. "How did

it go?" she asked, as much to Ralph as to me.

"Not very well," I admitted. "There's a regular shooting gallery down in the basement."

"Could I try, too?"

Ralph was amenable. "Might be a good idea."

"I've done some hunting with my Dad," she said, something I hadn't heard about.

"I'll have someone pick you up after breakfast."

Ivy was feeling better, not nauseous, and dug into the buffet with a vengeance.

In spite of the ear muffs, I felt a bit deafened and defeated by my failure as a marksman, so wasn't much for conversation.

While Ivy went for a shooting lesson, I was taken back for another session with Vladimir Putinsky. Ralph suggested I concentrate on questions about Katya. I had a different idea for my first line of inquiry.

Putin was glad to see me, as if I were a pal from the good old days, but I couldn't tell if it was just an act or his way to disarm me. I looked up at the one way glass and the invisible watchers, nodded as if to indicate they could turn on the recording machines, and got down to business, in Russian, of course. "Someone was looking for me back in Michigan. It might have been the same man who showed up at the Riggs bank sniffing around my account."

If that worried Putin, he didn't show it. "Someone went to the bank?"

"Do you know any Russian who is about six feel six inches tall, wears a long leather coat and snakeskin boots?"

In spite of his usually cool poker face, Putin telegraphed a startled emotion. "It is possible. What else about him?"

"I don't know. Maybe you know someone like that?"

"Maybe."

It's hard to extract anything from that man.

"How about this? I got an email in Russian from someone with an address Ivan-G. Said I was missed."

Putin didn't get it, or was pretending. "You are missed?"

I tried again. "In Russian it said, 'I miss you—Ivan.'" I corrected myself. "Signed Ivan."

"Ah."

That was it? "Ah?" "Ah, what?"

"What do you think?" Putin asked, turning it back around to me. Nothing like answering a question with a question.

"I think it's a message from Katya. She has a teddy bear named Ivan."

Putin actually smiled then looked serious. "That makes two Ivans."

"What does that mean?"

"I do not know this teddy bear, but I do know a tall Ivan. He could be your visitor."

"So who is he?"

"Russian mafia. A killer. Perhaps it is he who is missing you."

Two Ivans. That added ambiguity. "You think the message came from Ivan the Mafia killer, and not Ivan the teddy bear?"

Putin was enjoying this. "You lead a complicated life, Irvin."

It was like fencing with an opponent who might be concealing a dagger in the hand behind his back. "Tell me more about this mafia Ivan."

"He is very dangerous. He is very jealous of his money."

"Is the money in my account money you stole from him?"

Putin shrugged. He wasn't going to admit anything.

Wherever the money came from, and whoever put it in my account, I was sure it wasn't wages Putin had earned. Running from Ivan the mafia guy was a pretty good reason to go to the United States on the pretext of asking for political asylum.

"So, Ivan. Maybe you could describe this man for your keepers here," I suggested.

Putin shifted his shoulders. He wouldn't commit himself.

I tried another approach. "Back in Moscow, are you still with the police?"

Putin said, "I was not police."

I sighed with frustration. "What about State Security?"

"I was with State Security."

Emphasis on past tense. What was he lately? Fired? If

Putin had been canned, maybe before he left he had used his access to draw money out of the state coffers for his own use, sort of a personal, prepaid pension fund. Or maybe his investigation into the Russian mafia got him a means to tap into their assets. Or he might have infiltrated the Mafia as part of his job and then gone over to crime.

Whatever the reason, he'd had to leave the country.

At this point, I was convinced that finding Putin's Katya was secondary to his saving his own hide. Parlaying his KGB history in exchange for a US government stipend was a good idea.

I shifted my questioning to Katya. "Tell me about Katya." I then went though what I could remember of the questions Professor Melamed had asked her when we were at dinner at the fish restaurant. Where did she live in Moscow? What school did she go to? And so on.

Near as I could remember, I got the same answers. In fact, the answers sounded like exactly what Katya had told us. What was this, a rehearsed script? A memorized cover story? I decided to ask something different. "Did you send her to America, or was it her own idea?"

"Is safer for her to be in United States."

Was that an answer? Not exactly, but it did reveal something. Safer from what? Katya had not come to the states just to find her birth father. I had provided a potential destination or an alibi, but I was not the only reason for her leaving Moscow. Katya had said she was estranged from Putinsky, that he was a "very bad man." If the estrangement part was true and she had no contact with him, he had nothing to do with her leaving. If she was afraid of him, she didn't have to travel across the Atlantic to escape. She could have gone anywhere in Europe. Weren't borders open now?

Did Katya know about the money put into our joint account? I wondered. The account may have been only for Putinsky's convenience, but then we had found an envelope she had left behind from the Riggs bank. There was no telling what it had contained. It might have been junk mail, some sort of offer as banks frequently made, or a statement.

At that point I shook my head in frustration and stood up from the table. "This isn't getting us anywhere," I

286

confessed. "Do you know why money was put in my account in the Riggs bank?"

"The money is not for you."

Ah, now we were getting somewhere. "For who, then? For Katya?"

"It was only temporary, to be moved later."

"Except I moved it first, thanks to the IRS."

Putin didn't know IRS.

"Internal Revenue," I explained. "The tax office. I was billed for taxes on the interest on the account."

Putin showed embarrassment. "An oversight."

"So?"

He wouldn't elaborate. It was a small triumph for me to get him to admit he'd made a mistake, a chink in his armor. If I found out his other weaknesses and played upon them, maybe he would tell the truth. I was beginning to understand why some interrogations took months. Interrogating prisoners was not my expertise. I was happy enough to get a student to confess to having cheated on an exam.

"Time to take a break," I announced to whoever was listening. I stood up, ready to leave as soon as the door was opened.

Putin was taken away and the gang of four came in, Ginger, Ralph, and the two unnamed men in suits. "Time we compared notes," Ginger said, her frowning mouth stiff with determination. She was clearly impatient.

One of the two gray men, the one who appeared older, addressed me. "What do you think, Glass? What's your assessment?"

"Putinsky's hiding something, but I sense that he's vulnerable. He's in some sort of trouble or he wouldn't be asking for political asylum. I still can't figure out what's with Katya. She told me they were estranged, that when he was told by Svetlana..."

"Svetlana?"

"His wife. Katya told me that Svetlana was abused. I can understand that, if she was forced to pose for naked blackmail photos. That would be enough. Svetlana might have told her husband Katya was not his child just for spite. Then they divorced. Katya said Svetlana died of breast cancer, which left her at loose ends. That's one version of the story, what Katya told me to justify her search for me as her birth father."

Ralph pursed his lips thoughtfully. "Sounds plausible."

Ginger didn't buy it. "It's a cover story. I don't think they were estranged at all. I think he coached her. For all we know she's not his daughter at all, but a trained agent playing the role."

I didn't believe that.

The younger of the two men in suits had his hair cut military style. In an authoritative voice, he reported, "We got a notice that the Russian government wants Putin, or Putinsky as you call him, extradited. We are assured it's not political and they make a good case. He's wanted for criminal prosecution. I do not believe he qualifies for political asylum."

Ginger agreed. "When we've interviewed him he only hinted at being able to provide us with sensitive material. So far he's given us nothing of any substance."

"He's too cagey for his own good," I commented.

Remembering how we went to war in Iraq on two unsubstantiated nuggets of trumped up information—biological warfare factories that didn't exist and yellow cake uranium on a forged document-- maybe all Putin needed was one state secret to reveal at the right moment. That would be his hole card in this game of international poker.

Ginger didn't appreciate my interruption. "In any case, he's past history. The Soviet Union is no more, nor is the KGB he once worked for still in existence, not as he knew it."

As an academic I agreed that there was little hope for Putinsky to find a job at an American university. Hell, even with my fluent Russian I couldn't find a school that needed me to teach the language. The best he could get would be an adjunct position, not tenure track, and subject to budgetary whims and internal politics.

"So we send him back?"

They all agreed, except me, but I had no authority. They would deport Putin as a less than desirable irritant. Throw him on the mercy of the Russian prosecutor, if any such mercy was to be had, or worse yet, throw him to the mafia wolves if that was the reason he had fled.

Putin would be worse off than I was when I was dumped back in the States in the clothes I stood in, no money, a cancelled passport, no job, and a change of underwear in a plastic garbage bag. I felt a great kinship for him. He was, after all, family. Sort of.

It was too bad. For all his sneakiness, I kind of liked Vladimir. He was a cool adversary, but in spite of his devious nature I could live with that. Some people you just don't ask questions.

"How long does it take to deport him? Does he have to go through months of appeals with INS, or do you pack him in a crate and fly him to Moscow along with a case of Jack Daniels in the back of the military attaché's old C-46?"

They wouldn't say. The old "need to know" argument.

"Then I'm done here," I said. "So when do I go back to Michigan?"

Ginger gave me a cold look. "We're not done with you, Glass. There's still that business with Katya to clear up, and a business of money laundering, in case you forgot."

"That's not why I was asked to come here," I complained. I suspected that all along it was Katya they were after and Vladimir Putinsky was only an excuse.

"We'll talk about it later," Ginger said.

So it was going to be my turn to be interrogated. I thought they knew everything about me already, down to the brand of underwear I wear and, damn them, even the size of my cock. "It's a waste of your time," I pleaded. "I'm not anybody. I'm just a loose thread in all this alleged business."

Ginger's rare smile showed her teeth. "Sometimes when you pull on a loose thread a whole seam comes loose."

"I assume my sessions with Vladimir Putinsky are over. Can I say goodbye to him?"

Ralph thought that was OK.

I left the room feeling like a criminal who's been arrested but doesn't know yet what charges are being brought. We went outdoors into the steaming Virginia summer and walked about a hundred yards to one of the cottages where visitors were sequestered. It was like an old tourist cabin. No porch, but just enough overhand to provide shade for the guard sitting outside in civilian clothes and reading a Sachs mystery novel.

"Just having a word with Putin," Ralph explained to the guard, and whispered to me, "Not a word about what was discussed at our meeting."

I nodded.

The cabin was simply a bed-sit with an adjoining bathroom. There was a TV set, windows on three sides with views of the grounds, minimal furnishings—a bed, chest of drawers—similar to an average motel room, but no ubiquitous mirror over the bureau. I presumed that if there were watchers, there were hidden cameras.

It was an uncomfortable visit, like a final farewell to a man on death row. Putinsky was sitting at the desk, writing what looked to be a letter. I said, "I'll be going back to Michigan. If Katya shows up, I'll tell her about our conversations," I said it this time in English so Ralph wouldn't think I was concealing anything.

I had to assume everything we said was recorded. Somewhere down in the basement of the lodge there must be an army of people transcribing bugged conversations, stamping them "secret" and putting them in folders. Some world we live in! Back in Moscow it was the KGB snooping. Here in the States it was our own people.

Putinsky gave me a look that said he understood he was finished. He looked older, beaten. He gave me a wan smile and extended his hand. He said in English, "May you live well, Irvin."

Surprised, I shook hands with him and realized he had slipped me something. I held it in my fist and put it in my pocket and as soon as we went out the door.

"Lunch?" Ralph suggested.

"Sure. I'd like to freshen up, first. That interrogation room makes me feel unclean."

In a stall in the lodge bathroom, hunched over and fairly certain I wouldn't be observed, even by the intrusive eyes that were everywhere, I took out what Putinsky had slipped me. It was a note scribbled in Russian. "Get me out of here."

How was I supposed to do that? Even if I had the

means, why would I do it? It would only cause me more trouble. Sometimes I thought trouble was my middle name.

I was so suspicious I considered that it might be a setup, a trap to test my loyalty. Maybe I had appeared to be too friendly to Putinsky. Again the government, for all the perversity, was likely to dump on me.

Ivy was waiting for me in our room. She was excited, her eyes shining. I've never seen her so hyped up. "Say hello to Annie Oakley," she said.

"Hello to Annie Oakley."

"Seems I'm a crack shot," she said.

"Really?"

"They even let me try out an assault rifle. Bam, bam, bam bull's-eye!"

"Did you get the prize? I mean, do they give you a souvenir Glock to take home in your checked baggage?"

"No. We'll have to buy one. I hear they're pretty expensive."

"Don't you need a license in Michigan?"

She already had the explanation in the form of a brochure. "No, but you need a background check and a five day waiting period. You have to register the weapon with the sheriff's office. If you have a training certificate that says you are not likely to shoot yourself in the foot or your neighbor and don't have a police record, haven't been convicted of a felony, and haven't been served with a no contact order— stuff like that—you get a permit to carry a concealed weapon."

"Me? I don't think I can do that. Government records still suggest I'm a paid Soviet agent, a security risk."

"But I can. There's a fee, of course," Ivy said. :"Sixty bucks."

"I guess that's to keep out the riffraff." So much for the second amendment. "Are you going to do it? Buy a firearm?"

"Might be a good idea, considering the dangerous life you lead, Irwin."

"Will they give you the training certificate here?"

Ivy laughed. "Are you kidding, sweetie? They'd have to write it in invisible ink, stamped secret. To the outside world this place doesn't exist."

Made me feel more inadequate than ever. Not only could I hardly hit a target, but even though it was false, with my record I probably couldn't even buy a firearm of any kind unless it was a Red Rider BB gun. Portage Lake wasn't Detroit, home of the twenty-five dollar Saturday Night Specials.

"Not to belittle you or anything by changing the subject," I said, "but my talks with Putinsky seem to be over. I thought we were done here, but now they want to question me. Seems it's Katya they're after." Then I whispered, "Don't say anything. Look at this."

I showed her the slip of paper Putinsky slipped me. Of course, she couldn't read it. "What is it?"

"A plea for help. Putinsky wants out."

"What are you going to do about it?"

I shrugged. What could I do? I couldn't even leave the farm myself without someone like Ralph tagging along.

Were we being watched from outside our room? I looked out the window. Someone in a big straw hat was pretending to be gardening, perfunctorily snipping at a bush beyond the flagstone patio. At first I thought it might be some illegal alien working off his probation or something, but then he looked right at me. I recognized him. It was Robert in another disguise. No waiter's white jacket this time. Now he was a grounds keeper. Man of many guises.

I motioned him to come to the window.

He looked to both sides, and cautiously approached.

I held Putinsky's slip of paper tight to the glass. I knew he could read it. I'd done my reports for him in Russian back in Moscow and he had no trouble reading them.

He pantomimed "You?"

I shook my head, and he understood.

Maybe Robert could get Putinsky away from the farm. Just so I had no part of it. Whether Putinsky's chances were better if he worked his way through a hostile bureaucracy or if he went underground I couldn't know. My own tactic would be to play the agencies against each other but I wasn't Vladimir Putinsky. How did you win in the old Soviet Union? Latch onto an important figure and be bootstrapped to the top? Or did that risk losing your sponsor and mentor in the next purge? In our society elections were our own form of revolution and ours were bloodless. Defeated officials became highly paid CEOs or consultants to think tanks.

In Stalinist days people disappeared, were banished to the Gulag Archipelago of Siberian prisons, or simply shot in the back of the head with or without a show trial. But here?

Putinsky might fight through the courts, stretch his appeal for asylum out for months. But we also had our black operations. He might get the treatment I got. I had no opportunity for appeal when I got in that trouble in Moscow, no grievance committee. I just got hustled anonymously aboard that old C-46, what the flyboys called a flying coffin. Gone. Maybe Robert would spirit Putinsky away, but to where? Back to Russia?

Robert motioned that I should come outside and talk to him.

I whispered to Ivy, "Come along. Let's take a little walk in the garden before lunch." I needed a cover.

Ivy joined me. Wearing our guest badges we passed the gatekeeper at the front entrance and went around the building to the patio outside our room. The lodge was air conditioned and the heat in the garden was oppressive. Too bad we couldn't just lounge by the pool under an umbrella with a nice, iced drink. So far this had been no vacation.

Robert motioned that we should follow him to the hedge. Maybe the trees weren't bugged.

I spoke first. "Is it still Robert, or do you have a different code name nowadays?"

He was, of course, much older than the Marlborough smoking security guy who had ruined my life in Moscow and shipped me out on the military attaché's plane. He was deeply tanned and there were crow's feet wrinkles around his eyes. He had one of those upper lips that can look good sprouting a thin, trim mustache. He'd put on weight in the twenty years since I'd seen him last, most of it in the middle, and his cheeks were full, signs of too many heavy meals.

"Robert will do," he said. "And this would be...?"

"My wife, Ivy."

"Hartshorn," he added.

So he already knew. What else did he know?

"I looked for your mug shot on the farm file," I said. "Didn't find you. Why not?"

"I'm ex-officio."

"What does that mean?"

He adjusted the rim of his gardener's straw hat. "I'm here and I'm not here."

"Not with the same department or agency as before?"

"Past history," Robert said. "Thanks to you. You fucked me up."

That was a shock. I could feel my blood pressure elevate a few points. "I fucked you up? You've got to be kidding. You ruined my career. Said I was a paid Soviet agent."

"An exaggeration. Chalk it up to being overzealous. Mistakes tend to follow you around."

"You're telling me? I even got put on the No-fly list, thanks to you."

Robert obviously didn't care or didn't want to hear it. I persisted. "So you admit you were wrong in reporting that I was a paid Soviet agent."

He nodded. "Mistakes happen."

"Then how about if you make a retraction? Expunge my record."

Ivy chimed in, "That would be the right thing to do, Mr. Robert. You have no idea what trouble you caused with what you admit was a mistake."

It's hard to get some people to admit that they were wrong. Everyone else's fault. Robert's excuse? "I don't know if I can. I have no access. I left the agency and joined Whitewater."

Left or was fired? "The mercenaries." I said it with contempt. I didn't like the gun toting Blackwater bullies that got kicked out of Iraq for shooting innocents, only to be reorganized under a different name. I knew those guys were paid a thousand bucks a day like that CIA agent who shot two alleged robbers in Pakistan, claimed to have diplomatic immunity and had to be bailed out with blood money to avoid prosecution. "What's Whitewater doing here at the farm?"

"Can't say."

"No doubt."

"How about you?" Robert asked. "Still up to your old tricks?"

"I never had any tricks," I said. "Came to check out Vladimir Putinsky, now called Putin. He wants to make some kind of a political asylum deal with immigration."

"That what the note's about that you showed me?"

"Could be."

Ivy was listening uncomfortably. She knew most of the story of my debacle in Russia and I'd told her about Robert. I wasn't prepared to forgive Robert for ruining my career, but if he overstepped his own limits and got canned for it, he got what he deserved. I handed him the bit of paper Putinsky slipped me. My mother has an expression, "Let's you and him fight." "Putin wants out. I think he realizes he's about to be deported. I suppose he wants to go underground. He's a slick operator. Might steal an identity. He has resources."

Robert cocked his head thoughtfully. "If I get him out of the farm, maybe he'll lead me to his contacts."

Getting a good grip on Putinsky would be like a fisherman trying to hold onto a slimy bullhead. Grab it in the wrong place and get punctured by a poisonous spine.

Just so I had no part of it. Some people can't let go of their old job. Must be the thrill of being an insider working under cover. They go on in the life style even though they are no longer on the payroll. Robert, the one man counter intelligence agent? Or was Robert working with the government? Was this Whitewater a rogue organization? Maybe he was really FBI hoping to play good cop, pretend to rescue Putinsky from the INS or whoever those men back there in suits were, and follow that lead to the source of the mysterious cash.

It would be amusing if Robert's actions got him arrested for aiding or abetting and thrown in the slammer as offenders called prison. Couldn't happen to a nicer guy. That would be a sweet revenge for me. Screw you, Robert. "Why don't you try it?" I suggested.

I think Robert took the bait. He said "Thanks" and slipped away.

Ivy gave me a searching look. "What are you up to, Irwin?"

"I'm just trying to stay out of trouble," I said.

She laughed.

"We may need help getting out of this place ourselves, honey. I didn't say anything about this before, but I suspect they let you come along so they could hold you as a hostage in case I don't cooperate to their satisfaction."

"You're scaring me." She did look scared.

"When we do get back to Portage Lake, I think you'd better get a concealed weapon permit."

"To use against what enemy, Liebchen?"

She doesn't call me Liebchen unless she's being ironic. "I wish I knew." It would be a relief to get back to peaceful Portage Lake. I might have had a dispute with the Dean of Students, but university intrigues didn't end with gunfire or bodies in the trunk of an abandoned car at the airport.

"Do you think he can clear up your record?"

"I don't know if he's willing. The folks here at the farm think I'm a suspicious character. When I was questioned by the FBI years ago they said they didn't have enough evidence to charge me, so maybe they're looking for more. Let's get some lunch. Sure your morning sickness will tolerate it?"

We went back into the cool. The dining room was crowded, but we found a table in the corner where we had a modicum of privacy. It didn't last. Without an invitation Ralph joined us. He'd ditched the yellow tie. Weather was too hot. Ralph wasted no time but asked, "Who was the guy you were talking to out there?"

"You don't miss a thing, do you? That would be Robert," I said. "The guy who didn't show up in the roster of mug shots. He was the one who delivered our food when we arrived, only then he was wearing a waiter's jacket, not a straw hat."

"Really?" Ralph's skepticism suggested that he, like the others in that house of spooks, didn't believe any story.

I caught the drift. "He's a Whitewater mercenary. Who the hell do they work for, anyway? I thought Whitewater did security work in Afghanistan and Iraq, not Virginia."

"You making this up? Been listening to conspiracy radio?"

Irritated, I picked up the photocopied menu listing the

daily specials to show him I was more interested in food than his prying curiosity. "When I tell you Ivy and I are space aliens waiting for the mother ship, then you can assume I'm making it up."

"Don't be so sure," Ivy chimed in. She gave Ralph the evil eye. "We might be picked up any time. You ever been probed?"

Ralph stood up. "I get it. Sorry to have asked."

Mercifully, he left us to have a meal in peace. Ivy and I shared a Denver with a heaping side of French fries suitably dipped in ketchup.

Ivy considered, then declined sharing a piece of Black Forest cake. Her stomach was upset again.

I asked, "Morning sickness?"

She nodded. "I wish I could call my folks. Mom would be so pleased that we're pregnant. She's been bugging me about a grandchild for years."

We're pregnant? I hadn't thought about it that way, but I guessed she was right. She wasn't the only one having this baby. We were, though I didn't have the benefit of morning sickness. When I looked at Ivy's face closely, I could see what I think they call the mask, the subtle change in facial features that comes with pregnancy.

This was adding a new dimension to our lives. It was too bad that we had no access to a phone at the security obsessive farm. I wondered when they'd return my cell phone and Ivy's iPod.

Our privacy wasn't to last. Ginger, the frowning lady, came by, leaned over the table, helped herself to a French fry, and told us they wanted to discuss Katya. Since Ivy had been in on the story from the start they wanted both of us in the hot seat. "Informal, of course," Ginger promised.

Fat chance of that.

Well, I'd set something in motion. I'd got Robert off my back with the assignment of spiriting Putinsky off the farm. Maybe Ralph would set up a night watch for space aliens. Everybody's entitled to his own conspiracy theory. If it weren't so serious, I could enjoy this.

Seriously, I hoped I could enlist government resources in the search for my daughter. Wilson of the Marquette FBI wasn't interested in a runaway kid, what with potential spies and terrorists on the Tech campus. The spooks on the farm seemed determined to prove Katya might be a spy, not just a kid needing a Dad. Were they that paranoid about every foreign student? But of course, not every foreign student had a father who was in state security, or had been.

I was sure Katya was innocent, caught, like me, in the grinding gears of government subterfuge. To find her I had no resources beyond my Facebook appeal. I didn't have many Facebook "friends." As long as the government spooks helped me find her, that would be enough.

If Katya wanted to have her own life, that was her right. Her abrupt disappearance was such a shock and a disappointment that I needed closure. That might be the most I could hope for. Once I had that, we could move on with our lives.

The room we were taken to for the "discussion" about Katya was a comfortable lounge. A big, white sectional, U-shaped sofa was set up around a coffee table complete with a tray of mugs, a big Thermos pump of coffee, and even a plate of assorted cookies--chocolate chip, peanut butter, and oatmeal.

Ivy, never shy, pumped herself a cup of coffee and picked a chocolate chip cookie. Her appetite had returned.

The room was different, but the agency participants were the same. The two men who had worn suits had left their jackets behind and were down to short sleeved white shirts, ties, and the usual ID tags on lanyards. The informal appearance was superficial. They had not become friendlier, didn't introduce themselves.

Ivy was having none of it. She went around the room, extended her hand, and said, "I'm Ivy Hartshorn, Irwin's wife. And you?"

Good for you, Ivy. She wormed names out of them, Rick and Charles. Rick was the older one, the one with the military haircut. Of course, there was no telling whether those were their real names.

"And I'm Ivar Gregorovich Lenin," I said, "Master Soviet spy."

"You're not being funny, Glass." the one called Rick

said.

Ginger put the banter to rest. "Tell us how you first met...' she consulted her notes..."Katarina Volodna Putinsky."

Ivy had been the first to notice the Russian girl outside our office, so she began the story. Ivy thought I had a groupie, a student with a crush on her instructor, except Katya wasn't one of my students.

I explained the non-fraternization agreement and how I couldn't meet with Katya privately without risking my job at the university.

I grudgingly had to accept the likelihood that copies of the six incriminating photos taken at the Metropol were in the files and that our interrogators had all read transcripts or heard Putinsky's remark, that Svetlana thought I had "a nice cock." I skipped to the business of the recognition signal, Katya's upper half of one of the photos of me having sex with her mother.

So far whatever I said seemed to fit the record Ginger and the others had. I didn't know how much information the agencies shared. I puzzled over the possible interagency connections. Maybe they got the story from Wilson, the Marquette FBI agent. He had interviewed Katya himself.

Then I told about the DNA test, the evidence that proved Katya was my daughter after all, and the process we went through to get her US citizenship.

Rick, the man with the buzz haircut would have lit a cigarette but Ginger reminded him that the farm was a smoke free establishment. I guess booze was OK, but not tobacco. That told me Ginger was farm cadre and Rick was an outsider. He put the pack in his pocket and gave me a hard look. "Just for discussion, Glass. What if Katya is not your daughter after all?"

He was trying to revive my old doubts. "The DNA test proved it," I said. "I was there when the doctor took the swabs to send to the lab."

Rick nodded. "And the lab report came back positive."

I looked at Ivy. What was he getting at? "Right."

"What if—just for the sake of argument, I'm saying— what if someone at the lab made a mistake? Or if the lab was penetrated and the technician's report doctored. What if Katarina is not your daughter after all?"

That floored me. "I don't know." Who would have known about the test outside the university? I assumed only my department head and the dean of students knew, but I didn't trust Mrs. Houghton, the department's busybody secretary. She always regarded me as low level junior faculty. Suspicion, suspicion.

Ginger was eager to follow up on the theory. "What if the girl posing as Katarina Volodna Putinsky is actually a trained Russian agent who memorized and rehearsed the cover story?"

I remembered how nervous Katya had been, how uncertain, how vulnerable. There could be lots of reasons for her vulnerability, one being that her cover might be blown. I stammered, "I suppose that might be possible."

Charles had his own two cents worth. "Another possibility, Glass, is that you're a sleeper agent waiting for your partner to show up with that recognition signal."

Ralph got into the act. "We know from your conversations with him that you are actually friendly with Putin or Putinsky as you call him. You just told me that you were conspiring with a Whitewater agent to spirit Putin away from the farm."

Ginger exclaimed, "What?!"

"That's not exactly true. Putin slipped me a note asking me to get him out of here. There's no way I could help him escape if I wanted to. I passed the note on to Robert."

Rick was furious about that. "You had no authority..."

"Of course not. I have no authority to do anything. You guys asked me to question Putinsky, like you thought I knew him. I only met him three times and that was twenty years ago."

"Still..." Charles started to say.

I wasn't finished. "Look. I don't work here. I'm not on anybody's payroll. I haven't taken any oaths of secrecy." I turned to Ralph. "Ralph here was present when I told Putinsky goodbye. That was the sum total of our conversation."

Ralph had to agree.

"But you passed the note to this Robert fellow," Ginger said, like it was some sort of a crime.

"So what?" I wasn't about to reveal that, since he wasn't going to retract his claim that I was a paid Soviet agent, I hoped Robert would be arrested for aiding and abetting Putinsky's escape. One has to have some secrets.

Ivy's eyes were wide open with astonishment. She gave me a look that said she wasn't sure the accusations weren't true.

"And you've been laundering money Putin got into your Riggs bank account," Charles added. "We know about that."

I was still reeling from the suggestion that the DNA report might have been falsified. I couldn't believe it. I didn't want to believe it. The qualification that the theory was "Just for the sake of argument" was unnerving. God, these guys were skillful at breaking people down. Had I been betrayed again? This was too much.

"I don't know anything about that," I insisted. I remembered how Katya tearfully called me her papa. Was it all an act? If so, she was a convincing actor.

I shook my head to clear my thoughts and studied all their faces. "Do you actually believe that I struggled to rebuild my life for twenty years, moving from one academic shit job to another, to build a cover story as a sleeper agent? Are you all nuts?"

Rick sat back on the couch and smiled. "Just testing you, Glass."

I was really confused. If they were trying to shake me up, they'd succeeded. I tried to pump myself a cup of coffee but I couldn't hold the cup, had to settle for a peanut butter cookie which I nibbled while I tried to cover my confusion.

Ivy took my hand in a gesture to calm me down.

Rick's was a bewildering suggestion. I went back to the Katya business. "Suppose someone did deliberately falsify the DNA test. Who would do that? Why? Do you actually think some foreign agent would know the test was being done and change the results, or pay someone at the lab to do it? That's preposterous."

If Katya was planted by Putinsky, I couldn't believe he had the ability to engineer a false DNA report. They all admitted it was an unlikely story.

I tried to turn the tables. I could plant a seed of distrust and confusion, too. "If one of you were aware of what was going on in Portage Lake and at the university, would it be an advantage to you to assist Katya, to support her cover story? Who are you guys working for, anyway? Is there a mole in here who wants Katya's alleged role as a spy to succeed?"

They all looked at each other. I could see that no one in the place was sure of anyone else. I went on. "What purpose could there be for a Russian spy to pose as my daughter? If she's a spy, what's her mission? She doesn't have any access. She's just a student."

Charles corrected me. "You mean she was a student, until she split."

He was right. I still had no idea why she left us so abruptly, no explanation, just gone.

Rick pumped himself a cup of coffee, stirred in two of those little packets of cream, and studied me. "You teach English as a second language."

"Right." Of course, he must already know that, along with my brand of tighty-whities.

"Tell me about your classes."

I wondered what Rick was getting at. "Foreign students. Some are very good, though they learned British English in their home countries. Others struggle, particularly the Chinese students. We have a special section for them."

"Why's that?"

"Chinese tend to learn language by rote, to read and translate, not to speak aloud, and they have trouble with pronunciation. We have a Chinese professor the Yooper kids can't understand."

"Yooper?"

"Kids from the Upper Peninsula. Dey talk like dat dere, hey," I said, imitating the localisms.

Charles asked, "You have Moslem students?"

"Sure. Kuwaitis, Pakistanis, a couple of Palestinians, even a Saudi prince. Our foreign students are impressive. Some will end up in high public office when they return to their home countries." I was reminded that many terrorists had actually gone to American universities.

Rick had his own agenda. "You think you could spot a foreign student who might be of service to us?"

"You want me to be a spotter for the CIA?" If personal contact with Katya had nearly cost me my job for fraternization, what trouble would I get into if I got too cozy with other foreign students? "I don't think so."

At that point we were interrupted. Someone I had never seen before knocked, quickly entered, and whispered something to Ginger, then left.

Ginger seemed upset at first. With some difficulty she n recovered to announce, "I just learned that Vladimir Putin has left the farm."

"Hah!" I exclaimed. The announcement threw me. It didn't take Robert very long. I wondered how he did it. Did he kill the guard, distract him? With his paunch and at his age Robert didn't look like he was in good shape for hand to hand combat. Maybe Robert had other Whitewater cronies on the farm, waiting to assist.

An instant later I suspected the announcement was a trick, a staged theatrical ploy to get me to reveal something. Just goes to show how you can be so confused you don't believe anything.

If Putinsky had actually slipped out, I reasoned that our interrogation would be over as Rick and Charles went off in pursuit. If the announcement were genuine, they'd leave at once. If it were faked, they'd sit tight and watch for my reaction. On another hand, maybe they counted on farm security to go in pursuit.

Ivy was confused. She whispered to me, "Do you think it's true?"

I didn't know. "If we assume it's true, that Putinsky is gone and Robert got him away, I guess the next step is to figure out where they've gone. If I know Robert, he's going to try to get Putinsky to lead him to Katya."

Ivy was thinking, too. "And Putin will lead him on a wild goose chase to win time until he can get away on his own."

Ginger wasn't about to lose control of the proceedings. "That leaves us with only you two to track down this Katarina Volodna Putinsky."

I was tired of all this sparring. I simply wanted to leave.

303

Being on the farm was an interesting foray into the dark side of our conflicting government agencies, but I didn't enjoy being in the hot seat. I'd had a fantasy about a nice trip to Washington, to visit the Smithsonian, the Holocaust Memorial, and other tourist stuff. Instead, at the farm we were virtually under house arrest. "For sure Katya's not going to try to contact me here at the farm. If she does at all, it will be back home in Michigan. It's time Ivy and I flew back to Portage Lake."

"And do what?" Ginger asked, her frown as stern as ever.

"And wait," Ivy said and squeezed my hand in solidarity.

I thought all that nonsense about me being a sleeper agent needed to be put to rest. "Yes. She waited twenty years for the contact, which is pretty good considering she's only eighteen herself. Must have been born to the task. Maybe she'll wait another twenty years to reconnect." How old would I be then? Sixty-five? I shook my head in mock despair. "Being a sleeper agent is so tedious."

Ginger was like a pit bull that never lets go. "We still haven't talked about that account you have at the Riggs bank."

The money was something I had a weak alibi for, an unconvincing story. I realized that moving it out of savings into a separate checking account was a mistake. My reasoning was that if I had to pay tax on the interest, I could draw on it, at least for the tax and penalty. What I could not explain was where it came from, who put it there, why it came to me, and what it was for.

"I couldn't say." It was the truth.

"You mean you won't say?" That was Charles. I could imagine him reaching for his rubber truncheon to beat a confession out of me.

"I don't know. Anybody can deposit money to your account. Maybe it was a mistake, like in Monopoly, 'bank error in your favor'." I explained the bit about the hundred dollars Putinsky was supposed to deposit for me, which hadn't happened, at least not by the time I visited the bank to ask. "Any guess I might have would be pure speculation."

Ginger followed with, "And you knew nothing about the

304

driver who was killed."

"Nothing at all. Mystery to me."

There was a break in the discussion. Ivy helped herself to another chocolate chip cookie. I was suddenly weary. It was time for my after lunch nap. We had talked long enough.

Ralph had been quiet most of the time. Now he suggested, "I think you should move the seven hundred thousand back to the savings account. We can track any withdrawals."

"You mean, find out what ATM machines are used for withdrawals and get the surveillance photos?" That was something I couldn't do to find Katya. It was a good reason for me to go along with the suggestion.

"Right."

I agreed.

"Can we go now?" Ivy asked. She was ready to split, too.

Ginger asked, "You mean, back to Michigan?"

"Yes," I said. "We've told you all we know and if Putin is gone, there's no point in my sticking around. My conversations with him didn't yield much."

"We'll talk about that." Ginger turned to Ralph. "Show them back to their room."

I was confident that this would end our time at the farm. When we got back to the room I told Ivy, "Let's pack. I think they've had enough of us."

Ivy reminded me, "What about the bank accounts?"

"I suppose I could fix that with a phone call, if they let us make one. Being in this place is like being in a convoy at sea under radio silence."

Ivy had settled into the mentality of the spooks. "I suppose they'll think you'd phone some other number and pass on a coded message."

"Oh? And drop some password? Like saying I hear it's going to hit a hundred? Or where can I play a round of golf?"

"More subtle than a phrase like 'the cock crows at midnight.'" She laughed.

That sounded like something I once heard over East German radio. Maybe she had heard the same when she was a student in Berlin.

"We'll have to wait until we get out of here." I could

305

hardly wait to get away from the eavesdroppers, people who had no business knowing anything about our private lives. It would be a relief to get back to our rented house, knowing that nobody was listening to what we had to say.

Then I remembered we'd had a break-in and the house was a designated crime scene. The snoops were supposed to go through it looking for clues, fingerprints, which was why they had taken ours. What if they also planted hidden cameras and microphones? Paranoia is a terrible affliction.

"They didn't ask about one thing," Ivy reminded me.

"What?"

"Snakeskin boots."

"We've never seen the guy. Couldn't identify him. Kostinsky was the one who thought he was Russian mafia. Putinsky thinks his name is Ivan, like Katya's teddy bear."

"Ivan the Awful. What about the bank clerk?"

I'd told Ivy about that. "Might not have been the same person. There's more than one very tall, sinister character. Look at the NBA." I was alluding to overpaid basketball players who got in trouble with the law.

We packed and waited for the next development. CNN had a story of another congressman caught in a lie and another EU country going bankrupt. The world was full of turmoil.

To our relief, Ralph came in with a pair of vouchers for our air travel back to Michigan. He had another official letter permitting me to fly. I'd hoped the permission letter I'd used to get to Washington was open ended, that with it I might fly to Ocala and visit my parents. No such luck. It was like my old passport, stamped valid only for immediate return to the United States. We were to leave the next day.

Eager to escape the watchful eye of our keepers, I asked, "What about the morning shuttle? Can we take it into the District?"

"I think that would be OK," Ralph said. "One leaves at nine AM after delivering the morning shift."

That was OK. "Why don't we take advantage of the swimming pool while we're still here?" Ivy suggested.

"Great idea." We changed to our bathing suits, mine a minimal Speedo and Ivy's a scanty two piece. I wondered how long she would be able to wear it as her pregnancy progressed. Should she be swimming, now that she was pregnant? I didn't know.

We grabbed bath towels, and passed the receptionist. She didn't insist we were accompanied, which gave me the idea that if we wanted to escape the farm, we could do it in bathing suits, pretending to head for the pool. But of course, where do you go in just a bathing suit? I'm not cut out for daring do escapes.

Nobody at poolside bothered us. It was great, an hour of sun and a swim to cool off, to try to forget the turmoil going on inside my head. I enjoyed watching Ivy swim. She has a great body and can do those flip turns that always leave me dizzy with water up my nose.

Ralph still wouldn't leave us alone. He insisted on joining us at dinner, offered to buy us wine from the cash bar. Ivy would have accepted until I cautioned her about pregnancy and alcohol. I declined, too, because I'm still wary of anything alcoholic. I've never forgotten that fatal glass of vodka at the Metropol.

"So what are you going to do when you get back to Michigan?" Ralph asked, being friendly.

Ivy said, "We're still settling in. And we don't know what happened with the burglary."

"You think you'll follow up on that firearm suggestion?" He was referring to Ivy's success at the firing range in the basement of the farm.

"I might."

Ralph turned to me. "How about you, Glass?"

"I'd probably shoot myself in the foot," I admitted. Even if I wanted to buy a firearm, I wasn't sure my incriminating record would pass the background check.

To celebrate our impending departure, I smeared shaving cream all over the mirror in our room to confound anyone behind it if it was one way glass. We had sex but kept ourselves concealed under the sheets.

Of course, there might be cameras, and microphones, so I put on a show of making loud groans and cries of ecstasy. If those gossips joking about my "nice cock" were still at it, I'd give them something to write about in their reports.

Ivy had a great idea for our airline reservations. If we set up our flight to Chicago so it arrived too late for the only evening flight to the Houghton County airport, we could stay overnight and visit her parents.

We might get some personal benefit out of all this madness after all. The Hartshorns would be delighted to see us and Ivy could tell them about her pregnancy. Neither of us have much family, having no siblings. It's a sad consequence of small families, kids with no uncles or aunts, no brothers or sisters, and all too often only one present parent.

Ginger joined us at breakfast. I figured she must be on a diet, just coffee and whole wheat toast. Ivy's morning sickness was back and she had oatmeal and tea to settle her stomach. We were ready for the shuttle when it arrived. The receptionist returned my cell phone and Ivy's I-pod. We'd failed to turn them off and the batteries needed to be recharged.

The shuttle was a nondescript, white, twelve passenger bus similar to the ones used by nursing and retirement homes to shuttle patients and old folks on outings. Ralph gave the Hispanic-looking driver instructions and stayed aboard as far as the gate, then left.

Once in town we took a cab to the Riggs bank to transfer most of the mystery money out of checking and back into the savings account. I tried not to look suspicious myself as I checked out the bank security guard and anyone who might be watching for us. I knew already that it could be anybody, that woman filling out a deposit slip or a guy in a polo shirt and slacks who seemed to be taking a long time getting a cup of free coffee. I couldn't tell if we were being shadowed. In B movies the followers always looked sinister, trench coats and fedora hats, but in real life the pros were so slick you could never spot one.

The bank kid remembered me. He was wearing the same jacket and tie he had on the first time I saw him. I guessed maybe it was his only work uniform.

I asked, "Any more signs of a very tall man wanting to know about my account?"

None.

That was a relief. At least, I hoped it was.

Had there been any withdrawals from the savings account? I'd left a small balance just to keep it active.

"No, but there was a deposit."

"You mean, before the deposit I just made?"

"Yes. Ten thousand was deposited yesterday."

"Cash? Check?" I asked, my heart thumping with excitement or trepidation. I couldn't be sure which.

"Wire transfer."

So whoever had made deposits before was still at it. Maybe the dead chauffeur had been replaced.

That news distracted me. I had trouble focusing appropriately on our sightseeing. We had most of a day in Washington for touring. I had never had enough time when I was passing through years ago. Instead of flying out of Dulles, we opted for a Chicago flight out of Reagan National, an easy connection using the subway system.

There was a delay at the Union Station stop. Some kind of disturbance. Maybe there'd been a report of a suspicious package, something like that. Ever since 9-11 Homeland Security is justifiably hyper. Uniformed cops walked through the car. I was glad I don't look like an Arab in case they were racially profiling.

At the airport, waiting in the long line at the check in, we were both suddenly very tired. Our vouchers were approved, seats found for the next flight to Chicago where we would have to change.

Using a pay phone Ivy phoned her parents saying we could be staying overnight and could they pick us up? Her mother was overjoyed at the news of Ivy's pregnancy. It was hard to get her off the phone.

We made it through security with no trouble and proceeded to the gate, grateful to be on our way. The attendant started boarding the first class passengers. Naturally, we'd be in coach.

Then there was an announcement over the PA system. "Will Irwin Glass come to the reception desk?"

Oh, shit. Now what? I reported to the check-in desk. "I'm Irwin Glass."

There was a uniformed cop waiting there. "You can't leave. Come with me."

"Both of us?" Ivy asked, shocked.

"You can go," the policeman said to Ivy.

When Ivy saw the policeman she joined me. "I'm not leaving without him," she insisted.

"What's this about?"

"What man over there." The policeman pointed.

Damn it, it was Ralph again.

"What is it this time?" I demanded. "Ivy's folks are meeting us at O'Hare."

Ralph was actually apologetic. "Sorry. I'm afraid I need you for an identification."

"What is it?"

Ralph wouldn't say. Ralph's old Camry was parked illegally at the curb, guarded by someone whose appearance spelled detective, that air of arrogance that goes with immunity from parking tickets. Ivy and I piled into the back seat.

"I think I should have stayed in Portage Lake," Ivy complained as we slipped into Washington's evening traffic.

"Just think," I suggested, "You might have met our burglar—or burglars."

Ivy muttered, "Good reason to buy a gun."

"Good reason not to be at home."

Our destination turned out to be a tourist destination suitable only for crime writers or people with a macabre taste. It was the morgue.

An identification? I didn't know anybody in Washington. If it was Putinsky, the people at the farm could identify him.

We went through a sign in procedure and Ivy and I were led into a cold room smelling of disemboweled corpses, a combination of formalin and feces. I'd smelled it once in a hospital when someone was doing an autopsy. Cutting open someone's rotten bowels is an affront to the nose.

The body was under a sheet. The middle-aged, Asian-American attendant, to my astonishment, was eating a Mounds candy bar. Though the smell in the morgue was revolting to me, I realized your olfactory senses would soon be deadened. I guess you can get used to anything. Like Dr. Kostinsky used to joke about Russia, even get used to hanging if you hang long enough.

The sheet was pulled pack to show the face.

The pressure of a bullet entering a head can cause the eyes to bulge. It was an unnatural look, but there was no mistaking who it was.

"It's Robert," I said. "At least, the man who calls himself Robert. What happened?"

The attendant was still chewing on his Mounds bar, but crumpled the wrapper and put it in the pocket of his lab coat. "Typical hit. Two pops to the head. Probably a silencer."

My shock quickly changed to a sense of guilt. Was this my fault? Robert was my old nemesis, the cause of many of my troubles, but I didn't wish him dead. I'd needed him to somehow cancel out that old paid Soviet spy accusation, but now that would never happen.

I'd passed Putinsky's note and suggested Robert might help the Russian escape from the farm. Did this mean that Putinsky had somehow got hold of a gun and shot him? Or had Putinsky led Robert into a trap? Maybe there was a dead drop somewhere in the District. I could imagine a hidden key to a luggage locker or a safe deposit box. There was no knowing. Had Putinsky been with Robert? Or told him where to go and set him up? Was there a stakeout watching the place? There were all kinds of scenarios for someone with my fertile imagination. "Where did it happen? I mean where was he found?"

Ralph tucked his yellow tie inside his shirt so it wouldn't drag over the body as he examined Robert closely. "In the subway. Weren't you on the subway at Union Station today?"

How did he know that? Why wasn't I surprised? How foolish of me to assume that we were free, not shadowed to confirm or deny continued suspicious about me! "We were sightseeing. The train was delayed."

"Yes," Ivy added. "Our car was searched. We thought maybe someone had suspected a bomb."

Ralph actually told us something, a departure from his usual evasions and non-committal neutrality. "He'd been at the back of the train, last car. The victim wasn't noticed at first."

"Pretty bold," Ivy commented. "Shoot someone in a public place."

"There are surveillance camera in all the cars," I suggested. "Maybe the tapes will catch the shooter."

Ralph gave me a suspicious look. "Did you kill him Glass?"

"With what? I haven't seen Robert since the farm."

Ralph's smile was sardonic. "Just trying to rattle you, Glass."

"I'm already rattled. So who is Robert? I mean, really? Did he carry any ID?"

Ralph had a mental list. "Several passports. Swiss, German. In the name of Michael Mitchell, Frances French. Seems to have had a penchant for alliterative names. Makes them easier to remember."

"Drivers license?" I asked.

"Virginia license in the name of Ronald Rudolph."

I wondered if Robert knew who he really was himself. Maybe he was like Peter Sellers who played so many diverse roles that he was unsure of his own personality. How many cover stories did Robert have to memorize?

Ralph shook his head. "It's stupid to carry more than one ID at a time. Cops do get suspicious."

"No doubt," I agreed.

"Can we get out of here?" Ivy asked. "I'm going to be sick."

The attendant started to lead Ivy out of the room to a toilet. She didn't make it, puked in a bucket already full of something unspeakable. She was so upset she started to cry.

I tried to gather myself as the three of us left the room. I suggested, "If you review the subway surveillance tapes, look for a very tall man."

"Thanks for the tip," Ralph said. "Sorry you've missed your flight. We might get you on a red eye."

Back at the airport Ralph gave me a worried look. "Take care of yourself, Irwin." It was the first time he called me by my first name. "Whoever got this Robert character is probably after you, too."

"And Putin," I added, using the name Ralph was used to. "Maybe the subway tape will show whether Putin was the killer, whether he was with Robert or not."

"We'll find him," Ralph said.

"If you do, maybe he'll lead us to Katya. I still have no idea where she can be or what she's up to."

"Who would she know?" Ivy asked as we stood in line again at security screening.

I took off my shoes and dropped them into one of the plastic bins. "If she really is a Russian spy like Ginger and the others think, maybe she has some contacts."

"I don't think so," Ivy said. "She might go to Florida."

"What?"

"To Ocala, to meet her grandparents."

"Geeze, I never thought of that. I'd better warn them."

Just to make me worry even more, Ivy added. "If mister snakeskin boots, Ivan the Awful, has the same idea, your folks could be in danger."

Wasn't it enough that I had all those bad feelings about possibly sending my old nemesis, Robert, to his death with my little ploy about getting Putinsky away from the farm?

I couldn't fly to Ocala. My permission letter from the government was good only for the flights back to Michigan.

We settled into our seats on the late plane to Chicago. Ivy sat with a barf bag at the ready on her lap. It was one of those jumbo jets. As soon as the seat belt signs were turned off I walked the aisle looking at faces, hoping not to find a very tall man with the look of a Russian mafia killer, whatever that was.

We arrived at O'Hare on what must have been about the last flight of the day. The airport was strangely silent and deserted, very different from the gauntlet of jostling passengers we had struggled through to get to the Washington flight.

Ivy's parents met us. They both looked exhausted. Her father asked why we had missed the original flight. I didn't want to explain.

Ivy explained, "We got bumped."

I hoped the smell of formalin and putrefaction at the morgue hadn't permeated our clothes.

We were all so tired that there was no conversation as we made our way to the parking garage and the Hartshorns' station wagon. I fell asleep in the back seat on the way to their house.

It had to be a short visit. Ivy and I tumbled, exhausted, into the small double bed in the Hartshorns' spare bedroom. It had once been Ivy's room, but any mementos of her childhood or adolescence had long since been removed. At least her parents still lived in the old family home. The house I had grown up in in South Bend, Indiana had been remodeled by the new owners. I had revisited it, a mere drive by, when I first got the job at the IU-PU South Bend campus. The place looked different with plastic siding and fake shutters decorating the windows. You can't go home again.

In the morning Mr. Hartshorn proudly showed me his well-appointed basement workshop where he had created that wedding gift cuckoo clock we had mounted on the kitchen wall back in Portage Lake. A frugal man, he prides himself on making wonderful things out of scrap lumber.

Ivy dodged her mother's questions about what we did while in Washington. I went as far as to say we stayed at a resort in Virginia where we could lounge by the pool. That wasn't so far from the truth. You don't have to tell people everything.

"Wasn't that expensive?" Mr. Hartshorn asked. He's a man who watches his pennies.

"We were guests," I said, hoping that wouldn't lead to more questions. If he were really inquisitive, he would ask, "Guests of whom?" I would have had to say something like "old associates from my work in the State department," which wasn't exactly true, unless you counted Robert. It's a slippery slope into deception. 'Oh, what an ugly web we weave,' my mother used to say, 'when first we practice to deceive.' Fortunately, like most people Mr. Hartshorn didn't follow up.

The paranoia of life at the farm had affected Ivy, too. She cautiously asked, "Has anybody been around asking for us?"

Her father shook his head. "No."

"Any phone calls?"

"Why should there be? You don't have any debt collectors after you, do you? No unpaid credit card bills?"

Ivy reassured them that we were paid up. At least for now we were a couple of DINKs, Double Income, No Kids.

Ivy's father reminded us. "But you do have a kid, your Russian daughter. When do we get to meet her?"

"I don't know. She got her US citizenship and disappeared."

Now I had to go through the whole business again, about discovering she was gone, packed up, fled, and our finding my truck at the airport. It revived my old pain, a worry made worse by the assumption, rightly or wrongly, that some people in Washington thought she was a spy using me for her cover story.

That shifted the conversation away from the doubtful explanations of what we did in Washington to plans for the coming baby, the likely date, would Ivy have ultra sound to determine the baby's gender, etc. It was too early for that.

What a relief it would be to be in a normal life after those days of continual surveillance and all those questions. Others doubted us, but we knew who we were. We didn't have to justify our existence. We didn't need an alibi or a cover story to be just Irwin and Ivy, a couple of teachers in the humanities department of a Michigan engineering school.

The only moment that nearly blew my cover came when Mr. Hartshorn said, "I thought you didn't fly."

Ivy hastened to explain. "The ban's been lifted,"

I gave her a sharp look. I'd have preferred she say something else. So far as I knew, I was still on the No-fly list, our current trip being a one time exception.

The Hartshorns were affable, but I sensed they were uncomfortable, that they instinctively felt we were hiding something, not telling the whole story. Maybe they suspected there was something in our relationship with Katya we might be ashamed of or wanted hidden.

Ivy's mother, it turned out, like to read true crime stories. The Chicago newspapers were full of wild stuff about sexual abuse, incest, and murder. Would Mrs. Hartshorn think Katya hadn't run away but was buried in the basement? Good grief.

There was nothing salacious about our relationship with Katya. We hadn't actually lied about our trip to Washington, either. The farm was a sort of a resort, if you looked it that way, and we were sort of guests, even though we'd felt like prisoners under house arrest. I don't lie to anyone, but some

315

things don't need to be told. There was validity to that old "need to know" policy.

To tell the truth, I was glad to get away from the Hartshorns. Not that I don't like them, but I don't like having to be evasive. It makes life too tense.

We arrived back in Portage Lake on the afternoon flight, paid the parking fee, and returned to our rented house with its crime scene yellow tape across the front door. We wondered what to expect when we got inside.

Except for a broken window pane at the vulnerable back door, there was no damage. Someone had gone through my school papers, leaving a mess, and our clothes had been dumped out of the drawers in Ivy's old chest of drawers.

Nothing seemed to have been stolen. The only item of value, besides our laptop computers, was the cuckoo clock mounted on the kitchen wall. It was powered by a couple of weights shaped like pine cones. I had to pull the weight back up and restart the clock. It had to be done every day. The mechanism would run about thirty hours between pulls. I restarted the clock. Cuckoo-cuckoo. I wished Ivy's father had installed a shut off for that mechanical bird so at midnight it wouldn't wake up everyone in the house. That was why I set it up in the kitchen.

We had to restock the larder, throw out milk that had soured while we were away. The town felt strangely different. I realized it hadn't changed, but we had. Life on the farm was like being on a different planet. Washington was crowded, noisy. Though Portage Lake wasn't immune to murder, those were not a daily occurrence like our crime-ridden capital. The UP was peaceful and laid back; Ivy and I were still wound up.

On our way home from the Wal-Mart super store Ivy said, "I think we should stop at a gun shop."

"You're taking Ralph's suggestion seriously?"

"You betcha. What's a Yooper without a gun in the house?"

"You're not exactly a real Yooper."

"Might as well play the part, now that I have tenure."

"Don't rub it in." I hadn't achieved tenure at any of my teaching jobs. Everything about my tenuous teaching career had been temporary. In spite of being married and hired at

Da Tech as the locals called the university, I still felt insecure.

There's a gun store across the Keweenaw Waterway in Hancock. We drove over the massive lift bridge, the tires singing on the steel grating, and parked across the street from the gun store.

This was foreign territory to me, racks of shotguns and rifles on the wall behind the counter. The display counter showed a confusing array of handguns, revolvers, semi-automatics, holsters and the like under the heavy glass top. There were gun cleaning kits with little wire brushes, stuff like that, and a cabinet with drawers holding a variety of ammunition of all sizes. This was not my world, or was about to become my world whether I was uncomfortable with it or not.

I hung back, apprehensive. Even though the multitude of rifles, shotguns, and handguns on display would not have been loaded, they still struck me as menacing. I admit I'm gun shy. That may explain why I was such a poor shot in the firing range in the basement of the farm. I was plainly afraid of the Glock, an irrational anxiety that, instead of the bullet flying out the business end, it might explode.

Ivy, on the other hand, handled weapons as if she were familiar with them. She showed her ID and filled out the necessary papers. When the five day waiting period was up, she could pick up a semi-automatic hand gun.

Ivy was carefully handed a 9 mm Glock, which I recognized from my disastrous experience at the basement range in Virginia. She saw that the chamber was open. She did not have need for an extended clip, which had been made illegal anyway after that senator was shot in Arizona.

What did the regular clip hold? Nine bullets? I guess you could have ten if you started with the chamber already loaded.

I wondered what caliber weapon had been used to kill Robert on the Washington subway. With all the ambient noise of the subway train, a silenced pistol would not be noticed. What did it do? Instead of pop-pop, just a pfft-pfft?

I shuddered when I found out how expensive the weapon was.

"Want to heft it?" Ivy asked as she handed the Glock

over to me.

I declined. I didn't want to touch the damned thing.

She gave me an admonishing look, "Why, Irwin, I think you're afraid of guns."

"You could shoot your eye out," I said, a lame allusion to the Christmas story movie about the kid who wanted a BB gun.

"And your head with it," the gun shop owner added, taking the weapon back. He was dressed in an appropriate costume for a gun shop owner—a khaki jacket with lots of pockets. The only thing missing was a bandolier of ammunition over his shoulder like some Pancho Villa bandit.

Ivy had a suggestion. "Since Ralph recommended that we have a gun, why don't you pay for it out of the Riggs account? Chalk it up as a business expense."

"Chasing old KGB agents and spies is not our business."

"Some people are great," Ivy said, quoting someone. "Others have greatness thrust upon them."

I didn't feel so great. I was glad to be back in Michigan. We should be safe, away from the spooks and those sometimes menacing bureaucrats with ID tags, no names. I was reminded that we'd been told the house would be checked for fingerprints not ours. For all I knew, they'd also planted bugs and we were still being watched and recorded. Why did all this stuff happen to me?

Once the Wal-Mart groceries were put away and we'd thrown away the junk mail that accumulated while we were away, I plugged in the power supply and inspected my laptop computer.

I didn't notice anything unusual, but then, if someone had loaded some kind of sophisticated malware into the system I wouldn't have found it. I logged onto the university system to check my email.

Sure enough, amidst the spam and junk there was another message from Ivan-G@hotmail.com. No subject line. Russian text. "How is Ivy?"

I assumed this was sent by Katya and not Ivan, her stuffed teddy bear. "I have talked with Vladimir," I wrote. "Please come home and I will tell you all about our visit."

I was hoping Katya would return, but after I hit the send

button I realized the mail could have come from that other Ivan, the Mafia killer Putinsky had identified. Nothing like sending an invitation to someone who might have been the man who popped Robert, a.k.a. Michael Mitchell or Ronald Rudolf or whoever. Why do I do these things? I just keep falling into shit.

The next morning I walked the few blocks to the campus to check in with my department head. I breezed by Mrs. Houghton, his hostile secretary, and found Waarala in his throne room, behind the big desk. His is the only office with a carpet. Waarala has his degrees in prominent display on the wall, not that a degree from anywhere non-techncal would impress the engineering faculty at Michigan Institute of Technology.

Without asking, I closed the door behind me. I didn't want Mrs. Houghton snooping. "Ivy and I are back from our trip," I began.

"I noticed." Waarala closed the manila folder he'd been consulting. It's the time of year when they screen candidates for the few vacancies created when the old timers retire--for every opening a couple of hundred applicants desperate for a job. I know that feeling well.

I didn't know where to start and how much Waarala needed to know. "I want to thank you for making that call to let us know the house had been broken into."

"That number you gave me was kind of odd. The person who answered wouldn't say who she was or where. Where the heck were you, Glass?"

I swallowed. "At a place they call the farm. It's in Virginia. The government wanted me to help with the interrogation of an old KGB officer."

Waarala's eyebrows went up. "You?"

I didn't want to invite more questions but I was stuck. I could trust Waarala, but not his secretary. "Old story. Vladimir Putinsky is the parent of record of my Russian daughter."

"The girl who took off?"

I nodded. "Right. He's asking for political asylum but Immigration wants him deported. It's one of those interagency squabbles."

319

Waarala shook his head. "Glass, you come up with the most amazing stories."

I took a deep breath and tried to make light of it. "Irwin Glass, Man of Mystery." I clearly had too many connections for being a mere instructor of English for foreign students.

Waarala was amused but not necessarily a believer. "Next you're going to tell me the FBI wants you to write reports on all those students studying English as a second language."

I thought he was joking. "Not yet," I assured him.

It wasn't a joke after all. "You wouldn't be the first."

So there was more to the Humanities department head's job than shuffling class schedules. "That's not all I came to see you about," I added. "There was a murder while we were in Washington."

This was trying his patience. The amusement was gone from Waarala's demeanor.

"It's important that you keep all this confidential," I cautioned. "Whoever did the killing in Washington..." I paused and swallowed. Just saying this made me weak in the knees. "May be after me, too. Your neighbor, Professor Kostinsky, said a tall Russian came to his house. Might be after Katya, who if course isn't here, or me. Did your wife by any chance notice him?"

Waarala didn't know.

"If someone calls asking for my new address, will you let me know? I could use fair warning."

"I'm not likely to be asked. Those calls go to Mrs. Houghton."

Mrs. Houghton. As the executive secretary she was supposed to keep her mouth shut, but I suspected she was a key department gossip. "Could you tell her that you don't give out the addresses or home phone numbers of the faculty?"

"That's already our policy, but anybody can look that up in the directory." Waarala was referring to the university's staff directory. It was distributed only to the staff. Even the university switchboard operators didn't give out that information. The system was automated anyway. If Snakeskin boots Ivan called in, he wouldn't know the routine. I hoped that, as a foreigner, he'd be even more befuddled than we were, having to go through those automated systems that told us to push one for English. There was no push number for Russian.

Waarala made a half-hearted promise to let me know in the unlikely situation that he was asked for my address. "Any word from your Russian daughter?"

I shook my head. Everyone knew she had disappeared.

As I turned to leave Waarala tried to reassure me. "She'll call, Irwin. She may come back."

I walked back to the house. Ivy was on the phone to the sheriff's office, asking about where she could get the certificate from a local gun club saying she was qualified to apply for a concealed weapons permit. She was going whole hog on that gun business.

"I think I'll call Ralph at the farm," I said, when she hung up. "Maybe he can send the film clip from the DC subway surveillance cameras. Might show who shot Robert."

"You're playing detective?"

"Self defense," I pleaded.

"You think Putinsky shot him?"

"Can't imagine. If Robert got him away from the farm, why would he? And where would Putinsky get a gun? He probably escaped in just the clothes he stood in."

"Ah," Ivy said, putting on a sarcastic conspiratorial pose. "Maybe Putinsky knew where a weapon was stashed, waiting for him to pick it up, along with money and a forged passport."

I protested. "You're making fun of me,".

In spite of Ivy's intention, it was possible. There was no telling what Putinsky's resources were at the Russian embassy. If the chauffeur had secretly made those bank deposits it couldn't be official embassy business. Putinsky might have a network of allies. I had to admit I couldn't rule anything out.

I'd have to gamble that Ralph or someone at the farm would be able to get hold of the surveillance tape from the DC subway system and send the file as an email attachment. If we were really lucky, the image would be clear enough to make an identification. It was just a thread, but it was all I had.

Ivy made a connection with the Chassell Sportsman's Club where she could obtain the necessary certificate that said she was competent to qualify for a concealed weapons permit. I didn't go along. I heard they have beagle contests there, wild game dinners in deer season, stuff like that.

I did know from stories in the local Mining Gazette that the sportsmen were opposed to the out of state hunters who came to the Upper Peninsula with packs of radio collared dogs to track down bears while the hunters themselves sat drinking in a local tavern until the radio signals indicated that the dogs had treed their quarry. It wasn't sportsman like. The local hunters hated it.

The gun lovers and hunters are a culture different from mine. My father, a South Bend teacher of Social Studies in Northern Indiana, never had interest in hunting. We never even had a dog, though Mom had a cat once that got bitten by a raccoon, contracted cat leukemia and had to be put down. In Florida she had a parakeet until it flew away and joined a flock of feral budgies. Ours was not a successful animal household.

My tenuous contact with the farm, that innocuous telephone number, paid off. I got an email addressed to iglass@mit.edu and the hoped for attachment.

The surveillance camera on the Washington, DC subway didn't take streams of action but a sequence of still pictures. The camera was mounted at the front of the car, and Robert had been sitting at the back. I finally did spot him, though he was largely obscured by other passengers. There were some people standing, too, so the view of people at the back was not very good. It helped that the one very tall man at the back of the car was probably our man. It certainly wasn't Putinsky, who was a shrimp by comparison.

The quality of the images was pretty good. Two of the pictures did show a very tall man at the back of the car next to Robert. You couldn't tell what he was doing back there, but there was one clear shot of his face. Was it enough to make an identification?

In the sequence the subway must have stopped, for there was a shuffle of passengers and the tall man was gone. The last picture showed Robert slumped against the window, apparently asleep. I knew he was dead.

That was it. Was it enough?

Using Photoshop I enlarged the head portion of the only image that might be useful and made several prints.

I showed them to Ivy. "What do you think?"

She thoughtfully bit her lip. Ivy doesn't wear makeup. The only time I ever saw her wear lipstick was at our wedding at the Super 8 motel. "It's not conclusive."

"Sure, it would be better if the cameras caught him pointing a pistol at Robert's head. He might have concealed it under a jacket carried over his arm."

"Robert was on the left side of the car," Ivy said. "The tall man is facing forward. Could he be left handed?"

"Too bad we can't see his feet in the pictures." I was thinking about the notorious snakeskin boots.

We were only guessing.

"I'll take these up to the airport. If he is the one who came to Kostinsky's door looking for me or Katya, he probably came in by plane."

Portage Lake is six hundred miles north of Detroit, about five hundred from Chicago, farther from Detroit than Detroit is from New York City. When I drove up in my pickup it took me ten hours from Chicago, but now the truck is old, what the locals call a beater suitable for bashing through the old logging roads to hidden beaver ponds and fishing holes deep on the woods. I have to keep the truck under the speed limit for fear of blowing a gasket. The alignment isn't so hot and at sixty the Ford starts to shake and threaten to dance off the pavement.

To tell the truth, most of the Copper Country vehicles look like hand-me-downs, the dregs of the down state used car auctions. It's not uncommon to see a pickup truck with fenders and body panels that look like lace rust. Unless our quarry rented a spanking new SUV or something like it, I couldn't see this Ivan the Awful, Russian Mafia killer, driving up from Chicago or Detroit. If I were a hit man, I'd want to get in and out again as quickly as possible, but then, it's not my line of work. What do I know?

It was a chilly summer day, even for the Copper Country, my first full summer in the U.P. I drove up to the

323

Houghton County airport with the photoshopped pictures of our suspected killer. When I saw the United Airlines clerk on duty I thought I was in luck. It was Mrs. Kiusku, Ivy's once German student, who had checked us in on the flight to Washington via Chicago O'Hare.

It was the quiet time of the day between the rare flights. There was no one at the Hertz car rental desk.

"Hi," I said. "Remember me? Dr. Hartshorn and I flew out of here a week or so ago."

She remembered the government travel vouchers and the special letter permitting me to fly.

I showed her the pictures from the subway. "Does this guy look familiar? The tall one? Did he come in here?"

Mrs. K studied the photos, shook her head. "I wouldn't notice the arrivals."

"What about departures?"

"Sorry."

"I was told he wore a long leather coat and snakeskin boots." Women pay attention to shoes.

She shook her head. "I'd have remembered snakeskin boots."

Again no hit. I wasn't feeling so lucky after all.

She had an idea. "Why don't you ask at operations? He might have come in on a private plane. We have plenty of those."

I hadn't thought of that. I went around the corner to the operations office and knocked at the closed window. A man in his late fifties, grey hair, eyebrows that needed a trim. The name on his badge was Waatia. Another local Finlander.

About forty percent of UP residents are of Finnish descent, the largest such population in the country. There's even a Finnish college in Hancock, Finlandia University, known innocuously as FU.

I introduced myself and showed the pictures. "Do you remember a very tall Russian, might have worn a leather coat and funny boots?"

"Yes. He came in on a twin engine turboprop. "

Bingo. The date matched the approximate time Kostinsky had given me.

"Charter or rental? If he had chartered a plane, wouldn't

324

it have a pilot and co-pilot? Did he fly it himself?"

Waatia had been interrupted at his work and found my questions an intrusion. "We have about forty families that fly in here all the time. Some have pilots, but most fly themselves."

Forty fly-in families? From what I'd seen of the Copper Country it was the Appalachia of the North. In the days before the automobile mining companies built houses near the mine shafts so people could walk to work. The mines are long since closed, but most of the old houses remain. The hamlets like Baltic and Florida Location consist of old company houses that were sold off for a dollar a room when the copper mines closed. Some of those old houses still have the original clapboard siding. Who were those people who were rich enough to own airplanes?

"What was the Russian guy like?"

"Smart ass," Waatia said. "Didn't like the price of our fuel. Left without topping up."

What did that tell me? That our Russian was cheap? Maybe he didn't like being ripped off. If it were the latter and the seven hundred grand was his, that might explain the dead embassy chauffeur. I had to admit it was all speculation. There might be no connection between the dead chauffeur hanging from a bridge over the Potomac and the hit on Robert in the subway. I knew nothing except that the photos from the subway showed someone very tall next to Robert.

"Name?"

"Don't remember. He signed in." Waatia thought a moment. "He had to file a flight plan."

I wasn't familiar with flight plans. Talking down to me like I was some school kid doing research for a class, Waatia explained that pilots had to file flight plans so in case they went down the air patrol knew about where to start looking. That the Russian refused to pay the Houghton price for fuel probably meant that he would have to set down somewhere on his way, possibly Grand Rapids. What was his ultimate destination? Washington?

With great reluctance, Waatia dug out the flight plan and showed it to me, never letting go of the page, like he thought I'd steal it and run off. The flight plan gave me the tail number of the plane. The signature was illegible.

I didn't know anything about renting an airplane. It wasn't like walking up to Hertz, showing your credit card, and driving away. Whoever rented the plane had to have a pilot's license. Did our Russian have the right documentation? Maybe he was like Robert, with multiple identities and IDs.

I'd suspected the birth certificate Katya had might be a forgery. The KGB could produce any document. What about the Russian mafia--if this really was a mafia guy? I didn't know that.

I had to admit I knew nothing. I didn't know Robert's real name. I didn't know if Katya was for real. I felt so dumb sometimes when I looked in my mirror I wondered, "Who's that?"

OK, I had learned something. Though the photos from the subway weren't exactly studio portraits, I had a good idea of what the man looked like, now tall he was, his odd choice of footwear, that he had a thing about money, and—of course—that he was a killer.

And he was after me.

I began to wish that I only had Robert or Putinsky to worry about. Robert was dead, and Putinsky was turning into family. Strange how relationships can change.

I paid Waatia five bucks to make me a copy of the Russian's flight plan with information about the plane. As I turned to leave the terminal, Waatia showed he was actually curious about my questions. "What's this all about?"

"The photos were surveillance pictures from the subway in Washington, D.C. The tall Russian is a suspect in a murder, maybe even two murders. He came here looking for me and didn't find me, but he might be back."

Waatia looked like he thought I lived in fantasy land.

"If he shows up," I continued, "maybe you could phone me. Give me fair warning." I gave Waatia my phone number. As an afterthought I added, "Don't tell him he's expected."

"You want me to call the state police, too?"

If Waatia thought mine was a cock and bull story, he wouldn't be able to convince the state police at the post in nearby Calumet. "I'll check with them myself. This is really police business."

Mulling over my next course of action, I drove the seven miles back to Portage Lake. The only stations I could get on my radio played screaming rock, evangelical harangues, or tedious classical music on WGGL, the local public broadcaster.

As I drove, I reasoned that the Russian had to take a taxi from the airport. Would the Neil's Cab driver remember the tall Russian? I was willing to bet there'd be no tip. I'd call them just to confirm the identification, like, where did the driver let him off? Was it at Kostinsky's house? Did the Russian stay overnight in one of the motels? Or did he just turn around and fly back to wherever he came from?

The Ford's engine had developed an alarming knock. With a growing certainty that it was time to have it towed to Manninen's junk yard, I parked in the driveway.

Still on the trail, I called the cab company, but hit a dead end.

I phoned Prof. Kostinsky, first at his office in the Electrical Engineering building—not there—then at his house which Katya had shared with me until she split.

Kostinsky was glad to see me. "How are you, Irvin? All moved in to your new place?"

We still hadn't unpacked all the books. "Is one ever done?" I changed the subject and showed him the photos from the Washington subway. "Is this the Russian who came looking for me?"

Kostinsky was thoughtful as he held the copy. "Is possible. Where did you get photograph?"

"It's a surveillance picture taken in Washington, DC We believe this man killed someone on the subway."

Kostinsky handed it back like it might blow up in his hands. "I told you be careful, Irvin."

"I just hope he doesn't come back."

"Any word from your Katya?"

"Maybe. I got an email from Ivan-G. Like Ivan Glass. That would be the name she gave her teddy bear."

"Did your daughter say where she is?"

"No. I told her to come home. Her father is in the country."

Kostinsky's eyes widened with surprise. "Her father? But

you are her father."

"I am her papa. Her Russian father is Vladimir Putinsky, ex KGB. Now he's in this country asking for political asylum."

Kostinsky laughed. "It is like Bolivia after the great war against the fascists. Some Jews went to Bolivia and who did they meet there? Old Nazis also escaping."

"Yes. It's a strange world. In Moscow I thought Putinsky would kill me. I was in Washington to interrogate him. He is old now and in trouble. Now we are like family, sharing a daughter. It is strange."

A refusenik, Kostinsky had seen almost everything. "Like you say, politics make strange room mates."

"Bedfellows," I corrected.

I did not want to go into the business with Robert, the Whitewater rogue agent, or my visit to the DC morgue. Kostinsky had obviously never gotten over his old Soviet fears and didn't need a flashback.

At least Kostinsky affirmed the identity of the tall Russian.

Next step? Call the farm and tell Ralph, or whoever he was, how far I'd gotten. I could fax a copy of the flight plan and Ralph could turn it over to the FBI if he wasn't already FBI himself.

Even though we had been introduced, Mrs. Kiusku, the United clerk, Ivy's ex-student, had not been able to help. I was lucky to get something out of Mr. Waatia. Could I canvas the local motels, in case the Russian had stayed overnight? Visit all the restaurants to see if he had eaten someplace? If I were the police I could get away with bothering people with questions, but I'm not an official of any kind. Anyone could just blow me off, saying the information was confidential. The clerks at the local motels were not likely to be as cooperative. A motel registry could be filled in with false information. I was rapidly running out of steam.

I called the farm. The gatekeepers in the government bureaucracy reminded me that the farm wasn't like the Keweenaw. You couldn't just walk up casually and actually talk to someone in authority. All I got was to learn Ralph wasn't there. With growing frustration, I explained, "I've got a lead on the man who shot the Whitewater agent on the Washington subway. Who do I send it to? Do you people have an actual address?"

I was told I could hand over what I had to the local FBI, which meant Mr. Wilson over in Marquette, or I could send an email with a jpg image of the flight plan as an attachment. If my message made it through the spam filters all it took to nullify my investigation was to hit the delete key. Some people never opened attachments. They were afraid of viruses.

I showed Ivy the copy of the flight plan. She couldn't read the signature, either.

The printer Ivy and I share can also scan documents. I booted up my laptop, hooked into the printer/scanner and made a jpg of the flight plan.

When I logged onto my email account at the university there was a surprise message in the midst of the junk. Another hotmail tickle from Ivan-G. Could Katya be using her teddy bear's account name, or was it from that other Ivan, the one who killed people?

In Russian: "Where is Vladimir?"

My reply: "I don't know. Are you Katya? If you are, please come home." I hit the send button and hoped for a reply. In case it wasn't Katya, I didn't send our new address.

Ivy was standing behind me with her hands on my shoulders. Biting her lip, Ivy said, "I think you'd better talk to the Portage Lake police."

I knew the Portage Lake police kept banker's hours. At night there was no one on duty. Twenty-four hour protection was the venue of the Houghton County sheriff.

Actually, we were served by three police agencies: the city, the county, and the state. As for the FBI, agent Wilson was a hundred miles away in Marquette. He might be involved in under cover investigations checking on people who grew marijuana in the state forests or who cooked meth in the trunks of their cars, but those activities were invisible to me.

The five day waiting period was up so I went with Ivy in her Tracker to the gun shop in Hancock where she picked up the Glock, a cleaning kit, and a couple of boxes of 9mm ammunition. She even bought a holster and a heavy belt. With it slung on her hip she'd look like something out of a western cowboy movie, except they used six shooters. I wrote the check on the Riggs bank account. If this firearm thing was caused by the Putinsky business, let whoever pay for it.

The gun shop owner was leery about the out of town check, but Ivy assured him. "We're in town. Irwin and I work at Da Tech. If there's any problem with the check you know where to find us."

She packed the Glock in its box and put it and the rest of her purchases in her backpack. Since she was driving the Tracker I ended up with the heavy backpack on my lap. I was uncomfortable being around firearms even with the weapon in its box. If we were stopped by the police, was it considered a concealed weapon? I hoped not.

"You have that diploma from the gun club?"

"Sure."

"Then let's go to the county sheriff's office, get it registered, and you can apply for your concealed permit." Then we'd be legal.

The Houghton County sheriff's office is in a single story building alongside the remarkable, yellow brick county courthouse. The courthouse looks like one of those little castles you put in the bottom of a goldfish tank. Built in about 1885 it once housed a couple of jail cells on the top floor. Now the jail is behind the sheriff's office next door.

The deputy was another local. He had a badge, a uniform, and a paunch but no name tag. He was suspicious. "Why do you need a concealed permit?"

It was my turn to explain. "We just got back from Washington where I was asked to help with interrogation of a Russian who asked for political asylum. He was being kept at a government location, but got away. The man who I think helped him escape was murdered on the DC subway. I have his picture, taken from the surveillance tapes."

It was a long speech that was obviously too much information for the deputy. I doubt if he heard anything after the words "Washington" and "interrogation." He asked, "You making this up?"

I pretended not to hear that. I showed the deputy the

photo from the Washington subway. "He's a very tall Russian. He's been in town before. Flew in looking for me. He was probably the person who broke into our house while we were away."

"But he didn't find you?"

"Obviously not," I admitted, and wondered why the Russian had simply left. Maybe he'd found out that Putinsky was in Washington. All that would require would be a cell phone call from an informant. If Putinsky was a higher priority victim, that might have been a reason to skip me. Lucky break. "I think this character's name is Ivan and that he's Russian mafia. We were advised to buy a firearm for protection."

I included myself in the "we" but my crazy record as a "paid Soviet agent" could turn up in a background check. I wasn't going to buy any guns. Not that I wanted to even touch a Glock again after my fiasco at the firing range on the farm.

The deputy was skeptical, which was understandable. Portage Lake gets the occasional home invasion, quite a few drunk drivers, and even had its own serial killer, but my story was so far off the map that he couldn't relate.

There was no reason to reject Ivy's application for a concealed weapon permit unless the deputy thought I was a nut case and of course it wasn't Irwin Glass making the application. It was Dr. Ivy Hartshorn, assistant professor at Michigan Institute of Technology.

Ivy filled out the application form, swearing that she'd not been convicted of a felony, wasn't insane, and a long list of other qualifications that might cause her application to be turned down.

As we turned to leave, I explained about the picture. "I just wanted to give you a heads up. If this Russian guy comes back. We may have to call you."

As we got back in Ivy's Tracker, I reminded myself. "I guess I have to call Wilson in Marquette again."

"He won't be happy to hear from you, schatzy," Ivy said, mocking me with her German again.

"Why not? We're practically pals. Didn't he come to our wedding?"

She just laughed.

I had to leave a message on Wilson's answering machine. He was probably checking on some foreign students at Northern Michigan University or some such routine matter. In his job one can easily imagine there are spies everywhere, just as xenophobic about foreigners as the Russians were when I was back in Moscow.

Well, I had done my duty. All I could do then was hope Katya connected. I was still confused by the suggestion that the DNA test had been altered and that she was not my daughter after all. There had to be some motivation for that. I couldn't imagine it was mere carelessness, some clerk marking the wrong box on a form.

Who could benefit from Katya being my birth daughter? I remembered that Mohammed kid in Oregon who had basically been egged on by the FBI until he thought he was setting off a car bomb by the town Christmas tree. If the FBI wanted to grease the rails so Russian agent Katarina Putinsky could move freely in the country as a US citizen, that might suit someone's nefarious purpose. On the other hand, if it was a KGB operation and somehow a Russian agent got to the DNA lab personnel, it would strengthen Katya's cover story. Even in my paranoid state, that option seemed an unlikely stretch. I could not rule out Robert and his rogue Whitewater mischief. God knows what that outfit of mercenaries might be up to. Who knows what evil lurks in the hearts of men?

That was all speculation. I believed--I wanted to believe that the DNA report was true, that Katya really was my birth daughter. I just loved that kid. She was vulnerable and sweet. That she was not forthcoming I put down to shyness and the anxiety of being a stranger in a strange land. Some kids won't talk about themselves, maybe because they haven't decided who they are and don't want to reveal their vulnerability and uncertainty.

My trouble was that the spooks at the farm had planted a seed of doubt. They left me completely confused. They were so skillful that if they suggested I was not the child of my parents, that I was adopted from the planet Krypton, I would not be sure it wasn't true. I guessed that was an interrogation method used all the time, as in "We've already interviewed your partner and he says you were the trigger man," a trick to trip someone into a confession.

If the DNA test turned out to be a scam, how much responsibility lay with the Dean who insisted I have it done, and Agent Wilson who pointed out that if Katya was my birth daughter she was entitled to US citizenship? Maybe it was all a complex conspiracy. It's that kind of thinking that can push you off the deep end.

Something was bound to happen. I was anxious, felt an impending sense of doom. When we got back to the house I set about replacing the broken pane of glass in the kitchen door. "Maybe we should replace the door completely," I suggested.

I had never been a glazier. It couldn't be hard. Measure the hole, dig out the broken bits, buy some of that window putty. I had never owned a house or an apartment. I was always a tenant. I began to admire home owners who can do everything, replace shingles, and fix chimneys.

"I can do the glass bit," Ivy said. She's so handy and self-reliant. I'm just a bumbler always getting into trouble.

I watched Ivy measure for the glass and went with her to McGann's hardware in Hancock to buy a pane and the putty. In no time she had the window replaced, this time with heavier glass. Instead of one blow to the window another burglar might need two to break in. So much for burglar insurance!

A dead bolt would be better, something that couldn't be opened just by reaching through the broken window. We bought a lock set. As the owner of an aged truck, I have a bag of rudimentary tools. I followed the instructions and installed the dead bolt. Not that I felt much safer. If someone wants to break in, they always can. I once read about a man who had every door and window alarmed, so the thieves took a chain saw and cut a hole through the wall. The idea behind those safeguards is to make it more difficult and time consuming to break in, giving the inhabitants time to run off, defend themselves, or call the cops.

There were other things to do to bring the old house up to speed. The doorbell didn't work, for instance, and I didn't know how to wire one. That had a low priority.

"It's time we got ourselves a real bed," Ivy said.

We'd been sleeping on a mattress on the floor, our wedding gift quilt from my mother serving as a full size coverlet. Ivy's old futon was in the sparsely furnished living room. We had slept on it together when I lived in Kostinsky's house, but the futon frame was so rickety one risked a collapse. Nothing like being tangled in the frame of a cheap folding bed.

For the next couple of days we were busy getting into credit card debt. We bought a basic queen size mattress and metal bed frame from Kirkish furniture across from the Wal-Mart, carrying it home in the bed of my pickup. Getting it up the stairs to the bedroom was a feat. Now if we wanted to fall out of bed instead of just rolling off the mattress, we could. We were making progress.

Wilson didn't call back. Maybe he was out of town on a case. There was no email or phone call from Ralph or anybody at the farm in response to my report of what I found out at the airport. I hoped we were out of the loop. That was Washington and the farm. This was Portage Lake, far away in the U.P. Whatever had happened in Washington, the whole business of Robert's murder, was really none of my business. I wasn't there. I had never met or even seen the tall Russian suspected of the hit. Maybe we could get on with our lives without hassles.

If Putinsky was on the loose in Washington, that was not my responsibility. We had no idea where Katya was or what she was doing. She was a free agent. If she chose not to communicate, that was her decision. Much as it pained me, like a person in mourning for a lost loved one, I would have to learn to let go of it. Like that AA oath: "Lord, let me know the things I can and cannot change and the wisdom to know the difference." I could not change Katya's status.

At least this time I was not alone. In past years I'd been on my own, a single guy in crappy jobs. Though I was often lonely, at least I never let myself get utterly depressed. It was different now. Now it was Ivy and me. Our life in Portage Lake looked like it was going to be normal. We had a baby on the way, something to look forward to, to plan for.

I was a peripheral person. I hadn't stolen anybody's money, hadn't killed anyone, wasn't on any wanted list. I didn't have anything to worry about until the fall term. The only unknown quantity was that menacing Russian mafia guy, but I had no quarrel with him. If it was the money in the Riggs account, he'd have to settle that with Putinsky, wherever he was. Like the kid in Mad Magazine, I could say "What, me worry?"

That turned out to be wishful thinking.

It was about six o'clock in the morning when we were awakened by a banging on the front door.

Ivy sat up, startled. I headed downstairs in my pajama bottoms. Ivy, in just the top and a pair of cute panties went for her bathrobe.

I stood behind the front door off to one side. "Who is it?"

"Irvin! Let me in."

Irvin? Not Irwin? I half expected it to be Professor Kostinsky. Who else tended to call me Irvin?

I heard Ivy command, "Don't open it yet," and the click of something metal.

I turned to see her in firing position, holding the Glock steady in both hands and aiming at the front door. Was she overreacting or was she getting into that macho I'm a gun owner thing?

I unlocked the front door and cautiously opened it, half expecting to see a tall Russian. Our visitor wasn't tall. He was a small guy, in a Detroit Lions baseball cap, with bloodshot eyes and a very weary look.

I was speechless.

Ivy, seeing no threat, lowered the Glock, but didn't put it in the holster. "Who's this?"

I realized she had never met him. "Vladimir Putinsky, or Putin. Katya's Russian father."

Putinsky's half hearted smile showed teeth needing a dentist. He spoke in Russian. "Irvin. I am so glad you are safe." He caught a glimpse of Ivy with the gun, which she was putting back in its new holster. She looked incongruous, a pistol packing mama in a pink bathrobe and fuzzy slippers. "Who is this?"

"My wife, Ivy. She was with me at the farm."

"And she has a pistol. How very American."

His sarcasm wasn't wasted. "What are you doing here?" There was no flight that arrived early in the morning. I realized if he was on someone's wanted list he couldn't get on a plane. With only two flights a day into the Houghton County airport, he had to arrive in the afternoon or late at night. "How did you get here?"

"What's he saying?" Ivy demanded.

I told him to speak English.

"On the dog bus," Putinsky said.

"You mean the Greyhound?"

"Yes, the Greyhound. It is very long ride. Eighteen hours from Detroit."

"But you're coming from Washington. Did you fly?"

Putinsky had a small roll-on bag and pulled it inside, closed the door behind him and, after some fumbling to figure out how it worked, made sure it was locked. "You have poor security on trains and busses. I am not terrorist."

"Where did you get the hat?"

He gave me a toothy smile. "I found it. Very suitable. Nobody cares about old immigrant Russian in hat like this." He touched the baseball cap's bill. At least he hadn't worn it backwards like some kid from the hood.

"What about the people at the farm?"

He fell back into a more comfortable Russian, leaving Ivy bewildered. "I am not a criminal, at least not in this country. But I cannot risk being extradited to Russia. I have enemies there."

For Ivy's benefit I stuck to English. "But why come here?"

"Are you not family?"

"Well…" He sort of had me there.

"How about some coffee?" Ivy suggested. "I bet you haven't had anything to eat."

"A sandwich in…" he hesitated. "Esca something, I think. At midnight."

"Escanaba," I explained. "All the UP busses meet up at Escanaba about midnight."

Putinsky shook his head, bewildered. "Strange people."

"Yoopers," I explained.

"I saw an Indian," Putinsky said, his voice tinged with awe.

"They are Yoopers, too. The originals," I explained.

Ivy set about making an early breakfast. She filled the coffee maker. "I'm going up to get dressed."

That reminded me that I was still only in pajama bottoms and barefoot.

"I still don't understand why you would come all the way to the UP," I said. "You should settle your business in Washington."

"Too dangerous."

I understood that. I fetched the pictures Ralph had sent as email attachments. Without explanation, I showed him the un-cropped surveillance shot. "What about this man?"

"Da." Vladimir pointed to the tall man. "That is him."

I didn't want to give him all the details just yet. "How did you get away from the farm?"

"Your friend. Robert."

"Not my friend," I insisted.

"It was very simple. He spoke to the guard, showed some paper, and took me to a big car. Dark windows."

"An SUV." Ivy said.

"Yes. What you call SUV."

"Then what?"

Putinsky clammed up. He didn't like questions and he was back in his pattern of avoidance and dissembling.

"The man who got you away from the farm was shot on the Washington subway."

"Very bad." He pointed to the enlarged, cropped picture I had extracted from the subway photo. "Is Ivan. Mafia."

"Did you steal from the Russian mafia? Is that where the money in my Riggs account came from?" Not that it mattered much. Like they say, money is fungible. It has no loyalty. It is just a commodity.

Putin didn't explain.

Ivy came downstairs. She'd changed quickly into a pair of cut off shorts. For modesty's sake she wore a bra under a blouse I recognized as one of her better ones but she still had the fuzzy slippers. Ivy was trying to reconstruct Putin's story.

"So you came here on the bus? Why?"

I supposed she was going to worm out of Putinsky a step by step scenario, like where he got money, how he found out how to get to the UP, how he learned our new address. He would never reveal his secrets.

Instead, through a mouthful of toast and scrambled eggs, he said only "Katya."

That didn't satisfy Ivy. She was not happy that we suddenly had an uninvited guest she had never met, a man who would be pursued by the spooks from the farm, incriminating us as possible conspirators in his escape. "Katya's not here. We don't know where she is."

That didn't faze him. "She will come."

Again I was snared in someone else's web. "How do you know that?"

"It is my business to know these things," he said, secretive as usual. He could be so maddening.

"I think I'll get dressed." It would have been nice to crawl back into bed with Ivy. She seemed to be over the worst of that morning sickness, but now was not the time for lingering between the sheets. I went upstairs and got dressed, leaving Ivy to her own try at worming information out of the elusive Vladimir Putinsky.

We were not prepared to have a house guest and had no idea how long Putinsky would hang around. If his being in our house was adequate inducement to lure Katya out of wherever she was, it should be worth it, at least for the time being.

Apparently Ivy, too, had reached a dead end questioning Putinsky. Always the practical, thoughtful person, Ivy told him, "You'll want a bath."

"Yes. Thank you."

Wondering how to cope with this new development, I shook my head. At least, I didn't have to worry about Robert showing up unless as a ghost. Maybe he had some Whitewater cronies, but I doubted it. Robert had never alluded to having partners or associates. I was convinced, perhaps wrongly, that he worked alone as some sort of rogue agent with his own agenda.

Having Putinsky in the house was bad enough, a magnet

338

for trouble. I was sure to hear from Ralph or the other spooks at the farm determined to track him down. They would no doubt assume correctly that he might come to me. I could almost hear the thundering hooves of the posse coming over the hill.

Ivy showed Putinsky the upstairs bathroom and gave him a towel so he could freshen up after his long journey. While he showered, we discussed the situation. Ivy asked, "Should we notify the police?"

"You mean like Wilson in Marquette? I don't think Putinsky's really a fugitive. He wasn't under arrest at the farm. I think he came to the States for his own safety and asking for political asylum is a ploy to give him some currency. They wanted to debrief him. If he left, it wasn't like a jail break."

He reminded me of those scum bag amateur informants who cooked up the story of Saddam's fictional biological warfare factories and imaginary purchase of yellow cake uranium, both of which had been used as excuses to get us into war in Iraq. Putinsky wasn't a freelance informant cooking up stories for money. He was the real thing, even though his motives were different.

That sounded reasonable to her.

"He's not a wanted man. I doubt if there's a warrant out for his capture. I think he entered the country on a visitor's visa. So here he is, visiting. Nothing illegal about that."

"Except he's visiting us," Ivy said with some resentment.

Knowing something about how the bureaucrats at the farm thought, I assumed they considered Vladimir Putinsky a prize. If a bunch of biologists caught a rare species they'd want to keep it for study. How often did an old KGB officer land in their laps?

"So now we have a house guest?"

I put a slice of bread in the toaster. "I guess so. It's not going to cost us anything, if that's what you're worried about. He must have assets or he couldn't buy the bus ticket. God knows how many bank accounts he has stashed away. I can't imagine that the Riggs account is his only source."

Ivy smiled with reluctant admiration for the guy. "Resourceful. Always helps to have a little nest egg tucked away in some foreign bank."

"Maybe we should send an email to Ivan-G. Tell Katya he's here."

Ivy shook her head. "If, and that's a big if, Ivan-G is Ivan Glass, the stuffed MIT mascot bear and not Ivan the Awful."

"It would have to be something cryptic. Like those State Department memos that mean all things to all men." I booted up my laptop, logged in to the university server, set the keyboard for the Cyrillic alphabet, and sent Ivan-G this in Russian: "Come home at once. We have a big surprise for you." If anything, that should do it.

"Then what?"

I took the toast out and smeared on some butter. "Then we wait."

When Putinsky came back downstairs, freshly shaved and in a change of clothes, he still looked tired. Eighteen hours on the Greyhound from Detroit is not exactly restful. "You need some sleep," Ivy suggested.

I flipped the old futon couch into single bed mode while Ivy fetched him a blanket. Actually it was my sleeping bag, unzipped into a flat coverlet. While Putinsky sat on the edge, taking off his shoes, I asked, "If Katya shows up, what are your plans?"

"I must fight extradition."

"For that you need a lawyer." I didn't imagine there were any lawyers in Portage Lake with experience in fighting extradition to a foreign country, particularly Russia.

"I know some people," he said, not volunteering anything further. "It is all political."

As complicated as I found the labyrinth of interlocking and conflicting agency interests I detected at the farm, I could not imagine what went on in Moscow or at the embassy in Washington. It was as mysterious to me as the workings of Swiss watch might be to a kid who opens up the back and sees all those cogs and springs.

Putinsky had the audacity to suggest that there might be a chance for him to lecture at Michigan Institute of Technology. That would be in my department, but Dr. Waarala hardly had room in his budget to take on an adjunct in Russian history or international relations. Michigan

Institute of Technology is not that sort of a school. The most he might hope for would be an honorarium for an open lecture for the student body. That was another budget I knew nothing about.

Ivy and I simply had no idea what to do with our uninvited house guest. We were like the family suddenly saddled with a dead beat relative who has no job, no prospects, and whose only plan is to stay on indefinitely for free room and board. This was not good.

I looked in on him and saw that he was already fast asleep. He looked like a harmless, tired old man. That sinister aura he radiated when I saw him years ago in Moscow had disappeared along with the now splintered Soviet Union. If he had ridden the busses all the way from Washington, how many nights was that? The Detroit bus went to Sault Ste. Marie, the Chicago bus to Calumet. He must have changed where they met at Escanaba and where he had seen his first Indian.

It was late in life for him to start over. Pushing the limits myself, I knew that after the age of forty-five it was hard to find a job in the United States. It was that health insurance thing. Older people tended to have what the insurance companies called "preexisting conditions." The insurance companies didn't want high risk employees on any payroll. I had no idea what Putinsky's medical condition was, but his age alone was against him. He should be back in Russia living on a comfortable pension, but obviously his activities, whatever those were, precluded that.

I shut the door to the kitchen as quietly as I could and reminded myself to oil the hinges.

"Think positive," Ivy whispered to me as we sat at the rickety kitchen table and discussed our Russian problem. "You are a resourceful guy, Irwin."

"I think Katya should show up and whisk him away."

"Didn't Katya say her father hated her because she was not his real daughter?"

"That's what she said. The way he talks, that's not the case. Maybe they are reconciled. She also said her mother is dead, but I no longer know what to believe."

"Maybe he needs her, just as he needs you, Irwin."

341

I hadn't thought about that. At the farm Putinsky obviously looked at me as an ally in his sparring with the hostile government agencies. That might have been just a pose, Putinsky playing good cop. I was still bewildered by the confusion that resulted from the discussions at the farm. It was as if a psychiatrist asks you "How do you know you are sane?" You begin to doubt, and then you don't know what to believe.

Ivy poured herself a second cup of coffee. Before she went up to get dressed she had taken off the heavy belt with the holster and Glock and set them on top of the refrigerator. "Can you believe anything either of them says?"

"I don't know. In some cultures people will tell you what they think you want to hear. What we consider lying is to them merely being polite."

"It's not merely being polite for Katya to say you are her papa."

"Well, I am her papa."

"That's what you want to believe, Liebchen. You told me one of the spooks suggested the DNA test results might have been tampered with."

This was like a recurring migraine. "Don't confuse me any more, honey."

Ivy leaned toward me, both elbows on the table. "I think, sweetie, that the whole thing is an elaborate cover story to plant an agent inside the United States. You are the convenient peg to hang the story on."

"I don't want to believe that."

I had told Ivy the story of what happened at the Metropol. Now, recalling it, Ivy sat back in her chair and put on a seductive face, glowed at me. Speaking in her version of a Russian accent, she said, "You are such a nice boy, Irvin. I like you."

"You'd better, since you are married to me."

We needed to be rescued somehow, and a sort of rescue materialized on cue.

Standing at the front window I saw a silver-grey, two door car pull up at the curb. I didn't recognize the make, but it might have been a Honda Civic. A blond girl I didn't recognize got out. As she came around the car toward the house I saw she was wearing a barely decent short skirt, one of those it takes practice to sit down in without showing your panties, if you wear them. She had good legs and a full figure. She wore a Tee shirt stenciled with a message I could not make out. She was wearing sandals and carrying a big purse on a shoulder strap.

When she opened the passenger door and took out the teddy bear, I knew who it had to be.

She looked uncertainly at the little house we'd rented. It's an old place and the worst looking on the block. My Ford and Ivy's red Tracker were parked in the driveway. That must have convinced her.

Of course, the doorbell didn't work. Before she could knock at the door I opened it. Not wanting to wake Putinsky, I spoke softly. "Katya?"

She threw her arms around me and kissed me on both cheeks, Russian style. "Papa."

I just melted. All those doubts thrown at me evaporated. "Come in, but be quiet. Vladimir is asleep."

"He is here? Already?"

I gestured toward the futon and the sleeping Vladimir, bundled in my sleeping bag coverlet. I whispered, "He's very tired. Don't wake him up." We tiptoed into the kitchen.

So she expected Vladimir to be at our house. Somehow, without informing me or Ivy, the two had arranged a rendezvous. Perhaps they didn't want us to have fair warning in case we'd notify the spooks at the farm. That was a fair assumption, since it's always been my instinct not to conceal. Ivy says I'm too open. When that business in Moscow occurred the first thing I did was report to embassy security.

Coming to Portage Lake must have involved some risks, for Katya was uncertain. I didn't believe she didn't want to see me, her "papa," so why worry? What was she apprehensive about? Seeing her Russian father? I couldn't tell.

I spoke softly to Ivy, who had stood up at the kitchen table. "It's Katya." That was not as obvious as it sounds, considering how much she had changed her appearance. She had dyed her hair and had it cut short. Even this early in the morning she was wearing eye makeup. Where had she come

343

from? Had she driven all night from somewhere?

Not knowing what else to say to Ivy, I stammered, "She's brought Ivan." Ivan, the mascot pillow bear with the red star pin I'd brought back from Moscow, looked a bit tired.

"Where were you?" Ivy asked, getting right to the point.

"Not far," Ivy said. It was a non-explanation.

"Coffee?" Ivy suggested. There was still some in the pot.

We sat across from each other at the Goodwill store table, not knowing what to say next. After a long silence, I asked, "Why did you leave? You didn't stay long enough to take your exams."

Katya lowered her eyes. She sounded ashamed. "I was afraid."

I remembered that the policeman had come to the door because our engagement party was too noisy. "Afraid of the police? You have nothing to be afraid of."

"It is complicated," she said.

Again with the 'complicated.' It was starting to sound like a standard excuse for saying nothing.

I decided to try another approach and showed her the photograph from the subway camera. "Is this man what you are afraid of?"

Katya shook her head. "I do not know him."

Well, so much for that. "Did you send me emails from Ivan-G?"

"Yes." She cradled the teddy bear. Odd, how a stuffed animal can bring out the kid in us. "You send papa email, right, comrade Ivan?" She made the teddy bear nod in agreement like a hand puppet.

I refused to be distracted. "How did Vladimir contact you?"

"Telephone."

Ivy knew we could not accommodate two house guests. "You and Vladimir can't stay here. We have no beds."

"Yes. This is a small house, not like Professor Kostinsky's."

"We leave soon," Katya explained.

"Then you're dropping out of school?" To me that would be a serious mistake. In my family education was

344

everything.

We were interrupted by the telephone. It was in the living room, and I hurried to answer it, afraid to waken Putinsky. "Yes?"

"Dis here Glass?"

"Yes. What is it?"

"Dis is Waatia at the airport. Dat guy you wanted me to call youse about if he showed up?"

"Yes."

"Just flew in."

"Is he alone?"

"Pilot, him, and another guy. Asked about a rental car."

"Thanks."

He was about to hang up, but I stopped him. "Hang on a second. I think maybe you should notify the State Police in Calumet."

"What for?"

"The tall Russian is a suspect in a murder in Washington."

"Da state trooper ain't gonna arrest some guy just because you say so."

Of course. The State Police would need a warrant. In this country we don't use preventive detention and arrest someone if they might commit a crime. We have to wait until they do it, and then arrest them. If I expected police protection if the tall Russian showed up I was out of luck. "I guess not. Well, thanks for letting me know."

I hung up.

Putinsky was stirring, sat up on the futon, the sleeping bag coverlet still around his shoulders. "What is it, Irvin? You are worried."

"Ivan. I think he is on his way here. He is not alone."

"So quickly?" Putinsky bent to put on his shoes.

"What's he want?"

Putinsky smiled, showing that stainless steel tooth. "His money, of course."

"What's he expect me to do? Write him a check?"

Putinsky's laugh was feeble. "I do not think so."

I could not get out of my mind the sight of Robert laid out in the morgue with two bullets in his head.

345

Ivy came to the kitchen door. "Who called?"

"Waatia, the guy at airport operations. Said the Russian just flew in. I bet he's on his way here."

"Didn't Kostinsky tell him he didn't know our new address?"

Katya had the answer. "I telephone your office yesterday. The secretary tell me your address."

"Did you tell her you are my daughter?"

"Da. Yes."

"That would be Mrs. Houghton." So much for protocol.

Ivy retrieved the Glock from the top of the refrigerator and set it on her chair. "Let's just sit down and have breakfast. We don't know if that Russian, if he does show up, has evil intentions. He may just want to ask some questions. No harm in that."

Putinsky took a seat and settled himself like an actor getting into the role of an innocent.

Katya sat down in view of the back door with that heavy purse in her lap. Ivan the bear sat up on the table like a centerpiece. It was all very domestic, a family gathering, complete with mascot.

I watched from the front window. Sure enough, a red four door car pulled up across the street and two men got out, one of them unusually tall. Both men wore jackets, unnecessary in the Copper Country summer weather unless you wanted to hide a shoulder holster. I reasoned that if you wanted to take a firearm on an airplane, you didn't fly commercial. Private planes didn't have to pass through Homeland Security. The two men could have carried a bazooka of a machine gun if they wanted to.

The two split up. The tall man came to the front door. His partner waited by the kitchen door. They had us boxed in.

I had an impulse to call the sheriff, but like the state police, unless something nasty happened, there was no valid reason to call.

I took a deep breath, swallowed, and got up to answer the front door to open it. The tall Russian was a frightening figure, a bony face, cruel mouth, and cold eyes full of hatred.

Normally the only strangers who came to my door in the

Copper Country were Mormon missionaries. This was no Mormon missionary. He didn't look like he was collecting ten cent deposit pop cans for the hockey team, either. I put on a cordial demeanor. "Good morning. If you're selling something, we don't need anything."

The accent was unmistakable. "You are Irvin Glass?"

"Yes. Who are you?"

"You do not need to know."

Again the "need to know" mantra. Must be a universal slogan among people with secrets. "Then I'll just call you Ivan. That OK?" I left out the "Awful" nickname.

He was surprised. It was good to catch him off guard. I was beginning to learn the technique of the spooks. Hadn't I seen those guys in action? This was my chance.

"Ivan," he said, as if accepting the name whether it was his or not.

"I was expecting you," I said in Russian. That should confuse him a little more.

Now he was puzzled, startled that I knew the language. "Really? Why?"

"Professor Kostinsky said you'd been looking for me."

"Oh." That seemed to satisfy him.

"And I have your picture."

Now he was surprised. "My picture?"

"Wait here." I fetched the photographs from the Washington subway surveillance camera and held one up. "Isn't that you?"

"Where did you get this?"

I was determined to maintain the upper hand in this. "Look, Ivan. We know you murdered the Whitewater agent on the subway. The police are looking for you. They are on their way now, so if you have any business here, I suggest you get it over with quickly and leave. I suspect your plane at the airport will be impounded."

Ivan stood speechless for a moment. After a pause, he asked, "How do you know this?"

I bluffed. "We Americans know everything. You have walked into a trap. We have been waiting for you."

Now I really had him puzzled. He looked around, expecting to see a swat team.

I continued. "Don't you realize this is a police state? So what do you want?"

"Vladimir Putinsky has stolen money from me."

It was as I suspected. "I think Vladimir has stolen money from a lot of people. You will have to wait your turn in line."

"You are too late." It was Putinsky standing in the kitchen door. "The money is gone."

"You bastard," Ivan said.

Quicker than I could blink he pushed me aside and produced a pistol from under the jacket, took careful aim, and shot Putinsky in the knee.

I remembered it was a favorite IRA punishment. Shoot your adversary in the kneecap. The patella, a floating bit of bone, is not useless but anchors the tendons and muscles that the leg depends on. Kneecapped victims are crippled forever.

At the sound of the shot the man at the back door kicked it. It didn't give at first. He kicked it again and burst into the kitchen, gun drawn.

I turned in time to see Katya dive under the table, getting out of the way. I heard three quick shots, so close together they were almost as one, and the man dropped.

Vladimir was on the floor now, groaning in pain. And there was Ivy in the doorway, the Glock aimed at the tall Russian. "Put down your weapon, tovarish," she demanded.

Ivan set it down on the floor and stood up with his hands behind his head. He obviously knew the routine. "Not tovarish. That was for old Soviet Union. Communism is dead."

"You'll be dead, too," Ivy said. "Pick up his gun, Irwin," and to Katya who was leaning over the body of the man in the kitchen doorway, "Call 911. Vladimir needs an ambulance." A pause and Ivy told me, "Search him, Irwin. He may have another weapon."

I'd been patted down by Homeland Security when we boarded the flight from Washington to Chicago, so knew something of the routine. I told him to "do the airplane thing," arms out to the side. While Ivan held his hands up I checked inside the jacket, found the empty shoulder holster.

When I reached behind him to check the small of his back I had bingo, a very small hand gun. I pulled it out and held it up to show Ivy. "Ta-dah!"

That was a mistake. Ivan snatched the gun, which turned out to be a palm-sized .22 caliber Beretta, with his right hand while he encircled me with his left arm in a hug. I felt the cold metal of the little automatic against my temple.

What was he going to do? Shoot me and then Ivy? Or shoot Ivy and then me?

At that moment the cuckoo clock in the kitchen chirped, "cuckoo-cuckoo." Ivan was distracted and I let my self go dead weight. Even for a tough guy like Ivan the Awful my middle-aged sluggard body was a bit much. I slipped, and before he could get his head up again for a new position, I heard another crack and he went down in a heap on top of me.

There's a lot of blood pressure inside a head, and the bullet caused a red gusher. My face was suddenly hot, wet, and sticky. I tried to wipe it out of my eyes and nearly fainted with shock. I didn't know if he had shot me or what. I struggled to get the Russian off me and rolled him over to discover that, with his head slightly bowed, Ivy's bullet had entered just at the hair line on his forehead. He was dead, of course.

I was still trying to focus on all this when I heard Ivy throwing up in the kitchen. Was it her morning sickness coming back or the shock of having killed two men?

Katya was tending to Vladimir. She found a kitchen knife and cut away his slacks. She was not hysterical as I might have expected, nor in shock. She attended to him like an EMT trained in dealing with horrific injuries.

The sheriff deputy arrived, the same guy we had met when Ivy registered her Glock and filled out the forms for a concealed weapon permit. When he saw the two bodies he blinked a lot, like he didn't know how to proceed. Then the Portage Lake police arrived and the no nonsense city detective. He questioned everyone to get our versions of what had happened.

The ambulance arrived, too. The medics rushed Vladimir to the emergency room in Portage View hospital in Hancock. They let Katya ride along.

Ivy was arrested. What would the prosecutor charge her

with? Second degree murder? I doubted it. I mean, she had killed two would-be assassins, hadn't she? I was sure she wouldn't be charged with anything and if she was we could plead self defense. Real life isn't like the movies. James Bond never got arrested for all the bad guys he disposed of or he would have spent his life in the courts. We were in for a lot of explanations, red tape, etc.

Ivy was in shock, herself. She had reacted instinctively, like some kid who plays computer shoot 'em up games and loses the sense that those Russians were real targets, not images on a screen, but Ivy doesn't play those games.

At that point, if one of the spooks from the farm had told me that Ivy was secretly a trained CIA shooter I wouldn't have known what to believe. Things were so confusing I was losing my own grip on reality.

The city detective took photos of the bodies. It was a clear case: Ivy had prevented the home invasion by shooting the guy at the back door, then saved my bacon by knocking off Ivan. An arraignment and grand jury would no doubt decide no charges would be filed. It's one of those American rights: you can shoot dead a burglar or home invader as long as he dies inside the house. It has to be spontaneous, not premeditated. You're also not supposed to keep on shooting and shooting until you run out of bullets. Getting him in the back as he's running away down your driveway is something else.

While a second ambulance took the bodies away, leaving a mess of blood in the kitchen and inside the front door, a mess we weren't allowed to clean up because the house was again an official crime scene, Ivy was taken to the court house to be interviewed by the county prosecutor.

The prosecutor, a young law graduate named Haka, another Finlander elected because of his local connections, didn't strike me as being too bright. I went along to corroborate Ivy's story. After all, it's not every day that a couple of college teachers from Michigan Institute of Technology are involved with the KGB, the CIA, and whatever other agencies we tangled with at the farm in Virginia, not to mention shooting dead a couple of Russian mafia assassins.

The story had to be backed up, of course. I had the photos taken by the subway surveillance camera and the government agency letter permitting me on an airplane in spite of my no-fly status. The letterhead helped.

Haka was clearly out of his depth on this case. The county jail next door has only one cell for women, and it was already occupied by a couple of rowdy women. Where would he house Ivy?

While we were in the prosecutor's office I borrowed his phone and called the farm. Again Ralph or whatever his real name was wasn't in, but when I gave the person who answered my message the story that the Russian who had killed Robert—whoever he was—in the DC subway was now dead, I got her attention.

Case closed. All those interrogations and speculation had solved nothing, led nowhere. It ended in our old house in the remoteness of Michigan's Upper Peninsula. I wondered if, having done the Washington cops' job for them, I would be awarded a junior G-man's badge. Better, maybe I'd be reinstated as an innocent citizen permitted to fly. Retribution.

Ivy was badly shaken by the whole thing, obviously more than I was. I still keep replaying the scene in my mind, the shooting, and the fear afterwards, the fear I'd been able to suppress in my confrontation with Ivan. Afterwards I was numb, unable to process the whole thing. I guess that's what they call PTSD.

It was like that joke about the granny whose grandson is rescued by the lifeguard and is so upset that all she can tell the lifeguard is "he had a hat." When I first got back to the house, stepping over the bloodstains on the kitchen floor, I looked at the broken door. It had taken two strong kicks to undo the dead bolt I had installed. The door jamb was nothing but jagged splinters. What would our landlord say? "There goes our damage deposit," I mumbled, and then realized I was being stupid. Two men dead and all I can think about is our damage deposit? Irwin, when are you going to get a life?

I drove up to the hospital to see Vladimir. Katya was with him, of course, tight lipped and worried. Putinsky was drugged up with pain killers, but reasonably cogent.

351

"What now, Vladimir?" I asked. "What will you do when you get out of here?"

His non-committal answer was a shrug. Getting an answer out of him was always tougher than winkling a bit of flesh out of a snail. I discussed his predicament with the feds. There was that extradition thing, of course. He might be able to fight that, but political asylum was going to be a tough call. I suggested that if he wanted to stay permanently in the United States, Katya could sponsor him. He was a parent of record.

That was a confusing argument, of course. As a citizen, under the immigration laws she could sponsor a parent. But if I was her birth father, the reason for her US citizenship, maybe Putinsky didn't qualify as a bone fide parent. That would make for some confusion.

Well, confusion in the government seemed to be de rigor. Bureaucratic infighting was the norm, wasn't it?

What about Katya and Vladimir? They couldn't move in with us. While Vladimir was in the hospital Katya had the futon. It made for a strange family reunion broken by many trips up to the hospital. Vladimir would probably need a knee replacement. My immediate thought was "Who would pay for that?" But then I remembered the hefty Riggs account. That bank balance could easily pay for two knee replacements.

Vladimir had his own plans. When he had sufficiently recovered and was ambulatory again, they would drive west to Portland, Oregon. There's a large community there of Russian immigrants. Maybe he'd go into business. It was something I didn't need to know.

I asked him where he'd get the money, beyond the seven hundred thousand, of course. He laughed at me. "You think you are the only one I opened an account for?"

I don't know if there are more mafia hit men assigned to his case, but I'm out of it.

Ivy was changed by the whole episode. That teasing, kidding aspect of her nature had been tempered by the horror of actually killing someone. Something happens to your soul when you kill someone, even it's in defense of your husband. Her reflex action had consequences.

It had all started sort of innocently, a quirky paternity

case of a possibly fixated student who turned out to be my birth daughter—unless you bought into the theory that the DNA test was falsified. As a parent, even a surrogate, I had to face up to the transition every parent has to face the moment when their offspring leaves the nest. Katya is her own person, blond or brunette, whatever color she chooses. I told Ivy, "She's a smart kid. I know she'll do the right thing."

Ivy's not so sure. After Katya and Vladimir headed off into the sunset, driving west in her used Honda Civic, Ivy had a confession to make.

"You remember when Katya came back, just before Ivan the Awful showed up?"

"Yes. How could I forget? And the cuckoo clock startled Ivan."

"You remember the coroner's report on the Russian who kicked in the kitchen door?"

"Yeh. Three quick shots to the heart. You're an incredible shot, honey, I never thought it possible. That was quick thinking."

"That it took two kicks at the kitchen door to break in gave me time to get out my Glock."

"Lucky I installed that dead bolt."

"But I didn't shoot him."

"What?"

"When we got back from the courthouse, before the arraignment, when Katya was still up at the hospital with Vladimir, I found her purse on the kitchen floor."

"So?"

Ivy licked her lips. She didn't want to tell me this, but she can't resist an "I told you so" moment. "She killed that Russian. She had a gun in her purse. Besides her American passport, she had two others--the original Russian passport she came here with and a Swedish passport with her picture."

We do live in a complex world. I suppose Svetlana would be proud of her daughter. I shook my head in wonder and, I have to admit, admiration. "That's my kid," I said.

I wonder what she's up to now.

Book Three: Burnt Out

Chapter One

My name is Irwin Glass. I'm like the guy who wanders unwittingly into a gay biker bar by mistake and gets beat up. I don't look for trouble; it finds me. I started out as an unsuspecting kid from South Bend, Indiana, son of a k-12 teacher of social studies and history. I'm also the grandson or maybe great-grandson of someone named Isaac Melamed whose letter turned up in our attic in an envelope with an indecipherable postmark and no stamp. When I showed the letter to my dad he said he couldn't read it, but it looked like Russian. "It's a piece of history," he said, naturally, since he taught the subject. "Why don't you find out what it says? It's what we call a primary source. Old letters can be windows into the past. Maybe your past, Irwin."

So how could a Russian letter be part of my past? I got hooked on that mysterious letter. Nobody in our household could read it. You know how kids are with mysteries and secrets.

My Dad said when he was a kid you could send in a cereal box top and a dime and get a secret decoder ring and unlock the message dictated at the end of the Little Orphan

Annie radio broadcast. Turned out the message was "Drink more Ovaltine."

Impressions we get at age ten can stick with us all our lives. With me it was that letter. The Melamed letter wasn't in code. It was just Russian in Cyrillic. I just had to find out what was in it, like one of those puzzles you turn around and twist and tinker with until you get the solution. There was no box top and ten cent solution.

The Melamed letter set me on a path to a world beyond South Bend. There were people out there who were not Hoosiers. I was determined to learn the language, which I did, and eventually got a BA in Russian at Indiana University in Bloomington. So what do you do with a degree in Russian when you live in Indiana? Not much.

My professor encouraged me to go on for a Masters in international relations and take the Foreign Service examination. All that was because of a faded piece of thin, foreign paper. When I finally could decipher the Russian letter, it turned out to be a plea from Isaac Melamed's sweetheart for a ticket so she could join him in America. Did he ever do it? Did they get together? There was no way of knowing. It was only a link in a chain; all the rest was lost in time. At least it didn't say "Drink more Ovaltine."

By the time I could read it, it no longer mattered. Following the dictates of my karma, I got a job in Moscow at the American Library as a promising, I hoped, member of the Foreign Service. At last I could use my Russian language. Thanks, grandpa Isaac Melamed.

Then everything fell apart.

My seduction was a textbook honey pot case, almost a cliché. It's too embarrassing to go into detail but the upshot was that my hopes for a government career were ruined. I had to start over, build a new career on my limited skills. All that graduate study went down the drain.

What skills did I have? I might teach Russian, but with the cold war over, nobody needed teachers of Russian. Chinese was the new thing, or maybe Arabic, neither of which I knew. I was reduced like some expatriate abroad forced to fall back on teaching his native language to foreigners, like James Joyce in Paris, only the foreign place I landed in was Michigan's Upper Peninsula, about as far from the beaten path as you can get in the United States unless you choose Alaska.

At least Portage Lake Michigan, home of Michigan Institute of Technology and the birthplace of professional hockey, was safe. There were no KGB officers lurking in the bushes, no CIA spies ready to betray me as happened before. In spite of false claims that I had been a paid Soviet agent, I was not a spy come into the cold. I was just another MA struggling to make a living at a university that grants tenure only to Ph.D.s. Hell, I figured, a job's a job even if it's not tenure track. At least an instructorship at Michigan Tech was a step up from being an adjunct at IU/PU in South Bend or part time at Southern Illinois. Could be worse.

When I met Ivy Hartshorne, my smart and sexy office mate, things got better. Ivy's the sporty type. You can tell by her walk. It exudes self-assurance and confidence, that she's happy in her own skin and knows who she is. She drives a little red Tracker with a ski rack on the roof. She taught me how to cross country ski, an appropriate outdoor sport in the Copper Country where there's snow for six months of the year. After a couple of hours on the Tech trails we'd go back to her place for hot cocoa and a cuddle. So here we are: married. We're both too mature for puppy love and too calculating to pass up an arrangement what benefits both of us.

Ivy's not foolish or desperate enough to say, heck with it, husband or no husband, "I want a baby before my clock runs out." And I'm not so testosterone driven that I pursue everything in a skirt with boobs. Ivy and I have an arrangement that suits us both. I like to call it mature love.

Everything was working out fine until that cute Russian student, Katarina Volodna Putinsky, showed up and claimed I'm her father, result of that one night stand in Moscow twenty years ago. That should be a lesson to all young men. It could happen to almost anyone. In my situation it was an international paternity case. An additional surprise was that, since I am her biological father, she's a US citizen. Anyway, Katya'd gone her own way for the time being.

People in Portage Lake will find other things to gossip

about besides the shoot out in our kitchen. That's past history. Most people have short memories. Ivy and I could concentrate on our new married life and the coming baby.

It was a new chapter. Instead of worrying about sinister Mafia types lurking with guns we could think about prenatal care and baby clothes. We're both teaching, Ivy her classes in German for Yoopers, me in what used to be called bone head English. In the new fall term I had three mundane sections of English for foreign students, an easy teaching schedule. Life was good. Just me and my sweetie with her baby bump as they call being pregnant these days. I could look out the window of the second floor office Ivy and I shared in the Humanities building, watch the fall colors the Copper Country is known for, and be content.

A new crop of students was milling about, meeting new people and getting to know the map of the campus. The beginning of term is an exciting time, full of suspense, like what is my professor like, will there be exams and term papers, stuff like that. For me it was getting the syllabus worked out and the lesson plans. There's nothing as bad as the professor who has no plan, walks into a classroom clueless and has to wing it. If you plan ahead you get fewer unpleasant surprises, you hope.

It was a Wednesday morning when I got a surprise visit at the office from Mr. Wilkins, the FBI guy from Marquette. I thought it was a social call, but Wilkins's style can be oblique, friendly only to a point.

Wilkins isn't your stereotypical FBI guy in dark glasses with a long coat to conceal god knows what arsenal of firearms. Wilkins is a Yooper, a lifelong resident of the Upper Peninsula, stationed in Marquette a hundred miles to the east. He has a droopy mustache and wears a tarnished brass American eagle belt buckle the size of a saucer, an old fashioned, checkered mackinaw jacket and a knit wool cap that warms his balding forehead. In the parlance of detective stories he's good cop most of the time. I like him, especially if I'm not charged with anything or being investigated for laundering Russian money or caught in a riddle of who shot Ivan the Terrible in our kitchen with a 9 mm Glock.

Wilkins was the one who pointed out to me that if Katya

357

really was my daughter she was entitled to US citizenship. I'm still not sure that was a good thing to know. On that point I'm ambivalent.

"Oh, Mr. Wilkins," I said, putting on my friendly smile but feeling a tad uneasy. "What brings you to da Tech?"

"Da Tech" is the local abbreviation for Michigan Institute of Technology.

"Thought I'd check up on you." Wilkins's tone was friendly, almost joking, the kind of tease meant to disarm and rattle at the same time.

"Katya's out in Oregon, if you're looking for her."

It wasn't that. Wilkins paused, waiting for me to confess, I suppose.

I was compelled to say something. "You're not wondering if I'm laundering Mafia money? That's settled."

"Nothing like that." He almost said "dat," the local Yooper dialect.

"You didn't drive a hundred miles just to say hello."

Wilkins admitted, "It's a nice drive at this time of year."

We call it color season in the UP. Forty different species of trees make for a glorious kaleidoscope of autumn leaves.

Wilkins closed my office door, sat down in the guest chair and unbuttoned his red and black Mackinaw jacket. I glimpsed his ever present shoulder holster. "I could use your help in something. Nothing major. Just a courtesy."

That did not sound innocent. "If you're trying to recruit me, I don't do stakeouts or stuff like that. You know how I am with guns."

"Mildly incompetent," he affirmed.

"Don't rub it in."

He got to the point at last. "I see that you've got three sections of English for foreign students."

"That's right. You must have read the catalog." Michigan Tech has over a thousand foreign students and they come from about a hundred countries, most in need of engineers so the graduates can go home and whip our butts making things we used to while Americans are reduced to service jobs like burger flipping at MacDonald's. While our local kids are getting into perpetual hock with student loans the foreign students are subsidized by their governments or their rich families. The university needs the cash for tuition even if the foreign students' English is not up to speed. That's where I come in.

"What I'd like," Wilkins said, leaning forward and lowering his voice, "is a copy of your class lists."

I was reluctant. What did he want the lists for? I didn't want to know. "I'm sure you could get that from the department head, Dr. Waarala or maybe the Dean of Students."

"Waarala says it's an issue of academic freedom. What goes on in your classes is your territory."

Waarala will always fall back on the rules and regulations and let someone else stick his neck out. I guess that goes with being a Humanities department head at an engineering school where teachers of literature rank just above the janitorial staff that cleans the toilets. "There's not much left of academic freedom these days," I said. I was thinking about all the rules about discrimination, sexual harassment, non-fraternization, privacy, and so on.

"Just say it's a courtesy between friends," Wilkins said.

We are hardly friends or even colleagues. We're bound by our joint past history. Rather, I'm bound because I owe him. Wilkins knows how to lever a guy.

I tried to rationalize. Class lists? What harm could there be in that? For one, the information is confidential. For identification purposes, each name has a student ID number. In the case of the American students it's the Social Security number. When we posted exam grades we used to use those numbers instead of names. Now because of confidentiality, we can't even do that. "It's confidential stuff," I protested.

"This is FBI business," Wilkins said.

What was he going to do if I refused? Get a subpoena for a class list? Cause me trouble with the department head and the dean of students? "I guess I can make you a copy," I said. "Just don't say you're paying me and depositing the money in a Bahamian bank."

It was an allusion to a KGB trick that got me pegged as a paid Soviet agent.

Wilkins may be a Yooper with a disarming laid back nature, but he's also a government employee. "No budget for that."

I took the class lists to the office copy machine and handed him a set. "That all?" I asked, expecting more and afraid of what he might say.

Wilkins studied the sheets before he folded them and put them in his pocket. "For now. Thanks Irvin." That rascal pronounced the W like a V, his subtle reminder of my Russian connection.

He was playing with me. That kind of teasing can be amusing as long as it's not sinister.

I couldn't avoid explaining something about my class lists. "You'll see that one of the three sections is all Chinese students. They have specific problems with pronunciation. They're eager, but don't know our idioms."

"And the other two sections?"

I hadn't met the classes yet. "Looks like a mixture. Couple of German names, some Scandinavians who probably know English better than I do, and a bunch of Mohammeds. You know, most Moslems are named Mohammed."

"Any Pakistanis?"

I didn't know.

"No Afghans?"

"I can't imagine any Afghan has the money to send his son to study in Michigan."

"How do you pronounce the Chinese names?" Wilkins asked.

"I don't. They usually assume American sounding names like Mike or John. You've probably heard some of those. You call for technical assistance for your computer, get connected to Bangalore and talk to someone whose working name is Larry but whose real name is mumbledypeg." I imitated the Indian accent. "Just what is your problem, Mr. Wilkins?"

Wilkins laughed. It made his handlebar mustache jiggle. "You should be a comedian, Irvin."

"So what are you going to do with the class lists?"

He didn't answer directly. "We'll be in touch. Or I'll send someone."

"Oh? Someone carrying a folded copy of the New York Times and speaking in pass words?"

"You've been reading spy novels again." Wilkins left.

Hell, my life is a spy novel except I'm no James Bond or Jason Bourne. I had the feeling that this was going to lead to trouble.

Chapter two

Wilkins had hardly left when Ivy came in. She was wearing a light jacket over a long sweater that covered her stomach. Already she wasn't able to zip up the jacket. She'd have to invest in an oversize storm coat if she was going to do any cross country skiing. I didn't know if that was allowed when you're expecting. I'm still an amateur on the baby stuff.

"Guess who was just here?" I asked.

A flash of apprehension passed over her face. "Not Katya."

"No. Wilkins, the FBI guy."

Ivy slipped the book bag off her shoulder and sat down at her desk. "What'd he want?"

"Copies of my class lists."

"I hope you didn't give them to him. I'd tell him to piss off."

Ivy's more aggressive than I am. Maybe that's why she's such a good shot while I'm afraid to shoot myself in the foot or worse.

"Did I have a choice? It's not smart to give the FBI a hard time. I didn't want to wait until he reminded me that I've taken an oath to defend the Constitution against all enemies."

"You're not working for the government now, Irwin dear. That was years ago."

"But I'm still a law abiding citizen," I protested.

Ivy frowned. Her face has taken on that recognizable mask when women are pregnant. "What's Wilkins think? That one of your students is a terrorist?"

"Might be."

Ivy shook her head. "I should think that the government already plants an agent or two among the students to keep an eye on them."

"They probably do, as far as I know," I said. "But I don't

know anything. For all I know there's already someone in my class reporting on anything I say that's political."

"You're being paranoid."

"Hey, Honey, you hate it when students record your lectures or aim their cell phones at you."

I was alluding to the possibility that a video of a professor might turn up on U-tube. So much for the sanctity of the classroom.

She admitted that since 9/11 there was a resurgence of national paranoia. We both knew about the McCarthy period in the 1950's when the Wisconsin senator suspected everyone of being a communist. Now it was Moslems.

I already regretted giving Wilkins the copies. "If the FBI has agents under cover on campus, what does Wilkins need me for? If Homeland Security is that nuts they can run background checks on every foreign student."

"I thought that was the job of INS. Immigration wouldn't give just anyone a student visa."

Ivy didn't know what INS did with visa applications, nor did I. "I hear the Chinese students have their own watchers planted by their government. Or maybe that's just a rumor."

Ivy shook her head. "And we thought we were just teaching language classes. We weren't hired by Da Tech to spy on students. There's nothing political about basic German grammar, *nicht wahr*?" Ivy did a year in Berlin as part of her studies and little German expressions pop up now and then.

I was thinking out loud. "I wonder why Wilkins wanted the lists. Maybe he's after somebody specific." I thought about last term's roster. In some countries it's acceptable to lie and cheat. The only ones that really irritated me were a couple of Kuwaitis who cheated on tests. Cheating on a test wasn't grounds for denunciation to the FBI.

"Could be. Just don't cooperate with him," Ivy insisted. "Screw Wilkins."

I almost said "I'd rather screw you," but that would be rude and, well, we'd already done that.

Ivy started working on her own class stuff, but she was clearly thinking about Wilkins's visit. She looked up and asked, "Does the department head know about this?"

"Wilkins told me that Waarala said what goes on in my classes is my business."

"Waarals's weaseling."

"I'd better talk to him," I said, getting up from my chair.

Ivy nodded. "Right. Cover your ass."

She was being sarcastic but it was also good advice.

I went down the hall past a few confused freshmen. Waarala's secretary, the gossipy Mrs. Houghton, let me pass.

Waarala is the only Humanities faculty who has to wear a jacket and tie. The rest of us don't have to conform to any dress code. In the Copper Country the main reason for clothing is to keep from freezing to death when the winter socks in. Waarala had taken off his jacket and loosened his tie.

Waarala's office is the only one with a carpet. It's like entering a throne room. The bookcases behind the desk are full and his diplomas are framed and posted on his brag wall with other awards.

I closed the door and got right to the point. "I had a visit with Wilkins, the FBI guy from Marquette."

Waarala nodded. "So? You in trouble again, Irwin?"

"I try to stay out of trouble. Did Wilkins ask you for my class lists?"

"I told him your class lists are your territory. I don't interfere."

"Ivy thinks Wilkins might want me to spy on my students. That would violate student confidentiality. We can't even post grades. We can't tell parents how well their kids are doing."

Waarala agreed.

"What if Wilkins invokes Homeland Security? Am I covered?"

Waarala may be a Yooper, descended from the Finlanders who originally came to the Copper Country to work in the mines, but he's sophisticated. The politics of university life, with all the committees and cliques have made him cautious. "That's a grey area."

I tried to put it another way. "What if, for instance, Wilkins wants me to probe some Chinese girl?"

"Probe?"

I was embarrassed. "I didn't mean it that way. Investigate. Remember that business about non-fraternization?" I was alluding to my meetings with Katya that got me in trouble with Dean Sheldon.

Waarala looked at me over the tops of his glasses. "You planning some hanky panky?"

"God no."

"You don't have any other coeds claiming to be your daughter?"

"One was enough."

Waarala put his hands together in body language that said he was negotiating. "Write yourself a memo to file."

"A CYA memo? Cover your ass?"

Waarala nodded. "Just in case. As long as nothing major comes up I don't want to hear about it. I don't want any more trouble with the dean of students."

That didn't help me much. The only ass Waarala worried about was his own. A headship of Humanities was not exactly a rock solid job at Michigan Tech.

"You don't want me to keep you informed?"

Waarala shook his head. "Just don't let anything the FBI wants interfere with your teaching. You're on my payroll, not theirs. Or are you?"

Alluding to my past history, I said, "I am not a paid FBI informant." It was a little like Clinton insisting he did not have sexual relations with that woman.

So much for that. Clearly I was on my own and couldn't expect much backup from my department head.

I returned to the office.

Ivy asked what had happened.

"He told me to write myself a memo to file."

"Bureaucratic spineless jerk," Ivy said, fairly spitting out the words. *Scheisskopf.*"

I wouldn't be that vindictive. I'd seen too much of office infighting and betrayal to be surprised. I didn't know what a *scheisskopf* was exactly, but it didn't sound very good.

I tried to put Wilkins's visit out of my mind and returned to the lesson plans. After a new minutes of confusion and indecision I took a break and looked out the window again. It was the same scene of students and the falling leaves of autumn, but it had taken on a sinister undertone. Every student had their own story, their own secrets. It was well known that some of the 9/11 terrorists and their masterminds in Egypt and Afghanistan had studied in American universities. Those were well educated, some of them doctors, not your run of the mill deranged arsonist lurking on a street corner with a Molotov cocktail.

Why couldn't life be simple? I hoped Wilkins would leave me alone and let me and Ivy get on with our lives, have the baby, and be normal, none of that intrigue, but it's like that old trick, "Don't think of an elephant." You can't resist. You do think of an elephant. When someone even hints that one or more of your students is a terrorist in training, you can't help but be suspicious.

Anticipating the worst, I made a slight alteration to the lesson plan. As an exercise in Basic English I selected a subject that every student knew something about. They would be asked to write a paragraph or two about themselves, where they came from, and why they chose to study at Michigan Tech. My excuse would be that I wanted to get to know them individually, which I did.

It's essential to know your audience. For each student to give me a sample of their writing would tell me how far they'd come in the language, what they needed to learn, and how I might approach their problems. Of course, I could expect a mixed bag, and I could not expect someone to write, "I came to Michigan Tech from spy school in my country and I am studying chemistry so I can learn how to make bombs."

Nobody's that stupid, but sometimes a student who claims to need the subject reveals that he already knows it and is taking the class for an easy A to boost his GPA. For an FBI plant, writing too well in a bonehead English class might blow his cover. It was going to be like looking for plagiarism in a student term paper. I would have to do a serious analysis, not just check for typical errors in grammar and spelling.

I rationalized that it would be more interesting than watching for sentence fragments and comma splices, but it takes time. I had nearly ninety students on those class lists. Searching through their work would be like going through a carload of apples looking for one rotten one.

365

In the meantime, I'd wait to see if Wilkins turned up again, or if there really was an FBI agent planted among the students and could I spot him?

Chapter Three

I got a surprise call from Professor Kosinsky, my old landlord from when I first came to Michigan Tech and rented his house while he was in Israel at the Technion. He wanted to see me and suggested we meet at the student Union cafeteria. It was Wednesday, the day they offer pasties, the Copper Country version of the Cornish dish copper miners carried with them for lunch underground. The mines have long since been closed but the pasty remains as an Upper Peninsula tradition.

A pasty is essentially a portable stew. Like the food of any poor ethnic community, the filling consists of whatever was in the larder, in this case usually rutabagas, potatoes, some sort of meat, maybe carrots, all cubed and baked in a crust. Wrapped in a linen cloth, a pasty could be carried in a miner's pocket. That and a can of tea was lunch. In the Union cafeteria one also has the option of gravy or ketchup. Otherwise a pasty tends to be pretty dry.

Kosinsky is a Russian Jew who teaches Electrical Engineering. He's a bit paunchy, wears a favorite tweed jacket over a mismatched, baggy sweater, and doesn't bother to comb his hair. He considers me a landsman because we both speak Russian and I worked briefly in Moscow.

"Hello, Irvin," he said and held out his hand. Since it was a public place he restrained himself from the usual Slavic hug with air kisses on both cheeks. Yooper students wouldn't understand. "How are you?"

I wasn't going to tell him the FBI was after me again. Besides, in this country everyone asks "how are you?" when they couldn't care less. It's just a formality, like Germans when they say *wie gehts?* That much Ivy's taught me. "How's your cat?"

"Getting old like her owner," Kosinsky said with a deprecating smile. "She sleeps a lot."

We both went through the cafeteria line. I asked for a

pasty with gravy and Kosinsky, who hasn't become that assimilated to Copper Country life, bought a hamburger, no cheese, and a cup of coffee. Even though he doesn't keep kosher like his cousin, he abstains from mixing meat and dairy.

That reminded me of his cousin's visit. After emigrating from Russia to Israel Melamed had turned Orthodox, phylacteries and all. He had stayed at the house a couple of nights when he was in town for a job interview at Michigan Tech. As Kosinsky and I settled at a table for two amidst the noise of scraping chairs and clinking tableware I asked, "How is your cousin Melamed? Did he take the job at Stanford?"

"*Da*, yes. He said Stanford is a more prestigious university and they pay him more than Tech."

I remembered Melamed's farewell remark when I took him to his plane. "He thinks my daughter Katya is KGB."

Kosinsky's eyes squinted at me. "Is she?"

I shrugged. "I still don't know. She's in Oregon now with Putinsky." Putinsky, her Russian father, was once a KGB officer who prefers the abbreviated name Putin. Maybe that gives him more status or power to intimidate.

Kosinsky shook his head. "Strange."

I had to assume that he had read all about the incident with Putinsky in the Daily Mining Gazette. Ivy, Katya and I were now all public figures who were the subjects of news reports in the Gazette for about a week until we were mercifully blown off the front pages by a Japanese earthquake and bombings in Afghanistan and Iraq. A couple of the local kids who had enlisted to get money for college had been sent abroad and blown up. I was glad to no longer be the subject of news stories or bothered by the TV crew from Channel 6 in Marquette.

Kosinsky apparently realized I wasn't going to tell any more of my story and changed the subject. "My cousin Melamed is interested in the story of your letter."

"The letter that set me off studying the Russian language?"

"Yes. My cousin is now Israeli citizen. You know, Law of the return."

It's a peculiar law that assumes all Jews not in Israel are

367

exiles and are welcomed back to instant citizenship even if they never set foot in the place. It's similar to the German policy of welcoming ethnic Germans from Poland and other eastern countries. "Why is he interested?"

Kosinsky rearranged the slice of tomato and lettuce on his burger. The ketchup at the Union comes in little plastic packets. Kosinsky had taken two and fussed with the resistant plastic, finally squirted some ketchup on the meat patty. After taking a bite, deciding that it was OK, he continued. "You know that a Melamed is a teacher."

I didn't know that.

"You are also teacher, Irvin. My cousin says it runs in the family, in the blood."

I looked up from my pasty. I was having trouble cutting the crust which was hard and over baked. "Does that mean that all teachers are related? That's silly."

"My cousin is interested in genealogy. In Israel the holocaust survivors always look for who is a relative, who might have escaped the Nazi death camps."

"I'm sure my grandfather or great grandfather Isaac Melamed has no connection. He came to this country before the war." I was thinking World War I.

"My cousin thinks there is a connection."

I doubted it.

Kosinsky wasn't about to let go. It's probably a quality that makes him a good researcher. "You are not Jewish, Irvin?"

"I'm not anything," I explained. "My parents are Methodists. I don't go to any church."

"You should ask your parents if there are any Jews in your family."

"Why? What difference would it make?"

Kosinsky smiled apologetically. "It is a culture thing. What you call, I think, tribal. We are always sensitive to who is a Jew. Perhaps it is because so few of us are left."

"I'll ask my father."

"Ask your mother also. For Jews it is the mother that determines the religion."

What was Kosinsky trying to do? Make me out to be a Jew? I didn't know anything about Jews or their religion. I didn't believe that stuff about the Jews killing Christ. I vaguely remembered that the Pope himself had declared the Jews didn't kill our Savior.

Kosinsky took a sip of his coffee and grimaced. "I think they make this with kitty litter. Did you know, Irvin, that your Elvis Presley was Jewish?"

"What?"

Kosinsky explained. "Presley's grandmother was a Jew, which make his mother a Jew, and by inheritance, made Elvis a Jew. Did you know he wore a Mogan David, the Jewish star?"

I didn't know that. Being a Jew by any stretch of the imagination didn't fit with Presley's role as a sort of red neck who played his own brand of black music. To peg Elvis as a Jew had to be a peculiar quirk. I couldn't imagine Elvis Presley in a prayer shawl and skull cap.

"It is strange," Kosinsky said. "In Soviet Union I was not a Russian, but a Jew. The Union of Soviet Socialist Republics declared Jews to be one of the nationalities. To the Soviets I was Jew even if I never practiced the religion. Here in America I am Russian and to be Jew I must go to synagogue."

"Do you go to a synagogue?" I didn't even know if there was a synagogue in Portage Lake, Michigan, or whether there was a Jewish community at all. I thought the Copper Country consisted of Yoopers, most of them Apostolic Lutherans.

"I? Only once or twice a year for the High Holidays. Not like my cousin Melamed."

I remembered how his cousin had a Hebrew blessing for all occasions. "Your cousin Melamed is quite a character."

"He is entitled to his beliefs. He thinks I should be Orthodox."

I smiled. For a moment I imagined Melamed as a Jewish missionary knocking on doors of strangers with a bible in his hand like one of the Mormons. Except in Melamed's case it would be to convert secular Jews to his own orthodoxy. Was Melamed after me, too?

First it was Wilkins looking for terrorists in the bushes. Now it was Kosinsky's cousin looking for clues to Jews. What a crazy world.

Now Kosinsky was apologetic. "Pardon me for asking, Irwin. My cousin is…" He groped for the right word. "Persistent."

If Melamed could smell Katya as KGB, what next? Was Melamed with the Mossad? I shook my head as if to ward off a Copper Country deer fly. This was all getting to me. This was worse than not thinking about an elephant. I could just imagine Melamed first trying to make me out as a Jew and then trying to recruit me as a Mossad agent. It was nuts.

It was even more crazy than Waarala suggesting that I might seduce a Chinese coed. Just because I'd had an infamous one night stand in Moscow Waarala pegged me as a womanizer.

I suddenly lost my appetite for my pasty. I stood up. "I have to get back to the office."

"Yes. I, too," Kosinsky said, abandoning his coffee.

As I walked back to the Humanities building the planted thought grew on me. Reluctantly I resolved to ask my mother if there were any Jews in our ancestry. I hoped not. I didn't need any more complications in my life. And if there were Jewish ancestors, what difference would that make? None.

Back at our house Ivy put on a pot of home made chili for supper. It was pretty hot for my taste, but since her pregnancy she's had some peculiar cravings, like pickles and ice cream in the middle of the night. That must be some baby in there. Between gulps of fire quenching ice water I told Ivy about my lunch with Kosinsky.

Ivy was sitting at the table in her "Baby on Board" apron, which was just as well, for she'd thrown herself into the task of cooking dinner and there were splashes of chili on the lettering. "So Professor Kosinsky thinks you're Jewish?"

"No. His cousin Melamed thinks we are related because of my grandfather. He says I should ask my mother about family history."

"So ask. What harm could it do?"

It's funny how little we know of our own parents. Children of veterans never ask what their fathers did in the war. Even if they do, the vets don't want to remember or talk about it. We don't show an interest in family history until it's too late and the sources are dead.

My folks retired to Ocala, Florida to a double wide manufactured home. Ocala, being in the Eastern time zone, is the same time as Portage Lake, which logically should be on Central time. It wasn't too late to call.

After I cleared the kitchen to give Ivy a break I got on the hooter and phoned my folks. I didn't mention Wilkins' visit, but when I got my mother on the line I asked if there were any Jews among our ancestors.

My mother sounded a bit defensive, like this was a taboo subject. She admitted, "Your great Aunt Mary married a Jew and converted."

"Really? I never heard about that."

"The family was prejudiced against Jews. Nobody would ever mention her."

"Maybe she could tell me something," I suggested.

"She died years ago."

"Oh." A dead end.

But it wasn't quite. "Your grandmother once did a family tree. She thought our family went back to Scotland and the days when the land owners drove the crofters off the land."

"But grandma's dead, too."

"Yes, but I think I have a copy of her family tree around here someplace."

That was a possibility. "See if you can find it, Mom. I'm looking for a Melamed."

She remembered the mysterious letter. "Why?"

"My old landlord's cousin is also named Melamed. He thinks we might be related."

"I don't think so."

"Stranger things have happened," I offered. "Remember Madeline Albrecht, the secretary of state who found out that her parents had secretly converted to Christianity to escape the Holocaust? It was a closely guarded secret that wasn't revealed until some Jewish organization checked on her family history."

My folks have a speaker phone and Dad chimed on to say, "Son, when it comes down to it, we're all related somewhere down the line."

That was one of the most liberal things I ever heard him say.

Well, I figured I'd done what I could to satisfy my half-hearted promise to Kosinsky. I doubted if Mom had grandma's family tree tucked away among her clippings, patterns, and junk, if she could find it at all. I'd passed the ball to her and if she dropped it, who cared?

Chapter four

Classes began. The first session is like the moment the cards are dealt for a round of bridge. You don't know what hand you've been dealt. Though I had the class lists, those were just names, no faces. When the students were all Americans there weren't any cultural complications. With internationals, it was different. To the Chinese with their five thousand years of history and culture I was a barbarian. To the Moslems, Shiite or Sunni, I was an infidel. Saddled with that kind of categorization, I was at a disadvantage even though, as the instructor, I was supposed to be the authority figure.

I also had to be sensitive to cultural differences and body language. I couldn't sit on the desk and cross my legs or show the soles of my shoes. In some cultures when an instructor walks into the room the students all stand up and sit only when given the signal. I made a point of arriving early to avoid that. I wasn't going to be so intimate as to have them call me by my first name, especially since many couldn't pronounce the W. I was also uncomfortable being called Doctor Glass, since I have only an MA. What should they call me? Master Glass? Hardly. I'm not a professor, so calling me "professor" isn't accurate, either. Just call me Mister.

There were always a few latecomers who missed the first session and a few others who took one look at the syllabus I handed out and changed sections or dropped the course. I'm the only one teaching that basic course, but it's just pass/fail for one credit even though it meets three times a week, so students don't take it seriously.

The first time I taught it I had a Korean professor in one section, Dr. Park, who was forced by the administration to sign up, but what he really needed was private English elocution lessons so students could understand his lectures.

He obviously felt that was beneath his dignity.

Park didn't like to teach. Research was his interest and since it was the grants he got that were his ticket to the job, the administration let him do his thing. It was the money that mattered, not whether Yooper kids could understand a Korean's version of English syntax.

One nice thing about teaching foreign students is they are generally more mature than the local kids who had never been below the bridge as they say in the U.P., the bridge being the Mackinaw bridge that connects Michigan's two peninsulas. The foreign students have come a far distance, some half way around the world. Many in my class were engineering graduate students who just needed to brush up their language skills.

The second most spoken language in Portage Lake, Michigan isn't Spanish but Chinese. There's even a Chinese church. In the Econo Foods grocery you can find free copies of Epoc Times published in Oakland, California but entirely in Chinese. There are very few African-Americans in this otherwise white bread community, but there are a hundred Hindus from India, so the campus is pretty international while the town is provincial Yooper.

I set up seating charts and gave the assignment that would help me get to know my audience and might be useful to Wilkins: write a couple of paragraphs, not more than three hundred words, telling where you come from and why you chose Michigan Tech. I'd done that before.

I'd heard that in one class of American kids one of the boys wrote that he'd chosen the mostly male college because he was uncomfortable around girls. He must have been surprised when he discovered that female students now constitute nearly half the engineering student body and in the humanities programs are the majority.

I collected quite a stack of the assignments. Going over ninety students' papers is time consuming. Was there anything suspicious among those clumsily written submissions? I doubted it. Among the Chinese students there were a couple that were laced with patriotic balderdash one might suspect an applicant might write when asking a communist government for permission to study abroad. Say anything to get out of the country. But how do you distinguish between that kind of pose and the real thing? I couldn't tell.

Wilkins had an advantage over me. He had access to the government agency that granted the student visas. He phoned me and got right to the point. "You have an Afghan student from Kabul," he said.

I knew Kabul was the capital, but in spite of Afghanistan being in the news every day, I didn't know the geography of the country. I'm not as bad as those American kids who couldn't find the United States on a map if the name weren't printed on it, but I don't know all the provinces and cities in Afghanistan. When I was offered the job at Michigan Institute of Technology I had trouble finding Portage Lake on the map. I thought it was near Detroit. Big mistake.

"If you say so," I said.

"His name is Mohammed."

"That doesn't tell me anything. All of the male Moslems are Mohammed."

"He's in your two o'clock section," Wilkins said. "Does that help? You do have a two o'clock section, don't you?"

Now he was being sarcastic. I got out the class lists which were now all marked up with annotations and a few strikeouts. "What about it?"

Wilkins spelled out the name. It called up a somewhat older student with a ruddy face that suggested he'd shaved off his beard to better fit in among the American students. On the seating chart I'd drawn up he sat in the third row near the window. Wilkins asked, "What do you know about him?"

"Nothing." I had collected the assigned papers but hadn't gone through all of them. I had asked the students to write their self-descriptions by hand rather than print them out with a computer or send them by email. With computers the result might be more legible, but it was harder to cut and paste from each other if they wrote by hand. There was a certain risk that they're cook up a stock answer and copy from each other.

After struggling through a few of them I realized that even having assignments written in block letters and not some foreign version of cursive was going to be a real burden. I'd spend all my evenings trying to decipher handwriting. On the other hand, in spite of multiple choice exams where the students only filled in the little spaces with a pencil, some professor would demand essay answers. That would about kill a foreign student's chances.

I went through the two o'clock class submissions. The kid from Kabul hadn't turned his in.

Getting some students to do their homework on time was a royal pain in the ass. After a long delay while I sifted through the folder of papers from the two o'clock class I told Wilkins, "He hasn't done it."

"Good reason to call him into your office and talk to him," Wilkins insisted.

"I don't think so. You telling me how to run my class?"

Wilkins voice took on a hard edge. "I thought you were going to cooperate, Glass."

So now it was Glass, and not Irwin. I could see a real conflict brewing. "If there's a good reason to have a talk with him, I'll do it but a late paper the first week of class is no big deal." Many students are lackadaisical and simply blow off the assignments.

"I want to know how this Afghan guy ticks."

"What are you going to ask next? That I write a report? I don't have time for this stuff." It gave me a queasy feeling in my stomach. Putinsky, the KGB officer, had asked me to write a report on my boss at the American library in Moscow and look where it got me. Ruined. I certainly didn't want to start writing reports on my students. That wasn't my job. It would also be a violation of student/teacher confidentiality

"Make time," Wilkins demanded.

"*Screw you,*" I thought and hung up. But Wilkins had done it. Like it or not, now I was suspicious of the kid from Kabul.

There was another way to handle this problem: make copies of the homework and dump the entire set of submissions on Wilkins. Overload him with useless information. It would be a bigger pain in the ass for him to have to sift through all ninety homework submissions than it was for me. Those were my job. Presumably Wilkins had other things to do in the one man FBI office in Marquette, like check out students at Northern Michigan University, which has a larger student body than Tech.

There must be other issues for the FBI to pursue in Marquette, like people smuggling bear organs in from Canada, or five gallon flush toilets which, to conserve water, were prohibited in the USA. Imagine going through all the education and training for the FBI to chase toilet smugglers. But maybe that was the problem for US Customs. The US has so many policing agencies that it was no surprise that some terrorist might slip through. It would be ironic if someone tried to smuggle explosives or drugs in a five gallon commode tank only to be caught because the commode itself was illegal.

Of course NSA was watching the email traffic and for all I knew cell phone signals were being screened for key words, too. The old rule against wire taps had fallen by the wayside under the George W. Bush administration. No wonder criminals of all stripes used code words, like the Mafia calling a hit man a painter or a carpenter. If Ivy called me and asked me to pick up some bread at Jim's grocery would someone think that was a code word for ammo? Was the entire country hysterical?

Maybe we should call bread ammo and eggs grenades just to drive the watchers crazy.

I took the whole stack of nearly ninety homework submissions to the copy machine and ran off a duplicate set, stuffed them in a large, padded envelope, and mailed them to Wilkins.

Then I had second thoughts. This was a violation of student/teacher confidentiality. I shouldn't do that any more than I should publish samples of their work in a scholarly paper without permission. Wasn't what my students wrote automatically under their copyright? Hell, I wasn't publishing them; I was just sharing the papers with our own secret police. What Wilkins did with them was not my problem. Or was it?

But it was too late. I'd already mailed them. If my sending the whole bundle to Wilkins made him mad, he'd find ways to get even.

I'd made that kind of rash mistake before when, to provoke Katya into contacting me, I shifted what turned out to be stolen Russian Mafia money to a separate account. Ivy said I was laundering money. The Mafia thought I was stealing it and nearly killed me. Moving the money was nearly a fatal mistake. Dumb me.

Hell, sending Wilkins the student papers wasn't dangerous. I'd have to be ultra paranoid to believe that.

To make amends in advance I'd better scrutinize those student assignments and come up with something legitimate or substantial just to mollify Wilkins.

Unfortunately, the Afghan student hadn't done his homework. He wasn't the only one. The term before I had a couple of snotty Kuwaitis who didn't want to do anything and were shocked when they got a "fail." They came into the office and demanded, "How could you flunk me?"

"Because you didn't do the work," was my polite answer. Ass holes. They weren't Turks. I'd read that a Turkish major at the American War College killed himself because he didn't get the highest grade in the class. So much for cultural differences when teaching foreign students. Getting some of them to knuckle under in a pass/fail course was tough, especially when, for all I knew, back home they were princes or the scions of top government officials used to lording it over everyone around them.

How was I to find out anything about potentially suspicious students in my class?

Chapter Five

The surprise was that Ivy came up with a lead to all this on her own. It was the Muslim Students' Association. Would Wilkins expect me to attend their meetings like the FBI did when they planted agents in meetings of the US Communist Party? The joke was that there were so many FBI agents paying dues back then that they were the largest contributors to the CP. If the FBI wanted to plant someone in the Muslim Students' Association at Michigan Tech it wasn't going to be me.

As for the Afghan and others who didn't turn in their

homework, I'd ask them to see me during my office hours. That should take care of it.

I'd forgotten about Kosinsky's query on behalf of his cousin when I got a phone call from my mother in Ocala. Damned if she hadn't located that family tree.

"Really?" I said.

"I had it in a box of old quilting patterns."

My mother's hobby is quilting. She can't throw anything away. The spare bedroom in their Florida retreat is cluttered with quilting materials, boxes of bits of cloth. Last time I visited them I suspected she was a hoarder, but my Dad insisted she keep all the quilting materials in one room or the entire house would be choked with stuff. "You must have spent days searching."

Her voice took on a defensive tone. "It may look messy, Irwin, but I know where things are." She added, "More or less."

"So is there anything in the family tree about a Melamed?"

"Yes. It's not complete. No date of birth or death, Just that your great grandfather Isaac Melamed came from Odessa."

"I thought he came from Moscow. There was a photograph, too, taken in Moscow."

"Might have been the same, maybe someone else."

"When did he leave?" I knew enough of Russian history from my studies that some Jews left the country to avoid the twenty-five year conscription into the Cossack army. Others fled the pogroms of the eighteen eighties. Then there was the 1905 revolution. Melamed wouldn't have been around for the big one in 1917.

Mom wasn't sure, which means she didn't know when he left Russia.

"Can you send me the family tree?"

"The whole thing? It's pages and pages."

I realized I'd asked something inconvenient. To send a big document meant my folks would have to obtain an oversize envelope and pay extra postage. Dad would have to take it to the post office. He joked that a retiree shouldn't go to the post office and the bank the same day or he wouldn't have anything to do. On the other hand, he'd calculate how much gas it took to drive to the Windixie grocery store. I worried about him. He played golf at the municipal course because he couldn't afford greens fees anywhere else. My Dad was feeling pinched, living on a fixed income, no COLAs, and inflation. He complained that he was losing purchasing power every year. If it weren't for golf he'd sit at home all day and ruminate over his declining resources.

"Just make a copy of anything with Melamed's name on it," I suggested. "If Dad doesn't have a scanner for his computer he can get free copies made at the bank. Can't be more than a page or two, right?"

That seemed a satisfactory solution. As soon as she could persuade him to take the family tree to the bank, she'd send the key pages.

Here I was, buried in nearly a hundred student papers every week and my folks had trouble with a page or two. It was like the Peter Principal, work expands to fill the time available to do it, so a maiden aunt may take a full day to write a postcard.

"Should be interesting, if they do it," Ivy said.

Then I confessed to her that I'd sent the whole packet of student papers to Wilkins.

"What are you doing, Irwin? Spying on your students?"

"I'm not spying. Wilkins is spying."

"You're enabling."

"It's not like I'm sleeping with the enemy," I pleaded. "Wilkins is not the enemy."

"He's not exactly your friend, either."

I felt obliged to defend him. "He came to our wedding."

"That was business."

"I owe him a favor," I said. "He could have put the screws to us when we had that shooting."

I regretted the reference immediately. Ivy still has some PTSD because of that incident. Unless you're homicidal, you don't kill somebody, even in self defense, without some trauma. She sometimes has nightmares about it.

"I still don't like it," Ivy said. "You're on a slippery slope, honey. Please no more *lebensgefahr.* "

I didn't know what *lebensgefahr* was but I got the drift.

What cut off that discussion was a funny look on Ivy's face. She said "Oops! I think the baby just kicked me."

She put my hand on her stomach, but I couldn't feel anything.

I would wait and see what Wilkins said and postpone my curiosity about the Melamed ancestry until the papers arrived.

Chapter six

To my surprise the copies from the family tree arrived a few days later in a priority mail envelope from the post office. Grandma had tried to elaborate, write vignettes about each known ancestor. The Melamed name appeared on only two pages, but there were other sheets. She had actually obtained a copy of the manifest of the ship a Yitzak Melamed had arrived on and the page from the Ellis Island entry. Yitzak is an alternate spelling for Isaac. I guess my mother hadn't bothered to read those photocopied pages or she'd have known about when Melamed left Europe. You'd think that anyone who could puzzle through the patterns for quilts could read the copy of an old manifest, but people are selective.

It was remarkable. There was the name of one of my great grandfathers, age seventeen. The record shows he spoke Russian and Jewish. He'd been traveling alone. Imagine, as a teenager, leaving your country and crossing the ocean to a country where you didn't know the language. That took courage, or maybe desperation. But he was only one of four great grandfathers, of course. The farther back you go, the more relatives you have and the more distant the connection.

Except for that letter in Russian I'd never had much interest in family history. I guess that's something that comes when you reach a certain age, maybe when you realize that there's more of your life behind you than in front of you and you yourself are history. I wasn't at that stage, not yet.

I had reached that critical passage in life. I was past forty, the age when you realize your life is half over, that this is probably the last chance to get that Ph.D., sail around the world, or get married. For me it was marriage. For Ivy it was that critical age is when you can no longer have a baby. We had both taken the plunge, so to speak.

We have many passages in life, times when we are absorbed by graduations, then by weddings, then baby showers. I suppose the day comes when most of your life passage events are funerals. My Dad talks about it, that most of his old pals are dead.

I phoned Professor Kosinsky, told him that I had the Melamed information, such as it was, made a set of copies on the office machine, and dropped them in the campus mail. I presumed he'd pass the information on to his cousin at Stanford. Maybe that Melamed would figure it out. I had more important things to do.

Half a dozen of the foreign students hadn't turned in their assignments. Not the Chinese, of course. They are devoted. I never saw such highly motivated people.

Klaus Hitz, a kid from Stuttgart, Germany, was in my class only because his student advisor had recommended it. The German schools were so thorough that he didn't need a brush up of his English. Klaus has been studying English since the third grade. He felt doing the assignments wasn't necessary. He'd just take whatever tests I gave and breeze through. That made me feel like I was wasting my time.

From past experience I knew that cultural differences made American habits rude. You didn't call in an Arab-speaking student for a conference and get to the point immediately. There was a ritual to it. "Sit down. Eat or drink something." I didn't offer coffee or a Coke, but I kept a bowl of M&M's on my desk as an ice breaker. Like the Arab practice of handing out mints at a funeral to have a sweet association with death, a bit of candy might sweeten what could be a forbidding conference with your college instructor. The risk was that Ivy or I would nibble them all. At least I might. Ivy in her pregnancy suddenly had an aversion for chocolate.

The student from Kabul came in as commanded. He was short and swarthy, with heavy eyebrows that met in the middle of his forehead. I could tell by the two-toned color of his face that he'd been tanned with a beard but that the beard had been shaved off. As the tan faded in the Copper Country winter the difference would disappear. The M&Ms didn't sweeten his disposition.

The Afghan wanted to be called Michael because his name was hard for Americans to pronounce. Was he using Michael as a pseudonym? He was surly and I took a dislike to him. The feeling was mutual. I didn't know if I'd used the wrong body language in class, or whether I had inadvertently and unintentionally talked down to him or what. It could be that I was suspicious. If I projected suspicion, he could be reflecting it, being suspicious of me. It was not a good beginning. I rationalized that maybe he didn't like the M&M candy. These intercultural communications problems can be subtle.

I also got the impression that Mohammed—Michael—was a liar. I couldn't know whether he lied because it was convenient, whether it was habitual, a cultural thing, or a manifestation of disrespect. In some cultures lying comes naturally. They tell people what they think they want to hear, not the truth.

In some countries, like South America, you never tell someone "no." A tourist who asks, "Is this the way to the railway station?" might be told "Yes," even if that's not the way at all.

That's not my style. If I think someone's choice of furniture is ghastly, I'd rather say nothing than fake some praise. When Michael from Kabul finally turned in his paper he wrote that he thought America was an ideal country and the people wonderful but the tone wasn't sincere, like he wanted me to think that while in reality he felt something else. It was a pose.

I suppose we all do that to some extent. We wear masks, take on roles like actors. It's human nature to adapt to the expectations of others. If they laugh, you laugh. At meetings of the Humanities department I try to appear just as legitimate as the senior faculty, the ones with tenure, when we all know I'm a second class citizen teaching a course none of them would want to sink to.

The Afghan said his father was a government official in Kabul, which, considering the culture of bribery and corruption, might have been the reason he could afford to study at Michigan Tech.

Several of the Chinese students turned in their papers late and were sincerely apologetic. One of the girls actually cried in my office. God, dealing with these cultural differences was complicated. If I didn't lay down the law, some wouldn't do the work at all. If I embarrassed a student from one culture would he go out and kill himself? It was bad for a Chinese student to lose face. It would have been a lot easier if I just blew off the assignments myself, but then they'd all get the point and do nothing at all. I'd lose control of the class.

The other students who hadn't done their homework on time pretended to be appropriately chastened. I'd know if my message got through if they complied on the next assignment.

I waited until the last one was in before making a copy of the late papers and sent them to Wilkins. By that time I knew enough to jot down a few words of explanation if the content was so vague that the nationality of the writer wasn't clear.

As for Michael the Afghan, being unpleasant didn't mean you were a terrorist. I suspected that the fifteen mainly Saudis who did the 9/11 attack seemed to their neighbors to be a bunch of nice guys even if they did keep to themselves. I was reminded of how neighbors described some of our worst serial killers: "He's a quiet person, keeps to himself, very polite" et cetera. Then he goes out and commits mayhem.

Chapter seven

A few days later Kosinsky called me at home. He was amused. "Hello, Cousin Irvin!"

"What do you mean, 'cousin'?"

"My cousin in California says there is a family connection."

I couldn't believe it. Kosinsky's explanation was so convoluted that I immediately lost the thread. Was I a third cousin twice removed of a grand nephew? I thought about Melamed's extreme orthodoxy. He wore one of those skull caps like the Pope. When he stayed over as my house guest I'd seen him praying with phylacteries, those little leather boxes, one on his forehead, the other on his arm, the leather thong wrapped around his left arm. He even wore some kind of garment with fringes that hung out under his jacket. "Does your cousin think I'm Jewish?" That would be a stretch.

"Oh, no, Irvin, but you are *mishpucha*."

"What's that?"

"Yiddish for a relative, no matter how distant."

That made Kosinsky a relative, too. That Prof. Kosinsky could be related I found amusing, but he, living alone with his cat in a place far distant from his roots, clung to the idea. I was no longer his ex-tenant. I was by some stretch of his Jewish imagination, part of his family. Maybe that's what Kosinsky meant by the tribal connection. What had he called it? MOT? Member of the Tribe? Like the Mormons and their recognition signal, "LDS?" for Latter Day Saints.

It was a foreign idea to me. Though raised Methodist, I didn't feel any special kinship with other Methodists. I was a generic, non-sectarian, Christian, not one of those slack-jawed evangelicals who are so enthralled by having Jesus as their personal Savior that they bore everyone they meet with the news. Mulling over the idea of tribal association, I saw a similarity to some of the other cultures in my classes. It was natural for the Moslem students to have their own association.

During my brief stint in Moscow years ago it was clear that Americans at the embassy associated with other Americans. There was some interaction with personnel from other embassies, but in those Soviet days everyone had to be cautious. You never knew who you met from whatever organization might be political. Hadn't my brief foray with the locals, namely Vladimir Putinsky and his wife, been fatal to my career? It wasn't only normal to hang out with your own kind; it could be dangerous in that situation not to. That was what was meant by "sleeping with the enemy." Boy, I sure knew about that!

When Hemingway was in Paris, for instance, who did he hang out with? French people? No, with other expats.

That didn't mean your connection with people from your own country was particularly close. Did the Muslim Student Association at Michigan Tech break down into Sunni and Shiite factions? The enemy of my enemy is my friend? It was that sort of relationship, until it broke down and became brother against brother, father against son.

So I was-- what was the word?-- *Mishpucha* to Professor Kosinsky. I suppose that would be grounds for Ivy and me to invite him for a food ritual, to dinner or at least coffee. That's the way humans form bonds. They eat together.

No wonder I had to keep some candy in the office to break down communication barriers with my foreign students. It made sense.

I told Ivy, "Professor Kosinsky says we are *mishpocha*."

"What's that?"

"Relatives. His cousin studied the family history and says we are related."

Ivy gave me a smile that said she was thinking of far away things, sort of contemplative. "It would be nice to have some family close by."

She was thinking that her parents were down in Chicago, more than four hundred miles away, and mine were in Ocala, Florida. With an infant coming it would be nice to have a doting granny close by for moral support and the occasional baby sit. I couldn't imagine Kosinsky cooing over a baby, but Russians love children. Might happen.

It suddenly occurred to me that if our kid was a boy, would Kosinsky suggest a circumcision? That would be a stretch. We're not Jewish.

The whole business gave me pause. I would have to mentally rearrange my relationship with my ex-landlord. This was beyond being fellow speakers of the Russian language. It was like I was being admitted to a new fraternity.

I wondered if this would have some bearing on other relationships, Wilkins, for instance. He's a Yooper, of course, and FBI. I'm neither, but all that business in Washington with the CIA, NSA, or whatever agency I'd been involved with when we interrogated Putinsky gave me a kind of kinship with the undercover world. I wasn't a paid Soviet agent as I'd been suspected of being, and I wasn't part of one of our many police agencies, but I had worked for the State Department, the Foreign Service, and taken the oath. I was in a sense part of the brotherhood, like those veterans who might have fought in different theaters of war but had all worn the uniform.

What I realized was I was arriving at a new definition of myself, of Irwin, or Irvin, Glass.

What impact did my role as an FBI informant on potentially suspicious foreign students have on who I was and how others might see me if they knew?

Chapter Eight

At breakfast one morning Ivy and I discussed ultra sound to see whether she was expecting a boy or a girl. "I don't need to know. I just want it to be healthy," I insisted. "Let it be a surprise." Being an only child, I hadn't had a little brother or sister. I'd missed out on a sibling relationship. I wasn't into that stuff about blue baby clothes for boys and pink for girls, but Ivy was already lingering over the kiddy clothes when we shopped at the Wal-Mart super store. Just looking at those tiny shirts and baby shoes made me feel that I was totally out of my depth. This fatherhood thing was going to take some adjustment.

Ivy was full of anticipation and anxiety. Should she have a natural birth or have an anesthetic? She pored over magazine articles and checked the internet, learned about the frequency of C sections. There was a big debate about that. If you look enough you can find arguments on all sides of an issue, even people convinced that the earth is flat.

I was disturbed to learn that having a baby is more dangerous than having an abortion. Not that we would ever consider terminating a pregnancy Ivy wanted so badly. But a C section had its dangers, too. Any time you get a general anesthetic there's a risk that you won't come out of it. Any time you're cut open in a hospital there's a risk of infection. When I saw the statistics about infant mortality in the United States compared to other countries, we were way down the list, worse than countries like Nigeria. So much for the glories of the so-called American health system. The best place for

Ivy to have our baby would be Finland, but we weren't going there. No wonder she was apprehensive.

Ivy attended a prenatal class for expectant mothers. She wanted me to go along, but I could see that the women were uncomfortable to have a man present when they were discussing all that female stuff. I suspected that though caesarian birth might net doctors more fees, it was necessary only in certain cases. I was learning new things, like the fact that some women had pelvises that made natural birth dangerous for the baby. I was feeling overwhelmed and I was only the father. I wasn't the one carrying a fetus, so I relented. We'd get the ultrasound, which should remove one of the uncertainties.

Ivy made an appointment and we drove up in her Tracker to the Portage Lake hospital. We were now a one vehicle family. In spite of my sentimental attachment to the old truck, my Ford Pickup had finally proved too expensive to repair. Faced with an engine rebuild I'd had it towed to Manninen's junk yard at the top of the hill and said goodbye to it. While Ivy looked at the Penny's catalog for baby clothes, I studied car ads for the day when we'd need something bigger, preferably with four wheel drive for getting around in the Copper Country snow.

The technician at the hospital was so young looking to me that I wondered if she was a recent graduate. The ID tags have only first names, I suppose to protect the identity of employees. The med tech was "Charlotte" and had a Yooper accent. I suspected she was a graduate of the local Finlandia University nursing school. Instead of the typical white lab coat that sets some people off, she wore a smock with a friendly flower print.

I watched with curiosity as Charlotte rubbed Ivy's stomach with some sort of slippery gel and then applied the ultra sound gadget. We watched the grainy, ghostly image on the monitor. There it was, a tiny creature all cozy in a chamber of warm amniotic fluid. That anyone could see the elusive shape as a baby took training and practice. For me it was the first time. How could anyone tell anything?

"It's a boy," Charlotte announced.

Ivy gave me a teary smile. "A boy."

I could imagine that she was already rearranging her shopping plans for the layette. In light of my own recent adventures in genealogy I started thinking about names. Maybe we should call the kid Isaac, after the elusive and long dead Isaac Melamed.

"We should tell Katya that she's going to have a brother," I said.

"A half brother," Ivy corrected, wiping the gel off her stomach and rearranging her clothes.

"Sure." I'd have to send Katya an email, for I didn't know her address, she's that difficult to keep track of. Ever since she took off with her erstwhile Russian father, the enigmatic Vladimir Putinsky, now Putin, "Not that Putin" as he always said, I hadn't had a chance to speak with her.

We have a strange relationship. I'm her biological father, as the DNA test proved, providing the results were genuine, and we are as close as one might expect from such a short-term, stressed relationship. What has never been proven one way or another is whether she was sent from Russia as an agent to take advantage of the cover story of her being my daughter, or whether she had simply taken the advice of her dying mother and fled the clutches of her KGB father. Those were only two of the possibilities. People in trouble will grasp at any straw, and my connection to her, however tenuous and problematic, could have been enough to get her all the way from Moscow to Northern Michigan.

In the story she first told me, Katya said Vladimir was a very bad man, but he's obviously a complex personality. He abused his wife, Katya said, and I was proof enough of that, since he'd forced her mother to pose for those nude pictures at the Metropol hotel. Nobody is all bad. Even Hitler was fond of his German Shepherds. Now that Vladimir's fled Russia and his enemies there, I have more sympathy for him. In spite of our early history, I like the man. I'm not saying I trust him, for you never know what he's thinking or planning, but he's old now and demoted to the status of ordinary refugee. I suppose he's like the Vietnamese war criminal general who ends up in Louisiana on a shrimp boat.

As soon as we got back to the house I booted up my laptop and sent Katya an email at her hotmail address. "Must talk with you. Please call or send your phone number. Love, Papa." She calls me papa, a more affectionate alternative than the formal "father". She doesn't call Putinsky by his first name, either. He is not Vladimir to her and certainly not Vlady. Maybe his mother called him Vlady. It's one of those Russian name things like you run into if you attempt to read "War and Peace" which is published with a glossary of names of the fifty some characters.

Of course, we have numerous names, too. I could be Irwin, Irv, or Irwin Glass, or Mr. Glass. Like I said, not Doctor Glass or Professor. Katya, more formally Katarina Volodna, which means daughter of Vladimir, could also be Katarina Putinsky or Katarina Volodna Putinsky, the whole nine yards.

She replied right away with a number and I phoned.

Like most cell phone connections, the conversation began with "Where are you?" except, of course, I spoke Russian with her.

I was hoping for a real address. She said she was on a bus, which could mean anywhere.

"I have news," I said. "You are going to have a baby brother."

She was excited to hear that. "When?"

I told her the estimated time of arrival and added, "You must come and see him when he arrives."

"I will do that," she said.

Ah, that was a relief. I needed to see her. She is, after all, my daughter, sort of, anyway. "How is Vladimir?" There was good reason to ask, as he had a knee replacement after the wound he got from Ivan the Awful, the Mafia killer.

"Better. He had some rehab." She had picked up the English word for it and used it in the conversation. It was a word she'd had no occasion to use in her native language. That's how our language develops as we adopt foreign words and mix them into our vocabulary. Ivy is always howling about how many English words have been adopted by the Germans. Their equivalents of the grocery store gossip tabloids are full of awkward Americanisms like "weekend house."

"Are you in Oregon?" I asked. Getting details out of

her was as bad as interrogating Putinsky. It was like pulling a lion's teeth without anesthetic.

"Yes, Portland."

I wondered why she and Vladimir had ended up there but remembered that there were five thousand Russian émigrés in Oregon's largest city. He probably had some ex-KGB contacts there, or maybe some shady characters like himself. "So how about an address?"

She told me something but before I could write it down she added, "It is only temporary."

"You're moving?"

"Maybe to be student at Portland State University."

That immediately put me into faculty advisor mode. "But you're not an Oregon resident. The out of state tuition must be a killer. Why not come back here to Portage Lake. As daughter of a faculty member you can pay in state tuition at Michigan Tech. I might even get you a deal for a discount." A discount? Was I starting to talk like a Jew who never pays retail? Maybe Kosinsky's assertion that, as a descendent of Isaac Melamed, I had Jewish blood, was real.

I hadn't thought about the cost of sending a kid to college. I remembered the huge stash of cash Putinsky had hidden in my account at the Riggs bank. With that kind of support, I wouldn't have to worry about school money for Katya.

"I'll think about it," she said, but didn't sound persuaded.

I was going to add that she'd probably have to stay in the dorms, as our little rented house had only one bedroom and a futon in the living room, but she rang off with "This is my stop."

I heard bus noises in the background and she was gone. When I tried to call her back, there was no answer.

Chapter Nine

It was mid-September, a Tuesday. Since our classes are Monday, Wednesday and Friday, Ivy and I were at home, working on class preparations. The house was quiet except for the cuckoo clock in the kitchen doing its hourly thing. A cuckoo clock is one of those noisemakers you either learn to ignore or it gets on your nerves. Ivy's father made it for a wedding present and it nearly saved my life, so, irritated or not, I wasn't going to disable the cuckoo.

It was a tranquil, domestic moment. Ivy was propped up on pillows on the living room futon with her homework and I was at the used desk we'd found at the Goodwill. It was getting to be difficult for Ivy to make herself comfortable and baby's date was months away. The phone rang. It was Dr. Kosinsky.

"What's up?"

"Do you know, Irvin, it is a Jewish holy day, Rosh Hashanah. Would you like to see the synagogue? I'll give you a tour."

"I'll ask Ivy." I put down my work sheets and turned to her. "Want a tour of the local synagogue?"

"I didn't know there was one."

"Apparently there is. Kosinsky says it Rosh something or other."

Ivy put down her German textbook. "Why not? I need a break."

I agreed, but I wasn't so sure I wanted to see the synagogue. What was Kosinsky up to? Just because his cousin claimed I was a distant relative didn't make me Jewish. Did he have some ulterior motive now that he considered me by some stretch of the imagination a member of his tribe, as he put it? Maybe he felt he needed some companionship, that he, because of his secular bent, needed motivation to get himself to the services.

Ivy was curious. I was suspicious. Any time someone invites me to their church I think they're looking for a new congregant.

It made me feel uncertain, vaguely threatened, as if I feared that the tour would set off a sequence of disturbing events. Our lives were settling down, in spite of Wilkins, and I didn't want any more complications.

I didn't know there was a synagogue in Portage Lake, Michigan or that there were any Jews. How would I know? It turns out that there is a synagogue there and I'd driven past it every time we drove across the lift bridge that connects the two halves of the consolidated town of Portage Lake.

Kosinsky picked us up in his dark blue Camry. I think he acquired some bad driving habits during his year at the Technion in Israel, because he doesn't seem to understand that red traffic lights mean stop. "The temple was built in 1910," Kosinsky explained as we crossed the steel grating of bridge. Having been built before the automobile, the synagogue has no parking lot. Kosinsky had to drive past it and pull into the lot at the bank about half a block farther up the highway. There's no proper sidewalk, but a narrow shoulder.

The architecture of the synagogue is different from any other building in town. It has a domed roof like you'd expect in a warmer climate where summer heat is supposed to rise and be vented, which is why the capital and other Roman-looking buildings from days before air conditioning are built with domes. I'd never noticed the six pointed start at the peak.

"Looks Byzantine," Ivy commented as we shuffled up the rather dilapidated concrete steps leading up from the highway.

It certainly isn't Copper Country gothic. Instead of being constructed of pink Jacobsville sandstone, like many of the buildings in town, the Jewish church was built of glazed brick. Sandstone weathers badly. Aside from being pointed up by a mason every fifty years or so, glazed brick never needs painting and keeps out moisture. The synagogue was built to last.

Other churches in the Copper Country tend to be badly weathered sandstone or merely clapboard, needing paint. A few new ones have plastic siding.

I'd never been in a synagogue before nor had Ivy. I was curious. I knew Kosinsky wasn't particularly religious, at least not like his cousin from Israel, so I was surprised to find out something different about him. Until then, I'd pegged him as just another Russian emigrant, what they called a refusenik, one of the professionals who escaped the Soviet government's clutches as soon as exit vises were permitted.

I knew that leaving the Soviet Union wasn't easy for those Jewish professionals. The government sometimes demanded payment for the free college education they'd received.

There was something in Hebrew cut into the stone above the front door. "It says 'Adat Israel,'" Kosinsky explained. "The House of Israel."

"I thought you weren't religious,"

Kosinsky and gave me an apologetic look. "It is tradition."

I was reminded of the song in Fiddler on the Roof. "Tradition! Tradition."

I have no particular tradition. Until the recent investigation into the family tree I'd had little interest in family history beyond who the heck was Isaac Melamed. Being from South Bend, Indiana was no tradition. My parents didn't stem back to the Mayflower or the Civil War.

The service was already under way as we entered the sanctuary. The congregation praying inside was pretty sparse, little more than a dozen people. At the raised pulpit in front a small, grey haired man in a dark suit and a prayer shawl was leading the worshippers.

Though there was a gilded lion above the curtained cabinet which I later saw contained the Jewish holy scrolls, there were no statues like you find in Catholic churches and of course no depictions of Jesus. The only decorations, if you could call them that, were two flags, an American flag to one side and an Israeli flag on the other.

I reminded myself that I was a tourist, not a worshipper. I was impressed by the stained glass windows, something I thought you found mainly in Catholic churches, except at the Portage Lake House of Israel the stained glass doesn't depict Jesus or any aspect of Christianity. I recognized one of them had Noah's ark, another a Jewish star.

Kosinsky handed me a skull caps from a cardboard box in the pew near the entrance. This hat wasn't black like Kosinsky's cousin wore. It was blue and printed to commemorate some kid's bar mitzvah.

People turned with curiosity to see who had come in and one of the men shook hands with Kosinsky. He quietly introduced me, "Irwin and Ivy Glass, also at Michigan Tech."

The guy's face lit up like he had found long lost relatives.

Ivy and I sat near the back at the side and were handed a couple of prayer books. Kosinsky asked what page they were on and we fumbled though the books, discovering that the pages were numbered backwards, from right to left. Much of the service was in Hebrew but the passages were translated on facing pages of the prayer book. The Hebrew was all mumbo jumbo to me, but there was something friendly and homey about the place. For someone like me who feels like an outsider at faculty department meetings, painfully aware of my junior status, I felt strangely like I belonged with these people.

I whispered to Kosinsky, "Do you come to these services very often?"

He shook his head. "Just a few times a year. They don't have a regular rabbi."

When everyone stood up we followed suit, wondering what happened next. Then the visiting rabbi opened the cupboard behind the pulpit and took out one of those scrolls, what the Jews call the Torah, and I had a flash of déjà vu. I'd never been in a synagogue in my life, but it suddenly seemed familiar. Reading from the Torah scroll was the high point of the proceedings. I felt oddly touched. Maybe it was Isaac Melamud grabbing me by the collar like some ghost drawing me into his world.

When the service ended and everyone wanted to meet us, to know who this strange couple was, and I told them I was Irwin Glass, they simply assumed that I was a Jew, as if the name "Irwin Glass" was like a password, what the spies I'd read so much about called a recognition signal.

Was I now pegged as Jewish? I hate to be categorized. Everyone thinks I'm something or someone else.

"We're just visiting," Ivy explained. Maybe she was also afraid they'd want to sign us up as new members. We were obviously strangers.

What do we really know about each other? I didn't know Kosinsky went to a synagogue or even if one existed, but why should I? Our relationship, even though he'd been my landlord, was superficial.

Hell, I didn't even know my erstwhile daughter Katya very well, and some of the things she told me about herself weren't true. Ivy was always coming up with different things about herself. I suppose that even when we are married fifty years there will still be some surprises.

So some people were now under the impression that I was Jewish. Did that matter? It was just a misunderstanding.

After the service everyone went downstairs to the party room where there were snacks set out, bagels and some vegetarian dishes. The rabbi led a blessing over bread and wine. I felt uncomfortable and awkward. Ivy has better social skills than I and mingled. Everyone was friendly and welcoming, like maybe they thought if we weren't actually Jewish we might be potential converts, not that I ever saw a Jewish missionary in my life.

I was introduced to a few people I immediately forgot, but one made an impression, a stocky grad student Kosinsky introduced as one of his grad students in electrical engineering. Arya Katz had done his stint in the ADF, the Israeli defense forces, and now he was finishing his PhD.

I asked, "What did you do in the army?"

His answer didn't invite a follow-up. "I was in intelligence," like don't ask me anything more or I have to kill you.

It made me wonder if, besides Wilkins' possible watchers among the students, the Mossad had its own man on campus. Seemed unlikely.

When we left and Kosinsky dropped us off at the house Ivy was troubled. "What did you think of the synagogue?"

"Interesting architecture for the Copper Country. Or do you mean the people?"

"It's not handicapped accessible," Ivy said. "There's just that one entrance to the sanctuary, and you have to go up stairs. What if someone yelled 'fire' like happened at the Italian Hall?"

She was referring to a local tragedy. At Christmas during the infamous mine strike about 1914 there was a party upstairs in the Italian Hall in Calumet, ten miles north of Portage Lake. Someone yelled 'fire" and in the panic that resulted there was a crush of people on the stairs and a lot of people died, mostly children. "It's just a few steps," I commented.

I remembered there was only one entrance to the sanctuary, though there was a downstairs exit from the party room.

"Your FBI friend Wilkins would see Adat Israel as a potential target for terrorists."

"I suppose so, but there aren't any terrorists around here in spite of Wilkins' paranoid fantasies."

"There are crazy people everywhere."

"They don't go around to churches yelling 'fire.'"

"Even so, I think the Portage Lake Jews should be prepared."

I brushed her off with, "Maybe they are," but I couldn't help having misgivings. It was like that "don't think of an elephant" thing. First I found an unexpected affinity for the local Jews and now I was already worried that they'd be the target of terrorists. Thanks, Ivy. I sure didn't need that.

It's an old building. There's no fire exit.

Well, Isaac Melamed, what do you think of that? I wondered, and almost instantly I thought I knew why he had left Russia. How many Jews had been burned alive in the pogroms?

Of course I was only speculating. I didn't know anything. That I might be channeling the spirit of a great grandfather was something for charlatan spiritualists. It was all imagination, like Wilkins thinking there were terrorists among the foreign students at Michigan Tech. Of course, damn him, he might be right.

Chapter ten

I was convinced Wilkins was wrong. There were a thousand foreign students at Tech and all of the students in my three sections added up to less than a hundred. If Wilkins wanted to sniff out the whole foreign student population he'd need more than one willing informant. Not that I was willing. He had to have others planted on campus.

Surely not, I reasoned. Wilkins was a one man FBI office in Marquette. Marquette, the largest town in the UP, had fewer than thirty thousand inhabitants, including nearly ten thousand at Northern Michigan University. The FBI couldn't have the manpower to cover all the colleges. Homeland Security must be watching big city targets. It had to be easy to hide a foreign agent. Hell, the United States was supposed to be housing sixteen million illegal immigrants. If we couldn't identify them, how could we find one terrorist on the campus?

Then I remembered that NSA, the watchful agency in their black box building in Washington, had programs to scrutinize emails and even, thanks to George Bush bending the Constitution, domestic phone calls. I'd read that many cell phones recorded every text message keystroke and every call, supposedly so the phone companies could keep tabs on the efficiency and effectiveness of their towers. Did the government have access to those records?

Ivy and I had so-called club cards at Econo Foods grocery to get the members only discounts, but the real reason the store had those was for their computer to track purchases by people in certain age brackets and maybe even addresses. With that information they could manage which products should be stocked for certain populations. Thanks to the bar codes and computers the store manager no longer had to do an item by item manual inventory of the stock. Did Wilkins have access to that, too? Did he know what we ate? Raisin Bran instead of Corn Flakes? I suppose if we were buying lots of Sudafed that might suggest we were cooking meth.

The electric company checked out abnormal power usage to expose people cultivating marijuana in their basements with power guzzling grow lights.

Getting down to it, we had no secrets and no privacy. You can learn a lot about someone simply by what groceries they buy, people on food stamps buying snacks, for instance. With all that traffic it was no surprise that nobody could connect the dots until after a terrorist attack like 9/11 had happened. The snoops were overloaded, crushed by a mass of meaningless information. Would Wilkins care if Ivy and I switched to Special K breakfast food? Never. But he might notice if she was stocking up on ammo from Wal-Mart for her Glock.

A bomber in Tacoma, Washington had been tracked by his purchase at Wal-Mart of fishing weights used as shrapnel, paid with his debit card, and a single hair found in the bomb matched DNA from the perp's military record from Desert Storm! With detective work like that, we could conceal nothing.

So what did Wilkins need me for? I guessed he wanted me as a pointer to help sift through the information snowstorm. It came down to potential informants like me. What they called in that awful jargon "humint," human intelligence. But me?

People like Wilkins must be clutching at straws, or maybe Wilkins was playing some bureaucratic game of brownie points, counting me as one of his assets. He didn't strike me as the bureaucratic type, like some university department head bean counting, but I didn't know him, either, beyond that mustache, belt buckle, and Yooper exterior.

But Wilkins was tenacious as a bulldog. Just so he wouldn't bother me I thought I'd bury him in uselessness with that stack of student papers, but he came back at me. "You've got to penetrate the Muslim student association," he suggested when he phoned.

"That's ridiculous I'm not a Moslem, I don't know anything about it."

What's he think I am? His go-fer employee? I have a job and it's not with the FBI. I'm just a flunky instructor teaching make-up Basic English. "I don't have time for that. What do you expect me to do? "

"Just show them that you're interested."

"What? You want me to convert to Islam?" I'd just been to Adat Israel and the Jews would be glad if I were one of them.

"Just show an interest. Don't you have an intellectual curiosity?"

"About Islam? I'm not shopping for a religion. That's not for me, Wilkins."

"Buy a copy of the Koran. Homework. I'll reimburse you."

Wilkins buying me books? He must be desperate. Is there an FBI budget for books for informants? Of was I filed under "miscellaneous"?

While I hesitated, thinking of what he might come up with next, Wilkins added, "What about your daughter Katya?"

Did he know she was coming back to Portage Lake? How did he know that? It gave me a sick feeling in my stomach to think that Wilkins might be tapping my phone.

"Katya's not here. She took off with Putinsky after the shootout in our kitchen. She's in Portland, Oregon now."

"What's she doing there?"

Did I really know? "She says she's thinking about enrolling at Portland State University. I told her she should come back to Tech. She can pay in-state tuition or maybe get a deal as the daughter of a faculty member."

"Sounds like a good idea. Call her."

I could almost hear the little wheels and gears in Wilkins' mind clicking away.

"You telling me that you want my daughter to be an FBI informant in the Muslim Student Association? Give me a break."

"I already gave you a break, Glass." So now it was Glass again, and not Irwin or even Irvin. Wilkins was referring to his willingness to look the other way. I didn't think he knew what actually did happen when we were home invaded, but I suspected he talked to the judge or prosecutor about not pursuing charges of manslaughter.

A prosecutor can actually choose not to charge someone who commits a crime. There are other factors, like can the perp be an asset to the state, or do we want to reveal secrets likely to come out in a trial? That's how some people get off without being charged or get probation or community service while someone else gets hard time. That was what Wilkins was alluding to. Even if the government would have a hard time making a case, the possibility of facing a trial would be intimidating. That was how they got people to take a plea bargain so the government avoided the cost of an expensive, risky trial they might lose.

So now it was on my head. Cooperate or else.

I knew what he was up to, even though Wilkins, that shrewd bastard, hadn't spelled it out. He made me feel like Raskolnikov versus the detective in Dostoevsky's "Crime and Punishment" that I read when I was majoring in Russian at Indiana University. Not that I had anything to confess, but I knew what he was up to.

I changed the subject. "Did you find any person of interest in those student papers I sent you?"

"Yes. Two."

"You wouldn't tell me which they are? Did that include Michael, the kid from Afghanistan?"

"I'm not going to say. That would risk your not doing your own home work. If I told you, you'd automatically reveal that you were suspicious of them."

Am I that transparent? "You're saying I should be suspicious of all of them? All ninety? Even the Chinese girls?"

"Well, not the Chinese girls or even the wives who are taking your class."

That was something at least. "You're not helping me much."

"You're a smart guy, Irwin. You can figure it out."

Now he was resorting to flattery. I suspected he was telling me to profile the potential trouble maker. It was the American bent to be politically correct and frisk grannies and babies at the airport to avoid the accusation of racial profiling. The Israelis knew better. They knew what to look for, what body language would give away the evil intentions of someone getting on a plane. So far as I knew, Homeland Security had never caught a terrorist at the airport even though we had to take off our shoes and be patted down. It was all for show. The fact that, just to test the system, people had smuggled weapons in their luggage without detection was proof enough of that.

And Wilkins wanted me to get my daughter Katya into his game of find the terrorist?

Maybe it wasn't such a bad idea after all. She grew up in a household with Putinsky, a KGB officer, and even her mother was involved, which was how I got screwed in more ways than one. Katya was not an innocent. Ivy and I knew that. Katya, the daughter I'd come to love as her American papa, was an enigma. Not to mention that she turned out to be a crack shot with a nine millimeter Glock.

"OK, Wilkins," I said. "But I need to be up front with Katya. I don't want her to be in danger."

"You're in danger every time you get on an airplane," Wilkins insisted.

"Maybe I'll tell her to drive from Oregon."

"That, too."

I guess we gamble on the odds. Even being in bed can be risky. What if you fall out? You could break your neck.

Chapter eleven

I called Katya and got her on her cell phone. I didn't want to jump right to the point. I had to ease into the problem, like offering M&Ms to the foreign students who visited my office. I spoke in Russian. How else could I have a private conversation? If someone was listening in, their job would be that more difficult. "How is Vladimir?"

"*Horoshaw*. He is very good." Even with a cell phone connection she sounded evasive, suspicious. Must be in the blood. I knew from my brief time in Moscow that you never knew who was listening in to your conversation. Our own country was approaching what life was like in the old Soviet Union.

We don't have a gulag archipelago, but we have hundreds of internment camps for illegals awaiting deportation. Michigan's Upper Peninsula is our local equivalent of a gulag, with a number of prisons ranging from minimum to maximum security. Not that the UP has so much criminality, but folks in Detroit don't want a prison in their back yard, and in the UP with the copper mines closed and high unemployment, prisons mean jobs. I'd learned that the biggest item in the state budget was the penal system. Education came second.

The United States has more prisoners per 100,000 than any other country. People don't disappear like what happened in Argentina, drugged and dropped into a river from helicopters, but the CIA has whisked people away to secret torture places in accommodating countries.

401

"How's his leg?" I was referring to Vladimir Putinsky's knee replacement.

"Good. He will soon stop using a cane."

"What about his status with the government? Is he going to get political asylum? Now that there's been a new election in Russia maybe they will forget about extradition."

"Maybe."

I reasoned that there was a way to motivate Katya into coming back to Portage Lake, besides reuniting with her American papa. "Mr. Wilkins, the FBI agent who helped get you your American citizenship, needs some help."

"What kind of help?"

"He is looking for foreign students who might be terrorists."

At that I heard Katya laugh. "What does he think I am? Soviet agent?"

Ouch. I'd heard that before, except it was about me. Maybe that's what Wilkins thought. I wasn't so sure myself. That Katya tracked me down in Northern Michigan might not have just been to escape from a bad situation in Moscow when her mother died. She might have been sent by Putinsky to lever me into working for him after all, in spite of that past history.

"Did Vladimir come in on a visitor's visa? What's his status? He is no tourist." If he overstayed his visa he'd be just one more in the roughly forty percent of undocumented population, the millions who came to study or visit and never left.

Katya didn't know or wouldn't say.

"You know, Katya, if it is in our government's interest, a Federal judge can make Vladimir an instant US citizen." That would take away the cloud that hung over Putinsky's status. Because of his Mafia ties, Vladimir was *persona non grata* in Russia. Katya's cooperation might help leverage the government. I scratch your back; you scratch mine.

"I will ask."

"Let me know. What is he doing in Portland? I mean, besides getting used to his new knee?"

"Things."

She was as evasive at her KGB father.

"Let me know soon." Without consulting Ivy first, I offered, "You can stay with me and Ivy until we find you a place."

"When will baby come?"

I told her the anticipated date.

"*Horoshaw*, very good."

That didn't mean Katya would join us, but that she might even consider working with Wilkins on the student thing was as close to an admission of her real identity as I had ever come.

Breaking the news to Ivy was a bit tricky. Having Katya as a boarder might be an unwelcome invasion of our privacy. The house had only the one bedroom and one bathroom. We'd had to share the bathroom when I was renting from Kosinsky. It had been crowded. Katya had an array of lotions and potions, the paraphernalia of being a woman. All a guy needs is a toothbrush and a razor. Oh, and maybe a bar of soap and deodorant. Some students, away from supervision of Mama, skipped all of those.

"I'd love to see her," Ivy said.

"You don't mind?"

"She cooks."

I hadn't thought about that, but I remembered that Katya knew how to make piroshky, the Russian equivalent of a hamburger, except deep fried. All that cholesterol. That plus vodka must be why the life expectancy of Russians had fallen to fifty-five.

I would be glad to see her. For me Katya has not only a discovered daughter who turned up out of nowhere. She was a puzzle. One minute she was the pretty, innocent kid with her dark hair, ample bosom, and mouth that reminded me of that brief encounter with her mother. The next minute she could switch to someone shrewd and calculating. She had a hard edge to her under that disarming, even alluring exterior.

Wilkins wanted me to buy a copy of the Koran. I guessed that was my next step.

Chapter twelve

Unfortunately the university bookstore didn't stock

copies of the Koran, and the local Book World store deals in popular literature, best sellers, and books of local Copper Country interest. I had to turn to Amazon.com on the Internet and was bewildered by the number of English translations. I chose the one with the most pages and the greatest number of footnotes. Then there was the choice of a pricey new copy or a used one. Wilkins said he'd reimburse me, so what the hell, I ordered new.

When it came to Islam I didn't know where to start. I'm not big on religion and view it as the cause of war and slaughter. In Iraq it was suicide bombers and mosque massacres. In Sunday school our teacher was a bit of an iconoclast. Mr. Jones, who I figure must have been coerced into teaching a bible class because his wife was the organist and he couldn't stay home, focused on the prurient passages in the Bible, dismissing the Old Testament as a chronicle of dysfunctional families, brother killing brother, adultery, seduction, deceit, betrayal, and murder. The psalms, the Songs of David, were to his mind erotica. As for the New Testament, Jones dismissed the Jesus story as a myth. As proof, he pointed out that the Jesus story had been overshadowed by Santa Claus at Christmas and the Easter Bunny at Easter, both bogus and irrational.

I discovered that there wasn't just one Bible. The Catholics had their own version, as did the Protestants, and the Jews. So which was the so-called word of God?

We graduated as a bunch of agnostics. Maybe that was Jones' revenge for having been forced to teach Sunday school.

As for Islam? I knew virtually nothing except that, like the Protestants killing the Catholics in Northern Ireland, both allegedly Christians, and in Iraq Shiites and Sunnis killing each other, both allegedly Moslems, nobody seemed to be loving their neighbor like themselves. Then there were the stories in the *Daily Mining Gazette* about honor killings, Moslem fathers slitting daughters' throats because they dated someone outside the faith or even the clan. In some Moslem countries the victim of rape was considered an adulteress, likely to be stoned to death, the videos viewable on the Internet. So much for religion!

How could I carry on a conversation with those people?

I suspected that the Arab obsession with Israel and the Palestinians was a diversion from the real home issues like the lack of freedom and jobs. In Egypt or Iran to be openly critical of the government meant arrest, imprisonment, torture, and even worse. It would be safer to stick with the Israel-Palestinian issue in discussions.

Of course, in the old days of Edgar Hoover of the FBI to be openly critical of our own government risked being labeled a communist and investigated. That was before my time. Now if you looked up on the Internet how to make bombs in your kitchen you might get a visit from the Secret Service.

A bomb can be easy to make. Some kid in one of our dorms put baking soda in a large soft drink bottle, added vinegar, and left the device on the stairs for the fizz to blow the bottle up. Whoever did it was not exactly a terrorist, but risked expulsion for the injury it caused. When I was in college, flushing a cherry bomb down a toilet could blow up the plumbing. No sensible adult faced with plumbing bills would ever do that.

That's dumb stuff people do before they reach the age of good sense, which, according to the insurance companies' actuaries, is about twenty-five. People under twenty-five tend not to understand that stupid acts have bad consequences. That's why car insurance rates are higher for drivers younger than twenty-five.

That age of good sense issue was being exploited in Middle Eastern and African countries where the average age of the population was as young as nineteen. Millions under twenty-five meant instability. Add unemployment to the mix and you got a pool of frustrated, potential gullibles who could be persuaded to blow themselves up for the cause.

This reminded me that all of my students were under twenty-five. Maybe that's why Wilkins was nervous. I had been under twenty-five and never set off any bombs, but then, I wasn't fired up for any causes. Put religion in the mix and dumb fanatics go crazy.

The only really dumb thing I did was to follow Katya's mother into the Metropol Hotel. I hoped I was smarter now.

And Wilkins wanted me to study the Koran? Before the book arrived, I checked it out on the encyclopedia and the Wikipedia and learned that the Koran was a compilation of verses attributed to Mohammed the Prophet who claimed to have received the word in revelation, but were not written down until so long after his death that scholars disputed the origins. In Saudi Arabia, the seat of Islam, you could not even bring in a translation of the Koran. Only the Authorized Version in classical, Koranic Arabic was permitted, and most of the billion Moslems in the world couldn't read Arabic. They memorized verses from the Koran and recited them.

It reminded me of that Jewish service at Adat Israel. How many of those Jews understood those Hebrew prayers? At least their prayer book had the translation on the facing pages.

You could just be cynical and dismiss all religion as hogwash, except people might kill you. Salmon Rushdie had made fun of Mohammed's wives in his *Satanic Verses* and the irate Moslems put out a fatwa on him, a sentence of death, so he had to go into hiding. The message was "Don't criticize Islam."

With my cynical attitude toward religion I was definitely the wrong guy to visit the Muslim Students' Association at Michigan Institute of Technology. I might say something critical and end up with a fatwa myself.

Just how fanatical might my foreign students of Moslem faith be? Would the Muslim Students' Association be a hornets' nest of zealots or just a friendly fraternity of co-religionists? Even if I did own an English translation of the Koran, would it be safe to bring it to a meeting? Portage Lake, Michigan was not Saudi Arabia.

If I did attend one of their meetings, I'd better not risk saying anything that might be construed as being critical of their religion. I should stick with a religiously neutral topic they'd be amenable to, like Israel and the Palestinians. Talk about playing catch with hand grenades.

I was cautious enough not to walk into a Muslim meeting without learning something about them first. Who could I ask about the Muslim Students' Association? Dean of Students Sheldon would know.

I had had a run-in with Dean Sheldon over Katya. Sheldon had recommended a DNA test to dispel all of Katya's notions that she was my daughter, but that had backfired. I didn't know what Mrs. Sheldon thought about that, now the encounter was over.

It wouldn't hurt to talk to her. Couldn't risk anything, could it? I walked across campus to the dean's office in the basement of the administration building, got past her secretary.

Dean Sheldon had changed to different eyeglasses since I saw her last. Hers now had large-size horn-rimmed frames, some kind of style statement I was ignorant of. Sheldon wears severe pants suits that add to her authority. She is not a huggable house mother. In her territory she's the Boss. At least she doesn't wear neckties suggesting an alternative lifestyle.

Still, it wouldn't hurt to ask a few simple questions. "Remember me, Irwin Glass in Humanities?"

"I remember you," she said, with an edge that said it was not a pleasant experience.

"I have quite a few Moslem students. What can you tell me about the Muslim Students' Association?"

Sheldon gave me a patronizing look. "Where have you been? The Muslim Students' Association has a web site. Look it up yourself."

Having had no connection with any student organization, it never occurred to me. Boy, Glass, are you dumb or what? "I thought I'd get your impression first."

"Why the sudden interest?"

"I'm really not interested, but I'm getting some heat from the Marquette FBI agent, Wilkins."

Sheldon shook her head. "What does Wilkins think? That all Moslems are terrorists?"

It sounded to me like she knew him. Maybe when Wilkins was in town he didn't just make social calls to me. "You know Wilkins?"

"We do get queries from time to time."

Wilkins must think there are terrorists hiding behind every bush. I remembered the days I taught at Southern Illinois and at IU/PU in South Bend when we had to sign a loyalty oath. But back then it was communists that were the bogey men. "So tell me about the Muslim Student Association."

"They meet in one of the classrooms."

"Who's their faculty advisor?" Every student organization had to have a faculty advisor to prove they were legitimate and could book a meeting room on campus. Besides visiting their web site, which had to have been sanitized, I figured that my next source would be the faculty advisor.

"At the moment they're looking for a replacement. Dr. Sayid used to be their advisor but he's on sabbatical."

Nuts. There went that lead. "Too bad." Was I going to have to track down Dr. Sayid? Where? I didn't even know him.

"Why don't you volunteer to replace Professor Sayid? It will only be temporary until he comes back to campus."

"Whoah. Wait a minute. I only came in to ask a few questions."

Sheldon gave me a wicked look. "What better way to find out about them than to be their faculty advisor?"

Wilkins would love that. I would not. Being a faculty advisor meant one more responsibility. Running ninety students plus the usual department committee meetings was work enough. On the other hand, being such a responsible and willing junior faculty member might make points with the administration that I was a good guy worth keeping on campus. Of course, that could backfire if the Moslem students got into trouble and I got the blame.

I stood mute in front of her desk, wondering what I should do next, how I should phrase my refusal. She took some papers from the file cabinet behind her.

While I hesitated, trying to come up with an appropriate excuse besides an uncooperative "No," she slid a form across her desk at me.

"Sign there." I read the form with some trepidation. What was I committing to? Dean Sheldon was squeezing me between a rock and a hard place. Was this her subtle way to get even with me for beating the accusation of fraternization with Katya? Or was she just solving another minor administrative problem? Maybe she didn't care who the Moslem student advisor was as long as the position was covered.

I signed on as faculty advisor, God help me.

Dean Sheldon should be selling used cars, I thought, or tricking gullible wannabe home owners into signing bad mortgages. All I wanted was some information and now I was already the faculty advisor. Good Grief, Charlie Brown.

She told me that the name of the president of the organization was David ibn Saeed and he lived in Smith Hall, the old dorm just near the Humanities building. In fact, I could see that dormitory with its traditional ivy covered walls from the office Ivy and I shared. I wrote down his name and phone number and staggered out of Sheldon's office like I'd just been cold cocked. As I left I thought I saw her grinning.

Chapter thirteen

Ivy was not amused when I got back to the office and told her what had happened. She put down the papers she'd been grading and gave me the look that sees through walls. "Why didn't you just tell her 'no'?"

"That was my intention, but I was thinking that Wilkins would want me to do it."

"You're not working for Wilkins."

"No, but I told Katya that Wilkins might be of some use for Vladimir. Fix up his status with the government."

"You mean send him back to the Farm?" She was alluding to our visit to Washington when I was to help interrogate Putinsky who had asked for political asylum. Before the spooks had finished with him I'd helped him to escape, what they call aided and abetted. "If they're really looking for him he shouldn't be hard to find."

I wasn't so sure the government still cared. The FBI, or whoever, had more important fugitives to search for than a burnt out old KGB officer. Putinsky could simply fade into the background, disappear into the subcultures of the undocumented, live off the grey market, paid in cash, no social security, no tax. "If he doesn't get in trouble with the police, like a traffic stop or something, how would they?"

"They could track Putinsky through use of his bank account, in case he uses an ATM, for instance."

"I don't think so. He wasn't on my joint account with Katya." Putinsky had stashed a large sum on my account at the Riggs bank. Katya's name was on the account, too, and I had foolishly moved the money to a separate account to force her to contact me when she needed money. It had been a mistake.

"He could have other accounts. Vladimir Putinsky could have many accounts where he hid stolen money. Think ahead, *liebchen*."

"I guess you're right." Ivy is a quicker thinker than I am.

Ivy remembered our encounter with the party that wanted the money back. "I think Putinksy has more to fear from his own people."

"You think the Russians still want to extradite him? I doubt it, what with the regime change in Moscow."

"You don't know that. You're just guessing, Irwin."

"As for the CIA, any information Putinsky might have isn't worth much now. Not that I'm a judge of what the spooks do with what they wheedle out of people."

"They might know where he is all along and watch him from a distance to see what he does, who he contacts. Use him as bait."

The thought of anyone having to live under cover makes me uncomfortable. I thought about the few escaped convicts who came forward after leading new lives, having families, and being law abiding citizens for years, but conscious stricken, coming forward and confessing. A few got pardons. He shouldn't have to live like someone in the witness protection program, forced to never contact old family or friends for fear of someone taking revenge. Maybe that was Putinsky's situation, hiding from everyone. I'd rather see Putinsky legitimized. "I'd rather see him settled with a green card without INS hanging over him like the sword of Damocles. Wilkins might put in a word."

"You think being the faculty advisor of the Muslim students would help? Vladimir Putinsky's status with the government is none of your business Irwin, dear. You're trying to game the system. What's the point?"

"Well... I was thinking about Katya. It's family business." Besides the odd circumstance of Katya having two fathers, we were entwined with our involvement in a couple of shootings. If Wilkins decided to play hard ball we might even be forced to testify against each other. I wanted to stay in his good side.

I didn't want to get into that with Ivy. I wanted whatever went on on campus to be separate from our personal lives. I preferred it to be just me, Ivy, and the baby to come. But I had invited Katya to come and stay with us. Life gets complicated.

Ivy clicked her ball point pen against her teeth, the kind of gesture she uses when scheming a valuable word at Scrabble. It was what poker players call a tell. "I think you're confused. Let me get this straight, Irwin. You've given Wilkins copies of your class lists. Then you provided him with copies of student papers. Now you're willing to be faculty advisor for the Moslem Students?"

"Not willing."

"You're turning into a collaborator, Irwin."

"I'm not a collaborator. Wilkins is not the enemy."

"Neither are our students who happen to be Moslems."

I admitted that she was right. "Maybe I need to prove that our students are not the enemy."

"It's hard to prove a negative, *liebchen*."

I shook my head, not knowing if I was doing the right thing or not. "I have to call this David ibn Saeed."

"Who's he?"

"President of the Moslem Students' Association. Can't do any harm to sit in at one of their meetings."

Ivy gave me a knowing smile. "Being Moslems, at least they won't be having any beer parties."

I remembered that Moslems weren't supposed to drink alcohol or eat pork. "Maybe they're not devout. Maybe they're like Jews who eat bacon when no one's looking."

Ivy was alluding to my aversion for alcohol. It was a glass of vodka that ruined my career in Moscow and I've had sort of a phobia against alcohol ever since.

I wondered how their dietary restrictions affected their

eating in the dorms. Hadn't there been something in the student newspaper about a demand for halal, the Moslem equivalent of Jewish kosher food? No pork chops, ham, or bacon and tomato sandwiches. Did this David ibn Saeed have to live on peanut butter? I would soon find out. It would be a non-political way to start a conversation.

I checked out their professional-looking web site. Sure enough, they had solved that problem of halal food. The local Econo Foods grocery store stocked a few frozen items, like chicken and beef stew. If the remodeled Smith Hall had suites with kitchenettes or microwave ovens, the Muslim kids could cook.

If I was reading the web pages correctly, they didn't seem to pray five times a day, but different students held prayer meetings in their rooms on campus. Interesting.

I phoned David ibn Saeed.

The voice that answered the phone had a slight English accent. Maybe he'd been taught British English in his home country or even studied in Britain before heading for Northern Michigan.

"I'm Irwin Glass. I'm to be the temporary faculty advisor for the Muslim Students' Association."

"Is this a joke? We have a faculty advisor, Professor Sayid."

"The Dean of Students says he's away on sabbatical. I'm just a substitute until he comes back."

If David ibn Saeed didn't know his advisor was away, the professor couldn't have taken an active part in the organization. Maybe being the faculty advisor meant no more than having your name on Sheldon's sheet of paper to give the group official legitimacy.

I hoped the professor would come back. Sometimes they don't. The Faculty Handbook rule says that if you go on sabbatical you have to come back for at least a year. I didn't know if Prof. Sayid was away for a year at half pay or for a term for full pay. I hoped the latter.

"What did you say your name is?"

"Glass, Irwin Glass."

"Professor Glass? What department?"

"Humanities. I'm just an instructor."

412

David ibn Saeed was suspicious. "Irwin Glass? That is a Jewish name. Are you a Jew?"

"No. I'm nothing. I have no religion."

"Not even a Christian?"

"Nominally." I needed to change the subject. Whether I was a Jew or not by any stretch of the genealogy was not something I wanted to go into with the president of the Muslim students.

"What do you teach?"

"I have three sections of English for foreign students. Many of them are Moslems. Some might even be members of your organization."

There was a pause as ibn Saeed's light bulbs lit up. "Oh, yes. Professor Glass. A couple of the students mentioned you."

I wondered what the context was. Did I have a reputation for being a hard ass because I flunked those two Kuwaitis for cheating?

"How about you?" I asked. "What's your home country? Where are you from?"

"Alexandria. My father is an eye doctor."

"Are you premed yourself?"

"No. I'm civil."

That was Tech shorthand for Civil Engineering. "I'd like to introduce myself to your membership. When is your next meeting?" I'd seen a notice on the website but didn't understand what it meant.

"We are celebrating a religious holiday. I don't think it would be appropriate for you to visit then."

I supposed not. I felt uncomfortable enough sitting in at Adat Israel during the Rosh Hashanah service, even having what Kosinsky claimed was a Jewish connection among my ancestors. "If some of your group are in my classes, maybe one of them could help me keep in touch. Then I wouldn't have to intrude. Could you give me a list?"

"You want a list?" David ibn Saeed was suspicious.

"For the Dean of Students." I didn't know if Sheldon kept such records, but she probably did have rosters of everyone. "You can send it to me by email. Iglass@mit.edu."

"I can do that."

413

"Good." I added, "I look forward to meeting you." I was just being polite. I didn't want to meet him. I fumbled for an excuse. "I take this faculty advisor thing seriously and want to do a good job."

"You are interested in Islam?"

"I'm curious."

"Perhaps you would consider converting?"

Boy, he didn't waste any time. That's all I needed—to tangle with Muslim evangelicals. "You never know," I said. "Life is full of surprises." If he thought I was a potential convert, I'd be more welcome.

I rang off, thinking, *What the hell, Glass? You pretending to be a potential convert to Islam? Are you nuts, or what?*

Well, what else was I going to do?

Send Wilkins the roster or the Muslim Students' Association, for one.

Chapter fourteen

I didn't have to ask David ibn Sayed for the list of the members of the Muslim Students' Association. They had it posted on their web site. To my surprise, there were thirty-eight members in all, and half a dozen were girls. The names weren't familiar because the Muslim students didn't use their English names when among their co-religionists. Apparently they lived double lives, one face for each other, another for us infidels. It was like living with an alias. Michael, the Afghan, was on the list.

Did they take on English-sounding names because Arabic names are hard for us to pronounce or spell? I find it mildly irritating when foreigners call me Irvin instead of Irwin. Maybe for the Moslem students it was the same.

It isn't so different for Katya. Anyone who has read *War and Peace* will understand. Tolstoy has about fifty characters, each with about three names. My Katya is, formally, Katarina Volodna Putinsky. In Russia she'd be called by her name and patronymic, Karatina Volodna. On some papers she might sign as Katarina Putinsky, or Putin as she calls herself. Her so-called familiar name is Katya, of course.

It's the same thing as a Joseph being called Joey.

That name thing would make for an interesting class exercise. If I made a real effort to use my students' native names and pronounce and spell them correctly they would find me respectful of their culture. Not that I was disrespectful. My job was to improve their English, but in a sense I was also an ambassador to these foreign visitors. The exercise would improve rapport with my audience.

I was surprised that Wilkins hadn't looked up the Internet list of members of the Muslim Student Association himself. If he was such a hot shot FBI detective, why hadn't he? Or was this some sort of a test to see if I had any smarts? The roster posted on the Association web site had the native names, not American aliases plus their home countries. For instance, David ibn Sayed was from Egypt. Others were from Iran, Indonesia, Pakistan and even India. The Internet is wide open. You can find out almost anything, providing you trust the sources. If Wilkins didn't look them up, maybe he was too busy chasing smugglers of five gallon flush toilets from Canada.

Wilkins phoned. He was not satisfied with the copy of the member list I sent him. "Thanks for the list, Irwin." Was he being ironic?

So it was Irwin again. Wilkins being friendly. "Glad to be of service," I said, not meaning it. "Michael, the Afghan, is on the list. Is he one of your suspects?"

His time Wilkins let something slip. "Michael's brother was a translator for the American forces. He was killed by an IED while riding along in a Humvee. As compensation for the loss, the government gave Michael a visa to come to the United States for his own safety."

"So is he helping in this hunt for terrorists?"

"Can't say. As for the Association, I need something more than just the names. Don't these kids have email addresses? I thought you twenty-first century faculty did everything by email, submitting homework and such."

"They do have email addresses. My students do, but the Moslem email addresses weren't posted."

"The class lists you gave me just have names, not email addresses."

"You need those, too? What are you going to do, spam

them?"

Wilkins sighed, showing impatience. "I need to do some matching up."

"What do you mean?"

"If you must know, Glass," (now it was Glass again, unfriendly) "I need to see if any of your students have emails that match the Muslim association list."

"And?"

"Figure it out. We can connect the emails to the traffic, see who is visiting the militant web sites, who subscribes to Arabic news, who asks for what information."

"Like how to make bombs, for instance?"

"You always leave a trail, Irwin. Amazon does it. By the way, did you order that Koran?"

"Yes."

"Then you'll see next time you go to the Amazon site that they know what you read and will suggest books of a similar nature. We do the same thing, only it's to track people by their internet interests."

"Must take a lot of time," I thought, impressed by he bulldog nature of the man.

"Not so bad," Wilkins explained. "Marketing people do it, now that they have access to computer files. It's fast. There's plenty of information out there. You betcha."

"OK," I admitted, convinced. "So are you going to let me know which students to watch?"

"Maybe. Depends on what I find out."

Remembering my discussion with Ivy, I made a tentative inquiry. "Is the agency still looking for Vladimir Putinsky?"

"Not my case."

That didn't mean he wasn't interested. "I'd like to see him have legitimate status, green card or something."

"Why?"

"Family business," I said.

"I'll give it a thought," Wilkins said, and hung up.

Chapter fifteen

Wilkins request that I get into the name business sidetracked me from my lesson plans. Frankly, it was a

416

welcome diversion from the routine. Teaching the same thing in three sections may be efficient because there's only one preparation, but it's boring. By the time you get to the third iteration you think you hear the echo of yourself and don't know what you already said. It's confusing.

I plunged into the name thing. Names were an amazingly interesting subject, especially surnames. I didn't know, for instance, that in Europe nobody had surnames until Napoleon required it. Suddenly Jews who previously were known by names like Isaac the son of Jacob, were arbitrarily forced by the anti-Semitic Christian authorities to take surnames like Goldstein or even Tannenbaum. Imagine the humiliation of a Jew being forced to be called Christmas Tree!

I wanted my three sections to be as much as possible on the same page. I decided to get all the students involved in that problem of names and their meaning. I explained that if they looked up common names in their English dictionaries they'd discover that some had roots in mythology. Harold was heroic, Diana the huntress, Jane or Janet from Juno, goddess of love. Your name by some twist of pseudoscientific astrology was your karma. God help the boy whose parents saddled him with a silly name like Sue.

I don't know the root meaning of Irwin but wouldn't be surprised if it meant someone who gets dumped on. In class I mentioned that, in the News of the Weird syndicated column in the newspaper, murderers often had the middle name Wayne. Why someone with a middle name Wayne might be a murderer was a mystery.

To the Chinese students, the plethora of names in the United States was bewildering. With a conglomeration of immigrants from many countries, our phone books were filled with a kaleidoscope of surnames.

Some of my Chinese students thought our names were funny and laughed. There were only a few family names in China, like Chan or Wong

I have one student from Norway who explained that in Norway your name was that of the farm where you lived. If a young man married into a farm family and lived there his name was changed to that of their farm.

According to Native American tradition, I explained, as I understood it, when a baby was born the parent looked outside the teepee and named the child for something going on at the time, so a baby might be named "Running Water," "Flying Cloud, or "Little Bear."."

So I asked my students what is your name at home and what is the meaning of it? Were you named after a flower, or what?

When it came to Arab names I was quickly bewildered. A sample in the Wikipedia went like this: Muhammad Saeed ibn Abd al-Aziz al-Filasteeni, muḥammad saīdi-bni abdi l-azīzi l-filasṭīnī

> *Ism* - Muhammad (Proper name). Muhammad: praised.
> *Nasab* - Saeed (Father's name). Saeed: happy
> *Nasab* - Abd Al-Aziz (Grandfather's name). Abd Al-Aziz: Servant of the Magnificient.
> *Nisbah* - Al-Filasteenee (The Palestinian). Filasteen: Palestine.

So David ibn Saeed of the Muslim Students' Association had a much shortened name. His meant David, from King David of the Bible, and ibn Saeed meant the son of Happy. You could learn a lot from his name, just as Katya's formal name meant Katarina, daughter of Vladimir, family Putinsky.

This was going to be an enlightening exercise. Would it help Wilkins in his search for a potential terrorist? I wondered. If karma had anything to do with it we might look for someone named "Killer" or "Assassin." To complicate things even further, the students were using pseudonyms. If Katya's Russian father could change his name from Putinsky to Putin, was that official, affirmed by a judge, or was it simply the name he chose to be known by?

By comparison I am simply Irwin Glass, no middle name. I didn't know if any relative was also named Irwin.

A Korean student explained that there were only five surnames in Korea. The family name always came first, as in Glass Irwin. And in China millions of people were Wong.

American gangsters had nicknames like Louis the Lip or Homerun Harry.

I was beginning to acquire a genuine curiosity about my students' names.

The result was mind boggling. Faces I thought I'd put a name to suddenly acquired different meanings. It was a puzzle worthy of a New York Times crossword. I waited in suspense for the results of my class assignment

As for the Moslem students, I'd let Wilkins figure it out. The newspaper stories of terrorists had reported on some of the *nommes de guerre*. Was David ibn Saeed his real name, or a pseudonym? And why did the Muslim students ask on their web site that members use their home country names? Was using those long, drawn out Arabic names like Muhammad Saeed ibn Abd al-Aziz al-Filasteeni a way to confuse non-Moslems who might visit the web site?

I had seen in the newspaper that some home-grown terrorists who converted to Islam took on Muslim names. It was like Jews who, when they moved to Israel from Poland, for instance, changed their names to something Hebrew, like Ben Gurion. Was Arya Katz born Arya or Moishe? If he were born in Israel, he wouldn't have changed his name from something Russian or Polish.

Wilkins had suggested that he might have two suspects. Apparently Michael wasn't one of them. What did he base his opinion on? If I had a student with the middle name Wayne, did that mean he could be a murderer?

Or was Wilkins, in his pursuit of names, grasping for a thread that might unravel a major plot?

It remained to be seen.

It gradually dawned on me that Wilkins was going to link the made up English names the students used with their given names by comparing email addresses. David ibn Saeed would probably use the same email address no matter what he was called. Of course, someone could set up many email addresses, separate accounts, not only with @mit.edu but with hotmail or any other server. If I were afraid that my mit.edu address were compromised or hacked, that's what I could do.

It was up to Wilkins. He had the resources. The best I could do was ask David ibn Sayed if he'd send me the email addresses of his members.

Of course, not all the members of the Moslem Association were my students. David ibn Sayed, the Egyptian, was a senior and obviously didn't need a review of bonehead English. Though I got those brief autobiographical sketches of my own students, I didn't have any information on the others on the Association list. They were a mystery and I had no idea how I could learn their backgrounds without interviewing them personally, something I didn't want to take the time to do.

Chapter sixteen

My copy of the English translation of the Koran arrived from Amazon. It was a handsome edition, the hard cover decorated with geometric designs. When my class preparations were complete for the next day I settled down on the futon to study it.

To my relief, the Koran was not as prodigious a volume as the King James edition of the Bible. Unlike the Old Testament, the length of the Koran was similar to the shorter New Testament. It was broken down into sections called Suras and, the introduction explained, had been written at two different times, the early one revelations to the peasant Muhammad, the later one influenced by Muhammad the warrior. The propagation of the Muslim religion had been bloody. Conversion by the sword.

As such, it wasn't so different from Christian history. Religious wars were horrible. Cromwell pillaged and destroyed the castles of Catholics, seized Irish lands from them and handed them over to Protestants. The legacy was the continued animosity in Northern Ireland between Protestants and Catholics. Under Oliver Cromwell I guess it was "convert to our religion or lose your property."

In history the Jews didn't proselytize and refused to convert, or if they didn't, as happened in the Spanish Inquisition, were driven out of the country. That had to be the underlying basis for anti-Semitism and the Nazi Holocaust. In Moslem lands those who were infidels were dhimmis, second class citizens. That's what you got for not being in our church.

So here I was, a Christian American. Well, Christian in name only. Though they might not come right out and say it to my face, to the Moslem students I would be an infidel. To the Chinese whose history went back five thousand years, I would be merely a barbarian, and to the Jews and Mormons a gentile. No wonder I didn't want anything to do with any religion.

Of course, Chinese was a nationality and not a religion. In the old Soviet Union I had been a foreigner, and in that xenophobic place, a suspicious person, maybe a spy.

Do we fear, and maybe hate people simply because they are different? Speak a different language? Worship God by another name?

So what was it about Islam, anyway? As I read in the Koran, I found discrepancies and contradictions. Islam claimed to supercede both Judaism and Christianity, both respected as descendents of Abraham, yet Jews were to be killed. Was this the difference between the early revelations and later ones? I was in unfamiliar territory.

I'd seen that the Student Association's web site spoke of a religion of peace. If that were so, why did Sunnis and Shiites kill each other? I would have to visit the Association and ask for an explanation.

As Agent Wilkins had pointed out, sure enough, I got an email from the savvy marketers at Amazon suggesting other books on Islam, the *Hadith* or *Traditions, The Life of Muhammad*, and *Why I am not a Moslem*. The last might be informative for me, but sure to cause trouble if I mentioned it to our local Muslim students.

To criticize Islam in Saudi Arabia could mean a sentence of death. Luckily I was not in Saudi Arabia, but I didn't want to cause trouble. Now that I was the alleged faculty advisor I should be on the other side, defending those students and be their spokesman and defender to avoiding confrontations and trouble. I wasn't prepared for that.

Did I need this? I had a job and I wanted to keep it. I had lost too many jobs in the past and this time around I had a wife and a baby on the way. What had Hamlet said? "Conscience makes cowards of us all"?

This promised to be a mess. I'm no agent provocateur.

What did Wilkins expect me to do? Provoke the hidden terrorist to expose himself? It reminded me of the monkey who teases the boa constrictor and gets eaten. I had to figure out a way out of this.

Chapter seventeen

When I got home from my afternoon class I found Ivy in a house dress furiously vacuuming the threadbare carpet in the living room. It was getting to be an effort. Being pregnant had, for me, unexpected consequences. Her posture had changed to balance the growing weight in front. That our only bathroom was upstairs was turning out to be a problem, as she had to pee more often because baby left less room for her bladder. "You shouldn't be doing this," I said, and tried to take the heavy, second hand vacuum from her.

"She's coming home," Ivy announced brightly.

"Katya? When?"

"On tonight's late plane."

That explained the sudden burst of house cleaning. I was delighted that she was coming but we didn't have much warning. Last time she simply showed up. Not that she's like the proverbial dead-beat relative who turns up at the door broke, out of a job, and inviting himself to move in for an indefinite period. We had talked about her returning to resume her studies, but there was nothing definite beyond that.

Either Katya is a poor communicator or secretive or simply lacking in etiquette. I'd vote for secretive, because I was still unsure about her story of her past relationship with Vladimir Putinsky, now Putin. I never knew what to believe. For a time I even doubted that her mother, my nemesis, had died of breast cancer.

My suspicions might be unfounded. Katya was, after all, still a teenager. Though she was in some ways inexplicably mature, in other ways she was as erratic as a self-absorbed kid. Katya had a way of making abrupt decisions like when she left town without any notice at all. "That doesn't give us much time to prepare."

I wondered if Vladimir was coming, too. He had shown

up once unannounced, arriving on the Greyhound from Detroit, a choice he made because one didn't have to show a picture ID to get on a bus. Vladimir was a fugitive. With planes there were manifests and security searches at the airports. On a bus he could be anonymous. Katya, with her US passport, didn't have to worry about Homeland Security.

Then again, if she packed her 9mm Glock, maybe she did. Teenaged girls don't carry guns in their baggage, or do they? What do I know?

There is no direct flight from Oregon to our little airport which is always on the brink of losing service and FAA support because of inadequate boardings. The regional service plane from O'Hare in Chicago arrives at the Houghton County airport about midnight. Though there is an afternoon arrival, anyone traveling from the West Coast, three time zones away, would be hard pressed to catch the earlier connection in Chicago.

Ivy opted out. "You meet the plane, Irwin. I'll stay here and make her something to eat. You don't get anything on those planes."

That was just as well, for if Katya came with lots of luggage there was minimal space behind the driver's seat. It was cluttered with stuff, like a shovel to dig the car out if we got caught in a snow drift, a tow rope, and other junk that simply accumulates.

While I waited through the long evening I tried to get some advance preparations done for my next classes. I watched the ten o'clock news on TV for the weather report. Snow expected. What else in the Copper Country? Then, for sentimental reasons, I put on the worn out jacket I'd bought at Gum in Moscow and headed out.

As predicted, it was starting to snow, a flurry of soft flakes swirling in the blackness beyond the headlights of Ivy's Tracker. It's dangerous, driving in the dark. Until deer season sends the wildlife into hiding there is always the chance of getting a skittish buck through your windshield. . Once the real snow comes, it would never be dark. Starting in September, we get six months of snow in the Keweenaw. This was early stuff, a promise of things to come.

People who work at the Houghton County Memorial

Airport have goofy jobs. It's a split shift. The security screeners have nothing to do between the flights. They have to be in their crisp white shirts and uniforms for the very early flight departure, and then show up again in the afternoon many hours later. I wondered, what did they do in between? The plane that comes in at night is the same one that leaves early in the morning, giving the crew a minimal night's sleep.

What a job! Between the midnight arrival and the early departure there would hardly be time to get to a motel, tumble into bed, and get up again. How much sleep did the flight crews get? Six hours at the most. Then do it all over again, shuttling back and forth like a bus driver except up here there's some nasty weather for flying.

There was already a crowd of people waiting in the terminal for friends and family to arrive. It was a mixed bag, but a clear division between older locals waiting for family and students in their twenties. I thought I recognized one of them as one of my students.

Sure enough it was... could I remember his name? After all the poring over the class lists and the brief biographies they had written, I identified him—Albenasir. I remembered the name from the paper he wrote about his family in Iran. Except that wasn't the English name he had chosen. I walked up to him and asked. "It's Al, isn't it? Aren't you in my two o'clock class?"

He was pleased to see me. "Professor Glass. Are you meeting someone?"

"My Russian daughter," I explained.

"You have a Russian daughter?"

"It's a long story." Meaning I'm not about to tell it. "What about you? Do you have family visiting?"

"A speaker for our club."

Oh? But Al didn't explain. What club was that? Then I made the connection. Albenasir was on the Moslem Association list.

The plane landed, a powerful Canadian-built jet I remembered as small but comfortable. Through the dark windows of the secured area I could watch the drama as the ramp was wheeled up to the door. Near the tail end of the plane the two baggage handlers, bundled up against the cold, wheeled the wagon up. One climbed into the baggage compartment and started handing down the luggage.

The passengers started to deplane.

I almost didn't recognize Katya. Actually, what I did notice was those red boots she'd bought when I thought she was broke. Though she had once told me she had no money, I had found out she was on my secret account at the Riggs bank in Washington, the account where Vladimir had stashed the loot he stole from the Russian Mafia and almost got us all killed. Katya, freed of her "I'm just a poor student" cover story, shopped. It's an activity I dread, having been so frequently broke and out of work.

The last time I saw her Katya had dyed her hair blonde. Now it was black again. She's gorgeous and has a confident attitude that say's she's game for anything. She was wearing a dark lipstick smile and planted an imprint on my cheek as she kissed me hello. "Papa! I am glad you are coming to meet me."

"How could I not?" I was thrilled to see her again and full of questions it might take days to ask and she might answer only with evasions.

"Where is Ivy?"

"Home, making you something to eat."

My student was watching closely, which was no surprise. Katya is what some people would call a stunner, just like her mother.

Sensing an opportunity, I turned to him. "Katya, this is Al, one of my students. He's from Iran."

Katya was polite, but not interested. "Hello."

Al nodded.

I explained. "Al is in the Moslem Students Association at Michigan Tech."

"Oh?" Mild interest. "Excuse me. I must get my bag and make sure nothing is stolen."

Al didn't ask, but I could see he wondered why this girl who spoke with a Russian accent was afraid something might be stolen from her baggage.

Al's own visitor came in through the arrival door. He was a heavily bearded man in his thirties and dressed in a suit with a foreign cut I couldn't identify. What do I know about clothes, anyway? Maybe some haberdasher could identify a jacket by the cut, the lapels, the cloth, or whatever. To me, it just looked different.

Al hurried up to him, identified himself, and they engaged in quiet conversation while Katya and I watched for her luggage.

There was a crowd at the baggage rack. I didn't know what to look for, but Katya spotted her new, hard sided, stylish suitcase in hard plastic with a surface resembling fish scales. She hadn't had that when I saw her last.

She wouldn't leave the terminal without inspecting it first. Trying not to be noticed, she opened the neatly packed bag, found the locked gun case, saw that the contents were there, and closed it up again.

I'm not a gun guy and the sight of one gives me stomach palpitations. I knew that Katya had, sometime in her mysterious past, become a crack shot. So she still had it, what could be the twin to Ivy's own equalizer as they used to call them in the Wild West. I understood from past experience there might have been a reason for her to be armed, but I hoped that was all over.

I'd never known until after we married that Ivy had hunted with her father, Mr. Hartshorne, when she was a kid and that she had a knack for sharp shooting. Ivy even has, as they say, a permit to carry. Did Katya? It was just another of those things I didn't know about my recently legitimized daughter.

As we moved into the parking lot and loaded her suitcase behind the seat of Ivy's Tracker I was still thinking about the gun. I switched to Russian and asked, "It isn't going to go off, is it?"

She laughed. "Of course not. You think I am foolish girl?"

"Sometimes I wonder what you are." I started the engine. "Anyway, I'm glad you are here. I was worried about you. Ivy can hardly wait to see you."

"I, too," she said affectionately and put her arm around my neck, her head on my shoulder like a little girl. Her hair brushed against my cheek. "My papa."

426

It gave me a sensual flashback to that ride in the taxi with her mother in Moscow, my ride to perdition. Katya, I realized, could be as manipulative as her mother had been.

Chapter eighteen

The snow was starting to stick on the way back to Portage Lake, but it wasn't yet slippery. There would soon be enough on the ground for deer hunters to track their prey. Though it was past midnight when we got to the house, Ivy had set our wobbly kitchen table with a plate and a sandwich for Katya. The fragrance of freshly brewed coffee was welcoming and homey.

Though she was not hungry, saying that she'd had time in a long layover at O'Hare to get something to eat, Katya made an effort. Of course it was not so late by Pacific Time, not ten o'clock.

In deference to Ivy, whose second language is German, not Russian, Katya stuck to English. She looked around the room, clearly glad to be back in familiar surroundings. "You have that funny clock," she said.

As if on cue, the cuckoo bird popped out of its little house to sound the half hour. The clock is a wedding gift from Ivy's father, whose hobby is making them in his well-appointed basement workshop. He's threatening to give us a full size grandfather clock, complete with gong and pendulum. It would be out of place amidst our second hand furniture.

Ivy asked Katya how the flight was, the usual perfunctory stuff, before getting to, "How is Vladimir? His knee replacement?"

"It is very good," Katya replied after swallowing a mouthful.

I couldn't tell if she was talking about Vladimir's knee or the sandwich.

"He walks well. Sometimes with cane."

"What's he doing now, out in Portland, isn't it?"

"*Da*, yes. He has job. It is very good."

"What sort of job?"

Getting information out of her is like pulling teeth from

a lion that might wake up at any moment.

"At shopping mall. Lloyd Center."

I couldn't imagine what sort of job skills the immigrant Vladimir Putinsky, now Putin, a retired or fired KGB officer, might have that was suitable for work in a mall.

Seeing that we were still curious, Katya explained. "He is security guard."

"Doesn't that job require a background check?" I didn't need to remind her that Vladimir was technically a fugitive, having released himself—someone would call it escaped—from the Farm in Virginia.

"Is no problem," Katya said brightly after a sip of coffee. "He is now Vlady Pushkinsky. New identity."

That had to be an inside joke only a Russian would appreciate. Being a naïve person, I asked, "How did he manage that?"

"Is no problem. Security firm is Russian. Many Russians in Portland. Five thousand. Security company is good business."

I knew there were more private rent-a-cops in the United Stats than official police officers. They might wear intimidating uniforms and badges, but did not carry guns, could not even make an arrest. "Well, I suppose so." Was this something I should pass on to Agent Wilkins, or was that none of my business? A private rent-a-cop company was a legitimate business, and the experience of being in the old Soviet secret police was a genuine qualification. "Vlady Pushkinsky," I said with a chuckle.

I remembered that people taking on aliases often used the same initials as their real names. I didn't know if it was a conscious memory device or an inadvertent psychological link to one's real identity. If I were to make up an alias for myself it might be Isaac Griffin or something like that with the same initials. Vlady, of course, was the familiar version of Vladimir, but not all Americans hiring at the shopping mall would know that.

I couldn't imagine someone with a knee replacement able to stand for long hours patrolling a shopping mall, and I also didn't think Vladimir needed a job. He had plenty of money stashed away. He must have some ulterior motive, or it might simply be that he liked to be among people. He'd told me at the Farm that he might get a job lecturing at a university on Russian history or politics. Lecturing isn't the same as teaching. I didn't think he had the patience to teach his own language to foreigners, as I was doing for the students at Michigan Tech. Maybe the mall job was just temporary.

"And what have you been doing in Portland?" Ivy asked.

Katya shook her head in an offhand gesture. "I look at colleges. There are many colleges in Portland, but my papa has best idea. Stay in Michigan and finish degree here."

She'd left town abruptly before the term was over. "Come to the office with me tomorrow," I suggested. "You don't want those grades to go down in your record as F's. Maybe we can fix up incompletes or late drops. We can talk about it tomorrow."

We were all tired. When the cuckoo announced it was 1 AM, Ivy set Katya up with bedding for the futon in the living room and we all turned in for the night.

Chapter nineteen

I was still groggy when I got up and had to wait my turn at the bathroom. With guys the three S morning routine is quick, but we don't have to put on our faces. Ivy doesn't wear makeup, but she does have hair.

We were too tired from the late night visit to talk much over breakfast and walked the five minutes to campus together. The flurry at midnight had turned into a couple of inches of snow, not enough for the plows to bother with. It was just as well that we walked for the first snow is the worst for driving. There's not enough for tires to grip and no snow banks to cushion the cars if they slide off the road.

Ivy and I both had nine o'clock classes to teach so I parked Katya in my office to hold down the fort.

The nine o'clock was the Chinese section. They have difficulty pronouncing some English words and by the time I tried to go from the Chinese to English a few times I was tongue tied myself and the class turned into a laugh fest. A slight mispronunciation in Chinese and you get a totally different meaning. It was a bit like that movie routine when the French detective is trying to say "I want to buy a hamburger" except in Chinese it might come out as "I want to eat a dead cat." I was still laughing when I got back to the office.

I had a visitor.

Katya was sitting at my desk, having taken over like she owned the place and there was a good looking young man, a bit older than the usual student, and wearing a jacket too thin for the winter that was coming on. His hair was unruly and he looked like he couldn't afford a haircut or a comb. I thought the current style was to shave your head bald and save on barbers.

Katya introduced him. "This is David…"

He stood up "David ibn Sayed. We spoke on the telephone."

We did a little chair shuffle, I regaining mine behind the desk and Katya sliding into Ivy's visitor's chair. Warrala keeps promising us some new furniture, but Humanities is at the bottom of the list and there are always budget problems to deal with.

"Oh, yes, the Moslem Student's Association." That might explain the messy hair. I wondered, did Moslems, like ultra-orthodox Jews, follow the bible story of Samson and not cut their hair? There are all sorts of superstitions about hair, like some Moslem and Jewish women not showing theirs and Orthodox Jewish women wearing wigs. I explained the Moslem Student Association to Katya, "I've been made their temporary faculty advisor."

David was not in my class and, with so many in a section, I wasn't sure if he had been the year before. He got right to the point. "Al said he saw you at the airport last night."

Small world, but no surprise. Though Chicago's O'hare might have thousands of hurried and harried passengers, by the time Ivy and I got to the gate for the flight to the U.P. she recognized people. The community is that small. It's not so small that you know everybody's business, but small enough. I waited for David to continue.

"We have a guest speaker, an American convert to Islam.

430

We did not know until the last minute that he was coming. I need some help to arrange one of the bigger classrooms for him to speak."

"But you are a small group. A classroom should be big enough for all your members."

"We want this to be for the public."

That could be a bit tricky, for the department is cautious about religion. We can't teach the Bible except as literature. Though local ministers would love to make the campus their pulpit, it's a potentially explosive issue. "Depends on the subject of his talk," I said. "If he plans to preach it must be off campus."

"But you have freedom of speech in your country."

I countered with, "We also have separation of church and state. Michigan Institute of Technology is a state school."

"Our speaker wishes to speak on international relations."

That might be OK.

Ivy came in from her German 1 class with her heavy book bag, set it down on her desk, and did a quick assessment of our now crowded office.

I introduced David and explained that he needed a room assignment for his off campus speaker. I'd never done that but Ivy knew, as she'd set things up for the German Club.

"I'll call Scheduling," she explained.

Ivy is a take charge kind of person. She makes up for my timidity. Maybe it's because I've been burned before by quick, thoughtless decisions. A few minutes on our shared telephone and it was arranged, a lecture room in the Hellman Chemistry building to take place at 7:30 the next day.

Ivy explained, "It's short notice, but you can have his talk posted on the campus TV monitors. What's his name?"

"His Moslem name is Abdul ben Zarko."

I would have to check him out on the Internet. You can find out almost anything now. When I was an undergrad you had to mine the library stacks and probably find nothing. Now with Google you might get a thousand hits on a name.

Ivy wasn't finished. "If you want to go whole hog you can tweet everyone."

"Whole hog?" David didn't understand the expression.

"Send everyone a message on their cell phones."

431

That was all a bit too quick for me. "Tell me about this speaker."

"He's an American but he lives in Yemen now."

I remembered seeing him at the airport. An American convert to Islam living in Yemen? That might explain the different cut of the bearded man's clothes. "Does he have a web site?"

David confirmed that ben Zarko did.

"Where's he staying?"

"With one of our members who has an apartment."

Interesting. I asked, "Did the Moslem Association pay his air fare?"

David shook his head. He had to brush the hair out of his eyes to look at me. "No. We have a grant from the IMS, the Institute for Moslem Studies. It is in Washington."

"They must be loaded if they can afford to send a speaker all the way to Portage Lake, Michigan," I commented.

"It is Saudi oil money," David said with a superior smile.

Of course. I'd heard that that Saudis had financed mosques all over the country. If they could build a huge mosque in Chicago, the cost of sending a speaker to northern Michigan would be chump change. It was ironic. Our greed for oil was financing the potential Islamification of the United States. I reminded myself that Abdul ben Zarko's topic was not supposed to be religion.

"You should also notify the editors of the *Nugget*," Ivy suggested. "They'll send a reporter and a photographer."

The *Nugget* is our weekly campus newspaper. A bigger school might have a daily, but the student editors and writers do a good job. The *Nugget* got an award for one of the best student papers in the country for a school the size of Michigan Tech. "You could also send a news release to the *Daily Mining Gazette*." That's our daily newspaper, the only place local advertisers can reach the area, so it's a cash cow for the owners of the chain.

As David got up to leave our office I added, "Since I'm your faculty advisor, I'll be there."

That pleased him. "You can introduce him."

Oh, great. I thought agent Wilkins wanted me to sit in on

the sessions of the Moslem Student Association. Now I was going to introduce a visiting speaker who was financed by a foreign power with who knew what nefarious intentions.

Ivy was amused. After David left she said, "First you hand over your class lists. Now you're the faculty advisor about to preside over a meeting with the whole campus invited. *Schatze*, you do get yourself into a pickle."

Katya didn't understand. "You are a pickle?"

"No. It means I'm getting in trouble. Again."

I'd better find out who this Abdul ben Zarko was all about so I didn't make a fool of myself. David said he had a web site.

Chapter twenty

Some students don't adjust to college and drop out in the first two weeks. Others, separated from the discipline of home and suddenly on their own, go out of control, stay up half the night with computer games or parties, and fail. Until she'd left town abruptly with no explanation I thought Katya had been doing all right. Now that she was back in our household she would have to refocus.

The education at her Moscow technical gymnasium, as Ivy called it, was superior to the dummied down curricula in American high schools and was equivalent to the first two years of college here. She should have no trouble getting back up to speed.

I advised Katya to put together a plausible reason for having left town, more correctly fled, without finishing her course work last term, so she could make a plea to her instructors for a late drop or, to save money, an incomplete to be changed to credits when she took the final exams for the four courses she's skipped out on. No point in losing the tuition money if you'd put in at least some effort already. If she had all failing grades she'd be put on probation, possibly expelled.

Katya didn't understand the system. The courses she had walked out on were all obligatory first year introductions. Someone should have told her she could have taken the exams and passed out of them so she could advance to the more advanced classes. That usually meant you didn't get the credits, but avoided taking stuff you already knew. If she followed the path I advised she'd also get the credits toward her degree. I told her I could add my own endorsement and sent her down to the computer lab so she could compose a formal letter.

I also wanted her out of the office when I called Agent Wilkins at the FBI office in Marquette. Just as I'd had to write a CYA memo to myself, also called a "memo to file," I realized I'd better notify Wilkins of the latest developments in his, I suspected, unjustified and ill conceived hunt for a potential terrorist among my foreign students.

I remembered the case that was widely publicized of a kid, conveniently named Mohammed, who had been aided and abetted by the FBI in a plot to blow up the Christmas tree lighting ceremony in Portland, Oregon. I believed it was a case of entrapment and that the FBI could have stopped the kid long before the scheme got to the point where he tried to detonate a dummy bomb in a conveniently parked vehicle. I suspected someone in the agency wanted some brownie points. The kid could go to prison or, worse, Guantanamo, where he might languish for years without a trial so someone could get a promotion for saving America from terrorists.

I have to admit I didn't want the same thing to happen to myself if, by some perverse stretch of someone's paranoid imagination, I introduced Abdul ben Zarko or whatever his original American name was and it was construed as being part of a scheme to recruit terrorists for the Islamic jihad.

You can call it paranoia, but I'd been tagged as a paid Soviet Agent for money I never received, and I wasn't about to take any chances.

By luck, I caught Wilkins in. "Hi," I began in a voice intended to sound like an old chum, "It's Irwin. Got some interesting developments here in the Copper Country."

Wilkins was interested. "So?"

"First of all, my daughter Katya has returned from Portland, Oregon. She says her Russian father Vladimir Putinsky, now Putin, has changed his name again. Now it's Vlady Pushkinsky and he's working at a mall as a security guard for a Russian agency. Cute, hey?" I realized I'd fallen into the Yooper vernacular. "KGB officer reduced to watching for shoplifters and rowdy kids in a shopping mall. How about that?"

"Interesting," Wilkins said. I could sense that he was writing all this down. "You know the name of the mall or the security company?"

"No." Wilkins had his lead. Let him do the digging.

I heard him grunt his disapproval. What did he expect? A detailed report in triplicate? I'm not his employee.

"More important, I've been made the reluctant faculty advisor of the Moslem Students Association just in time to introduce their visiting speaker, Abdul ben Zarko who is speaking on campus tomorrow night, seven-thirty, in the Hellman Chemistry building. Do you know anything about this ben Zarko?"

"Never heard of him."

"He's supposed to have a web site."

"I'll check it out."

"I will, too. Sometimes, like on Facebook, people say things they shouldn't." I was reminded of the stupid kid who, after robbing a store, posted a picture of himself on Facebook holding some of the loot. Some people should never be criminals.

"Thanks for the tip, Irwin. I owe you one." Wilkins hung up.

Good, I thought. *I hope he does "owe me one." I hope he doesn't forget.* I also hoped there'd never be a need to cash in those good guy points.

The folks at Scheduling were on the ball. On the way to my next class when I glanced at the monitor mounted high on the wall near the elevators, the screen flashed, announcing the appearance of Abdul ben Zarko, a guest speaker for the Moslem Students Association, everyone welcome.

Well, maybe not everyone was welcome.

By the afternoon when the Tweets had gone to all the cell phones and closed circuit monitors, the morning snow had melted. On the sidewalk in front of the union building someone had chalked "Ragheads out!" and another, in a handwriting that might have come from a third grader's work book, "No kamel jockys here."

The dean of students was going to raise hell about that. I could just see the stream of editorials and letters to the editor in next week's *Nugget*.

We'd had a sidewalk chalking incident when I first got to Tech. That time it was gay bashing. Turns out there had always been an in the closet circle of gay and lesbian students on campus, and when they outed themselves out of pride or obstinanteness they smoked another bunch out of another closet: skinheads and racists.

It must have been a bit awkward for the rather narrow-minded Dean Sheldon to have to publicly preach tolerance and multiculturalism, but she did. It was odd that in a country composed of immigrants from all over the world there'd be an outcry against multiculturalism. What did Americans think we all were, anyway? Wonder Bread? People one or two generations from steerage acted like they were the founding fathers while the real Native Americans languished on reservations.

Al, the Iranian student, was in my last class of the day. He'd already been told that I was to be at Abdul ben Zarko's talk and asked me after class, "Will your Russian daughter be there, too?"

"She might." I sensed Al's pecker was up. Ivy and I hadn't talked about that. Katya is a stunner and though there are many more female students at Michigan tech than when I was told it was like in the olden days, Katya would no doubt be a magnet for testosterone-pumped males.

Suddenly I was feeling protective of my daughter's virginity, if she was one. Certainly I wanted her to stay out of trouble. I had seen the horror movie "Not without my daughter" about an American woman who married an Iranian Moslem who turned into an Orthodox control freak. I didn't want Katya go get into that kind of trouble.

I was being ahead of myself, of course, but we are sometimes prisoners of our own imaginations-- too many "what ifs" that never become realities. Just so I never had to say, "I told you so."

Chapter twenty-one

My class schedule has lectures three days a week so I was free the next day to walk Katya through the drill of trying to resurrect her aborted studies. It was a bit awkward for me to be with her when she saw her instructors in their offices. I don't like parental interference in my own relationship with my students. I certainly wouldn't feel comfortable if the Sheik of Araby dropped in with his robes and retinue because I'd flunked his kid. It wasn't inconceivable that it could happen. I envisioned a gold plated private jet from some Arab emirate country swooping in to our miniscule airport to intimidate the administration and force me to change a grade. That would never happen. My classes were pass/fail, for Christ's sake. But I didn't like being there when Katya made her plea for leniency.

The story of my mysterious Russian daughter and the encounter with the Russian mafia had been hot gossip and not forgotten even though it was almost eclipsed by an unrelated drug bust on campus. Like it or not I was, at least among the faculty, a reluctant public figure with a measure of celebrity clout. People were willing to talk to us if only to get a chance to ask questions unrelated to Katya's grades. In the end it looked like Katya might be given two incompletes and a late drop. At least she had a chance to stay off the list of students on probation.

She'd have to study pretty hard, but Ivy was confident Katya could do it.

We get home delivery of the *Mining Gazette* mainly for the grocery ads. The news coverage outside of the sports was provincial and not interesting but the Econo Foods coupons are easily worth the cost of the newspaper.

David had beat the journalists' copy deadline and the announcement of the public meeting of the Moslem speaker made it into the column of local happenings along with a notice of the Lake Linden pinochle club. I hoped nobody would see it. If there were Moslem haters in town besides the couple of nut cases among the students, there might be hecklers.

I had time to do some exploring of the Internet to learn about this Abdul ben Zarko. Turns out there were plenty of Google hits. Most mentions were incidental but at last I found the web site.

There was a disturbing video clip. Ben Zarko, in some sort of white turban and robe gesticulated and earnestly ranted at the camera like a protégé of Fidel Castro in one of his four hour harangues. Stripping away some of the rhetoric, it boiled down to a simple message, "America is at war with Islam and it's all because of the Jews."

And I thought our sidewalk chalkers were bigots!

Well, if that was his message, what were his listeners supposed to do about it? If Abdul ben Zarko preached on how to make bombs and blow up synagogues that would be an actionable offense Wilkins might take umbrage to. You can preach hatred all you want in this country, but if you actually foment a riot you might be in trouble. Look what happened at the Haymarket riot in Chicago. People who hadn't rioted themselves ended up hanged. That was a long time ago. People didn't get hanged anymore. Now we had interdiction and Guantanamo. So much for the evolution of justice.

But virulent or not ben Zarko in his video clip stayed just this side of the law. You can scream "Kill the Jews" or the Catholics or the Christians all you want, and you can burn someone's bible, but you can't pass out burning torches and lead the march, at least, not if you are in America. But I was reminded of the evangelical bigot down south who threatened to burn the Koran, caused a world-wide uproar in Moslem countries, and got himself a fatwa, a sentence of death.

They say what goes around comes around. Love your neighbor and you get love back. Burn his holy book and there's hell to pay.

I'm not a praying sort of person, but I did pray that Abdul ben Zarko didn't misjudge our student audience. You can scream at the video camera and froth at the mouth on U-tube and watchers can hit the delete key, but in front of a real crowd you might get rocks thrown at you.

I didn't share all these misgivings with Ivy and Katya. I would have to sit in the front of the lecture hall, but I advised them to sit in the back so they could escape if things got ugly. Ben Zarko's intended audience were the Moslem students, after all. We were just to be observers.

I wondered if, having been forewarned, Wilkins might have sent one of his own plants to be on hand. You never knew who was taking photos at public gatherings and what was done with the pictures. Nowadays a cell phone picture might appear instantly on the Internet.

Chapter twenty-two

All that worry wasn't good sleeping medicine. I lay in bed alongside Ivy and tossed and turned. Finally she snapped on the bedside lamp. "Can't sleep?"

"I'm worried about tomorrow."

"You'll be OK."

Ivy was wearing a nightgown that had crept up to her belly. Under the blanket I gently caressed her stomach, wondering if a fetus slept in there. Cozy there in the dark womb there was no daytime or night. Floating in amniotic fluid must be comfortable and warm. If we watched TV or played jazz music could the unborn baby hear it? Did our baby sense that I was there on the outside awaiting its appearance?

"He's quiet tonight," Ivy said as she struggled to find a comfortable position.

Her face was an inch from mine. "Relax, honey. I know you can pull it off tomorrow. Just be neutral and formal. No big speeches necessary, *nicht wahr*? You're technically not even the host. The Moslem Association is."

"But my being there will be considered an endorsement. You should see the guy's rant on his web site. Inflammatory as hell."

Ivy tried to reassure me. "Maybe in front of an American audience he'll be tactful and make nice. Deliver one of those oily peace and love and brotherhood speeches. How nice Moslems are and all that sort of window dressing."

"You think he's that kind of con artist?"

"I don't know. Just go to sleep. Don't worry about tomorrow. It'll come whether you worry about it or not."

I didn't feel reassured. I always fear the worst.

Ivy raised herself up on her elbow. "Just say, 'I'm Irwin

Glass, the association's faculty advisor. David will introduce our speaker' and be done with it."

"You always have good advice," I said.

"Good. Now go to sleep," she said and turned off the light.

I had been sent internet photos of Moslem demonstrators with signs saying things like "to hell with your freedom" and "anyone who criticizes the Koran should be beheaded."

Fanaticism was horrible in all stripes. In Israel the haredi, the black hatted ultra Orthodox Jews, forced women to sit at the back of the bus and threw stones at women on the street that were not modestly dressed.

How different was that from the Saudi religious police who would beat up a woman who didn't cover her hair? Or from the American white supremicst skinheads with their swastika tattoos and Aryan nation aggression? The last lynching of an African-American had not been that long ago.

Now it could be gays who were beaten up outside of bars.

For that matter, what about political demonstrators who put Hitler mustaches on pictures of our president? Fanaticism bred hysteria, violence, and ethnic cleansing.

The United States was not immune. Some Native American Indians had been hunted like varmints. Abdul ben Zarko had better be careful. The United States was just as capable of ethnic cleansing of Moslems as Germany was against the timid and defenseless Jews.

No wonder I couldn't sleep.

Chapter twenty-three

The impending evening event put me off my teaching rhythm. I was distracted. I knew some of my foreign students were Moslems and certain to attend. I could not make any comments about it in class. English as a second language was my subject. Politics, race, and religion were taboo topics in my classrooms. I knew some faculty members might ramble, get off the subject, and express their political opinions to students who were afraid to object for fear of being graded down. That would be unethical.

I almost forgot to make the assignment for the next session to my last class of the day.

At supper I had no appetite even though Katya had shown off her culinary ability by whipping up a pot of traditional Russian borscht. Borscht, like all ethnic dishes prepared by poor people, could include almost any ingredient depending on what was in the larder. For poor Mexicans it was corn meal and beans: hence tacos. For Russians it might be cabbage or beets, and, as Katya explained, even fish heads were cooked up. We didn't have any fish heads in hers.

I would have gone to the meeting in the same clothes I wore to class, a pair of jeans and a turtleneck, but Ivy insisted I change. "It's a big deal, Irwin. All that publicity. You have to look good."

It was true. Though people might have gossiped about me, Ivy, and my mysterious Russian daughter, not many had actually seen me. It's a big campus and outside of the Humanities building no one really knew me personally.

I didn't have much wardrobe to choose from. I'm not much for clothes and dressing up. I had the jacket and a red power tie I wore for the wedding. The outfit might look ludicrous with snow boots, what we call waffle stompers because of the pattern left by the footprints, but this is the Copper Country, hey, as the locals would say.

We elected to drive the short distance to campus. The core buildings at Tech are built in a row along the top of a bluff overlooking the Keweenaw waterway but they don't face the view. The access road is along the edge and the parking lots behind the buildings. Ivy parked in the lot behind the Hellman Chemistry building and we walked in half frozen slush to the side door. We didn't see whatever was going on in front of the building until later.

We were early. It was one of the medium-sized lecture rooms with a capacity of about one hundred. Unlike Humanities, the Chemistry building was well appointed with tables that allowed students to set up laptops and spread their papers around, not like the old style seats with little, folding arm rests. The only exits were up at the back of the room.

Katya hadn't carried many clothes in her luggage but she

441

and Ivy had shopped in the few stores still open in the depressed and nearly deserted Copper Country Mall. Katya had on heavy tights suitable for winter and a long sweater that covered her behind for a modicum of modesty. Ivy had bought a pair of those maternity slacks with an ever expandable waist band, but it was a squeeze when she and Katya took seats at the back of the room. As the faculty advisor introducing David, the Moslem Student Association President, I had to be down in front at the side.

David conferred with the sound and lighting technician to make sure the microphone worked. David hadn't put on a jacket and tie for the occasion. He wore a hoody with the Michigan Tech mascot silk screened on the front. Very casual. I guess he didn't have a mother or a wife to dress him.

The members of the Moslem Student Association came in in a body and sat in the front rows. I recognized two of them: Michael, the kid from Afghanistan, and Al who had been at the airport. I didn't know the others and probably wouldn't recognize my own students if they weren't in their positions on my seating chart. Ninety faces is a lot to become acquainted with when you see them only three hours a week.

Other students came trickling in until it was, to my surprise, a full house. There were even a number of curious local senior citizens who perhaps thought the event was more intriguing than the pinochle game also advertised in the events column of the *Gazette*. There's not that much going on in the Keweenaw. You have to take advantage of what opportunities there are, especially the free events.

I looked at my watch and scanned the room for someone with a full, black beard. Where was Abdul ben Zarko? I had seen him briefly at the airport. He was late.

Ivy came down front at whispered to me, "You'd better take a look in the hall outside."

"What?"

"You'll see."

I followed Ivy up the ramp.

Outside in the hall there were some tough-looking kids that might be the hockey team. I recognized Arya Katz, the electrical engineering grad student from Israel who I'd met at the synagogue. He'd brought an Israeli flag, possibly the one I'd seen at Adat Israel beside the pulpit. At a safe distance someone else had a Palestinian flag. I didn't get a good look at him. There was bound to be some sort of confrontation. The air was full of tension.

Apparently I was not the only one who had visited Abdul ben Zarko's web site and watched his diatribe against America's Jew-sponsored crusade against Islam.

There was going to be trouble, and I was bound to be in the middle of it.

I didn't support Abdul ben Zarko's opinions but as long as he didn't foment riots or encourage suicide bombers he had a right to speak and I would have to defend that.

"This is not your problem," I told myself. "Just introduce David who will introduce the speaker and be done with it."

I wondered if campus security had been warned that their presence might be needed.

Finally Abdul ben Zarko showed up accompanied by a couple of students I did recognize, one from India, the other one of the two Kuwaitis I had flunked for cheating. Fortunately ben Zarko had chosen a normal jacket, shirt, and tie. No turban as he'd worn for his Internet video. He was tall, an imposing figure. I supposed whoever chalked the comment about rag heads on the sidewalk by the Union would be disappointed.

Though I had glimpsed Abdul ben Zarko briefly at the airport when I picked up Katya, I hadn't been introduced. I walked up to him. "I'm Irwin Glass, the Moslem Association's faculty advisor."

He didn't like the name. Maybe he thought I was one of those Jews conspiring for world domination. He looked down at me with a superior attitude and almost a sneer. "What is it you advise? Are you a Muslim?"

I had expected a foreign accent, but of course this was an American now living abroad. "I'm not anything."

That's about the same as saying I am nothing or nobody, an evaluation ben Zarko seemed to have already settled on. I was of no more consequence to him than a bug. He made an attempt to classify me. "Irwin Glass?" He said it like it tasted unpleasant on his tongue. "That's a Jewish name."

Was I to be forever haunted by my name? "So is George M. Cohan, but he wasn't Jewish, either."

"I should think the Moslem Student Association would have a Moslem faculty advisor."

"They do, but he's away on sabbatical. I'm just a substitute. Every student organization has to have a faculty advisor, and for the time being I'm it. I'm just window dressing."

'Window dressing' is an idiomatic description but ben Zarko, being a native American convert to Islam, understood. To him, I was not important, an infidel.

He was preoccupied with how he was to address the audience, started to take what might be his written speech out of his inside jacket pocket, thought the better for it, and put it back. I would have liked to have a copy. I didn't trust my note taking. One had to be accurate. I hadn't thought about it and supposed it would have been wise if I asked Katya to record everything on her cell phone camera.

When I looked at the audience I saw that a number of cell phones were in action. Students were constantly texting or playing games or whatever. Everyone is wired these days.

A student with a heavy single lens reflex camera came up to us. "I'm from the *Nugget*. Can I take your picture? The two of you?"

I stood next to ben Zarko. "Like this OK?"

"How about shaking hands?"

Ben Zarko rose to the occasion and took my hand. His hand was cold and sweaty but the grip strong enough to throttle someone if it was around their throat. The flash went off.

The photographer looked at the little screen. It was a digital camera. "Can we do another one? You blinked, Professor Glass. Looks like you're asleep."

This time ben Zarko put an arm around my shoulder like he was taking possession, not a hug, more like a preliminary to a wrestling hold.

Another flash and I thought we were done, but then, to my dismay, I saw someone moving up the aisle with a heavy television camera on his shoulder. My God, it was Channel 6,

WLUC, all the way from Marquette. We were getting the full treatment.

We had entered the Hellman Chemistry building by a side door. Otherwise we would have seen the TV truck parked on the sidewalk out in front. I wanted to hide under my chair.

To David I whispered, "Ready? Let's get on with this."

He nodded and I walked up to the podium with its Michigan Tech logo. I blew into the microphone, listened for the speakers, and waited for the crowd to settle down. "I'm Irwin Glass of the Humanities Department. I'm the faculty advisor for the Moslem Student Association. This is David ibn Saeed, the Association president who will introduce tonight's guest." Well, that was easy. I took my seat.

More camera flashes. I dreaded this. Was I going to be on someone's blog?

David wasn't going to miss a chance for some PR and led off with an explanation of what the Moslem Student Association was, what its charter stated, and that its purpose was to provide a support group for the Moslem minority on campus, to hold prayer meetings, to have pot lucks where they served halal foods, foods suitable for the Moslem diet. They were not missionaries, but if someone were interested in the religion, instruction was available for potential converts.

When he sensed interest was flagging, he introduced the speaker.

Abdul ben Zarko stepped up and took out the speech but he did not read from it. I guessed it was just an outline. He was an adept speaker, a natural. He thanked everyone for coming, for the Moslem Association for inviting him, and even gave a nod to the faculty advisor though he had already forgotten my name. Like some black Baptist minister he started off on a low key, talking about peace and brotherhood and world-wide mutual understanding. He knew that in the world there were over a billion Moslems, about the same number as Christians.

As he warmed to the topic he pointed out that Christianity was on the decline, church attendance in some countries like Scandinavia, almost nil. Only ten percent of Christian Norwegians, for instance, ever went to church, but

Islam was on the rise. It proved that Islam was the superior religion, transcending the other Abrahamic Jewish and Christian religions which were its antecedents. Christians might call their religion the New Covenant, surpassing Judaism, but Islam was the religion of the future.

At that point some of the audience grew restive. Since I sat in a chair at the side of the room I could watch the speaker and the audience and saw some of the old folks get up to leave, muttering their disapproval.

Ben Zarko was not to be deterred. He was hitting his stride now, leading up to the vitriolic intensity I had seen on his web site video. America was intolerant. America was at war with Islam. Look at what happened in Iraq and in Afghanistan. It was not just about oil, but a crusade, an inflammatory, hot button word George W. Bush had once used (much to the horror of the State Department, I remembered, and never mentioned again).

Then he shifted to the Israeli/Palestinian question. There should be no Jewish state, he insisted. Once land was Islamic it would be forever Moslem. All the land would be returned to the Arabs. The Jews would be driven into the sea and Palestine would be the only state.

Someone at the back of the room shouted "Bullshit!"

Ben Zarko went on as if he didn't hear the heckler. He had worked himself up but the audience was not with him. No one was going to rush forward and convert like you might see at a Billy Graham prayer fest. Instead there were shouts of disapproval. Whatever polite interest the audience had shown at the start had evaporated. Now they were hostile.

I regretted being at the front of the room. I would have preferred to grab Ivy and Katya and slip out the back myself, but I was supposed to be present and observe and report to Agent Wilkins whether I liked to or not.

I didn't see who threw it, but suddenly a shoe bounced off the logo on the podium. It must have been someone who had seen a shoe thrown at George Bush. Showing the soles of your feet was an insult, which was why I was careful never to sit on my desk in the classroom and cross my legs, signs of disrespect. Ben Zarko didn't flinch.

I was afraid the place would turn into a riot but David took over the microphone and said, "Mr. Zarko will take a few questions."

He should have planned better, arranged for people to pass written questions up to the front where they could be screened.

A hand went up. "Can you explain Sharia law?"

Ben Zarko regained his position at the microphone. "That is easily explained. It is not so different from your Bible. You are all familiar with the Ten Commandments, thou shalt not commit adultery, for instance, but do you know the penalty for breaking those commandments? In your Bible the penalty is death.

"Your bible also states that all males shall be circumcised. Are you circumcised? Moslem males are. Islam is a pure religion, it is not corrupted. We live by the letter of the Koran. You cherry pick from your bible and ignore the laws you find inconvenient."

I would have countered by saying that Christianity had evolved. No Christian or Jew, for that matter, was stoned to death for adultery. But these replies are what we think about afterwards. "What I would have said." But it was not my business to say anything. I was not part of the audience and I was not present to debate with that fanatic. There was no point to it. You can't persuade or even argue with someone who has already made up their mind. Anything I said would not have changed anything.

Another question: "What about honor killings?"

At that ben Zarko smirked behind his black beard. "Remember your biblical commandment, Honor thy Father and Mother. If a Jewish girl marries outside the faith she is shunned, declared dead by her parents and never spoken of again. But the Biblical commandment states that the child who does not honor her parents shall be put to death. Read it. It is in your Bible. The Sharia law of the Koran is immutable. You do not change the word of Allah."

I had done some perfunctory reading in the copy of the Koran I'd ordered from Amazon, but hadn't seen anything about that. I was beginning to understand ben Zarko's mind set.

Others in the audience were better informed than I was. Someone asked about dhimmis, the second class status of non-Moslems in Islamic countries. Someone who was not a Moslem in some Moslem countries could not hold public office, had to pay a special tax. Ben Zarko shrugged it off. "You have discrimination in this country. In this country you exterminated whole tribes of Native American Indians. You lynched black people. You deport undocumented Mexicans without even notifying their American families. Your civil rights laws are a joke. And less than half of Americans vote anyway. American democracy is a farce, a charade."

I had to admit ben Zarko had a point. To his mind, Americans had no right to criticize Moslems. Both sides were guilty which made us all equally culpable. He was taking facts and fitting them to his own purpose.

Of course, that didn't justify blowing people up in cafes or crashing hijacked airplanes into buildings.

This was neither the time nor the place to have a reasonable, peaceable discussion. It was too late.

Another shoe went flying through the air, this one bouncing off David's shoulder. The entire membership of the Moslem Student Association stood up in a body and the fists started flying. Someone shouted "No one criticizes Islam!"

There was no way I was going to get this under control. Where were the campus cops? Maybe someone was calling on a cell phone. Certainly there were lots of cell phones trained on the podium. How many pictures or video clips were already being posted on U-tube and Facebook?

I saw that the Channel six camera man was filming everything. We were sure to be on the ten o'clock news. And what about the picture of me being hugged by ben Zarko? It would look like I was responsible for the whole thing. Irwin Glass embraced by a Moslem fanatic. It would be guilt by association.

I worked my way to the back of the room, staying out of the center of the action, and found Ivy and Katya in the hallway, but the shouting was going on there, too, and the hockey players were ready for a fight. The students who had carried the flags were nose to nose.

I was worried about Ivy and the baby to come. "Let's get

out of here."

We escaped through the front door of the building, and passed the Channel 6 TV truck just as the police arrived. Damned if there weren't a couple of students with anti-Moslem signs.

"You should have done something," Ivy said breathlessly as we slogged through the slush toward the parking lot.

"Never try to break up a bar fight," I said as we squeezed into Ivy's little car. "You end up in the middle and get beat up by both sides." It had happened all too often. The good Samaritan gets a knife in the ribs or a chair over his head.

We drove home glad to have escaped unscathed, but my bruises were yet to come.

Chapter twenty-four

The crew in the WLUC camera truck had wasted no time. There was a dish antenna on the roof and they must have had an up link to Marquette a hundred miles and two hours away, for they made it to the ten o'clock news broadcast. Ivy, Katya, and I sat on the futon in our living room and watched our television screen with intense interest.

In spite of Yoopers' obsession with the weather reports, the Moslem Student Association event got first billing, but the girl who read the report from the teleprompter had not been at the meeting. The text she read had been cobbled together hastily to go with the edited film clip and the result was a distortion. I could hardly believe that what we had been part of was what was in the report. For a few seconds there I was, being embraced by ben Zarko. Then ben Zarko's remark about Islam being the superior religion was included but taken out of context.

The upshot was it looked like I was the sponsor of a riot.

I hadn't noticed if anyone from the *Daily Mining Gazette* was in the audience and wondered how the story would appear in the newspaper. And of course, there was the *Nugget*, the campus weekly.

I was in for a shit storm.

The broadcast had hardly moved on to sports when the phone rang. Nobody calls us so late in the evening. We don't have caller ID, so who was it? I picked up. "Hello?"

"Irwin Glass?"

"Yes. Who's speaking?"

"You son of a bitch. I didn't go to Iraq so you could invite some rotten bastard to come in and attack my religion. I hope you die."

"Wait a minute. I didn't invite anybody." But the caller had already hung up.

Ivy asked, "Who was that?"

I sighed. "If I can make any sense out of it I'd say someone who came home from Iraq with PTSD is venting his anger and frustration on me."

Katya asked, "What is PTSD?"

"Post Traumatic Stress Syndrome. Comes from the continuous stress of war. In World War II they called it battle fatigue. In World War I it was called shell shock."

Commenting on the television report, Katya said, "They think you are Moslem?" She thought that was funny.

"No. They think I am Jewish or a zombie or a space alien. What do I know? These people are irrational."

Katya laughed, an expression that squinted her dark eyes and wrinkled her nose. "My papa is space alien."

"If this keeps up, I think I'll go back to my home planet," I quipped, but of course this is my planet and I'm stuck with it, nutty reporters and crazy callers or not.

"I wouldn't worry about it unless he calls again. Let's get to bed," Ivy said. "We'll see what fallout there is tomorrow."

In bed I wanted to read something that would put me to sleep. I had a bedside book that generally paralyzed my brain, the heavy prose of Adam Smith, but even that didn't work.

I was still at my turn in the shower the next morning when ivy called me out. "Phone call for you Irwin.."

"I hope it's not that crazy veteran again," I said. Wrapped in a towel I came out, my hair still dripping, and took the call. The person at the other end claimed to be a reporter from the *Daily Mining Gazette*. "Our editor needs me to fill in some information about the riot on campus last night."

"I can't tell you much. We got out of there as quickly as we could. So what happened?"

"There were some arrests. One student is in the hospital with a head wound from being hit with a flag, possible concussion."

"A flag? How do you get hit with a flag?"

"It was on a pole."

I remembered the two flags, one Israeli, one Palestinian. "Which flag?" Did it make any difference?

If one of our burly hockey players had pounded the Palestinian, that could easily lead to a concussion.

The reporter didn't know. "How is it that you invited this ben what's-his-name to speak at Da Tech?"

Da Tech? Must be a local reporter. "I didn't invite him. He was invited by the Moslem Student Association. His trip was paid for by some organization in Washington. I think they send speakers all over the country, financed by Saudi oil money."

"So you're part of this international program?"

He made it sound like a world wide conspiracy. Jesus, have someone come to campus to give a talk on international relations and all of a sudden it's a conspiracy. "No. I'm just the faculty advisor for the Moslem Students Association. Temporarily. The regular advisor is on sabbatical."

"When you know nothing about this?"

"That's right. I'm a non nothing. I had nothing to do with the guy's invitation. Maybe he invited himself. My job was just to introduce David ibn Saeed to the audience. He's the group's president."

The reporter was taking notes. I could hear a keyboard clicking. "Sounds foreign."

I was getting exasperated. "Of course he's foreign. Most of the Moslem students are. They come from all over the world. David's a grad student. Can't remember off hand which department or even what country he's from." It was too early in the morning. I might have something in the files I'd shared with Agent Wilkins, but I wasn't about to do the reporter any favors.

"Uh, huh."

"So what are you writing about this?"

"Can't tell you. That would be prior restraint."

That pissed me off. Gets me out of the shower and then

451

wants me to write his story for him. "If you libel me I'll sue you and the newspaper." Not that I had a lawyer or the money to pay for one. The whole thing was ridiculous.

That sort of shut the guy up. Now he had to be cautious. If I sued the paper he might be fired. I asked, "Who is this speaking?" It was my turn to take notes.

"Keranen. Eino Keranan."

"Well, Eino, you go ahead and write what you want. Just make sure it is factual. "I'm only the faculty advisor and temporary at that. I had nothing to do with the riot. Nothing at all. Get it?"

"Got it." He hung up.

I feared what might be published in the *Nugget*, a name dating back to the university's origins in mining. Since it's a weekly, I figured I'd have a few days for the story to stop boiling and settle down.

It didn't. I didn't have to be on campus that day, though I was supposed to hold some token office hours. I wanted to lie low after all the commotion, but it pursued me at home. Wouldn't you know, but the dean of students called.

I feared for the worst.

After Dean Sheldon identified herself, I pretended that all was normal. "Good morning. How's life in the Ad building basement?" That's where her office was.

"You owe me an explanation," she said, a hard edge to her voice.

I was all innocence. "For what?"

"Don't be funny, Glass. I have to go down to the jail and see about bailing out a couple of hockey players. The coach is furious. This is not a job I enjoy."

So the dean was caught between the local cops and the hockey coach. Hockey being Michigan Tech's primary sport and as important to Michigan Tech as football was to Notre Dame, the hockey coach had more clout than some deans. Made me smile.

"I thought that was what deans do, like when some students gets nabbed for hunting in the Huron Mountains." The Huron Mountains are an enormous tract of private land owned exclusively by a group of millionaires, mainly from Chicago, who have armed guards patrolling their property.

452

From time to time some Tech student gets nabbed and thrown in the clink in Marquette, necessitating a trip by the dean or even the college president to try to smooth things over in a case of trespassing.

"Don't remind me," Sheldon said. "I'm getting all kinds of conflicting reports about the disturbance in the Hellman building last night."

"It's pretty cut and dried," I said, making as little of it as possible. "The Moslem Students Association had a guest speaker paid for by a Washington group. I think he misjudged the audience."

"My take on it is that he deliberately provoked the audience," Sheldon said.

"Might have. Have you seen the film clip on ben Zarko's web site?"

"No."

"I suggest you see that before you go down to the jail. Ben Zarko stays just this side of the line where he could be arrested for fomenting terrorist acts and the site taken down. He has a right to his opinions, of course."

"Hmm."

"If this were some other country ben Zarko would be arrested, tortured, jailed, or maybe just disappear. Ain't America great?"

"And you let this happen?"

She was clearly trying to lay the whole thing on me. "Hey, you made me the faculty advisor. If you hadn't done that I'd probably have stayed home and watched South Park on television."

"Did you do this deliberately to embarrass me?"

I guess Sheldon thinks she is the center of the world's attention. "Why would I do that? Of course not. All I did was introduce the association president. He made a pitch for his group and introduced ben Zarko. End of story."

"If this goes to trial, you might be called as a witness."

"A witness to what? As soon as shoes started flying through the air Ivy, Katya and I left. I didn't see what happened after that."

I paused and she said nothing.

"So who got arrested?"

She named a couple of the hockey players.

"Who were the kids with the flags? One Israeli and one Palestinian?" I wasn't about to tell her that I had recognized Arya Katz with the Israeli flag.

She didn't know.

"And who got hurt?"

"A Palestinian student. Abdul. He's in the Portage Lake hospital. Concussion."

"Well, Mrs. Sheldon, I wish you luck at the jail. This is not my problem."

Of course, saying it wasn't didn't make it go away.

It was as if someone had opened the flood gates for pent up hatred and frustration. Ben Zarko had blamed the Jews who, of course, are your standard scapegoat. They're even blamed by some for the 9/11 attack even though the hijackers were all Moslems and, except for one, all Saudi Arabs.

Next thing I knew I got a call from Professor Kosinsky.

"Irvin," he began. "Someone hung a Palestinian flag on the railing outside Adat Israel."

How many Palestinian flags could there be in Portage Lake, Michigan? I knew only one. "Are you sure?"

"I could show you."

Partly as a favor to him, and partly out of curiosity I agreed to go over and have a look. Kosinsky picked me up in his blue Camry and we drove over on icy streets to Adat Israel. Had to park down the street by the local bank and walk the slippery shoulder of the highway. There's no sidewalk there and every time a car passed we got nearly doused with slush and dirt.

There were several sets of footprints in the snow on the synagogue steps and I suppose we shouldn't have walked on them, for the police might have been able to take molds or whatever police do with footprints for evidence. I doubted if the Portage Lake police were that sophisticated.

Sure enough, a Palestinian flag had been tied to the pipe railing at the top of the stairs. "I guess it's a warning," I said.

"This is not good, Irvin."

"We should take this flag to the police station."

"First I take pictures," Kosinsky said and got several.

The light wasn't very good. Days are short, the latitude of Portage Lake half way to the North Pole, and it was overcast, clouds pregnant with more snow.

We untied the flag. I noticed there was a brown stain on it that looked like blood. Might be that kid Abdul. We took the flag to the police department. Portage Lake is not a crime-ridden place. Drunken driving and parking tickets, drunk and disorderly, the occasional car prowl in the university parking lot by someone stealing speakers or GPS gadgets are what gets in the Gazette news. Hate crimes, which is what this was, are unknown. I didn't think anything would come of it, but the police chief reluctantly took the flag as evidence. He looked like he didn't know what to do with it. Probably stick it in the bottom of a file drawer someplace. Unless something else happened, there wasn't much point in investigating. You didn't get fingerprints off a flag.

Kosinsky was troubled, as you'd expect. You would be, too, if you were black and someone burned a cross on your lawn. It was too bad the congregation at Adat Israel hadn't set up a surveillance camera.

When I told Ivy and Katya about it Katya was very serious. "In Moscow Muslims took over a theater full of people. What if they do that in the Jewish church?"

From what I'd seen there was seldom anyone in the synagogue. The congregation was so small they didn't have a rabbi. As Kosinsky had explained, they were only open for major holidays.

I remembered the incident in Moscow. Moslem women in the audience had worn bomb vests under their clothing, and the men, armed with AK47s, had held everyone hostage. It was a disaster. Afraid to storm the place, an act that would cause the women to trigger their bombs, the Russian security force had gassed the whole place with a deadly sleep gas that killed almost everyone. Then they went in and shot every one of the Moslem women in case they might wake up and detonate themselves. But seven hundred people died. What a fiasco.

People don't go to a theater expecting a siege. None of the audience was armed. What would happen if someone did that in a church or a synagogue?

"I have gun," Katya reminded me.

I was suddenly afraid that Katya might carry her Glock on campus. "You can't just walk around carrying a gun unless you have a permit," I said. "Ivy has a permit to carry, which is what they call it."

"How do I get permit?"

Ivy, knowing my aversion for firearms, volunteered. "At the sheriff's office. I'll show you." She explained the procedure and the fee. Katya wasn't worried about the fee.

I reminded her, "Just don't tell the sheriff what happened at the home invasion." That was our secret. The police and not even Agent Wilkins knew the real story.

I wanted to know how Katya learned to shoot, but her only answer was "Vladimir teach me."

Therein lay an untold tale of some KGB shooting range or whatever. I didn't bother to ask more. She can be as close mouthed as Putinsky.

We got another phone call, but this one was for Katya. It was Al, the Iranian kid who'd seen her at the airport when he picked up ben Zarko. He must have seen her again at the ill-fated lecture. Al seemed to me to be a nice kid, but at this point, after all of Agent Wilkins's intimations, I was suspicious of all the Moslem students.

It's too bad how we categorize people. Just because ben Zarko was a near lunatic didn't mean there was anything wrong with the Moslem students. They were on campus to earn degrees, usually in engineering, not to make trouble. In a sense they were like me in that they were magnets for trouble.

Katya talked with Al for a few minutes. When she hung up she said, "He wants to meet me for a coffee at Union building."

I wasn't surprised. "I think he has the hots for you."

"Hots? What is hots? He has fever?"

Ivy laughed. "Irwin means that Al thinks you are beautiful."

"So do I," I said.

"But not hots?"

I had to laugh. "No." I had had "the hots" at one point, years ago, but it was for Katya's mother, and look what trouble it got me.

In the meantime, Ivy explained to Katya the regulations and paperwork required so our daughter wouldn't be arrested for carrying a concealed weapon. I didn't know what the rule was for firearms on campus. That's not the world I lived in, or hoped I didn't. The idea of students walking around packing heat gave me the willies. It was bad enough if a disgruntled student's parents showed up because they didn't like their kid's grade in my course. If someone showed up in my office with a loaded weapon, well, I didn't want to think about it.

Knowing that Katya was already a crack shot gave me some comfort. You just never knew what might happen, what with some disturbed and distressed army veteran making threatening phone calls. God knows what else might happen as this campus riot story spread all over the Copper Country. It was drawing every nut case of any stripe out from the woodwork.

The country was in such disarray and crisis what with congress deadlocked and reduced to screaming instead of legislating, it was no wonder that the natives were restless. Angry people might lash out at any time out of frustration and anger. For lack of a better target, they might go after me.

Chapter twenty-five

I didn't know if he watched the ten o'clock news on WLUC, but it didn't take long for the story to get to Agent Wilkins. I expected him to phone, but he turned up at the house that afternoon while Katya was off on her date at the Union with the Iranian kid.

I couldn't tell whether Wilkins was troubled or pleased by the incident. If what he wanted to do was ferret out potential terrorists among the student body, the ben Zarko incident might be construed as a happy event. If his job was keeping the lid on trouble, the riot was an unwelcome disruption.

I took Wilkins's red and black mackinaw jacket and hung it on a hook beside the front door. Under the shoulder holster he wore a shabby looking old sweater that might be suitable for a disguise as a homeless bum, but he seemed to

me to be uncomfortable to show his armament. For all I
knew, he might have a derringer in his boot top, or the hand
gun might just be for show.

I beat him to the first question. Like I told my students,
no basketball player could score if they didn't have the ball.
He who asked the question had the hammer, so to speak. It
put the questioned person on the defensive. So I asked, "Did
your assistant on campus get good pictures?"

"What?"

Ivy wanted to be a witness to anything that went on
between me and the FBI and stayed in the room at her desk,
pretending to prepare for her German class. She gave me a
cautionary look that told me to lay off, but I kept at it. "I
assume you had someone filming the whole event, the ben
Zarko speech and all that."

Wilkins shook his head. "You think I have that many
resources?"

"I was thinking maybe Michael, the Afghan whose
brother was killed. You told me Michael got a visa for his
own protection."

"The Afghan's been cleared," Wilkins said.

That didn't mean he wasn't working for the FBI. "So
you depend on volunteers like me?" Not that I'm a volunteer.
I'm coerced into being his informant, an unwilling participant
in his search for the campus bogy man, if there was one,
which I doubted. Ivy's potted plant in the window might
have some weed seeds in the soil. That doesn't mean they'll
sprout. Being a potential terrorist was not a crime. We don't
have preventive detention in this country. In this country you
have to commit a crime first before you are arrested, but
sometimes I'm not so sure. People get racially profiled.
African American drivers get stopped for DWB, Driving
While Black, the assumption being that any black person
driving a fancy Cadillac had to have stolen it or be a pimp.

Blacks were not the only ones suspected. Get on a plane
while wearing a Moslem headdress and kneel down to pray at
the prescribed hour and the passengers might demand an
emergency landing. It's happened.

Hell, some Jewish kid on a plane was praying with
phylacteries, those little black boxes with leather thongs for

the head and arm, and some lady panicked. What language was the boy mumbling? What was in those boxes? A bomb?

Lucky for devout Catholics, rosaries don't look threatening. Hail Mary, full of grace.

I guessed Wilkins was only slightly less hysterical when it came to Moslem students. And I had to deal with this, too?

Wilkins took a conciliatory tone. "I appreciate your help, Irwin. The country needs you."

Flattery and appeal to patriotism. Wilkins knew what he was doing. I wondered if they learn that in FBI school.

If I'd been a paid informant who needed the money, which I wasn't, I might feed him stuff just for the cash. Someone else might tell lies just to please him. I didn't have to please Wilkins, but I also didn't want to provoke him, either. It was a narrow path I had to tread, cooperative, but not committed to satisfying his prejudgments.

I shifted to my own report mode. "You must have seen the video of the riot on WLUC. They gave the report a whole two minutes. Now Dean Sheldon has to negotiate bail for the two hockey players that were arrested, so she's getting heat from the coach. She'd like to blame me for the whole thing."

It was a long speech, but Wilkins listened patiently. He smiled under his bushy mustache. "You can handle it."

"What's to handle? I wasn't even in the building when the police arrived. My wife and I split right away. But you're right. I got a phone call last night."

Wilkins leaned forward. "What phone call?"

"Some veteran who'd served in Iraq. He was pissed off. I'd guess PTSD, but coming out of a war zone he's probably angry at all Arabs and Moslems for killing one of his buddies. I'm only guessing."

"Hmm. Fair assumption. Hey, if you'd like, we can put a trap on your line and trace every call."

"I thought you already do that for everybody."

Wilkins shook his head. "Come on, Irwin. This isn't a police state."

"If you think it's important, go ahead. I have nothing to hide." My denial sounded like a confession. Of course, I had plenty to hide. Nobody but Ivy, Katya and I knew exactly what happened when we were home invaded by the Russian

Mafia. I wanted to keep the facts secret, especially from the police.

Wilkins may have been suspicious, but like the detective in Dostoyevsky's *Crime and Punishment*, he could wait until I hanged myself. That case wasn't the issue at the moment. I realized I was beginning to act like a convicted felon. Talk to the inmates at the prison and you'd hear that they are all innocent. Convictions notwithstanding, they tell themselves their alibis so often that they believe it themselves.

As for the threatening phone call, it might be helpful if every threat could be traced.

Wilkins was compliant. "I'll check with the phone company."

"With all the stuff I gave you, do you have any real suspects, potential or real?" I wanted to plant the idea that Wilkins was only imagining things.

"I have two possibles," Wilkins admitted. "NSA is tracking the internet traffic. That David ibn Sayed has been logging on to Islamic agitators' sites."

"So have I. Hey, just because I own a copy of the Koran doesn't make me a Moslem," I said. I knew, thanks to the Homeland Security law instigated by George W. Bush, the government could track your lending habits at the public library, which was why the librarians purged their patrons' records every twenty-four hours. What you read should be your own business. Did they also track your book purchases the way Amazon did? After I ordered my copy of the Koran they offered similar books.

It was just crazy. If a parent had pictures of their babies in the bath tub with their rubber duckies or toy boats, it could be construed by some as child pornography. Possession of child pornography might be grounds for a conviction as a sex criminal. A registered sex offender couldn't live within stalking distance of a school. It went on and on.

Did Wilkins have any real evidence of potential terrorists? "David's the president of the Moslem Students' Assocation. Anyone else?"

"There's an Iranian."

Was he thinking of Al? The kid Katya was at that moment having a date with at the student union? "You mean

Al? I've met him."

"As you know, our country is having trouble with the government of Iran."

"That doesn't make him an agent of some ayatollah."

"Tell me more about him."

I shook my head. "I don't know any more than that. Katya has a date with him today."

"Ask her for an assessment," Wilkins said.

What did Wilkins expect? That I enlist Katya as some sort of sub-agent in his witch hunt? And if she were aware of it and refused? Did that put her on some blacklist like happened during the McCarthy era when actors and Hollywood authors who refused to name others who had attended a Communist Party meeting were barred from future employment? Wilkins wasn't a congressman or a judge, but he was FBI and I was afraid of what he might report.

Hadn't I been falsely accused of being a paid Soviet agent? What happened to me in Moscow haunted me forever afterwards. The accusatory reports written about me were something I could not defend against. We're supposed to have a right to face our accuser, but some judges can agree that such revelations might jeopardize the government's methods or expose their agents. Then the denunciation hangs over your head like an invisible sword of Damocles.

I agreed to sound Katya out about her date. Any parent might do that. "How was your date?" was casual enough, and knowing Katya she'd shrug it off with a non-committal OK and go no further. She'd be as hard to interrogate as Vladimir.

"Anyone else?" Wilkins asked. "I mean, beside the Iranian?"

"There's a Palestinian. He's the one who got beat up by the hockey players. He's in the hospital."

"You know him?"

"No. Name's Abdul something. The report said he has a concussion."

"Check him out."

It looked like I'd have to make a trip to the hospital. I didn't know if anyone but a relative could be allowed in.

Wilkins decided he'd got as much out of me as he could

461

for the moment. He stood up, made polite departure remarks, and fetched his old jacket.

In the kitchen our wedding gift clock cuckooed.

Wilkins smiled. "You have a cuckoo clock?"

"My father makes them," Ivy explained. "It's his hobby."

I could see Wilkins tucking away that bit of trivia in his mental file.

It was an opportunity to tell how the sound of the cuckoo clock probably saved my life, but I didn't want to go there. That was a taboo subject.

As Wilkins drove off, Ivy said, "You could at least have offered him a cup of coffee."

"It wasn't a social call."

"If he gave us fair warning I could have put up a pan of brownies."

"I don't want to get too chummy with Wilkins," I said. "I'd just as soon keep my distance."

Ivy shook her head. "I don't think you can do that, *shatze*. You're in this up to your neck."

"I guess we both are."

"Not me, white man," she said. It was our inside joke about Tonto and the Lone Ranger surrounded by hostile Indians. "Don't ask me to start spying on your students."

"What if Katya likes Al, invites him home for supper or something?"

She admitted that might happen.

"Who knows?" I suggested. "We might invite the Moslem students here for a pot luck of halal food. Wilkins would like that."

"Don't go off half cocked, Irwin."

Half cocked. That was an appropriate expression for someone who kept a loaded Glock beside the bed. I didn't know if you cocked a Glock. I stayed away from guns as far as possible. Here I was living with two armed women. It does make you very, very polite. "Inviting the whole club wouldn't be out of bounds for their faculty advisor, now would it?"

"I guess not." I could almost see her thinking about recipes and wondering what a student who lived in the dorms could possibly bring to a pot luck.

Chapter Twenty-six

Since it was a date only for coffee, Katya hadn't dressed up. Portage Lake in Michigan's U.P. is not a dress up place. The female students wore only slacks and storm coats. We wouldn't see another short skirt until May. I hadn't seen Katya leave and was surprised when she came back she was wearing a scarf to cover her hair. "You pretending to be a Moslem?"

"It is respect." She corrected herself. "Respect-ful."

I hadn't expected that. Was she being compliant, or playing one of her deceptive games? Katya was still an enigma. Growing up in a household with Vladimir Putinsky maybe she'd picked up the ability to be a chameleon, to melt into a crowd unobtrusively. That was why I could never be hundred percent certain who she was.

I didn't want to think about that. I was more comfortable with Katya as my Russian daughter, not with Katya as a potentially trained agent groomed to assume a disguise, a false identity. Never asking was my way of going along with the story just for the sake of being with her. I couldn't look at her without thinking of her mother in spite of all that trouble. So what was I seeing? Katya? Or her mother in Katya? It was a peculiar bond, a game of let's pretend that made a comfortable but fragile reality. I'd been smitten by her mother, but I hadn't loved her. I did love Katya, but I wasn't smitten. There was no incest here. We'd become family, Ivy, Katya, and I.

"So how was your coffee date with Al?" I expected her to give me a non-committal "OK" but she didn't.

She took off her red boots and left them on the mat inside the front door vestibule so the snow would drip off. She hung her hooded jacket on one of the hooks beside the door, dropped down on the futon and arranged a pillow behind her back.

Ivy put away her German textbook and turned in her chair to ask, "So?"

Katya's expression showed amusement and disbelief. "He wants me to convert to Islam, marry him, and move to Persia."

463

"What? That must have been some strong coffee. What did you put in it?"

Ivy had a possible explanation. "There aren't that many beautiful girls on campus, Irwin. He must have been carried away."

"So what did you tell him?"

"I let him think I saw it was joke. You must find Moslem girl, I tell him. I am no Chechin."

She must have been thinking of that incident in the Moscow theater.

"Was he offended?"

"Disappoint. Al is nice boy."

I wondered how nice. Coming from a strict Moslem country where dating was forbidden and women could not leave their homes without the company of a male relative, the United States college campuses with the immorality now called "hooking up" for casual sex must be a paradise for the testosterone frustrated young Arab men.

"He says next time maybe we go to dinner at Library Bar."

The Library Bar is a hangout in downtown Portage Lake. I was told it originally had a lot of books so patrons could say they were going to the library instead of out for a beer. There's a micro brewery in the place, but since I don't drink any alcohol, I never go there. "Does he drink?"

"Sure."

"I thought Moslems were forbidden alcohol. No wine, no liquor."

"I ask him that. He said maybe in their home country, not here."

I shouldn't have been surprised. Once away from strict parents many students cut loose without restraint. Binge drinking was a serious problem at Michigan Tech and other colleges. Occasionally some out of control freshman could die of alcohol poisoning. One of the fraternities got busted for serving beer to students who were minors, especially the local high school girls. There'd been a story in the *Nugget* about a girl who claimed she was gang raped in one of the fraternity houses because she was drunk. The fraternity was disenfranchised from its national organization.

Free sex and unrestricted alcohol made a dynamite combination. For a frustrated, male Moslem student coming out of a strict Sharia environment, the reaction might vary from pure joy at the sudden freedom to utter revulsion at the decadence and immorality of our society. No wonder America was seen as a threat to Islamic culture. Having both reactions at the same time could make for near schizophrenic confusion. No wonder the Dean of Students had her hands full.

As a single junior faculty member I hadn't paid that much attention to the situation. What went on inside the heads of my foreign students wasn't my problem. My problem was helping them improve their English language skills. I wasn't personally involved in their lives.

Al's hasty and probably irrational marriage proposal broke that barrier. I had a daughter with all the parental anxieties that went with it.. "So you think you'll go to dinner with him?"

"Why not ask him here?" Ivy suggested.

That surprised me. Would Ivy seriously consider Al as a suitor for our daughter? I couldn't believe that.

Katya only shrugged at the suggestion.

Ivy caught my look of skepticism and explained, "We could see how serious he is. See how he reacts with your family present."

Katya was thoughtful. "My family…"

Ivy turned to me, "And that might serve your purpose and satisfy Wilkins."

"Wilkins?"

"The FBI man was here," Ivy explained. "You remember him. He thinks there may be a terrorist on campus."

Katya fell right into it. She didn't have to say anything. Her nod told me she had switched into what Kosinsky's Israeli cousin would have identified as KGB mode. She was suddenly something other than a bright eighteen year old. She was something else, a glimpse behind the veil of her identify as my daughter. Finally she said, "Very good. If he calls again I will say have dinner here. OK?"

"*Haroshaw*," I said, reverting to Russian. We were now all co-conspirators.

Chapter twenty-seven

I didn't know the Palestinian Abdul, and wouldn't have gone to the hospital to see him, but Wilkins wanted me to, so I drove Ivy's Tracker up Quincy Hill to the portage hospital. I asked the blue-uniformed volunteer gatekeeper where I could find the Palestinian kid.

The volunteer was a grey-haired local man without a name tag. "Are you a relative?"

I hoped he would refuse to let me in. That way I'd have an excuse to give Wilkins. "I'm the faculty advisor to the Moslem Student's Association."

That seemed to be enough. I hadn't seen anyone named Abdul on the Association roster, but maybe the kid wasn't a Moslem. There are Christian Palestinians, too, of course.

I was directed to his room.

Abdul was in a bed with a view of a snowy landscape stretching all the way to the Huron Mountains, but he was in no shape to look out the window. His head was bandaged and there was an IV hooked up to his right hand and a white hospital ID band on his wrist.

"You are Abdul?"

His voice was weak. "Who are you?"

"Irwin Glass. I'm the faculty advisor for the Moslem Student Association."

"I am not a Moslem."

"Neither am I. I was the one who was at the Hellman building and introduced David. He was the one who introduced ben Zarko."

Abdul had no answer. He was in no condition to be questioned.

"Who hit you? The hockey players?"

"The man with the Israeli flag. I think he broke the flag pole over my head."

"But it was the hockey players that got arrested."

Abdul shook his head, a movement that made him wince. "They, too."

I wondered how Arya got away from the melee, but Abdul had obviously been unconscious and couldn't tell me

466

anything more.

I wondered what had happened to the Israeli flag. Was it the one I had seen at the synagogue?

There was nothing more I could learn from Abdul, except that Wilkins might be mistaken in looking only among Moslem students for a trouble maker. I thanked Abdul, who was fading out on me, and I left.

Should I try to contact Arya Katz? I'm no detective. I also didn't want to involve Adat Israel in this mess. I felt an odd kinship to the local Jews, thanks to Professor Kosinaky whose cousin was convinced that my ancestor, Isaac Melamed, was a Jew and presumably by some obtuse connection I was a half Jew or a quarter or whatever.

The whole business was a puzzle. So far all there was to it had no substance. No crime had been committed other than a brawl in the Hellman Chemistry building. So far as I could tell there was no Moslem conspiracy and no terrorists hiding in the snow banks of Portage Lake, Michigan. As far as I was concerned, Agent Wilkins was barking up the wrong tree, as the cliché goes, and if Arya Katz happened to be an Israeli PhD candidate in electrical engineering, even if he was an IDF veteran, that didn't make him anything sinister.

Still, the whole business nagged at me. It didn't help that Al the Iranian or Persian, if that's what he preferred to call his country, wanted to marry my daughter Katya and carry her off to his homeland as some kind of a trophy.

The publication of the riot story in the *Daily Mining Gazette* bought out all the local evangelicals and other well-meaninged but ill informed letter writers. We took the paper primarily for the grocery ads, but the editorial page provided some wry amusement. There was an ultra right wing Mrs. Sawyer whose self-righteous bible pounding always led to the same conclusion: that the answer to everything lay in Jesus. Another writer down in the next hamlet cherry picked the Bible for quotations taken out of context and misinterpreted.

Applied to the situation where a foreign student is hospitalized with a concussion after a brawl with a couple of our heroic hockey players who were only defending American freedom and you got demands that the Arabs go home, that this was a Christian nation, and on and on.

The personal attacks against me in the letters to the editor page were more disturbing. People could be as nutty as they liked, but the suggestion that Michigan Institute of Technology's administration shouldn't be hiring faculty who sponsored—that was the word—a Moslem speaker who attacked the United States and fomented terrorism was a threat to my own job. I was named. I had become a public figure.

The letter writer stopped short of libel. Suggesting that I resign or be fired was in the realm of fair comment, except that I had not sponsored Zarko, who had left town on the next early morning flight, by the way, having poisoned all our wells with his brief appearance. With the cause of the trouble away from the scene, I was left standing as the unwilling and innocent target: Irwin Glass, faculty sponsor of virulent anti-Americanism, not the unwilling recruit as temporary faculty advisor.

I got called onto Warrala's carpet, which is not a mere figure of speech. Warrala's department head office is the only one with a carpet, a status symbol Ivy and I did not enjoy, being mere faculty. It made me think I might find some carpet remnant and install it in our own office just for spite, a small man's gesture of protest.

Warrala had several clipping from the Gazette spread on his desk blotter for reference. "What the hell is this about, Irwin?"

I tried to make light of it with a ridiculous exaggeration. "It's a conspiracy between the FBI guy, Wilkins, and the dean. You were the one who told Wilkins that handing over my class lists was my business, and Dean Sheldon made me the faculty advisor, the *temporary* faculty advisor, of the Moslem Students Association. All I had to do was introduce the Association's president and he introduced ben Zarko. I had no idea what he was going to say. I certainly didn't expect a riot."

"Now I'm getting heat from the President," Warrala said.

I knew his status as head of the Humanities department wasn't that great. I might end up being the scapegoat or the sacrificial lamb, depending on your choice of clichés. All I could do was stand mute, like some guilty drunk driver in front of a judge..

"Fix it," Warrala said, dumping the situation on my head.

Nobody was going to back me up. I would have to redirect all the anger to save my own skin.

Chapter twenty-eight.

It looked like if I didn't fulfill Wilkins' request to root out the terrorists on campus, real or imaginary, it would mean my own job. I'd beaten bushes for years, a gypsy itinerant teacher of quasi-courses, drifting from campus to campus, no tenure track, no seniority, and no benefits. Jobs were beastly hard to find. If I lost this one, what would happen to my marriage? What about Ivy and the baby? If I left portage Lake, Michigan, could Ivy follow? She had tenure. Teachers of German were not faculty in high demand any more than teachers of Russian.

Americans are notoriously poor at foreign languages, so xenophobic that there are periodic attempts to declare English as the national language. The Christian evangelicals want this declared a Christian country, but which Christians? Houghton County with thirty-five thousand inhabitants, not counting the students at Michigan Institute of Technology, had about one hundred different churches including the one synagogue. All the intermittent uproar was in spite of the fact that, because of sheer demographics, in a few years the dominant language in the United States might be Spanish, the primary religion Catholic, and white people a minority.

Because of this damned business with the Moslem Student Association, our whole future could be at stake. No thanks, Agent Wilkins.

What was I going to do?

When I got back to the office I confided with Ivy. "The shit's hit the fan. Warrala's getting heat from the President over this riot business. I'm really afraid I might get fired over this."

"You worry too much, *liebchen*. They won't fire you. It wasn't your fault. You worry too much."

I was too glum to say anything more.

"If you do get fired, when baby comes you can be the

stay at home dad."

That put me on another path of speculation: Irwin Glass changing diapers, heating up baby bottles, and making baby noises. If I were twenty years younger it might seem more natural. I was going to be an old father. By the time our kid was in college I'd be retirement age. Worse things than that could happen, I hoped not.

Then I got a surprise visit from my old Jewish landlord, Professor Kosinsky. He showed up at the door with what might potentially be the murder weapon, providing the Palestinian kid up in the hospital died of malpractice or his concussion.

Kosinsky was apologetic and pleaded with me in Russian like I was an old comrade. "I'm no carpenter. Can you fix this?"

I didn't see at first what it was until he unrolled the Israeli flag that was wrapped around the broken staff.

"Come inside," I said, and looked at the two pieces. It was the flag I'd seen beside the pulpit at Adat Israel. I remembered the brass Jewish star ornament at the top. For ease of transport, the flag staff had come in two pieces, joined by a brass sleeve. The bottom bit fit into the sleeve, but the pole had broken at that joint, leaving a splintered stub inside and a raw end on the lower half.

I tried to jam the broken bits together, but the splinters simply stuck out. "I don't think it can be glued," I said. "How did you get this?"

"Arya borrowed it for the Parade of Nations."

I remembered Arya, the Israeli who had been in the IDF in "intelligence" and the annual event in which Michigan Tech showed off its international student body with a parade. I hadn't watched the parade. I imagined that there would be a company of Chinese and a platoon of Moslem students from various countries. So, Arya Katz and possibly one or two other Jewish students had marched in solidarity with Israel.

"So Arya gave it to you to fix?"

"*Da*, yes. He is one of my graduate students. No tools."

I guessed that having borrowed the flag he was embarrassed to return it broken. "When do you need it back?" I knew that the local Jews, having no rabbi, seldom

470

held services. Maybe they wouldn't meet again until next year, or Passover, or whatever holidays they celebrated.

"For Hanukah. There is a Hanukah party soon."

I didn't know anything about Hanukah, which I thought was the Jewish Christmas. "Leave the flag with me. I'll see what I can do."

Kosinsky was effusively grateful and left me to puzzle over the problem.

Ivy had been in the kitchen and came out asking, "What is it?"

"It's the synagogue's flag. Remember we saw that Israeli grad student, Arya, in the crowd at the Hellman building? I think he broke it over the Palestinian's kid's head."

"I thought the hockey players beat him up."

"That, too. For all I know, they were the ones who clobbered the kid with the flag pole. Anyway, it's broken."

"Let me see it." Ivy examined the broken pole. "My father could fix this in a minute."

I remembered Mr. Hartshorne's extensive basement workshop where he made our cuckoo clock. "We're not going to ship the flag to Chicago." I imagined trying to wrap the pieces and sent them by UPS.

"Of course not." She showed me the broken bits. "All you have to do is fish out the stub from inside the sleeve and saw off the splintered end. The pole will be about four inches shorter. Nobody will notice."

"You're a genius," I said, and gave her a kiss.

She had it fixed in no time at all.

Unlike houses in more temperate climates with entrances that open directly to the outdoors, homes in the Copper Country have an air lock, a vestibule with front storm door. Ours was a good place to leave our skis and poles. Since the space isn't heated, I don't leave my winter boots out there. Putting on a pair of frozen boots is a short cut to cold feet. Having no good place to store the Israeli flag until Kosinsky picked it up, I just stood it in the vestibule with our skis and basically forgot about it, not realizing how much trouble it would cause later.

Chapter twenty-nine

Just as Katya expected, Al, the Iranian student who said he wanted to marry Katya and take her back to Persia, called to follow up his invitation to a meal at the Library Bar.

Katya remembered our conversation and told him to come to our house instead. She didn't say whether it was a dinner for two or a family affair.

It was an opportunity for a major miscommunication. In some countries if a suitor is invited to the parents' home, it means there are serious plans for a wedding. If Al's hasty proposal was simply an impetuous joke, but we were serious, he was in trouble. If he actually was serious about marrying Katya, which we were not, maybe we were in trouble. We didn't want to lead him on. I had never been invited to a girl friend's parents' home for a dinner. I'd have been nervous, too. It was the kind of a situation depicted in that old movie, "Guess who's coming to dinner?" except in that case the guest was a black man, not an Iranian the FBI suspected might be a terrorist in training.

I wasn't as suspicious as Wilkins. I didn't think any of the Moslem students were sinister. They were just different from us. I didn't know Al personally beyond that brief encounter at the airport and what Katya had told me about their date at the Union. True, Al was in one of my classes, but with a class of thirty students you only got to know the best and the worst. He was neither. The rest were a blur. I dug my copy of the paper he'd written about himself out of the files. It was just a paragraph. He was from a city I couldn't find on the map and his father was some kind of a government official, but it was all vague. Was that on purpose? A report that meant all things to all men?

I didn't take his marriage proposal seriously. Katya had joked about it, so we only got it from her. It would have been different if I'd been there myself to hear it from him. I decided to chalk it up to immature, adolescent impetuosity. Still, this would be an opportunity to sound him out, learn enough to scratch him off Wilkins' list of possible suspects.

It didn't work out that way.

Ivy and Katya got into a huddle about what to serve for the dinner. Since Al was a Moslem, that ruled out any pork dish. Ivy suggested broiled lake trout. Portage Lake is on the Keeweenaw Waterway connected to Lake Superior. The lake wasn't frozen yet and the Indian fishing boats must still be doing their thing with nets. Ivy drove up to Petersen's fish store on Quincy hill near the hospital and bought a couple of pounds of trout filets.

We didn't have a proper dining room and would eat in the kitchen on that wobbly Good Will table. It was hardly the milieu for a formal meal, but Ivy has a couple of nice table cloths in her hope chest.

Katya's Russian repertoire of cooking didn't include broiled lake trout, but she suggested an entrée of cold borscht. There was discussion about the appropriateness of borscht served at the same meal as broiled lake trout, but I stayed out of it. If I'd had anything to say about the menu I'd do spaghetti and meatballs, but I didn't think the accommodating Econo Foods halal offerings included frozen ground beef.

Al showed up on time with a box of English cookies he'd found at Jim's Foods near the campus. Jim's Foods caters to the foreign students, especially those from India, and has bulk spices we don't find at Econo or the Wal-Mart super store.

Al stood in the doorway. He'd bought a Husky booster jacket with the MIT logo and, except for what a study of ethnic faces would identify as definitely not of Finnish extraction, looked like any first year student. He was a couple of years older than our typical Yooper freshman. He was a bit uncertain about who to give the box of cookies to, Katya or Ivy, finally decided and the cookies, more correctly what they call digestive biscuits, to Ivy. "For you, Mrs. Glass."

"It's Hartshorne," Ivy corrected. Though we're married Ivy's one of those emancipated woman who always uses her professional name.

Al, confused, looked at the three of us in turn. "Then is Katya a Hartshorne or a Glass?"

"Putin," Katya corrected, amused. "It used to be Putinsky."

Al ruminated about that one. "Hartshorne? Glass? Putinsky?"

473

"A modern family," I suggested. "Katya was born in Russia." I didn't want to go into our peculiar history. "How about you? Do you have any brothers and sisters?"

"Two sisters and one brother. I am the oldest. I had an uncle who was killed in the war with Iraq."

I remembered the protracted war Saddam Hussein and the Iranians had fought to a sort of stalemate. Because of our long history of conflict with Iran, the hostage business that brought on the defeat of Jimmy Carter, the United States had been an ally of Iraq, providing Saddam Hussein with the makings of poison gas. Then we'd gone to war with Saddam on the false rumor that he had weapons of mass destruction. The Iraqi army disbanded, the regional balance of power had passed to the Iranians. So much switching of sides could confuse anyone. Both countries were oil producers, but American companies had their eyes on the Iraqi resources. To Iranians, the United States was the great Satan, which made me wonder why an Iranian student would choose Michigan Tech.

At first Al was reluctant to talk about America as the great Satan and enemy of Islam, the message we'd heard from Zarko.. He'd rather talk about Israel. Had we seen the broadcast video of the riot? There's been an Israeli and Palestinian in the fight.

"Of course we've seen it," I told him. "It's all over the news and in the newspapers. People think I brought ben Zarko to campus and am in cahoots."

"Cahoots?"

Neither Katya nor Al knew the word. "In league with, sympathetic to, whatever."

We hadn't gone directly to the kitchen and were talking in the living room, Al and Katya on the futon, me on a Lay-Z-Boy recliner chair we'd recently bought. Ivy wheeled her desk chair over, but went into the kitchen to fetch some glasses of juice and a little plate for the crackers Al had brought so he'd know we appreciated his courtesy. "Irwin has had threatening phone calls."

Al's eyebrows went up. "Really? But you had nothing to do with the fight."

"Thanks. At least somebody believes me."

Al was curious. "What did you think about Zarko's talk?"

"You mean, do I think the United States is at war with Islam?"

Al nodded, and Katya leaned forward, interested.

"I think it's the other way around," I said. "I think some Moslems are at war with the United States. It's a cultural thing."

Al didn't understand.

"Obviously American movies, violence, nudity, immodesty, pornography, and so on are a threat to the old guard conservative Moslems."

"But Persia is a modern country. We have television, cell phones, computers."

"It's also a theocracy ruled by the ayatollahs," I said.

Al agreed. "And the United States is ruled by the big corporations."

I admitted that since the Supreme Court gave corporations the right to be involved unimpeded in elections, the balance had shifted away from what had been our democracy.

"And America supports Israel, the oppressors of the Palestinians."

Ivy tried to present the official line of the American government. "Isn't Israel the only real democracy in the region?"

Al insisted that his country was a democracy, too, but admitted that opposition party leaders might be imprisoned. He wanted to talk about Israel's bullying of the Palestinians, taking their land for a "Greater Israel," an allusion to Hitler's concept of "Gross Deutschland" and the Third Reich. Zionism, he said, was the same as Nazism.

It was what George Orwell once called duckspeak, the quacking of meaningless catch phrases passing for political speech.

"You think Israel wants to conquer the world?"

"The Jewish bankers control the world economy," Al insisted. "I have read the Protocols."

"What is Protocols?" Katya asked.

Al looked at us as if we were ignorant. "The Protocols of

Zion, of course. Everyone has read it. It reveals how a secret organization of three hundred Jews controls the world."

None of us had read the Protocols, so didn't know what to say.

Ivy asked, "What Jews would those be?"

Al squirmed because he didn't know. "Jews everywhere."

It's always revealing when you dig at people's premises and they don't realize they are false, like asking someone how Saddam was a threat to our freedom. No one has an answer to that one and when asked people usually change the subject.

At that point I made a mistake. "You mean, like the Jews here in Portage Lake?"

"There are Jews here?" he asked.

"Sure. A small congregation. There's even a synagogue."

"You have been there?"

"Yes," I admitted, my eyes inadvertently turning toward the front entrance where the rolled Israeli flag stood with our skis. If Al had noticed it he didn't say anything. "Once. There are maybe a half dozen families, a couple of kids. None of them look like they are part of a secret committee that rules the world."

"They are masters of disguise,' Al insisted. "Snakes. Evil people."

I thought about Professor Kosinsky who had fled the Soviet Union when it broke up, and his cousin who had escaped to Israel, still haunted by memories of the Secret Police, the KGB he thought Katya smelled like. "That's propaganda," I said.

True to form, Al changed the subject. He was suspicious. "Glass. That's a Jewish name, isn't it? And you have been to this synagogue?"

"As a visitor. I'm not Jewish."

Al's silence was an invitation for a further explanation.

"It is possible that one of my ancestors was a Russian Jew. My family is Methodist Christian."

Al didn't think much of Christians, either, though his attitude told me that we were simply backward and ignorant, not slimy, Nazi snakes intent on world domination.

If world domination was what he feared he had reason

to believe it. Moslems had long memories. The Crusades were an attempt at Christian world domination. South America had been invaded for gold and to spread Catholicism. Now it was the United States in Afghanistan on a mission of so-called nation building, working on the principle that everyone needed to live in a democratic country whether it suited them or not. That was our form of arrogance.

I figured at that point there was no risk Katya would have any interest in Al as any kind of suitor or even a boy friend. On the other hand, Wilkins would, for Al was thoroughly indoctrinated in the anti-Israel, anti-Zionist, and by extension anti-Jewish line. He could be a potential recruit for someone with violent intentions.

Al was really not very different from the white supremacists who get fired up with slogans and phrases that fuel their hatred, except in this case it wasn't "mud people" he hated, to use one of those racist terms, but Jews and their allies. Allies included the United States, of course. Al was already indoctrinated and could be prey for someone like ben Zarko.

Ivy, ever tactful and conciliatory under the right circumstances, changed the conversation to lake trout, a non-political topic. Al hadn't eaten broiled lake trout and was eager. He hadn't eaten Russian borscht, either, so talk turned to food, the universal subject for which there was no political argument.

Al stayed only long enough to be polite. He asked if Katya wanted to go to town for a beer afterwards, but she declined and he left. It was not a very satisfactory evening. I guess politics and religion do not make for laughter or congeniality.

Chapter thirty

Agent Wilkins would be interested in our dinner with Al. I called him the next day and he asked me to write a report. That was awkward. I had nothing personal against the Iranian student. His attitudes were essentially his country's party line. He repeated it without thinking very much, and if he did think for himself, he didn't reveal his views to us. If you lived in that kind of regime, when you talked with strangers you didn't reveal what you really thought.

It reminded me of my brief time in Moscow when political discussions with the citizens were taboo. It wasn't that we Americans weren't interested. It was because Russians were afraid. Only the most indoctrinated Young Komsomol wanted to push the joys of Marxism-Leninism or dialectical materialism, whatever that was. I suspected those subjects were no longer taught. Katya never mentioned them. She was a science student, not a social engineer.

For my report to Wilkins I tried to reconstruct what Al had said. His views of Israel, of the mythical committee of three hundred Jews who ruled the world, of Zionism which he said was the equivalent of Nazi racism, were all out of the official Iranian party line. He'd said that he liked Americans, but not our government, something not far from what the Tea party libertarians might say. That didn't make him a terrorist.

You can shout indignations about the government, camp out in front of the White House, but that doesn't make you a Timothy McVeigh who blows up government buildings.

That didn't explain why Al had chosen to study at a small engineering school in Michigan's remote Upper Peninsula. People's motivations are complex. Maybe he hadn't been accepted anywhere else. Maybe he liked snow. Maybe we offered the curriculum he wanted.

Hell, I had majored in Russian because of a letter I found in the attic as a kid. How about that for motivation? Not everything we do is rational. At the time studying Russian was as good as anything else, and look what it got me: a beautiful Russian daughter. Did that make sense? I'd stumbled through my life like a ball in a pinball machine, knocked in all directions. So why couldn't Al choose Michigan Institute of Technology? It could have been a fluke, and I regretted not having asked him.

Wilkins saw something sinister in everything. I was convinced that the FBI agent was looking for someone who had been deliberately groomed to go to the United States and pose as a student. It wasn't a far fetched absurd idea. The FBI had caught ten sleeper agents sent from Russia to live quietly until activated. Kosinsky's cousin had suspected something similar about Katya, a theory I myself could not totally discount. For all I knew, Katya could be a sleeper agent posing as my daughter, DNA evidence notwithstanding. I didn't want to go there.

Because of his views, Al's identity and purpose were all the more questionable.

Look at it this way: if you are accused of molesting a child, all you can do is deny, deny, deny. Guilty or not, the accusation sticks. In Minnesota a mere accusation would blacklist an inocent teacher. So how could Al, if accused, prove he was not a terrorist?

Not trusting the security of email, I did not save the report to my computer hard drive but simply printed it out and mailed it. I did not want a record of it and, to my perpetual regret, forgot what I had actually written and how it might be misunderstood.

Chapter thirty-one

The madness of the aftermath of the fight in the Hellman building was not over. The story that came out in the *Nugget* included the photo of me being hugged by that bearded Moslem fanatic. It looked like we were buddies.

The event sparked an editorial by Dean Sheldon pleading for better understanding among our students. The many nationalities represented in the student body were an opportunity for otherwise provincial Yoopers and Michiganders to be exposed to broad world views. She hadn't been present for the speech and if she did know what ben Zarko said, she judiciously avoided mentioning it.

Dean Sheldon's editorial was counteracted by a letter from one of the locals who had followed the event on television and in the *Mining Gazette*. Some guy named Ahola ranted about the evils of multiculturalism. He made it sound as evil as Communism or any other ism, which is odd when you think about it in a country populated by immigrants from all over the world. This country is a mixture of Italians, Germans, Scandinavians, Jews, African Americans, Asians,

Greeks, Mexicans, etc. The historic pattern was that the most recent immigrants were looked down upon with distrust and aversion. At times it had been the Irish or the Italians or the Jews. Most recently it was the Mexicans, and now, thanks to 9/11 and our wars, it was Moslems.

The difference was that the Italian and Jewish immigrants were determined to assimilate, to become real Americans, not greenhorns. The Moslems were different. In Dearborn, Michigan, the largest Moslem city in America, there was a rumored attempt to make Sharia law official. To some fearful people it was as if Dearborn was an advance outpost in the Islamification of America. That's what people like Ahola believed.

And of course, I was the collaborator, having personally invited ben Zarko to the campus. "Personally invited." That was a stretch.

Ivy and I discussed whether I should respond in a statement to the newspapers and the local radio stations. I hoped the excitement would simply go away. To be fair to the Moslem Students' Association, as their faculty advisor, even a temporary, stand-in advisor, I felt it necessary to defend them. Anyone could be duped. Being able to host a speaker on campus could be a good thing. Unfortunately, ben Zarko was an agitator, not a conciliator. His wasn't special pleading for tolerance and understanding, but a heavy handed attack on American culture and politics.

I didn't think that was David's intention in accepting to offer of a Chautauqua-like speaker. The Moslem students were like any small group of outsiders who hang out together as co-religionists. The Lutherans on campus had their organization and for all I knew there might even be a formal group of Jewish students, though I didn't know of any. Hell, there was even an outspoken gay club whose agenda wasn't to recruit people into the gay community but to say, "Look at us. We are real people, too." The Americans in Moscow had also grouped together, not because of religious or sexual preferences, but because of the language problem and certain justified fears of being infiltrated by the Soviet secret police. Hadn't it happened to me? Unfortunately, most people wouldn't see the parallel.

If I defended the Moslem students I might be pegged as some sort of traitor to our good Christian society. What a dilemma.

I tried several drafts of a letter and deleted them one after the other. What could I do but deny, deny, deny like some politician accused of infidelity only to have the proof come out and blow up in his face. If I were really unlucky, and I feared this would happen, someone would somehow find out that I had at one time been accused of being a paid Soviet agent, that I had been part of a scheme to launder stolen Russian Mafia money. I was tainted. If that came out I would be painted as a scurrilous traitor to all things American, shifting from being pro Communist to pro Islamification.

Unable to produce evidence to the contrary in a form readily understandable in a couple of paragraphs in a public letter, I was in a precarious position.

I discussed it with Ivy and Katya. Katya knew about the Mafia money. Ivy knew about my off and on relationship with her Russian father Vladimir Putinsky, now Putin. Though Katya didn't about the business that began with handing over the class lists, she and Ivy both knew that FBI Agent Wilkins was involved in our lives. He'd been the one who told me that Katya, being my biological daughter, was entitled to US citizenship.

Not only could I be fired from my precarious position at the university, but this business could blow our fragile family apart. This wasn't just about me. It was about us.

Ivy understood very well, but Katya, in spite of her maturity, was still a teenager. If she felt like it, she could just split as she had before. She didn't have to hang around with a disgraced papa and her step mother. With access to the money Vladimir had pilfered from the Russian Mafia, Katya could be independent. Katya wasn't at risk. Ivy and I were.

I finally settled on a simple letter to the *Nugget* and to the *Mining Gazette*. As the stand-in faculty advisor to the Moslem Students' Association I had no part in the invitation of ben Zarko to the campus and no knowledge of what he might say in his presentation. The Moslem Students' Association had done nothing illegal. They were entitled to hold meetings on campus and to invite the public if they so wished.

I attempted to draw a parallel. Sometimes local clergy would get political in their sermons; even though they had to know that, under the constitutional rule of separation of church and state, to use the pulpit for political purposes could jeopardize the tax free status of a church. The lecture hall we used in the Hellman building was not a church and the event was not a religious service. Ben Zarko was free to discuss anything short of sedition. I guess it wasn't a parallel situation after all.

Freedom of speech gave us lots of latitude, but nobody said democracy was a bad thing. No one argued for the return of the monarchy.

The only positive note was news that Abdul, the Palestinian who'd been hit over the head with the Israeli flag, was out of the hospital. There had been no permanent damage. He apparently had no memory of or had forgotten who hit him in the head, or with what. Only the hockey players had been arrested.

When this all blew over, there would be no permanent damage to me, either. I hoped.

In the middle of the night Ivy nudged me and woke me up.

"What?"

"You're grinding your teeth."

"Am I?"

She snapped on the bedside lamp and turned toward me, hampered by her stomach.

I wondered if a fetus slept, and if Ivy's movements woke up our baby. No man can have the same kind of intimate relationship that a woman has when she carries her child.

"If you keep it up you can actually crack your teeth. You know that?"

I didn't.

"You might have to see a dentist and sleep with a retainer."

I could only grunt.

"What's bugging you, Irwin?"

"This whole business. I don't know what to do next."

"Like what?"

I evaded the real issues. "It's not fair to Katya to have to sleep in the living room on a futon. She has no privacy."

"Coming from Moscow, maybe she's used to it," Ivy said. "I read someplace that it was common for three families to crowd into a three room apartment."

I'd seen something of that myself, a two burner kerosene stove in the hallway and schedules so people could cook their meals separately. But Vladimir had been a KGB officer. I was sure he'd had a decent apartment. Before Ivy and I got serious she had her little apartment on Fifth Street near the campus and I rented Kosinsky's big old house. There was a spare bedroom for Katya there. Then she disappeared. "We need a bigger place. With Katya here and the baby coming, we'll need three bedrooms."

She saw through me. "That's not why you're grinding your teeth."

I admitted, "I feel torn. I'm not a Moslem, but I feel responsible for those kids in the Moslem Students' Association. They're getting a lot of heat. It's not fair."

Ivy brushed the hair out of her eyes and kissed me. 'You're a very loyal person, Irwin. Think about it: after 9/11 the Arab population in this country was too silent. It was as if they agreed with the attack on the World Trade Center. They needed to speak up in protest, to show that they want to be good Americans. They didn't."

"Maybe they were afraid. Like the Afghans who are terrified of Taliban retaliation. It's like people who witness a gang drive by shooting and are afraid to speak up."

"9/11 wasn't a drive by shooting."

"No, but a lot of the Moslem immigrants have families abroad. They might be in danger."

"I don't believe it."

"Even if they don't, the American Moslems need to be more proactive. I don't mean in proselytizing or demanding Sharia law, but in showing that they want to be loyal Americans like the rest of us."

"Maybe they don't," Ivy said.

I had to admit that there were strong cultural differences and some people did not want to assimilate. Our students would go back to their home countries after they got their degrees. They didn't have to become Americans.

"I'll call David and arrange to meet with the student association to explain to them." In this society they needed to be tactful, especially in a society where hostility lay just beneath a thin surface of tolerance. This could be explosive, too, but I would talk with them in a private meeting, not open to the madding crowd.

"OK. Now go back to sleep. And stop grinding your teeth."

Even so, I lay awake a long time listening to the snow plows grinding by on the street. I would have to shovel in the morning.

Chapter thirty-two

David lived on campus in the classic old dorm with its ivy-covered walls that I could see from the window of my office in the Humanities building. He told me the next meeting of the student association would be in an apartment off campus and I was welcome to come. He gave me the address, which wasn't far from our little rented house.

The older homes in Portage Lake come in three distinct classes: nearly identical workers' houses built by the mining companies, were originally clapboard, some still with old, weathered siding. Others had siding that dated them, depending on what material was in vogue at the time. There were phony asphalt bricks of red grit in panels or slabs of gritted asphalt siding of sugar cane fibers. More recent homes had Masonite that had to be painted from time to time. The latest fashion was plastic.

The middle class houses were more elaborate with fancy shingling on the upper walls or decorative wood trim. The old mining captains' Victorian places usually had towers and even back stairs for servants. All had steep roofs to keep them from being crushed by the heavy U.P. snows.

The place where the Moslem Student Association was meeting was off campus in one of the big old houses that had been broken up into apartments. It had a big, unheated porch, storage place for bicycles, skis, and assorted junk.

Inside, I saw the spacious dining room was now a

bedroom separated by sliding pocket doors. The living room was furnished with several couches in disrepair and one current luxury: a large flat screen television set. I suspected that was the only item owned by the tenant students.

About a dozen showed up. Some I recognized for the previous year. Al, the Iranian, was there. I didn't see the two Kuwaitis I had flunked. Kuwaitis are rich. Maybe they eschewed the other Moslems as being inferior. From the paragraphs my students had written about themselves, I knew some were wealthy scions of important people in their own countries. Others were making do on what funds their parents could scrape up for an expensive college education in the United States. Compared with bigger, more prestigious schools, Michigan Institute Technology was relatively cheap. That might answer my question of why on earth anyone from India or some other warm place would choose the sub arctic of Northern Michigan. There were no women present.

Though all Moslems, they came from so many countries that their common language was English.

I hadn't attended any of their prayer meetings or dinners and hadn't met the members formally, so I introduced myself. "I'm Irwin Glass. Dean Sheldon asked me to fill in as your faculty advisor while your regular advisor is away on sabbatical leave. Now, as you probably know, I'm getting a lot of heat because of the fight in the Hellman building."

There were murmurs but I couldn't tell if they were sympathetic or whether they simply didn't like me because I was not one of them.

I took a deep breath before continuing. "I guess it's obvious that there's a lot of suspicion and even animosity among the locals. They think that all Moslems are Arabs, which of course you are not—(a nod to a student I recognized as Indonesian)—and some think that all Moslems are terrorists. This is unfortunate, because I'm sure you are all here to study and get an education so you can go home and be assets to your countries. You are the cream of your society, but Americans are pretty ignorant of other countries and cultures."

At least on this point there was general assent.

"Even though you were not responsible for what

happened in the Hellman building, I need your help to mend some fences."

They weren't certain what I meant by mending fences. I had to remember to purge my language of idioms others might not understand.

"It would be helpful," I suggested, "if you as a group put together a statement disavowing ben Zarko and his vitriol against the United States. You didn't know what he was going to say, did you?"

The agreement was half hearted. Maybe some of them did.

I let myself go out on a limb in my determination to please them. "I see from your web site that you sometimes have a pot luck when you can all share halal food. How about having your next communal meal at my house?"

Al hadn't given up his interest in Katya. "Will your daughter be there?"

"I'm sure she will. And my wife Dr. Hartshorne, too, of course. I'm not much of a cook. At a pot luck everyone brings something. We'll count on you to come up with appropriate recipes."

It was impetuous and thoughtless of me to invite the whole Moslem club to our house without first consulting Ivy, but I was sure she would agree. I wondered if the others had similar political views to Al's. I needed to get to know them better if I was to provide Wilkins with meaningful commentary. Getting to know the young men better couldn't do any harm, could it?

I almost regretted my hasty invitation. The logistics were going to be tough. We didn't have a dining room. We had four kitchen chairs. In the living room we had only the futon, the Lay-Z-Boy recliner and Ivy's desk chair. We couldn't seat ten or twelve visitors. I knew Professor Kosinsky played bridge. Maybe we could borrow some folding chairs from him.

That we only had tableware and dishes for six shouldn't be a problem. We could buy some paper plates and plastic knives and forks. It would be a picnic.

Chapter thirty-three

I should have known better, for Ivy was furious that I'd invited the whole Moslem Students' Association to our little house. Katya thought a party was a cool idea, but she had never entertained a houseful of guests and wasn't aware of the logistics. Even when Vladimir and Katya were both with us, Katya bedding down on the floor in a sleeping bag while Vladimir had the futon, we were only four people.

Ivy wasn't happy about having to do a thorough housecleaning and I wondered about the food. It was to be a pot luck, right? So what would Moslems bring? When he came to dinner Al had brought a box of digestive biscuit crackers for the host, a token. In some cultures fresh flowers would have been appropriate, or maybe a box of chocolate, but the nearest grocery to campus was Jim's Foods and they didn't sell flowers. Someone among the Moslem students must have a car to get them to Econo Foods west of town or to the Wal-Mart super store.

It was thoughtless of me. My invitation put a burden on everyone, except Katya who thought it would be fun.

When I broke the news to Ivy she took a deep breath to keep from flying into frenzy. "You'll have to clean this place," she demanded. "I put you in charge of the bathroom."

The small bathroom, with its tired, iron tub and old plumbing, would never shine. The house was a hundred years old. We'd put down a shag throw rug on the cracked linoleum bathroom floor. Katya and Ivy would have to stow their lotions and potions on the shelf in the bathroom closet. And no hanging tights or underwear, please!

Ivy looked up some halal recipes on the internet and printed out several. She and Katya conferred on what was easy and possible. Not all the ingredients were available locally. I didn't know what lemon grass was or who might sell it. The two women in our little family balked at wearing head scarves. Moslem women didn't do that indoors, did they?

The Moslem students arrived and took off their shoes and boots in the vestibule where our skis were stacked. There was soon a pile of footwear that would have to be sorted out when they left.

My fears were unfounded, as it turned out. The students were nice kids. I call them kids because I was old enough to be their father, but of course they were young men. They had never been invited as a group to an American home before, and a party at their faculty advisor's house was a treat. They plunged into it with enthusiasm.

They had all been at the Hellman building lecture. David was the only one whose American name corresponded to his native one. David came dressed casually. It looked like he'd had a haircut, no more hair coming down into his eyes. Al, whose correct name was Ali, actually wore a tie, though it was badly knotted. I guessed he wanted to make a good impression in spite of the strained conclusion of his dinner with Katya and us.

Al, having been at our home before, introduced all of his co-religionists. I tried to remember which was which and to mentally connect their American names with the names on the club's roster. They quickly got over their initial awkwardness and plunged into the cooking bit. It got pretty crowded, but Ivy is a take charge sort of person. She instructed two of the boys to set up sort of a buffet on her desk which had been cleared of paperwork.

They were able to make a halal dish of lemon rice and potato wedges. Another meal called for papaya, something Katya had never tasted and wasn't available in Portage Lake.

It was a bit crazy with all those people crowded in the kitchen around the old gas stove. We didn't have a frying pan large enough to make a portion big enough to all those mouths, but we managed.

I was aware of the rules on alcohol for minors and the Moslem dietary laws, so there was no beer or wine, which would have been expensive if allowed. We had lain on several bottles of juice cocktails and disposable plastic cups. Our little coffee maker was put to the test to keep up with the appetites.

Everything was going along smoothly and I was enjoying myself until one of the students, an Indonesian, noticed the flag I'd left in the vestibule along with our cross country skis. "Is that an Israeli flag?"

The room went silent.

"Professor Kosinsky brought it in to be repaired. The shaft was broken. He'll take it back to Adat Israel tomorrow. There's a Hanukah party."

"Adat Israel?" someone asked.

"The synagogue," I explained.

"Hanukah?"

"I think it's Jewish Christmas." Though not accurate, it was the simplest explanation I could muster.

Al came to my rescue. "Professor Glass is not a Jew. He is Methodist."

Thanks, Al, for remembering. I suspected that some of the Moslems didn't know what a Methodist was, there being so many Christian sects, like Catholic, Baptist, Lutheran, Apostolic, and others I couldn't distinguish from one another any more than I could tell the difference between a Sunni and a Shiite Moslem. Some people claim that Mormons aren't Christians and some Christians, like Seventh Day Adventists, eschew what they call Trinitarians. I wasn't going to get into a theological discourse on the differences between the various churches, even if I knew. I'm not into religion.

To my relief, they didn't press the point, though I sensed the mere presence of an Israeli flag in the house placed me in the enemy camp.

With all the traffic, talk, joking, and socializing I didn't pay any attention to who went upstairs to the bathroom.

At last it was over. In spite of the sour note about the flag, I thought it was a success. A couple of the boys, Al, in particular, stuck around to help with the washing up. The paper plates and plastic tableware went into a big garbage bag.

When they were gone I rearranged the furniture and relaxed. Katya made up the futon and unrolled the sleeping bag she used as a blanket.

It was my turn in the bathroom when Ivy knocked at the door. "We've got a problem."

I was brushing my teeth and must have looked like I was foaming at my mouth when I let her in.

Ivy was frightened. I'd never seen her frightened before, not even when we had that fatal home invasion. Then she was steely steady, cool and focused. Now she was shaking.

"What is it?"

"My Glock. It was in the drawer next to the bed. It's gone."

"You sure?"

"Sure, I'm sure. I'm not careless about guns."

"Is it loaded?"

"Of course, it's loaded. You think I'd have time to load it if we had another home invasion?"

"Did you ask Katya?"

"Yes."

"She has a Glock, too. Is hers safe?"

"Yes."

I rinsed out my mouth and spit in the sink. "I guess we'll have to call the police."

Having to quiz all of our now departed guests about the missing weapon was going to destroy any rapport we'd achieved. It was best to leave that up to the Portage Lake police, and not get into any confrontations myself. I didn't want to appear hostile. I had to be Irwin Glass, good cop, except I wasn't.

I'd forgotten that Portage Lake has only about three policemen and the office is closed after five o'clock, like all criminals must keep regular office hours. Late calls had to go to the Houghton County sheriff's office where Ivy and more recently Katya had registered their hand guns and got their licenses to carry concealed weapons. They made me feel like I was in some sort of Wild West show, except it was the women in our family that were packing heat, as they say in the hood.

I got the sheriff's office on the line. "I want to report a stolen hand gun."

The deputy on night duty asked for the particulars and Ivy provided the serial number, make and model of her nine millimeter Glock. At least it didn't have an extended magazine.

The deputy was skeptical. No, there wasn't a burglary. The gun was probably stolen by one of our party guests. Could I provide a list of whoever had been at the party?

That's where I had a problem. I had the roster of the Moslem students' Association which listed them by their native country names. I knew Al and David, by their American names. I hadn't sorted out the others and didn't take notes.

"You mean they all have aliases?" the deputy asked.

"Foreign students take American sounding names we can pronounce and spell. How would you spell Mahatma, for instance?"

"I wouldn't."

"So you might call him Mike, just for convenience," I explained.

"OK." He didn't sound very convinced.

"I'll have to print out the whole roster and check off the names of the boys who were at the party."

"You have a roster? You mean an invitation list? That's a help. You betcha."

"They are all members of the Moslem Students' Association at the Tech. I'm their faculty advisor."

Clearly, the deputy wasn't friendly to Moslems and, by extension, to their faculty advisor. "I can't do anything for you tonight. I'm the only one in the office. The other deputy is out on patrol. You want him to stop by?"

I didn't see that there'd be anything to gain in that, not at that hour. "I'll bring the list by tomorrow. I suppose you'll want to question all of them."

"How many are there?"

"Ten."

The deputy was reluctant. "Why don't you call the Portage Lake police in the morning?"

"OK. I'll do that." I hung up and turned to Ivy who was standing there in her bathrobe and bare feet. The house was chilly. "This is not going to be easy."

Chapter thirty-four

Before going to class the next morning I called the Portage Lake Police, told the officer on duty about the theft and promised to send over the list of potential suspects.

My first class was the Chinese students, all eager, but struggling with their pronunciation as usual. A couple of our guests from the night before, Michael and Al, were in the two o'clock class. I didn't know if I should take them aside and discreetly ask about the missing Glock. How could I? What should I say, "Did you steal my wife's gun?" That would be too aggressive. I'm not a confrontational sort of a guy.

I wasn't sure about Michael, but Wilkins had said he was OK. Maybe he knew something I wasn't supposed to. If Michael's brother had worked as an interpreter, my student might be the FBI plant.

With the possible exception of Michael who, being the only Afghan, seemed to be suspicious of the other Moslems, we had all been having a good time at the party. If anyone did snoop in our bedroom upstairs, did they share the experience with the others? "Look what I got?" and a sly peek at their trophy? It's fairly common for teenagers who are guests to go through their host's medicine cabinet in search of pain killers and other prescriptions. All we had in ours was some Tums, aspirin, and stomach medicine for Ivy's morning sickness. That, thankfully, was all over now that she was settled into a more advanced state of pregnancy. As far as I knew, no one had stolen any of our medicine.

I didn't know if Katya took birth control pills. There were none such in our cabinet. It was a subject I wasn't prepared to ask her about. I guess I wasn't being a good parent, but I figured it was a mother daughter thing.

Anyway, I printed out the Moslem Students Association roster, checked the names of those I recognized as having been at our party, and faxed it to the Portage Lake police as the list of possible suspects.

Then I phoned Agent Wilkins in Marquette. He'd want to know about this.

To my surprise, Wilkins was actually glad to hear about the theft. "So, you're smoking them out. Good."

"I wasn't trying to smoke anybody out."

"You know what I mean, Glass."

So it was Glass again. At least it wasn't Irvin. When Wilkins was being tough guy it was Glass, when friendly it was Irwin, and sometimes, when he was being cute just Irvin, an allusion to my Russian connections. "I'm going to leave the smoking out to the Portage Lake police."

"You probably won't get the hand gun back. If this was

Detroit, your wife's piece would be sold by now. That's what usually happens wit dem stolen firearms."

"I don't think any of our students would steal it to sell it." Most of the foreign students, especially the Chinese, came from wealthy families.

"I don't, either. They're probably planning something."

They? Did he assume more than one? I shuddered. I had fearful recollections of campus shootings. Some kid who flunks or is mad at his professor goes into a classroom and starts firing. I was glad those Kuwaitis I had trouble with were no longer in my class.

It's hard to read some people. The killers who committed those campus crimes fell into a pattern of being strange loners, sometimes with a record of psychological problems. Maybe Dean Sheldon would have information on whether any of the Moslem students had a past record of psychological problems. If they were, I had to know, if only for our own safety.

I didn't want to talk to Dean Sheldon, but I'd have to. We are not buddies. I called her and asked, "Have any of the Moslem students needed psychological counseling?"

Dean Sheldon is not a friendly person, at least not to me, especially after that business of my being accused of fraternization with Katya which turned out to be legitimate. "That sort of information is confidential."

"I had to ask, because one of them probably stole my wife's gun."

That got to her. "Has anybody threatened you? Acted strangely?"

"Nope. We had a halal dinner party. Ten members of the Association were at my house. You know how some people are. They snoop. They swipe stuff."

"What kind of a weapon are you talking about? Hunting rifle?"

"Nine milimeter Glock. It's no toy. It's a deadly weapon. Cops use them. Katya has one, too, but hers is safe."

"Your Russian daughter has a handgun?"

"She has a permit to carry."

"Well, I hope she doesn't carry it around on campus. We have a rule about that."

I didn't know if Katya did. There are lots of things about her I don't know. Sometimes I wonder if she is really my daughter after all, but the thought is so troubling I have to put it out of my mind. Sometimes we hope that if we don't think about something, like cancer, it will go away.

My conversation with Dean Sheldon got me nowhere. If anything, it reinforced her opinion that I was some kind of trouble maker. I'm not. Trouble just follows me around. I suppose Professor Kosinsky would call me a schlemiel, whatever that is. Someone not very effective.

That reminded me of that darned flag. Kosinsky was going to pick it up and return it to Adat Israel.

Chapter thirty-five

Professor Kosinsky called us at supper time. He loves the opportunity to speak Russian, as there aren't many in Portage Lake who share his native language. Sometimes he likes to tease me and call me "comrade" though the use of the word is an anachronism, a throw back to the old Soviet Communist days. It's a jibe because of my own past history as an alleged paid Soviet agent. "*Tovarish*. I need to pick up the Israeli flag. It is Hanukah. Party time. You should come along."

"I'm not Jewish." It seems the more I protest the more Jewish I feel. "I don't know anything about Hanukah."

"Good reason for to come. Have you had latkes?"

"What are latkes?"

"Potato pancakes. And there will also be jelly donuts."

"I don't get it."

Kosinsky explained the tradition. "Jewish history. They tried to kill us. We won. Let's eat. Hanukah is about the miracle of the holy oil that burned for eight days instead of one. In those days lamps were oil, not candles, so we eat foods made with oil. Latkes, and in Israel jelly donuts."

"What else besides eating?"

"We sing songs. It is party. You should come. Bring Ivy and Katya."

Ivy and I had been to Adat Israel at the Jewish New Year. That was before the serious snow. She remembered

494

that there is no sidewalk at the side of the highway. We had to park at the bank lot and walk along the edge. "It's too slippery for me," she said. "I'm afraid to fall. In my condition…"

"Right." I turned to Katya. "How about you, Katya? Are you game for a party?"

"Game?"

"Hanukah. Jewish Christmas. Potato pancakes."

"Sure." 'Sure'? Her American was improving.

I told Kosinsky, "OK. Will you pick us up? We can't all fit into the Tracker with the flag, too. Do we bring anything, I mean, besides the flag?"

"I will buy the jelly donuts."

"Fair enough." We got ready and about seven o'clock Kosinsky's car was waiting beside the snow bank out on the street. I disassembled the flag pole so it would fit inside the car and we rode up the hill to Econo Foods.

It was snowing a little, just enough to put a fresh coating of wet stuff on the four lane highway. There had been a blizzard for Thanksgiving weekend, typical, I was told, for the Copper Country, but now it was December. Most of that November snow had melted and all that remained were banks beside the road where the plows had pushed it. I was told that sometimes there wasn't snow at Christmas. Ivy looked forward to it, but I hoped she postponed cross country skiing until after the baby arrived.

Kosinsky bought a dozen jelly filled donuts.

We had to park in the bank lot and stumbled along the side of the highway like a little parade, me with the flag and Kosinsky with the donuts. I had a fleeting image of the three wise men bearing gifts. Luckily there wasn't much traffic for we'd be sitting ducks for an inattentive driver.

The front steps to the synagogue had not been shoveled but the Hanukah celebration wasn't in the sanctuary upstairs. It was in the ground floor party room where I'd been before. The path to the ground floor back door had been cleared. Inside, there were only half a dozen adults and a couple of little girls in cute party dresses. The whole place smelled of hot oil and frying potato pancakes.

Arya, the Israeli student, ex-IDF, was chief cook. I hung

around in the kitchen and watched. He had two iron skillets going at once on the electric stove. "Aren't you afraid of a fire?"

Arya was wearing a borrowed, frilly apron that looked a bit ludicrous, and handled a metal spatula like a conductor's baton. He nodded toward the entrance where I stood. Mounted beside the door was a hefty fire extinguisher, just in case one of those pans of hot oil reached the flash point.

Katya and I stood around watching while the two little girls lit the Hanukah candles, one they called the shamas which they then used to light the others. It was the third day of Hanukah, so there were, including the shamas, four candles. Then they sang some cute songs, the parents joining in.

Professor Kosinsky tried to explain to me the little, four sided Jewish top, what he called a dredel, and the Hebrew letters on the sides. He explained that Hanukah was the only time Jews gambled, usually for hazel nuts or chocolate Hanukah geld. The only time Jews got dunk was at Purim. I didn't know Purim, either.

Then I remembered the flag. "Look, I'll just take the flag upstairs, OK? I know where it stands."

I took the Israeli flag and climbed the stairs up to the darkened sanctuary. The place was empty and forbidding, like somewhere you might encounter a ghost, but it may have been history talking to me. I fumbled for the light switch, found it, and the place lit up memories of the Rosh Hashanah service, the men in prayer shawls, the prayer scroll, the Torah. The sanctuary was cold. It's an old building, its Byzantine architecture an echo of ancient times. The heat comes up through air ducts in the floor. I could hear the singing of "Oh, Hanukah..." from below.

The heavy, metal base the flag normally stood in was at the side of the pulpit. I assembled the flag pole, saw that it was almost as good as new, and set it in the stand.

It was at that moment that I heard a whoosh from downstairs and a scream. As I rushed back to the stairs I saw a little puff of smoke coming from the air duct in the floor.

As I reached the top of the stairs one of the little girls who had been playing dredel came screaming up from below.

Her hair was singed and her party dress had caught fire. I grabbed her, trying to smother the flames, and tried to exit through the front door. It was locked, but it was old.

On the second crash against it, the lock splintered and I pushed the door open against the snow that had accumulated in front. Then with the kid in my arms, we rolled in the snow to put out the flames. I lifted her up just as her father came out after her. He was distraught and frightened.

"She's OK," I said, handing her to her dad. "She's probably in shock." Her screaming was now just a whimper.

Then I heard Katya shouting, "Stop or I shoot!"

I looked down over the railing where we're found the Palestinian flag. Katya was in the road, holding her Glock, aiming at someone.

I could just make out a dark figure in a hoodie running away. He turned and hesitated, pointed something at Katya.

There was a sharp report as someone fired a gun. I didn't know who. The figure spun around just as the headlights of what turned out to be a logging truck appeared in the blur of falling snow. It rumbled past, the compression brakes a roaring rattle, but it didn't stop. Probably the driver never noticed, what with all that falling snow, that he'd hit someone.

I stumbled and slid down the snow covered synagogue steps to the highway. Katya was ahead of me.

It's not a pretty sight when an eighteen wheeler runs over your head, which is what happened. When I caught up with Katya she was bent over the body, what there was left of it.

"Who is it?" I asked.

Katya said nothing, but picked up something out of the snow and handed it to me. Though it was filthy with snow and slush, when I wiped it off to put in my pocket I recognized it.

I could not recognize the body. If a loaded logging truck runs over your head, what's left is mush.

I remember the wisps of steaming vapor as the hot blood spread into the snow and the faint smell of gasoline. We flagged down the next vehicle before we became casualties ourselves. Katya got out her cell phone and dialed

911. She put her gun back in her shoulder bag before the police and firemen arrived. I asked, "Did you shoot him?"

She wouldn't say.

I left Katya beside the body. While she explained to the people in the car that had stopped what had happened I picked my way up the snow-clogged front steps up to the front door of Adat Israel. Smoke was coming out of the building, but not as much as I'd expected. I assumed it was a kitchen fire, right?

Choking on the smoke, I went down the stairs and found that all of the Jews, except the father who had pursued his daughter up the stairs, had escaped out the side door leaving Arya in his ludicrous frilly apron, standing with the extinguisher, coughing, putting out the last of the fire on the carpet. It was one of those bicarbonate of soda extinguishers that put out streams of white powder. Though the carpet was charred, the fire hadn't taken hold of the flooring itself. There was white powder all over the place. It was going to be a mess to clean up. At least the synagogue hadn't burned. That would have been a tragedy for the community. There wasn't enough capital in the congregation to build another and I doubted if fire insurance would cover a replacement in the grand, Byzantine style of the place.

Why the carpet? I had thought the potato pancakes had caught fire in the kitchen, but that wasn't it. Someone had pushed open the back door and thrown in a Molotov cocktail. Whoever it was wanted to incinerate the congregation, what little there was of Jews in Portage Lake, Michigan.

Strange how the far away conflict in the Middle East reached all the way to the wilds of Northern Michigan.

The fire department, the ambulance, and then the county sheriff's car arrived at the scene. A little while later the state police showed up, having driven down from Calumet. The vehicles and people created a traffic jam. The state policeman immediately set out flares and diverted what traffic there was to detour west bound cars down to the waterfront and the marina. They could follow the service road around to the lift bridge approach on the other side.

The paramedics scooped up what was left of the arsonist

on a gurney. The girl I had rolled in the snow had minor burns. Her pretty party dress was ruined, but she'd worn wool tights under it, not nylon or polyester which melts as it burns and adheres to the skin. The little girl and her father rode along to the hospital. There's only one ambulance service in Portage Lake. Must have been pretty sickening to sit beside the corpse during that ride. I bet the kid will have nightmares forever.

Katya was badly shaken, but though I had with difficulty suppressed the impulse to vomit at the sight of the mashed body, she didn't. Katya is one tough kid. We were both cold, standing there in the snow and slush without our coats. My hands were burned from holding the little girl and smothering her burning dress. Putting my hands in the snow helped. They were red, but the burns were first degree like a very bad sunburn.

Later, when Ivy cleaned her Glock, she found it had been fired once, but there was no telling when. If it had been fired just before the logging truck hit, the ejected shell was lost in the snow and roadside deleterious. It might turn up in the spring when the snow finally did melt.

The fire was out before the firemen came, so there was no need to soak the place, which would have buckled the flooring and done more damage than the brief fire. After the firemen left Katya and I stuck around with Professor Kosinsky to tidy up the place.

Professor Kosinsky was badly shaken. "I thought maybe in America I would escape this." He would have been too young to experience the German invasion of Russia, but he knew the history and what happened to the Jews.

Katya found the vacuum cleaner in a closet and made an effort to clean up all that white powder. Arya shook his head at the remains of his efforts in the kitchen. There were donuts left. He held up the flat, white bakery box to Kosinsky. "You want these?"

I had lost my appetite. I never did get to eat a jelly donut or taste a potato pancake.

We were the last to leave. Our winter coats which we had hung on the rack beside the door had not burned, but reeked of smoke. We mushed along the roadside back to the bank parking lot, passed the dark stain in the snow. The flares on the highway had 400and the state police had left. There were only two cars left in the bank lot, Arya's and Kosinsky's. Arya drove off. Before getting into Kosinsky's car, I stopped and looked around the bank lot. Ours was the last car to leave.

How had the arsonist got there? He'd been running toward the bank lot. When we arrived a few cars were already there. If the arsonist had driven himself, his vehicle should still be there. It wasn't. Someone must have driven him and waited, but when the fire department and police arrived, had taken off, unnoticed. Who was the accomplice?

By the time we were ready to leave snow had covered all the tire tracks.

Ivy freaked out when we got in the house. "What happened to you? You smell awful."

"Smoke. Someone tried to incinerate the Hanukah party."

Katya explained. "I saw him and run after. He try to shoot me with your gun."

She nodded to me and I handed the Glock to Ivy.

"What about you, Katya? What did you think you'd do if you caught up with him?"

Katya was hanging up her coat beside the door. She turned with a knowing smile. "I shoot him. Not to kill. Just to stop."

So she did shoot. "Did you hit him?"

Katya nodded apologetically. "Only in leg. Here." She tapped her thigh.

"Then the autopsy will show that he'd been shot."

"I not think so."

"Oh, you mean that since his head was mashed by the truck further examination won't be necessary."

Katya nodded, but it was a loose end. If he'd been hit in the head, there'd be nothing to find. In the leg? Maybe. Considering the obvious reason for the arsonist's death, I didn't think an autopsy would be performed.

I called the Portage Lake police in the morning to say the missing Glock had been found. I feigned embarrassment. It was a false alarm, I said, sorry to have caused so much trouble. I didn't mind if the cops thought I was a hysteric who called the police the first time something went missing.

The story I told Agent Wilkins was different.

"So who was it?"

I had no idea. I hoped it wasn't one of my Moslem students, but that was wishful thinking. "He had to have had an accomplice to drive him there."

Wilkins was thoughtful. "Sometimes the perp hangs around to watch the action."

"There were some bystanders, people from the congregation and a couple that drove up right after the accident. They couldn't just mill about. It's the side of the highway. The hill comes right down to the edge. Whoever drove the perp, as you call him, must have left right away."

"You didn't see who it was?"

"Not a chance. It was dark and snowing. There's a dusk to dawn light by the bank, but it's too far away."

"Hmm. Well, Irwin, just keep me informed."

So it was Irwin again. I was in his good graces.

If whoever drove the arsonist to the synagogue was a member of the Moslem Students' Association, who could it be? Few of the Moslem students owned cars. The only one I was sure of was David ibn Sayed, the president. He'd told me that when the Association needed halal food from the Econo grocery, he drove. But it could be someone else.

The more one mulls over these things, the wider the field of possible suspects.

Chapter thirty-six

I had to call Dean Sheldon back to tell her what had happened and as a post script, not connected to the synagogue incident, to say, incidentally, that Ivy's gun had been found. I didn't say it had been found in the snow on the highway beside the arsonist.

That the missing gun was a false alarm only reinforced Sheldon's view that I was some kind of a jerk, but that was alright. That I didn't know who the arsonist was and feared it was one of my Moslem students, was a different matter.

One of the local radio stations, the Bear 98 I think they

501

call it, broke the story first. Someone had tried to burn down the Portage Lake synagogue while there was a Hanukah party going on, but was run over by a truck while running away. The only serious casualty was the arsonist, but he had carried no identification. So far, nobody had come forward to identify him.

He must have some ID, I thought. No wallet? Maybe there were laundry marks on the clothing, the sort of thing detectives look for, but I'm no detective.

The radio announcer, it turned out, was himself Jewish, and made a comment that burning Jews alive in their synagogues was something the Germans and the Poles did during the Holocaust. He also mentioned that a Palestinian flag had been hung on the railing some time ago and wondered if there was a connection.

It occurred to me that the radio announcer was a better detective than the Portage Lake police, except nobody had ever found out who hung the flag on the synagogue's railing. This might have been the same person or persons. Maybe not.

I called the Portage Lake police, identified myself, and said I was concerned that the arsonist might be one of my Association members. Had they made an identification?

The police chief said, "We don't normally release that information until the next of kin have been notified. We don't want parents to read in the newspaper that their kid's been killed without their being informed officially."

"I'm the faculty advisor of the Moslem students. You know, *in locus parentis*. I need to know."

The chief didn't understand what *in locus parentis* meant. Copper Country folks don't learn Latin unless maybe they went to Catholic parochial school. He did accept that my request was semi-official.

"Well, Professor Glass, if you keep this confidential, I'll tell you, but keep it under your hat, hey? Don't announce this to anybody."

"So who is it? Who set the fire?"

"Kid named Abdul something I can't pronounce."

"How'd you find that out? I was there when he was run over. He didn't have any ID on him."

"Seems he did. He was wearing one of those plastic, hospital bracelets."

He must have forgotten to cut it off when he was released, or kept in on as a reminder. It was the same student who'd been hit on the head, breaking the Israeli flag pole.

It was a relief to me that Abdul was a Palestinian Christian, not one of my Moslem Students' Association. My Moslems? Odd that I'd taken on a possessive point of view. My students, my Moslems. None of them had thrown the gasoline bomb.

But someone who had been at our halal party and stolen Ivy's hand gun had given it to Abdul. Someone who knew there was a Hanukah party had driven him to the other side of the waterway and waited for him to come out.

But why would a Moslem help a Christian fire bomb a synagogue? Perhaps to avoid being identified. It was typical of al Quaida to enlist someone gullible to wear a bomb into a café. The leaders didn't do that stuff themselves. They were too smart, too cynical, or too valuable. What I was looking for was someone who was a leader. The only one I knew who had a car was David ibn Sayed, the club's president.

David ibn Sayed was an Egyptian. He said his father was an eye doctor. Some of Osama ben Laden's advisors were Egyptian doctors, but that didn't mean that all Egyptian doctors were al Quaida, and certainly not that their sons would be part of a plan to burn down a synagogue anywhere. Such an assumption was absurd. I didn't want to rush to judgment. I didn't have any evidence.

Still, I had to report to Agent Wilkins. I phoned and told him that the perp, as he called him, was Abdul, the same kid who'd been injured in the fight at the Hellman building. He was a Palestinian and a Christian, but he had to have help, someone who had given him Ivy's hand gun, which had to be one of the Moslem students who had been at my house.

"Cute," Wilson commented. "Get a Christian to do the dirty work for a Moslem."

I had to agree.

"Do you realize, Irwin, that in Iraq the Christians are being driven out of the country?"

Ever since the US declared the Iraqi war over and had

withdrawn I hadn't paid much attention.

"Not only that," Wilson continued, "But the Christians are leaving the West Bank as well. Bethlehem, the birthplace of Christ, has hardly any Christians left. It's ethnic cleansing."

"Terrible."

"How does it feel to be the faculty advisor of a group whose goal is world domination?"

That was too much for me. "They're just a bunch of kids far away from home," I pleaded. "It's natural for them to stick together."

"Don't be naïve, Irwin. Tell me, were any of the Moslem girls at your halal party?"

"No."

"It's Sharia law. They want to make it the law in Dearborn. Don't you understand any of this?"

"I guess not."

"Write me a report."

I didn't want to buy into Wilkins' islamophobia. I'd write a report for him and resign from my role as faculty advisor of the Moslem Student's Association.

Writing reports of something as traumatic as being fire bombed and seeing someone mashed by a logging truck is tricky. If you write too soon after, your emotions color your story. If you wait too long, you forget details or your incomplete memory gets filled in by your imagination, what they call false memory. Take ten people who observe the same incident and you get ten different versions. All I could do was give mine.

I didn't want Katya to write her own version. I wanted her to stay out of it. She had been in the room when the flaming bottle of gasoline had been thrown in. I wasn't. She saw the one who did it. She also told me she shot the guy. I wasn't going to tell Wilkins that, for sure.

I divided my report into two parts: what I knew, and what I speculated about. I speculated that David had taken Ivy's gun and given it to the Palestinian kid. Still shaken by his head injury and angry at the Jews—I assumed he knew it was Arya who hit him with the Israeli flag staff, though I didn't know if that part was true---he might have been easily persuaded to take revenge. The Moslem political world view

504

was to wipe Israel off the map, an agenda held in common with the Palestinians, most of whom agreed. That was Al's point of view, too. The enemy of my enemy is my friend.

That was speculation. I had already told Wilkins of Al's vitriolic view of Israel and the West, pale repetitions of the scrod we'd been dished out by that visiting speaker.

I didn't know what Wilkins would do with my report, but in a cover letter I blamed him for my troubles. "It was you who got me into this," I wrote. "First with the class lists, then copies of the student biographies."

Of course, Wilkins hadn't made me faculty advisor to the Moslem Students' Association. That was Dean Sheldon's doing. From that moment, for whatever motivation I had in agreeing to hand over the class lists, the daisy chain of circumstances led to a student being killed and I was an inadvertent, unintentional key figure in the whole mess.

I could not have anticipated the result of my report. In my haste to get out of the whole business I forgot something vital to the outcome. There are facts and there are suppositions, but with repetition suppositions become facts. Facts lead to consequences. I faxed the report to Wilkins, kept no copy in my CYA file, and sent a note to Dean Sheldon. "I hereby resign from being faculty advisor to the Moslem Students' Association." End of story.

God help me, so I thought.

Chapter thirty-seven

The firebombing of the Adat Israel synagogue was big news, not only in the *Daily Mining Gazette*, but in the wire services. The Anti-Defamation League made it one of their cases for fund raising in their campaign against anti-Semitism. WLUC in Marquette sent a video crew, but there was nothing to show besides a charred carpet. The building was not reduced to smoking rubble. None of the stained glass windows had been broken. It was simply not a visual story. The only one who actually died was the arsonist. There were no morgue photos of a crushed corpse. Maybe some day someone would get hold of one of those grotesque, regurgitative pictures and publish them in a true crime magazine, but not now and maybe not ever. The video crew had to fill in with a few exterior shots of the synagogue. Somewhere they found a file photo of Abdul, the dead Palestinian. Nobody had any information about his background. The local Jews didn't want any publicity. They wanted the story to simply go away as if it never happened.

I stayed out of it. Though I got a call from the *Gazette* reporter, I didn't admit to having been at the synagogue when the fire bombing occurred. I insisted that I had no knowledge.

I wanted to be invisible.

Wilkins tried to follow up on my report, but I declined. "Look, I don't want any more of this, Wilkins. If you think one of those kids is a terrorist, it's your job to find him, not mine." That one of the students had stolen Ivy's hand gun brought this theoretical hunt for international terrorists too close to home. I had a wife, a baby on the way, and a lovely daughter with a questionable past I didn't want anyone digging into. Whatever our status quo was, I wanted to hang onto it. I wanted the problem to go away.

Somewhere Wilkins had got hold of my own past history. "You think you can just back out, like you did in Moscow when you told that KGB officer Vladimir Putinsky to go fuck himself? He said you were a dead man."

"This isn't the same. I was never a paid Soviet agent and I am not a paid FBI informant, either."

"Glass, do you think you can release the brake of a car parked at the top of a hill and just walk away while it rolls down toward a crowd of people?"

"I don't get it."

"You will."

This time I avoided being interviewed and quoted. The Jewish radio announcer at the Bear 98 station must have had a friend in the Adat Israel congregation who told him that Katya and I had been at the Hanukah party, but I declined a radio interview. I wasn't going to say anything about repairing the broken flag pole used in the assault on the Palestinian. Deny, deny, deny.

Things looked like they would settle down. Dean Sheldon accepted my resignation as faculty advisor of the

Moslem Students' Association, but I got a call from one of them.

He identified himself but I immediately forgot who was calling. It was one of those long, foreign names. "David and Ali have disappeared."

"Disappeared?"

"Yes. Nobody knows where they are. Do you?"

"I know nothing," I insisted. The tone of my voice made me sound like Clinton saying he "never had sexual elations with that woman." I had a sinking feeling in my stomach that somehow something had happened and I had been responsible.

I felt compelled to phone Wilkins. "I hear David and Al, those Moslem students, have disappeared. You know anything about that? Were they arrested?"

Wilkins chose his words carefully. "Not by me. Immigration and Naturalization may have revoked their visas."

I wasn't convinced. "Wouldn't that take time? Involve a lot of paperwork?"

Wilkins admitted that it would. There'd be lawyers and delays.

"But they're both gone, like in thin air."

"They may have been interdicted."

"What?"

"It's not my department, Glass." (So it was Glass again.) "Why don't you call the CIA?"

"I'm not going to call the CIA. They wouldn't tell me anything anyway."

"Don't you have friends back in Langley?"

I had to laugh at that one. "You must be kidding. No."

"I think this conversation is over." Wilkins hung up.

He must be mad because I got cold feet. I felt like an agent who'd been burned, as they say in the spy books, recognized, his cover blown. I didn't want the Moslem students to think I was their enemy. I didn't want anybody throwing a fire bomb through my front door. I couldn't forget that terrified, screaming kid I hugged and rolled in the snow to stop her hair from burning off. I admit it. I was afraid.

507

It took a long time for the rest of the story to come out. David and Al, whose real name was Ali, had been picked up in the middle of the night, snatched, and flown out of the country to destinations unknown. They'd fallen into a black hole.

Ivy and I were in our office in the Humanities building when I got a surprise visit from a foreign gentleman. He was very distinguished, wearing an expensive suit and an overcoat too thin for our mid-winter, Upper Peninsula climate. His flat shoes were unsuitable for the deep snow that had accumulated on the campus sidewalks. His face was frozen in an expression of heartbreak and grief. The name on his gild-edged visiting card was Mustafa Martael in the Iranian Ministry of Agriculture.

"I believe you knew my son, Ali," he said once he was certain he had the right man. "He wrote me about you and your daughter Katya."

"Oh?"

"I have come to pick up his things from his room in the dormitory."

Until then I had not met any parents who had the painful experience of collecting the effects when a student dies of an accident, heart attack, suicide, or drug overdose. That was what Dean Sheldon encountered in her job. I did not envy her.

Mr. Martael handed me and Ivy some photographs. They were somewhat pixilated enlargements of cell phone shots showing Katya having coffee with Al in the Student Union.

"Where is Al now?" I asked.

Mr. Martael had to take a deep breath to control himself and sat down weakly in one of our visitors' chairs. "You do not know?"

Ivy said, "We only know he disappeared."

"He was kidnapped by your government, taken to a foreign country where he was tortured."

"Water boarded?"

"I do not know. When his body was returned to us he was covered with bruises. They say he killed himself."

"My God."

"Perhaps your daughter would like to keep these

photographs?"

We could not refuse to take them.

Looking across my desk at Ali's father, I realized we were both about the same age, except I was wearing blue jeans and a turtleneck. I was just a second rate instructor of English for foreign students, and he was a high government official in his own country. But we were also parents of children about the same age. If Ali's foolish fantasy about marrying Katya had come to fruition we would all have been family.

As I studied the photographs, Ali's father continued, "Ali wrote to me about how you and your family welcomed him into your home. He was very grateful for your hospitality and friendship. It meant very much to him, and to me. It is not so easy to fit in when you are in a foreign country."

His comments only added to my own depression. I could not help but realize, to admit, that something I had reported had been misconstrued. When I reported to Wilkins I had divided my message into two parts, the facts and the possibilities. The only facts were that someone had taken Ivy's gun from the bedside stand. It could have been any one of the Moslem students. Someone had passed it to Abdul, the Palestinian kid. I didn't know if it was Al who had taken Ivy's gun. I didn't know that for a fact. I didn't know if it was David who then gave the gun to Abdul. I had said, if I remembered correctly, that it was a possibility, not even a probability or a supposition. But with the retelling a possibility becomes a probability, becomes a fact. Hadn't we gone to war in Iraq on a rumor that became a certainty that led to a decision and a hundred thousand dead people? Had Al confessed? If so, to what? Under torture people will say anything to make the torture stop.

I had difficulty imagining that Al, for all his repetition of Moslem political quackspeak, those hateful catch phrases used to incite people, was anything but vapid talk. Had my own irritation about what he said colored my report to Wilkins? Even if Al had been the one who stole the hand gun and given it to the Palestinian, all he might be guilty of was theft and being an accomplice to arson in a building. These were not capital offenses. They did not justify interdiction, torture, and such a breaking of spirit that he killed himself, if that's what really did happen.

I had a sudden, disturbing recollection. Susan Lutz, my old boss at the American Library in Moscow had written a report on me. Perhaps she was jealous of my having left the party with Katya's mother, or was angry or vindictive because I had turned up in my underwear on that Moscow street, drunk or drugged. Perhaps it was out of anger she had accused me of being a drunk and a womanizer, just to get rid of me. The only fact she had was that I had left with a Russian woman and turned up drunk and nearly naked. She had no other facts, but she reported that I was a drunk and a womanizer. Lutz had informed on me. It ruined my career. Now I had informed on the Moslem students. Had I become one of the bad guys? Had my report on the Moslem students been the cause of this horror?

I wanted to believe that they were all innocent. People like Wilkins thought they were all guilty. We were both wrong. But I had Ali's death on my conscience and, it turned out, also David's. His story, which came out later, was that he allegedly had a heart attack under interrogation, but these things never come out in official black and white.

I could not help but feel tainted by the whole affair, burnt out like that carpet on the floor at Adat Israel. Ivy says I should not be depressed. It was not my fault. She reminds me that pretty soon the baby will arrive. We're going to have a boy. We have already settled on a name: Isaac.

I think I know why my ancestor Isaac Melamed fled the pogroms. Jews had been burned alive in their houses and their synagogues. I now knew how that felt, even though I insisted I was not a Jew. Deny, deny, deny. But something's in the blood. Isaac Melamed Hartshorne-Glass. There's a name for you. How about that for karma? I hope he handles it better than I have.

About Harley L. Sachs:

Harley L. Sachs is the author of many novels, short stories, magazine articles and newspaper columns. His short stories have been broadcast on the BBC World Service short wave and on Oregon Public Radio's Golden Hours. His awards for writing are too numerous to list as are his over 1000 publications. He and his wife now live in Portland, Oegon.

Here's a list of books by Harley L. Sachs:

MYSTERY NOVELS

The Mystery Club Series

THE MYSTERY CLUB SOLVES A MURDER
First and most popular of the Mystery Club series. Mary Higgins finds the body of Dora Reed on the roof of the Plaza retirement building, notifies the police, then tells the Mystery Club. They assume several suspects: the manager of the Plaza, Dora's son Donald, or a Plaza employee. Dora's husband, Ed Sutherland, is in Hawaii on board the yacht Miss Chief with an all girl crew. Carrying on their own investigation, the Mystery Club finally suspects Sutherland, though he seems to have a perfect alibi. If they can prove it to their satisfaction, will a court ever convict him-- if he can be found somewhere in the Pacific?

THE MYSTERY CLUB AND THE DEAD DOCTOR
Second in the Mystery Club series. The Mystery Club

consists of five elderly women who live at the Rose Plaza and discuss mysteries written by women. The Mystery Club ladies have no idea of the consequences when Viola Cartwright, their blind member, asks them to go over her Medicare bills. That leads to suspicion about the identity of her personal assistant, Dorothy Anderson, who turns out to be using a stolen identity. Viola's doctor runs a phony clinic owned by a member of the Russian Mafia. Soon the investigation of Medicare bills leads to murder and tragedy, stopped only by the courage of Mary Higgins.

THE MYSTERY CLUB AND THE HIDDEN WITNESS
Third in the Mystery Club series. The ladies of the Mystery Club discover one of the residents is a crook under WITSEC, the witness protection program. He apparently keeps dipping into the employee gift fund. The Mystery Club bands together to track down the missing money, but what they discover is danger.

THE MYSTERY CLUB AND THE SERIAL WIDOW
Fourth in the Mystery Club series. Caroline Kostinsky, new resident at the Rose Plaza, is a widow four times over and she's looking for a fifth husband in retired General Hardcastle, but when drunk she says she killed all of her husbands. Except for her confession, there's no evidence. Now what?

DELIVER ME FROM EVIL
Responding to a posted invitation for new members for the Mystery Club, Judge Ira Kahane and Ursula Besette show up. Ursula, at a turning point in her life as a new Rose Plaza resident, is interested in Wicca and Kabala. Roberta Nelson believes one should not suffer a witch to live. Judge Kahane tries to lead Ursula on the right path, but there is conflict and tragedy coming.

WHITE SLAVE
Sequel to *The Mystery Club Solves a Murder*. The appearance of Ed Sutherland's gold bracelet in a Portland pawn shop revives retired detective Casey's interest in the cold case. He

doesn't know that Sutherland has been picked up and is a slave on a Korean fishing boat. Sutherland, penniless, .without clothes or identification, is stranded in New Zealand. Can he find his way back to Portland and be somehow redeemed or face a death sentence for first degree murder?

The Irwin Glass Series

BETRAYAL

Prequel to *Retribution*. Irwin Glass, BA in Russian, MA in International Relations, has a promising career in the Foreign Service in Moscow until he is snared in a classic "honey pot" seduction. He's young and naïve, honest, always wants to do the right thing, but at every turn he is betrayed. The incident in Moscow destroys his career. He is accused of being a paid Soviet agent and is pursued by the consequences of his encounter with the KGB twenty years later. Some enemies never let go

RETRIBUTION

Sequel to *Betrayal*. Newly married to Ivy Hartshorn, Irwin Glass gets a dunning letter from the IRS for taxes on interest at the Washington, DC account he didn't think he had. It's a joint account with his missing birth daughter and the balance is huge. Assuming it's money Katya's KGB father of record, Vladimir Putinsky (now Putin) deposited for her living expenses, Irwin moves it to force her to contact him. But Ivy warns him that he is laundering money and the people it belongs to will come after him. Irwin's complicated life is catching up with him, but this time he will find retribution.

BURNT OUT

Irwin Glass is approached by FBI Agent Wilkins who asks for Irwin's lists of foreign students. Not satisfied he wants more and is looking for potential terrorists among the Moslem students. Gradually Irwin is sucked into the role of FBI informant on the Michigan Institute of Technology's Muslim Students' Association and the results are tragic.

Other mystery novels

MURDER BY MAIL

German exchange student Klaus Hitz is more interested in making money than in asking questions about his work assignment. He doesn't know that the industrialist father of his punk girl friend is using him in a terrorist conspiracy to kill everyone in the United States with a mass mailing of a scratch and sniff virus. The plot begins to unravel when a Polish nurse brings blood samples from Libya and alerts a CIA agent. While the CIA and FBI track down the terrorists, Klaus Hitz gradually figures it out. How can he avoid being murdered or imprisoned for being naive?

MURDER IN THE KEWEENAW

CIA agent recovering from Post traumatic Stress after failed missions in Finland and a divorce is fishing in Lake Superior when he snags a corpse. He thinks he has seen the girl before and his attempt to identify her leads him to a ring of deadly pornographers. It almost costs him his own life.

CONSPIRACY!

Technical writer Tom Godot can't believe his luck when CONSPIRACY!, the book he has co-written with the elusive Harold Stevenson, is a hit. The book details a plot to hijack communication satellites. As Tom crosses the country on his book tour, he is disturbed by people interested in early drafts and dogged by an NSA agent. Communicating by fax with his editor and by encrypted e-mail with the mysterious Stevenson, Tom reaches out in his loneliness to his California girl friend Sylvia Hanson who turns out to be a pivotal figure. There is another conspiracy, and Tom is part of it

THE GOLD CHROMOSOME

When Adam Rottman's childless Aunt Sadie Gold died, the eight cousins learned her estate was in an irrevocable trust, the proceeds going to Adam's sister Sarah while she lives.

After Sarah's death, the money would go to the last surviving cousin. It's a fatal tontine Adam's lawyer brother Harold set up. Would the cousins kill each other for one million dollars? Sarah's car is found in the river, but not Sarah. That begins a series of mysterious deaths. Coincidence? Or Murder? Who will be next? Adam and his psychologist wife Deborah must stop the chain before he, too, is eliminated.

BEN ZAKKAI'S COFFIN
Born of a Jewish father and a Catholic mother, Herman Bachrach insists he has no religion, but he is drawn by circumstance into a holocaust vendetta over gold stolen by a Swiss bank from Jewish depositors. Seduced by a woman who calls herself Diana, no last name, Herman is suspected by detective Sheehan to be her murderer. Someone else wants him dead. His Jewish boss provides him with a lawyer, but sends him to Switzerland to finish the job "Diana" started. It's an assignment he can't refuse. The result is an epiphany of identity that changes Herman's life forever.

THE LOLLIPOP MURDER
A warning for wannabe novelists! What happens when a stable of neurotic novelists who live in their pseudonyms and are bound by iron clad contracts are invited aboard their miserly Florida publisher's yacht for the Miami Book Fair only to find that they have no hope of ever earning a dime of royalties for their books? All this as Hurricane Gerta threatens to sink the yacht at the dock. It's grounds for murder

A ROMANCE

SAM IN LOVE
A coming of age romance for mature young adults. U.S. Army life in Europe in the 1950's was an equivalent of the Grand Tour of the eighteenth century when young men traveled and sowed wild oats. Marty, roommate of Sam Logan, a PFC draftee serving in the US Army in Munich, Germany, says all Sam needs is to get laid. Sam is not a virgin,

but has a Midwestern ethic and believes in love. He doesn't know quite what that is. No Casanova, Sam, through a series of tentative encounters, thinks he's found the love of his life.

SCI-FI AND FANTASY

NEVER TRUST A TALKING HORSE
The narrator of this dystopian novel escapes preventive detention into a world he discovers has gone mad. Hungry, he is told he can eat for free at Lachumba's supper club, only to discover that he might be the main dish. He rescues Iris I. Iris from the ovens and in a series of episodes explores the insane world in search of a livelihood. He gradually realizes why he was incarcerated in the first place, but by then it is too late. His and Iris's roles have been reversed. Arrested, they are given a sadistic sentence which is their final challenge.

THE SEARCH FOR JESSE BRAM
Jesse Bram, the young hero of this metaphysical science fiction adventure, is unaware of his Jewish roots. An Eldre of mixed breed, he is marooned on the post apocalyptic shunned planet URth where technology and books have been destroyed. The URthlings variously view Jesse as a bringer of cargo for the half-breed prefect Hrod, as the reborn Savior by crypto-Christians, and as a link to the past by a remnant of Jews. The Galactic Federation suspects him of treason and he is pursued by an enigmatic Trinian policeman. If Jesse survives, will he be convicted? If acquitted, what next?

SHORT STORIES

THREADS OF THE COVENANT: THE JEWS OF RED JACKET
A collection of twenty-one short stories about Jewish life in small town America centering about two main characters, David Katz, the only Jewish boy in Red Jacket, and Richard

Goldman, the only Jewish professor at Copper country Community College. Each story depicts another aspect of what it means to be a Jew in a small town as each character comes to realize his own identity.

MISPLACED PERSONS
Though set in different locales what these stories have in common is a central character who is out of his element, in the wrong place, coming to grips with cultural, generational, or physical displacement.   In PROBLEM FOR THE TEACHER an expatriate fumbles for a living; in LIMBO an ex-G.I.   is adrift in Copenhagen; in TRIUMPH OF THE WILL   a   nervous   wreck   seeks   recuperation;   in MISCALCULATION a would be tax evader succumbs to his own fears; in THE LIE a drunk gets himself into difficulties, and in THE GIRLS OF FREDERIKSHAVN an old man is trapped by girls looking for action.

YOOPER TALES AND OTHER FUNNY STUFF
Extracted from the massive volume of Sachs's published Essays and Columns: 1992-2011, this collection of stories related to Michigan's Upper Peninsula, known as the UP, home of Yoopers, reveals the truth about snow fleas, ice worms, the humungous fungus (world's largest living thing) and the rigors of winters in the remote north woods. You can also learn how to catch and cook the Mosquito Giganticus and why visitors won't come. Sachs has several awards for his humor.

AHOY! QUARTERDECK!
Originally published as IRMA QUARTERDECK REPORTS but re-released with new illustrations and, in the paperback edition, with sea shanties, this funny book is a series of boating anecdotes about Irma and her bumbling husband Ralph ("I can't believe I lost the anchor") Quarterdeck in their many boating adventures and mishaps.   One reviewer says the book is as informative as Chapman's famous manual, but more fun.   Readers will find plenty of laughs in this book

and at the same time learn a great deal of boating fundamentals.

ANNA-LENA'S TROLL AND OHER STORIES
Each of the three Sachs daughters has a story in this children's book. "Anna-Lena's Troll" explores the nature of trolls, which represent the dark side of human behavior as Anna-Lena's nasty letter to Santa is rewarded by the gift of a nasty troll. "The Return of Baby Suzy" is the true story of Cynthia's worn out doll and its resurrection. "The Stars for Christmas" is the remarkable surprise Belinda got along with her new eye glasses. Other family stories are Christmas related.

NON-FICTION

THE MISADVENTURES OF CPL. SACHS
Adrift through college at Indiana University, author Sachs was drafted at the end of the Korean War. Physically unfit for combat, he was sent to Queer Company for basic training, then by a fluke was shipped out to Germany instead of Korea. Thus began his own version of the traditional Grand Tour.

FREELANCE NONFICTION ARTICLES
This third edition of a monograph on freelance writing first published by the Society for Technical Communication is newly updated. This little manual provides tips for interviewing, article structure, article preparation and submission, photography, and business practice.

CHILLY-CHILLY-BANG—HOW WE FREELANCED THROUGH EUROPE'S COLDEST WINTER IN A VW WITH A KID
Companion piece to *Freelance Nonfiction Articles*. The former is a how to book. This is a "how we did it" memoir. The author knew nothing about Volkswagens when they set off, but as they worked from VW dealer to dealer getting the old Combi fixed, he learned! It's as much a book for VW enthusiasts as it is for writers.

The Irwin Glass Trilogy

Both FREELANCE NONFICTION ARTICLES and *Chilly-Chilly-BANG! How we Freelanced Through Europe's Coldest Winter in a VW with a Kid* are combined in a double volume, *The Writing Life*.

THE 1957 SACHS ARCTIC EXPEDITION
After military service in Germany the author took the GI Bill to Sweden. With no income in the summer, and not even sure there was a road to the far north, he set off hitchhiking to North Cape, the northernmost point in Europe in search of the midnight sun. Illustrated.

FROM TENT TO CASTLE: MEMOIR OF A YEAR LONG HONEYMOON
Setting off from Stockholm, Sweden on rebuilt one speed bicycles, Harley and Ulla embarked on an open-ended honeymoon with no fixed destination and equipped with a tent, a thin double sleeping bag, a tiny gasoline stove, and $3000. After arriving in Britain, Ulla discovered she was pregnant. Tired of unrelenting rain, they advertised for a cheap place to spend the winter. They were offered the gatehouse to Borthwick Castle outside Edinburgh, Scotland for $25 a month by British author Theo Lang.

"IS"
As Bill Clinton said, "It all depends on what the meaning of "is" is."
A problem we all have is distinguishing between what is real and what is not. This is in fact an age-old question. This volume switches between classical instances of the problem to the author and his psychiatrist and his wife. What is real? That all depends on the meaning of "real."

QUEER COMPANY
Not a gay novel, this is a fictionalized memoir of an experimental basic training unit at the end of the Korean War. All the draftees were physically unfit for combat but the army didn't want to discharge them. Instead they got

modified training in a company unfortunately designated Q. In the Army phonetic alphabet Q is Queen, but Q company was called queer.   A copy is in the US Army historical archives.